MOUNTAIN VIEW
PUBLIC LIBRARY
Mountain View, CA
P9-ELQ-326

SPYMASTER

Books by MARGARET WEIS and ROBERT KRAMMES

DRAGON BRIGADE

Shadow Raiders

*Storm Riders**

*The Seventh Sigil**

DRAGON CORSAIRS

Spymaster

*Oath Breaker**+

*Kingmaker**+

*A TOR BOOK

+ FORTHCOMING

SPYMASTER

Margaret Weis
and Robert Krammes

A TOM DOHERTY ASSOCIATES BOOK / NEW YORK

This is a work of fiction. All of the characters, organizations, and events portrayed in this novel are either products of the authors' imaginations or are used fictitiously.

SPYMASTER

Map and family tree by Ellisa Mitchell

Edited by James Frenkel

A Tor Book
Published by Tom Doherty Associates
175 Fifth Avenue
New York, NY 10010

www.tor-forge.com

Tor® is a registered trademark of Macmillan Publishing Group, LLC.

The Library of Congress Cataloging-in-Publication Data is available upon request.

ISBN 978-0-7653-8107-1 (hardcover)
ISBN 978-1-4668-7795-5 (e-book)

Our books may be purchased in bulk for promotional, educational, or business use. Please contact your local bookseller or the Macmillan Corporate and Premium Sales Department at 1-800-221-7945, extension 5442, or by e-mail at MacmillanSpecialMarkets@macmillan.com.

First Edition: March 2017

Printed in the United States of America

0 9 8 7 6 5 4 3 2 1

For Mary, with love

—Bob

To Christi Cardenas, literary agent and friend.
We have been through a lot together!
Thank you!

—Margaret

King Lionel II

Ester of Travia (D) — M — King Lionel II — M — Blanche Hunsman

Osric (D) Died with Queen Ester
Frederick M Elizabeth
Oswald I M Caroline

Victoria M Michael
Bridgett
Oswald II M Ann

Richard M Margaret
Mary M Oswald III (K)
Phillip M Martha

Lucia M James I (K)
Oswald (K)
Mortimer (K)
Alfred I M Susan

Vincent M Evelyn
Margaret
Thomas (D) Died as a Baby
Marjorie M William I
Jonathan (D)
Richard

Elanora M Henry
George I M Caroline

Giovana M Joseph
Anne M George II

Constanza M Alistair Oberlein
Godfrey I M Jane

Thomas Stanford (Prince Tom)
Michael Owens M Mary I
Elinor

(D) Osric
Jonathan

Bastard Line

Godfrey M Honoria
Elise M Hugh
Martha
Susan
Claire M Jeffrey
Henry M Ann
Henry E.

House Stanford

House Chessington

(M) Married
(D) Died
(K) Killed

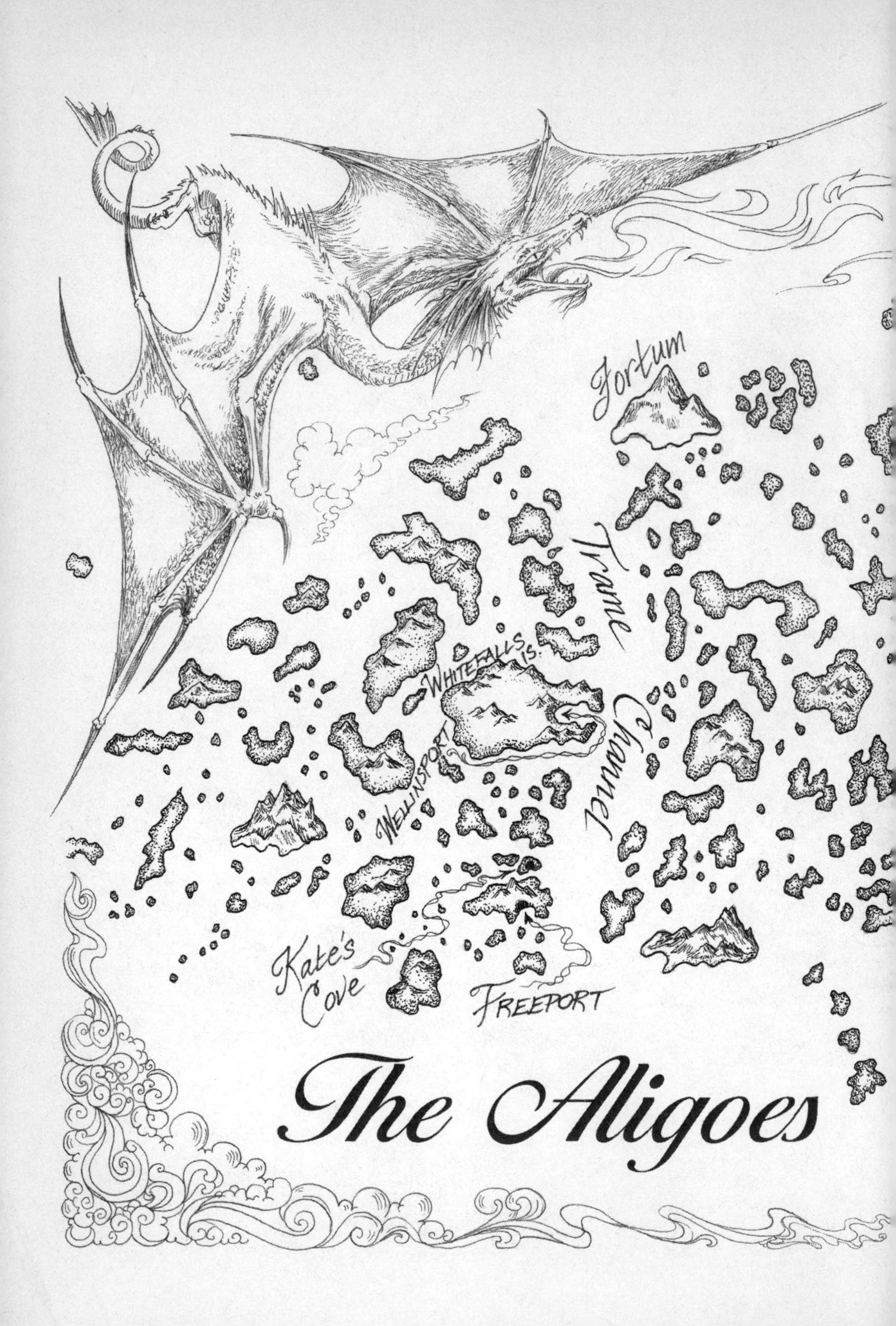
Fortum
Trame Channel
Whitefalls Is.
Wellinsport
Kate's Cove
Freeport
The Aligoes

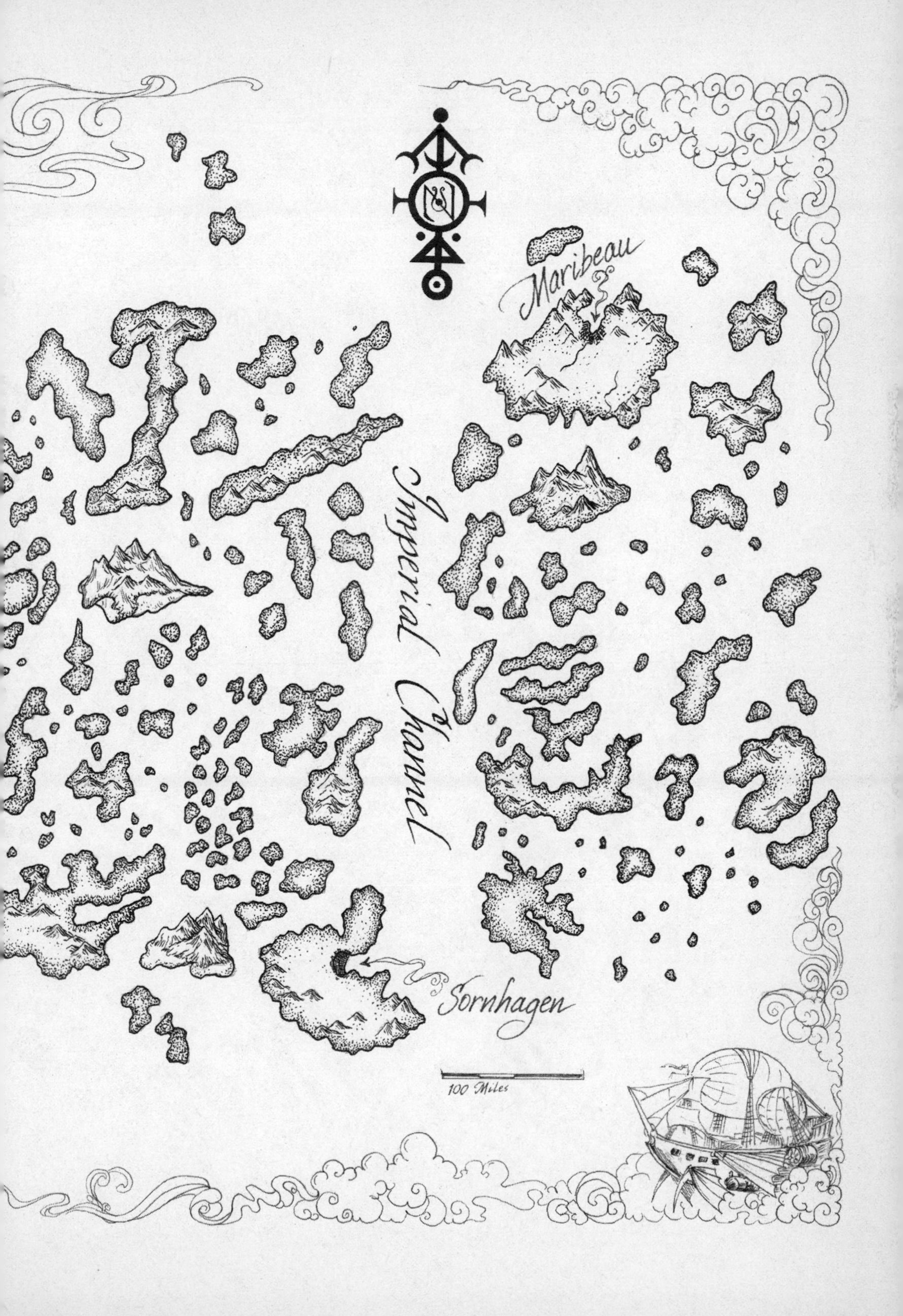
Maribeau
Imperial Channel
Sornhagen
100 Miles

SPYMASTER

PROLOGUE

Kate sat on the deck, her back against the lift tank, playing at a game of knucklebones and watching her father meet with the revenue agent, who had come aboard to inspect the ship for contraband. The ship's crew, old hands at their business, went about their duties as normal—lowering the sails, deflating the balloons, making ready to dock the ship—while those who had no work leaned over the railing to barter with Trundlers offering to sell their potent liquor, Calvados.

"Hey, little boy, want to be a man tonight?" a shrill voice called out.

"You talking to me?" Kate demanded, turning to see a gaily colored barge filled with enterprising whores nudge alongside the ship. The woman stood up in the barge and lifted her skirt to display her wares.

"Come to the Perky Parrot, little boy," she said. "I'll give you a closer look."

"Did you say the Poxy Parrot?" Kate shouted back.

The crew roared and even the revenue agent laughed, as the offended whores sailed off.

"You tell 'em, Li'l Captain," added one of the sailors, who were regarding her with the fond pride of parents whose child has done something clever.

Kate grinned and went back to her game, surreptitiously watching her father and the revenue agent. She didn't have to concentrate on the game; she was an expert at knucklebones, having quick reflexes and deft hands. The crew had stopped playing with her for money when she was ten. This meant she could keep an eye on her father, ready to spring into action if something should go wrong.

Her father and the agent shook hands and then exchanged pleasantries. Watching closely, Kate saw that after the handshake, the agent slid his hand into his pocket, no doubt depositing the five silver rosun coins given to him to keep his inspection brief.

The ship, an older design, had two masts and a wide beam made for sailing the open Breath. The short wings, swept back along the length of the hull, ended with a large airscrew on either side. A cargo hold ran the full length of the ship, with a smaller hold under an old-style sterncastle.

The revenue agent was sweating in his blue uniform beneath the midday sun and seemed glad to make quick work of the inspection so that he could retire to his cool office on shore. He smiled at Kate, who jumped to her feet and knuckled her forehead. Dressed in loose-fitting trousers and shirt, her curly sun-bleached blond hair cut short and her skin burned brown, Kate was just another ship's boy, and she knew how to act the part.

"Clever lad," said the agent.

"Thankee, sir," said Kate.

The agent walked on and Kate cast a sly glance at Olaf, ship's crafter and mechanic, who had been loitering nearby, ready with his magic in case the revenue agent had taken it into his head to ignore the bribe and inspect the lift tank. Olaf winked at her and nodded. All was well.

The revenue agent glanced down into the hold, saw a great many barrels marked "tar," noted that they were on the manifest, and gave Captain Fitzmaurice permission to enter the harbor. The agent departed, jingling coins in his pocket.

The *Barwich Rose,* named for Kate's late mother, sailed into the Rosian harbor city of Westfirth, joining the traffic in the busy harbor. Kate's father celebrated by buying a bottle of Calvados from one of the Trundlers. Walking over to Kate, he clapped her on the shoulder.

"I heard you give the Perky Parrot a new name," he said, grinning. "The Poxy Parrot! Agent Rouchard was most amused."

Morgan reached out to cup her face with his hand, turning it to the sun slanting through the mists of the Breath.

"Damn, but you are like your mother, Kate. Poxy Parrot!" Morgan gave a rueful grin. "A girl your age shouldn't talk of such things or even know about them. Your mother would skin us both if she were alive. Damn if I know what to do about you, though."

He took off his hat and ran his sleeve across his forehead while he regarded Kate with a look of mingled regret, fondness, and perplexity.

"I suppose you could go to school back in Freya," he said vaguely. "You're a fair crafter. The Crown would pay for your schooling . . ."

Kate felt a chill. Her father had talked of sending her off to school ever since her mother died. So far, he hadn't carried through on his threat, but she noticed he was starting to bring it up more often now that she was growing older. He had not known what to do with his daughter when she was six; he was completely flummoxed over what to do with her now that she was developing into a young woman.

Born to a family of merchant seamen who had used their influence to gain him an officer's commission in the Royal Navy, Captain Morgan Fitzmaurice had lost his commission and barely escaped court-martial when it was suspected, though never proved, that he was using naval ships to transport contraband.

A handsome man with a ready smile and glib tongue, Morgan had one goal in life, and that was to make as much money as he could, with as little effort as possible. A fondness for baccarat always seemed to prevent him from achieving that goal, but he was optimistic and never failed to believe that the next voyage would make his fortune. Kate had adored her father when she was little, and she had tried hard to keep on adoring him even after she was old enough to know better.

She knew how to disarm him, however. She grabbed a section of silk from a balloon that was being mended, wrapped it around her slim body, and then went mincing about the deck.

"My dear sweet papa wants to send me to school to learn to be a fine lady," Kate shrilled, talking through her nose. "I'm to be presented to the queen."

Her clumsy curtsy drew hoots of laughter from the crew. Morgan joined in, and Kate dropped the balloon to run to him and throw her arms around him.

"I don't need school," she said persuasively. "Mama taught me to read and write and cipher. I'm better at keeping the account books than you are. I can do everything there is to be done around the ship, including taking the helm. I'm as good a crafter as Olaf—"

"You are not!" Olaf roared, grinning.

"Well, almost," Kate amended. "I know how to use a sextant, I can read navigation charts. I know the weather signs, when there's going to be a storm and when it's going to be fine for sailing. And, most important, I'm your luck, Father."

"She is that, Cap'n!" called a member of the crew. Others said "Aye" to that.

"She brings us fair winds and a prosperous voyage," said another.

"And revenue agents who take bribes!" said a third.

"Remember when I was sick with the measles and you had to leave me with the nuns at Saint Agnes and sail on without me. You remember what happened?"

Many in the crew dourly shook their heads.

"Only time we was ever boarded," said one.

"Had to dump the cargo," said another.

Kate gave her father a kiss on his cheek. "You're the best father a girl could have and you know you can't get on without me, so don't talk nonsense."

Morgan allowed himself to be persuaded, particularly in the matter of luck. No one is more superstitious than a sailor, and the crew firmly believed that Kate was their lucky charm. The one voyage she had missed had ended in disaster.

"You're a good daughter to me, Kate," said Morgan, adding with a shrug and a grin, "You're growing up wild as a catamount and God knows what will become of you, but you are a good daughter."

He clapped her on the shoulder again and went off to take over the helm to steer the ship into port. Kate gave a sigh of relief as she neatly folded up the silk and stowed it.

"Come here, Katydid," Olaf called, using his pet name for her. "Come look at this."

Grateful for the distraction, Kate joined her friend at the rail. The sights of Westfirth were new to her.

Morgan's usual smuggling runs took him to remote and isolated coves along the coastlines of Rosia and Freya. He had recently been in contact with a notorious Westfirth gang who didn't like the bother of having to travel long distances to obtain their contraband. They had made all the arrangements for delivery of their cargo, including making certain the right revenue agent was on hand to clear them and telling them which dockyards the police didn't bother to patrol.

Kate was enthralled by the huge gun emplacement guarding the harbor. She had not imagined there could be that many cannons in the world, and she kept staring at them until Olaf nudged her elbow and pointed to the top of the enormous cliff that towered high above the coastal city of Westfirth. Kate craned her neck to see.

"Oh, Olaf, those are dragons!" she said breathlessly, awed.

All her life she had heard of dragons, but she never had seen any before now, for there were no dragons in her native Freya. And here were three of the magnificent creatures, flying in wide circles above the cliff.

"Those aren't just any dragons," said Olaf. "Those are members of the famed Dragon Brigade. The Brigade has its headquarters atop that cliff, known as the Bastion. Those would be young recruits, I'm guessing. Probably in training."

"You're talkin' heresy, Olaf!" said one of the sailors, scowling. "Don't pay heed to him, Kate. Dragons are evil creatures. Foul serpents. Minions of the devil. That's why they do the bidding of the damn Rosians."

Kate looked questioningly at Olaf and saw him roll his eyes. She turned her gaze back to the dragons—huge, monstrous beasts—yet so graceful in flight. The sunlight glittered on their scales and shimmered through the membrane of their wings.

"No creature that beautiful could be evil," Kate said softly. "Look, Olaf! There's a man riding on the back of a dragon!"

"He'll be one of the officers," said Olaf.

They watched as a fourth dragon flew into the air with the officer riding on the back, seated just below the neck, atop the massive shoulders and ahead of the flashing wings.

"The riders sit in specially designed saddles that keep them strapped in, even when the dragon flips over in midair," said Olaf. "Saw it myself at the Battle of Daenar when I was a gunnery crafter. Let me see, that must have been nigh on forty years ago.

"We were holed up in this fortress when the Dragon Brigade attacked us. It was a terrible sight, Katydid, to see the beasts fly so close their wings sliced through the clouds and you felt the heat of their fiery breath. Worse yet to watch their magical fire burn clean through all our magic constructs, see walls start to crumble. Terrible, but, as you say, beautiful."

Olaf fell silent, watching the dragons, leaning on the rail, his chin resting on his hand. He was a small man, about five foot, with large shoulders and arms and undersized legs. He had worked for a blacksmith when he was a boy, and his face and hands were black from the soot that was ingrained in his skin. He had grizzled hair and a gap-toothed smile. He didn't know his age, but had a vague idea that he was somewhere above sixty.

He had been a ship's crafter employed by the Fitzmaurice Shipping Company until it had gone down in financial ruin. Then he'd joined Morgan's crew, and he'd known Kate since she was born. Most of what Kate knew about her family—or at least the truth of what she knew—came from Olaf. He was fond of her father, but free to admit that Morgan "tended to shave the truth" a bit on occasion.

"How do you suppose people climb to the top of the cliff?" Kate asked.

Olaf gave her a sharp glance, which she met with a look of wide-eyed innocence.

"Those who have permission to be in the Bastion fly on the backs of their dragons," said Olaf. "The area is restricted. They don't encourage visitors."

"Pooh, there must be another way to reach it besides dragons," said Kate, taking a practical view of the matter. "What if someone was hurt or they needed to send an urgent message to the dragons? I know you know, Olaf," she added in wheedling tones. "You know everything."

"I know you could charm a wyvern with those brown eyes," Olaf said, pretending to grumble. "That big building is the Old Fort. The building surrounded by the *wall* with the *guard towers* near the gun emplacements. The admiral of the Western Fleet lives there now and I've heard tell that there's a walking path that leads from his garden to the Bastion."

Kate heard him lay emphasis on the words "wall" and "guard towers," but dismissed that as unimportant. She differed from her father, who tended to be easygoing and take life as it came. Kate was stubborn, like her mother. When Rose Gascoyne had decided to do something, she had let nothing stand in her way.

The buyers for the contraband would arrive at midnight. Kate had to be back on board ship then, to ensure her father kept money enough to pay the crew and make the repairs the ship needed for the voyage home. Otherwise the profits would end up on the baccarat table. But for now, she had the afternoon and evening free.

The *Barwich Rose* slowed as a harbor tug took over the final maneuvering. The tug pushed the merchant ship into a berth barely larger than the ship itself. As soon as it was secured to the dock, the harbor tug sailed off to the next ship, and Kate was down the gangplank before it touched the dock, making the leap from the plank to the shore with ease.

She heard her father calling and Olaf yelling that Westfirth was a wicked place and she should stay on board ship. Ignoring both of them, she made her way among the barrels and crates and boxes stacked on the wharf, and ran into a street lined with warehouses, markets, and taverns.

The street was named Canal Street, and although Kate had never been to Westfirth, she knew that almost every city had a Canal Street that ran along the ship channel. Since they had seen the Bastion while sailing down the canal, she figured she had only to follow Canal Street and it would lead her to back to the Bastion. She didn't want to waste time getting lost, however, and so she stopped to ask for directions.

She spoke fluent Rosian, and although the fishmonger appeared to wonder why a ship's boy needed to know how to get to the Old Fort, he told her to just keep following Canal. When it ended, she would be there.

She was so eager to reach her destination that she ran past the shops and market stalls and street vendors that would have otherwise drawn her interest. Canal Street ended at the Old Fort, and Kate stood on the sidewalk, gaping.

As Olaf had pointed out to her, the Old Fort was surrounded by a wall with guard towers. Although known as the Old Fort, the beautiful building resembled a palace more than a fortress, and was now, as Olaf had told her, the living quarters and offices of the admiral of the Western Fleet.

Kate was impressed. She considered the manor house on her family's estate—Barwich Manor, where she had lived when she was little, until the bank took it—to be more beautiful, but she allowed that this building would come in second. Looking at it now, she was somewhat daunted by the prospect of trying to sneak inside. The women emerging from the carriages or walking about the streets outside the front gate were elegantly dressed, wearing elaborate hats. The men were, for the most part, officers in the Rosian navy, splendid in their uniforms. Kate wasn't even wearing shoes.

She pilfered an apple from a vendor, and ate it while she walked around the wall, searching for a solution to her problem. She found it in the form of a large oak tree growing near the wall. The lowest branches were far above her head, but she had been climbing the ship's rigging since she was little, and she dug her bare feet into the bark and shinnied up the trunk with ease. After crawling along a large branch that extended over the wall, she dropped down into the garden.

She was annoyed to find that the garden was occupied; a great many rich people were promenading up and down the paths. Kate was forced to hide in the shadows of trees and hedges as she circled about the ornamental fish ponds, always keeping her goal—the Bastion at the top of the cliff—in sight.

She had no trouble locating the stairs that led up the side of the cliff. The steps had been cut into the stone in a zigzag pattern and were both decorative and functional. Climbing stairs that went back and forth, ascending gradually, would be far easier than climbing straight up.

Kate ran up the hundreds of flagstones with the strength and energy of her twelve years, fueled by her eagerness to obtain a close-up view of the dragons. Arriving at the top, she stopped to catch her breath, gaze, and marvel.

The Bastion was built in a circle; halls and rooms radiated from an enormous courtyard made of stone. A mosaic of glittering tile in the center of the courtyard portrayed a blue-green dragon in flight, wings extended, against the background of a red and golden sun.

Some of the buildings must be barracks for the humans, Kate guessed, for she could see men walking about on business or pausing to talk and observe the maneuvers being performed by the dragons.

Having located the enemy—those humans who might catch her—Kate crouched behind a tree. From here, she was free to admire the dragons, one of whom was standing at the edge of the cliff, poised to take flight along with two of his fellows.

The three dragons were being observed by an officer and another dragon. The officer would gesture to the three, making comments to the observing dragon, who either nodded in agreement or answered the officer. Kate couldn't hear what they were saying; the wind was far too strong, for atop the cliff, it blew continuously. But she was enthralled to know that dragons could talk with humans. Wyverns hitched to carriages pulled them through the air, but they couldn't talk; not that wyverns would have much anyone would care to hear, being stupid, nasty beasts. Griffins—which carried individual riders and were half eagle, half lion—could talk, according to her father. They mostly chose not to, thinking themselves above having to communicate with humans. Kate would have given her knucklebones, her most precious possession, to be able to talk to a dragon.

The beasts had looked small as birds from down below. Viewed up close, they were enormous. She could not fathom the height of the dragons, but she guessed that if the dragons were standing alongside the cathedral of Saint Agnes, their heads would be about level with the vaulted roof.

Their shimmering scales shifted colors in the sunlight, sometimes looking blue and sometimes green. Their heads, with elongated snouts and sharp fangs, were mounted on long, graceful necks. The spiky mane started at the top of the head and ran the length of the neck, ending right at the shoulders, leaving a gap for the saddle, then extending down the back to the tip of the tail.

One dragon, Kate noticed, had a twisted spike on top of his head, an oddity, for all the rest of the spikes on his mane were smooth, as were the spikes on the other dragons.

Kate chose him for her favorite, naming him Twist, and waited impatiently to see him fly. She watched in awe as the dragons took flight, one after another, spreading their wings, pushing off with their powerful legs, and sailing effortlessly off the cliff.

She made herself comfortable, sitting down on the ground, hugging her knees to her chin, to watch the dragons dip and roll and turn somersaults in the air. She thought they were playing the way she played in the rigging, until she saw the officer closely observing them and making notes in a book he carried. The dragon standing at his side would sometimes bellow at the three in the same sort of tone Olaf used when reprimanding one of the crew. Kate concluded that Olaf had been right; the three dragons, including Twist, must be in training.

After about an hour of maneuvers, the officer said something to his companion dragon, who gave a hooting, booming call. The dragon recruits started to spiral downward. Kate realized they were going to land. The next moment she saw, with a thrill, that they were going to land in the courtyard with the mosaic, which was only a few yards from her.

She held her breath when the lead dragon landed, hitting the ground with its tail and back legs first, then dropping down on its front legs. The dragon folded his wings, shook its mane, and then walked off, as the officer nodded in approval and pointed toward the barracks.

The second dragon followed the first, landing with ease, and got a nod from the officer. The dragon standing with the officer began hooting again. Kate was excited to watch Twist land. She looked up into the sky, but was disappointed not to see him. Wondering where he was, she left her tree and ventured out into the open. She searched the skies, not watching where she was going, and not realizing she had strayed out into the courtyard. She also did not notice that the wind had shifted.

The dragon who had been hooting suddenly gave a deafening shriek. The officer whipped around, dropping his book and shouting a warning as he ran toward her. Kate turned to see Twist swooping down on top of her, preparing to land right where she was standing.

At the last moment the dragon saw her and frantically beat his wings to gain altitude. The officer was close to her, ordering her to run. Kate bolted, tripped on a loose flagstone, and fell flat on her face. The officer flung himself on top of her and the dragon soared past them, coming so close that Kate felt a blast of air, followed by a jarring thud. She couldn't see, for her face was plastered against the stone, but she knew by the sounds that the dragon must have crashed into the ground.

The officer picked himself up and turned to help Kate.

"Are you all right?" he asked, speaking Rosian.

Kate nodded a little shakily. She was scraped and cut and bruised and had the wind knocked out of her, but was otherwise unharmed.

She managed to squeeze out, "Yes, sir," as she scrambled to her feet. She was far more worried about the dragon than she was about herself, and she tried to peer around the officer to see what had become of him.

The dragon had managed to avoid smashing into them, but he had been unable to stop his forward momentum. She gathered, by the shaking of the ground and the enormous dust cloud, that he had come down in a heap, tumbling and rolling.

"What happened to Twist, sir?" Kate asked, trying to see.

"Twist?" the officer asked, puzzled.

"The dragon. Is he all right?"

The dust settled and Kate saw Twist lift his head and start to move, albeit a little unsteadily. The dragon who had been hooting at him hastened over, along with his two comrades and some of the men who had been in the barracks, to check on him. The officer turned from Kate to shout to the hooting dragon.

"Lady Cam, how is Dalgren?"

Before Lady Cam could reply, the dragon himself responded, "A few bumps, Lieutenant. Nothing broken. I remembered my lesson, sir," he added with faint pride. "Tuck in the wings, go limp, and roll."

"Well done, Dalgren," said the officer. "Don't move until Lady Cam has examined you."

Reassured that Twist was uninjured, Kate shifted her gaze to the man who stood in front of her. He was perhaps in his mid-twenties. He had removed the heavy uniform coat in the heat and was in his shirtsleeves, uniform trousers, and high, black riding boots. He wore his blondish brown hair tied back from his face and was regarding her sternly.

"It was my fault, sir!" Kate said breathlessly. "I was trying to see Twist land and I didn't realize the wind had changed direction. He won't get into trouble, will he?"

The officer glanced over his shoulder, saw the dragon staggering to his feet, watched over by Lady Cam, and looked back at Kate. Her question seemed to have gained his favor, because the stern expression relaxed.

"I'm glad you're thinking of the dragon," he said drily. He crossed his arms over his chest. "You realize you could have been killed, son. The Bastion is a dangerous place, which is why access is restricted to the dragons and their riders. You've broken the law, young man. I could have you arrested."

Kate had been thinking fast and she had a lie ready. She would whimper, adding a few tears, that she was lost and had wandered up here by accident. She would have lied to her father and not thought twice, but she found she couldn't lie to this man, who was looking down at her with cool, appraising eyes. The realization suddenly came to her that he, a fine gentleman, had been prepared to sacrifice his life to save hers.

Her father never put much stock in a man's honor, saying that only the wealthy could afford to indulge in it.

Kate learned a lesson in that moment. Her father was wrong. This man had been honorable enough to be willing to die to save her, and she was bound, in honor, to repay him. She had nothing to give in return except the truth.

Hanging her head, she lowered her eyes.

"I . . . I wanted to see the dragons, sir."

He said nothing, and Kate was frightened. Peeping up, she saw his lips twitch.

"I see," he said finally. "What's your name, son?"

"I'm a girl. My name is Katherine Gascoyne-Fitzmaurice," she said and, remembering her lessons from her mother, she gave a bobbing, awkward curtsy.

The man's smile broadened. "A girl with a name that's bigger than she is."

"They call me Kate, sir."

"Very well, Kate. You're Freyan by your accent. Not a spy, are you?"

"Oh, no, sir!" Kate assured him. "My father is a merchant seaman, Captain Morgan Fitzmaurice. He has his own vessel, the *Barwich Rose*. We're in port making a delivery."

"You are a sailor," said the officer. "That's how you knew about the shift in the wind. I am Lieutenant Stephano de Guichen of the Dragon Brigade."

"Pleased to meet you, sir," said Kate with another curtsy. "Thank you for saving my life. You didn't have to do that."

"Well, of course I did," said Lieutenant de Guichen, laughing. "Otherwise you would have left a big, ugly splotch of blood all over our nice clean flagstones."

He grinned at her, and Kate, now perfectly at ease, grinned back.

"Since you're not a Freyan spy and you've come all this way, would you like to meet Dalgren?" Lieutenant de Guichen added. "I'm sure he's worried about you."

"Oh, yes, sir!" said Kate. "I'd like to apologize."

"You speak Rosian well," said Lieutenant de Guichen, as they walked toward Dalgren, who had been watching them all this time.

"My father does business with people from all over," said Kate and hurriedly changed the subject. "What is that picture?"

She pointed to the mosaic that portrayed the dragon.

"The emblem of the Dragon Brigade. Dragons and humans working together, living together, fighting together for our country."

Kate sighed with longing. "Would someone have to be Rosian to join the Dragon Brigade?"

"I'm afraid so, yes," said Lieutenant de Guichen. "Lord Dalgren is a young dragon, perhaps about eighteen in human years. He is one of our new recruits, hoping to join the Brigade."

"*Lord* Dalgren?" Kate questioned.

"Dragons and men must be of gentle birth to be officers in the Brigade."

Kate supposed she was of gentle birth, although she never concerned herself much about her station in life. Her mother had been the daughter of a viscount. Upon his untimely death, she had inherited two things: his debts and Barwich Manor. Kate remembered her mother's sorrow over her "comedown" in the world. The servants had called her mother "my lady" until they had left because they hadn't been paid.

Kate was content to be a smuggler's daughter, with only one regret: that her mother and father had lost Barwich Manor, her dearly beloved home.

Her one dream in life was to buy it back. She now added another dream to that: to join the Dragon Brigade. Why not? she reasoned. Both were equally unattainable.

Dalgren stood stiffly to attention as they approached. Kate noticed that he was favoring a back leg, trying not to put his weight on it, and she felt horrible.

"At ease, Lord Dalgren," said Lieutenant de Guichen. "May I introduce Katherine Gascoyne-Fitzmaurice, the young woman you almost flattened. You will be glad to know that although shaken up, she was not injured."

"I am so sorry, mistress," said Dalgren, lowering his head to speak to her. His voice was gravelly, as though he were talking around boulders in his throat, but she was thrilled to find that she could understand him. "I did not see you standing there."

"It was all my fault, Your Lordship," said Kate. "I wanted to watch you land and I didn't realize the wind had shifted—"

They were interrupted by someone shouting from the barracks. "Stephano! Officers meeting!"

"I have to go," said the lieutenant. "Lord Dalgren will show you the way out of the Bastion. A pleasure meeting you, Mistress Katherine. Please, *don't* come again."

He grinned and she grinned back; then he walked off. He had taken only a few steps when he stopped and turned back. "Fight for your dreams, Kate! Never sound retreat!"

He waved, then hurried back to the barracks on the run, motioning for Lady Cam to join him.

"I know the way out, Your Lordship," Kate told Dalgren, embarrassed. "Your leg is hurt. You don't have to show me."

"But I'd like to," said Dalgren. He ducked his head to say in a low voice, "Otherwise I have to return to the barracks and endure Lady Cam's reprimands."

They walked together, the dragon crouching down and moving at a crawl in order not to outdistance her. Kate was surprised to find herself talking to a dragon as easily as she could talk to Olaf.

Dalgren explained what he had been doing, practicing maneuvers used in attacking ships and fortresses. Kate listened, fascinated.

She expected him to leave when they reached the wall, but Dalgren flattened down on his belly and laid his head on the ground, to bring himself almost to eye level with Kate. They continued talking until a bugle call caused Dalgren to raise his head.

"That's the evening mess call. I have to go. You should leave, too, Kate, before it gets dark."

"Good-bye, Dalgren," said Kate. "This has been the best day of my life. I wish we could meet again."

"I'm afraid that's not likely," said Dalgren regretfully. "If you ever came back here, the lieutenant would have no choice but report you to the authorities. We could write letters."

"Can dragons write?" Kate asked, awed, trying to picture Dalgren holding a pen in an enormous claw.

"Well, no." Dalgren rumbled deep in his throat, which Kate took for laughter. "Humans do the writing for us."

"The problem is that I don't have an address," said Kate. "We live on our ship and we never stay in one place very long and we don't generally know where we're going."

"Sounds like a wonderful life," said Dalgren, adding in rueful tones, "I *always* know where I'm going. I have no say in the matter."

Kate thought he was just being kind, and didn't respond. She was busy thinking.

"We do stop in one place a few times a year," she said. "The Abbey of Saint Agnes. The nuns are kind to us and whenever we are in Rosia, Father stops to exchange news and visit with them. They'd hold the letters for me."

"What a good idea! I'll write to you care of the Abbey of Saint Agnes," said Dalgren. "And you must write me back. I'll send you my address."

She waved to Dalgren and then hurried down the path, reliving over and over every glorious moment of this wonderful day. Not paying attention, she ended up getting lost in the admiral's garden and was nearly caught by one of the gardeners, who chased her until she reached the oak tree, and then stood beneath it shaking his fist at her. Kate paid attention to where she was going after that.

She longed to tell Olaf about her adventure. But although he was her friend, he was also Morgan's friend and might tell on her. Her father would be alarmed over the fact that not only had she almost been killed, she could have ended up in the hands of the police just when he was about to turn over smuggled contraband. Her father would talk again about sending her off to school, and this time he might actually go through with it. Kate decided to keep her adventure secret.

Late that night, the customers arrived to collect their goods. They were satisfied, and not only paid, but wanted to order more. Kate managed to wheedle the money she required out of her father, and he took the rest and went to the gambling dens.

After he had gone, Kate sneaked into her father's cabin. She cut a blank page from the ship's logbook, sat down at her father's desk, opened the ink bottle, dipped her pen, and began to write. When she was finished, she let the ink dry, then carried the paper with her to the storage closet that Olaf had transformed into a room of her own. Kate lay down on the bed to read what she had written. Folding the paper, she tucked it under the pillow and thought over all that had happened until she fell asleep.

Fight for your dreams. Never sound retreat.

Book 1

ONE

Sir Henry Wallace sat at a table in the small cabin aboard the Freyan ship HMS *Valor,* dunking a ship's biscuit in his coffee in an effort to render it edible and reading the week-old newspaper.

"Ineffable twaddle," said Sir Henry, scowling. He motioned with his egg spoon to an illustration and read aloud the accompanying tale. "'The gallant Prince Tom, heedless of the many grievous wounds he had suffered in the course of the fearsome battle, raised his bloody sword, shouting, "If we are to die today, gentlemen, let history say we died heroes!"' Pah!"

Sir Henry tossed aside the newspaper with contempt.

"Your Lordship is referring to the latest exploits of the young gentleman known in the press by the somewhat romantic appellation of 'Prince Tom,'" said Mr. Sloan. "I have not read the stories myself, my lord, but I understand they have garnered a great deal of interest among the populace, such that the newspaper has trebled its circulation since the series began."

Sir Henry snorted and, after tapping the crown of the soft-boiled egg with his spoon, removed the shell and began to eat the yolk. At that moment the ship heeled, as a gust of wind hit it, forcing him to grab hold of the eggcup as it slid across the table. He looked up, frowning at Mr. Sloan, who had rescued the coffee.

"I haven't been on deck yet this morning," said Henry. "Is there a storm brewing?"

"Wizard storm, my lord," said Mr. Sloan. "Blowing in from the west."

Henry heard a distant rumble of thunder. "At least those storms are not as frequent or as bad as they used to be when the Bottom Dwellers were spewing forth their foul contramagic."

"God be praised, my lord," said Mr. Sloan.

"A dreadful war that left its mark on us all," said Henry, falling into a reflective mood as he drank his coffee. "I think about it every time there is a storm. We wronged those poor devils, sinking their island and dooming them to the cruel fate of living in relative darkness at the bottom of the world. Small wonder that even after hundreds of years, they sought their revenge on us."

"I confess I find it hard to feel much sympathy for them, my lord," said Mr. Sloan. "Especially given the terrible fate they intended to inflict on our people. Thank God you and Father Jacob and the others were able to stop them."

"I will never forget that awful night," said Henry. "I thought we had failed and all I could do was wait for the end. Alan, bleeding to death . . ."

He fell silent a moment, remembering the horror, the pain of his wounds. He had spent months convalescing and months beyond that battling the nightmarish memories. Not wanting to give them new life, he shook them off and managed a smile. "And there you were to save us, Mr. Sloan, your face 'radiating glory' as the Scriptures say of the angels."

"You were delirious at the time, my lord," said Mr. Sloan with a faint smile.

"I was not," said Henry. "You saved our lives, Mr. Sloan, and I do not forget that. As for the Bottom Dwellers, we couldn't let them continue sacrificing people in their foul blood magic rituals and knocking down our buildings with their contramagic."

"Indeed not, my lord," said Mr. Sloan.

"Even if the war did bankrupt us," Henry added somberly. "Fortunately the crystals will help ease that burden."

The ship rocked again, causing Mr. Sloan to stagger into a bulkhead.

"Please sit down!" Henry said. "You stand there hunched like a stork and being tossed about. I cannot function if you are laid up with a cracked skull."

Mr. Sloan sighed and reluctantly seated himself opposite Sir Henry on the bed, a shocking liberty that was harrowing to the soul of Mr. Sloan, who normally would have been standing or respectfully seated in a chair as he attended to his employer, but for the sad fact that the cabin was small with a low ceiling. Being above average height, Mr. Sloan was forced to stand with his head, back, and shoulders bent at an uncomfortable angle.

HMS *Valor* was a massive warship, with three masts, eight lift tanks, four balloons, and six airscrews. Her two full gun decks carried twenty twenty-four-pound cannons, thirty eighteen-pound cannons, and twenty nine-pound cannons, as well as thirty swivel guns on the main deck. She was a ship designed for war, not for the comfort of those who sailed her.

Having finished his egg, Henry left the past to return to the present. "If all these fanciful stories about Prince Tom did was to increase the circulation of this rag, I would not mind. But these stories are doing considerable harm, not the least of which is forcing you to sit on a bed with your chin on your knees."

Mr. Sloan was understandably mystified. "I am sorry, my lord, but I fail to see the connection between the prince and the bed."

"The reason we are on board Admiral Baker's ship is directly related to this so-called Prince Tom," said Sir Henry. "Her Majesty the queen complained to me that her own son, the *real* crown prince, comes off badly by comparison to the pretender. She ordered me to take His Royal Highness on this voyage in order to show the populace a more heroic aspect to his nature. Thus here we are: I have to play nursemaid to HRH while he is on board the flagship, and we find ourselves in these cramped quarters instead of our usual more commodious accommodations aboard the *Terrapin.*"

The ship heeled, this time in a different direction. The thunder grew louder and the room darkened as clouds rolled across the sky, blotting out the sun.

"I must confess I wondered why His Highness was traveling with us, my lord," said Mr. Sloan, deftly whisking away the empty eggcup and pouring more coffee. Henry kept a firm hold on the coffee cup. "I am sorry to say His Highness does not appear to be enjoying the voyage."

"Poor Jonathan hates sailing the Breath," said Henry. "He was sick as a dog the first two days out. He's being a damn fine sport about it though. He knows what his mother is like when she fusses and fumes. Easier to give way to her fancies, though I'm sure he'd much rather be back home in his library with his books. He's found a new obsession: King James the First. Says he's discovered some old letters or something about the murder of King Oswald that reveal James in an entirely new light."

Mr. Sloan shook his head. "A match to gunpowder, my lord."

"The whole damn powder keg could blow up in our faces," said Henry. "This blasted Prince Tom craze put the idea into Jonathan's head. I warned His Highness to drop the matter, but Jonathan gave me that professorial look of his and said history had maligned his cousin and that it was his duty as a historian to seek the truth. Once HRH has made up his mind to proceed, nothing will budge him. He's like his mother in that regard."

"Perhaps Master Yates might be of assistance in the matter, sir," suggested Mr. Sloan. "Simon could offer his help in the research."

"By God, there's a thought!" said Henry, wiping his lips with his napkin. "Simon could stop His Highness from going off on one of his tangents or, at the very least, keep whatever Jonathan discovers out of the press. I can see the headlines now: 'The Crown Prince of Freya Proves He Has No Claim to Throne.' "

"Let us hope it will not come to that, my lord," said Mr. Sloan.

"We will put our faith in Simon, as always. He did not let me down in the matter of the crystals. He has discovered the formula and knows how to produce them. He only needs access to the Braffan refineries. Once the Braffans grant us that, he is ready to launch into production. Soon the Tears of God will be powering our ships. The navies of other nations—including Rosia—will have to buy the crystals from us, and we will charge them dearly!"

Henry drank his coffee. "Speaking of Braffa and the negotiations, I suppose we had better deal with these dispatches. How old are they?" He eyed the pile of letters and newspapers with a gloomy air.

"Some were delayed more than a fortnight, I fear, my lord," said Mr. Sloan. "The mail packet only just caught up with us."

"One would think we were living back in the Dark Times," said Henry irritably.

"Sadly true, my lord," said Mr. Sloan. "I have placed those I deemed most urgent on top."

He held out a small packet of letters that smelled faintly of lavender. "I thought you would like to read these from your lady wife in private."

Sir Henry Wallace, spymaster, diplomat, assassin, trusted advisor to the queen, member of the Privy Council, and long considered by many to be the most dangerous man in the world, smiled as he took his wife's letters and thrust them into an inner pocket.

He then perused the dispatches. His smile changed to a grimace as he read the first, which was from an agent known simply as "Wickham" living in Stenvillir, the capital of Guundar.

Henry slammed down the coffee cup, spilling the liquid. Mr. Sloan reacted swiftly, jumping off the bed to mop up the coffee before the small flood reached the remaining dispatches.

"The Guundarans are moving on Morsteget!" Sir Henry exclaimed, waving the dispatch. "According to Wickham, their parliament passed a resolution proclaiming Guundar's right to the island and voting to establish a naval base there. Fourteen ships set sail for Morsteget weeks ago and I am just now learning about it! These delays in receiving mail have to end, Mr. Sloan. I am seriously considering employing my own griffin riders."

"The expense, my lord—"

"Hang the expense!" Henry said savagely. Jumping to his feet, he promptly cracked his head on the low ceiling. "Ouch! Bloody hell! No, don't fuss. I am all right, Mr. Sloan. The devil of it is that we cannot stop Guundar from annexing Morsteget and King Ullr knows it."

"As bad as that, my lord?"

"Oh, we will make a fine show of being outraged," said Henry, seething. "The House of Nobles will pass a resolution in parliament, Her Majesty will send a strongly worded protest, and we will boycott Guundaran wine, which is so sweet no one drinks it anyway. But that will be the extent of our fury."

Henry resumed his seat, rubbing his sore head. Lightning illuminated the cabin in the bright purple glow that was the hallmark of the wizard storm: the clash of magic and contramagic. The thunderclap was some time in coming; Henry judged that the storm was going to miss them, probably passing to the north.

"At least I can use this move by King Ullr to impress upon the Braffan council that Guundar is a dangerous ally. He has gobbled up this valuable island and has his eye on the Braffa homeland," Henry said. "I wonder if those damn Guundaran ships are still skulking about the coastline."

He sifted through the pile of documents, picked up another dispatch, this one from his agent in Braffa, and swiftly read through it. "The two Guundar ships remain in port in the Braffan capital. The Rosian ships have departed. Not surprising. King Renaud is planning to turn his attention to the pirates in the Aligoes. And speaking of the Aligoes, make a note that I need to speak to Alan about finding a privateer to take his place, since he has quit the trade and become respectable."

Mr. Sloan made the notation with a smile. After years serving his country as a privateer, Captain Northrop had finally been granted his dearest wish: a commission in the Royal Navy.

"But what to do about Guundar?" Henry muttered, returning to his original problem. "I made a mistake advising the queen to request King Ullr's help in freeing the Braffan refineries from the Bottom Dwellers. We have given that minor despot delusions of grandeur."

"You had no choice, my lord," said Mr. Sloan in soothing tones. "You could not allow the Bottom Dwellers to continue to hold those refineries and after the war, neither the Freyan forces nor those of the Rosians were strong enough to oust them."

"You are right, of course, Mr. Sloan," said Henry. "Thank God for Simon and the crystals. Without him Freya would be in dire straits."

He sifted through the dispatches. "I suppose we must let King Ullr have his little island, at least for the time being. Our people will grouse, but once we have this treaty with Braffa and we put the crystals into production, money will flow into the royal coffers, our economy will improve, and our people will forget about Guundar and continue to waste their time reading about the fictional exploits of Prince Tom."

"Might I play devil's advocate, my lord?" Mr. Sloan asked.

"One of the many reasons you are in my employ, Mr. Sloan. Please, do your damnedest."

Mr. Sloan smiled. "If we make a secret treaty with Braffa to produce the crystals, won't we be breaking the Braffan Neutrality Pact?"

"Not so much a break as a hairline fracture, Mr. Sloan," said Henry. "The other signatories won't like it, but if we keep the agreement secret until the crystals are ready to come to market, it will be too late for them to protest."

The two continued to work their way through the dispatches and letters. Henry longed to read the letters from his wife, to hear about young Henry and his recent exploits, but duty called and he forced himself to concentrate on official business. Mr. Sloan handed him a letter from his rival spymaster, the Countess de Marjolaine of Rosia, ostensibly written to the gamekeeper on her estate. One of Henry's agents in Rosia had intercepted the letter, and Henry was trying to figure out if the missive was in fact to her gamekeeper and did in fact refer to poachers or if it was a message of a more sinister nature to someone with the code name "Gamekeeper."

Henry had long suspected the Rosians of supporting the Marchioness of Cavanaugh in her ridiculous attempts to make her son—the Prince Tom of whom the newspapers were so enamored—king of Freya. King Renaud of Rosia had said publicly that Rosia had no business meddling in Freyan affairs, but Henry had discovered that the Rosians were privately funding the prince's cause, hoping to destabilize the Freyan monarchy.

Henry was interrupted in his code-breaking by a stentorian bellow from the deck above. Henry raised his head.

"Was that Randolph shouting for me? What the devil—"

He could hear drums beating to quarters, feet pounding on the deck above, men running to their stations. The next moment someone was frantically pounding on the door. Mr. Sloan opened the door to find a breathless midshipman.

"The admiral's compliments, my lord; you're wanted on deck."

Henry and Mr. Sloan exchanged alarmed glances. Admiral Baker was known by the men who served under him as "Old Doom and Gloom" for his pessimistic outlook on life. He also was known to keep a cool head in a crisis.

"Randolph would not bellow without cause. This does not bode well," said Henry.

Mr. Sloan assisted Henry with his coat. Henry slipped his arms into the tailored, dark blue wool frock coat, which he wore over a blue waistcoat and white shirt. He grabbed his tricorn as he was leaving and firmly clamped it on his head, mindful of the strong wind gusts.

Mr. Sloan followed. The private secretary wore the somber, dark, buttoned-up, high-collared coat preferred by those who observed the conservative beliefs of the Fundamentalists. He then checked to make certain his pistol was loaded. Having served as a marine in the Royal Navy, Franklin Sloan was well aware of the dangers of sailing the Breath.

When the two arrived on deck, Mr. Sloan remained discreetly in the background, while Henry advanced to join the admiral, the ship's captain, and His Royal Highness on the quarterdeck. None of them immediately noticed Henry. The captain and the admiral were both focusing their spyglasses on the distant shore. Crown Prince Jonathan stood nearby, muffled in a long boat cloak that was whipping in the wind. His face, visible above the tall, turned-up collar, was tinged with green.

Henry bowed to the prince, then glanced at the sky. Clouds roiled overhead, gray and ominous and flickering with purple lightning. A smattering of rain was falling, but he could see that the worst of the storm was, as he had thought, heading north, bearing down on the Braffan city of Port Vrijheid.

He cast a look around the horizon. From the ominous tone of Randolph's bellow and now the sounds of guns being run out, he expected nothing less than a Rosian man-of-war bearing down on them. The only other ship in sight was their own escort, the *Terrapin*.

Henry looked toward Port Vrijheid. The city appeared quite peaceful. No pirate ships attacking, no thundering of cannon fire, no smoke billowing into the air. The port was almost empty, but that was not unusual. Prior to the Bottom Dweller War, he would have seen the large freighters that carried the liquid form of the magical Breath setting out for various parts of the world. Only a few small merchant ships were in port today and none of the freighters, for the refineries had suffered severe damage during the war and were still being rebuilt.

Henry wanted to go speak to Randolph, to find out the nature of the emergency. Protocol demanded that he first greet the prince, however.

Jonathan appeared relieved to see him, for he gave Henry a faint smile and a nod.

Jonathan, Crown Prince of Freya, was twenty-two years old, was married, and had done his duty by already producing an heir. The only living child of Queen Mary of Chessington, the prince was an affable, serious-minded young man far more suited to a career as university professor than future monarch.

Passionately fond of history, Jonathan had even written a book, titled *The Six Sigils of Magic as the Foundation Blocks of the Sunlit Empire,* much to the chagrin of his mother. Queen Mary had never read a book in her life and seemed to feel there was something plebeian about writing one, rather as if her son had taken up bricklaying.

The queen was an active woman, fond of shooting grouse and chasing foxes. She found it difficult to understand a son who would rather read in the library than go galloping about the countryside.

The ship lurched at that moment, causing the prince to hurriedly grab hold of a mast.

"How are you feeling, Your Highness?" Henry asked.

"A bit queasy," Jonathan replied with his customary frankness. "Never been in a wizard storm out in the Breath. Damn fine sight. Wouldn't have missed it. Don't fret over me, Sir Henry. I believe the admiral needs you. Trouble of some sort."

Henry bowed and hurried over to join his friend.

"What's going on, Randolph?" Henry asked. "Judging by your bellow, I thought we were sinking with all hands."

In answer, Randolph took the spyglass from his eye and thrust it at Henry.

Randolph Baker had never been handsome, and his bald head and florid face were not improved by scars from burns he had suffered during the war, when he had dragged a burning sail off one of his officers. His face was redder than usual, verging on purple; his perpetual scowl was grimmer and deeper.

Henry put the spyglass to his eye. "What am I looking at?"

"You'll see," Randolph growled.

Henry swept the shoreline just north of the port. He suddenly stopped, stared, and then moved the spyglass slowly, concentrating, making certain he was seeing what he feared he was seeing.

"Damnation!" Henry muttered.

He should have been looking at two old-fashioned Guundaran warships, sent to Braffa to try to convince a skeptical world that King Ullr was a leading actor, no longer a spear-carrier. Instead, Henry counted ten ships of the line, six frigates and two massive troop carriers, all in full sail and all flying the blue and gold ensign of Guundar.

A bitter taste filled Henry's mouth, a taste to which he was not accustomed: the taste of defeat. He tried telling himself he and Randolph were both jumping to conclusions, but he knew quite well they weren't.

"Morsteget, my ass!" Henry said. "That was a bloody ruse! Ullr is here to snap up Braffa! Damn and double damn!"

He shut the spyglass with a snap and handed it back to Randolph. The Guundaran ships had sighted the approach of HMS *Valor.* Observing that one of the ships was flying the Freyan royal arms, indicating that royalty was aboard, the Guundaran flagship, the HMS *Prinz Lutzow,* fired a salute.

Henry saw that the *Prinz Lutzow* was also flying the royal arms of Guundar, which meant that some member of their monarchy was on board. He swore beneath his breath. King Ullr, without a doubt. Come to claim his conquest. Randolph had noticed as well.

"I suppose we have to salute the bastard," he said.

"Unfortunately, yes," said Henry.

"Signal from the *Terrapin,* sir!" shouted a midshipman.

"That will be Alan, wanting to know what's going on," Randolph remarked.

The *Terrapin* was raising and lowering signal flags at such a furious rate that the midshipman on board *Valor* responsible for reading them could scarcely keep up.

"What do we tell him?" Randolph shouted as the *Valor* fired her cannons, returning the salute.

A gust of wind almost took off Henry's hat. He grabbed hold of it as the smoke from the cannons blew past.

"*You* tell Alan he is not to start a war," Henry shouted back.

"Must I?" Randolph asked, frowning. "We could sink three of those frigates before they knew what hit them."

"Not even you and Alan can take on the entire Guundaran naval force," said Henry. "We don't want trouble. I will handle this with diplomacy. Once this storm ends, I will go ashore and meet with the Braffan council as planned."

Randolph looked grim. "I'd like to give that bastard Ullr diplomacy—in the form of a broadside!" He glanced sidelong at the prince and lowered his voice. "What about HRH? You were planning on taking him with you."

"To be humiliated? I won't give the Braffans or Ullr the satisfaction," said Henry. "Besides, I still have one card to play—Simon and the crystals.

We know the formula and the Braffans don't. Something may come of that."

"Not bloody likely," Randolph grunted.

"Always the optimist," said Henry.

"Realist, old chap," said Randolph. "Realist."

"I have to tell the prince about the change in plans," said Henry, sighing. "Let me know when the wind has died down and you think it's safe to go ashore."

Randolph nodded and turned back to closely observing the Guundaran ships.

Henry signaled to Mr. Sloan, who had remained discreetly in the background and now advanced to meet him.

"You heard the news, Mr. Sloan?"

"Yes, my lord. Most unfortunate."

"I have been outwitted by King Ullr, a barbarian whose mental processes are taxed by trying to decide what to have for dinner!" Henry said bitterly. "He fooled us into thinking his blasted fleet was sailing to Morsteget, when in reality they were sailing for Braffa. And now I will have to go ashore and meet the old fart and listen to him gloat."

"We *do* have the crystals," said Mr. Sloan.

"That we do, Mr. Sloan. The Tears of God. Tears that are more valuable than diamonds."

"Will I be accompanying Your Lordship?"

"Yes, Mr. Sloan. I'll need you to take notes when I meet with the Braffans. You prepare for the journey. I must go speak to His Highness."

The rain had stopped and the wind had shifted. The storm had passed, though a few ragged clouds still boiled overhead. Henry was crossing the deck when a blinding flash of purple lightning streaked down from the sky, striking so close he could smell the sulfur. The lightning was accompanied by a nearly simultaneous thunderclap and the sickening sound of rending and cracking wood.

The mainsail boom crashed down onto the deck. Prince Jonathan disappeared beneath a tangle of rope, splintered wood, and sailcloth.

TWO

Time distorted for Henry. He watched the broken boom fall, the sails crumple, the rigging twist and cascade downward, all with such agonizing slowness that every moment was imprinted on his brain.

The prince vanished amid the wreckage, and suddenly time accelerated, with subsequent events happening in a confusing blur. The sight of Mr. Sloan rushing past him, shouting for help, jolted Henry to action.

He ran to join Mr. Sloan and the others as they worked frantically to free the prince. Some grabbed axes and knives. Seeing this, Randolph shouted that no one was to start chopping until they knew what had become of the prince, and try to determine his location.

Henry peered through the wreckage and thought he caught a glimpse of the boat cloak the prince had been wearing.

"I see him," Henry cried. "He's not moving. Your Highness! Jonathan!"

Everyone waited in anxious silence. There was no response.

"Clear away this bloody mess!" Randolph ordered, grabbing hold of a length of rope and hauling it off.

They worked feverishly to remove the tangle of sail and rope and splintered wood and eventually found the prince lying beneath the boom, which had fallen across his chest.

Jonathan was unconscious, his face deathly pale and covered with blood. For a terrible moment Henry feared he was dead. The ship's surgeon felt for a pulse and announced that His Highness was alive. The good news caused the sailors to raise a cheer. Randolph summoned the strongest men on board ship, and together they lifted the heavy boom and held it steady until Mr. Sloan, under the surgeon's direction, was able to grasp the prince by the shoulders and gently and carefully drag him to safety.

They placed Prince Jonathan on a litter and carried him to his cabin. Henry stood by, feeling helpless, while the surgeon and his mate stripped off the prince's clothes. Henry noted that the surgeon looked grave as he poked and prodded. The prince had an ugly cut on his head and a large purplish red bruise on his chest.

Completing his examination, the surgeon was more optimistic.

"His Highness is very lucky. He has two broken ribs, but his skull remains intact," the surgeon reported. "His lungs were not affected."

Prince Jonathan regained consciousness moments later, wondering where he was and what had happened. When the surgeon asked him if he could move his feet, the prince obliged.

"No damage to the spine, Your Highness," said the surgeon. "I predict a full and complete recovery. I will give you laudanum for the pain and to help you rest."

"I will remain with His Highness," said Henry.

The surgeon eyed him. "No, you won't, my lord. Not with those hands of yours resembling sides of beef. You come below with me."

Henry looked at his hands and was surprised to find he had ripped most of the skin off his palms, leaving them bloody and raw. He accompanied the surgeon to the sick berth. The surgeon applied a healing ointment, bandaged his hands, and recommended rest and brandy.

Mr. Sloan accompanied Henry to his cabin, then left in pursuit of brandy. He returned to find Henry attempting to change clothes and having a difficult time of it.

"What are you doing, my lord?" Mr. Sloan asked.

"Dressing for my meeting with the Braffan council," said Henry. He scowled at the bandages on his hands, which prevented him from doing the simplest tasks, such as buttoning his trousers.

"Be reasonable, my lord," Mr. Sloan said. "You have missed the meeting which was scheduled for ten of the clock. The time is now almost noon. And the surgeon said—"

"Devil take the surgeon and the clock!" said Henry angrily. "I must speak to the Braffans. Help me on with this blasted shirt and give me some of that brandy."

Mr. Sloan frowned his disapproval, if he didn't speak it. He assisted with the shirt and waistcoat and frock coat, wrapped a boat cloak around Henry's shoulders, then poured some brandy into a tin cup. Henry drank it at a single gulp.

"Have the pinnace waiting for me, Mr. Sloan. I will pay my respects to His Highness and then join you on deck."

Henry found Jonathan sitting up in bed. The prince made light of the accident.

"My own damn fault, really," said Jonathan. "I should have gone below when the storm hit. As it is, the surgeon says I shall be up and about in a few days."

"I am thankful to hear that, Your Highness," said Henry. "With your permission, I would like to proceed to my meeting with the Braffan council. I can remain here, if Your Highness has need of me—"

"No, no, carry on," said Jonathan. "I saw all those Guundaran ships in port. I gather something is amiss."

"Hopefully to be set to rights, Your Highness," Henry replied.

"Do you think the Guundarans are breaking the neutrality pact, Sir Henry?" Jonathan asked, frowning.

"I should not like to venture to say, Your Highness," said Henry.

"But you think it likely," said Jonathan. "Good luck and a safe journey, my lord. Report to me on your return."

Henry bowed and took his leave. He found the crew of the pinnace waiting for him. Mr. Sloan had already boarded, and he assisted Henry to his seat. The boat was small, designed to ferry supplies, crew, and passengers to and from shore. The helmsman inflated the single balloon and then sent magic flowing from the brass helm to the air screws and the lift tanks. The pinnace rose from the deck of the ship with a slight lurch and then sailed toward the pier.

Henry thrust the shock and the upset and the stinging pain of his palms out of his mind. He would need all his faculties to deal with the Braffans. He did not say no, however, when Mr. Sloan offered him another gulp of brandy from a small pocket flask.

As they approached the harbor, Henry saw two people, both of whom he recognized, standing on the pier in the shelter of a boathouse. One was a middle-aged woman in a rain-soaked bonnet. The other was a tall, broad-shouldered man in a military uniform and a plumed gold-braid-trimmed bicorn. They had apparently been about to board a pinnace of their own. Seeing Henry's approach, they had seemingly decided to wait.

"What are those two doing on the dock?" Henry wondered.

"I would hazard a guess that since you did not attend the meeting, they were about to sail to the *Valor* to speak to you," Mr. Sloan suggested. "Do you know them, my lord?"

Henry grunted. "The woman is Frau Aalder, a member of the Braffan council. She was with me at the refinery the day the Bottom Dwellers attacked. She formed a bad opinion of me during that incident—not entirely unwarranted I must confess, given that Alan and I threatened to sink the ship on which she was sailing.

"The tall man with all the medals and gold braid and plumed bicorn is His Majesty, King Ullr Ragnar Amaranthson of Guundar. I have no idea how he came by the medals. As far as I know the man has never seen combat, if you don't count the duels he fought in his youth."

The pinnace docked, the crew lowered the gangplank, and Henry and Mr. Sloan stepped onto the pier. Henry walked across the dock to meet Frau Aalder and the king. Mr. Sloan remained at a distance, yet keeping close enough to hear the conversation. Mr. Sloan could not take notes, for this conversation would be unofficial and off the record. But he had an excellent memory and would make a record of it later.

Henry bowed to the king and gave Frau Aalder a curt nod.

"I apologize for my late arrival," Henry said. "Our ship was struck by lightning with the result that I was unavoidably delayed. We can now proceed—"

Frau Aalder interrupted. "The meeting is over. Ullr and I were coming to tell you. You know Ullr, of course. What the devil did you do to your hands?"

Henry stared at the woman, disgusted at her gauche remarks, and pressed his lips together to keep his rising anger in check. He saw no need to reply. Frau Aalder was considered rude, even by the relatively relaxed mores of the Braffans. King Ullr cast her a glance of disdain and tried to make up for her crudeness.

"We were sailing over to the ship hoping to visit Crown Prince Jonathan," said King Ullr, speaking passable Freyan with a thick Guundaran accent. "We were going to invite His Highness to dine aboard the *Prinz Lutzow* this evening."

"I am certain His Highness would have been glad to come, Your Majesty, but unfortunately the crown prince is indisposed," said Henry.

"I am sorry to hear that," said King Ullr. "Perhaps another time. We wanted to tell His Highness how much we enjoyed reading his book. Perhaps you can pass along—"

"Never mind about books now, Ullr!" said Frau Aalder, who had been impatiently tapping her foot during the niceties. "The council originally agreed to meet with you, Wallace, to discuss Freyan offers of help to rebuild our refineries. Such help is no longer required. Braffa is now a protectorate of Guundar."

"Protectorate!" Henry repeated, amazed.

"As you know, we have no standing military of our own," Frau Aalder continued. "Our nation is too small to fund one. Guundar has offered to establish a naval base on Braffa, and to assist us to build up our defenses. During that time, their ships will patrol the refineries and our coastline."

Henry saw triumph gleam in the king's eyes. In that moment, he would have given a great deal to see a boom fall on King Ullr.

Henry kept his face expressionless as he considered his response. An outward show of anger could reveal Freya's desperate need for the money from the sale of the crystals. To say nothing of the fact that the Freyan navy required the liquid form of the Breath of God in order to condense it down to manufacture the crystals. Anger could hurt his cause. He decided to respond with the sorrow of someone who has been betrayed by a friend.

"I trust the Braffan council realizes, Frau Aalder, that such an agreement breaks the terms of the Braffan Neutrality Pact," Henry said. "Freya made that pact in good faith which, I am sorry to discover, was apparently not shared."

King Ullr gave a derisive snort. "Neutrality pact be damned! You came to Braffa, Sir Henry, hoping to persuade the council to allow *your* government to take over the refineries. We have simply beat you to the punch, as your Freyan pugilists say."

Henry turned a cold eye upon the king. "Since I am not to be permitted to speak to the council, you will never know, will you, Your Majesty?"

Frau Aalder intervened with the exasperated air of a governess separating naughty boys. "As for breaking the neutrality pact, that's rubbish. Guundar is acting to *enforce* the pact that you planned to break. So, you see, Wallace, you have no reason for complaint and so you may inform your queen." Frau Aalder plucked at King Ullr's gold-braided sleeve. "We should leave now, Ullr. I am certain Wallace is eager to return to his ship before another storm hits."

"We see no storm in the offing, madame," said King Ullr. Stepping away from her reach, he walked closer to Henry. "And our business with Sir Henry is not concluded."

"Yes, it is," said Frau Aalder irritably. "I have nothing more to say to Wallace."

"But we do, madame," said King Ullr, fixing her with an imperious stare.

Frau Aalder glowered and fumed, reminding the king that he wanted to make an inspection tour of the refineries. King Ullr was not to be deterred from speaking to Henry, who found this altercation between the two intriguing. Frau Aalder was clearly trying to whisk King Ullr away. Henry wondered why, and the next moment he had his answer.

King Ullr, brushing aside Frau Aalder, drew near Henry until they were practically toe-to-toe, attempting to use his height and bulk to intimidate him. "We have heard rumors that the Braffans developed a crystalline form of the Breath known as the Tears of God. What do you know about such crystals, Sir Henry?"

Before Henry could reply, Frau Aalder literally pushed her way into the conversation, shouldering between the two men. "I have told you, Ullr, that those rumors are completely unfounded."

As she said this, she shot Henry a warning glance from beneath the brim of her bedraggled bonnet and very slightly shook her head, urging him to silence.

Henry responded with a derisive smile, reminding her that he knew the rumors were not all unfounded. Frau Aalder grew grim.

"We did conduct some research," she admitted. "But the experiments failed and the program was halted. No need to ask Wallace. He knows nothing about it. And now we really must leave, Your Majesty. We have that inspection tour scheduled . . ."

King Ullr had seen Henry's smile and was not to be deterred. "Our agents tell us that the Rosians unexpectedly came into possession of several barrels of these crystals that do not exist. I suppose it was a coincidence that the appearance of the crystals in Rosia occurred immediately after you, Sir Henry, and your friend, Captain Stephano de Guichen, visited one of the Braffan refineries. The captain is reputed to have used the crystals to raise an enormous fortress off the ground and sail it Below. And yet you claim to know nothing of any of this."

"I was in Freya at the time, fighting my own battle with the Bottom Dwellers, Your Majesty," said Henry grimly. "As for Captain de Guichen—now the Duke de Bourlet—he is a Rosian and thus no friend of mine. He is, however, a close friend to King Renaud and a hero to the Rosian people."

Henry paused, then added in milder tones, "Perhaps I should remind Your Majesty that King Renaud is a signatory to the Braffan Neutrality Pact and that His Majesty will be extremely displeased to hear of Guundar's interference. The Rosian navy is dependent on the liquid form of the Breath to fuel their ships. I doubt King Renaud will be pleased to hear of this new 'protectorate.' "

"I find it hard to believe that you know nothing about these crystals, Sir Henry," King Ullr insisted stubbornly. "Captain de Guichen could not have flown a massive stone fortress to battle at the bottom of the world without them."

"And I find it hard to believe that you are coming perilously close to calling me a liar, Your Majesty," Henry said angrily.

"Actually, Ullr, you are calling *me* a liar!" said Frau Aalder, glaring at both men. "I told you Wallace knows nothing about the crystals! We are late for our appointment."

Frau Aalder might be rude and crass, but she was also clever, counting on the fact that King Ullr could not afford to offend her, the representative of his new ally. King Ullr realized he had gone too far and he was forced to let the matter drop.

"Forgive me, madame," King Ullr said in frozen tones. "Such was not my intent."

"I should hope not," said Frau Aalder, sniffing. She was actually almost cordial to Henry. "We will be in touch, Wallace. The council knows the importance of the Blood of God to the navies of the world and we hope to resume production as soon as possible and get it out on the market."

"At an exorbitant price, no doubt," said Henry, his lip curling.

"If you find the liquid too expensive, perhaps your navy could go back to sailing using the old-fashioned means," said King Ullr. "Although I doubt even God's Breath could float that monstrosity."

He cast a glance at HMS *Terrapin,* sailing in the Breath alongside the *Valor.* The hull of the *Terrapin* was covered with specially designed magical metal plates that gave the ship her name. Their magic made the ship practically impervious to gunfire, but the sheets of metal were extremely heavy. The "old-fashioned means" to which the king referred were tanks filled with the Breath of God. The magically enhanced gas could not provide the lift needed to keep the *Terrapin* afloat.

Henry was aware he had lost the battle and he could do nothing now except claim his wounded and retire from the field. He could at least fire a final parting shot.

"I will take this news back to Her Majesty," he said. "In the interim, I urge you, Frau Aalder, and the other members of the Braffan council to recall what happened when King Ullr's forebearers took their neighbors 'under protection.' "

King Ullr stiffened, his face flushed an angry red. The ancient Guundarans were reputed to have been barbarians who preyed upon their neighbors, looting, burning, and plundering. The Guundarans had long sought to live down this reputation; King Ullr was so outraged Henry thought the king might actually challenge him to a duel on the spot.

As the king advanced, his hand on the hilt of his sword, a gust of wind left over from the storm chose that moment to carry off the king's tall, plumed bicorn and send it bounding along the pier.

Henry kept a straight face as one of the king's aides ran to fetch the wayward hat, though he did allow his lips to twitch. Frau Aalder was not so kind. She laughed out loud. King Ullr cast Henry a furious glance, turned on his heel with military precision, and, retrieving his hat, thrust it under his arm and angrily stalked off.

Henry removed his own hat for dignity's sake, lest the wind blow it off, too. He joined Mr. Sloan, and the two slowly walked back to the pinnace.

"What did you think, Mr. Sloan?"

"Frau Aalder is an extremely unpleasant woman, my lord," Mr. Sloan replied.

"I wish I'd let the Bottom Dwellers shoot her," Henry muttered. "At least the meeting ended on an amusing note."

"If you are referring to the wind gust carrying off the king's hat, I have always said God is a Freyan, my lord," Mr. Sloan observed.

Henry smiled. "So you have, Mr. Sloan, but that wasn't what I meant."

He paused a short distance from the pinnace and lowered his voice. "The matter of the crystals. Frau Aalder and the council are lying to their new 'protector.' She was there when Captain de Guichen and I seized the crystals. And I am certain Ullr knows she's lying, though he can't prove it."

"Why would the Braffans lie about the crystals, my lord?" Mr. Sloan asked.

"I am wondering that myself," said Henry. "At a guess, I would say they don't want King Ullr to know that the crystals exist. She must know that both we and the Rosians are studying the crystals in our possession, trying to learn how to manufacture them. The Rosians have failed thus far and, from what my agents tell me, they are going to cease working on it in order not to waste any more of the crystals."

"It would seem King Ullr has bought a pig in a poke, my lord."

"I believe you are right, Mr. Sloan. Let us say that we start manufacturing the crystals in Freya. Three crystals can lift a frigate off the ground, replacing several barrels of the liquid form of the Breath. All the navies of the world would flock to purchase crystals from us. The price of the liquid would plummet and Ullr would realize he had made a bad bargain."

Henry was grim. "Unfortunately, to make the crystals, we need the liquid form of the Breath. King Ullr will see to it that we pay through the nose, such that we will not be able to afford to manufacture the crystals. This is a disaster, Mr. Sloan. An unmitigated disaster."

"I am certain you will find a way to remedy the situation, my lord," said Mr. Sloan.

Henry only shook his head and boarded the pinnace.

The journey back to the *Valor* was rough. The gusty winds that had carried off the king's hat blew the pinnace all over the sky and made landing treacherous. The coxswain in charge knew his business, however, and safely brought the boat down onto the deck. Sailors rushed to secure it.

Randolph was on hand to meet them. When he saw Henry, he raised an eyebrow. Henry shook his head, letting him know he had failed. Randolph shrugged. With his customary pessimism, he had been expecting nothing else. The flag captain of the *Valor* ordered the crew to weigh anchor and prepare for return to Freya.

That evening, Captain Alan Northrop of the *Terrapin* sailed to the *Valor* to join his friends for dinner.

Alan, Henry, Randolph, and Simon Yates had been friends for over twenty years, since their days at university. They had called themselves "the Seconds," for they had discovered that each was a second son, meaning their older brothers would inherit the family fortunes, leaving each of the younger brothers to fend for himself.

In their numerous adventures during their university days, Henry had been the cunning schemer, Randolph the dour pragmatist, Simon the swift thinker, Alan the bold, daring rogue. Their friendship had remained strong through the years. Although Simon was not present, being confined to a wheelchair in his eccentric house in Haever, his friends always kept a place for him at the table and drank a toast in his honor.

The three dined in the admiral's spacious cabin in the ship's stern. Conversation was desultory, none of them able to discuss international intrigue in the presence of the servants. Henry had finally found time to read his wife's letters; he recounted a few of young Henry's three-year-old exploits to proud smiles from the "uncles," as his friends considered themselves. After dinner, Randolph dismissed the servants. Mr. Sloan served brandy, cheese, and walnuts, and at last they were able to discuss the day's events.

"How is His Highness?" Alan asked.

"The prince is resting comfortably," Henry reported. Not wanting to risk dropping one of Randolph's fragile crystal snifters with his bandaged hands, he was drinking the brandy from a tin cup.

"Thank God for that," said Alan.

They had drunk the traditional toast to the queen, but now Randolph raised his glass to the prince. "To His Highness. Long may he reign."

"I fear the news isn't all good," Henry said, holding out his mug for a refill. "The surgeon told me privately that he is worried about the ugly bruise on the prince's chest. He fears his heart may be damaged. He detects a slight irregularity in the prince's heartbeat."

"Damn sawbones! Always making a fuss," Randolph said in disgust.

"Of course the prince's heartbeat is irregular. Goddamn boom fell on him! Good stiff drink, that's what he needs. I shall send him a bottle of the '88 port."

"How did the meeting go with the Braffans?" Alan asked, finally asking the question that had been on everyone's mind. "What is Guundar up to?"

Henry gave a morose shake of his head.

"As bad as that," said Alan.

"Worse," said Henry.

He described his meeting with Frau Aalder and King Ullr. "Braffa is now a protectorate of Guundar."

"Protectorate!" Randolph repeated with a bellowing laugh. "Might as well ask the goddamn wolf to protect the goddamn sheep!"

"By God, Henry, Guundar broke the neutrality pact!" Alan exclaimed, flushed with excitement and brandy. "This means war!"

Alan had lost his right hand during a fight with the Bottom Dwellers, when his rifle had exploded after being hit by a blast of contramagic. The loss had not slowed him down, nor did it seem to overly concern him. He had practiced until he could wield a sword and shoot with his left hand almost as well as he had with his right.

Three years since the war ended, Alan was growing bored with peace. Henry suspected his friend missed his days roaming the Breath as a privateer, hoping to snap up an Estaran treasure ship or capture a rich Rosian merchantman.

"Keep your voice down, Alan, for God's sake!" Henry said, annoyed. "Rumors spread like the yellow jack aboard ship! I don't want half the fleet thinking we're going to war."

He tried to set the mug down on the table, but dropped it, spilling brandy. Henry swore, kicked the mug, sending it flying. Mr. Sloan silently retrieved the mug and mopped up the brandy.

Henry muttered an apology, then rose to his feet. "We will talk in the morning."

"Henry, this is *us,*" said Alan earnestly. "You can tell us anything."

"Bloody damn right," said Randolph.

Henry knew he could. He knew he must tell them someday that Freya was teetering on the edge of a financial precipice. But not tonight. His bandages were stiff and uncomfortable, and his hands burned.

"Good night," said Henry.

As he left, he heard Randolph remark, "Poor old Henry. He looks like the goddamn boom fell on *him.*"

Henry gave a bitter smile. In a way, he felt as though it had. A boom by the name of King Ullr.

THREE

Six months after the accident on board the *Valor,* Crown Prince Jonathan was dead.

The royal physician said he died of a bruised heart muscle suffered when the boom struck his chest. To compound the tragedy, the prince's little son and heir died a fortnight later, a victim of the diphtheria epidemic currently sweeping through Haever. The two were buried side by side in a vault in the great cathedral.

The nation of Freya, having lost both heirs to the throne in a span of weeks, was in shock and mourning. Queen Mary was a widow, past the age of childbearing. The tragic double loss meant that suddenly, the line of succession was in serious jeopardy.

Henry recalled terming the Braffan takeover by Guundar a "disaster." He reflected grimly that he had not then known the meaning of that word.

He and his wife, Lady Ann, attended the lavish funeral. Heads of state the world over had come to pay their respects. Among them were King Renaud of Rosia and his sister, the Princess Sophia, who had spent time in Freya following the war as a gesture of friendship between the two nations. King Ullr had come, as had a representative of the Braffan council (though not Frau Aalder, for which Henry was grateful!), as well as the monarchs of both Travia and Estara and a host of princes, nobles, bishops, and foreign dignitaries.

Surrounded by a suffocating mass of humanity, Henry was conscious only of a small white casket and the body of the little prince, looking like a waxen doll. The sight of the dead child, who had been the same age as his own son, badly unnerved Henry. During the service, he went down on his knees to pray to a God in whom he didn't believe to bless and keep his dear boy.

The service was beautiful, sad, and solemn. Henry and his wife escaped as soon as decently possible. They were well aware that with all the dignitaries crowding around her, offering their condolences, Her Majesty would never miss them.

Arriving back home, Henry handed his black top hat and cloak to the footman. His wife removed her black veiled bonnet and her cloak, then rested her black-gloved hand on his arm.

"What a dreadful time this has been," she said. "You look exhausted, my dear. You haven't slept in a week. Shall I have tea served in the drawing room?"

"Always thinking of me, little Mouse," said Henry. "I should be the one worried about you, especially in your condition."

Lady Ann smiled and placed her hand on her swollen belly. She was six months pregnant with their second child.

"You must be upset," Henry continued, taking her hand. "You and the prince were cousins. Her Majesty told me you two played together as children."

His wife was close to the same age as the dead prince; she had only just turned twenty. He was in his forties and he could still not believe his good fortune in obtaining such a woman as his wife. The queen had given Lady Ann to Henry in marriage as a reward for his loyal service, making him Earl of Staffordshire. He had been astonished beyond belief to learn that in addition to the money and the title and the manor house, she brought him love.

Ann was pale and slender, with large eyes and brown hair. The queen had deemed her niece "a sweet child, but mousy," and "Mouse" had become Henry's pet name for her. Twenty-five years older than his wife, he marveled every day that she should have fallen in love with him and, more astonishing, that he—hard-bitten and cynical—had fallen in love with her.

"Jonathan was never one for childish games," said Ann, making a face. "All we ever did together was play checkers. He would very politely beat me and then leave to go read a book. I never really minded, though. He had the most wonderful rocking horse. I loved riding it. He kept it for little

Charlie. I suppose it had to be burned with all the rest of his toys, poor lamb."

Ann wiped her eyes with her handkerchief. Henry gripped her hand.

"Our son is well, isn't he?" he said with a catch in his voice. "No sign of contagion."

"He is fine," Ann replied with a reassuring smile. "We are taking every precaution. Nurse keeps him indoors, away from other children. He doesn't like being cooped up, though, and I'm afraid he's been very naughty. He jabbed one of the maids in the leg with that wooden sword Captain Northrop gave him. Hal told her he was a pirate and he was going to make her eat macaroons."

"Eat macaroons?" Henry repeated, mystified.

"Nurse and I believe he meant 'marooned,' " said Ann. "Now don't you laugh, Henry! You and Captain Northrop encourage him to play pirates, but he cannot be allowed to stab the servants."

"No, no, of course not," said Henry hurriedly. "I will speak to him. And now I'm going to change my clothes. You should rest and put your feet up."

He kissed her and hastened upstairs to his dressing room. He did not employ a valet, knowing better than most that servants make excellent spies. Shutting the door, Henry sank down in the chair and let his head fall into his hands. His laughter at his son's exploits had brought him near to tears.

Henry was, as Ann had said, exhausted. During the last month of the prince's illness, Henry had spent much of the time at the palace, dealing with physicians and the Privy Council and attempting to calm the fears of the House of Nobles. After Prince Jonathan's death, Henry had been obliged to assist in planning the elaborate funeral and to urge the grief-stricken queen to make a decision about the heir to the throne. Queen Mary refused to even discuss the matter.

Henry rose, splashed cold water on his face, changed his clothes, and joined his wife in the drawing room. Ann poured tea and, at Henry's request, told Nurse to bring young master Hal to visit his parents. Remembering the small white casket, Henry clasped his son in his arms so tightly that Hal protested.

"Papa, stop! You're squishing me!"

Henry released the child and studied him anxiously. Hal did look healthy. No sign of a runny nose or fever, the early symptoms of the disease known as the "Child's Strangler," so named for the membrane that grew in the throat, causing children to suffocate.

"Henry, you promised you would speak to him," said Ann with a reproving look.

"I did, indeed." Henry sat down in a chair, placed his son on his knee, and undertook to lecture him. "Now, young man, I have received a report that you stabbed one of the maids—"

"Polly," said his wife.

"You stabbed Polly with your toy sword," Henry continued, trying to sound and look stern. "That was very wrong of you, Hal. A gentleman respects his servants. He does not mistreat them."

"But Polly wasn't a servant, Papa," Hal argued. "We were playing pirate. I was Captain Alan and Polly was a dirty Rosian dog."

Henry dared not look at his wife or he would have disgraced himself by bursting into laughter. Nurse was standing by, looking grim, and he recalled a rainy afternoon when she had caught him and Alan and young Master Hal playing "pirate" in the nursery.

He explained to his son that the Rosians were now their friends and that it was not polite to refer to anyone by such a derogatory appellation as "dirty Rosian dog."

Hal listened to the lecture with wide, solemn eyes and then said, "Can I have my sword back, Papa? Nurse took it away from me."

"I think the sword should remain with Nurse for a time," Henry said, trying to sound severe and probably failing, for his wife's lips were twitching.

Young Master Hal gave a philosophical shrug. "That's all right, Papa. Captain Alan promised next time he'd bring me a pistol."

"My dear!" exclaimed his wife, casting Henry a look of alarm, while Nurse's eyebrows shot up to the edge of her white cap. Henry would have to speak to Alan. Meanwhile, he decided it was time for diversionary tactics.

"Would you like one of these little tea cakes, son," said Henry, presenting Hal with a treat from the tea cart.

This indulgence proved too much for Nurse, who advanced to rescue her charge. Seeing her coming, Hal crammed the small cake into his mouth before she could snatch it away.

"Such rich food before bed will give him nightmares, Your Lordship. Now, Master Henry, tell your mama and papa good night."

Hal presented his mother with a sugary kiss, and Nurse carried him off, scattering crumbs and waving to his father over her shoulder.

Once Henry was certain his son could not hear, he threw back his head and roared with laughter.

"Dirty Rosian dog! Ha-ha! Wait until I tell Alan!"

"I am glad to see you more cheerful, my love," said Ann.

"I must either laugh or break down and cry," Henry replied, chuckling and wiping his eyes.

He picked up the newspaper, took one look at the hysterical headline ranting over the succession, and threw the paper to the floor. Flinging himself into his chair, he closed his eyes with a sigh.

Ann laid down her embroidery and came over to sit in his lap, resting her head on his shoulder. He put his arm around her and drew her close.

"Aren't you afraid the servants will see us?" Henry asked. "A husband and wife aren't supposed to be in love—at least not with each other."

"The servants won't come until I ring to take the tea tray," Ann replied. She patted her belly. "And as for showing that I love you, I'm afraid we have let that particular cat out of the bag."

Henry smiled, but his smile didn't last. "I am glad to have a chance to talk. I have been thinking of giving Her Majesty my resignation."

"Henry!" Ann sat up straight to stare at him. "You're not serious!"

"I am very serious, my dear," Henry replied. "We could move away from the city with its plagues and bad air and assassins, retire to our country estate in Staffordshire. You could go about the tenants with a little basket, doing good works. I could be a country squire and raise prize hogs. I think I would like that. Pigs are quite intelligent creatures. Far smarter than humans."

"There, I knew you weren't serious," said Ann, snuggling back down with him.

"I am, though not perhaps about the hogs. I am serious about a life where I could be home with my family at night. Hal could run about the lawn with a huge, slobbering dog. Our daughter will have her own pony to ride."

"First, we do not know that we are having a daughter. Second, our country house also came under attack from assassins, which makes the country just as dangerous as the city. Third, you would die of boredom and leave me a widow."

Henry shook his head, not convinced.

Ann smoothed the frown lines from his brow with her fingers. "Tell me what this is about, Henry. Is my aunt being more difficult than usual?"

"I have been trying to talk to Her Majesty about the line of the succession," said Henry. "She *must* make her wishes known, although I fear her silence on the subject is partly my fault. When she did finally deign to discuss it with me, she hinted that she was thinking of naming her younger sister, Elinor, her successor. I was so shocked she would even consider that horrible woman that I may have overreacted."

"I know I am also on the list," said Ann. "But I always forget exactly where. Far down, I hope."

"Very far down," said Henry. "Your father and his brother are sons of the late King Godfrey, which makes them Mary's half brothers. But they both carry the 'bar sinister' so they can't inherit. Damn Godfrey and his philandering. This is all his fault. And to think I saved his life when I was young!"

"Godfrey was hopelessly in love with Lady Honoria, so my father always told me," said Ann. "She was the love of his life."

"Godfrey was fortunate the lady was married and that her husband was a fool. As it was, he had to pay an enormous sum to hush up the scandal. I've always stated love was the ruin of a man," Henry added, shaking his head in mock sorrow.

Ann punished him by kissing him on his long nose and then slid off his lap. Returning decorously to her chair, she rang for the servants to remove the tea tray. After the servants left, Henry drew his chair close to hers to continue their conversation, while Ann took up her embroidery.

"Godfrey made matters worse by claiming your father and his brother as his sons," said Henry. "He gave them titles, land, et cetera. Your uncle, Hugh, expected the throne and he was furious when Godfrey named his legitimate daughter, your aunt, as his heir."

"My father said Godfrey couldn't do anything else," said Ann. "Mary had the support of the most powerful nobles. He and Hugh did not."

Henry was silent, remembering. Seventeen years ago, he had been the one to make certain Mary had the support of the key members of the House of Nobles. He had been the one to make it clear to the dying Godfrey that in order to ensure the stability of the realm, he had to name Mary, not his bastard son, as his heir.

Henry had been twenty-eight years old then and he had discovered the power of secrets. He had learned how to ferret them out, how to keep them, how to use them to his advantage and the advantage of those whom he served.

Henry had ostensibly worked in the Foreign Office. His true job was spymaster to the king. Ever since he and his friends had helped thwart an assassination attempt against Godfrey when he was crown prince, Henry had handled various matters of a delicate nature, including concealing Godfrey's secret liaisons with his mistress, Lady Honoria.

Godfrey had ruled only a few years when the physicians told the king that there was nothing more they could do to treat the malignant growth in his stomach and that he had only weeks to live. Henry had coolly considered where to place his allegiance. He could have aligned himself with the bastard, Hugh, and his faction, for Henry knew that Godfrey wanted to name his son as his heir. Or Henry could side with Princess Mary.

Henry recalled discussing the matter with Alan, Simon, and Randolph.

"My loyalty is first and foremost to Freya," Henry had told them. "Mary is the legitimate heir. Hugh is a bastard. If Godfrey were to name Hugh his heir, we would be embroiled in civil war. Our enemies would like nothing better."

Ann nudged his foot with her own.

"My dear, you have wandered off and left me," she said.

Henry smiled. "Sorry, my love. I was woolgathering."

"I was saying that it was too bad my father is the younger son. He would make a good king," said Ann.

"He would, in fact," said Henry. "Sadly, your father would never consider it. Jeffrey is devoted to the Reformed Church and he has enough to do as bishop, trying to save the Church from the scandal following the war and the growing popularity of the Fundamentalists."

"Why don't you like Uncle Hugh? He is a good man, I believe," said Ann, frowning over her embroidery, counting her stitches. "Is it because he's an ironmonger or something like that?"

"An ironmonger sells kettles and horseshoes. Your uncle owns a coal mine and a steel mill," Henry said. "I have no objection to his occupation. I don't like him because he is brash and insolent and has radical ideas, such as abolishing the House of Nobles—"

"No! Truly?" Ann regarded him with consternation.

"That said, I may be forced to support him," said Henry, adding with a grimace, "I prefer Hugh to the devout Elinor and her Rosian husband. I can manage Hugh. I could do nothing with Elinor."

"My aunt will never agree to name Hugh her heir," said Ann, shaking her head. "She dislikes him *and* my father."

"Mary and her sister never forgave them for being born," said Henry drily. "I suppose that is natural. Godfrey made it clear he loved his bastard sons more than he did his legitimate daughters. Poor Godfrey. He may have been a good king, but he was not a very good man."

Ann was shocked. "Henry, don't say such things. It's . . . sacrilegious. Godfrey was God's anointed."

Henry wisely kept silent. Ann had been raised in a pious household, her father being the Bishop of Freya. He had taught his children to believe that monarchs derived the right to rule directly from God and therefore were subject to no authority except God's.

Henry did not believe in the divine right of kings, but he did believe that a strong monarchy overseen by the nobility was the best form of government. He had witnessed firsthand the chaos that resulted when ordinary citizens, such as Frau Aalder, tried to rule a nation.

Ann was regarding him with an anxious air, undoubtedly convinced he was going straight to hell. Henry assumed he probably was, but he doubted it would be for thinking that kings and queens were human, could make mistakes like other mortals.

Knowing he had upset his wife, Henry looked for some way to make amends. He reached into her work basket and drew out a folded section of the *Haever Gazette* he had noticed hidden under several skeins of yarn.

"Ah, now I understand," said Henry, indicating the article on the fold. "My wife is no doubt going to advance the claims of the dashing Prince Tom who believes himself to be divinely chosen to rule Freya."

"I would do no such thing, Henry!" Ann protested. "How can you think that of me? This Prince Tom comes from a family of traitors. His forebearer James stole poor King Oswald's throne, then murdered him and his sons!"

"King Oswald's own claim to the throne was not the strongest," Henry reflected. "His grandfather, Oswald the First, stole the throne from his older half brother, Frederick—the true and rightful king. Oswald did not murder his half brother, but he did lock him up in some godforsaken castle for the rest of his life. Thus, I suppose one could say Oswald the First began this trouble by deposing an anointed king. Perhaps God is punishing us by sending us Prince Tom."

His wife lowered her embroidery to her lap and turned to her husband with a troubled look. Seeing him grinning, she relaxed. "Henry, you have been teasing me."

"Just a trifle, my dear," he admitted. "But if you don't approve of Prince Tom, why have you been reading about him?"

"Not him," said Ann. Blushing deeply, she took the paper and turned it over to indicate another story on the other side. "I have been reading 'The Adventures of Captain Kate and Her Dragon Corsairs.' "

"Subtitled 'The Tales of a Female Buccaneer' by Miss Amelia Nettleship," said Henry, glancing at the story with a smile.

"Kate has such wonderful adventures, Henry, and she is so bold and free and not afraid of anything," said Ann, her eyes shining with enthusiasm. "Lady Rebecca introduced me to the stories. All my friends talk about Captain Kate far more than Prince Tom."

Henry read a passage aloud. " 'Captain Kate shook back her beautiful mass of shimmering gold hair, drew her cutlass and leaped onto the deck of the Rosian warship. Pointing her cutlass at the throat of the cowering Rosian captain, she shouted, "Surrender or die, you scurvy dog!" ' "

Henry shook his head in mock sorrow. "I see how it is. The day will come when Nurse will be devastated to inform me that my wife stabbed Polly with a sword and ran off to become a pirate."

"A corsair, my dear," said Ann. "'Captain Kate and Her Dragon Corsairs.' Kate is a real person and her adventures are true. She lives in the Aligoes. I wonder if Captain Northrop knows her? I will have to ask him the next time he visits."

"And Alan and I are blamed for being a bad influence on our son!" Henry said, heaving a deep sigh.

"I will make you a bargain, Henry," said Ann. "I will not run away to be a pirate if you will not resign. My aunt needs you."

"No prize hogs?" Henry asked.

"No hogs of any sort," said Ann firmly.

"Very well, my dear," said Henry. "I will not resign. And you will not join Captain Kate's bloodthirsty crew."

Ann laughed. She looked so charming when she laughed that Henry was obliged to kiss her, and for a time he was able to forget about the cares of state.

He kept the newspaper, however, folding it and tucking it into his coat pocket when Ann wasn't looking. She had given him an idea.

FOUR

Captain Kate edged her way among the rocks and boulders, careful where she put her feet, for she was perilously close to the edge of a cliff. The undergrowth was tangled, wet, and slippery and she had to be mindful of rockslides. Edging her way as near the edge as she felt was safe, she stopped to survey her surroundings, to see if she had missed anything worth taking.

She had received a report that a Travian merchant ship had been caught in a wizard storm and sunk. Some of the crew had managed to escape in lifeboats and reported hearing sounds of a crash, which meant that the ship had likely slammed into the side of Mount Kaius, one of the six mountains in the Aligoes. Kate and her crew of "wreckers," as they were known, had been searching for the valuable wreck for a week, ever since they'd heard about the sinking.

Kate had an advantage other wreckers did not. She had a dragon. Her friend Dalgren could fly beneath the Breath to search the Aligoes Islands floating in the Deep Breath—a chill, damp, and fog-bound realm beneath the surface of the Breath.

The Aligoes consisted of a thousand islands or more, clustered together, and six mountains, known as the Six Old Men, whose peaks thrust up above the Breath and thus were often mistaken for islands. The Aligoes were a treasure trove of natural resources, from indigo and logwood to sugarcane and cotton. Every major nation on Aeronne had staked out a claim to one or more of the larger islands, founding cities and establishing lucrative trade routes.

Merchant ships from all over the world passed through one of the Aligoes' two major channels. Although the channels provided the fastest means of travel, they were unfortunately subject to an odd natural phenomenon known as "tides," because the magic of the Breath ebbed and flowed much like tides in an inland ocean. During ebb tide, the magic decreased to the point where a ship could be in danger of sinking. During high tide, the magic increased, touching off violent wizard storms that—ironically—could also sink a ship.

Shipwrecks were therefore not uncommon and, by the international Law of Finds, a ship abandoned by the crew became the property of anyone who managed to find the wreck.

Katherine Gascoyne-Fitzmaurice, known to her friends and crew as Captain Kate, had loftier ambitions, but for now she was a wrecker. It was a difficult and dangerous job, and often thankless, too, for wreckers had the reputation of being little more than scavengers.

Ships generally crashed on islands below the Breath, which meant Kate had to contend with the cold and the fog and the damp, all the while crawling among wreckage that might be, like today's wreck, teetering precariously on the edge of a cliff.

And while Kate hoped for the day she would discover the wreck of an Estaran treasure ship packed to the bilge with gold and jewels, she was far more likely to find cargo such as she had found today: barrel hoops, shovels, a cask of iron nails, and rotted bags of rice.

Shivering in her thick peacoat, Kate pulled her stocking cap down more closely about her ears. She envied Marco and her crew, who had already returned to the ship. The *Barwich Rose* rode at anchor, moored to two mahogany trees on an island far above. Her crew would be sweltering in the heat of an Aligoes afternoon, while she was down here in the Deep Breath, freezing in the cold and the damp.

"Akiel's magic spell must be starting to wear off," Kate muttered.

She reached into a pocket of the peacoat and drew out a timepiece she had found on a corpse in one of the wrecks. She should probably have felt guilty about robbing the dead. Her lady mother would have been horrified. Even her father, Morgan, would have been shocked. Kate didn't have the luxury of sentimentality. The dead had no use for rings or watches and she did.

They had been down here since dawn. Kate decided that she had found everything worth finding and began to climb back up the steep hill, crawling among the broken planks, splintered masts, and tangled rigging.

"Dalgren!" Kate shouted, waving her arms to draw the dragon's attention as he circled overhead. "I need you to haul up this lift tank!"

Dalgren flew closer, saw the lift tank, and gave a disdainful snort. He could see that the lift tank was beyond repair. Dented and battered, the tank would leak lift gas like a sieve.

"Are you sure you want that piece of junk?" the dragon asked.

"I can sell it for scrap," said Kate. "Take it to the ship, then come back. I have one more thing for you to carry."

Dalgren scooped up the lift tank in one of his left front foreclaws. He rarely used the right leg. A member of the famed Dragon Brigade, he had been hit by cannon fire during the Battle of the Royal Sail, shattering his shoulder joint. Dragons used their own magic to heal themselves, but for some reason, Dalgren's wound had not healed properly. His right foreleg hung at an odd angle to his body.

The right leg worked as well as the left. Dalgren had no difficulty leaping into the air to take flight or walking on it. He claimed his right leg was weaker, but Kate told him that was because he favored it. The right leg would grow stronger if he would only exercise it. Dalgren refused. He was a noble dragon from the Dragon Duchies in Rosia and was sensitive about his appearance. He was embarrassed when he walked on his leg, believing he looked awkward and ungainly.

"As if I were eight hundred years old," he would grumble.

Kate hadn't been able to argue with him on that point. She hadn't given up scolding him, either.

Dalgren disappeared in the mists as he flew the lift tank to the *Barwich Rose*.

Kate shivered again and turned up the collar on the peacoat to stop the chill from flowing down her back. She had dressed in boy's clothes when she was a girl, and she still adopted men's clothing, finding it far more comfortable and utilitarian. Skirts and petticoats were not suitable for crawling among wreckage and debris. She particularly favored the loose, baggy trousers sailors termed "slops," adding a touch of color with a red sash and red kerchief around her neck, blue calico shirt and blue knit cap. She wore men's boots and thick wool stockings, and carried a cutlass on a leather baldric slung over her shoulder.

Both cutlass and baldric had belonged to her father and neither was in very good shape. She used the cutlass for chopping down vegetation, slicing through rigging, and occasionally for defending a find against fellow wreckers.

Dim gray sunlight filtered through the mists. Overall she was pleased with the day's work. She and her crew had salvaged what remained of the cargo, which wasn't much. When the ship crashed, it had broken apart and a good portion of the hull had tumbled over the cliff, taking most of the cargo with it.

Kate would make more money off the carcass of the ship itself, selling the scrap at the auction in Wellinsport. Balloon silk, wood planks from the hull and deck, sailcloth, a few spars that hadn't been smashed to splinters, and pots and pans from the galley would fetch a fair price and would, as her mother was wont to say, "keep body and soul together" for a time yet.

Kate's best find was a brass helm. It was smeared with blood, but mostly undamaged, having sustained only a few dents in the fall. Kate hadn't had time to test the magic yet, but she was hopeful that the constructs on the helm were still able to function.

The helm was a large square brass tablet engraved with complex magical constructs that sent magical energy to the air screws that steered the ship and to the lift tanks filled with the Breath of God. Although the Breath itself was magical, the small quantities in the lift tanks required magical "sparks" to generate enough lift to float a ship. The liquid form of the Breath, known as the Tears of God, was more powerful, but the cost was far more dear. Few could afford it.

Kate crouched down beside the helm, studying it and thinking back to the first lessons Olaf had given her in using the helm's magic. She had been eight years old and needed to stand on a crate to reach it.

Kate took off the red kerchief she wore around her neck and used it clean off the worst of the blood, then wadded up the kerchief and stuffed it in her pocket. She reached out to touch the central construct. Before she could even bring her fingers close, some unseen force struck her hand, knocking it aside.

"What the hell?" Kate frowned down at the helm.

The magic must be malfunctioning, probably owing to the wizard storm. She had never heard of such storms disrupting the magic on a ship's helm, but then she wasn't a magical scholar. Given that wizard storms were created by the magic of the Breath running amok, she supposed such disruption could be possible. She tried again to touch the construct.

The force that struck her this time was stronger.

"Damnation!" Kate swore. "Akiel! I need you!"

She stood up, looking for him. He was here on the island somewhere, but she had lost sight of him in the mists. She heard his heavy footfalls before she saw him, seeming to swim his way out of the mist.

Akiel was about thirty, a big man, tall and muscular with skin the color of warm dark rum and brown eyes. He came from Bround, but had moved to Freya when he was older to ply his trade: back-alley prizefighting.

He had fled Freya because he had killed a man, or so he had told Kate when he signed on to the *Barwich Rose.*

"I think you should know the truth about me, mum," Akiel had said. "I did not mean to kill. He was my opponent in a fight and he was winning. My manager had wagered a lot of money and he told me to use my magic to beat him. I only meant to knock the man down, but sadly I killed him."

"Your magic killed him?" Kate had asked.

"No, mum," Akiel had said patiently. "My fist killed him. Spirit magic does not kill."

"Spirit magic," Kate had repeated, frowning. "That's also known as dark magic and that is illegal."

"My magic is not dark. It is called so by people who are ignorant—no offense, mum. In fact, I believe I can use my spirit magic to help you with the wrecking. I can cast a spell that will keep you warm, let you work longer in the Deep Breath."

"You don't have to sacrifice anyone to do it," Kate had asked. "Not like blood magic?"

"No, mum," Akiel had replied with a smile, and so Kate had hired him.

"I found two bodies, mum," Akiel reported as he came up to where she was standing.

"I thought I heard you talking to someone," Kate said, frowning down at the helm. "What do you and the dead find to talk about anyway?"

"Sometimes spirits are confused by the sudden change in their situation. For some, death comes as a shock and they do not know what to do or where to go. I give them advice, but only if they ask. Some of the dead do not like to be disturbed. They consider it an imposition."

Kate had seen death enough in her twenty-four years to know that dead meant dead: cold, stiff, silent. She changed the subject.

"You're a crafter, Akiel, albeit a strange one. I need your advice. Something is wrong with the magic on this helm. I've never seen the like. Whenever I try to touch it . . . this happens."

Kate demonstrated, placing her hand near the central construct engraved into the brass. As before, something seemed to strike her hand away.

"See there?" Kate said, exasperated. "You try it, see what happens."

Akiel gently touched the helm.

"I do not need to try it, mum," he said. "I know what is wrong. The spirit of the captain is guarding his ship."

Kate started to laugh; then she saw he was serious.

"Oh, come, now!" Kate protested. "The magical construct has been damaged. I just need to know how to fix it."

"You see the blood on the helm," Akiel said, pointing to the red smears that remained. "That is the captain's blood. He did not leave his ship with the rest of his crew. He stayed with her until she crashed. He must have loved her very much."

Kate gazed at the blood splotches and pictured herself clinging to that helm, fighting to the end to save her ship. The *Barwich Rose* was her dearest possession. She had been raised on the ship. The *Rose* was all she owned, as perhaps this ship was all this captain had owned. She accorded him a moment of silent respect.

"But you are gone now, Captain," Kate told him. "And I need this helm."

"You plan to sell it to pay off your debt to that bad man," said Akiel in an accusatory tone.

"No," said Kate. "I'll find some other way to pay Greenstreet."

She didn't really believe in what she was about to say, but she was desperate. "Akiel, could you use your magic to . . . uh . . . talk to the captain? Tell him I'm going to keep his helm. I'm not going to sell it. I'm going to use it in my own ship."

"That old derelict you are trying to restore, mum?" Akiel asked, frowning.

"She isn't a derelict!" Kate retorted, annoyed. "Just tell the captain what I said. And make it quick. We've been down here all day. I'm tired and I'm hungry and your warming spell is starting to wear off. I can't feel my toes."

"I will try, mum," said Akiel. "Did you find the body?"

Kate shook her head. "The helm broke off from the base. I think the captain's body must have gone over the edge of the cliff with the rest of the ship."

"That will be a more difficult task," said Akiel. "I will have to cast a very powerful spell. You should keep your distance, but stay nearby, in case the captain has any questions."

Kate rolled her eyes and obligingly backed off a short distance, thankful Olaf couldn't see her. He would be scandalized. Jamming her hands into her pockets, she stood shivering and stomping her feet, trying to get some warmth into her toes.

Akiel drew out the stub of candle from the pocket of his peacoat. Pinching the wick between his thumb and forefinger, he began to sing in a deep, gruff voice. Kate spoke a smattering of most languages of the world. She couldn't understand this one. When Akiel let go, a flame appeared. He held the candle over the helm, letting some of the wax drip onto it; then he placed the candle firmly in the wax.

He gently cupped his left hand over a clump of grass and weeds, not harming them, but simply touching them. He thrust his right index finger directly into the flame of the candle and held it steady.

Kate gave a cry, expecting to see him burn himself. Akiel paid no heed to her. Still singing, he drew back his hand. Flame blazed from the tip of his index finger, and using the flame he swiftly began to draw what looked to be sigils in the air. Kate could briefly see the afterimages and she recognized some of the sigils, though not others.

After a moment, Akiel stopped singing. He cocked his head, appearing to be listening. At length he nodded and turned to Kate.

"The captain said his ship was everything to him. He was both captain and owner, sailing under contract to the Travians. He had no family and thus his crew became his family. He is glad to know so many survived."

"Fine. Good," said Kate. "Will he let me have the helm?"

"He wants to know why you need it, mum. What you plan to do with it."

"Is that really necessary?" Kate demanded.

"If you want the helm, yes, mum."

"Oh, very well!" Kate grumbled, resigned. "Tell him I found an old Rosian warship, the *Victorie,* that had crashed on one of the remote islands during the Bottom Dweller War. The ship sank when a direct hit of contramagic struck the helm, destroying the constructs. I wanted to replace them, but Olaf said only a crafter who specialized in that field could do that and I can't afford to hire anyone, nor can I afford to buy a new helm. That's why I need this one."

Akiel waved his blazing finger in the air.

"How do you do that?" Kate demanded. "Keep from burning yourself?"

Akiel frowned at her and shook his head. He began to sing again. Kate sighed. Her feet were numb. She began to hobble back and forth to bring some feeling into her toes. Akiel quit singing.

"Well?" Kate asked impatiently.

"The captain says you may have it," Akiel reported.

"Thank God! Dalgren!" Kate shouted.

She walked back over to the helm. Akiel had doused the flame on his finger and let go of the plants he had been holding, gently smoothing them to straighten any he might have bent. He blew out the candle, removed it, and tucked it back into his pocket.

Kate eyed the helm. Crouching down, she cautiously reached down to touch the central construct. This time, her fingers actually made contact. She felt the familiar tingle of the magic, and the construct began to glow blue.

"You fixed the magic!" Kate said, pleased. "Thank you, Akiel."

"I did not fix anything, mum," said Akiel. "The captain's spirit has departed. He is at peace."

Kate wasn't listening. A drop of cold water had hit her on the back of her neck, running down her peacoat. She looked up to see Dalgren hovering overhead. Water from the thick mists was dripping off his scales.

"What now?" Dalgren shouted down.

"I need you to carry this helm to the ship," Kate called.

Kate and Akiel scrambled out of the way to give Dalgren room to maneuver. He flew as low as he dared and reached down with his forefoot.

"Be careful," Kate said, watching anxiously as the dragon's claws closed over the helm. "Don't scratch the brass or you might damage the magic."

Dalgren rumbled deep in his chest, muttering something about a waste of time and energy. He lifted the helm off the ground.

"I heard that remark. I'm not wasting my time. I'm not going to be a wrecker all my life," Kate told him.

"You're not going to impress Captain Northrop, either," Dalgren said. "Not with a forty-year-old ship and a salvaged helm."

"He'll be struck by my ingenuity," said Kate. She tried to grin, but her face muscles were stiff from the cold. "That's the last load. Tell the crew to send down the bosun's chair."

Dalgren flew back up to the ship. Despite his grousing, he was carrying the helm as carefully and gently as he would have carried a baby dragon. He vanished through the mists. She could not see either him or the ship.

She stood with her neck craned, impatiently watching, and gave a sigh of relief when she saw the bosun's chair come into view, dangling from a long length of rope.

Once the chair was in grabbing distance, Kate caught hold of it and took her seat. The bosun's chair aboard the *Rose* was crude, little more than a plank attached to ropes attached to a block and tackle thrown over the yardarm. With Akiel's help she settled herself and, tugging on the rope, gave the signal to start lifting.

She could hear the screeching of the winch and feel ropes tighten as the crew hauled the chair up through the mists. She was about halfway to the ship when the chair came to a sudden stop, leaving Kate dangling in midair.

"What the hell is going on?" Kate yelled.

Her shout was drowned out by the boom of a cannon. The next moment, Dalgren came plunging down through the mists.

"What's happening?" Kate gasped.

"A Travian patrol boat," he reported. "They've come to collect their cargo."

"They can't!" Kate said angrily. "We found the wreck first. It's ours."

"That's what Marco told them," Dalgren said, hovering near her chair, barely moving his wings for fear the breeze would cause the chair to start swinging. "The Travians don't agree. The captain laughed when Marco mentioned the law. The patrol boat is armed. Twelve nine-pound guns. That boom you heard was a warning shot across the bow."

Kate swore roundly. The *Barwich Rose* was also armed, but only with a couple of swivel guns. The *Rose* had been built during a more peaceful era, when the biggest threat merchant ships faced was pirates. Following the depredations committed by the Bottom Dwellers, who captured merchant ships and either slaughtered or enslaved the crew, merchant ships had been refitted to carry cannons.

Kate gave an angry shout to the crew, and the bosun's chair started to rise again.

"Did they see you?" she asked.

"I don't think so," said Dalgren. "I've been keeping to the mists."

"Good," said Kate. "Stay out of sight and wait for my signal. I'll try talking reason to them, but I might need your help. I'm not letting them take what's legally mine!"

"So far no one in the Aligoes knows I'm here. If people see me, rumors will run rife. People will think I'm a wild dragon," Dalgren grumbled. "They'll send out hunting parties."

"People were bound to see you sooner or later," said Kate. "After all, you're bigger than some of the islands. I'm surprised you've stayed hidden this long."

"If I have it's because I've take precautions!" Dalgren retorted, glowering. "And I won't harm a human."

"No one is asking you to," Kate said.

The chair continued to rise. She could now see her small ship looking ghostly in the mists. The sails, masts, and balloons of the larger Travian vessel were just beyond.

Dalgren was looking stubborn. The scales between his eyes bunched up. His twisted horn quivered and small puffs of smoke rose from his nose.

"Please, Dalgren," Kate pleaded. "I'm not giving up that brass helm!"

Dalgren sighed, and smoke gushed from his nose. "You're always landing me in trouble, Kate. Starting from that time I nearly flattened you when you were little. I'll watch for your signal."

As he flew off, he shouted back, "It's funny to hear you talking about the law. What was it your father always said? 'Laws are only for those who get caught.' "

"I like the law when it's on my side," Kate shouted back.

Dalgren made a rumbling sound in his chest like rocks rolling down a cliff and disappeared into the Breath.

When Kate reached the ship, the crew was waiting for her. Two sailors grabbed hold of the chair and swung it over the deck. Kate jumped out.

"Send the chair back down for Akiel," she said. "And get ready to release the lines."

The mists drifted about the Travian ship, the *Hortsmann*. The Travians were expecting trouble. The captain had ordered the gunports open and the guns run out. Kate's own crew lined the rail, armed with muskets and pistols, all aimed at the Travians.

"Put down your weapons and return to your posts," Kate ordered. "This is just a misunderstanding."

The men did as she told them, some of them winking as they stuffed their pistols into their belts.

Kate was headed for the quarterdeck when she caught a glimpse of her reflection in the brass helm.

"Good God!" she muttered. "I look like something that crawled out of a Westfirth sewer."

Her face and ears were scarlet from the cold and covered with dirt. Her peacoat was muddy and so were her slops and her boots. She needed to look like the captain, not the loblolly boy.

She hurriedly pulled off the seaman's cap and used it to scrub her face. Her hair, flattened by her hat, hung in lank, sodden curls. Her mother had disparagingly termed her hair color as "dishwater blond." Kate grunted. Today her hair just looked like dishwater.

She raked her fingers through her curls and shed her dirty peacoat and the baldric. Reaching beneath the helm, she grabbed one of the pistols that she kept there and thrust it into the belt at her waist, making certain the pistol was visible.

The helmsman watched approvingly.

"Give the bastards hell, Captain," he told her.

"I plan to," said Kate. She ducked under the rigging that supported the balloon, and mounted the stairs that led to the quarterdeck.

The Travian vessel was a merchant ship out of the city of Sornhagen, the only Travian stronghold in the Aligoes. The two-masted ship was a hundred feet long with a single balloon and short stubby wings over two large airscrews.

"What's going on, Marco?" Kate asked.

Her first mate, Marco, was the best officer she had ever known. Levelheaded, cool in crisis, he had served as a midshipman on an Estaran brig during the war with the Bottom Dwellers. He had challenged a superior officer to a duel—a court-martial offense. Rather than spend years in the brig, Marco had run.

He was tall, lanky, and gangly with black hair, a swarthy complexion, and big ears. His ears and his broad grin made him look closer to sixteen than his twenty-one years. He was aiming a pistol at the Travians.

"They want us to hand over the cargo, Captain," Marco reported, his voice loud enough to carry. "They are threatening to blow us out of the Breath if we don't. I told them by law we have a right to it. They took exception to that."

"They think that the sight of a cannon will make me turn tail and run," Kate scoffed. Lowering her voice, she asked softly, "Did they catch sight of Dalgren?"

"Not a chance, Captain," Marco whispered back. "They wouldn't be so damn cocksure of themselves if they had."

"Good," said Kate. She studied the two men standing on the Travian quarterdeck. Judging by his uniform, one was the captain. "Who is the other man?"

Marco pointed. "The tall man is the captain of the *Hortsmann.* The other is the head of the cartel that owns the cargo on the *Marie Elaine,* the brig that sank. He's hopping mad. Literally hopping. Up and down. Look at him."

Marco was right. The head of the cartel was so angry he was stamping his feet on the deck. Seeing her look at him, he began yelling and waving his arms.

Kate ignored him and addressed the captain.

"There appears to be a misunderstanding, sir," she said, speaking in Freyan, her voice ringing across the misty gap between the two ships. "As my lieutenant has explained, we are wreckers and we have every right to claim this wreck."

The captain blinked at the sound of her voice. He had apparently mistaken her for a man; a forgivable error, seeing as she was wearing men's clothes.

"I asked to speak to the captain of this wrecker," he said, his lip curling. "Not his trollop."

"And I want to speak to a gentleman," Kate shouted back. "Not a son of a bitch!"

Her crew roared with laughter. The captain was now livid.

"Come now, Captain," said Kate, in mollifying tones. "We don't want trouble. I am Katherine Gascoyne-Fitzmaurice, captain of the wrecker, *Barwich Rose.* And I repeat, sir. I have done nothing illegal, I assure you."

The captain managed to master his anger. "I am Captain Schmidt and

I am here to recover the cargo and whatever is salvageable from the merchant vessel the *Marie Elaine*. We know she sank in this vicinity."

The head of the cartel barged in, furiously jabbing his finger at Kate. "Don't deny it! I see some of our cargo and that . . . that's the ship's helm! I demand that you hand over everything!"

"The crew abandoned ship, Captain Schmidt," Kate said, still ignoring the head of the cartel. "They sailed off, leaving her, and thus, by the international Law of Finds, I have the right to the wreck's cargo and anything else I manage to recover."

Captain Schmidt pointed at his guns.

"And by the law of my twelve nine-pound guns, I say you hand over the cargo."

Some of the sailors on board the *Hortsmann* began to pick up grappling hooks. Others were arming themselves with cutlasses and pistols. Kate understood the captain's plan. He wasn't going to sink the *Rose.* He didn't need to. He had only to fire a few shots to cripple her, then he and his crew would board her.

The sun was starting to set, looking like a ball of glowing red flame through the thickening mists. Kate drew the bosun's whistle from beneath her calico shirt and held it to her lips.

"Is Akiel on board?" she asked Marco.

He glanced over his shoulder to see the men hauling in the bosun's chair. "He's just setting foot on the deck now, Captain."

"Good," said Kate. She yelled across the gathering gloom. "I think you should reconsider, Captain! The law is on my side. I could bring you up before the maritime court!"

"Stop wasting time listening to that female vulture and sink her, for God's sake!" roared the head of the cartel.

"I give you one more chance, Madame Wrecker," said the captain. "Tell your crew to stand down and prepare to be boarded and all this will end peacefully, without bloodshed."

"Damn right, it will!" Kate muttered and blew the whistle.

Dalgren materialized out of the mists, only a few yards from the *Hortsmann,* his snout level with the open gunports. His lips curled back, revealing his fangs. Flames flickered from his jaws. His claws flexed as though he could hardly wait to snatch up a few humans and hurl them into the Breath.

Sailors aboard the *Hortsmann* cried out in alarm and pointed. Captain Schmidt had been concentrating on Kate and missed seeing Dalgren until the terrified crew brought his attention to the fact that a dragon was within spitting distance of their ship. Hearing the shouts, the captain turned in time to see the outraged cartel head draw his pistol and aim it at Dalgren.

"Are you mad, sir?" Captain Schmidt knocked the pistol from the man's hand. "If that beast breathes fire on us, he could hit the powder magazine and blow us into eternity!"

"You can't let her get away with this!" the head of the cartel howled, gesturing at Kate. "Think of the money we'll lose!"

"Your crew should have thought of that before they abandoned ship," Captain Schmidt said coldly.

He spoke that last in Travian, probably thinking Kate could not understand. Her father had been an educated man, however, and he had seen to it that his daughter learned to speak what he termed the languages of commerce: Travian, Estaran, Freyan, and Rosian.

"So you admit, Captain, that we have a right to the salvage," Kate called out in Travian.

Captain Schmidt fixed her with a baleful glare and made a stiff bow. "I wish you joy of your spoils, Captain."

He gave the orders to return to Sornhagen. The *Hortsmann* started to rise out of the thick mists, sailing into the clearer air of the ship channel above. Before the ship could depart, Dalgren spit a gout of molten fire onto the deck.

"That's for the trollop insult," the dragon boomed.

The crew of the *Barwich Rose* cheered and hooted in derision. The last they saw of the *Hortsmann,* the sailors were dashing about with buckets, trying to put out the blaze.

"Well done, Dalgren!" Kate shouted to the dragon.

"I have to admit I enjoyed that," Dalgren said, flames flickering from between his teeth. "But all this work has made me exceedingly hungry. If you don't need me, I'll go find dinner."

"Good hunting!" Kate called.

Dalgren dipped his wings in salute and flew off.

Kate gave Marco orders to sail to Freeport, then headed below to warm up. Akiel trailed after her, shaking his head.

"Did you see that, my friend? I won!" she told him.

"By making an enemy of the Travian cartels," said Akiel. "Trouble will come of this, mum, mark my words."

"Don't be so gloomy!" Kate said, laughing. "Wrap my new helm in sailcloth. I want that ghost captain to see I'm taking care of it."

Kate retired to her cabin, planning to celebrate as her father had always celebrated a victory—with a bottle of Calvados.

Pouring the liquor, she thought about what Akiel had predicted.

"'Trouble will come of this,'" Kate repeated.

She remembered an old mariner's lay her father used to sing. *"There's no luck about the house. There's no luck at all."* Morgan had always sung it with a laugh, as though by daring Fate, he could force her to smile on him. Kate raised her glass in a mocking salute. "'No luck at all.' The family motto."

FIVE

The Foreign Office, located in Haever, the capital of Freya, was located about three blocks from the palace. The massive, stolid building with its squat fluted columns flanked by rows of long, narrow windows was completely devoid of charm. The dignified façade was intended to symbolize Freyan stability and security, symbolism that was somewhat lacking at the moment, for the façade was covered by scaffolding. Stonemason crafters had recently discovered that the magic which kept the building standing had been weakened by the Bottom Dwellers' contramagic bombardment. The crafters were currently working to repair the magic before the building collapsed.

Entering through the bronze double doors, ducking beneath the scaffolding, a visitor found himself in the grand hall. By craning his neck, he could see the ceiling, seven stories above him. With its balconies and murals, a painting meant to depict God, and an enormous sun made of shining gold mosaic tile, the hall was meant to inspire awe and a feeling of pride. As with the exterior, however, repair work marred the effect. God was forced to peer through the scaffolding while bits of the sun dropped onto the heads of the unsuspecting.

The irony was not lost upon Henry.

The fate of the nation rested on the shoulders of those who worked here. Even the lowliest clerks went about their business with an air of importance, talking together in hushed tones, giving the impression that they were engaged in the most urgent business that could not be interrupted, or the nation would fall.

The great men who ran the Foreign Office from their offices on the seventh floor—directly beneath God and the sun—were rarely visible. If anyone asked to see them, they were far too busy with matters of state. Two people were the exception to this: Her Majesty the queen and Sir Henry Wallace. If Her Majesty sent for the great men, they would attend her. If Henry sent for them, they came on the run.

Henry's office was not close to God or the sun. It was off by itself in a corner on one of the lower levels. No one was ever certain precisely which level, for visitors had to go up three stairs and then down six, traverse a hall, and round a corner to reach it. The office had a front door and a back door, though few people knew about the back door, which led down a flight of stairs to a dark and dismal alley.

The casual observer could have mistaken the office for that of the clerk to some very minor functionary, for it was small and nondescript, with but a single window that looked down into the alley. What the casual observer did not see was that both the front door and the back were guarded by an elaborate system of magical warding constructs designed by Simon Yates. He had also created the illusion that made the back door appear to be a wall, so that Henry's visitors—and Henry himself—could come and go without attracting notice.

The office furniture consisted of a single desk and three chairs, one for Henry and two for visitors, although the visitors' chairs were currently the repository for documents, folders containing documents, newspapers, reports, letters, books, and missives, all stacked on the chairs because there was no room on the desk, the shelves, or the floor.

The clutter pained Mr. Sloan, even though he knew Henry left his office this way on purpose. If he wanted a visitor to stay, Henry would clear a chair. If he did not, he kept them standing.

The morning after the funeral, Henry was seated at his desk, contemplating how to help his beloved country. He would develop ideas, examine them, think them over, then discard them. The death of the prince was just the latest in a series of blows. If Freya had been in a pugilistic contest, his country would be lying bleeding in the dirt with the referee standing over her, giving the final count.

He heard someone removing the magical locks, and looked up to see Mr. Sloan enter the office, carrying an envelope.

"This was delivered to your club, my lord," said Mr. Sloan.

He made his way through the piles to hand the letter to Henry.

"It's from Simon," said Henry. Opening the envelope, he drew out a small sheet of paper that had been torn from a ledger.

Henry glanced over the letter, crumpled the paper, swore, and threw it on the desk. "Look at that, Mr. Sloan."

Mr. Sloan was forced to smooth the paper. He read aloud, "'Prince Tom, confirmed. Dragons, solution. Lunch.' Typical of Mr. Yates's style. I must confess I am at a loss, my lord."

"Simon has been studying the late Prince Jonathan's research into King Oswald. We all fondly believed that Oswald's line died out following the death of King James. Sadly, it seems it did not. This Prince Tom's claim that he is a direct descendant and therefore the rightful king of Freya is true. Jonathan even drew up a family tree! I take Simon's use of the word 'confirmed' to mean that Simon has confirmed Prince Jonathan's findings. Prince Tom has a legitimate claim."

"That is most unfortunate, my lord," said Mr. Sloan. "If the newspapers were to discover this—"

"They won't," said Henry with a grim smile. "The question is, what to do about this young man."

"He could meet with an accident, my lord . . ." Mr. Sloan suggested.

Henry shook his head. "His mother is an Estaran princess married to a Bheldem marquis. In addition, they both have close ties to Rosia, personal and financial. This young man's death under suspicious circumstances would cause an international incident."

Henry paused, then said, "To tell the truth, Mr. Sloan, I find that I no longer have the stomach for such wretched deeds. I look back on some of what I have done in my career with deep regret. I think to myself, 'What if Hal finds out I sent innocent men to their deaths?' I fear my own son will learn to despise me . . ."

"You did what you had to do for our country, my lord," said Mr. Sloan firmly. "You have risked your own life on more than one occasion for the sake of Freya. Your son has every reason to be proud of his father."

"Thank you, Mr. Sloan," said Henry. "And forgive me for my piteous ramblings. I have been feeling a trifle despondent lately, that is all."

"Perfectly understandable, my lord. You have been beset by many problems. What will you do about Prince Tom?"

"I have an idea," said Henry. "I need to think on it. As to the dragons, I have no notion what Simon is talking about. I hope he does not mean that we are having dragon chops for lunch."

Henry drew out his pocket watch to check the time. "Do you happen to know the location of Simon's house today?"

"Yes, my lord. I saw it this morning floating above the Cooper's Square market, traveling in a northeasterly direction. I will arrange for a carriage."

Henry and Mr. Sloan located the famous flying house, known as Welkinstead, punctually at noon. They had no sooner descended from their wyvern-drawn carriage than they were joined by Randolph and Alan, arriving in their own carriage. Simon's manservant, Mr. Albright, appeared at the entrance and silently ushered them inside.

Welkinstead did not actually fly. According to its late owner, the Duchess of Elsinore, the house "drifted with panache." The late duchess had been a gifted crafter, a renowned scientist, and an artist. Her friends deemed her eccentric. Everyone else termed her a crackpot.

The original house had started out as a marble villa. The duchess, who had more money than sense as the saying went, had added on wings, domes, flying buttresses, steeples—whatever took her fancy. Not content with having turned her house into an architectural monstrosity, she had decided she was bored with the view and wanted a change of scenery, though without leaving her house.

To achieve this goal, she designed powerful magical constructs to fortify the villa's structure and hired hundreds of workmen and crafters to jack up the house and remove it from its foundation. The duchess had stood on her porch, waving to the crowd as lift tanks filled with the Breath of God and several enormous balloons carried Welkinstead into the air.

The duchess and the Seconds had become friends when she aided them in their investigation into the assassination plot against the late king Godfrey. When Simon was felled by a bullet that severed his spinal cord, the duchess designed a special magical chair for his use and brought him to live with her in her wondrous house. She had bequeathed both the house and her immense wealth to him.

The duchess had been content to let the house drift about Haever, hiring tugboats to assist her if the house ventured too far out into the Breath. Simon had deemed such aimless travel annoying. Much to the ire of the tugboat captains, who had made an excellent living off the duchess, he had added sails and airscrews to the house. Now either he or Mr. Albright could steer it.

Alan had once described Simon as "preeminent scientist, genius crafter, renowned detective, and the world's most inveterate busybody."

Henry termed Simon "Freya's secret weapon."

Mr. Albright silently took their hats and indicated with a gesture that Simon could be found upstairs in his office. They made their way through the first level of the house, which was an homage to the duchess's penchant for collecting. Her taste was eclectic; the collection included stuffed tigers, birds' eggs, more than a hundred crystal chandeliers that swayed perilously with the movement of the house, and works of art of varying quality all hanging at tilted angles on the walls.

Simon's office took up the entire second floor, with the exception of a small bedroom and a water closet. He had placed his desk in a turret surrounded by windows that provided a magnificent view of Haever and the orange mists of the Breath beyond.

His enormous desk was the repository for newspapers, pamphlets, and gazettes from across the world, as well as correspondence from his many informants. He read everything from major news stories to the agony columns and obituaries. He absorbed information, sorted and compiled and considered, then used the results to thwart the plots of their foes, solve crimes, catch criminals, and gather intelligence on friends and enemies without ever leaving his house.

Seeing that the chairs apparently had migrated to various parts of the room due to the listing of the floor, Mr. Sloan and Mr. Albright went to fetch them, while Henry, Alan, and Randolph visited. They had not seen one another since the funeral.

Simon was examining a small painting in an ornate frame, peering at it through a magnifying glass. He did not look up, but waved to his friends, motioned to them to be seated, and kept studying the painting. At last, he raised his head and set his glass aside.

Henry walked over to look at it. "A Brandess?"

"A forged Brandess," Simon declared. "The forger used magic to obtain the delicate shade of blue for which Brandess was renowned. He would have succeeded, but he then attempted to erase the magic using contramagic, only he didn't know what he was doing. I can still detect faint traces of the sigils. I will send a note to the museum curator. She was right to be suspicious."

He jotted down a few words on the back of the curator's letter, then handed the letter and the painting to Mr. Albright, along with instructions to wrap them up and deliver them by messenger.

This done, Simon leaned back in his chair and smiled at his friends. "You've come about the dragons."

"And lunch," Alan added.

"Never mind lunch or the goddamn dragons," said Randolph. "We've come to make plans to go to war against Guundar."

"We can discuss that over lunch," Alan said.

"Ah, yes. Regarding lunch, I'm afraid there's nothing in the house to eat," said Simon.

"You never have anything in the house to eat," said Henry. "Mr. Sloan has brought sandwiches."

"Now, about that war . . ." said Randolph, rubbing his hands.

Henry stood with his hands clasped behind his back, gazing out the window at the city drifting by.

"You haven't told them," said Simon, looking at Henry.

"Told us what?" Alan asked warily.

"That we can't afford another war," said Henry, turning around. "Freya is on the verge of bankruptcy."

"I know things are bad," Alan said. "But are they really as bad as that?"

"Worse," Henry said. "I could go into the reasons behind the financial collapse: the cost of the last war, the disruption in trade worldwide, inflation—"

"I believe you!" Alan said, raising his hands in defeat.

"Suffice it to say," Henry continued, "we have been spending money we don't have. Our creditors—among them the Travian cartels—are growing nervous and starting to demand that we pay them back. We can't. We have almost no revenue flowing into our coffers."

"Raise taxes," Randolph suggested.

"We can't keep raising taxes," said Henry impatiently. "The wealthy won't stand for it—the House of Nobles is already in open revolt. The middle class is being squeezed as it is and the poor can't pay what they don't have."

"There's been nothing in the newspapers," Alan said.

"Of course not," said Henry. "You don't think I want to publicize this, do you? I suppose we should consider ourselves fortunate that speculation about an heir has kept the newspapers from raising hell about the sad state of our economy."

"We don't need to fret over a goddamn heir. Her Majesty is in good health, God bless her," said Randolph gruffly. "What are you going to do about this economic mess, Henry?"

"I *was* counting on the manufacture and sale of the crystals to pull us out of the hole, but King Ullr put an end to that."

"Just tell our creditors we're good for it," said Alan, shrugging. Being fond of baccarat, he knew something about debts and moneylenders.

Henry gave a faint smile. "The problem is we're *not* 'good for it' and they know it."

"And this is why I asked you to lunch," Simon said. "I have the solution. Dragons. Specifically, Travian dragons."

"Good God! Simon, you've finally gone crackers," said Alan.

"I didn't know there were such things as Travian dragons," said Randolph.

"Be quiet, you two," said Henry. "Simon, speak."

"The Travian economy is in worse shape than ours, which is why the cartels are insisting we pay them back. King Henrick of Travia did what Randolph suggested. He imposed a hefty tax on wealthy Travian landowners. This tax was aimed specifically at the dragons, who own vast amounts of land rich in gold and timber."

Alan interrupted. "I cannot follow this on an empty stomach. Mr. Sloan, I believe some mention was made of sandwiches?"

Mr. Sloan distributed the sandwiches. Simon took his, set it down, and promptly forgot about it.

"Now, you must understand that dragons living in Travia are not like dragons living in Rosia," he explained. "The Rosian dragons have been an integral part of Rosian society for centuries. They attend court. Humans have established cities in the Dragon Duchies and live and work among them.

"The dragons of Travia, on the other hand, have never been considered a part of Travian society. The dragons live in mountainous regions and keep themselves apart from humans. Thus the Travian dragons do not believe they should have to pay this tax—"

Alan again interrupted. "Mr. Sloan, do you know where to find the aqua vitae? I believe it is in one of the filing cabinets. Try searching under 'V' for 'vitae.'"

Mr. Sloan ferreted out the bottle and poured the liquor. Henry refused. He had an idea where Simon was going with this and he needed a clear head.

"The Travian dragons are extremely wealthy. They could easily afford to pay the tax. They do not like being told to hand over the money and then have no say in how their money is spent. The king has decreed that they must pay or he will seize their lands."

Alan laughed. "What passes for an army in Travia couldn't take a toy from a child, much less threaten dragons."

"Still, the dragons are unhappy and I was thinking that if Her Majesty were to send an envoy to the dragons, offering them land in Freya and titles and a seat in the House of Nobles, she could prevail upon the Travian dragons to move themselves and their gold to Freya."

At this, Randolph flushed purple and snorted. "Dragons living in Freya! Not bloody likely! Remember the Battle of Daenar? Thousands of Freyans died in that battle, killed by dragons! My own uncle was one of them, God rest him!"

"Randolph is right, Henry, there would be trouble," Alan warned. "The hatred for dragons in this country dates back farther than Randolph's uncle. It goes clear back to the Sunlit Empire and the ancient Imhruns."

"Mr. Sloan, I see you looking somber and shaking your head," said Henry. "What are your reservations?"

"According to Scripture, my lord, dragons are the minions of the Evil One. I am not saying I believe that. We have dragons to credit for our defeat of the Bottom Dwellers. Unfortunately, many members of the Fundamentalist religion, as well as conservative members of the Reformed Church of the Breath, consider dragons evil. I agree with Captain Northrop and Admiral Baker. There would be trouble."

Henry had run out of patience. "There will be a damn sight more trouble if Freya goes bankrupt and we have to ground the fleet, lay off thousands of sailors, and put captains and admirals on half pay!"

Randolph sputtered. "Goddamn it, you don't mean that, Henry! You're not serious!"

"I have never been more serious in my life," said Henry.

"I can't live on half pay," said Randolph.

"Neither can I," said Alan, sounding troubled.

"Bosh!" Randolph snorted. "You could always go back to being a glorified pirate."

"No," Alan said quietly. "I can't."

Henry understood what Alan meant. The commission in the Royal Navy had made Alan respectable. Freyan lords and ladies gushed over the daring exploits of the romantic privateer, but they had never invited the "glorified pirate" into their homes. The handsome Captain Northrop of the Royal Navy, however, was a welcome addition to balls and dinner parties. After years of scandal and living as an outcast, Alan had finally restored his family's honor.

"I think Simon's idea is a good one," said Henry. "I will make the recommendation to Her Majesty. Do I hear objections?"

Alan turned away to pour himself another glass of aqua vitae. Randolph muttered something, but said nothing out loud. Simon gave Henry a sympathetic smile and handed over his report. Mr. Sloan brought Henry's hat.

Climbing into the carriage, Henry realized he had forgotten to talk to Alan about his idea for a privateer.

"Send an invitation to Alan to dine at my club tomorrow night," said Henry.

"Your Lordship is scheduled to sail for Wellinsport tomorrow afternoon," Mr. Sloan said.

"Damn and blast it!" Henry swore. "I forgot the voyage was scheduled for tomorrow."

"I could cancel the booking," said Mr. Sloan.

Henry was tempted. After a moment's consideration, he sighed and shook his head. "I must go, Mr. Sloan."

The Rosians were sending ships to the Aligoes, and while they claimed to be interested only in driving out the pirates, the Rosians had long coveted Wellinsport and its Deep Breath harbor and might decide to try to take it. The city was in desperate need of a vast sum of money to reinforce the batteries that protected it.

"Although where we're going to find the money for Wellinsport is another problem altogether." Henry spoke his thoughts aloud. "Still, we must come up with it. Wellinsport is too valuable to lose."

"Indeed, my lord," said Mr. Sloan.

Henry sank back into the leather cushions. "In addition, I promised Her Majesty that I would rein in the excesses of the governor, the Right Honorable Aldous Finchley. I have tried to convince Her Majesty to remove the viscount from office, but he's a great favorite and she won't hear of it."

Henry sighed and rubbed his forehead. "He sent her a monkey."

Mr. Sloan expressed his sympathy with a cough, then added, "Perhaps a restful voyage will do you good, my lord."

Henry fixed his secretary with a grim look. "I know you are trying to lift my spirits, Mr. Sloan, but stop it. I prefer to be miserable."

"Very good, my lord," said Mr. Sloan.

"Speaking of being miserable," said Henry. "I want you to book a passage for Miss Amelia Nettleship, the journalist and author of 'The Adventures of Captain Kate.' Then extend my invitation to Miss Nettleship to be my guest on this voyage. She will want to know why, of course. Tell her I would like her to write about the Right Honorable Aldous Finchley. Not the true reason, of course. If I have my way, Finchley will not be the Right Honorable for much longer. But that should do for the moment."

Mr. Sloan was so amazed he was momentarily struck speechless. At length he ventured a feeble protest: "A journalist, my lord? Captain Kate?"

"For the sake of queen and country, Mr. Sloan," Henry said. "Queen and country."

SIX

On board the *Victorie* a week later, Kate polished the newly installed brass helm. She was looking forward to tomorrow, which was when she would finally take her newly restored old brig into the Breath to see how she handled.

Dalgren had found the wrecked Rosian brig on one of his hunting trips among the small islands. The *Victorie* was an older model that had been brought out of retirement to join the fight against the Bottom Dwellers. The ship was small, only about one hundred ten feet long, with a thirty-foot beam, two masts, a single gun deck, two airscrews, and two balloons.

Kate recalled hearing about the sinking of the *Victorie*. The brig had come under attack by one of the Bottom Dwellers' infamous black ships and, according to reports, was severely damaged. Captain and crew had been forced to abandon ship. She and other wreckers had searched for the ship for years. The other wreckers didn't have a dragon working for them, however; a dragon who could inspect hundreds of islands from the air.

Kate and her crew had arrived at the site to find that most of the damage done to the brig had occurred when it had crashed into the jungle: broken masts, punctured balloons, a gaping hole in the hull. She saw no signs of explosions or fires; the powder magazine had not been breached.

Kate had been puzzled as to why the ship had gone down until she saw the helm.

The brass was blank, as though wiped clean with a towel. The magical constructs used to control the ship's lift tanks, balloons, and airscrews had been obliterated by contramagic, probably a direct hit from one of the Bottom Dwellers' green-beam weapons. The helmsman would have immediately lost control, leaving the ship to the mercy of the wind and the Breath until it fell out of the sky.

The way Olaf explained it, contramagic acted like acid on the magical constructs, destroying them without a trace. When Kate had tried to replace the constructs on the helm, the lingering effects of contramagic had eaten away at her magic.

"Most of the damage can be repaired, except for the helm," Kate had told Marco as they were inspecting the vessel. "Seems a shame to scrap the *Victorie*. In fact, I won't," she had added on impulse. "I'm going to claim her myself. All I need is a new helm."

Because they had no way to control the magic, Kate and Olaf had been forced to rely on their own crafting skills to keep the ship afloat. *Victorie* was so old that it used the Breath of God, not the liquid, to lift her off the ground. Olaf and Kate had crouched beside one of the two large lift tanks and placed their hands directly on the constructs, using their own magical energy to spark the Breath in the tank. They were exhausted by the end, but they managed to keep the ship afloat long enough for the crew to tow it to Kate's Cove, a secluded bay she had found not far from Freeport, on one of the innumerable islands floating in the Breath.

Kate had chosen it because it was close to Freeport, yet not close enough that anyone was likely to stumble across it. The island was home to tall cedar trees, which could be used to tie off the ship, and a stretch of cleared beach where they could sink the bollards on which to secure the anchor.

The iron bollards had cost Kate dear. The Aligoes Islands produced almost no iron ore, and thus nearly every object made of metal had to be imported. In addition, each bollard had to be specially made with a clamp on top to hold the anchor in place. She had searched for anchoring bollards at auction, but had not found any. She had purchased the bollards from an ironworks in Freya, borrowing money to cover the expense. Olaf had grumbled that she could have built *Victorie* for what the bollards cost.

Once they had the bollards, Olaf had blasted holes in the rocks with gunpowder. The crew sank the bollards into the holes, packed them with dirt and large chunks of stone on which Olaf had placed magical constructs, the same type used by stonemason crafters. The crew filled the holes with mortar and Olaf used the magic to fuse the stones together.

"Those bollards won't shift for centuries," he had proudly told Kate.

The two arms of the anchor fit over the bollards, held in place by the clamps so that the anchor could not accidentally break free.

Since the anchor was far too heavy to lift off the bollards, Olaf had rigged a metal bar operated by a modified well pump that sprang up out of the ground and knocked the anchor off the bollards. The crew could then haul in the anchor and the ship would float free. Kate held her breath the first time they lowered the anchor and attached it to the bollards and again when they raised the anchor. Everything worked as planned. Olaf was so pleased and proud he quit grumbling about the money it cost.

Kate and her crew had spent every free moment for the past six months refitting the *Victorie* and repairing the magical constructs that were essential to the operation of the vessel. Kate had done most of the repairs to the magic herself. Olaf, her instructor, had always insisted she was a talented crafter.

Kate knew better, rating her skill at fair to middling. She knew the workings of the constructs on the helm, how to repair the magical constructs on the lift tanks and inscribe protective constructs on the hull. Her true talent lay in being able to cast a magical spell "on the fly." She was quick-witted, quick to react. Magic seemed to sparkle at her fingertips.

She took pride in her ability, smiling when Olaf grumbled that she should think first and react second.

With the new helm in place, *Victorie* was ready to sail. Kate was eager and at the same time afraid to cut the cables that tethered the ship to the shore. If the *Victorie* sank, her dreams sank with it.

Kate ran her fingers over the constructs on the helm and imagined them glowing with faint blue light at her touch. She could hear the whirring of the airscrews, the whoosh of the balloons inflating; feel the thrill of the ship coming to life beneath her fingertips.

"We can do it, old girl," said Kate, giving the helm a pat. "We'll set sail first thing in the morning."

"Hail the *Victorie*!" someone called.

She heard the creaking of a rusty airscrew and turned to see a single red silk balloon bobbing along the narrow channel that led to her cove.

Kate was not expecting company. She picked up her pistol, which she kept beneath the helm, and aimed it at the wherry.

"Stand off!" she shouted. "I'm armed!"

"Mum! Don't shoot! It's me, Akiel! Olaf sent me to find you!"

The wherry emerged from the trees and she could see Akiel alone in the small craft.

Kate shoved the pistol back under the helm.

"What's wrong?" she asked as the wherry came up alongside. "Other than the fact that Olaf needs to oil that airscrew."

"Two of Greenstreet's men came to the tavern asking for you, mum. They said—"

Kate impatiently interrupted. "I know what they said, Akiel, and you can go back and tell them I haven't got the money now, but I will have it. Greenstreet needs to give me more time."

"The men did not say anything about money, mum," Akiel replied. "They said that Greenstreet says you are to come to his office. This evening at sunset."

"What's this about?" Kate asked, startled and uneasy. "What does Greenstreet want with me?"

"The men would not tell Olaf. Greenstreet is a bad man, mum," Akiel added. "A very bad man. You should not have borrowed money from him."

"I didn't have a choice," Kate snapped. "You like being paid, don't you?"

Akiel smiled. "You have yet to pay me, mum."

"Well, I will," said Kate.

"I am not complaining," Akiel assured her.

"I know." Kate sighed.

Entering the Perky Parrot tavern, Kate was relieved to see that Olaf was too busy washing the pewter mugs and getting ready for the supper crowd to scold her.

"You know I don't approve!" he called from the kitchen.

"Duly noted," Kate called back.

She went out back to a screened-off area she had rigged for bathing. She hauled water from the well and dumped it into a metal tub made from a cut-away lift tank. The water was cold and she didn't have time to warm it. She lowered herself into the water, gasping at the cold, and scrubbed vigorously to keep warm.

Kate was uneasy about this meeting. Greenstreet was the most powerful man in the Aligoes. Not only the most powerful; also the most feared. No one knew much about him. He had arrived in Freeport ten years ago, moved into the biggest house on the island, and set up shop. Within a year, he was financing nearly every illegal enterprise in the Aligoes. He was heavily involved in the black-market arms trade; he ran whorehouses, opium dens, and gambling casinos; he was also a moneylender, and Kate, needing materials to refit the *Victorie,* had availed herself of this service.

She had missed a few payments on her loan.

"I need to convince Greenstreet to give me more time," Kate muttered, wrapping herself in a towel and heading for her small room in the back of the tavern.

Kate considered what her father would have done in this situation. Morgan had spent most of his life in debt to someone or other and he had generally been able to placate even the most obdurate creditor with his roguish smile and silky promises.

Kate did not have a roguish smile, but she was an attractive woman and Greenstreet was a man. Her father would have advocated using her feminine wiles. Kate opened her sea chest and took out the only feminine clothes she possessed, consisting of an emerald green silk skirt and a green silk jacket with a tight fitted bodice and puffy elbow sleeves finished with lace. A lace petticoat, a cotton chemise, and silk stockings completed the outfit.

She had packed the clothes in linen and lavender; the fragrance now filled the room as she shook out each article and laid the clothes on the bed to admire them. Her father had ordered the ensemble from a dressmaker in Westfirth and presented it to his daughter on her sixteenth birthday. He had also given her a book on deportment, undoubtedly with the vague hope that feminine clothes and a book on how a lady should act would magically change his rowdy hoyden into a genteel damsel.

Kate smoothed the long silk skirt. Her mother had worn gowns such as this. Even after the servants had walked out and her mother had sold most of the furniture, she would dress in her fading silken finery every night, sit in the one chair they had left, and tell stories of the time she had been presented at court.

Kate had worn the clothes twice. She had put them on to show her father, who had laughed heartily to see her flouncing around the deck in her fine silk skirt and bare feet. The second time had been at Morgan's funeral, standing on the deck of the *Rose,* watching, dry-eyed, as Olaf and the crew wrapped her father's battered and bloody corpse in sailcloth and dumped it into the Breath in the dead of night.

Kate shivered and put the memories out of her mind. She didn't have time for them now. She put on the chemise and the petticoat, then stepped into the skirt. Buttoning up the jacket, she looked at her reflection in the cracked mirror.

Kate was above average height for a woman, strong and muscular. Morgan had always told her she was beautiful, but then he said that to all the women he met. Kate had no claim to beauty that she could see except, perhaps, for her eyes, which were a deep brown flecked with glinting specks of gold. A drunken longshoreman had once composed a song praising her eyes. The crew had never let her forget it and would still roar it out on occasion.

Kate had considered wearing the dress when Alan Northrop had visited the Parrot during the Rose Hawk days before the war. She had seen the way he smiled at other women dressed in pretty clothes and she had wanted him to smile at her the same way. Instead, he had always treated her like a kid sister, twitting her about wearing men's clothes, teasingly calling her "Nate" instead of "Kate." On reflection, however, she had decided that she preferred having Alan number her among his friends and share companionable laughter with her, even if he left the tavern with a woman in a skirt.

Kate took an experimental turn around the room and ended up stepping on the hem of the petticoat, nearly tripping herself. She remembered then the book of deportment telling her that ladies took small steps. On no occasion was a lady ever to "stride."

Kate hurriedly took off the skirt and jacket and bundled them back into her sea chest and slammed shut the lid. Once the green silk was out of sight, she breathed easier.

"The hell with feminine wiles," she muttered. "I don't know how to be a girl."

She sneaked into Olaf's room, pilfered one of his red calico shirts, and put it on over a clean pair of slops. She tied a red kerchief around her neck and shook out her wet curls. She knew better than to take a pistol. Greenstreet's men would only confiscate it.

Entering the common room, she saw Olaf and Akiel standing at the bar, talking in low voices. Both men fell silent when they saw her and she knew by their guilty expressions they had been discussing her.

"I'm leaving for Greenstreet's now," Kate called, not stopping to talk, knowing what Olaf would say. "Thanks for the loan of the shirt. Mine were both dirty."

Olaf had known Kate since she was born. He had held her in his arms when she was a baby and taken care of her when she had come to live aboard ship. Now in his seventies, Olaf walked with a crutch ever since his right leg had "given up on him," as he put it.

After Morgan's death, he and Kate had sailed the old *Barwich Rose* to the Aligoes. Kate had tried to carry on her father's career as a smuggler, but that hadn't worked out too well. Now she earned a living as a wrecker. Olaf had retired from sailing, though he still helped on board the *Rose* if Kate needed him. He had used his small savings to buy a tavern he named the Perky Parrot. Kate helped him when she could.

They worked hard and made ends meet, but Kate longed to earn more than a pittance and, like her father, she was always busy devising schemes to make her fortune.

"You shouldn't go, Kate!" Olaf called. "I don't like it."

"Very well, Olaf," said Kate, turning to him with a grin. "I will send my servant round with a note telling Greenstreet that I am indisposed. I shall call upon him another day."

"I've warned you time and again, you can't trust Greenstreet," Olaf said, not to be deterred. "You should have never gotten mixed up with him."

"And where was I supposed to go for money, Olaf?" Kate demanded irately. "Should I have walked into the bank in Wellinsport and asked the fine gentlemen in their fancy suits for a loan? Would they have given it to me, do you think?"

Olaf glared at her. "We didn't need the money. We were doing fine until you found that broken-down old derelict and got come crazy scheme into your head to sail off and make your fortune!"

"I won't be a wrecker all my life!" Kate shouted.

Picking up his crutch, Olaf stumped away, heading toward the back of the tavern. Kate sighed.

"Olaf, I'm sorry!" she called after him. "I didn't mean to lose my temper—"

"Akiel is going with you," Olaf yelled, and slammed the door.

"Fine," Kate muttered. Walking out of the tavern, she slammed the door.

She hurried off, only to find Akiel following her.

"I really don't need protection," Kate told him. "Greenstreet just wants to know when I plan to pay him back."

"And when do you?" Akiel asked, catching up to her.

I wish I knew, Kate thought. Aloud she said, "Soon."

"Olaf told me Greenstreet once threatened to kill you," Akiel said.

"That was just a warning," Kate said. She shrugged. "He threatens to kill everyone."

"And sometimes he carries out his threats. Olaf said I was to come with you," said Akiel.

"Suit yourself," said Kate.

She continued down the dirt road that led into the shore town of Freeport. The Perky Parrot was located on the outskirts of town, only a short distance from the docks. The road was lined with whitewashed stucco houses. Men and women sat on the stoops of some of the houses, fanning themselves, gossiping, and watching their children play. A few waved at Kate, who was well liked, mainly because she was a hard worker and didn't ask anyone for anything.

Their feelings would have been different if they had known she was the granddaughter of a viscount, but no one did. Kate made sure of that.

"Why did Greenstreet threaten to kill you?" Akiel asked.

"My fault," said Kate. "I deserved it. When Olaf and I arrived here with nothing except the *Rose,* I decided I'd carry on the family business and I began smuggling whiskey from Freya. I should have given Greenstreet his cut like Morgan always did, but I thought I could get away with it.

"Greenstreet confiscated my cargo and suggested I find another line of work or I would meet the same fate as my father. That's when I became a wrecker."

Akiel shook his head. "And you borrowed money from this man."

"It takes money to make money," Kate said defensively. "Once *Victorie* is ready to sail, I will make money. Lots of it. You've heard of Captain Alan Northrop, the famous privateer?"

"Of course," Akiel replied. "Everyone has heard of him."

"Captain Northrop was the leader a group of young Freyan noblemen who called themselves the Rose Hawks. Before the war, they would capture Rosian ships and raid Rosian and Estaran towns. Captain Northrop and the Rose Hawks would visit the Parrot every time their ship docked in Freeport. Alan promised me that if I ever owned my own ship, I could join up with him. Become a privateer."

"I do not recall ever seeing him in Freeport," said Akiel.

"He hasn't been here for several years, not since the war ended," said Kate. "But I know he'll remember me."

Kate certainly remembered Alan Northrop, his dark wavy hair and melting eyes and devil-may-care smile. He had the reputation of being a ladies' man, but there had been something in the way he looked at her that made her feel she was different from all the others.

"Look out for that puddle," Akiel warned.

Kate circled around a large area of water flooding a low point in the road.

"Captain Northrop pays a one-fifth share of the loot he captures to those who sail with him," Kate continued. "Once he captured a Travian shipment of gold that proved to be worth over eight hundred thousand Freyan eagles. Imagine!"

"A vast sum. What would you do with so much money?" Akiel wondered.

Kate glanced around to make certain no one was listening. "You can't tell anyone. I would use the money to buy Barwich Manor, my family's estate in Freya. I will be the lady of the manor, like my mother."

Akiel was amazed. "Your family owns a manor?"

"We did own it," Kate corrected. "We don't anymore. The bank has it now."

"What happened?" Akiel asked.

Kate shrugged. She thought of the family motto. "What always happens—no luck."

Reaching the outskirts of the town, Kate turned off the main road onto a path lined with flowering bushes and lime trees. The path was about half a mile long and led to a large two-story house, painted white, with a veranda that encircled the house, and a red tile roof. Palm trees and shade trees surrounded the house, planted to keep the interior dark and cool. Flowering hedges lined the walkway. A well-trimmed lawn extended from the path to the distant jungle.

Kate stopped at the edge of the lawn and turned to face Akiel. "Olaf will need you to start cooking supper. I will meet you back at the Parrot." Seeing Akiel start to protest, she added, "You know that the customers will leave if they have to eat Olaf's cooking."

The tavern served only one dish each night and that was either chicken stew or pork stew. Akiel livened up the plain fare with vegetables and spices such as ginger root and hot peppers. Ever since he had started cooking, the supper and dinner crowd had grown.

Akiel made his protest anyway. "Olaf told me to come with you."

"You may do the cooking for Olaf, but you work for me," said Kate.

Akiel did not budge.

Kate put her hand on his arm and looked up into his eyes. "When I said that Greenstreet threatened me, that wasn't exactly true. He threatened Olaf. He told me if I didn't stop smuggling, his men would beat him and burn down the Parrot."

"Olaf doesn't know about this?" Akiel asked, frowning.

"I never told him," said Kate. "He warned me about Greenstreet and he would say 'I told you so' and I would never hear the end of it. Don't worry. I can fix this. But if things do go wrong, you need to be there to protect *him*. I can take care of myself."

"What do I tell Olaf?"

"That I sent you back and if he doesn't like it, he can take it up with me."

Akiel mulled this over. "Very well. But if you are not home by suppertime, I will come looking for you."

"I will be back," Kate promised.

Akiel nodded, then slowly retraced his steps down the lane.

Kate proceeded on toward the house. Two of Greenstreet's men were lounging in rocking chairs on the veranda. Apparently they were expecting her, for as she stepped onto the veranda, one man wearing duck trousers and a dirty shirt stood up and opened the door for her. Once they were inside he grunted at her and pointed to a chair in the entryway. Kate sat down opposite a closed door

The man knocked on the door, called out, "She's here, boss," and walked over to stare out the window.

Kate glanced around. She had never been in Greenstreet's house before. She didn't see much of it. The hall was lined with doors leading to other rooms and they were all closed. The house was deathly quiet; the only sounds came from birds and animals outside.

A voice called, "Send her in, Jacob!"

The man—presumably Jacob—stood up, walked over, opened the door, and grunted once more. Kate assumed this meant she could enter. She walked into the room; it was empty except for a small chair, a large desk, a large chair behind the desk, and a large man in the large chair. The only object on the desk was a folded-up newspaper. The room was cool, with a slight breeze blowing through the open windows.

Kate recognized the large man in the chair. She had seen Greenstreet only once, but he was hard to forget, being so big that parts of him spilled out over the chair. He pointed to the small chair, apparently an invitation to sit down.

"Captain Kate," Greenstreet said, leaning back in his chair and peering up at her from beneath hooded eyelids. "You are properly addressed as 'Captain Kate,' I presume."

Kate had no idea what he was talking about. "My crew calls me 'captain.' I guess you can, as well."

"Thank you, *Captain Kate.*"

Greenstreet laid emphasis on the words and chuckled. A corpulent man, he was dressed all in white—a concession to the heat—wearing a white jacket, a white shirt, and a white waistcoat that did not button over his expansive middle. He liked to refer to himself as jovial. He was good-humored and always smiling. He had smiled the entire time he had warned Kate that he would have his men beat Olaf within an inch of his life.

"You have been holding out on me, Captain," said Greenstreet.

Kate was uneasy, thinking he must have found out about *Victorie,* afraid he might try to claim her ship to pay off her debt. She affected ignorance. "What do you mean, holding out on you? I'm good for the money I owe you. It will just take a little time. I made a fine haul a day or so ago—"

"The Travians. Yes. A piddling amount and you know it."

"Then what do you mean?" Kate asked.

Greenstreet shoved the newspaper across the desk.

"Read that, Captain."

Mystified, Kate picked up the newspaper, the *Haever Gazette,* dated several weeks ago. She glanced at the articles about the death of the crown prince, including a lengthy description of his funeral and speculation on the heir to the throne.

"What does this have to do with me?" Kate asked. She grinned. "Unless you think I'm one of the heirs. I can assure you I'm not."

Greenstreet smiled. "Most amusing. Page seven."

Kate opened the paper and turned to page seven. She saw a lurid illustration of a beautiful young woman, armed with a cutlass, riding on the back of a fire-breathing dragon. The illustration was part of an article titled "The Adventures of Captain Kate and Her Dragon Corsairs. A True Story."

"Bloody hell!" Kate gasped.

SEVEN

Kate read just enough of the story to know she was in serious trouble. Before she could say anything, Greenstreet confirmed her fears by playfully wagging his finger at her.

"You and your dragon have been raiding ships, stealing treasure, holding rich men for ransom. And all this time, you owe me money and claim you cannot pay."

"I swear I haven't done any of this, Greenstreet," Kate protested.

Greenstreet appeared to ruminate. "Let us consider this. Kate is your name. You are captain of the *Victorie,* which is the name of that derelict brig you borrowed money from me to restore."

"I know this looks bad, Greenstreet, but I can explain—"

"And you partner with a dragon. I received a complaint from the Travians who claimed a dragon acting on your orders attacked their ship and set fire to it. In addition to that, I have received reports that a dragon has been observed flying at night in the vicinity of Freeport."

Greenstreet leaned back and clasped his hands over his capacious belly. "A series of remarkable coincidences?"

"The Travians were trying to steal the wreck from me," Kate said.

"I should be the one to complain about them. The Travians threatened to sink my ship! Dalgren was only defending me—"

"Ah, you admit you partner with a dragon."

"He is a friend," Kate said. "And I'm not a corsair or a pirate—as you damn well know!"

She bounded up out of the chair, slammed her hands on the desk and leaned over it to look Greenstreet in the eye. "You keep yourself informed about everything that goes on in the Aligoes. You know this story isn't true!"

She jabbed her finger at the newspaper.

"Sit down, Captain," said Greenstreet. "I do not like to have to crane my neck to look up at you."

Kate hesitated, then threw herself back into the chair and crossed her arms over her chest.

"It's not true," she repeated.

"Then how did such a tale come to be written? Are you claiming this Amelia Nettleship made up the specific details? She just happened to use your name, the name of your ship, the name of your dragon friend? . . ."

"Miss Amelia didn't make it up," said Kate. She drew in a deep breath. "I did."

"I think you had better explain," said Greenstreet.

Kate felt her cheeks burn. "About six months ago I was in Wellinsport selling cargo. I was in the auction hall watching the sale when this woman came up to me. She said her name was Amelia Nettleship and she was a journalist. Someone told her I was captain of my own ship. She said she had never met a female captain before and she wanted to buy my story. She offered to pay me five eagles for it."

Kate's flush deepened. "I needed parts for my ship. I knew she wouldn't pay to hear the squalid tale of my real life, so I made up a story. I said I was one of the Rose Hawks, captain of my own pirate ship, and Dalgren was my partner. I told her a lot of crap about sinking Rosian galleons and stealing Travian gold. I just wanted the money! I never thought the fool woman would go ahead and publish it!"

Greenstreet chuckled. "Damn, Captain! Of all my clients, I do believe you are the most amusing."

"You know I'm telling the truth," said Kate, relieved.

"Of course I do," he said. "As you say, I know everything that goes on in these islands. I would have heard about a sunken Rosian 'galleon,' especially considering the fact that not even the backward Guundaran navy owns such a museum piece."

"I'm glad you understand, Greenstreet," Kate said. "I won't take up any more of your time. I'll soon have that money for you—"

She started to rise, hoping to escape. Greenstreet raised a hand, palm out.

"We are not finished, Captain. Sit down."

Kate sighed and sank back into the chair. She was fairly certain she knew what was coming.

Greenstreet sat forward and tapped the newspaper. "I find this story quite intriguing, especially the part about the dragon. You terrorized the Travians, Captain, set their deck on fire, threatened to roast them! I was most impressed."

"Dalgren helps me with the wrecking," Kate said. "We're not pirates."

"So what did you plan to do with this brig you salvaged?" Greenstreet asked. "Deliver the mail?"

He was smiling, but the smile did not reach his hooded eyes.

Kate couldn't very well tell Greenstreet that she had planned to slip out of Freeport before he knew she was gone. He would be furious that she had fled without paying him what she owed, but Kate figured that once she was working as a privateer for the Freyan government, she wouldn't have to worry about Greenstreet. He wouldn't dare touch her.

"It's just a story," she said insistently. "I made it all up. If you want to know the truth, I'm refitting the *Victorie* as a merchantman. I'm going to haul cargo. More money than in wrecking."

She started again to rise from the chair.

"Speaking of cargo," said Greenstreet, unperturbed, "I have it on good authority that the *Pride of Haever* is en route from Freya to Wellinsport. The ship is carrying valuable cargo and passengers."

"That's interesting," said Kate, sidling toward the door. "I hope they have a safe passage—"

"I trust they won't," said Greenstreet drily. "The infamous Captain Kate and her Dragon Corsairs are going to capture this ship, the cargo and passengers."

Kate gave an uneasy laugh. "You're not serious!"

"I assure you I am, Captain. Quite serious." Greenstreet pointed to the chair. Kate sighed and sat back down.

Greenstreet reached into an inner pocket of his jacket. "I have here the ship's manifest."

He slid the paper across the desk toward Kate. "You will note the date the ship is expected to arrive, as well as a listing of the cargo and passengers. The *Pride* will be sailing the Trame Channel—an ideal place for your attack."

"I told you I'm not a pirate. And I haven't completed the repairs to my ship, so it's not possible anyway—"

"You are being too modest, Captain," Greenstreet said. "You've done a remarkable job refitting the ship, or so my men say. They have been checking on your progress and they tell me that since you installed the brass helm, the *Victorie* is ready to sail."

Kate swore silently. She herself had said Greenstreet knew everything that went on the Aligoes. She should have been more careful.

"If you know that, you know I have yet to take my ship into the Breath," said Kate. "You also know that I have no guns, no gun crew, no powder or shot. So how do you expect me attack an armed merchant ship?"

"You threatened to attack the Travians," said Greenstreet. "You have a dragon. Who needs cannons? I will provide whatever you require including a crew—the best sailors in the Aligoes. Make a list of the supplies."

Kate did some fast thinking. She had two reasons she couldn't attack this Freyan merchant: Alan and Dalgren. Alan Northrop was a Freyan patriot, fighting for the glory and honor of his beloved country. If he found out that Kate had turned pirate and attacked a Freyan ship and stolen Freyan money, he would never forgive her.

As for Dalgren, ever since the battle that had left him severely wounded and killed one of his dearest friends, he had sworn to Kate that he would never fight again.

The answer came to her. She would let Greenstreet think that she was going to go along with his plan, and then slip out of Freeport before he knew she and *Victorie* were gone. Olaf would oppose such a dishonest scheme, but she'd deal with him when the time came. Greenstreet had offered to pay for supplying her ship. She might as well let him.

"Very well, I'll do it," she said, sounding reluctant. "Provided we can come to terms. What's my share of the loot?"

"The usual for those in the profession," said Greenstreet. "One-tenth of the value of the cargo and ransom money to be divided up between you and your crew as you see fit."

"One-fifth," Kate countered. "I deserve more. I have a dragon and Dalgren will want a cut."

Greenstreet smiled. "Very well. One-fifth. But you must capture the *Pride* intact, not sink her. I don't mind if the passengers and cargo are slightly singed, but they must not come to any harm."

"Agreed," said Kate, eyeing the man closely. Greenstreet was rarely so amenable. He smiled at her, but then he was always smiling. "I will come back with the list of supplies tomorrow."

She rose from the chair again, taking the manifest and the newspaper with her. This time she managed to reach the door and was about to open it when Greenstreet called after her.

"How is my old friend, Olaf, these days?" he asked pleasantly. "Business at the tavern brisk?"

Kate stopped with her hand on the door.

"Business is fine," she said.

"Excellent," said Greenstreet. "And that cook—Akiel. I hear his food is quite good. I must stop in for supper sometime. Did you know there is an arrest warrant out for him in Freya? He is wanted for murder."

Kate was silent.

"Then there's your dragon friend, Dalgren," Greenstreet continued. "Are you aware he is a deserter? The Dragon Brigade would give a great deal to have him returned to stand trial."

Kate gripped the door handle so hard her knuckles turned white. No one, not even Olaf, knew that Dalgren was a deserter. The dragon had sworn her to secrecy. She might not be a very good person, but she was loyal to her friends.

"And finally we come to you, Kate," Greenstreet continued, smiling. "I hear the Hollow Soul gang in Westfirth is still unhappy that you left without making good on Morgan's gambling debts."

Kate turned to face Greenstreet.

"I said I would do the job," she told him. "You don't need to use threats."

"You forget, my dear," said Greenstreet, leaning back and lacing his fingers together across his belly. "I did business with your father."

The setting sun gilded the Breath. Looking out across the mists, Kate could see other islands in the distance. As dark rain clouds rolled in, the islands vanished. A light drizzle began to fall. Kate hunched her shoulders against the rain and kept walking.

She had no idea what to do. She devised various plans and discarded all of them. Greenstreet was having her watched, having her ship watched. Apparently he was even having Dalgren watched, although how he was managing this—given that the dragon's cave was halfway up the side of a mountain—Kate couldn't fathom.

She slowed her footsteps as she drew near the tavern. The rain had changed from a drizzle to a downpour, but despite the fact that she was soaked, she did not want to go inside. She was planning to fix this mess, but at the moment she didn't exactly know how.

Like most buildings in the Aligoes, the Parrot was constructed of wooden slats covered with stucco and magic. During the years the building had been unoccupied before Olaf bought it, the magic had been allowed to deteriorate. Olaf had repaired the magical constructs and given the building a new coat of whitewash. Unable to afford a sign with the tavern's name, he had hired a local artist to paint a garish green and orange parrot on the outer front wall.

The parrot seemed to view Kate with a critical eye. Once again, she'd landed herself in trouble. Herself and her friends, in another scheme to make money.

She could rationalize her reasons, just as Morgan had always done. She needed the money. The Parrot had done well during the war, but now in peacetime the tavern was barely surviving. Rum and ale were plentiful, but whiskey had to be imported all the way from Freya. The cost was dear and Olaf was reluctant to pass it onto the customers, while Akiel gave away food to anyone with a hard-luck story. Without Kate and her wrecking business, they might all be in the workhouse or worse.

That much was true, Kate offered in her defense. But it was also true that she had borrowed money knowing she couldn't pay it back to fix up a derelict warship intended to buy a dream.

"I'll fix it," Kate told the parrot.

A flash of lightning drove her inside. Wooden booths lined the walls, and a few tables and chairs were scattered about the middle of the room. The bar was on the left near the back. She and Olaf each had their own small room in the rear of the building. Marco and the rest of the crew lived in town. Akiel lived on board the *Rose*, which was docked in the harbor, and did the cooking out back in a lean-to shack with a brick oven and a fire pit.

The tavern's regulars called out greetings to Kate as she walked in the door. The smell of Akiel's spicy chicken stew filled the air. Olaf was behind the bar, keeping ale mugs full, and Akiel was filling stew bowls. She noticed that two of Greenstreet's henchmen sat in a corner booth. They grinned at her when she entered.

Olaf flashed her a questioning look that she answered with a reassuring smile before going to her room. After shutting and locking the door, she picked up a bottle of Calvados, poured some into a mug, and took a gulp. Fortified, she sat down to read the story about Captain Kate in the newspaper.

Miss Amelia Nettleship certainly had a way with words.

Kate threw down the paper, poured herself another drink, and shifted her attention to the manifest Greenstreet had handed her.

Captain Northrop had always had access to ships' manifests, which was how he came to know what ships he and the Rose Hawks would attack. She had often wondered how he had obtained them and she guessed she now knew the answer. Greenstreet had provided them. Reading the manifest, Kate poured herself another drink.

She remained in her room until she heard Olaf shouting last call and the sounds of Akiel herding stragglers out the door. Kate picked up the newspaper and the bottle of Calvados and went into the common room.

The lanterns hanging from the ceiling were still lighted. Akiel was doing the washing up, dunking pewter mugs in a big tub of soapy water, while Olaf wiped down the bar with a rag.

"What happened, Katydid?" the old man asked. "What did Greenstreet want?"

Kate sat down at a table. "Do you have any of that stew left? I'm starved."

Akiel brought her a bowl of stew and a mug of ale. Kate ate rapidly, then shoved the bowl away.

"Come join me, both of you," said Kate.

"As bad as that, is it?" Olaf grunted.

Kate ignored him.

Olaf rested his crutch against the table and lowered himself onto a chair. Akiel took a seat alongside him. Kate opened the newspaper and spread it out on the table.

Olaf saw the headline, blinked, then looked at Kate in astonishment. "'Captain Kate and Her Dragon Corsairs'?"

"Read on," said Kate. "It gets better."

Olaf brought out a pair of old glasses, hooked them over his ears, and began to read. Occasionally he would pause, glance at Kate, shake his head, and sigh. Akiel looked over Olaf's shoulder.

"A lot of words," said Akiel, who had never learned to read. "What do they say?"

"The story says that I'm a pirate," said Kate. "I sail a pirate ship with a ruthless pirate crew and a dragon. We roam the Breath in search of treasure."

Akiel blinked at her. "But you are not a pirate. Why would someone tell such lies about you?"

"The lies are mine," said Kate.

She explained how she had met Miss Amelia Nettleship.

"She paid me five golden eagles and said there would be more money to come if her readers liked the stories. I never thought—"

"'I never thought,'" Olaf said grimly. "Now, where have I heard those words before?"

Kate began toying with her mug, pushing it back and forth.

"I do not understand," said Akiel, watching them both.

"'I never thought' was Morgan's mantra," Kate said. "'I never thought the constable would refuse a bribe.' 'I never thought the customs agent would inspect the hold.' 'I never thought that gang in Westfirth would bash in my skull!'"

Kate sighed, poured Calvados in the ale, and drank it. Olaf gave her a troubled look.

"So Greenstreet read this malarkey, Kate. What of it? He couldn't possibly believe it." Olaf slapped the newspaper in disgust. "This woman claims we sank a Rosian galleon off of San Artejo! I haven't seen a galleon afloat in twenty-five years. No one sails those tubs anymore. Even a lubber like Greenstreet knows that."

"He does know it," Kate said. "He doesn't believe the stories."

"Then why did he send for you?" Olaf asked.

"Because he wants to believe them," Kate said. "Captain Kate and her Dragon Corsairs are going to sail the Breath. He's even picked out the first ship we are going to attack."

"And you told him we would," Olaf said, glowering.

"Of course, I did. The idea is sound," Kate said, manufacturing a smile. "What do you think I've been planning to do all these months? Deliver the mail? Those stories I told that woman are my dreams. 'Fight for your dreams,' Captain de Guichen told me. Well, I'm fighting."

Kate ran her hand through her rain-damp hair, rumpling her curls. "What I *didn't* plan on was involving Greenstreet. Still, he's agreed to pay me a one-fifth share *and* provide the crew, supplies; anything I want."

Olaf whistled. "One-fifth! And he pays for everything?"

"He agreed to the deal without a murmur," said Kate. "Stinks, doesn't it?"

"To high heaven," said Olaf.

"Greenstreet gave me the manifest. Read the description of the cargo."

Olaf read aloud, "'Iron hoops, indigo, farm implements, whiskey, wool, turpentine, and hides.'"

"Would you call that cargo valuable?" Kate asked.

"All this would fetch a tidy sum on the black market," Olaf said. "Particularly the whiskey and the indigo. But I wouldn't term it valuable. Not near as valuable as the gold you stole from that Rosian galleon."

"I do not understand," said Akiel. "What stinks?"

"Greenstreet runs all the black markets in the Aligoes," Kate explained. "He knows what this lot is likely to fetch. He's going to a lot of trouble and expense to have me attack a ship carrying hides and turpentine. Something's not right."

Kate drank from the mug, then slammed it on the table. "And what really galls me is that Greenstreet thinks I'm so stupid I can't tell he's using me! What's the real reason Greenstreet wants me to attack the *Pride of Haever*? If I could figure that out, I would have a secret of our own we could use against him."

Olaf shook his head. "You're already in a hole, Katydid. Don't dig yourself any deeper. Here's an idea. Sell the *Victorie*. You've done a wonderful job on her. You'd make a tidy sum. You could pay back Greenstreet with money left over."

"The *Victorie* is mine! I won't sell her! Besides, Greenstreet now wants more than what I owe him," said Kate.

Olaf regarded her with concern, but he must have realized she was right.

"Bring me the registry, Kate," he said.

Kate lit a candle and went to Olaf's bedroom, which doubled as his office. Her father's old desk was covered with diagrams of Olaf's latest magical inventions. He kept his books here as well, including his well-worn copy of *A Seaman's Guide to Nautical Magic*, and several books that had belonged to Morgan, among them *Fairbanks Registry of Freyan and Foreign Shipping*.

Kate brought the book back to the table and gave it to Olaf.

Ships were listed in alphabetical order. He flipped through the pages until he came to the "P"s. He read through the descriptions; Kate read over his shoulder.

Pride of Haever:	***498/501DT (Owners only)***
Master:	*Captain William P. Bastian*
Rigging:	*Full Rigged*
Tonnage:	*1050 tons*
Measurements:	*Length, 157'6" (Keel, 130'1")*
	Beam, 41'3"
	Depth of hold, 15'4"
	Wings, Fore: 18'w×30'l
	Aft: 22'w×42'l
	Airscrews, Fore, 8' diameter
	Aft, 10' diameter
Flotation:	*2 6-chamber balloons*
	6 lift tanks
	3 ballast tanks
Construction:	*Tipton Yard, Whithaven*
Armament:	*28×12 lb cannon, 28×9 lb cannon,*
	36 swivel mounts

Owners: *Erlyon Shipping*
Port of Registry: *Haever, Freya*

"Bloody hell!" Kate swore.

She flung herself back in her chair.

"Always bad news," said Akiel. "Now you know why I do not learn to read."

"The *Pride of Haever* carries fifty-six guns!" said Kate. "She's as well armed as a ship of the line!"

"And all those guns means she has valuable cargo to protect," Olaf pointed out.

"That's for damn sure," said Kate. "But what? Freyan whiskey is good, but not that good."

"Whatever it is, they kept it off the manifest," Akiel pointed out. "They don't want the customs officials to know."

"What about the passengers?" Kate asked suddenly. "Greenstreet made a point of mentioning the passengers. Maybe there's a duke or a prince on board. Someone who would fetch a king's ransom."

Olaf picked up the manifest. "There is only one passenger: 'Henry Wallace, forty-seven, a gentleman of good character.' "

"I doubt if 'gentlemen of good character' are worth much these days," said Kate dispiritedly. "So what does Greenstreet want?"

"Whatever it is, he expects you to do the dirty work and he'll take the reward," said Olaf.

"And what will you do about Dalgren, mum?" Akiel added. "I do not think the dragon will want to be a corsair."

"Dalgren may not have a choice," Kate muttered.

"What was that?" Olaf asked, cupping his hand around his ear.

"I said—let me worry about Dalgren." Kate picked up the manifest to go over it again. "Greenstreet thinks I'm so stupid. He's the one who'll look stupid if we find the treasure first—"

"Kate, you're not thinking straight!" Olaf protested. "Even the Rosian navy would think twice about attacking the *Pride* . . ."

Kate looked up from her reading. "That's it!"

Olaf eyed her warily. "What is?"

"The Rosian navy!" Kate said.

"I know that grin," Olaf said, frowning. "That's the same smug, cat-that-ate-the-canary grin your father wore when he was plotting one of his crazy schemes."

Kate laughed and stood up. "No canary feathers in my teeth. I promise. Now I'm off to bed. I have lots of work to do tomorrow."

She kissed Olaf on the cheek. "You always say I'm my father's daughter."

Patting Akiel on the shoulder, Kate took the newspaper and the manifest and went to the back of the tavern.

Olaf shook his head and reached for his crutch.

"I don't mean it as a compliment," he told Akiel.

EIGHT

Kate returned to Greenstreet's house early the next morning. Jacob was on duty and looked surprised to see her.

"What do you want?" he grunted.

"I came to talk to Greenstreet," Kate said.

"He has someone with him," Jacob said.

"I'll wait," said Kate.

She did not have to wait long. The visitor departed, apparently by a different door, for Kate never saw him. The bell rang and Jacob grunted her inside.

Greenstreet, dressed all in white as usual, sat at his empty desk.

"Back so soon, Captain? I trust nothing is amiss."

"I have the list of supplies," said Kate. "Now tell me the truth about the cargo."

Greenstreet gazed at her in silence. He was still smiling, but light flickered in the hooded eyes. Kate smiled back.

"You presume too much upon my good nature, Captain," Greenstreet said at last. "I think you should leave. Go back to your wrecking."

Kate sat down in the chair opposite the desk.

"I am the one risking my life and the lives of my crew, Greenstreet. The

Pride of Haever could smash my brig to kindling. I need to know what cargo she is carrying that is so damn valuable you agreed to pay me a one-fifth share without so much as blinking."

Greenstreet regarded Kate from beneath his hooded eyelids. His pudgy finger traced a circle on the desk.

"She is carrying gold eagles from the treasury of Her Majesty, the Queen of Freya," he said. "The passenger, Wallace, is bringing the money to the governor of Wellinsport to pay for the repairs and reinforcement of the gun batteries in order to thwart an attack by the Rosians."

Kate concealed her surprise. She had not actually expected he would tell her.

"How much gold?" she asked.

Greenstreet shrugged. "I do not know. Thousands, certainly. Maybe hundreds of thousands."

Kate eyed Greenstreet. Once again, he had given in far too quickly. He still wasn't telling her the truth. Not all of it, at least.

"Obviously the fewer who know, the better," Greenstreet was saying. "Otherwise every pirate in the Aligoes will be after that ship. You would have to fight your way through a crowd."

"Believe me, for a share of hundreds of thousands, I will keep the secret," said Kate.

"And do not concern yourself over the *Pride of Haever,* Captain," said Greenstreet. "No captain—even one with fifty-six guns—would be so foolish as to fight a dragon."

Kate let that pass, and tossed over a piece of paper. "In addition to the supplies you mentioned, I need these items. And I need them fast."

Greenstreet picked up the paper, glanced over it, and raised an eyebrow. "Uniforms, assorted colors of balloon silk, bolts of cloth, paint . . ." He read on, then looked at her, amazed. "Three seamstresses and a tailor? I fail to understand—"

"This is secret, right," said Kate. "The less you know about my plans, the better. I assume you can lay your hands on all this."

"The uniforms will take some time," said Greenstreet. "I can have the rest to you by tomorrow, along with three women who are skilled in sewing. I am not certain I can find a tailor."

"I'll make do," said Kate. "Oh, and let your bullyboys know I'm going to be traveling to Wellinsport for supplies. I'll be there overnight. I don't want your men to think I'm trying to run."

"I will inform them," said Greenstreet. "No doubt they will continue to make themselves comfortable in Olaf's tavern while you are away. Just to ensure your return."

"I'll return. And I'll capture that ship," said Kate. "After all, you're paying me one-fifth. Tell your men to deliver those supplies to the Parrot."

She was pleased with herself and even wished Jacob a good morning as she left. He answered with a grunt.

Kate wondered whether or not to tell Olaf and Akiel about the gold. She decided she would keep the information to herself until she found out if Greenstreet was telling the truth.

It was midmorning and already the heat was unbearable. Shading her eyes against the blinding sunlight, she left the main street and turned onto a rockbound path that wound its way along the shoreline to what had once been a lighthouse. The path was overgrown with weeds, for few walked it these days. The citizens of Freeport had built a new lighthouse, closer to the entrance of the harbor. The old stone tower, its light extinguished, stood abandoned.

When Dalgren had arrived, he and Kate had needed a way to communicate with each other. She had come up with the idea of using the lighthouse, which had a flagpole from which different flags would be flown to alert passing ships to changing weather conditions.

The lighthouse had been left in a tumbledown condition, but Olaf had managed to repair the magical constructs on the stone exterior and the stairs that spiraled up to the top. Kate ran up the stairs and climbed through the trapdoor onto the roof. As always, she took time to admire the breathtaking view as she attached a flag to the halyard.

From this vantage point, on a clear day, she could see twenty or more lush green islands floating on the orange mists of the Breath. Some of the islands were lighter than others, particularly those formed of lava, and they ranged in altitude. Most of them were level with Freeport, but a few drifted above her and, looking down, she could see others below, partially obscured by the thicker mists.

She raised the flag—her private signal for Dalgren, telling him she needed to talk. Exactly what she was going to say to him to convince him to go along with her plan was still open to question. She had a three-mile-long walk to consider it.

Their meeting place was a large, empty patch of rock-strewn ground in the middle of the jungle. Kate had built a shed to house the dragon saddle, harness, and other gear Dalgren had taken with him when he had left the Brigade, telling Kate the Brigade owed him something for having ruined his life. He had presented them to Kate and taught her to ride—the fulfillment of one of her dreams.

Ever since the time when she was twelve years old and had sneaked into the Bastion to watch the dragons of the Brigade, Kate had longed to be a dragon rider. She and Dalgren had been practicing several times a week for over a year. They flew at sunrise, practicing their maneuvers over uninhabited islands where no one would see them.

Those moments spent soaring over the treetops, skimming the mists of the Breath, were the happiest in Kate's life. She was flying with her friend, and during those times she left her schemes and plans and dreams on the ground below.

She would revel in the exhilarating plunge out of a cloud bank as she and Dalgren swooped down on some imaginary ship or streaked upward to escape imaginary gunfire. She would gasp in stomach-lurching delight when the world tipped over as Dalgren rolled away from a phantom attack, or rest easy in the saddle, admiring the beauty of the islands drifting in a sea of mists, watching the sun spread red and gold light across the sky. At these times, she would think of telling Dalgren to fly eastward into the sunrise and never stop.

But the world was always right below her, and eventually she would have to come down. While she unfastened the complicated harness and removed the large, ungainly dragon saddle, she and Dalgren would talk over their flight, sometimes seriously discussing problems, but more often laughing. With his help, she would drag the saddle into the shed and shut the door, and the world and its problems were there to greet her.

Thinking about their flights together gave her an idea for how to persuade Dalgren to go along with her scheme.

The dragon must have been close by when he saw the flag, for she found him lying on the sun-warmed rocks, snoozing, the bloody remnants of a meal scattered on the ground. Dalgren had no difficulty finding food. Most of the nearby islands were teeming with deer and goats and wild hogs. He ate so well, Kate often accused him of getting fat.

Hearing her approach, Dalgren sleepily opened his eyes. He greeted her with a prodigious yawn. "I saw the flag. What's happened now?"

"We're famous," said Kate, waving the newspaper.

Dalgren raised his head, eyes narrowing. "I don't want to be famous."

"I am afraid you have no choice," said Kate.

She told Dalgren how she had met Miss Amelia and regaled her with tales of their imaginary adventures, how Miss Amelia had written the stories and published them in a Freyan newspaper and now everyone was reading about Captain Kate and her Dragon Corsairs.

Dalgren listened in growing shock and disbelief. He raised his head, jaws parted, eyes wide, smoke curling from his nostrils. Shock exploded into outrage when Kate added that Greenstreet had read the stories and now he wanted the Dragon Corsairs to capture a merchant ship.

"I am not a corsair!" Dalgren roared. "If I wanted to fight, I'd still be with the Brigade. You refused, of course."

Kate didn't immediately answer, and Dalgren regarded her with suspicion. "You did refuse."

"I couldn't, Dalgren," she said. "Greenstreet knows you are a deserter."

Dalgren stared at her, aghast. "That's not possible. The Brigade dragons handle matters among their own kind. They don't even tell their riders. Only another dragon could have discovered such information."

He eyed her. "Unless you said something . . ."

"I didn't, Dalgren," said Kate. "I would never betray you. You know that."

She was in earnest. She might and often did lie to her friends, generally telling herself that the lies were for their own good. But though she might lie to them, she was fiercely loyal to them and would never betray them. Her friends were family to her, all the family she had left.

Kate started to excuse herself by saying, "I never thought . . ." Hearing Morgan's voice in her head, she quickly changed the words to "Don't worry. I'm going to fix this."

"Where have I heard that before?" Dalgren muttered.

"I know," said Kate. "But this time I have a plan. I'm going to capture the merchant ship. This job is going to make our fortune, Dalgren! And just think of it," she said hurriedly, seeing by the glint in his eye that he was going to refuse, "we'll get to fly together! We don't need to hide anymore!"

Dalgren grunted and fire flickered from between his teeth, but at least he was listening. "I won't fight."

"You won't have to," Kate said eagerly. "You scared the wadding out of the Travians! One puff of smoke and you had the sailors bleating like sheep."

Dalgren had been trying to look stern and forbidding, but the memory of the terror he had caused on board the Travian ship was too funny. He gave a chortle that rumbled deep in his chest.

"They did bleat, didn't they?" he said, fangs showing in a grin. "You're saying that's all I have to do? Scare people?"

"That's all you have to do," Kate promised.

"And you and I will fly together?"

"Our first real mission as dragon and rider," said Kate. She rested both her hands on Dalgren's forefoot. "That will be the best part."

"Flying together, dragon and rider," said Dalgren. His eyes warmed. "I wonder what Captain de Guichen would say if he could see us."

"That we fought for our dreams," said Kate in softened tones.

"Dreams of being pirates!" Dalgren said, snorting out a gout of flame. "Speaking of pirates, what will your friend, Captain Northrop, say when he hears you and I seized a Freyan ship?"

"He won't say anything because he won't know you and I did it," said Kate.

Dalgren was dubious. "*You* might get away disguising yourself as a man, but I'm hard to miss. People have a tendency to remember me."

He indicated the newspaper. "I'm even in that disgusting illustration, although no one would ever recognize me! Whoever drew that monstrosity has never seen a real live dragon."

"That's because there are no dragons in Freya, so the artist didn't have a model," said Kate. "I have everything worked out, Dalgren. Trust me."

"Two words that with you are a precursor to trouble," Dalgren growled.

Kate laughed. "Not this time, my friend. Fate owes me. Now, make yourself comfortable and I'll read our story to you."

Dalgren rested his chin on his front feet, stretched out his hind legs, and folded his wings close to his body.

"You made me the hero, of course," he said.

NINE

Now that Kate had Dalgren's consent, she needed only to confirm the story of the gold on board the *Pride of Haever*. She had a contact in Wellinsport who might be able to help. That was why she had told Greenstreet she would have to pick up supplies there, so that he wouldn't be suspicious. To further allay his suspicions, she openly sailed in the *Barwich Rose,* when otherwise she might have taken one of the island jumper ferries.

Freyans had colonized the island of Whitefalls eight hundred years ago. Wellinsport, located on the Trame Channel, was the island's capital. One of the few Deep Breath ports in the Aligoes, Wellinsport had become a hub for international trade, some of it legal, much of it not.

Wellinsport had a thriving black market and was renowned for its gambling clubs, houses of pleasure, and opium dens. Captain Northrop and his famous privateers, the Rose Hawks, had been based out of the city before and during the war and were local heroes. Smugglers had never had a need to hide, and often shared berths with legitimate shipowners.

Money flowed from Wellinsport into Her Majesty's coffers, and if some of the coins ended up in the pockets of the governor, the Right Honorable Aldous Finchley, Viscount Claremore, Her Majesty turned a blind eye.

Known for its wealth and coveted for its Deep Breath harbor, Wellinsport had often come under attack, most recently fending off the Bottom Dwellers and their pirate allies. Menacing gun batteries guarded the harbor. As the *Rose* sailed beneath them, Kate tried to imagine what it would be like to come under fire from the massive forty-two-pound cannon.

Unfortunately, the batteries were not as formidable as they once had been. The green-beam weapons of the Bottom Dwellers had badly damaged the cannons, particularly the magical constructs that were used for everything from firing the weapons to protecting them from enemy fire. For two years, the Right Honorable had done nothing to repair them, despite angry letters from the Foreign Office in Haever.

With the Bottom Dwellers no longer a threat, Governor Finchley had found other uses for the money. He had completely remodeled the governor's mansion, thrown lavish parties, and entertained wealthy plantation owners. The residents did not begrudge him his fun and no one gave a thought to the crumbling, rusting guns.

Life in Wellinsport was good again. Trade had resumed. Markets and auction houses flourished. The taverns, whorehouses, opium dens, and gambling clubs were filled. And then one day, two enemy ships belonging to the Rosian "Rum" Fleet, as it was popularly known in the Rosian navy, had sailed into the Trame Channel.

Everybody in Wellinsport, including the governor, was convinced that the Rosians were here to prepare for a campaign to capture the city. Governor Finchley had dispatched an angry letter to King Renaud, demanding to know what the Rosians were doing in the Aligoes.

The king had sent a soothing letter to Governor Finchley, reminding him that the Rosians had a perfect right to be in the Aligoes and explaining that he was planning to stop the depredations of pirates on Rosian shipping. Governor Finchley did not believe him.

Panicked, the governor had belatedly ordered repairs to the batteries, and recently, in a fit of pique, he had placed an embargo on Rosian merchant ships.

The batteries were a hive of activity now. They were covered with scaffolding, and Kate could see men crawling about, probably stone crafters replacing and strengthening the constructs, which had been obliterated by the weapons of the Bottom Dwellers. Balloons were being used to lift and position new forty-eight-pound cannons, along with barrels of powder and shot. Soldiers lined the walls, keeping watch for the hated Rosians. Kate was in a good mood and she waved to the soldiers as she sailed past.

All that work must cost a lot of gold eagles, Kate reflected. Hundreds of thousands. She tried to picture that much gold and wondered how many strongboxes would be required to transport such a vast sum.

After a five-hour voyage, the *Rose* arrived in Wellinsport in the afternoon. Kate left Marco in charge while she and Akiel went into the city. They visited the markets and the auction houses, purchasing food and supplies.

By the time they were finished, darkness had fallen. Kate left Akiel and Marco to make certain everything was delivered and safely stowed. When that was done, she told the crew they could go ashore, so long as they were back on board ship in the morning.

Kate went into town on business of her own, planning to talk to one of Alan's former Rose Hawks, a young man known as Phillip "Jones." She had always assumed his name was a nom de guerre. The Rose Hawks had been formed by young gentlemen from good families who had come to the Aligoes in search of adventure and had kept their true identities secret so that their families might be spared embarrassment. Although in Pip's case, Alan had often said jokingly, his family might have changed their name in order to be spared Pip.

Pip, as he was called, worked as a clerk in the governor's office, and if anyone would know anything about the *Pride of Haever* and the truth about its cargo and passengers, it would be Pip.

She and Pip had first met in the company of Alan Northrop and the Rose Hawks during one of their visits to the Parrot. The youngest of the Rose Hawks, Pip had served as second lieutenant aboard Alan's ship, the *Royal Hawk*. Pip was not particularly handsome—not like Alan. Pip's mouth was too wide, he had one blue eye and one green, and his short blond hair was bleached almost white by the sun. He was fun-loving and charming, however, although he had an unfortunate tendency to squander his prize money on games of chance and Freyan whiskey. Pip and Kate had become friends, perhaps because, as Olaf said, Pip reminded her of her father.

Captain Northrop and the Rose Hawks had left the Aligoes to join the fight against the Bottom Dwellers, and Kate had lost track of Pip. She hadn't heard from him in years and she had therefore been astonished to run into him a couple of months ago in a market in Wellinsport.

Their conversation had been short.

"I didn't you know you were back in the Aligoes, Pip," Kate had said. "What are you doing here? Are you still with Captain Northrop? Are the Rose Hawks going into action against the Rosians?"

"I can't say what the Rose Hawks are doing these days," Pip had replied with a gusty sigh that reeked of wine fumes. "I got sacked, I'm afraid."

"I'm sorry, Pip." Kate had been sympathetic.

"My fault entirely," Pip had answered cheerfully. "Alan had every right to give me the boot. I had a bit too much to drink and fell asleep on watch.

He was decent about it. Court-martial offense, but he hushed it up. I had to quit the service, though, and seek gainful employment. I'm clerking for the governor."

"I thought clerks sat on tall stools with their fingers steeped in ink," Kate had said, laughing. "And here I find you at the wine merchant's."

"The Right Honorable is throwing a big party," Pip had explained. "He sent me to order the wine."

"You've obviously been tasting it before you buy it," Kate had teased. "How is Captain Northrop? What is he doing?"

"No idea, I'm afraid," Pip had told her. "I heard he got his hand blown off in a fight with the BDs. Oh, he's fine," he had added, seeing Kate's alarm. "Alan always did have the devil's own luck, you know."

Kate had wanted to ask more about Alan, but Pip said he must run; the governor was waiting to hear about his wine.

"Come see me the next time you're in town," Pip had added before rushing off. "We'll have more time to chat. You can find me at the Red Lion. Ask anyone. They'll tell you where it is."

Kate didn't need to ask. She was familiar with the Red Lion. The gambling club had been one of Morgan's favorite haunts.

On the off chance that Greenstreet was having her watched, Kate disguised herself as one of the locals, dressing in a long skirt, an apron, and a shawl tied around her shoulders, with her hair bound up in a colorful scarf.

She didn't see anyone following her from the ship, but she didn't dare take chances and so she went first to a tavern popular with the locals. Almost every woman there was wearing a shawl and a scarf. Kate mingled with them, then slipped out by the back entrance and walked to the center of the city.

The streets of Wellinsport were crowded. People slept in the afternoon during the heat of the day, and did business or took their pleasure after dark. The first few blocks, Kate kept careful watch. Seeing no one dogging her steps, she relaxed. The Red Lion Gambling Club was located in a well-to-do neighborhood, and was known for the eclectic nature of its clientele. The only requirement for admittance to the Red Lion was money; so long as you had that, you were welcome to enter. Merchants and plantation owners played cards with smugglers and pirates, soldiers, sailors and clerks.

The Red Lion had been a private house before it was converted to a gambling club. The house was made of brick and was three stories tall with long, narrow windows. Light streamed from the windows onto the street. Inside, men and women gathered around tables, drinking and laughing. Kate remembered standing on the street as a girl, wondering where her father was among that glittering crowd.

Morgan had been a good-natured gambler. He had played for the excitement, the thrill of risking all he had on the turn of a card. If he won, he was happy. If he lost, he smiled and shrugged it off. Kate often thought her father had become a smuggler for the same reason—the excitement, the thrill of risking all he had.

That had included his life. Kate turned away from the windows and walked up to the front door.

She curtsied and held out a note. "I have a message for a gentleman of this establishment, from my mistress."

The doorman saw the name, Phillip Jones, written in a feminine hand. He summoned a servant, who carried it inside. A few moments later, Pip appeared, dressed in evening clothes and smelling of whiskey.

The doorman pointed to Kate, who dropped another curtsy.

"Do I know you, madame?" Pip asked, peering at her uncertainly.

"My mistress is around the corner, in a coach, sir," said Kate. "She says you are to talk to her."

Pip was overcome with amazement. "Are you sure she meant me? Women don't, as a general rule."

"Just come, sir, please!" said Kate.

"Very well," said Pip with a good-natured smile.

Kate seized hold of him by the hand and guided him, swaying slightly, down the street and around a corner. Here she ducked behind a large flowering bush and pulled off her scarf.

"It's me, Pip."

Pip blinked, his confusion growing. "Kate? Where did you come from? I was talking to a servant. There was a woman in a carriage . . ."

"Yes, never mind," said Kate. "I need to talk to you. I'm sorry to take you away from your card game—"

"Oh, that's all right," Pip said. "I was glad for the excuse to leave. Have you ever played vingt-et-un? Don't. Wretched game." Looking downcast, he took a seat on a convenient door stoop. "Why did you want to talk to me?"

Kate sat down beside him. "I need information. What do you know about a Freyan merchant ship called the *Pride of Haever*? The ship is on its way to Wellinsport."

"Merchantman owned by Erlyon Shipping," Pip said promptly. "Makes regular voyages between here and there. Why? Are you hoping she'll wreck and you can claim the cargo?"

"Of course not! You know me better than that, Pip," Kate said, genuinely shocked. "You were a sailor. Even thinking about wrecks is bad luck, like whistling on board ship."

"Sorry, I didn't know," said Pip, looking anxious. "Should I turn around three times and spit?"

He started to stagger to his feet. Kate pulled him back down. "No, you'd just fall over. A man named Henry Wallace is one of the passengers on board the *Pride*. If this is the same Henry Wallace, he was a good friend of my father's."

Kate was lying, of course. Her father had never known anyone named Wallace. Pip wouldn't be aware of that, however. "Do you know anything about this Wallace? I'm trying to figure out if he's the right one."

"Wallace," Pip repeated, his forehead creased in thought. "The only Henry Wallace I know works in the Foreign Office."

"That sounds like my father's friend," said Kate. "Would he be likely to travel to Wellinsport?"

"He might, I suppose. . . ." Pip brightened. "Maybe he's come to sack the Right Honorable! The chappies in the Foreign Office aren't at all happy with the governor. Devilishly hard to get rid of the viscount, though. He's a friend of the queen's. Sent her a monkey."

Kate wasn't interested in monkeys. She had counted on the fact that in his inebriated state, Pip would let slip something about the gold. Unfortunately he appeared on the verge of nodding off. His head sank to his chest, his eyes closed.

Kate gave him a nudge in the ribs with her elbow. Pip blinked and jerked upright. "Is it my turn to lead?"

Kate sighed and decided she needed to take desperate measures before Pip passed out. He probably wouldn't remember anything she said to him by tomorrow anyway.

She leaned close to whisper, "The truth is, Pip, I heard a rumor that this Wallace is carrying a fortune in gold eagles."

"No! Really?" Pip whispered back, breathing whiskey fumes in her face. "Whatever for?"

"I heard Wallace is going to give the gold to your governor—"

Pip threw back his head, losing his hat, and burst into wild laughter.

"Stop it! Someone will hear you!!" Kate scolded. "What's so funny?"

"The notion of Wallace giving a fortune in gold to the Right Honorable!" Pip said, choking on his own mirth. He wiped his eyes and looked about vaguely for his hat. "That's a bloody good rumor. Where did you hear it?"

"Never mind," Kate said, disappointed. She picked up his hat and put it back on his head. "Are you sure it's not true?"

"Of course I'm sure. Her Majesty, God save her, is fond of the Right Honorable, but not that fond," said Pip. "She would never entrust a fortune to the governor, no matter how many monkeys he sent her."

He chuckled again at the thought. "And now, speaking of fortunes, Kate, I must be getting back to the gaming tables. My luck's bound to change. Give us a hand, will you?"

Kate hauled him upright and, seeing that he was a bit unsteady on his feet, she put her arm around him and helped him back to the Red Lion.

"Good-bye, Pip," said Kate. "Take care of yourself."

"I always seem to manage," Pip said, grinning. "Though I'm damned if know how."

He shook hands and with a bow and a cheery flourish of his hat, bid her good night. Kate watched to make certain he made it safely inside. The last she saw of Pip, he had bounded up the stairs and tumbled headlong into the doorman.

Kate slowly walked back to the harbor. With her head down and her arms crossed under her shawl, she was absorbed in her thoughts and not watching where she was going, bumping into people on the crowded streets without noticing.

At first she was inclined to believe Pip and was disappointed. Upon reflection, however, she grew more cheerful. Pip was a low-level clerk, responsible for buying wine and planning parties. What would he know about a fortune in gold? Greenstreet was reputed to have spies everywhere. He was much more likely than poor Pip to have reliable information.

"Greenstreet is going to a lot of trouble and expense," Kate said to herself. "The gold will be there. I know it!"

TEN

Sir Henry Wallace, on board the *Pride of Haever,* was thinking to himself that Miss Amelia Nettleship was certainly not what he had been expecting.

He reflected on this and other matters of no importance as he leaned against the rail, sipping his morning coffee. He found it pleasant to have the leisure to reflect on unimportant matters. He had any number of extremely important matters to worry about, but since there was no way he could possibly attend to them while sailing on a ship through the Aligoes, he dismissed them from his mind.

Mr. Sloan had been right. The voyage had been idyllic: calm weather, sunshine, amiable company. Henry had enjoyed himself. He felt more relaxed that he had in months.

He would undoubtedly find mail waiting for him in Wellinsport, but until then, he did not have to concern himself with reports from his network of agents and spies. He could trust Mr. Sloan to deal with those in his absence. If there was a true emergency, such as his beloved Mouse going into labor or the fall of the government, Mr. Sloan would send a griffin rider to find him.

Henry allowed himself to drink his coffee, watching the green-forested islands of the Aligoes slip past the ship and reflecting upon Miss Amelia Nettleship.

Having never met a female journalist, Henry had pictured a severe, formidable woman much like Matron, who ran the university infirmary. Matron had dealt with countless young gentlemen over the years and had learned their ways. She could spot a malingerer trying to avoid a test at fifty paces and with a look reduce him to a blob of pease pudding. Henry still shuddered at the memory of her cure for a hangover, a concoction that had caused many a young libertine to abstain from strong drink for the remainder of his life.

Henry found Miss Nettleship to be a strong-minded woman in her forties, outspoken, cheerful, and insatiably curious. She wore practical clothes with little care for the dictates of fashion, appearing daily in a brown tailored jacket and matching brown ankle-length skirt, a white linen blouse with a stand-up collar, and lace-up black boots. Her thick hair was of the same brown color as her clothes and she wore it knotted in a bun, "so as not to be a bother" beneath what was known as a "porkpie" hat.

Henry found himself liking her, despite the fact that she immediately attacked him, bombarding him with questions about everything from the succession to the Braffans and King Ullr to Prince Tom.

"Is it true, Sir Henry, that the queen supports her Rosian sister to be queen of Freya?" Amelia had asked before the *Pride of Haever* had even left the harbor. She followed up this question with "I was informed, Sir Henry, that the leader of the House of Nobles attempted to persuade Her Majesty to name her half brother, Hugh, as her heir. What was Her Majesty's response?"

After he had managed to avoid answering that, she asked, "Is it your opinion, Sir Henry, that the wildly popular young man known as Prince Tom has a legitimate claim to the throne?"

Accustomed to dealing with reporters, Henry had fended off her questions with his customary polite answers that appeared to say a great deal yet in fact said nothing at all. Amelia was not in the least upset by his refusal to provide her with a story; indeed, she could hardly be angry, since he had paid for her passage.

That said, she truly appeared to relish the challenge of trying to wheedle information from him. She made rather a game of it, pouncing on him at odd times—such as when they were dining with the captain—hoping to catch him unawares.

The daily Aligoes rainstorm drove Henry off the deck and back to his cabin. He wrote a letter to his wife and then took advantage of the solitude to read several more stories about Captain Kate.

He was smiling over these when he noted that the storm had ended. He went back on deck and found Miss Nettleship "taking the air," which meant she had cornered the captain on the quarterdeck and was asking him about the effect that sales of Freyan whiskey were having on the Aligoes rum trade.

Henry went to the rescue. Hat in hand, he bowed to Miss Nettleship, begged forgiveness for the interruption, and asked if she would like to join him in his morning constitutional.

"I owe you one," said Captain Bastian in a low voice as he beat a hasty retreat.

Amelia went armed with an umbrella, which Henry had never seen her without, and a beaded reticule, hanging by a chain over her left arm.

"Mrs. Ridgeway, of Mrs. Ridgeway's Academy for Young Ladies, used to say that a lady can go anywhere in the world with an umbrella and a sensible pair of shoes," Amelia had informed him.

Her shoes were most certainly sensible, being sturdy, lace-up walking boots with a small heel. As for the umbrella, she used it for a wide variety of purposes: shading herself from the sun, shielding herself from the rainstorms, as a walking stick, and, once, to jab at a rat as it scurried across the deck.

The reticule was a repository for all manner of objects: a brown leather notebook, pencils, a knife for sharpening the pencils, a handkerchief embroidered with the initials "A.N.," and, Henry was startled to see, a small pistol.

"Do you always carry a weapon, Miss Nettleship?" he asked.

"Indeed, I do, my lord," Amelia answered with a vigorous nod. "I will go anywhere in pursuit of a story, often venturing into unsavory locales."

"Where you obtain answers to your questions at gunpoint," Henry said, teasing.

"Keep that in mind, my lord, when I ask you about Prince Tom," said Amelia, with a wink.

She permitted him to examine the weapon, which featured two chambers and two barrels, each with its own trigger.

"Please be careful," she instructed. "I always keep the pistol loaded."

"Quite unique," said Henry, inspecting the weapon. "I've never seen one quite like this."

"My own design," said Amelia. "I employed a gunsmith to make it for me. The pistol has special magical constructs that enable each barrel to fire independently. Thus I always have two shots available without having to stop to reload."

"A formidable weapon, Miss Nettleship," said Henry, handing back the pistol.

"I have found it advantageous to be able to defend myself," said Amelia cheerfully. "I am quite a good shot, if I may so myself. During my years as a student at Mrs. Ridgeway's Academy for Young Ladies, I always received the prize for Expert Marksmanship."

Amelia returned the pistol to the reticule and drew out the brown leather notebook and the pencil. With these in hand, she snapped shut the reticule, hung the umbrella by its handle over her arm, and returned to the attack.

"And now, Sir Henry, on the subject of the heir to the throne, I have it on good authority—"

Henry interrupted. "I beg your pardon, Miss Nettleship, but I begin to find walking about in the sun fatiguing. Let us sit in the shade and enjoy the cool breeze."

He did not give her time to respond, but escorted her to two deck chairs the sailors had placed in the shadow of one of the balloons. Before Amelia could return to the heir to the throne, Henry launched a counteroffensive.

"I have been meaning to tell you, Miss Nettleship, that I have been enjoying your stories regarding Captain Kate. They were recommended to me by my wife, who is one of your most devoted readers. I do have one question for you. I trust you will not mind if I ask it?"

"Considering that I have been plying you with questions these last five days, my lord, I believe you have the right to turn the table on me, as we say in backgammon," replied Amelia.

Henry leaned close to ask softly, "Is Captain Kate real or did you make her up?"

Amelia was highly amused. "No need to whisper, my lord. Captain Kate is quite real, though I fear the tales she told me are not. She is captain of a wrecker, not a pirate ship, as she claimed."

Henry pondered this information. "Wrecking is a dirty and dangerous job. She must be an extraordinary woman."

"She is, indeed. Why are you interested in Captain Kate, my lord?" Amelia asked.

Henry was silent. Amelia regarded him with a knowing air, then leaned forward to tap him on the arm with her pencil.

"You asked me to accompany you on this voyage to talk about Kate, didn't you, my lord! I have been wondering about your true motivation. I didn't think you wanted me to write about the viscount. At least, not disclose the truth."

"You may disclose whatever you like about the Right Honorable Aldous

Finchley, Miss Nettleship," said Henry drily. "But, yes, I admit that I really wanted to know more about Captain Kate."

"And why is that, my lord?"

"I want you to keep writing stories about her, Miss Nettleship," said Henry. "You have a devoted following and I would like to see it grow. Stories about this courageous and patriotic young woman are of value to the public."

Amelia gave him a shrewd look. "More so than stories about Prince Tom."

"More so than stories about a pretender to the throne," said Henry, frowning.

"You are a cagey one, my lord," Amelia said. "I begin to think all the stories I have heard about *you* are true."

Henry fanned himself with his hat. "Tell me more about Captain Kate."

"I met her in Wellinsport at an auction house. I offered to pay her for her story. I gave her money and said if my readers liked it, I would pay for more."

Amelia smiled and shook her head. "I knew immediately she was embellishing her adventures. The tale about the galleon, for example, was quite preposterous. Still, I also knew that my readers—particularly my female readers—would enjoy them. Perhaps even be inspired by them."

"I have read the fictional account of her life," said Henry. "What is the truth about Kate? Did you find out?"

"I am a journalist, my lord," said Amelia with a look of reproof. "Of course I found out. The tale of her true life is far more tragic and sordid than anything I could make up. I happen to have my notes, if you will give me a moment . . ."

Amelia removed a pince-nez from the reticule, attached it to her nose, then flipped through her notebook. Finding the page, she peered at it through the glasses.

"Her true name is Katherine Gascoyne-Fitzmaurice. She is the daughter of Morgan Fitzmaurice, third son of a wealthy merchant. Morgan obtained a commission in the Royal Navy and was eventually promoted to captain. Those who knew him describe him as 'engaging, charming, handsome.' Unfortunately he was also a liar and a fraud. He was suspected of using his position in the navy to smuggle goods on board a naval ship. The admiralty could not prove their case, however, and he was never court-martialed. He resigned his commission. The family hushed up the disgrace and promptly disowned him."

Henry made a mental note to have Randolph Baker obtain the naval records regarding Captain Morgan Fitzmaurice.

"Kate's mother, Lady Rose Gascoyne, was the only child of Viscount Ferdinand Gascoyne of Barwich—"

"That name sounds familiar," Henry said, brow furrowing. "Why do I know it?"

Amelia glanced up from reading. "Perhaps you are thinking of the rumors regarding the death of the viscount, my lord."

"That's right!" Henry exclaimed. "The old boy died in a hunting accident. Though circumstances were suspicious, as I recall."

"The truth was he shot himself," said Amelia. "Although that didn't come out until months after his death. That and the fact that the viscount was heavily in debt. His only child, a daughter, Lady Rose Gascoyne, was seventeen at the time of his suicide. Poor girl. She had no idea of the desperate state of his affairs until his solicitor told her. He suggested that she sell the estate, Barwich Manor."

"Rose knew if she did sell the estate, she would be ruined. She had beauty and she had a title. She determined to marry a rich man and save her estate. Friends introduced her to Captain Morgan Fitzmaurice."

Amelia closed her notebook. "Fate played a cruel jest upon these two weak young people. In order to capture a rich husband, Rose told Morgan she was a wealthy heiress. Morgan wanted a rich wife and told her he was the son of a wealthy merchant. They began a passionate affair and within a month, Rose was pregnant with Kate. The marriage was hasty, and it was only after the wedding that Rose discovered her 'rich' husband was knee-deep in gambling debts and Morgan found out that his 'rich' wife had one foot in debtor's prison."

"A cruel jest, as you say, Miss Nettleship," Henry remarked. "What happened to them after that?"

"Morgan accepted the situation with good grace. He had gambled and lost, which for him was nothing new. But Rose never forgave him for lying to her; never mind that she had lied to him.

"Morgan managed to buy a ship—some say he won it in a game of cards. He left Rose and went back to smuggling. After Kate was born, Morgan at first sent home money enough to support his family. His reformation did not last long, however. Morgan could never resist the lure of the cards. The money stopped coming and when Kate was six, the bank took possession of Barwich Manor. Rose died not long after. The locals say she died of a broken heart.

"Morgan was left with a daughter. Not knowing what to do with the girl, he took her with him on his travels. Kate was raised on board his ship, which is where she learned sailing, among other less savory skills. Morgan and Kate were close, or so I've been told. Eight years ago, Kate turned up in the Aligoes, saying she was now owner of the *Barwich Rose.* No one knows what became of Morgan. He was never seen or heard from again. Since he was involved with the Westfirth gangs, it is easy to imagine he ran afoul of them in some way."

"Poor girl," Henry remarked, almost to himself. "No wonder she makes up stories. Is the dragon real? Or did she make him up, as well?"

"Ah, that I do not know, my lord," said Amelia. "Kate spent time in Westfirth as a child when the Dragon Brigade had their headquarters there, so she could conceivably have encountered a dragon. I could not find anyone in the Aligoes who had ever seen a dragon living there, although that doesn't mean much. A gathering of dragons could make their home in the islands and no one the wiser."

Removing the pince-nez, Amelia turned a stern gaze on Henry. "I quite like Kate, my lord. I trust you will not do anything to make her life more difficult. All she wants is to amass enough money to return to Freya and buy Barwich Manor."

"I hope to improve her life, Miss Nettleship," said Henry. "You make Captain Kate a household name and I will see what can be done about the manor."

"We have a deal, my lord," said Amelia, pleased. She picked up the notebook and the pencil. "And now tell me, is it true, Sir Henry, that you are traveling to Wellinsport to sack the governor?"

Henry smiled. "You never give up, do you, Miss Nettleship. This may seem an odd question, but how do you feel about monkeys?"

"On deck!" yelled the lookout from his perch in the crow's nest. "Ship to the south!"

Henry rose with alacrity from his deck chair. The captain and first lieutenant both grabbed their spyglasses and trained them in the direction indicated. The morning sun was starting to burn through the mists, but the air was hazy, and although Henry could see a ship in the distance, he could not make out details.

"Mr. Hawkins, take a glass aloft," said Captain Bastian, speaking to one of the midshipmen.

The young man scrambled up the rigging. Everyone on board the ship waited in tense silence to hear the report.

"Do you think it could be Bottom Dwellers?" asked Amelia.

Henry glanced at her. She didn't sound afraid. She seemed extremely eager. Probably had questions for them.

"I hate to disappoint you, Miss Nettleship, but no Bottom Dwellers have been in the Aligoes for years."

The Trame Channel was popular with pirates, but they were not feared as much as were the Bottom Dwellers, who had made this area a favored hunting ground. Although the war had ended, some of the more diehard followers of the late Blood Priest were said to attack ships and butcher the passengers and crew in their cruel blood magic rituals.

"I heard reports that people had seen them lurking in the jungle, my lord," said Amelia.

"A combination of Calvados and an overactive imagination, Miss Nettleship," said Henry. "This ship is likely another merchant vessel."

"Not even a pirate?" Amelia asked. "I would like some adventure on this voyage."

"I hate to disappoint you, Miss Nettleship, but even the most foolhardy pirate would think twice about attacking a ship of this size."

Despite his reassuring words, Henry thrust his hand into an inner pocket, glad to feel the reassuring presence of his pistol. He saw Amelia observing him with a knowing smile.

"Until we find out for certain, you might want to go below, Miss Nettleship," he advised.

"Stuff and nonsense, my lord," said Amelia. After collecting her reticule and her umbrella, she adjusted her hat, took out a pair of opera glasses, and walked over to the rail for a closer look.

Henry shook his head in admiration, then went to join the captain on the quarterdeck.

"What do you think it is, Captain?" Henry asked.

"The ship is not behaving in a suspicious manner," said Captain Bastian. "She's not hugging the shoreline or trying to hide in the mists. I imagine she is a—"

"Rosian brig, sir!" the midshipman called down. "The *Victorie.*"

"*Victorie*?" Captain Bastian repeated, puzzled. He trained his glass on the ship, then turned to his lieutenant. "Wasn't she reported sunk during the war, Mr. Hobbs?"

Captain Bastian had been a naval captain during the war, serving as a commander under Alan. After the war had ended, Bastian had found himself out of a job. Alan had persuaded Henry to use his influence to find his friend a ship. Henry owned shares in the wealthy merchant shippers Buchanans, Hasite, and Company, and was able to obtain a post for Captain Bastian.

Henry occasionally found it advantageous to travel abroad in the guise of a simple passenger, a "gentleman of good character." When he did, he would choose to sail with Captain Bastian, who had proved not only an able commander, but one who could also be trusted with secrets.

"I believe she was sunk, sir," said the lieutenant, training the glass on the brig. "The Rosians must have salvaged her and put her back into action."

"*Victorie* has changed course, sir," the midshipman called. "Heading for us."

"So we are going to play that game, are we?" Captain Bastian said, annoyed.

"What game is that, Captain?" Henry asked.

"Rosian ships out of Maribeau have begun harassing Freyan merchant ships. The Rosians claim this is in retaliation for Governor Finchley placing an embargo on Rosian merchant vessels—"

"He did what?" Henry demanded.

"He placed an embargo on Rosian merchant vessels. They're not allowed to enter Wellinsport."

"Damn and blast that fool to hell!" Henry swore. "When?"

"Almost a fortnight ago, my lord," said Captain Bastian. "You didn't know?"

"This is the first I have heard of it," said Henry grimly. "News has been slow to reach me these days."

Letters from his agents informing him of Finchley's latest debacle were probably lying on his desk in the Foreign Office this very moment.

"What exactly is the Rosian navy doing to harass our ships?" Henry asked.

"According to Captain Westfall of the *Emily Jane,* a Rosian frigate fired a warning shot across his bow and ordered him to anchor. The Rosians demanded to board and inspect the cargo to search for contraband. Captain Westfall told the Rosians they had no authority to make such a search. They exchanged heated words. Both crews grabbed pistols and cutlasses. At the last moment, the Rosian frigate sailed away. Westfall said the Rosian captain was laughing."

"Someone's pistol is going to go off by accident and start a war," said Henry. "Then no one will be laughing."

He tried to look on the bright side. This latest piece of lunacy spelled the end for the Right Honorable Aldous Finchley. Henry had been searching for an excuse to get rid of him and now he had one.

"I'm not going to play their fool game," Captain Bastian stated. He walked over to confer with the helmsman, ordering an increase in their speed.

The midshipman who had gone aloft gave a strangled yelp.

Henry couldn't understand him very well; the lad's voice was breaking.

"Did he say 'dragon'?" Henry asked in astonishment.

Captain Bastian glared up at the midshipman. "Quit skylarking, Mr. Hawkins!"

At that moment, the lookout gave a bellow and pointed.

"Deck, there! Dragon! And a rider!"

Henry and everyone else on board the *Pride of Haever* turned to stare at the dragon, who had emerged from a bank of puffy white clouds high above the channel. A rider sat on the dragon's back in a saddle positioned just ahead of the dragon's shoulders. Dragon and rider began making a slow descent, flying in the direction of the *Pride*.

"You might want to rethink your plan, Captain," Henry suggested. "That dragon is a member of the Dragon Brigade. You can tell by the emblem he is wearing around his neck. His rider is wearing a Brigade uniform."

Yet even as Henry spoke, he frowned.

The dragon was wearing the emblem of the famed Brigade—a silken sash in the colors red and gold—around his neck. But as far as Henry knew, Brigade dragons wore those emblems only on ceremonial occasions.

And as of the last reports he had received, the Dragon Brigade was still in Rosia. They had returned to their headquarters on the cliffs above Westfirth. He was certain he would have reports if they had been deployed.

Of course, he reminded himself glumly, given the delay in messages reaching him, the Dragon Brigade could have been deployed twenty times over and he wouldn't have known about it.

Still, a suspicion crept into his mind. He shot a glance at Amelia. She had her opera glasses trained on the dragon. She didn't appear the least alarmed. In fact, he thought he saw a smile playing about her lips.

The *Victorie* continued on course and the dragon and rider flew lower and lower on a course that would converge with theirs. Captain Bastian drew Henry to one side.

"My lord, Governor Finchley has been spreading news of your impending arrival, letting it be known you are sailing on this very ship. Have you considered the possibility that the Rosians might be seeking to capture you?"

Henry thought this over. He could have traveled in secret under one of his many aliases, but he had an important reason for making this journey under his own name. He had been aware he would be in danger because he was always in danger. He had enemies the world over, including in Rosia.

That said, tensions had cooled between the two longtime enemies since they had allied to defeat the Bottom Dwellers. Finchley's idiotic embargo might have changed that, though Henry doubted it.

As for his own personal Rosian enemies, the bishop's spymaster, Dubois, was involved in a desperate struggle to save the Church of the Breath. And

King Renaud's spymaster, the Countess de Marjolaine, had just sent Henry a friendly letter informing him of her son's marriage.

Henry had his agents spying on them, as they had their own agents spying on him. He knew it and they knew it and no one was offended. That was just how the game was played.

The threat did not come from one of his usual enemies. He had a new one; one who had taken the bait.

"I thank you for your concern, Captain, but I do not think I am the prize," Henry said. "I have diplomatic immunity. Capturing me would cause an international incident."

"I hope you are right, my lord," said Captain Bastian, sounding dubious.

The *Victorie* was now within hailing distance, and her captain shouted something in fluent Rosian.

Captain Bastian scowled. "I don't speak that infernal language. What the devil is he saying?"

"He wants you to shut down the airscrews and prepare for boarding," Henry translated.

The captain flushed in anger. "Tell him I will be damned—"

A large, hulking body slowly flew over the ship. Henry looked up to see the belly of the dragon. The beast was almost as long as the ship. Sunlight glittered on the iridescent green scales and shone through the membrane of the wings. Red eyes glared down on them.

The dragon roared, revealing razor-sharp fangs, and flexed his claws.

The Rosian captain on board the *Victorie* was shouting.

"He says if you don't surrender, the dragon will attack," said Henry.

Captain Bastian told him what the Rosians could do with their dragon.

As if the beast had heard, the dragon started spitting gobs of fiery drool onto the deck, setting any number of small blazes.

"Someone put those out!" Captain Bastian roared.

The sailors ran to obey, all the while watching the dragon. Most of the sailors had served in the Freyan navy, many under Captain Bastian. They had seen action and were not easily frightened, but none had ever fought a dragon. Undoubtedly every one of them was picturing being turned into a human torch.

"I think you should do as the Rosian asks, Captain," Henry said. "Many of your men are on the verge of jumping overboard."

"I suppose I have no choice," Captain Bastian muttered. "Goddamn Rosians!"

He gave orders to reduce the flow of magic to the airscrews and the balloon, slowing their speed, but not bringing them to a full stop.

The *Victorie* sailed over to join them, guarded by the dragon, who flew in large, lazy circles overhead. Henry noted Miss Nettleship observing the creature with intense interest, that same smile on her lips.

Henry raised his glass to look at the dragon's rider. He could not tell much about the rider, other than that he was wearing a long leather coat and a leather helmet—standard issue for those serving on the Dragon Brigade. Helm and coat would both be covered with magical constructs to protect the rider from magic, bullets, and flame.

"My lord, forget the dragon for a moment," said Captain Bastian. "Cast your eye on the crew of the *Victorie*. Doesn't that captain appear to be a bit youthful? I know the Rosians are lax and slipshod, but one would expect a naval captain to be over the age of fifteen."

Henry turned his glass to the ship to observe the Rosian captain. He was not perhaps fifteen, as Captain Bastian had said, but he was certainly very young. His double-breasted, gold-buttoned uniform coat was too large through the shoulders, causing the gold epaulets to sag, and his high black boots were too big. He nearly tripped over his feet when he walked.

Henry swept his glass over the rest of the crew. They were a scruffy lot, clearly unaccustomed to wearing uniforms, for they were fidgeting with the sleeves and tugging at the collars. One was actually barefoot.

Henry's suspicions were further confirmed by the sight of Amelia hastening onto the quarterdeck, her reticule wildly swinging from her arm, her cheeks flushed with excitement.

Henry turned to the captain.

"Those men are no more in the Rosian navy than I am," Henry told him. "They are pirates. Or rather, I believe the word you would use, Miss Nettleship, is 'corsairs.' "

"Dragon Corsairs, Sir Henry," Amelia stated in triumph. "And that is Captain Kate! What a surprise!"

"Isn't it," said Henry, smiling.

ELEVEN

Kate took off the helm she was wearing to gain a clearer view of the crew of the *Pride of Haever*. From her vantage point on Dalgren's back, she surveyed the deck below. She focused particularly on the captain and a man standing beside him on the quarterdeck. The man was dressed in civilian clothes. He must be the passenger, Henry Wallace. And there was someone else, a woman.

Kate wondered who she was, for she hadn't been listed on the manifest. Perhaps she was the captain's wife. Kate didn't give the woman any more thought.

Thus far, Kate's plans were going well. The captain had shut down the airscrews and lowered the sails. He couldn't bring his ship to a complete stop in the middle of the channel, but *Pride* had slowed enough that the crew of the *Victorie* could take the prize. Akiel was in command of the boarding party. He and the sailors Greenstreet had sent to fill out the crew stood at the rail, grapnels in hand, waiting to board.

Kate uncoiled the rope that was a standard part of every dragon rider's equipment and attached it to the saddle, knotting it as Olaf had taught her. Dragon riders often had to climb down ropes as their dragons hovered in the air, and she and Dalgren had practiced this maneuver. Because Kate had swarmed up and down ropes since she was a child, she had been confident she could manage.

But as the rope tumbled down, wildly swinging in the breeze, Kate gulped. Climbing down a rope onto a broad expanse of open field was far different from trying to hit the deck of a moving ship floating in the vastness of the Breath.

The *Pride of Haever* had appeared enormous until she thought about trying to land on it. Now she looked down into what seemed a jungle of masts, sails, yardarms, rigging, and the tops of two large balloons. The main deck looked smaller than the kerchief she had tied around her head. If she missed her footing or lost her grip, she wouldn't just suffer a few bumps and bruises from a hard fall. She would end up dead at the bottom of the world.

"Take me closer, Dalgren!" Kate called.

"I can't fly any closer!" Dalgren returned, his voice grating. "My wings will get tangled in the rigging or shear off the balloon stays!"

He twisted his head to regard her with anxious eyes. Smoke puffed out from between his clenched teeth. He was as nervous as she was.

"You don't have to board!" Dalgren shouted. "Let Akiel handle it!"

Olaf stood beside Marco, peering up at her. The sailors on board the *Victorie* were waiting for her. She could see Akiel craning his neck, watching. Her descent down the ladder was the signal for them to fling the grapnels and board the ship.

Kate clutched the saddle with both hands, her palms sweating inside the heavy leather gloves. The *Pride*'s captain and the man, Wallace, were also gazing up at her. They would know she was afraid. She imagined them smirking.

Drawing in a breath, Kate relinquished her grip on the saddle and released the safety straps that held her in place. She shifted in the saddle so that both legs were hanging over the dragon's flank, and grabbed hold of the rope. She then exhaled and drew in another deep breath. Gripping the rope, she pushed with both feet off Dalgren's flank, propelling herself clear of the dragon's body, and leaped.

Kate dropped through the air. The rope settled against Dalgren and she caught her breath with a gasp. She steadied herself, then began to climb down hand over hand, keeping her feet clear, as the sailors had taught her when she was a girl. She was wearing a dragon rider's long, split leather coat and the tails flapped in the wind. Her confidence grew as she descended. Seeing Dalgren watching anxiously, she gave him a reassuring smile.

Akiel shouted the command and the sailors on board the *Victorie* threw their grappling hooks and dragged the *Pride* close to the *Victorie,* then climbed over the rail, landing on the deck of the captured ship. Kate trusted Akiel to supervise the boarding party. She had to concentrate on reaching the deck safely before the strength in her arms gave out. As it was, she lost her grip, but fortunately managed to land on her feet on the main deck.

Kate took a moment to recover, calm her fast-beating heart, and revel in the realization that she was standing on board a ship she had captured. She looked around to see her crew carrying out her orders, rounding up the *Pride*'s crew and officers and marching them belowdecks.

She could hear a lieutenant swearing in Freyan, referring to "stinking Rosian turds." Kate was elated; her spirits soared. The crew of the *Pride* believed they had been attacked by Rosian privateers. Marco was on the *Pride*'s quarterdeck, accepting the captain's surrender, while Akiel held the male passenger, Wallace, at gunpoint.

The *Pride of Haever* was her prize. Kate pulled out the battered bicorn hat she had stuffed into a pocket and jammed it on her head, turning the brim to wear it "fore and aft," as the expression went, to hide her face. She would introduce herself as "Captain Henri Rossini" of the Rosian privateer *Victorie.*

Kate's voice was naturally low, and she could make it gruff. With her height and with her body concealed beneath the leather coat, she could easily pass for a man long enough to escort Wallace down to the hold, put a gun to his head, and demand that he tell her where to find the gold.

She waved to Olaf, who had remained on board *Victorie,* manning the helm, performing the tricky task of keeping the two ships close, but not so close that he risked damage to either one. Olaf couldn't take his hands off the helm to wave back, but he gave her a grin.

Kate rapidly ascended the ladder leading to the quarterdeck and noted that Akiel, by contrast, was looking grim. Kate raised an eyebrow, asking what was wrong. Akiel shook his head and jerked his thumb in the direction of the woman.

Kate sighed. She should have foreseen that the woman would be a problem for Akiel. Like many sailors, he believed the presence of a woman on board a ship was bad luck. Kate had pointed out to him that she herself was a woman, but Akiel had argued that Kate was different. She was not a woman, she was a captain. Kate could not see the logic in this, but if Akiel could, she was fine with his reasoning. Maybe now Kate could prove to him that he had no cause to believe in such a silly superstition.

Kate cast the woman a fleeting glance, long enough to note she was wearing a brown skirt and jacket and a hat, and she was carrying an umbrella and a reticule.

Kate paused. Something about that ensemble seemed familiar. Kate looked at the woman more closely and her elation seeped out of her, leaving her emotions as flat as a punctured balloon.

"Bloody hell!" Kate muttered.

The woman advanced, holding out her hand. "Captain Kate, how good to see you again. And I will be able to meet your crew and your dragon. How exciting!"

Akiel and Marco were both staring at Kate in astonishment.

"How does she know you?" Marco mouthed.

Kate didn't have time to explain.

"Keep an eye on both the captain and the passenger!" she ordered Marco. "Don't let them interfere! Akiel, come with me."

Grabbing hold of Amelia's arm, Kate marched her over to the rail. The captain took a step, thinking to stop her, perhaps believing she was going to shove Amelia overboard. Akiel made a gesture with the pistol and the captain halted.

"Don't you dare harm her!" he shouted.

"Shut up!" Kate growled. She turned to Amelia and lowered her voice. "What are you doing on board this ship, Miss Amelia? Your name wasn't on the manifest!"

"I came to see you, Captain," Miss Amelia replied. "Sir Henry Wallace was so kind as to invite me and pay for my passage. Your stories have been an immense success, you see, and I want—"

"Sir Henry Wallace! Did you tell him about me?" Kate gasped.

"Oh, yes, my dear captain. Sir Henry is extremely interested in your adventures. He did me the honor of reading my stories, you see, and he—"

Kate wasn't listening. She suddenly put the title before the name and remembered Alan talking about a friend—Sir Henry. His surname was . . . Kate groaned and clutched at Amelia.

"Does this Sir Henry Wallace know a man named Captain Alan Northrop?"

"The privateer?" Miss Amelia smiled. "Why, yes. The two are best friends."

Kate stared at her in dismay, then turned to Akiel.

"This is Miss Amelia, the journalist who wrote the stories about me, Akiel. Take her to her cabin, lock her inside, and stand guard."

Akiel was shaking his head in protest. "A woman on board a ship is bad luck, mum. I have always said so. You should not go through with this. We should leave this ill-fated vessel at once."

Amelia was adding her protest to his. "I assure you, Captain, I am not concerned about my own safety. I would enjoy watching you in action—"

Kate silenced them both.

"Akiel, that was an order," Kate said.

"Aye, mum," said Akiel, sounding glum. "You should know that the captain gave Marco his parole so long as you do not harm anyone. Also that I took this pistol from the other gentleman. He was carrying it inside an interior pocket."

Kate gave an absent nod, trying to think what to do. Akiel escorted Amelia, still protesting, belowdecks.

Once Amelia was out of sight, Kate took off her hat, which was hot and now useless, and flung it to the deck. She would have to think of some way to keep Sir Henry from telling his friend Alan, and, failing that, devise an explanation to give Alan about why she had pirated a Freyan ship. But she would worry about all that later. Right now, she had to concentrate on what was important: the gold.

Kate walked over to Henry. She took her time, closely observing him, judging how to deal with him. She tried to remember what Alan had said about his friend, but she hadn't really been paying that much attention. She had been admiring Alan.

Henry did not appear in the least afraid. He regarded her with an air of calm detachment, a faint smile upon his thin lips. He was a tall, spare man in his late forties with a long, aquiline nose and narrow face. He wore typical traveling clothes for a gentleman: coat, waistcoat, shirt, and trousers in a light gray linen suitable to the climate. His clothes were not ostentatious, no lace cuffs or cravat. His waistcoat was plain, not embroidered.

Yet Kate knew something about men's clothes from her father. Morgan had always dressed well. She remembered her father saying, "If you're going to borrow money from a chap, you need to look as though you can pay it back."

Henry was wearing clothes that were expensive, elegant, and covered in powerful magic.

Those who were crafters and gifted with the ability to use magic—about one-third of the world's population—could see magical constructs. Since almost every object in the world, from tea cakes to palaces, was constructed using magic, constructs tended to be ubiquitous.

Kate was not surprised to see the faint traces of magical constructs covering his coat. She was surprised to see the nature of the magic. Generally, magical constructs were used to keep the fabric from wrinkling or the lace from fraying. The magic on Wallace's coat essentially turned his clothes into a suit of armor. These constructs would deflect the blade of a knife or the tip of a sword, possibly even repel bullets.

"What have you done with Miss Nettleship?" Captain Bastian demanded angrily. "She is not to be harmed!"

"Precisely the reason I ordered my friend to keep her safe," said Kate. "I give you my word, Captain, that I will not harm her or anyone else on board this ship, so long as everyone cooperates."

She had brought several pistols, carrying them on her baldric and in the pocket of the leather coat. Drawing a pistol, she pointed it at Wallace, aiming for his head, not at the coat with the magical constructs.

"I am Captain Kate. Miss Amelia tells me that you know my reputation from the stories in the newspaper, Sir Henry. You should know, therefore, that it will be in your best interest to accompany me to the ship's cargo hold."

"I will gladly go with you, Captain Kate," Henry replied. "Though I confess I do not understand why."

"I will be happy to explain, my lord," said Kate. "Start walking!"

She gestured with the pistol for him to precede her to the hatch that led down to the hold, which was on the lowest deck of the three-deck ship. As they went, Kate looked around, taking stock of the situation. She had brought her own helmsman, not trusting the helmsman aboard the *Pride*. She needed to make certain the magic that kept the ship afloat continued to flow. Other members of her crew were attaching a towline, preparing to tow the *Pride* back to Freeport.

Dalgren continued to hover over the ship. His shoulders must be growing stiff. She signaled that all was well, and Dalgren gratefully rose on the breeze, flexing his wings and aching shoulder muscles. He began to circle the ship, looking fierce, his mere shadow menacing.

"We'll take that lantern with us," Kate said, gesturing for Wallace to pick it up.

The two descended into the bowels of the ship, Kate keeping her pistol aimed at the back of Wallace's head. He was being extremely cooperative, and that was making Kate uneasy. While she didn't want to have to pistol-whip Alan's best friend, she thought that he should at least appear more reluctant to surrender the gold.

When they reached the orlop deck, Kate located the hatch that led to the hold and found that an unusual amount of care had been taken to keep the hold secure. Generally a padlock was thought sufficient. In this case, the hold was locked with both a padlock and magical warding spells. Such an abundance of caution could mean the hold contained a fortune. Or it could mean that the captain simply wanted to keep his crew away from the whiskey.

Observing the lock, Henry shook his head. "We have reached the end of our journey, Captain. I do not have the key."

"What we are reaching is the end of my patience, Sir Henry," said Kate. "I have only to look at the magical constructs on your coat to know that you are a man who does not trust his fellow men. You are responsible for a fortune in gold that is stowed in the hold. You would have the key to open this lock."

Henry regarded her with interest. "Miss Nettleship was right when she described you as a keen observer, Captain. As regards the contents of my luggage, I fear you will be disappointed. I brought with me a change of clothes and some books. Nothing more."

"Then you will have no objection if I search for myself," said Kate. "Come, my lord, I know you have the key. I suggest you look through those hidden pockets of yours until you find it. I can put bullets in places that will not affect your usefulness to me."

Henry smiled. "I do seem to recall that I might have the key somewhere about my person. If I may put my hand beneath my coat? . . ."

Kate nodded permission, keeping the pistol aimed at him. Sir Henry placed the lantern on the deck and reached into his coat to draw out his pocket watch. A key hung from the fob. He removed the key and inserted it into the lock. He turned the key half a rotation to the right; then, taking hold of the bow, he rotated the bow on the shank a full rotation to the left. The key glowed blue. The warding constructs on the hatch flared and Kate backed up a step, just in case. The blue glow dimmed, however, and the padlock released and dropped to the deck.

At Kate's direction, Henry opened the hatch. She looked past him to see steps leading into pitch darkness, redolent with the smell of whiskey. The hold was dark and well sealed, for both sunlight and rain could ruin cargo.

"You go first, Sir Henry," said Kate. "Take the lantern with you. My pistol and I will be right behind."

Sir Henry did as ordered. Picking up the lantern, he descended the ladder leading down into the hold. Kate followed, holding her pistol.

"I'm leaving the hatch open," she told him. "My men will hear me if I shout for them, so don't be a hero."

"I would not dream of such a thing," said Henry. "I am the world's most inveterate coward. You can ask my friend, Captain Northrop. I believe you two know each other. Alan speaks quite highly of you."

Kate almost missed her footing on a rung and had to grab hold of a beam to keep herself from falling. She cursed herself for having let him rattle her.

"Alan speaks highly of you as well, my lord," said Kate coolly, hoping he hadn't noticed. "Take me to the gold and we can discuss our mutual acquaintances over a drink to celebrate my good fortune."

"I assure you once again, Captain, you are wasting your time," said Henry. "There is no gold on board this ship."

"Thank you for your advice, Sir Henry. But I hope you won't mind if I see for myself. Keep walking."

Henry shrugged and began making his way through the maze of barrels, bales, sacks, kegs, chests, and coils of metal hoops for barrels. He held the lantern high to make certain he didn't bump into anything. Kate followed closely, trying to keep her mind on her work, although she was intensely curious to know why he had mentioned her to Alan, and exactly what Alan had said about her. She considered asking, but she'd be damned if she would give him the satisfaction.

Henry came to a sudden halt, lowering the lantern.

"What's the problem now?" Kate asked, annoyed at the delay.

"My luggage is in the stern. This netting is in the way. I can't get past."

Thick rope netting hung from the beams, rigged to keep large, heavy sacks of grain from shifting. Some of the netting had come loose and tumbled down, blocking their route.

"Shove it to one side," said Kate.

Henry placed the lantern on top of a barrel marked "whiskey" and tried to move the netting. Kate stood behind him, impatiently waiting for him to proceed. The rope was heavy and he was having difficulty—or feigning having difficulty.

Fuming, Kate started to go to his aid.

She heard a faint creak, coming from behind her. Kate was familiar with the sounds of a ship: the creak of wooden planks expanding or contracting, the creak of the blades of the airscrews, the creaking of barrels rubbing against each other. The creak she heard was different, as of something heavy treading on a wooden step.

A shaft of sunlight slanted through the open hatch. By its light, Kate could see three men moving slowly and stealthily down into the hold. She stared, astonished. She recognized one of them, Greenstreet's grunting henchman, Jacob. She didn't know the names of other two, but she had seen them around Freeport and knew they too worked for Greenstreet. All three were carrying pistols.

They must have sneaked on board *Victorie* with the rest of the men Greenstreet had sent. But why the secrecy? What were they doing down here?

They've come to take the gold! Kate realized. Cheat me out of my share! No wonder that bastard Greenstreet was so damned generous!

She was furious and was prepared to storm over to Jacob, ready to tell him where he and his thugs could go and what they could do with themselves when they got there.

Before she could stir, Jacob pointed and shouted, "There! By the lantern!"

He and his friends turned toward her and raised their pistols.

"Jacob, what the hell do you think you are doing?" Kate shouted. And then she realized they were not aiming at her.

They were aiming at Henry.

Kate shifted her aim from Henry's skull to Jacob and his cronies. She couldn't take time to try to understand what was going on. All she knew was that these three were about to shoot her dream in the back. She fired at the beam over Jacob's head. Startled, he flinched and ducked, giving Kate time to give Henry a violent shove, knocking him to the deck. She flung herself down after him, landing on a sack of wool.

Shots slammed into the beams, one right where Wallace had been standing.

"Are you all right?" Kate whispered.

Sir Henry had gone down hard and was lying flat on his stomach. Stirring, he started to raise his head.

"Stay down!" she hissed. She dropped her empty pistol and drew the other from her belt. "There are three of them. All armed."

Henry nodded, keeping his head low. "I take it you are not in league with them?"

"I'm not planning to shoot you—at least not until you tell me where the gold is . . ." Kate paused in sudden, bitter understanding.

Jacob and his men weren't here for gold. They were here to kill Wallace. Greenstreet had used her, played her for a fool. He had concocted this whole elaborate scheme to assassinate Sir Henry Wallace and blame his death on pirates or—even better—on her. Greenstreet had known exactly the type of bait to dangle in front of Kate and she had been stupid enough to bite.

"There is no gold, is there, my lord?" Kate said.

"I am sorry, Captain," said Henry with a faint smile. "For your sake, I could almost wish there was."

"Bloody hell," Kate muttered.

Another shot rang out, hitting the whiskey barrel not far from where they were hiding.

"You need to douse that light," Kate said, indicating the lantern Henry had placed on top of the barrel. "I can't reach it."

"Agreed," said Henry.

Twisting around, he took off one of his shoes and flung it at the lantern, knocking it off the barrel. The lantern fell to the deck with a crash, breaking the glass and disrupting the magical constructs that gave off the bright glow.

The only light now was coming through the hatch, shining on Jacob and his henchmen. Kate raised her pistol, hoping for a shot, but they must have realized they made excellent targets, for Jacob slammed shut the hatch and jumped to the deck. Kate could hear the three talking, as they scrambled about in the darkness.

"Why the hell is that bitch shooting at us?" one demanded. "You said she was working for Greenstreet!"

"Shut up!" Jacob ordered angrily. He raised his voice. "Kate, this is none of your concern! You can leave. No harm done."

Kate couldn't see, but she could hear the three stumbling about. Then came the creaking sound of a pulley.

"What are they doing?" Henry whispered.

"They're going to light the lanterns, make the hold bright as day," Kate whispered back.

Cargo holds were lit by lanterns suspended on ropes from the overhead. In order to light them, the sailors would lower the lanterns one by one, activate the magic, then raise them back up.

"How many pistols do you have?" Sir Henry asked.

"One," said Kate.

"I have one, as well," said Sir Henry.

"No, you don't," Kate returned. "Akiel took it from you."

"He took the pistol he *found,*" Henry corrected. He flourished a pocket pistol. "Do you have any powder? Shot?"

Kate had brought a powder horn and bullets. She had made certain to pack them in a pouch on the dragon saddle. And that's where she had left them.

"No," she said, angry at herself.

"We have two shots for three men," said Henry.

Jacob must have lit the first lantern, for Kate could see the light, swinging back and forth, rising up to the ceiling. The lantern was not that close, but already it was having an effect. Dim light seeped around them.

"I suggest we move," Henry said, hunkering back into the shadows. "Ouch! Mind the broken glass!" he added with a curse.

"Wait!" said Kate softly. He had given her an idea. "Is that lantern close by? Can you reach it?"

Sir Henry searched for the lantern. He found his shoe, retrieved it, and discovered the lantern on the other side of the barrel. Broken shards of glass still clung to the brass frame and he took care as he lifted it.

He handed it to Kate, who was pleased to see the brass frame of the lantern still intact.

"I need big pieces of broken glass!" Kate whispered.

Henry raised an eyebrow, but did as he was told, plucking shards of glass off the floor. Jacob and his men were on the move, lighting the next lantern.

Kate used her cutlass to slash open a hole in the sack of wool, yanked out a handful, and stuffed the wool into the lantern. She added more wool until the frame was filled, then stuck pieces of broken glass into the wadding.

"Are you a decent shot with that thing?" Kate asked, indicating Henry's pistol.

"Fair," he replied with a smile.

"Then slow them down," she told him. "I need time!"

Henry crawled over to take cover behind the whiskey barrel. He raised up, peered over the top. Kate began sprinkling the gunpowder from her second pistol onto the wool.

"Why does Greenstreet want you dead, my lord?" Kate asked.

"I have no idea," said Henry. "I do not know the man. Who is he?"

"He's behind almost every criminal operation in the Aligoes," Kate said.

Henry rose swiftly and fired, then ducked back down. He must have hit something, for there was a cry and a crash and swearing. Someone fired back and then the men retreated, tumbling over things in their haste.

"I don't think that fellow will stand in the light anymore," Henry remarked.

Kate heard Jacob say, "How's Jo? Was he hit?"

"Shot dead," the other answered.

Kate stopped her work to stare at Henry in amazement.

He shrugged. "Lucky shot."

Kate shook her head and continued to work. She fished her knife from her boot and began to crudely etch a simple magical construct on the brass, whispering beneath her breath as she worked.

When she was finished, she said softly, "All right, be ready to run."

Henry nodded. "Good luck. Oh, and thank you for saving my life, Captain."

Kate grunted. "I haven't saved either of us yet." Raising her voice, she called, "Don't shoot, Jacob! Wallace is dead and I'm wounded. I'm coming out."

"Keep your hands where I can see them," Jacob shouted.

Kate stood up, holding her left hand in the air, carrying the wool-stuffed lantern in her right. Jacob could probably see just a shadowy form, if he made her out at all.

"You'll tell Greenstreet I never meant to hurt Jo, won't you, Jacob?" Kate said, creeping forward.

"Sure, Kate. I'll tell him," said Jacob.

"Liar!" Kate muttered.

Jacob had taken cover behind the ladder and she could see him start to raise his pistol. His friend was behind him, his pistol aimed at her. Kate needed to get close enough to throw the lantern, even if that meant walking into pistol range. She kept her eyes fixed on Jacob's hand and when he pulled back the hammer, Kate flung the lantern as far as she could, then dropped to the deck.

She heard the brass lantern clang on wood and for an instant nothing more happened. Just as Kate was about to start swearing, certain she had failed, magical blue light glowed, igniting the wool and setting off the gunpowder. The lantern blew apart.

Kate flung her arms over her head. Brass fragments and splinters of glass flew through the hold. Someone was screaming, horrible to hear. Kate jumped to her feet. Jacob was on his knees, moaning; his head and arms and hands were covered in blood. His companion was also bleeding, but not as badly. He was still holding his pistol.

Kate ran toward the man, waving her cutlass. At the sight of her, the man threw down his gun and raised his hands. A shot rang out, coming from behind Kate. The bullet passed so close by her cheek she swore she could feel the rush of air. The man dropped down, dead.

Kate gasped and turned to glare at Henry. "He was trying to surrender!"

"Was he?" Henry asked. "Hard to see through the smoke. I thought he was going to shoot you."

Kate frowned. "And I thought you said you had only one pistol."

"I may have found another," Henry replied.

Shaking her head, Kate climbed the ladder to open the hatch and peer out, fearing someone might have heard the shots and the explosion. She didn't want any interruptions. She was relieved to hear no sounds of a commotion, of someone running to find out what was going on. She looked back in time to see Henry pick up a pistol off the deck and hold it to Jacob's head. Jacob couldn't see for the blood in his eyes. He had no idea he was about to die.

"Don't!" Kate cried. "You can question him. He can tell you why Greenstreet wanted you dead—"

Henry fired and Jacob slumped over. A pool of blood spread from the hole in his skull.

"I have learned not to take chances," said Henry.

He drew a handkerchief from his sleeve and used it to wipe gunpowder and blood from his hands.

"For a coward, you are very cool under fire," Kate said, eyeing him.

"Alan taught me well," said Henry. "Would you still like to inspect my luggage, Captain?"

"I'll send my men to do that," said Kate.

She knew they wouldn't find anything. She would have to face her crew, her friends, confess that yet another of her grand schemes had blown up in her face. Literally.

"You are bleeding, Captain," said Henry, pointing.

Glass had cut her forehead and her hand. Blood was dripping onto the deck, mingling with the blood and bone and brains splattered about the hold and on Henry's clothing.

"Hand me your kerchief," Henry suggested.

She took it off and gave it to him. He mopped the blood from her forehead, then bound the kerchief over the wound on her hand, making a neat job of it. Taking out his own handkerchief, he coolly cleansed the blood from his face, then tossed the handkerchief to the deck.

"I would like to give you a reward, Captain," he said. "After all, you did save my life."

"What is your offer, my lord?" Kate asked dispiritedly, thinking he would toss her a few silver talons.

"A job," said Henry.

TWELVE

Sir Henry Wallace finally reached Wellinsport three days later than scheduled. Following the attempt on his life, he had sailed on the *Pride of Haever,* which Kate had returned to its captain.

"My first act as a privateer for Freya," Kate said, laughing. "I'm giving you back your ship."

Captain Bastian was not amused. He made no secret of the fact that he thought Henry had lost his mind, giving letters of marque and reprisal to a female and a dragon. Henry considered pointing out to Captain Bastian that without a shot fired he had surrendered his ship to this woman and her dragon. The captain was useful to Henry, however, and so he had merely smiled and kept silent.

Kate and Henry shook hands on their deal and Kate sailed back to Freeport, taking Miss Nettleship with her, for which Henry was grateful. He liked Amelia, but she never tired of asking questions, and he found that being continually under fire was exhausting. Amelia was going to stay with Kate to work on new stories about the Dragon Corsairs.

"With your permission, my lord, I will tell the public that Captain Kate and her Dragon Corsairs are now Freyan privateers," Amelia told him in parting.

"I think that is an excellent idea, Miss Nettleship," Henry said.

"I would also like to write your account of the attempt on your life, my lord," Amelia added.

"I have told you, Miss Nettleship, that no such attempt was made," Henry replied. "Captain Kate was forced to deal with some mutinous members of her crew. She fired a few shots over their heads and that was the end of the matter."

He could tell by her snort that Amelia did not believe him. She could not very well prove otherwise, however, for she had been locked in her cabin during the incident. Henry had sworn Kate to secrecy and told Captain Bastian to clean up the mess and remove the bodies.

The *Pride of Haever* sailed without further incident, arriving in Wellinsport at the south docks, constructed to accommodate large merchant vessels and naval ships. Small fry such as wreckers, barges, houseboats, and ferries tied up at the north docks, nine miles away.

Henry had visited Wellinsport on several occasions and he was familiar with the south docks. They were always crowded. Passengers bustled about. Stevedores operated the cranes and winches that unloaded the cargo from the holds. Dockworkers handled the complicated docking procedure, tethering the ships to their mooring stations. Families waited to meet loved ones or wave them farewell. Thieves and pickpockets circulated among the crowds, dodging the constables, while customs officials walked about looking important.

Horse-drawn carriages for hire lined up at the stands, waiting for fares. Wagons loaded with goods clogged the streets. Henry enjoyed the sights and he smiled to see an elegant wyvern-drawn carriage alight on the boardwalk.

"The governor's sent his carriage for you, my lord," said Captain Bastian. "What shall I tell the driver?"

"That he arrived late, much to my annoyance, and I found my own transportation," said Henry.

Captain Bastian smiled. "The pinnace is ready when you are, my lord. The crew has orders to deliver you to the north docks."

"Thank you, Captain," said Henry. "I will be back tomorrow. I have passage booked for two, I believe."

"Indeed, you do. Good luck, my lord."

Henry had never been to the north docks and he noted that they were just as busy as the south, only shabbier and on a smaller scale.

The ubiquitous Trundlers, who belonged to every nation and none, had established one of their floating villages nearby. A hundred Trundler houseboats, marked by gaily colored balloons and striped sails, were tied at the docks, bobbing up and down in the Breath. Today being market day, crowds of people went from boat to boat to view the Trundlers' beautiful hand-dyed silk or buy bottles of their famous Calvados.

Henry thanked the crew of the pinnace and disembarked. A few people glanced at him as he stood on the dock with his trunk and his portmanteau, but no one paid him much attention. He would visit the odious Finchley tomorrow. Tonight he had important business to conduct in private.

Henry paid a boy to deliver a message to a carriage driver of his acquaintance, then hired a horse cart to drive him and his luggage to a small apartment he kept in a quiet and unassuming boardinghouse.

Henry rented similar rooms in similar boardinghouses in cities the world over. In each he kept clothes, wigs, and travel documents suitable for whichever identity he happened to be using at the time, as well as pistols, pocket guns, and assorted cutlery, bandages and healing salves to deal with emergencies; in these pieds-a-terre, he also kept a certain amount of currency from all over the world.

He checked first to make certain no one had been inside his apartment in his absence. Finding that none of the magical traps devised by Mr. Sloan had been disturbed, Henry lay down to rest after the rigors of the journey.

He woke refreshed from his nap at around eleven of the clock at night and changed into evening clothes—a coat of expensive make and impeccable tailoring, a silk waistcoat, a linen shirt with lace cuffs, silk hose, and expensive leather shoes. He then kept watch out the window until he saw a coach-and-four driving slowly down the street, pausing now and then as though the driver were lost and searching for an address.

Henry signaled with a candle from his window, and the carriage rolled to a stop. He threw on a greatcoat to conceal his evening wear, which would have looked out of place in this modest neighborhood. He folded up the coat he had worn during the voyage, wrapped it in brown paper, tucked it under his arm, and departed.

The boardinghouse provided "Lodging for Single Gentlemen," according to the sign in the window, and it was dark and silent at this time of night. Most of the other single gentlemen had to work the next day and were already in bed. Henry met no one on his way down the stairs.

He spoke a word to the coachman before entering the carriage. Once he'd shut the door, he rested his back against the leather cushions as the carriage rattled off down the cobblestones. The journey to his destination took about a half hour. The carriage stopped outside the Red Lion Gambling Club.

Henry did not get out, but waited inside, keeping watch out the window.

The clock on a nearby church struck two. The door to the Red Lion opened, disgorging several young gentlemen who looked much the worse for drink, weaving arm in arm and singing a bawdy song at the top of their lungs. They paused to hold a discussion about where to go next and decided to move on to another club. One of the young gentlemen declined, saying he had lost money enough for one night. His friends bid him farewell and tottered off, leaving him to stagger down the street by himself, still humming the song.

When he drew near the carriage, Henry opened the door.

"Don't I know you, sir?" Henry called. "Aren't you Phillip Jones, clerk in the governor's office?"

The young gentleman came to a halt and peered at the carriage as though trying to bring it into focus. "You are correct, sir. Though you have the advantage of me. Damned if I know you, sir."

"Lord Winston," said Henry. "Would you like a ride, old chap? You seem rather the worse for wear."

"Very kind," Phillip said and endeavored to find the carriage door.

The coachman descended from his box and assisted him to enter, pushing him from behind while Henry grasped hold of his coat collar. Once the young man was safely inside, Henry gave the coachman his orders, shut the door, and lowered the curtains to cover the windows. The coachman mounted his box and slapped the reins, and the carriage started off.

Henry reached out to shake hands.

"Your Grace, I am pleased to see you again," he said warmly, then wrinkled his nose. "Despite the fact that you smell like a distillery. Do you bathe in the stuff?"

Phillip began to laugh. "Actually I dip my cravat in whiskey before going out for the evening. I need to smell the part of poor dissolute Pip as well as act it."

He regarded Henry with concern. "I must say I am extremely glad to see you alive and well, my lord. When the *Pride of Haever* did not arrive on schedule, I feared the worst. Were you attacked by Rosians or pirates?"

"Pirates disguised as Rosians, Your Grace," Henry replied with a wry smile. "They knew right where to find me *and* that I was carrying a 'chest filled with gold.' Thus I take it that Finchley walked into our trap."

"He didn't walk, my lord, he jumped in with both feet," said Phillip. "The day after the governor received word of your plans to travel here, Pip just happened to be cleaning out a closet in his office and managed to overhear a very interesting conversation."

"I take it the governor did not know Pip was cleaning the closet?" Henry asked, smiling.

"I fear Pip forgot to inform him, my lord," Phillip replied gravely. "Very remiss of the lad. Finchley was talking to a man I had never seen before. The governor called him Greenstreet—"

"Greenstreet!" Henry repeated, startled.

"Do you know him, my lord?"

"In a manner of speaking, Your Grace," said Henry. "Please continue."

"The governor told Greenstreet that you would be sailing on the *Pride of Haever* and that you would have a large quantity of gold in your possession. Greenstreet paid the governor a handsome sum for the information."

"We have got him, Your Grace!" said Henry, clenching his fist, as though he had Finchley in his grasp.

"'Dead to rights' as a pickpocket friend of mine would say, my lord," said Phillip. "How do you know this Greenstreet?"

"I know him only by name. Greenstreet didn't want just the gold. He also wanted me dead. He sent three men to assassinate me."

"Assassinate! Good God, my lord!" Phillip exclaimed, shocked. "What happened?"

"I'll tell you in a moment, but while we are speaking of the gold . . ." Henry tossed over the brown paper parcel. "You will find bank notes in the sum of five hundred thousand eagles sewn into the lining of my coat."

Phillip opened the parcel to regard the jacket with admiration. "The work of the inimitable Mr. Sloan, I take it, my lord?"

"That man is a marvel," said Henry. "I wore the coat the entire voyage and no one was the wiser. If Pip would deliver the funds to the fort's commander, General Winstead, he will put the money to good use. I noted he has already started the repairs to the fort."

Phillip rewrapped the parcel and placed it on the seat beside him.

"Pip will deliver this to the general this morning," said Phillip. "What do we do about the Right Honorable, my lord?"

"It will be my distinct pleasure to deal with the wretch myself, Your Grace," said Henry in grim tones. "I would like to have him tried as an accomplice to attempted murder, but Her Majesty would never agree. Still, after this, she must withdraw her support, no matter how many damn monkeys he sends her. Suffice it to say the Right Honorable will be on the next boat to Haever—a fishing boat, at that. Now, tell me what you know about this Greenstreet."

Phillip took a moment to arrange his thoughts. "I once did some research on him. He claims to come from Travia. He arrived in the Aligoes about ten years ago, making his home in the small town of Freeport. Rumor has it that he is behind most of the criminal enterprises in the Aligoes and other parts of the world. He has ties to the gangs in Westfirth, for instance. He smuggles arms, funds pirates, operates a number of houses of ill fame, opium dens, and crooked gambling clubs. Greenstreet has never been accused of murder, but people who cross him do have a nasty habit of turning up dead."

"I was almost one of those, Your Grace," said Henry. He went on to relate his adventures aboard the *Pride of Haever,* and concluded by adding, "This Greenstreet is good. I was caught unawares, Phillip. Taken completely by surprise. I was fortunate that the captain of the pirates Greenstreet hired was accompanying me at the time. She is a remarkable woman. Her name is Captain Kate. She knew Alan from his days with the Rose Hawks."

"Kate?" Phillip said, smiling. "She and Pip are old friends. She questioned me about the gold last week, come to think of it. I wondered how she had heard about it. I should have guessed she would have ties to Greenstreet. I tried to steer her clear. I told her the truth—that there was no gold. Obviously she didn't believe me."

"I owe my life to Captain Kate, Your Grace," said Henry. "How did you two meet?"

"Whenever the Rose Hawks sailed to Freeport, we visited a tavern run by her friend—the Perky Parrot. Kate had inherited her father's ship and she wanted to join the Rose Hawks. But she was only seventeen at the time and a bit too wild and impulsive for the dangerous work we were doing. Kate tried her hand at smuggling, but that didn't end well. She now makes her living as a wrecker when she's not pretending to be a Rosian privateer. You must do something to reward her, my lord."

"I have already made her an offer. Since Alan has his commission in the Royal Navy, I am in need of privateers of my own. I was quite impressed with the young woman's quick thinking and courage, not to mention her ingenious idea of teaming with a dragon. Captain Bastian was forced to surrender without a shot fired."

"I can well imagine," said Phillip, chuckling.

"In addition, the exploits of Captain Kate are the talk of Freya. Have you read the newspaper accounts of her adventures, Your Grace?"

"I haven't seen a Freyan newspaper in months, my lord," said Phillip. "The last mail packet was captured by pirates and the one before that sank in a wizard storm."

"That is why I began sending my messages to you by courier," said Henry. "Suffice it to say, Captain Kate is much admired, especially among the women. I fear my own lady wife has secret plans to run away to join Captain Kate and her pirate crew."

Phillip laughed. "Thus by hiring Captain Kate, you garner favorable publicity."

"For a change," said Henry with a bitter smile. "The news of late has all been bad and will only grow worse."

He was silent a moment, brooding, then shook himself out of his dark reflections. "Can I trust Kate? Her father was by all accounts a rascal and a rogue. Kate herself was quite eager to lay her hands on that gold. I shudder to think what might have happened to me if she had discovered I was carrying a fortune in the lining of my coat. You said she was reckless and wild when she was young. What is your opinion of her now?"

Phillip gave the matter serious thought. "Kate is fiercely loyal to those she considers friends, but she is also extremely ambitious and, as you say, eager to make money. Does she know you are friends with Captain Northrop?"

"Yes, we talked about Alan a good a deal," said Henry. "I think she fancies herself in love with him. I am afraid I led her to believe he remembered her with affection. The truth is that when I asked him about her, he hardly remembered her at all."

"Kate is but one more lovely woman to throw herself at Alan's feet so that he can trample on her heart," said Phillip, adding with an exaggerated sigh, "She never looked twice at poor Pip."

"Perhaps if Kate knew Pip was not a lowly clerk, but the immensely wealthy Duke of Upper and Lower Milton she would have looked upon him more fondly," Henry returned, smiling.

"I'm not so sure," said Phillip. "Kate has an odd code of honor, much like her father's. From the stories I've heard about him, Morgan would cheerfully swindle you out of every last penny, but he would have been horrified at the thought of robbing you at gunpoint. Kate would steal my money, but not my heart, if you take my meaning, my lord."

"Just as she was prepared to take my money, but could not bear to see me shot down in cold blood," Henry said thoughtfully.

"Speaking of money, may I make a suggestion . . ."

"I should be glad to hear your thoughts, Your Grace," said Henry.

"Kate values money for one reason—she dreams of buying back the family estate known as Barwich Manor. If I were you, my lord, I would obtain the deed to this estate. Offer half the deed to Kate now, with the other half to be given to her upon successful completion of her service to Freya."

"An excellent idea, Your Grace," said Henry. "I will have Mr. Sloan make the arrangements."

"So what are you going to do about Greenstreet, my lord?" Phillip asked. "I assume you will be interested in finding out why he tried to have you killed."

"I have given Kate the assignment," said Henry.

"I hope she understands the danger," Phillip said. "I would not want to see any harm befall her."

"We developed a plan together, Your Grace," said Henry.

"So long as she follows it," said Phillip, sounding doubtful.

"I find this Greenstreet business very odd, Your Grace," Henry said. "As far as I know, I am no threat to him or his business dealings. I have never had any involvement with the man before now."

"Were you able to question the assassins, my lord?"

"Sadly, no, Your Grace. I had to kill them," said Henry. "I couldn't risk letting them talk. I had no idea what they might say."

"I could ask around, my lord," Phillip offered. "That is, Pip could ask around."

"Thank you, Your Grace, but Pip is about to receive a stern letter from his father. Having been informed of his son's gambling debts, Pip's father is ordering him to come home."

"Ah, dear, that's too bad," said Phillip. "I've become quite fond of Pip—other than the fact that his clothes reek of whiskey and he is a dreadful card player. I shall be sorry to see him go."

"Yet go he must, Your Grace," said Henry gravely. "I have another assignment for you, if you are interested. You will have to travel to Estara."

"Gladly!" said Phillip. "Anywhere except my drafty old castle in Upper Milton where I would be bored out of my skull and slowly dying of mold and mildew."

"I have been your guest at the castle in Upper Milton, Your Grace," said Henry. "I never felt the hint of a draft and I should think a staff of some two hundred servants would be able to keep it free of mold and mildew."

"If you say so, my lord," said Phillip. "To me living there is like living in some elegantly furnished mausoleum. So what becomes of poor Pip?"

"He will disappear into ignominy. Once Pip has vanished, Phillip Edward James Masterson, fourteenth Duke of Upper and Lower Milton, will travel to Estara in order to advance a noble cause."

"I am intrigued, my lord," said Phillip. "What is this noble cause?"

"You will be supporting the cause of Thomas Stanford, descendant of James the First, known to many as 'Prince Tom,'" Henry replied. "His Highness needs a friend—a gallant young Freyan nobleman ready to pledge his life and his fortune to the true and rightful king of Freya."

"In other words, I am to spy on him," said Phillip. "So you perceive this young man to be a true threat, my lord?"

"I do, indeed, Your Grace," said Henry. "And I want you to give the assignment serious thought before you accept. We will not publicize it, but word will leak out, of course. Some in Freya will view you as a hero for joining with Prince Tom. Others will consider you a traitor. Her Majesty will be forced to denounce you in the strongest terms. And if the Estarans discover you are a spy, they will most certainly hang you."

"Does Her Majesty know the truth, my lord?"

"She does, Your Grace," said Henry. "She asked me to convey her gratitude and warm regard. She will do what she can to protect you. Unfortunately we can do nothing to help you once you reach Estara."

Phillip shrugged off his warning. "By God, Sir Henry, after spending these past months sitting on a stool, I feared my brain as well as my posterior were both going numb. An adventure such as you propose is a godsend!"

"I was hoping you would think so, Your Grace," said Henry. "You are admirably suited for the assignment."

"And what exactly *is* the nature of this assignment, my lord?"

"You will my eyes and ears, Your Grace," said Henry. "The prince's mother has supporters in Freya who are raising funds and providing her with sensitive information. I believe that some of these people are in positions of power. They call themselves 'the Faithful' and I fear they are plotting the violent overthrow of our government. My agents have been unable to find out who they are, however. Constanza is devilishly clever."

"Violent overthrow!" Phillip repeated, shocked. "I had no idea! Is Her Majesty in danger?"

"I have reason to think so, Your Grace," Henry replied gravely. "I would otherwise not ask you to risk your life."

Phillip extended his hand. "I am your man, my lord."

"Excellent, Your Grace," said Henry, shaking hands.

"How will you convince the prince to trust me, my lord?"

Henry smiled. "We are going to shoot you, Your Grace."

THIRTEEN

The night of her father's death, Olaf had been forced to lock Kate in her cabin to prevent her from roaming the streets of Westfirth in search of those who had murdered her father. Olaf threatened the same this early morning.

"Greenstreet tricked you. What did you expect? That you were dealing with an honest businessman? You knew better than that when you agreed to do his dirty work, Kate," he told her. "The truth is, Katydid, you planned to hoodwink Greenstreet and you failed. You thought you were clever, going after the gold like that, figuring you'd help yourself and Greenstreet none the wiser. You are damn lucky you're not dead!"

Kate held her tongue. She could understand why Olaf was upset. He loved her like his own child, which in a way she was, for Olaf had been more a father to her than Morgan.

Olaf had been horrified to hear that she had nearly been killed, and he had raved about that all day yesterday, and most of last night, and was starting in again this morning.

"You have your heart's desire, Kate: letters of marque and reprisal from Sir Henry Wallace himself and money enough to complete refitting *Victorie* and hire a crew!" Olaf continued, his face flushed. "We can sail away from Freeport and never look back."

Kate was sweeping the floor, wielding the broom with more energy than skill. She didn't like being scolded, especially when she knew Olaf was right. Turning her back on him, she surreptitiously whisked dried mud into a dark corner, hoping he wouldn't notice.

The tavern was closed and would not open until noon. Olaf sat at a table, hunched over his ledger, supposedly recording yesterday's sales. He had spent most of the morning yelling at her.

Akiel had ducked behind the bar and was making a racket rattling pots and pans. He never liked to hear people arguing.

The sun had only just risen and already the day was oppressive. The tavern was relatively cool, for Olaf had not yet opened the shutters, keeping the interior dark. The only sun allowed to enter came through slats in the shutters in the back, shining down on a table where Amelia was working.

The table was covered with sheets of her manuscript. Absorbed in her work, Amelia wrote at an extraordinary rate. Her pen made a scratching sound as it dashed across the paper.

Olaf had paused to draw breath, and now he added with a scowl, "And I see you sweeping dirt into the corner, Katherine Gascoyne-Fitzmaurice! Give Akiel the broom!"

Kate handed over the broom to Akiel, who rolled his eyes and shook his head. "Olaf is right, mum."

"Of course he's right," Kate said impatiently, flinging herself into a chair opposite him. "But I made a promise to Sir Henry Wallace."

"Promised His Lordship what?" Olaf asked.

"He asked me to talk to Greenstreet," said Kate.

"What about?" Olaf demanded. "Killing three of his men?"

"They died in a fight below deck when we boarded the *Pride,*" said Kate. "Killed by the ship's crew. Who's to say differently? There weren't any witnesses."

She glared at him, wishing he'd take the hint and keep quiet.

Amelia looked up from her work. "I should say, at a guess, that Sir Henry thinks Greenstreet sent those men to kill him. I know of a great many people who would sleep far more soundly at night if they knew Sir Henry Wallace had departed this life."

"You cannot write that in a story, Miss Amelia," Kate said, alarmed. "I promised Sir Henry I wouldn't say anything."

"It's old news anyway," said Amelia. "Someone is always trying to kill him."

"But why?" Kate wondered. "Sir Henry told me he works at the Foreign Office. He is some sort of low-level diplomat."

Amelia chuckled. "You are most refreshingly naive, Captain. Did you never stop to consider that a low-level diplomat would not be entrusted with granting letters of marque to privateers? Sir Henry Wallace may *say* he is a low-level diplomat. In truth, he holds the unofficial title of Her Majesty's Spymaster. He is thought by many to be the most dangerous man in the world."

Kate remembered watching Henry put a pistol to Jacob's head and then, with cool aplomb, blow out his brains. Admittedly Jacob had been prepared to shoot Henry in the back, but the poor bastard had been on his knees, no threat to Henry. She still felt sick to her stomach thinking about it.

At least Amelia's explanation effectively silenced Olaf's objection. He did not want anything to go wrong with this deal.

"I suppose if you promised His Lordship, you better see it through," Olaf said, subdued. "But use some diplomacy yourself, Katydid. Don't antagonize Greenstreet. He did give you money to make repairs to *Victorie.*"

"Never mind that his assassins would have killed me along with Sir Henry," Kate muttered, but she kept her voice low, not wanting to start another argument.

Akiel heard her, however, and shook his head. Olaf didn't. He was a little hard of hearing anyway and had gone back to working on his figures. Kate sat back in the chair and mopped her neck with a handkerchief.

"Speaking of the *Victorie,* Olaf," she said. "I need you to check the magical constructs on the lift tanks. They're starting to break down again and I can't fix them. They need your special touch."

"Contramagic destroying them!" Olaf snorted. "I can mend the constructs, but they'll only break down again. I was talking to a ship's crafter the other day and he claimed some chap in Rosia had found a way to stop the contramagic from eating away at the sigils. He couldn't remember his name—"

"Rodrigo de Villeneuve," said Amelia.

"There you go, Olaf," said Kate. "Ask Miss Amelia."

The writer wiped her metal pen and carefully set it in the holder of her inkwell before continuing.

"Rodrigo de Villeneuve discovered how to use what is termed 'the seventh sigil' to repair damage done by contramagic. He published a treatise on the subject, which later was made available to the public in pamphlet form. One of the bookstores in Sornhagen would likely carry it. I could purchase a copy for you the next time I am there."

"I would appreciate that, ma'am," said Olaf.

Miss Amelia picked up her beaded reticule, opened the clasp, drew out a small leather book, and made a note to herself. This done, she returned the book to the reticule and shut the clasp.

Olaf winked at Kate, then added politely, "The morning is a hot one. Could I bring you a mug of ale, Miss Amelia?"

"Water, if you please, Master Olaf," said Amelia, picking up her pen and dipping it in the inkwell to continue her work. "While some health benefit may be derived from the grains in the ale, I believe that to be negligible when compared to the ruinous effects of alcohol on the brain and liver."

"Stop teasing her, Olaf," Kate whispered, grinning.

"And miss hearing her talk? Don't take away one of the new joys of my life," Olaf whispered.

He picked up his crutch and propelled himself over to the bar, where he now kept a pitcher filled with well water for the express use of Amelia. Filling a glass, he carried it to her and received her thanks.

Kate felt hot just looking at Amelia, who was dressed in a stiff-collared white linen blouse with long cuffed sleeves, a long skirt, and a petticoat. By contrast, Kate was wearing a man's shirt, open at the neck, and slops, and was bathed in sweat.

"You should dress for the heat, ma'am," Kate advised. "Like I do."

"If I were twenty-four years old as are you, Captain, I would adopt your unorthodox attire," Amelia replied. "As it is, I prefer to dress as I have always dressed. With regard to the heat, I believe that one's comfort is the result of mind over matter. As you see, I am quite cool and comfortable."

Kate had to admit that while she saw Miss Amelia occasionally dab a few drops of what the woman called "perspiration" from her upper lip, she did not appear to suffer from the heat.

"You could at least shed the petticoat," Kate said.

Miss Amelia regarded Kate over the top of her pince-nez. "Mrs. Ridgeway of Mrs. Ridgeway's Academy for Young Ladies taught us that one can always tell a lady by her petticoats."

Olaf's face flushed red, this time from embarrassment, not anger. He was spared any more discussion of ladies' undergarments by loud knocking on the front door.

"We're closed!" Olaf shouted.

The knocking persisted.

"I'll tell them to come back later," Kate offered.

She went to the door, removed the bar, and opened it, letting in a flood of bright sunlight. Kate blinked at the two men standing in the doorway.

"We open at noon," she said and started to shut the door.

One of the men blocked it with his foot. "Greenstreet wants to speak to you. Now."

"As a matter of fact, I was just coming to talk to him," said Kate. She tied her kerchief around her head, tucked in her curls, and left the tavern in company with the two men.

The air was humid; water dripped off the leaves. The misty layers of the Breath lay motionless. Everything seemed to wilt in the heat, including the people.

Greenstreet's house was quiet, as always. Bright colored birds flashed among the leaves. The veranda was cool, shaded by the trees. Another man had replaced Jacob on porch duty. No one appeared to mourn Jacob's loss. Bullyboys were plentiful in the Aligoes. His replacement told her to wait, but Greenstreet must have been impatient to see her. He shouted that she was to come in.

He was in his chair behind his empty desk, his fingers laced over his broad middle. The room was cool and shadowy.

"Sit down, Captain," said Greenstreet, glowering at her. "And no more lies. I am not a fool. I know that my men did not die in a fight to take the ship."

Kate remained standing, arms folded.

"You were the one who lied to me, Greenstreet. There was no gold. The only reason you hired me to attack that ship was so that your men could kill Wallace—a job they bungled, I might add."

Kate slammed her hands on the desk.

"Why didn't you hire me to kill him? I could have done that job for you and succeeded!" she said, irate. "Not manage to get myself killed like the numbskulls on your payroll."

Greenstreet observed her through hooded lids.

"Are you quite finished, Captain?" he asked.

"Yes," Kate said.

"Then please be seated."

Kate sat down in the chair. Removing her kerchief, she shook out her curls and used the kerchief to mop her face. Then she retied it around her head. "Why do you want Wallace dead anyway? He claims he doesn't know you."

"He doesn't," Greenstreet said imperturbably. "I understand that he has given you letters of marque."

Kate was startled. She hadn't expected Greenstreet to hear about the news this fast, and she certainly hadn't expected him to mention it.

"What if he has?" Kate asked. "I can pay you what I owe you, if that's what you're worried about."

A sudden thought struck her. "And if you're thinking about asking me to kill Wallace now, Greenstreet, I won't do it. He is my future. When I set sail, you and the Aligoes will be my past."

Her voice trembled. Up to now, she had been acting a part, carrying out the plan she and Sir Henry had concocted. But when Kate spoke about Sir Henry being her future and the Aligoes her past, she was in earnest. She never wanted to see this place again.

"I am not satisfied—" Greenstreet began.

He abruptly stopped talking. His gaze shifted to a point past her shoulder and he barked out, "Trubgek! Damn it, don't sneak up on me like that! What the devil do you want?"

"Plans have changed," said a voice.

Startled, Kate turned to see a man entering through a secret panel in the wall. The man was about her height, of medium build, and wore an old leather jerkin over a worn shirt, leather trousers, and boots. Iron-gray hair fell to his shoulders, yet he did not seem old. Nor did he seem young either. His face was ageless, gaunt and smooth and empty. No emotion had left its mark, no laughter, no sorrow, no anger or tears. His dark eyes too were empty, devoid of life. When he looked at her, she might just as well have been the chair or the wall or the desk.

Kate started to jump to her feet, every instinct warning her to flee. Trubgek raised his hand and spoke a word, and Kate could not move. He walked over to her, slowly, without haste, and grasped her, unresisting, by the shoulders.

His two strong hands pressed into her flesh and he spoke again, garbled words, meaningless, but with a familiar sound.

A dreadful chill spread through Kate's body, as though her blood had congealed into icy sludge and then slowly frozen solid. She lost feeling in her hands and arms and legs. The paralysis spread to her chest and she had no thought of flight now. She had to struggle to simply draw a breath.

Trubgek seized her by the hair and yanked her head back. He prized open her jaws to tie a strip of cloth over her mouth, then dragged her limp arms behind her to bind her wrists. Kate was slowly suffocating, and she began to think this man was going to a lot of trouble for nothing, because she would soon be dead.

"Why did you interrupt me?" Greenstreet asked.

"He wants to speak to her in person," said Trubgek.

He pressed his hands on Kate's shoulders again, and spoke once more, and the debilitating chill started to seep away. Dizzy from lack of air, Kate could do nothing except sag in the chair, gasping, her heart thudding.

"Fine," Greenstreet said. "Saves me the trouble."

He sat back, again laced his fingers across his belly, and closed his eyes.

Trubgek jerked Kate to her feet and dragged her toward the secret panel.

"Close the door when you leave, Trubgek," Greenstreet added, without opening his eyes.

Trubgek: a strange and forbidding name. Few people would know what the word meant; only someone like Kate, who was familiar with the dragon language. The word was one of many dragons used for "human." But "trubgek" was different from most. The word was disparaging, a vile insult. Kate had heard Dalgren use the word only once and that was in reference to the Rosian naval officer who had ordered his men to fire on their own forces at the Battle of the Royal Sail, killing Dalgren's friend, Lady Cam.

She wondered how this man had come by such a name, and if he knew what it meant.

He thrust Kate toward the secret door. Her arms were bound behind her back, but she had the use of her legs. She could make a run for it . . .

"I know another spell," Trubgek remarked, as though he had read her thoughts. "One not so pleasant as the last. You will still be able to walk, because I don't intend to carry you, but you won't like it."

Greenstreet stirred and murmured, "If I were you, Captain, I would do as he says."

Kate kept walking. A series of stone steps led down below ground level.

Trubgek paused in the doorway to glance back at Greenstreet. "Any message for him?"

"No, none," said Greenstreet.

Trubgek nodded and walked through the doorway. He touched a magical construct on the wall, and the panel slid shut.

Kate descended the stairs first, with Trubgek following, his hand on her elbow. The stairs led to an underground passage with smooth-planed walls and a smooth floor. Magical constructs engraved on the walls glowed, lighting the way. They had walked about twenty paces when the passage split into two, one leading off to the right and another straight ahead. The passage to the right was dark. Trubgek ignored it and kept going straight. They followed the tunnel for about another hundred paces, then climbed more stairs, leading to another secret panel at the top.

Trubgek touched a construct on the wall. The panel opened into a shed filled with gardening tools: rakes, hoes, and shovels. Trubgek steered her toward the door to the shed, pushed it open, and walked outside.

Kate looked around, blinking in the bright sunshine. She was behind Greenstreet's house, facing the kitchen and the servants' entrance. There were several outbuildings, including the shed. A broad expanse of lawn ended at the edge of the jungle.

Trubgek escorted her in the direction of the jungle, a solid mass of trees, tangled underbrush, and other thick vegetation. Kate wondered where they were going. The jungle was impenetrable; she could see no trail.

Yet Trubgek kept walking. Reaching the tree line, he gave Kate a shove that sent her staggering off balance. With her arms tied behind her back, she couldn't catch herself, and she fell flat onto her belly.

Trubgek let her lie on the grass. He spoke a few words and this time Kate recognized the language, knew why it had sounded familiar. She stared at him in astonishment. She didn't know what the words meant, but she knew by the intonation, the way the words were pronounced, that Trubgek had spoken in the language of dragons.

Many humans could understand dragon speech, but Kate had never known a human who could speak draconic, not even the members of the Dragon Brigade, who had worked alongside dragons for much of their lives. The language of the dragons was rich and colorful and impossible for the human voice to re-create—or so Kate had always believed.

Trubgek had spoken the language crudely, like someone mangling a foreign tongue. The fact that he had spoken those words at all was astounding.

He reached down, grabbed hold of Kate, and dragged her to her feet. With the gag in her mouth, she couldn't talk, so she tried grunting her question, "How did you learn to speak draconic?"

"Talking annoys me," Trubgek replied. "That's why you are gagged. Keep walking."

He pushed her toward the tree line. Kate grunted again. "I can't! There's no trail . . ."

The trees shimmered in her vision and then seemed to shift and move, gliding to one side or the other, opening up a trail to let them pass. As she walked, she closely examined the trees, the dirt beneath her feet, the vegetation. After a moment's concentration, she could see the faint glow of eerie blue-green light.

She looked around, awed.

"Magic . . ."

The jungle seemed real, and in some sense, it was. She stumbled over the uneven ground, rolled her foot stepping on a stick, and felt the stinging slap of leaves hitting her in the face. Nature had no hand in the creation, however. The jungle had been created by magic, although no human, not even the feared priests of the Arcanum, had ever worked magic this powerful.

A dragon was the only being that could produce such wondrous magic; an immensely powerful dragon. Dalgren might be able to conjure up a few scrubby trees, but conjuring a jungle would be far beyond his skills.

Trubgek walked behind her, prodding her if she slowed. They must have covered a mile at least, going deeper and deeper into the jungle, following the trail that opened up in front of them. Kate had no idea where they were or how to find the way out. Glancing over her shoulder, she was relieved to see the trail was still there even after they had passed. She had been fearful it might vanish.

Kate had time to think, for Trubgek had nothing to say to her. She recalled the conversation between Greenstreet and Trubgek. Trubgek was taking her to speak to someone; he had said as much. She didn't know who or why or what this was about. At least she was still alive. Anyone who meant to kill her would hardly have gone to so much trouble to conjure up a magical jungle.

Kate couldn't make sense of it; after a while she was too exhausted to think or care. The heat was sweltering. The jungle might be magical, but the sun slanting down through the canopy of leaves was real. She was parched; the gag in her mouth made her jaws ache, and the ropes dug painfully into her flesh. Walking was difficult without the use of her arms. She stumbled and sometimes tripped and fell.

Trubgek didn't say a word. He simply dragged her to her feet and forced her to keep walking.

Kate was thankful at least that Olaf couldn't see her. He would never have stopped reminding her, "I told you so."

FOURTEEN

Amelia Nettleship was constantly on the lookout for the news story that would win her professional accolades and acclaim. She had acquired a devoted following with her fictional accounts of the Dragon Corsairs, but the journalist in her hungered to be taken seriously. Her goal was to write a story that would cause members of the House of Nobles to leap from their chairs, waving newspapers and shouting, "According to the prominent journalist Miss Amelia Nettleship, we face a crisis that will affect the fate of the nation!"

Despite what she had told Kate about the attempted assassination of Sir Henry Wallace being old news, the likely involvement of the mysterious man Greenstreet could make this just such a story. The problem was that according to Sir Henry, there had been no attempt. Henry had passed off the incident as a fight with the *Pride*'s crew when they boarded the ship.

Amelia knew better. She had been locked in her cabin, which was located on the deck above the orlop, and she had heard the gunshots, as well as the sound of an explosion. The moment she was freed from her cabin, she had sneaked down to the hold, taking advantage of the general confusion on the deck above as members of Kate's crew celebrated their good fortune.

Amelia had discovered the hatch locked and for a moment she had despaired. A quick examination proved her worries groundless. She had to contend with only a padlock. The magical warding spells that had been placed on the door were no longer working.

"Never forget, young ladies, that hairpins and hatpins can often be useful in a crisis," Mrs. Ridgeway had been fond of saying.

Amelia had drawn one of her long hairpins from her bun and thrust it into the lock. After a moment's work, the padlock released. She had crept into the hold, regretting that she had not thought to bring a lantern. As it was, she had to leave the hatch open in order to have light.

She had found the bodies at the bottom of the stair, as well as evidence of a blast that had left one of the men with a chest full of glass shards and bits of twisted brass. She had noted the position of the bodies, the location of pistols, and concluded that these men had come down here for the purpose of killing someone. And that someone had to be Wallace.

She did have to consider the possibility that they had planned to kill Kate, but Amelia discarded that. The men were members of Kate's crew; they could have killed her at any time with far less trouble and risk. No, they had been after Wallace. But why? Who was this Greenstreet? Therein lay the story.

Amelia looked out the window to observe the direction Kate and Greenstreet's men had taken. She wiped her pen, laid it down, rose, and stretched.

"Such a fine day," she said to Olaf. "I believe I will go for a walk."

She went back to the small room she was sharing with Kate, closed the door, and changed into a riding skirt, which was split up the middle, and a blouse with long sleeves to ward off insects.

She pinned on her hat, checked her pistol to make certain it was loaded, and placed it in her reticule along with the leather notebook and pencils. Finally, she picked up the umbrella, which was not at all an ordinary umbrella, but had been specially made for her with a magically reinforced steel shaft and a knife concealed in the handle. Thus armed, Amelia left the tavern and set off down the street.

Kate had a head start, but Amelia was not worried. She did not think it was likely they would rush in this heat and, besides, she knew where they were going. If she lost them, she could always ask for directions to Greenstreet's house. Amelia had not gone very far before she caught sight of them, about a quarter of a mile ahead.

Raising the umbrella to shade her from the sun, Amelia followed them and arrived in the lane that led to Greenstreet's house. She lowered the umbrella and darted into the shadows of the trees to reconnoiter. Kate had already gone inside, apparently, because she was not in sight.

Amelia considered sneaking up to the house to peer in the windows. Two men keeping watch on the veranda—the two who had escorted Kate—and thick oleander bushes planted around the house thwarted that idea. Amelia's next plan was to sneak around to the back. An estate this large must have a servants' entrance, and she had found that careless servants often left the door unlocked.

"I will enter through the back door," Amelia said, in the habit of talking to herself. "If anyone catches me, I can always say I came to apply for the housemaid's job and got lost."

Such a ploy had worked for her in the past and she didn't see why it wouldn't work now.

She studied the terrain. Several large oak trees near the dwelling provided shade. Since the trees were close together, she could move from tree to tree, staying in the shadows, until she reached the back of the house.

The two guards began playing mumblety-peg, a game that involved hurling knives. Amelia waited until they were engrossed in their sport. Keeping a firm grasp on the umbrella, she darted across the lawn, heading for the nearest oak and praying no one was looking out a window.

She reached the first tree and hid behind the trunk, pausing to catch her breath. No one had caught sight of her, apparently, for no one was raising the alarm.

The windows were wide open and she thought she heard voices. She hurried over to the house, planning to hide among the oleanders. The bushes, covered with pink and white flowers, were thick. She crouched down beside them to avoid being seen. The voices must be coming from another room, for while she could hear people talking, she couldn't understand what they were saying. She tried peeking inside, but the windows were too high. Returning to the original plan, she followed the line of oleander bushes until she reached the back of the house.

Here were more trees, a couple of outbuildings, and what once had been a kitchen garden, but which was now little more than a fine collection of weeds. The yard ended in thick jungle that looked as though it was biding its time, waiting to seize the land lost to mankind.

Amelia liked that description and, taking out the notebook, made a note to use it in the story.

She soon located the back door and found, upon investigation, that it was not only unlocked, it had been propped ajar, undoubtedly to let in air. No one was in sight. She was about to slip inside when a flash of red caught her eye.

Amelia looked in time to see Kate, wearing her red kerchief around her head, walk out of the shed, accompanied by a man dressed in leather. Kate was gagged and her hands were bound behind her back. She and her captor walked into the jungle and disappeared.

Amelia was too good a journalist to entirely abandon her plan to obtain a story on Greenstreet, but that plan must of necessity now change. Kate had obviously been taken captive. She was in danger and Amelia had a split second to go through her options and decide what to do.

"I could run back to the tavern for help, but by the time I explained to Olaf and Akiel what has happened, Kate and her captor would be long gone." Amelia rejected that idea.

"I am armed," she said. "And I have the advantage of surprise."

She hurried off in pursuit, searching for a trail and almost immediately finding it. The moment she set foot on the trail, however, a chill sensation came over her—a "frisson," as the Rosians would term it.

Some people have a primordial terror of forests and jungles, but Amelia was not one of them. She could not explain the shiver of apprehension and therefore she ignored it and moved deeper into the jungle, following the narrow trail. She kept her eyes on the ground, watching where she was putting her feet, and it was then she suddenly noted the ghostly glow of magic.

Amelia was not a crafter. She could not work magic. She was, however, a channeler, which meant that although she could not create magical constructs, she could direct the flow of magic into existing constructs and thus was able to see them. Amelia gazed around in awe. She doubted if even the saints who had discovered contramagic could have possessed such incredible power as the person who had created this jungle. She would have liked to stop to investigate, make notes and take samples for later analysis with a view to writing a paper for presentation to the Royal Botanists Association.

The report would have to wait, however. Her concern now was for Kate. Amelia needed to move quietly, which meant moving slowly and cautiously. She blessed Mrs. Ridgeway for her counsel regarding sensible shoes.

The trail ran straight, did not branch off, and although she could not see Kate and her captor, Amelia could follow the physical signs of their passing: broken sticks, trampled vegetation, a partial footprint.

Noting these, she was intrigued. A broken stick meant that the jungle was real, not an illusion.

"The jungle was not created by magic," Amelia remarked. "Magic is manipulating the jungle."

She also noted the absence of wildlife: no birds or snakes or wild boars, no bloodsucking leeches, flies, or mosquitoes. All the wildlife and even the insects had fled, not liking the magic.

She had walked about a mile when the trail began to slope, leading down into a valley. Amelia tried to catch some glimpse of the top of the mountain that formed the island, to determine where she was, but the foliage was too thick for her to see it.

The trail descended at a steep angle, diving into a crevasse, slicing through towering rock walls. Amelia was forced to cling to the walls to avoid losing her footing. The path grew narrower and narrower and then ended with a suddenness that took her by surprise.

She edged forward between the rock walls, and realized the path didn't end. It continued through a crevice in the wall. Amelia put her eye to the crack and saw the path extend on through the crevice about twenty feet. She couldn't see where it led, but she could see, at the end, the back of a leather jerkin.

Kate's captor must be standing at the end of the path, blocking the entrance, keeping guard. Amelia could not see Kate, but she could hear her voice and the voice of another. The other voice was big and deep and booming, and Amelia had no trouble at all understanding what was being said.

Amelia was no coward, but she was blessed with common sense, and even though she was armed, she knew better than to rush in to try to save Kate. If the owner of the big, deep, booming voice was as large as the sound of the voice, she could be facing a formidable foe—possibly the one who had the magical power to manipulate a jungle.

Amelia regretted that she couldn't see for herself what was going on, but she did the next best thing. She braced herself against the rock wall and settled down to eavesdrop.

FIFTEEN

Kate squeezed through the crevice, scraping the side of her face and ripping her shirtsleeve. The rock walls opened into pitch darkness. She felt smooth stone beneath her feet and had the impression she was in a vast cavern.

She stood still, concentrating on listening, since she could not see. She could hear movement, a sound as though a large bulky object was being hauled across the floor. Trubgek tore the gag from her mouth.

"He wants to talk," said Trubgek.

"Who?" Kate demanded, wincing at the pain in her jaws.

Trubgek didn't answer. He stood near her, close enough to remind her that he had only to lay his hands on her to work his magic. He did not remove the ropes.

Light flared, illuminating her surroundings, and Kate gasped. She was in a vast underground chamber, but this was no mere cavern. She might have been standing in the ballroom of a royal palace. The walls were adorned with friezes, paintings, tapestries, and marble statues. The light shone from a multitude of lamps.

Every object in the chamber was beautiful and valuable. Kate had learned something about art from her mother, and she recognized works of the masters. She first was awed by the splendor. Then, looking more closely, she saw that the great artworks were covered with dirt. The paintings were dusty and hung at angles. The marble statues were filthy; they needed scrubbing. The tapestries were shabby and frayed.

No one cared about them. No one admired them.

Kate looked up at the high ceiling, then took note of the immense area of empty floor space. She added that to the fact that the chamber was located beneath a mountain and that visitors had to traverse a magical jungle to reach it, and she began to understand.

"This is a dragon dwelling," Kate said loudly. "I know, because I have been a guest in a dragon house many times."

Actually, she was putting on a bold front to show she wasn't going to be intimidated. The truth was she had never been inside a dragon house in her life. She knew what their houses were like, however. Dalgren had often described his parents' fine mansion to her. Dragons were fond of human art and enjoyed collecting paintings and statuary. Most dragons loved and cared for their collections. These pieces reflected nothing except pride of ownership; even that had reached a limit, apparently.

"I am accustomed to being around dragons," she added. "I am not afraid of them."

"Perhaps you should be, Captain Kate."

The dragon emerged from the shadows and walked into the center of the chamber. He was large, although not as large as Dalgren, and he had the thick neck and short stature that denoted a "common dragon"—one of common birth. His scales were a uniform color of green, as was his stubby mane.

"My name is Coreg," the dragon continued. "My time is limited and we have business to discuss."

Coreg was in his prime, strong and vigorous, probably around four hundred years of age. He was powerful in dragon magic. Kate knew now who had cast the spell over the jungle. The dragon was obviously wealthy and covetous, with no care for the beautiful objects decorating his house, needing to know only that he possessed them.

A great deal began to make sense to Kate, mainly why Greenstreet always sat at an empty desk, never did any work. He was the mouthpiece. Coreg was the true master of the Aligoes.

"What do you want, Coreg?" Kate asked, tilting back her head to see. "Why bring me here?"

Coreg gazed down at her from his great height. He lifted a claw from the floor, twitched his tail. "I could kill you with a swipe of my claw."

"Yes, you could," said Kate. "But I don't think you will. You want something from me."

Coreg chuckled, a rumbling that shook the floor.

"You are not easily intimidated. But then, as you say, you are accustomed to being around dragons. I refer to your companion, Lord Dalgren, of the Dragon Duchies."

Coreg shook his massive head. His mane brushed a chandelier, causing the crystal bangles to faintly jingle.

"You ruined my carefully laid plan, Captain. I wanted Sir Henry Wallace dead. And yet he breathes."

"I didn't ruin anything," said Kate. "I can't be blamed for the fact that Greenstreet hired fools."

"I was angry at first," Coreg went on as though she hadn't spoken. "The governor of Wellinsport gave me free rein to run my business operations in that city and Wallace came here to remove him. I planned to remove Wallace, but now I find myself glad you saved the man's life. I have a new plan. Sir Henry has given you letters of marque, making you and your crew, including your dragon friend, Lord Dalgren, Freyan privateers."

"What if he has?" Kate asked, her nonchalant manner hiding her uneasiness. Coreg seemed to know a lot about her and about Dalgren.

"As it happens, I want you to work for me," said Coreg.

"I appreciate the offer, but I can't work for you," said Kate. "I am leaving the Aligoes. If I return, I would be glad to reconsider."

"You are your father's daughter, Katherine," said Coreg, amused. "Pity about his sudden death. Skull crushed, wasn't it? You always suspected the Hollow Soul gang. I wonder if I should tell her the truth, Trubgek."

Kate cast a startled glance over her shoulder at Trubgek. He stood with his arms crossed, his legs planted, his gaze fixed on the dragon, and his eyes empty.

"What do you mean?" Kate asked, scowling, turning back to Coreg. "What do you know about my father's death?"

"Only that he refused a simple request," said Coreg.

Kate felt her mouth go dry, her throat close. "You're lying. You don't know anything."

Coreg made a sudden dart with his head, so that his snout was only a few feet from her. Startled, Kate took an involuntary step backward and bumped into Trubgek. He put his hands on her shoulders and she froze, nerving herself to meet the dragon's slit eyes.

"You won't refuse a simple request, will you, 'Katydid'?" Coreg murmured.

Kate set her jaw. "You can threaten me all you like, Coreg. I'm working for Sir Henry."

"You must allow Wallace to think so, of course," Coreg agreed. "He must never know the truth. Don't worry. You will not find the tasks I assign onerous. You may capture all the Rosian treasure ships you want, keep Sir Henry happy. A year or more could pass and you might never hear from me."

Coreg thrust his head even closer. His fetid breath, stinking of blood, washed over her. Kate choked, struggled to keep from gagging.

"When you do hear from me, I expect you to do what I ask," said Coreg. "My reach is long—it can crush a man's skull in an alley in Westfirth."

The dragon drew back his head. Raising himself to his full height, he gazed down on her. "Have a safe and pleasant journey to Freya, Captain. I would warn you to say nothing of our conversation, but I won't bother. If you did, no one would believe you. I will be in touch. Trubgek, I need a word with you."

The lamps went dark; the only light now was sunlight filtering through the crack in the stone. Kate lost sight of both Trubgek and the dragon. She could hear them talking, but they were speaking draconic. Kate tried to figure out what they were saying. She knew a smattering of the language, but could understand it only if it was spoken slowly. Coreg spoke rapidly, though, and Kate gave up.

No one was guarding her. She could have escaped, but there was a reason no one was guarding her. She didn't have anywhere to go. Coreg had only to withdraw the magic to leave her stranded, lost, in the midst of the jungle. She did edge nearer the crack in the wall to get some fresh air, rid her nostrils of the nauseating odor of Coreg's breath, and was surprised to hear a scrabbling noise from outside, as if someone was beating a hasty retreat.

Kate concluded that the noise was probably made by an animal and thought nothing more about it. She went over everything the dragon had said, especially the threats. He knew a lot about her father's death, more than she had ever told anyone. She and Olaf were the only two who knew about the Hollow Soul gang. And she wasn't the only one he had threatened. He had let her know he was familiar with Dalgren's noble family and that he knew Olaf's pet name for her.

Kate leaned back against the wall. She was desperately thirsty. Her arms hurt, her shoulders ached, her spirits flagged. She couldn't believe this was happening. Or rather, she could. The family motto.

"I'll fix this," Kate vowed. "I will. I always do."

Hearing footsteps, she hurriedly straightened. Trubgek was walking toward her, holding the gag in one hand and a waterskin in the other. Silently he held out the water. Kate was thirsty, but she hesitated, thinking it might be drugged. Trubgek shrugged and started to toss the waterskin on the floor.

"No!" Kate said. "Please."

He removed the stopper and held the waterskin to her mouth. She drank some; then he took it away and started to gag her.

"You won't need that. I won't talk," Kate said. "I promise."

Trubgek paused and seemed to consider, then stuffed the strip of cloth into a pocket in his jerkin.

He pointed at the crevice in the wall. "That way."

"It would be easier for me to walk if you could free my wrists—" Kate began.

Trubgek reached for the gag. Kate pressed her lips together and squeezed through the crack in the stone. The walking was arduous; she was already tired and felt drained after the tense interview with the dragon. The water revived her, however. She had a lot to think about, decisions to make, and as she put distance between herself Coreg, her spirits rose.

I'm leaving the Aligoes, Kate said to herself. I'll be sailing the Breath, the world over. I'll be under the protection of the Freyan government. He can't touch me.

Nonetheless, she was uneasy. She had never before heard of a dragon engaged in villainous enterprises, criminal activity, sinking as low as humans. Dragons were intelligent, noble creatures with high standards and ideals. True, Dalgren had sunk beneath those standards by deserting the Dragon Brigade, but Kate knew that he was tormented every day by his actions. He never said as much, but that was the reason he refused to fight humans or dragons. Coreg would make a powerful foe. All very well to tell herself she would keep out of his reach, but that might prove difficult. And, as he said, if she told someone, no one would believe her.

Her worries carried her through the magical jungle, and for all her defiant determination, she was extremely glad to step onto the smooth, green, nonmagical lawn of Greenstreet's estate.

Kate wondered if Trubgek would take her back to Greenstreet. She looked back at Trubgek for instruction, only to see that he had stopped at the edge of the jungle. Startled, Kate turned to face him.

"Aren't you coming?"

Trubgek fixed his dark, empty eyes on her and she had the strangest impression he was studying her, engraving her image on his mind, never to be forgotten. Kate met his gaze. She'd never forget him either. She indicated the ropes.

"You need to untie me," she told him.

Trubgek stared in silence and then started to turn away.

"No! Wait! Where are you going?" Kate called, alarmed. "You can't leave me tied up like this!"

Trubgek said nothing. He walked back into the jungle, leaving Kate standing on the lawn, her hands locked behind her back.

"Why do you let Coreg call you by that horrible name?" Kate yelled after him. "You know it's an insult. You know that every time he says 'Trubgek,' he's sneering at you. Why do you put up with it?"

Trubgek stopped. He turned to face her, and Kate saw a flicker of life in the man's eyes, a feeling long suppressed. His expression did not change and Kate couldn't tell whether the emotion was anger or disdain or maybe even laughter. He turned away again. The glow of the magic started to fade. The trees closed ranks and the trail through the jungle vanished. Trubgek vanished.

Kate shivered. She was glad he was gone, although he had left her in a sorry predicament. She wondered what to do. She didn't want to have to grovel in front of Greenstreet, beg him to remove the ropes, but she couldn't very well walk through the town trussed up like a chicken.

And then she would have to face Olaf. . . .

Sighing, Kate started toward the house, thinking she would enter through the back door. A voice startled her.

"Hst! Captain! Over here!"

Kate raised her head to see Amelia standing in the door of the shed, waving to her.

"Miss Amelia!" Kate gasped. "What are you doing here?"

Amelia was red in the face and breathing fast. Her clothes were disheveled, and her hat was askew, her neat hair straggling around her face. She darted out, caught hold of Kate by the arm, and dragged her back inside the shed, then shut the door.

"Are you all right, Captain?" Amelia asked, concerned.

"I'm fine, except for these damn ropes," Kate replied.

Amelia swiftly set about removing the ropes.

Kate grimaced as she flexed her arms and rubbed her scraped and bruised wrists.

"How did you come to be here, Miss Amelia?" Kate asked, wondering uneasily how much she knew.

"I followed you, Captain, in pursuit of the story," Amelia replied, and added exultantly, "And what a story! A dragon criminal mastermind in the Aligoes!"

"Did you follow me . . . all the way?" Kate asked.

"To the dragon's lair? I did," said Miss Amelia. "I was unable to see inside. That man with the odd name had his back against the crevice, blocking my view. But you can describe it to me."

"How much did you hear?"

"Everything," said Amelia, sounding rather satisfied with herself. "That is, right until the dragon told Trubgek to take you away. It occurred to me that the dragon might remove the magic on the jungle once it was no longer necessary and that I needed to leave posthaste. I had to run most of the way to keep ahead of you and the Trubgek fellow. Thank goodness I keep myself fit. A brisk five-mile walk daily. The secret is to swing the arms vigorously, like this. Expands the chest."

"You can't write about this, Miss Amelia," said Kate. "You can't tell anyone. Please!"

"You are correct, Captain. I cannot write about Coreg," said Amelia, looking downcast. "At least, not yet. I don't have enough information. Editors would read the first paragraph of such an outlandish tale and eject me from their offices. I need proof. I did consider telling Sir Henry—"

"He'd think we were insane," said Kate, remembering Coreg's words.

"You do Sir Henry a disservice, Captain," said Miss Amelia. "He might believe us. The man has not lived as long as he has by rejecting even the most outré notions willy-nilly. But what would we gain if we did? We have no proof. Greenstreet will never talk, and we don't dare take a chance questioning him. I don't want to alert Coreg to the fact that I am planning to investigate him."

"Are you?" Kate asked. "Planning to investigate?"

"Of course. I must do thorough and exhaustive research into this dragon. By the way, I assume it was Coreg who cast that wondrous magic spell on the jungle?"

"Yes," said Kate, feeling dazed. "Dragons have the innate ability to magically alter their surroundings. Dates back to ancient times when humans hunted them and they had to hide their lairs."

"You must explain dragon magic to me, Captain. Most remarkable thing I ever saw."

"I'd love to talk about dragon magic, Miss Amelia," said Kate. "But right now we need to get out of Greenstreet's shed before someone finds us."

"Quite correct," said Amelia. After picking up the umbrella and the reticule, she opened the door to the shed and peered out. "I believe the coast is clear, Captain, as you sailors would say."

The sun was high overhead. Kate was surprised that it was only midday. She felt as though she had been gone a year. She and Amelia kept to the shadows of the trees, but they saw no one, not even men guarding the veranda.

Once they were safely away from Greenstreet's, Amelia wanted to talk about everything from the interior of the dragon's dwelling to what Coreg looked like and any other details Kate could remember. Kate was in no mood to answer questions. Pleading that her throat hurt from the gag, she said she would discuss things with Amelia on the voyage home.

Amelia cast her a sharp glance and said she understood. Taking out her notebook and a pencil, she began to jot down notes, occasionally glancing up to see where she was going.

Kate wanted only to put the dragon out of her mind. The less she thought about Coreg, the better. Her more immediate concern now was finding words to explain to Olaf how she had come by the bruises on her wrists.

Book 2

SIXTEEN

The tavern El Chancho Feliz, translated as the Happy Pork, was the favorite gathering place of the young officers of the Estaran Royal Military Academy. The officers would arrive in the late afternoon to drink sherry—the mother's milk of Estara—and discuss their classes, mock their professors, and flirt with the serving maids.

After a good deal of sherry, the young men would shove aside tables and chairs—and other customers—to practice their fencing skills. At these times, the tavern's owner would retire to his office in the rear and pretend not to notice the ensuing havoc.

When evening fell, the young gentlemen would leave to seek other entertainment, or to study . . . if they had nothing better to do. The owner would emerge from his office, sweep up the mess, and happily total the day's earnings. A wise man, he knew where his interests lay. The young men of the Royal Military Academy came from wealthy families. He had only to send bills to their parents to be reimbursed for the broken chairs and shattered glass.

Thomas James Stanford Oberlein was on his way to the tavern. Still a block from his destination, he could already hear bursts of uproarious laughter. He grinned and quickened his pace, placing his hand on the basket-hilted sword known as a schiavone to keep it from clanking against his leg. He wore the uniform of an officer-student with the rank of lieutenant in the Estaran army. The uniform consisted of tricorn hat, long-skirted coat in blue with gold braid trim, waistcoat, shirt and breeches in white, and white stockings.

The blue became Thomas, whose eyes were an unusually crystalline and intense shade of blue. Framed by black eyebrows and black eyelashes and contrasting with his black wavy hair, his eyes were truly striking and caught the attention of all he encountered, especially the women, while his wide and infectious smile charmed the women into smiling back at him.

Thomas's looks were enhanced, not marred, by the battle scar that slashed across his left cheekbone. He had received the scar and a medal of valor to go along with it fighting the Bottom Dwellers at the Battle of San Estevan. The single daughters of Estaran noblemen of marrigeable age were united in their belief that the scar gave him a romantic, heroic air.

Thomas doffed his hat to several of these young women, walking with their duennas, as he hurried down the streets of the Estaran city of Arcos, which were unusually crowded today. People had come from all over Estara to celebrate the reopening of the famous arched crystal bridge for which the city was named. The bridge spanned the river Artegar, but had been closed to traffic about five years ago, when it was discovered that the magical contructs that strengthened the bridge's crystal structure had been heavily damaged by contramagic during the war with the Bottom Dwellers. The crystal had begun to crack and the bridge had been declared no longer safe.

The beautiful bridge was famous the world over, for it shone like flame in the sunlight and disappeared completely on gray and cloudy days. In the early days of the war, no one knew how to repair the damage from contramagic. The people had feared it was irreparable.

The discovery of the seventh sigil by the priest of the Arcanum, Father Jacob Northrop, had saved the bridge. For the past two years, crews of crafter masons had been hard at work repairing and restoring the magic, and now the work had finally been completed.

The bridge had been reopened and the city fathers were planning a weeklong celebration. The King of Estara was attending, as were members of his royal court, including Thomas's mother, Constanza, Marchioness of Cavanaugh in the country of Bheldem and a cousin to the king.

Constanza was also Queen Mother of Freya, or so she had recently begun to style herself, firmly believing as she did that her son, Thomas James Stanford (he went by her family name, at her insistence)—more popularly known in Freyan newspapers as Prince Tom—was Freya's true and rightful heir to the throne.

Thomas was fond of his mother, but he did not take her obsession seriously. She lived for intrigue and was never happier than when forming schemes and plots involving her son.

He entered the tavern to cheers and invitations to come join in the swordplay. He was immensely popular among the young officers. Even those who longed to hate him because he was handsome and wealthy and famous were soon conquered by his warmth and self-deprecating good humor.

Thomas declined the swordfighting, instead joining a group sitting on stools at the bar, drinking sherry and eating walnuts, cheese, and olives.

"Thomas, I was just talking of you," said Hugo, motioning him near. They had to shout to be heard above the noise of clashing steel and smashing chairs. "We are getting up a group to go trout fishing this weekend on the Artegar River. We will be staying at Henri's father's country estate. You must join us."

Thomas longed to join them. He was fond of trout fishing and the rest of the day's activities that usually followed. After catching the fish, the young men would go back to Henri's beautiful mansion, play lawn tennis with his pretty sisters and their equally pretty friends. Nighttime would bring dancing with these same sisters and playing at cards with his friends. He was forced to shake his head in refusal.

"I would love to come, but I have been invited to the royal ball and I have orders to attend," Thomas replied.

"Whose orders?" asked one of the officers, who had not known Thomas long.

"My mother's," said Thomas, grimacing. "She has been invited to the ball as a guest of His Majesty and I must attend her."

His statement was received with mockery and good-natured jeers. Thomas only laughed.

"Trust me, my friends, I have been praying for another war to break out, so that I might escape atttending this ball. Sadly it seems all the nations in Aeronne appear to be firmly committed to peace."

"Is your mother so formidable?" Hugo asked.

"Let me put it this way," said Thomas. "Do you remember that night we were pinned down at the fort with hot lead zinging around our ears? I think of that fondly in comparison to attending a ball in the company of my mother.

"That is not to say I do not love her," he added, becoming more serious. "For I do love her with all my heart. But lately she insists upon introducing me as His Highness, the Crown Prince of Freya. Then people stare and no one will dance with me."

"I doubt that," said Hugo, grinning. "I have seen women stand in line to dance with the handsome prince." He raised his glass. "A toast to His Majesty, Thomas Stanford, King of Freya."

As the young men raised their glasses, Thomas playfully kicked Hugo's stool out from under him. Hugo retaliated by throwing olives at Thomas, who grabbed a trencher to use as a bat and struck the olives with skill, launching them into the swordsmen. The swordsmen turned their attacks upon the olive throwers and the fun became general.

Thomas ran out of ammunition and was forced to retreat behind the bar. He and his forces had begun tearing off hunks of bread with which to pelt the enemy when silence enveloped the room. The silence started at the entrance and rolled like a wave over the crowd.

Thomas peered over the bar. His first thought was that either an uncommonly beautiful woman had entered or perhaps—frightful thought—the regimental commander. Wondering if he should sneak out the back, he cautiously joined Hugo and the others as they crouched behind the bar, trying to see without being seen.

"It's a preacher," Hugo said in whisper. "What's he doing here?"

Thomas got a good look and sighed.

"He's not a preacher," he said, although the older man with the somber expression and close-cropped hair could have been mistaken for one. He wore a uniform that was as somber as his expression, consisting of a beige leather coat, gray breeches, a long-sleeved brown shirt with a wide white collar, and a broad-brimmed black hat.

"That, my friends, is Captain Jonathan Smythe," said Thomas. "The 'y' in his name is properly pronounced as in the word 'smite.' Do not call the good captain 'Smith' or, God forbid, 'Smithee.' You will never hear the end of it."

"Devil take me if I call him anything," Hugo said, laughing. "Is he one of those religious fellows who believes we're all going to hell for laughing and wearing the color red?"

"And for singing and dancing and indulging in any other pleasure you care to name."

"How do you know him?"

"He works for my father," Thomas replied. "He is head of the household guard."

An evasion, if not a lie. His mother would never forgive him if he told the truth. Thomas realized he probably shouldn't have said that much, but he was angry. Captain Smythe had no business turning up here among his friends. Hugo clearly had more questions, but Thomas wasn't inclined to answer them.

Leaving his friends to speculate, he made his way through the crowd. Smythe must have been asking about him, for various people were pointing him out. As Thomas approached, Smythe bowed.

"I hope I find you well, Your Highness."

"I am fine," Thomas said. "And I have asked you not to—"

"God be praised for your good health, Your Highness," Smythe said gravely.

"I have asked you *not* to call me 'Your Highness' in public, Captain," said Thomas in a low voice.

"Your lady mother has commanded I do so, Your Highness," Smythe said. "She sent me to find you. May we speak in private?"

Thomas sighed. "If we must."

When he went back to retrieve his sword and make a brief and unproductive search for his hat, his friends bombarded him with questions. Thomas answered with a shake of his head and left.

Smythe waited for him near the door, looking about the tavern. Thomas noted as he returned that the captain's eyes flicked from person to person, intently scrutinizing each one, undoubtedly hoping to ferret out some dastardly plot or foil an attempted assassination against the heir to the Freyan throne.

"Let us step outside, Captain," Thomas said, eager to be rid of the man.

Smythe inclined his head and the two walked out. By unspoken agreement, Thomas and the captain turned their steps toward a cemetery behind a church that was generally deserted at this time of day.

"Why did my mother send you, Captain?" Thomas asked when they were alone. He switched to the Freyan language, which he spoke as fluently as Estaran, his mother having hired the best tutors to teach the "future king" his "native" tongue. "And what are you doing here in Arcos? The last I heard, you were in Bheldem, training and equipping my mother's army, which I thought, by the way, was supposed to be a closely held secret. I had to tell my friends you were head of my father's household guard."

Captain Smythe stood ramrod-straight, as though on parade. His grizzled hair and weathered complexion made him appear older than his forty years. He had been a marine in the Freyan army, honorably retired, before coming to Bheldem to work for the marquis and the marchioness.

"I wish you would think of the army as *your* army, Your Highness. The army that will restore you to your rightful place upon the Freyan throne."

Thomas checked an impatient retort, not wanting to get into an argument.

"Well, Captain?" he said. "Why are you here?"

"I received a message from Her Ladyship summoning me to Arcos, Your Highness. Once I arrived, she ordered me to find you and escort you to her lodgings. Her Ladyship did not tell me why, only that the matter is one of the utmost urgency. She sent her carriage."

Smythe indicated the elegant horse-drawn coach adorned with the Oberlein family coat of arms that was waiting for them around the corner.

"Why did my mother send *you*?" Thomas asked. "She could have sent a servant."

Smythe gave a faint smile. "You are, of course, aware of Her Ladyship's feelings regarding the trustworthiness of servants, Your Highness."

Thomas was aware. He sighed, resigned, and turned his steps back toward the coach. "I suppose we should not keep my mother waiting. Do you know anything about this serious and urgent matter, Captain?"

"I do not, Your Highness," Smythe replied. "I confess I was myself surprised to receive Her Ladyship's abrupt summons. I was told to drop everything and travel posthaste to Arcos. I flew here by griffin, arriving only last night."

Thomas and Smythe entered the coach. The coachman closed the door, and the carriage rolled off down the street and across the newly reopened crystal bridge. The scaffolding was being dismantled and people were decorating the bridge with garlands, bunting, and Estaran flags. Captain Smythe sat gazing out the window at the bridge. Thomas had the impression the soldier was not enjoying the beauty of the crystal shining in the sun, but rather thinking how he would deploy his troops if told to seize and hold it against some foe.

"How goes the training of the army, Captain?" Thomas asked in order to be polite.

"The men are shaping up well, Your Highness," Smythe replied.

"What are their numbers?"

"The army consists at present of five hundred crack troops—trained mercenaries, the majority of which are Guundaran—and one thousand regular infantry. I plan to increase that number to fifteen hundred."

"Two thousand troops. Seems a rather small force to lay claim to a kingdom," Thomas said with a smile.

"I am a soldier, Your Highness," Captain Smythe said. "I obey orders and right now my orders are to raise and train an army. I know nothing of any plans for that army."

Thomas didn't believe him. Captain Smythe had been born planning incursions. He had probably ordered his toy soldiers to attack his sister's rag dolls. Still, Thomas reflected, Smythe couldn't be blamed for keeping his mouth shut. Constanza trusted no one, not even her own son, apparently.

Thomas considered it all nonsense, just like the stories about his supposed heroic exploits she fed to the Freyan press. She kept mailing him copies of the "Prince Tom" stories, which he promptly fed to the fire.

"What about weapons, then?" Thomas persisted, determined to make the captain tell him something more. "Rifles and ammunition and suchlike. Do you have enough to outfit two thousand soldiers?"

"One can never have enough, Your Highness," Smythe said.

Thomas gave up. Flinging himself back in the seat, he closed his eyes and pretended to go to sleep.

SEVENTEEN

Constanza owned a house in Verisol, the capital of Estara. She divided her time between Verisol and with her husband on their hereditary estate in Bheldem.

When Constanza visited her son in Arcos, she stayed at the home of a cousin, who rarely used his country house and was happy to open it to her. The manor house belonged to a Count Alfonse, who visited it only during shooting season.

He would have put his servants at her disposal, but she refused to rely on strangers. She brought her own servants. Thomas always wondered why, for she didn't trust them either, although most had been in her employ for years.

The chief steward answered the door and directed Thomas and Captain Smythe to the music room. Thomas was somewhat surprised, for his mother did not care for music.

"I didn't even know there was a music room," Thomas confided to Captain Smythe, who, of course, had no comment.

Uncertain where to find the music room, Thomas followed the tinkling sound of a pianoforte. The door was closed and he and the captain entered unannounced, for his mother had ordered the servants belowstairs.

Thomas walked in, followed by Smythe, to find his mother in company with an unknown gentleman. The two were seated on a couch, deep in conversation. The sound of the pianoforte, being played by a young woman in a far corner, drowned out what they were saying.

Constanza Celeste Stanford Oberlein, the Marchioness of Cavanaugh, was fifty-four years old, though she always claimed to be younger. She had married the marquis at the age of eighteen. After several miscarriages, she had given birth to her precious son, the first male child born to the Stanford line in over a hundred years.

A beautiful woman, with royal blood in her veins from both the Estaran and the Freyan sides, Constanza had been besieged by suitors. She had chosen an extremely wealthy nobleman from the small country of Bheldem. Many had wondered at her choice, for Bheldem was generally considered to be a country in chaos, more or less run by a confederation of nobles, some of whom were corrupt and at least one of whom was insane.

Thomas's father, Alastair Oberlein, the Marquis of Cavanaugh, was a man of power and influence with vast land holdings in Bheldem and in the Aligoes Islands. He was coolheaded and practical, the opposite of his fiery, emotional wife. Thomas had seen little of his father growing up. Alastair was deeply involved in Bheldem politics and spent most of his time traveling the countryside, bolstering allies and crushing rivals.

Alastair was well aware that Constanza married him for his money. He had told Thomas he believed he had done well out of the deal and he would do still better when his son became king of Freya. Alastair's goal was to unite Bheldem under a strong central leader, preferably himself. A son who was king would help further that goal. Thomas liked and respected his father, if he could not love him.

Embroiled in her own intrigues to make her son king of Freya, Constanza divided her time between Estara and Bheldem. Despite the fact that they lived separate lives—or perhaps because of it—Alastair and Constanza were a happy couple, united in ambitious goals for their son.

Constanza was so absorbed in her conversation with her guest, and the pianoforte music was so loud, that she did not hear her son enter. Thomas walked over to the couch, hoping to catch his mother's eye. As he did so, he caught a few words of her conversation and he groaned inwardly. Constanza was telling this man, a perfect stranger, the story of her son's miraculous birth.

"I was twenty-nine, my lord, and I had yet to produce a male heir," Constanza was saying. "I prayed to God and was told to make a pilgrimage to a long-forgotten shrine of Saint Celeste, my patron saint."

Thomas knew there would be no stopping her now and he resigned himself to wait in patience, even as he felt his face growing uncomfortably warm. Captain Smythe had the grace to retreat to a distant corner.

"To prove my dedication, my lord, I crawled on my hands and knees for miles up a rocky path," Constanza continued. "When I reached the top, I was exhausted. My dress was in rags, my hands and my knees were bloody. I touched the altar and I begged the saint to lift the family curse and send me a son. Then I fell into a swoon at the foot of the statue of the saint and lay there, half dead."

Constanza paused dramatically, putting her hand to her bosom and lowering her head as though in prayer. The unknown gentleman said something Thomas could not hear. To give the man credit, he was listening to her with grave attention.

"A woman came to me, my lord," said Constanza, her voice hushed in reverence. "She held me in her arms, tended my wounds and gave me water. When I came to myself, I looked for the woman to thank her, but she was gone. An old shepherd happening by with his flock told me that the shrine had been long deserted. No one ever came there. I was lucky to be alive. I knew then that the woman had been Saint Celeste and that the curse was ended. I found myself pregnant and my child was a strong and healthy boy."

"A remarkable story, my lady," said the gentleman, appearing to be deeply moved.

Thomas took this opportunity to make himself known by loudly clearing his throat. His mother caught sight of him, and her eyes shone. She smiled and rose to greet him.

Constanza had jet-black hair that she pretended she did not dye, and the blue eyes and fair skin that she proclaimed to be family traits of the Stanfords. She dressed in the latest Rosian fashion, wearing a gown of purple silk decorated with lace and a great many flounces. She was also wearing the Stanford family diamonds and by this Thomas knew she wanted to make a favorable impression on the unknown visitor.

Thomas returned his mother's kiss, smelling her powder and perfume. No matter where he was, the scent of gardenias would always remind him of her.

"My son, I am so happy to see you," Constanza said. "Are you well? You look pale."

She asked after his health every time they met, always with an anxious air, always fearful he was going to be felled by some dread illness. Thomas found her anxiety amusing, for she had been the one to urge him to enter the military, saying kings needed to be seen as strong leaders. She was deathly afraid he would succumb to measles, but not the least worried that a cannonball would take off his head.

"I am well, Mother," Thomas assured her. He cast a questioning glance at the pianoforte player, who was pounding the keys with extreme vigor, and raised his voice. "Could we talk somewhere quiet?"

"The music is necessary, my dear. I do not want our conversation to be overheard," Constanza replied, drawing him over to the couch. "I want you to meet someone."

The unknown man rose to his feet. He was tall, above average height. He had a thin aquiline nose, a thin, intelligent face, thinning gray hair, and a slight paunch. He was in his middle years, perhaps early fifties. He was dressed well, but without ostentation, in a rust-colored long coat, a russet waistcoat, and breeches. He had keen eyes and an earnest, serious air.

"Sir Richard, this is my son, His Royal Highness, Thomas James Stanford," said Constanza. "Thomas, this is Sir Richard. He has traveled here from Freya."

Thomas extended his hand.

Sir Richard did not shake hands. Instead, he made a deep bow, as to his sovereign.

"Your Highness, I am deeply honored to meet you at last."

Thomas flushed, embarrassed, not knowing what to do with his hand. Constanza saved him by clasping his hand and giving it a pat.

"I always think Thomas should be addressed as His Majesty, my lord, but I am told that is not proper."

"Indeed it is not, my lady," said Sir Richard earnestly. "Although there is no doubt His Highness is the true and rightful king of Freya, he must first be anointed king before he can claim the throne and the title."

"A pity," said Constanza coolly, obviously considering this to be errant nonsense. "As for Sir Richard's background, you need not concern yourself, Thomas. All you need to know is that His Lordship comes from a very old Freyan family which has been loyal to our cause through the years, never wavering in their support."

"That is true, Your Highness," said Sir Richard. "My great-great-great-grandfather was one of a group of loyal supporters of King James who called themselves the Faithful. They fought at his side and when he fell—savagely murdered—they rescued Queen Lucia and her children from the hands of the Usurper, who would most certainly have executed them."

"Sir Richard's ancestor smuggled James's widow, Queen Lucia, and her children safely to Estara," Constanza said, giving Sir Richard a grateful smile. "The Faithful hoped to be able to see James's son, Thomas—for whom you were named, my son—crowned king, but, alas, the crown prince died on the voyage to Estara."

"Only a baby, poor thing," said Sir Richard, his expression darkening. "The child could not stand the rigors of the journey."

"The Usurper killed him just as surely as if he had cut off his head!" Constanza exclaimed, quivering with indignation.

They both looked at Thomas, who had heard the story many times before, and found it difficult to become incensed over an incident that had happened one hundred fifty years ago.

"Sir Richard's family was made to suffer for their loyalty," Constanza went on. "The usurper stripped them of their lands and title. The count was arrested and held for years, barely escaping the block. The family was left impoverished."

"I am sorry to hear this, my lord," said Thomas, since it was clear he was expected to say something. "I trust you find yourself in more favorable circumstances."

Sir Richard bowed. "Thank you, Your Highness. My family has since managed to recover."

"God be praised, Sir Richard," said Smythe, who now advanced.

Sir Richard turned to him. "Rest assured I do, Captain Smythe. It is good to see you again, sir."

"And you, my lord," said Smythe, bowing.

"You two know each other," said Thomas.

"I had the honor of recommending the captain to your mother, Your Highness," said Sir Richard. "She was kind enough to seek my advice in the matter of a commander for your army."

"Ah, well, then," Thomas muttered. The reference to an army he had never seen, and about which he knew next to nothing, made him uncomfortable.

At that moment, the pianoforte player hit a wrong note. The sun was setting, the room growing dark; she must be finding it difficult to see the keys, and of course his mother would not allow the servants to come in to light the lamps. The musician paused, trying to find her place in the music. Grateful for the respite, Thomas started to speak, only to be silenced by a warning look from his mother. The music began again and Thomas was able to talk.

"I regret I did not bring a change of clothes for dinner, Mother, but I left Arcos in such haste—"

"Do not worry. You are not staying for dinner, my son," said Constanza. "You are setting off with Captain Smythe upon an important mission tonight."

"I am? Tonight?" Thomas repeated, astonished. "But I have had nothing to eat since breakfast and I am famished—"

"I will order the servants to take a tray to your room," Constanza said. "Come sit down and I will explain. Here, my son, sit close to me. Sir

Richard, bring your chair nearer. Captain Smythe," she said, pointing, "you will take a seat there."

They all arranged themselves, Thomas and his mother on the couch, Captain Smythe and Sir Richard across from them in chairs. Thomas imagined they must make quite a sight, all sitting in the darkness with their heads together, trying to hear over the pianoforte. The situation was too absurd. He wondered that a man of means like Sir Richard could be taking this so seriously.

"You are traveling to Verisol this night, Thomas," said Constanza in low, conspiratorial tones. "Captain Smythe will accompany you. I fear this means you will miss the ball tomorrow. I will make your apologies to the king."

Thomas found reason to bless the darkness, thankful that his mother could not see his smile. He had been trying to find a way to escape the ball and now he would not have to endure the flattery, his mother selecting his dance partners, and the embarrassment of her introducing him as the future king. He could not help but tease her, however.

"Mother, I am devastated," he protested. "You know I have been looking forward to the ball for a month now."

"I know you have been complaining for a month about having to go," Constanza retorted. "Now please pay attention, my son. Sir Richard will explain."

"I have received intelligence that a wealthy young Freyan nobleman is interested in advancing your cause, Your Highness," said Sir Richard, sitting forward. "His Grace, the duke, has become disillusioned with the current ruler of our country and seeks a change. He has been reading of your exploits and admires you greatly."

"I wish I could take credit for those exploits, my lord," said Thomas. "As it happens—"

His mother smashed the heel of her shoe onto his toes. Thomas winced and subsided.

Sir Richard politely pretended not to notice the interruption. "His Grace was particularly impressed by your actions at the Battle of San Estevan."

"My son was the hero of the battle!" Constanza proclaimed. "The Bottom Dwellers laid siege to the fort, which was held by only a small Estaran force, many of whom were mere students, young officers of the Royal Military Academy. Upon hearing that the fort was under attack, they bravely rode to the rescue, led by my son."

Thomas thought it best that he not mention the fact that he and his friends had been roaring drunk at the time they had decided to ride to the fort. His mother continued the tale.

"They found that the fort's commander had been killed and the Estaran troops were about to surrender to the enemy. Even though Thomas had been wounded, my son took command, rallied the soldiers, and held the fort until reinforcements arrived. He then joined the assault that drove the Bottom Dwellers from the peninsula. Show Sir Richard your scar, Thomas."

"Some other time, Mother," said Thomas, embarrassed. "I am glad this young nobleman of whom you speak thinks well of me, but why must I miss dinner on his account?"

"His Grace is sailing here to join your cause, Your Highness," said Sir Richard. "He will arrive tonight."

"He is, by God?" Thomas exclaimed in some dismay. He very nearly asked "What cause?" but he stopped himself in time. His mother would have been furious.

"His Grace is due to arrive at a secret location near Verisol this night," said Constanza. "You will travel by griffin under the cover of darkness to meet him. He is bringing with him money and a shipment of rifles and ammunition and I do not know what else. Captain Smythe will take possession of the money and the weapons."

Thomas was perplexed. "I beg your pardon if I appear difficult or ungrateful, Sir Richard, but what am I supposed to do with your Freyan duke once he arrives?"

"His Grace has publicly expressed an interest in attending the Royal Academy, Your Highness," said Sir Richard. "A patron has advanced his cause and he is to be enrolled as a student. This is not unusual, I am told."

"True, my lord," said Thomas.

Most of the young officers in the academy were there owing to patronage of some sort. He himself had been recommended by the king. The Estaran Academy, considered by many to be the best in the world in the teaching and training of young men for careers in the military, attracted its share of foreign students.

"Are you acquainted with His Grace, my lord?" Thomas asked Sir Richard. "What sort of man is he?"

"My dear, what can that possibly matter?" Constanza demanded, annoyed.

Sir Richard nodded in understanding. "I have not met His Grace, Your Highness, but he comes highly recommended by people I trust. He has been described to me as bold and courageous, if somewhat impetuous in his decision making."

"Impetuous!" Thomas said, laughing. "The fellow sounds barmy! All this fuss over a few stories in a newspaper!"

"Thomas!" Constanza said, shocked. Drawing herself up, she pierced him with an angry look. "How can you say such a thing when this young man risks his very life to serve you?"

"I fear you do not understand the gravity of the situation, Your Highness," Sir Richard added, frowning. "The queen has her agents on the watch for those who are known to favor the cause of the 'Pretender,' as Her Majesty terms you. Matters would go quite ill for this young man if he were discovered."

"As to that, Thomas, Sir Richard himself could be in danger if Her Majesty's agents find out he has traveled to visit us," Constanza said in a tone of rebuke.

"No, no, dear lady," said Sir Richard, making light of the matter. "I am perfectly safe. With my connections in the royal court, no one would dream of suspecting me."

"Still, we do not underestimate your sacrifice and the sacrifices of all our friends in Freya, my lord," said Constanza, overcome with emotion, her voice husky. "Do we, Thomas?"

"Forgive me, my lord," said Thomas, truly contrite. "I meant no disrespect. I look forward to meeting His Grace and I am proud and honored that he has chosen to help my cause."

He cast his mother a glance, seeking some sign of her approval. Constanza favored him with a smile, and the meeting ended shortly after, with Sir Richard saying he had another engagement and needed to be going.

It was probably just as well the meeting was ending, Thomas reflected. The musician's strength appeared to be giving out.

Constanza rose to her feet and the gentlemen rose with her.

"You and Captain Smythe have a long journey ahead of you, my son," she said. "I have provided clothing suitable to a clandestine mission. While you are changing, I will give Captain Smythe the details regarding the location of the meeting site."

"What is the name of this young nobleman, my lord?" Thomas thought to ask, accompanying Sir Richard to the door. He added jokingly, "Unless I am not to know it."

Sir Richard seemed not to notice Thomas's jape; instead, he replied gravely, "His name is Phillip Edward James Masterson. Note that he bears the name of our martyred king and your ancestor James the First. His Grace is the Duke of Upper and Lower Milton."

He bowed again to Thomas and expressed his pleasure in meeting him. Constanza kissed Thomas and told him to have a safe journey and to bring His Grace to meet her. Summoning Captain Smythe, she drew him off with her and the two departed.

"You can quit playing now, madame," Thomas called to the musician.

She gave him a grateful glance, stopped mid-bar, and began massaging her hands.

Thomas bounded up the stairs, taking them two at a time. He was in an excellent mood. A secret midnight ride to a mysterious location to meet a ducal gunrunner *and* an excuse to miss the ball.

His prayers had been answered.

EIGHTEEN

Thomas found that his mother had provided everything he needed for a swift journey and secret rendezvous: dark cloak, dark clothing, leather coat and helm that he presumed—knowing his mother—were covered with protective magical constructs. She had also provided two pistols, powder, and shot.

Thomas laughed out loud at the sight of the pistols. Nestled in a rosewood box, each had a long barrel of etched silver with a flower-and-vine motif and, of course, the Stanford coat of arms that continued with rosewood inlays down the handle. The powder horn was inlaid silver and matched the pistols. The shot was probably silver, as well, Thomas reflected. The pistols were beautiful, expensive, and completely useless for actual combat.

He changed his clothes, wolfed down his food, and gulped a glass of wine. He wasn't planning to take the pistols, figuring Captain Smythe would provide adequate weaponry, but then realized that the servants would find them and show them to his mother. He would have to endure questions, recriminations, and tears. He tucked them into his belt.

Having visited the manor only once before and that for just a single night, he was unfamiliar with the extensive grounds of the manor house.

He wondered where to find the griffin stables and finally asked a servant, who offered to guide him. His mother would have disapproved of involving the servants, but Thomas didn't want to waste an hour bumbling about in the dark.

When he arrived at the stables, he found that the ever-efficient Captain Smythe had two griffins saddled and ready. The captain introduced the beasts to Thomas, who greeted them politely. Griffins were touchy creatures who thought well of themselves, considering themselves to be equal to humans, if not slightly above. They deigned to permit humans to ride them, but only if the humans treated them with the proper respect.

Thomas took note of the army-issue saddles and harness, and the rather astonishing fact that the griffins observed a disciplined silence. He realized these were not griffins-for-hire, who generally complained about everything from their saddles to their food and the accommodations. He was not surprised when Captain Smythe indicated he and the griffins were acquainted.

"I thought it best to bring beasts that are military-trained, Your Highness," said Captain Smythe. "They are accustomed to the sound of gunfire. They do not participate in combat, of course."

Thomas understood. At the dawn of time, griffins had considered human flesh a delicacy, and no sane commander would ever allow the beasts to think that they could kill humans with impunity.

When one griffin made a legitimate complaint about the cinching of the saddle around its leonid body, Smythe was quick to alleviate the problem. The griffin acknowledged his assistance with a nod of its elegant eagle head.

"Are the griffins in your employ, Captain?" Thomas asked, checking over his saddle and harness as he had been taught. He did not want to be flying among the clouds only to feel his saddle start to slide off.

"The griffins are in *your* employ, Your Highness," Smythe corrected. "They are among six who accepted a commission to serve in your army."

Thomas shook his head. "*My* army again. You never give up, do you, Captain?"

"I should be a poor officer if I did, Your Highness," said Smythe with a faint smile.

Thomas was impressed. The man has a sense of humor. Who would have guessed?

He grinned. "I believe you almost made a jest, Captain. Now tell me, since you brought an extra griffin for me to ride and one for our duke, did you honestly have no idea what my mother was plotting?"

"The marchioness sent me a message to attend her posthaste, to travel by griffin, and to bring two griffins with me," Smythe replied. "That is all I was told."

"My mother certainly does have a gift for intrigue," said Thomas.

"Eminently wise, under the circumstances, Your Highness," said Smythe.

Thomas climbed onto the griffin's back and began the complicated procedure of strapping himself into the saddle.

"Oh, come now, Captain," said Thomas impatiently. "My mother is under the delusion that Freyan spies are everywhere. Our servants do not hide under the bed in hopes that they will hear something incriminating. I have never been followed down a dark alley, nor are people steaming open my letters."

"I pray God continues to preserve Your Highness," said Smythe, mounting his griffin. "Your lady mother is right to take precautions, as you should be doing yourself, if I may be so bold to advise. I have friends in Freya and I read their reports. All is not well inside that country. Your moment approaches. Are you armed, Your Highness?"

"If you want to call it that," Thomas said, laughing.

He showed off his mother's gift. Smythe regarded the silver-inlaid target pistols in silence, although Thomas thought he saw him cringe.

"I trust you can accommodate me with something more practical, Captain?" Thomas asked.

"You will find pistols in those compartments, Your Highness," he said. "Freyan-made, the pistols are the same used by the Freyan army. I have found them to be the best in terms of range and accuracy."

He pointed to one of several storage pouches incorporated into the military saddle, designed to hold pistols, shot and powder, water, and a couple of days' worth of rations.

"How do you come by Freyan military pistols, Captain?" Thomas asked. Opening the pouch, he examined the pistol with an expert eye.

"I have my sources, Your Highness," said Smythe. "Would you like for me to stow your mother's gift in my saddlebags? It will be quite safe there, I assure you."

Thomas handed over the rosewood box.

"You won't let me forget them, will you, Captain?" he said.

"Of course not, Your Highness."

Smythe put on his helm, lowered the visor, and waited for Thomas to do the same. Thomas checked again to make certain he was securely strapped in, then indicated with a hand signal that he was ready.

Smythe spoke to the griffins, not issuing orders, but speaking to them as one officer to another. "We are prepared to fly whenever it suits your convenience, gentlemen."

The griffins padded out into the open yard. Spreading their wings, they jumped into the air.

Thomas had flown on griffins before and he knew to be prepared for the stomach-dropping jolt as the griffins made a rapid climb to avoid crashing into the trees. He hung on to the saddle with both hands, his jaw clenched, legs braced. Once the griffins were safely above treetop level, they began to fly eastward toward the coastline.

Thomas settled down to enjoy the flight and put his mother and her scheming out of his mind. The night sky was clear, filled with stars and what was called a "smuggler's moon," which meant no moon at all. This duke might be barmy, but he had timed his voyage well. Thomas looked down on the city of Arcos, blazing with lights, and then the city was gone and they flew over inky blackness.

In his eagerness to leave, he had forgotten to ask Captain Smythe about their mysterious destination, where and how they were supposed to meet His Grace the Duke of Upper and Lower Milton. Somewhere along the coast, presumably. He wondered what he was going to do with this duke who had been so unexpectedly foisted on him. Thomas foresaw all manner of complications. He would have to find lodgings for the man, introduce him to his friends, and devise some sort of explanation for his sudden arrival in their midst. His mother would, of course, never think of such things.

Thomas mulled over the problems until he grew weary. Knowing he could leave the flying to the griffins, who were extremely reliable—unlike wyverns, who would bash you into a mountain out of sheer cussedness—Thomas fell into a light doze. Wakened some time later by the sound of the two griffins talking with each other, he yawned and shifted in the saddle to ease his aching muscles.

The lights of Verisol, the capital city of Estara, shone off to his right. Verisol was quite beautiful by day; by night, the city was spectacular. Like many large cities, Verisol was crisscrossed with canals to accommodate boat, barge, and ship traffic. What made Verisol unique was that her canals were filled with water, not the mists of the Breath. The canals were lined with streetlamps and, by night, the sight of the myriad lights reflected in the water was breathtaking.

The griffins veered away from Verisol, however. Thomas had been looking forward to seeing Verisol from the air, but he shrugged off his disappointment.

The griffins reached the Estaran coastline and headed north. There was no wind this night. The mists of the Breath drifted, white and ghostly, in the still air. A speck of light shining in the Breath was probably one of the many buoys in place along the coastline, warning ships they were nearing land.

The griffins flew for several miles more, then began to descend, flying low over the coast. Rock-bound and thickly forested, this part of Estara was not habitable. The fact that it was unpopulated and contained numerous inlets and coves made it an ideal location for smugglers.

He raised his visor to shout to Smythe. "How do we know where to meet this duke, Captain? Is there some sort of landmark?"

"A lighthouse, Your Highness," Smythe yelled back. "The meeting site is about two miles north of the lighthouse."

Thomas leaned over the griffin's neck to observe the coastline. The griffins were also searching for the lighthouse and their eyes were far keener than Thomas's. His griffin gave a caw and swooped downward. Thomas saw a beam of light stabbing out into the mists.

The griffins continued to fly past the tower, finally reaching their destination—a cove that appeared to have been specially designed for smugglers, for it featured a wide strip of barren shoreline large enough for a smallish ship to dock.

The griffins circled, awaiting instruction. Thomas looked out into the Breath and saw no sign of a ship. Smythe raised his visor and scanned the area with a spyglass. He consulted his pocket watch and then indicated to the griffins that they could safely land.

"We are early, Your Highness," he said to Thomas. "The rendezvous is slated for two of the clock and the time is now just a quarter past one."

The griffins landed on the shore, which was made of stone worn smooth by the incessant wind. Thomas dismounted and thanked the beast for its service. Smythe removed the gear he had brought from his saddle, including a dark lantern, and two pistols for himself.

Thomas took the Freyan pistols from the saddlebags, loaded them, and thrust them into his belt. He then strolled up and down the shore, looking things over. By now quite accustomed to the darkness, he could see where people regularly built bonfires. The place was littered with trash and empty bottles.

"Popular," he muttered, hoping they weren't interrupted.

Smythe was telling the griffins they were free to either rest or hunt, asking only that they remain within call. The griffins nodded their assent and departed.

"What is the plan, Captain?" Thomas asked upon his return. "I could point out that we have three people and only two griffins, but I assume you prepared for such an eventuality."

"We are to show a light at the proposed time to let His Grace know we are in position, Your Highness," Smythe answered. "When his boat lands, he will disembark. I will board the boat and sail to Bheldem with the rifles, leaving the griffins, which will carry you and His Grace to your mother's home in Verisol. Her staff has been told to expect you."

"Which gives the servants time to rush to their hiding places," said Thomas with a grin. "Speaking of hiding, it occurs to me we are highly visible on this white stone. We could conceal ourselves in those bushes over there."

Upon reaching the bushes, however, Thomas discovered a flaw in his plan.

"Brambles! Wouldn't you know? Ouch! Damn it!" Thomas dug a thorn from his hand. "Hiding in a bramble bush. Just how I wanted to spend my evening. Open that dark lantern a crack, will you, Captain? Let's have some light. I brought along a deck of cards to pass the time. We could play beggar-my-neighbor."

"Cards are the devil's picture books, Your Highness," said Captain Smythe. "Might I suggest that your time would be better employed in giving your thanks to God?"

Thomas was glad the darkness hid his smile. He returned the offending cards to his pocket and found a seat on a boulder. He could only hope this "impetuous" duke was different from most Freyans he had met. His mother had once described Freyans as being like their weather: chill and gray. In this, Thomas agreed with her.

Considering that his mother disliked Freya and Freyans so much, Thomas had once made the mistake of teasingly asking her why she was so determined to make him their ruler. His mother had not considered his question funny. She had responded by denouncing him as an ungrateful child and had refused to speak to him for days. She had not, however, answered his question.

Smythe remained alert, pacing back and forth, keeping watch. Thomas shifted restlessly, slapped at the mosquitoes, and began to regret not attending the ball. He hoped this blasted duke was worth the trouble.

The time seemed to drag. Thomas hummed a dance tune, thinking that even the ball would be better than this. The Lady Castila was going to be in attendance and he had promised to dance with her. She was married, but her husband, Count Castila, was proud of his beautiful wife and thought that when other men admired her it reflected well upon him. Being rather obtuse, the count didn't know that their admiration often extended into the lady's bedchamber.

Thomas had enjoyed her favors, and he just was thinking that he would like to deliver his apology for missing the ball in person when he saw Smythe pick up the dark lantern.

Thomas consulted his watch. The hour of two of the clock was approaching.

His pulse quickened and he eagerly rose to his feet.

"Please remain under cover, Your Highness," Smythe said. "I will signal you when it is safe for you to come out."

"And you can go to hell, Captain," Thomas returned good-naturedly, walking over to stand beside him.

Smythe opened the panel of the dark lantern. Magical constructs placed on an angled piece of glass, aimed at a small highly polished mirror, shone forth a bright beam of concentrated light. He left the panel open for a count of ten, then shuttered it. Another count of ten and he again opened the panel. He did this one more time and then shut the panel. They waited.

Thomas heard the boat before he saw it: the whirring of airscrews. Emerging from the mists, the boat came into view, and Thomas was startled to see the colorful striped balloon and gaily painted hull of a Trundler houseboat.

Upon reflection, he realized he shouldn't have been surprised. Trundlers were people who roamed the Breath, "trundling" along the coastlines of islands and continents, and tended not to attract attention. Because of this, smugglers sometimes used Trundler boats to haul their contraband, though in doing so they risked the ire of the Trundlers, who took a dim view of outsiders masquerading as their kind in order to perpetrate crimes. Those who did so might receive a visit from the "boys"—the Trundler version of law enforcement.

The Trundler boat chugged toward the beach. A man Thomas assumed was His Grace Phillip Masterson stood at the prow, holding a mooring cable, intending to throw it. He waved at Thomas, who started to walk over to grab the rope.

Orange flame shot out of the darkness, accompanied by the shattering boom of cannon fire. The Trundler boat seemed to disintegrate as cannonballs ripped through the balloon, sliced the rigging, and took down the mast. How Phillip escaped unharmed was a mystery to Thomas. The duke had been completely taken by surprise, apparently unaware that an enemy was creeping up on him. Standing amid the destruction of his boat, he half turned, instinctively raising his arm as though that would protect him from the next blast of cannon fire, which would tear him and his boat apart.

Thomas dove for the ground, along with Captain Smythe. Lying flat on their bellies, they could see what appeared to be another ship sailing through the mists.

"Of all the confounded luck!" Thomas said grimly. "An Estaran patrol boat looking for smugglers!" He half rose, intending to call them off.

Smythe grabbed him and pulled him down. "That is not a patrol boat, Your Highness. That is a naval frigate and by the looks of her, she is Freyan. They are in pursuit of the duke."

The duke was still at the helm, desperately trying to keep his damaged boat from sinking into the Breath before it reached the shore. Thomas wondered why the frigate didn't open fire again; then he heard the sound of a gunshot. The duke gave a cry and clapped his hand to his left shoulder. Thomas could hear a cool voice in Freyan giving the order to cease firing. "No need to waste gunpowder," said the voice.

That was true enough. The Trundler boat was not going to reach the shoreline.

Thomas leaped to his feet and ran toward the boat, ignoring Captain Smythe, who was shouting for him to keep down.

"Jump, Your Grace!" Thomas yelled to the duke. "Jump!"

The duke saw that he had only seconds to live. He managed to climb over the rail and then flung himself toward the shore. He landed on the edge, his legs dangling. Thomas grabbed hold of his hands and dragged him to safety. The Trundler houseboat disappeared from view. Long moments later, he heard it smash onto the rocks below.

Kneeling protectively over the injured duke, Thomas drew his pistol, waiting for bullets to splatter the rocks around him. Captain Smythe crouched beside him, a rifle in his hand. Those on board the frigate would find it difficult to see in the darkness. He had no idea if they had seen him rescue the duke, and he tensed. He was relieved to hear the same cool voice on board the frigate give the order for the helmsman to reverse airscrews.

"Take us out of here, Lieutenant, before that Estaran patrol boat finds us."

Airscrews whirred and the Freyan ship changed course and disappeared into the mists.

"They must think His Grace went down with his boat," Smythe remarked. He laid down his rifle and turned to examine the duke, who lay very still.

"He is unconscious. If you could assist me, Your Highness," said Smythe, sliding his arm around the wounded man's waist. "We should move him under cover of the bushes. We do not want to have to answer questions from an Estaran shore patrol."

Thomas and the captain placed their arms around the duke and managed to half drag, half carry him into the brush. Thomas laid him on the ground and eased off his blood-soaked peacoat. Smythe lifted the panel on the dark lantern and shone the light on the site of the wound.

The duke's shirt was soaked in blood above the left shoulder. He opened his eyes, winced, and started to reach for his wounded shoulder.

"You are safe now, Your Grace," said Thomas. "But you have been shot. Please lie still until the captain can determine the extent of your injuries."

The duke looked up at Thomas, and his eyes widened.

"Good God!" he gasped. "You are . . . the prince. Your Highness, forgive me . . ."

He struggled to sit up. Thomas smiled and placed a restraining hand on his chest.

"And you must be His Grace Phillip, Duke of Upper and Lower Somewhere."

Captain Smythe was probing the bullet wound, peering at it in the light of the lantern. Phillip gasped with pain.

"Not how I pictured our first meeting, Your Highness," said Phillip, managing something between a grimace and a grin.

"Your Highness, Your Grace," said Thomas, keeping his tone light. He didn't like the look of the wound, which was perilously near the heart. "We sound as if we have stepped out of the pages of *The Gentleman's Book of Etiquette and Politeness*."

Phillip laughed a bit shakily. "From the chapter 'How the Well-Bred Gentleman Behaves Upon Being Shot.' "

Smythe peeled away the blood-soaked shirt from the wound and probed the wound more deeply, with his fingers. Phillip shuddered, and gasped. Thomas clasped his hand and Phillip grasped hold of it tightly.

"I am honored to meet you, Your Highness," Phillip said in a whisper. He was extremely pale. Sweat covered his face.

"The honor is mine, Your Grace," Thomas said. He asked Smythe in a low voice, "How badly is he hurt, Captain?"

"The bullet missed hitting anything vital," Smythe replied. "You are extremely lucky, Your Grace."

"The devil's own luck, you might say," Phillip remarked with a faint smile. "Though I am sorry to have lost the rifles," he added, just before his eyes closed and his head lolled.

Captain Smythe stood up and motioned Thomas to walk with him. "His Grace has lost a quantity of blood and is in shock. If you will stay with him, Your Highness, I will summon the griffins."

Thomas agreed and went back to the patient. Smythe began blowing on a silver whistle, to summon the griffins. Within moments, Thomas heard the flapping of wings, and he watched the griffins land on the shore with feline grace.

Smythe rummaged through one of his saddle pouches and returned with a roll of bandages. Using his handkerchief to pack the wound, he began to bandage Phillip's shoulder.

"I will do what I can to stanch the bleeding, Your Highness, but His Grace needs a surgeon. The bullet is still lodged in the wound and may have chipped a bone."

"He will have the best surgeon in Verisol," said Thomas.

Smythe nodded, and glanced at the griffins, his brows lowering. Thomas guessed what he was thinking.

"You should return to your command in Bheldem, Captain. I will take care of His Grace."

"I do not like leaving you under such circumstances, Your Highness," Smythe said.

"Nonsense, Captain," said Thomas briskly. "I am perfectly capable of treating a bullet wound. I am a soldier, too, remember?"

"You are, indeed, Your Highness," said Smythe. "I was impressed with your coolness and courage. You acquitted yourself well under fire."

"Perhaps because they weren't shooting at me, Captain," said Thomas, grinning.

Smythe apparently did not find that funny, for he did not smile. He continued with the bandaging and helped Thomas drape Phillip's coat around his shoulders.

"I seem to have passed out," Phillip murmured, rousing. "Unforgivable lapse of manners. I do beg your pardon, Your Highness."

"I will demand satisfaction another time, Your Grace," said Thomas. "Now we must convey you to the griffin."

"I believe I could walk, if the stern-faced gentleman would lend me his assistance," said Phillip.

"I am sorry, Your Grace, I should have introduced you. He is Captain Jonathan Smythe." Thomas hesitated, then added with some embarrassment, "The captain is commander of my army."

Captain Smythe expressed his pleasure in meeting the duke; then he and Thomas helped Phillip stand. Putting weight on his foot, he bit his lip to stifle a groan.

"Are we causing you pain, Your Grace?" Thomas asked.

"Not my shoulder. I believe I have twisted my bloody ankle," Phillip replied. He added with a plaintive sigh, "Here I came intending to lend you my support, Your Highness, and thus far I've put you in danger of being blown up, shot, and God knows what else. I fear I'm more trouble than I'm worth."

"I will be the judge of that, Your Grace," said Thomas.

Thomas seated himself on the griffin's back and he and Smythe helped lift Phillip into the saddle. He sat in front of Thomas, who braced the nobleman with his arm. Smythe strapped Phillip securely and even provided him with an extra helm, which he said he carried in case of emergency.

Thomas and Phillip were a tight fit on the saddle, but fortunately the journey to Verisol was short. Captain Smythe saw them settled, then bid them farewell and went to mount his own griffin. He looked back at them, obviously intending to wait until they were safely in the air. Thomas was ready to depart, when his griffin, perhaps unhappy about having to carry two riders, stated irritably that one of the straps was too tight across its chest. Thomas had to unstrap himself, dismount, and work to loosen it.

"No need to wait for us, Captain," Thomas yelled.

Captain Smythe remained where he was. Thomas shook his head.

"Captain Smythe is presumably an excellent commander, or so I am told, but he is dull company," Thomas remarked, working the leather strap through the buckle. "He rarely smiles and never laughs. He belongs to some strict religious sect . . . I can't think of the name . . ."

"Fundamentalists, Your Highness," said Phillip. "They do not hold with laughing. To them, life is meant to be taken seriously. Does the good captain support your cause?"

"I suppose so. He is willing to fight and die for it, seemingly. Why do you ask, Your Grace?"

"He does appear devoted to you, Your Highness," said Phillip. "I find it odd. Most Fundamentalists do not believe in the divine right of kings. According to them a king is a mere mortal and should not hold God-given authority over his fellows. Men should answer only to God."

"In the case of Captain Smythe, he answers to my mother," said Thomas drily. "I am certain she is paying him enough to be devoted."

Having adjusted the strap to the griffin's satisfaction, Thomas again took his seat in the saddle behind Phillip. "Are you secure, Your Grace?"

The griffin began rustling its wings and stamping its feet, indicating it was ready to leave. Phillip managed with some difficulty to put on his helm. Thomas had just lowered his visor when the griffin began galloping over the ground, straight toward the edge of the cliff. The griffin spread its wings to catch the updraft and soared into the Breath.

The griffin's run was jarring and took its toll on Phillip. Thomas felt him sag back against him. The young nobleman had apparently lost consciousness again.

Thomas tightened his grip. He found himself liking this brave young nobleman with the ready quip and the frank, disarming smile.

"Not at all barmy," Thomas remarked.

Then he grew serious. Thinking of the risks Phillip had run on his account,

Thomas was humbled and dismayed. Phillip had been ready to give up his life for the sake of Thomas's cause: his claim to the throne.

"A throne I don't want," Thomas reflected somberly. "A cause in which I don't believe."

He sighed and spent the remainder of the journey deep in thought.

NINETEEN

For the first time in his life, Thomas blessed his mother's penchant for intrigue. She had selected her house in the city of Verisol for the specific reason that the stables were located in the back and were concealed by a high wall that separated them from their neighbors. Clandestine visitors were thus able to come and go without being seen.

The stable yard was bounded by the stables on two sides, the carriage house on the third, and a wrought-iron fence on the fourth. His mother had always claimed the yard was large enough to accommodate griffins, though Thomas had the feeling his griffin didn't agree. The beast was forced to glide until it came level with the treetops, then snap its wings close to its body so that it didn't clip them on the roof or the spiked fence.

The griffin plummeted like a stooping hawk, landed with a thud, and pitched forward, throwing its passengers against its neck. Once he had recovered from the harrowing dive, Thomas set about extricating himself from the straps and assisting Phillip, who remained unconscious.

The servants must have been wakened by the commotion of the griffin landing in the yard, for they came running. The first to reach him was the coachman, who had rooms over the stables. Armed with an old blunderbuss, he stood pointing it in a threatening manner at Thomas.

"Don't shoot, Falto!" said Thomas, hurriedly raising his visor. "It's me, Thomas. We need to get this man into the house. He's been shot."

The coachman stood the blunderbuss against a wall and assisted Thomas in lifting Phillip out of the saddle. Falto and two stable hands carried the wounded man into the house.

Thomas remembered to politely thank the griffin, and offered to accommodate it for the night. The griffin regarded him with a cold stare, declined the offer with a snap of its beak, and departed.

Thomas hastened into the house. The men had carried Phillip to one of the upstairs bedrooms and placed him in bed, under the direction of the housekeeper, who was shaking her head at the sight of the wound, which had started bleeding again. She ordered the maids to boil water and fetch clean towels.

"He needs a surgeon," Thomas said to the housekeeper. "Is there one close?"

"Father Ramone, Your Highness," the housekeeper replied. "I have sent the footman to fetch him."

"He needs a surgeon, not a priest," Thomas protested.

"Father Ramone is both," said the housekeeper. She added with a sharp look, "*And* he is a friend of the family."

"What does that have to do with anything?" Thomas asked impatiently.

"It is four of the clock in the morning, Your Highness. Your friend has been shot. Father Ramone will keep quiet," said the housekeeper.

"Ah, yes, of course," said Thomas, berating himself for not having thought of the fact that the situation would look extremely suspicious. Constanza had trained her staff well, even if she did think they were spies.

"Would you like a cup of tea, Your Highness? Something to eat?" the housekeeper asked.

"I don't want to leave him," said Thomas, pulling a chair up to Phillip's bedside.

The housekeeper said she would have food brought to him, and soon one of the maids returned with tea and sandwiches. The housekeeper cleaned the wound and sponged off the blood. Thomas had his first good look at Phillip in the light.

Thomas guessed him to be close to his own age, in his mid-twenties. He had white-blond hair and his face was frank and open and genial. The servants had removed his blood-soaked shirt, leaving him bare-chested, and Thomas was interested to see a large scar on his torso. At first Thomas thought the wound had been made by a sword, but then he realized the flesh had been burned.

Thomas was familiar with such wounds, which were made by the fiendish contramagic green-beam weapons of the Bottom Dwellers. Thomas himself had a similar scar on his back.

"So he fought in the war," Thomas said to himself, drinking his tea. "Sir Richard said he was adventurous."

Father Ramone arrived, carrying two bags, one containing his surgical instruments and another filled with herbs and potions in brown bottles. Thomas advanced to welcome him.

"Your Highness," said Father Ramone, extending his hand. "I am pleased to finally meet you. Your mother has told me a great deal about you."

"Thank you, Father," said Thomas. "If you would see to my friend. He is restless and appears to be in pain."

"Certainly, Your Highness," said Father Ramone.

He was a short man in his middle years with gray hair worn in the traditional tonsure and plain brown robes. He went to work with an air of quiet confidence that did much to reassure Thomas. The priest examined his patient, listened to his heart and breathing, and studied the wound.

"I think he is feverish," Thomas added.

"Yes, infection is setting in," said Father Ramone. "I must remove the bullet at once. How did he come to be shot?"

"An affair of honor, Father," said Thomas. "I was his second. I would appreciate it if you didn't mention this to anyone."

Dueling was against the law in Estara, as it was in most civilized nations. And, as in most civilized nations, the gentlemen of Estara continued to settle their differences with either pistols or swords.

Father Ramone nodded in understanding. Thomas guessed this was not the first bullet the priest had been called upon to remove in the dead of night.

"Your friend was very lucky, Your Highness," said Father Ramone. "Either that or his opponent was a very bad shot. I will need some assistance, preferably from someone with a strong stomach."

"I can assist you, Father," said Thomas. "I am not in the least squeamish. I have seen far worse, I can assure you."

The priest instructed the male servants to remove a door from its hinges to use as a litter. They carried Phillip to the kitchen, transferring him to a large table, much to the dismay of Cook, who began to protest. The housekeeper whispered something and nodded at Thomas. Cook flushed, dropped a curtsy, and offered to fetch more hot water, towels, and clean bandages.

Father Ramone began by running his fingers over the shoulder, murmuring to himself.

"Shouldn't you be removing the bullet, Father?" Thomas asked impatiently. "You can take time to pray over him later."

Father Ramone glanced at him with a smile. "Healing magic, Your Majesty. Very old. I am ensuring that your friend does not wake during the procedure. Also I find that if I use such magic prior to surgery, the wound is far less likely to putrefy."

"I beg your pardon, Father," said Thomas. "I am not a crafter, as you can no doubt tell."

The priest dug the bullet from the shoulder, with Thomas standing by to mop up blood so that he could see what he was doing. Father Ramone held the bullet up to the light.

"Perhaps your friend would like to keep it as a good-luck charm," he said. "He could wear it on his watch chain."

"Give that to me, Father," said Thomas.

He washed off the blood and studied the bullet closely. He could tell by the impressions on the bullet that it had been fired from a Freyan rifle, a long gun with a rifled barrel, a type of firearm that had been introduced during the war. He tucked the bullet in his pocket.

Father Ramone stitched up the wound, treated it with ointment from one of his jars, then bandaged the shoulder and placed Phillip's arm in a sling. Finally, he passed his hand over Phillip's forehead, whispering as he did so. The lines of pain faded from Phillip's face. He seemed to fall into a restful sleep.

The servants carried Phillip back to the bedroom. Thomas remained downstairs with the priest, receiving instructions.

"He will sleep for some hours now," said Father Ramone. "When he wakes, I have no doubt he will want to be up and about, but he should remain in bed for several days. Otherwise he could reopen the wound and it will start bleeding. He is to have a diet of beef broth, to replenish his blood, and milk toast. Nothing more."

"Thank you, Father," said Thomas gratefully. "A prayer would also be welcome now."

"I will pray for him and for you and your cause, Your Highness," said Father Ramone.

Thomas was about to laughingly say he doubted if God took much interest in his cause, but recalling his thoughts during the flight, he kept silent.

"You should get some rest yourself," Father Ramone advised. "I will visit our patient tomorrow afternoon to change the dressing."

Thomas thanked the priest. He would have sent him back in a carriage, but Father Ramone said that the way was not far and he would enjoy the walk.

By this time the sun was rising. Thomas yawned until his jaws ached. He suddenly realized he was exhausted. He retired to his room, leaving instructions that he should be wakened if Phillip needed anything, and was immediately asleep.

Thomas woke late in the day and went to check on his patient. He found Phillip sitting up in bed, eating eggs and bacon and tearing off hunks from a large loaf of bread.

"I gave strict orders to Cook to serve you beef broth and milk toast, Your Grace," Thomas said, trying to look stern.

Phillip shuddered. "The stuff brought back such horrifying memories of old Nanny Pritchard that I feared I might sucumb to my wounds, and I sent it away. Will you have something?"

"I usually skip breakfast, thank you. I won't ask how you are feeling," Thomas added. "I can see for myself. By the way, may we dispense with the formalities? I feel uncomfortable being called 'Your Highness.' My friends call me Tom."

"My friends call me Pip," said Phillip.

The two shook hands. The maids removed the tray and carried away the food, leaving the two gentlemen alone.

"The truth is," said Thomas, "I don't much like *being* 'Your Highness.' I need to be honest with you, Your Grace—"

"Pip, Your Highness," said Phillip.

"And I'm Tom, Pip," said Thomas, smiling. "The truth is that I think all this talk of 'my cause' and me being the anointed of God, destined for the throne, is like the plot of some yellow-backed novel. It has no basis in reality. I suppose I may have some claim to the Freyan throne—"

"*Some* claim!" Phillip interrupted. "My dear Tom, don't you know your own family history? You have *undisputed* claim and Her Majesty knows it. I admit it's all very complicated, but your thrice great-grandfather James the First was the son of the anointed king, and Queen Mary's foul ancestor, Alfred, was a blackguard cousin who rebelled against his ruler. If you want any proof that the queen is afraid of you, consider that she sent the Freyan navy to try to stop me from reaching you."

"Her Majesty did go to great lengths to try to keep you and your money," Thomas said with a smile.

"I am the wealthiest man in Freya," said Phillip in a cheerful, matter-of-fact way. "Given Freya's current deplorable financial situation, I could probably buy the country. Instead, I would much rather spend my money placing my country into better hands."

He leaned forward eagerly. "I can fund your cause, Tom. I can pay for soldiers, weapons, ships, supplies . . ."

"But won't the Crown seize your assets or whatever it is crowns do to punish . . . uh . . ." Thomas hesitated, not wanting to say the ugly word.

"Traitors?" Phillip said. "I do not consider myself a traitor, since my country is currently being ruled by the descendant of a traitor. I have placed my fortune in foreign banks. The Crown cannot touch it. And, I'll tell you this, Tom. I am not the only noble who backs your cause. I have friends who will watch out for my interests."

"I met one such gentleman," said Thomas. "Sir Richard."

"Sir Richard who?" Phillip asked. "Perhaps I know him."

"I wasn't told his last name," said Thomas. "My mother loves intrigue. She sees spies hiding under the tea cozies."

"She is right. You cannot be too careful," Phillip observed, sounding serious.

"I suppose," said Thomas. "What do you know of my family history?"

"I've made quite a study of your family," said Phillip. "When the newspaper stories about you began coming out—"

"Those were my mother's idea," Thomas said hurriedly. "You can't believe half of them."

"I know what to believe and what not," said Phillip, smiling. "I did my research. The story about the Battle of San Estevan was true."

He grew more somber. "I fought the Bottom Dwellers myself, Tom, and I can only imagine the hell you endured. You took command of the company and held that fort for three days against an overwhelming force. Half your number died in the first assault—"

Thomas cut him short. "We did what we had to do," he said, loath to remember those brutal three days, and uncomfortable hearing such praise. "I can tell you that I did *not,* as the story claims, kiss my dead comrade on his bloody forehead and then draw my crimson blade and shout, 'On, friends, on to victory or death!' "

"What did you say to rally your troops?" Phillip asked.

"I think it was something on the order of 'It's either them or us,' " Thomas said with a rueful grin.

"Pithy and to the point," said Phillip. He was silent a moment, then said, "I tell you straight out, Tom, I have not been happy about the situation in Freya for a long time. The country teeters on the edge of disaster. Since the death of the crown prince, God rest him, Queen Mary wants to make her sister queen. The woman is married to a Rosian merchant, for God's sake!"

"I could be married to a Rosian," said Thomas. "I don't suppose your people would like that in their king."

"What?" Phillip asked, looking worried. "Who?"

"The Princess Sophia. My mother is negotiating with some countess."

"The princess? Oh, she's different," said Phillip. "She is a Rosian, but my people adore her. She came to study at the university following the war. Everyone loves her, except you, apparently. You don't seem enthused."

"I've never met her," said Thomas. "And I am to have no say in the matter."

"The fate of princes, I fear," said Phillip, sympathetic.

"Go on with the history lesson," said Thomas. "I didn't mean to interrupt."

"Where was I? Oh, yes, I studied the reign of King James and became convinced you are the true heir. Don't you know the story?"

"I know what my mother told me," said Thomas. He stood up, thrust his hands into his pockets, and began to pace restlessly. "I never really believed her account. To hear her tell it, my ancestor was a saint who walked the palace grounds bathed in a glow of heavenly light. And that there seem to be a great many Oswalds."

"That part about the Oswalds is true," Phillip said, laughing. He watched Thomas pace the room with some concern. "You seem upset. Are you sure you want to talk about this?"

"I don't," said Thomas with a sigh. "But go ahead."

"The War of the Cousins, as it became known, started over two hundred years ago when King Frederick was forced by the nobility to abdicate in favor of his younger brother, Oswald the First," said Phillip. "All was fine until fifty years later when Oswald's grandson, Oswald the Third, suffered a disastrous defeat at the hands of the Rosians in the Blackfire War.

"James, the great-grandson of Frederick, claimed that his cousin, Oswald the Third, was not fit to rule, because *his* grandfather, Oswald the First, had deposed the true and rightful king, James's great-grandfather, Frederick. Since Oswald the First had no legitimate right to the throne, his grandson, Oswald the Third, had no right. Follow me so far?"

"I told you there were a lot of Oswalds," Thomas growled.

"The upshot was that James declared himself king and sought to depose Oswald the Third. The civil war lasted twenty years. At the end, James defeated his cousin. He imprisoned Oswald and his two sons and claimed the crown. The story goes that Oswald refused to acknowledge James as his king and James, in a fit of rage, ordered one of his knights to murder Oswald and his two sons in their prison cells."

"My mother maintains that James was innocent," said Thomas drily. "A saint, as I said."

"James wasn't a saint," Phillip said. "But your mother is right. He did not kill his cousin Oswald."

Thomas stopped, interested. "How do you know?"

"The late crown prince, Jonathan, discovered the truth when he came across some old letters. Oswald was murdered by his younger brother, who wanted to be king and hoped to implicate James to turn public opinion against him."

"Why was your Crown Prince Jonathan studying the reign of King James?" Thomas asked, frowning. "Did he hope to discredit me?"

"Quite the contrary," said Phillip. "Prince Jonathan was a scholar and, like every true scholar, interested only in the truth. He used to infuriate his mother. The queen once accused him of trying to prove you had a better claim to the throne that he did."

"I am sorry," said Thomas, seeing Phillip look downcast. "Apparently I misjudged him. Did you know him?"

"We were in school together. Jonathan was a good friend," said Phillip. "You would have liked him, Tom. The two of you have much in common."

"Meaning he didn't want to be king either," said Thomas. He regretted the words the moment they were spoken, and he turned to Phillip, who was regarding him with an air of gravity. "I am sorry, Pip. I shouldn't have said that. Especially after you nearly got yourself killed for my sake. You must think me a whining, ungrateful wretch!"

"You are not what I expected, Your Highness," Phillip admitted. "But I have to say I admire your candor. Honestly, I don't see why any rational man would want to be king, knowing the weight of the burdens he must shoulder."

"Such as James being accused of a murder he didn't commit," said Thomas. He had shared too much of himself and he wanted to change the subject, talk about something else.

Phillip took the hint and resumed his story.

"James was consumed with guilt. He didn't know the truth about who killed Oswald and his sons. He had not ordered their deaths, but he thought his supporters had taken it upon themselves to kill them in his name. When one of James's sons died soon after, he believed he had been cursed by God for having killed an anointed king.

"Matters went from bad to worse for poor James after that. I'm sorry to say, Tom, but your ancestor wasn't a very good ruler," said Phillip. "He turned a blind eye to corruption and let priests and nobles run the country. Oswald's nephew, Alfred, and his own powerful backers led the rebellion to overthrow James. One could almost make the case that they had no choice. Once again, Freya was plunged into civil war."

"My mother failed to mention most of that," said Tom. "According to her, James was a paragon of nobility and virtue."

"If it is any comfort, James may not have been a good king, but he *was* a gallant soldier. He died on the field of battle, leading his troops, when he could have stayed behind, safely ensconsed in his castle."

"I'm at least glad to know James wasn't a coward. But you left out the prophecy," said Thomas.

"A prophecy!" Phillip exclaimed. "I never heard of a prophecy. Tell me. Unless it's a family secret."

"No secret. My mother is happy to relate this tale to all and sundry," said Thomas. "According to family legend, the usurper Alfred sent men to arrest Queen Lucia and her children. Her priest held the soldiers at bay in order to give the queen and her children time to escape. Alfred had the priest arrested and tortured, then executed. Before the priest died he said that the true heir would return. The exact wording was 'A male child will return with the sign of the seven, to save Freya from an ancient evil.' "

"I do love a good prophecy," said Phillip. "When do you think it will come to pass?"

"According to my mother and her followers, the first part of the prophecy has already been fulfilled. They are just waiting for the other half."

"The first half," Phillip mused. "You would be the male child, of course. But what is 'the sign of seven'?"

"The discovery of the seventh sigil," Thomas explained.

"Good God!" Phillip said, startled. "You are right. Now you just have to save Freya from an ancient evil. I can't think what that would be."

"Not even my mother can find an ancient evil," said Thomas. "And, trust me, she has been searching."

Phillip seemed restless. He suddenly threw off the bedclothes and stood up. "I'm sick to death of lying about like a slug. Let's go for a walk."

"Absolutely not!" said Thomas. "I have strict orders from Father Ramone to keep you in bed. There, you see! You can't even stand."

He hurried to help Phillip, who had grown giddy and nearly fallen.

"I could stand if your bloody floor would stop jumping about," Phillip grumbled.

Thomas grinned. "What you need is beef broth and milk toast."

"Heaven forfend!" Phillip said with a faint smile. Thomas saw that he looked very pale.

"I should not have kept you talking," said Thomas in remorse. "I will let you rest. Is there anything I can bring you? A book to read? My mother has an extensive library. All for show, of course. She throws books on occasion, but I don't think she has ever read one."

"I'm not much of a reader myself. There is one thing you could do," said Phillip. "I promised a young lady of my acquaintance that I would— She was worried, you see, and I told her I would let her know . . ." He flushed. His voice trailed off in embarrassment.

"I will have servants bring you pen and paper," said Thomas. "Write your letter to this young lady and then take a nap."

Thomas rang the bell and ordered paper, ink, and a writing desk Phillip could use in bed. Seeing his friend settled, Thomas again admonished him to rest, then went to the stables.

Saddling the horse his mother kept for him, he set out for a ride in the park. He soon found friends who invited him to join them, but he was in a reflective mood and wanted to be alone.

"It's good to talk to someone who understands. None of the others do," Thomas said to himself.

He thought of the teasing about being "the Prince of Freya" he had endured since his mother had revealed to the world the secret that had been closely held for one hundred fifty years: The Stanford line had not perished with the death of King James. His direct descendant, Thomas Stanford, was the true and rightful heir to the throne.

If asked, his friends would have termed their gibes good-natured; their insults were "meant to be funny." He was the only one who heard the bitterness and jealousy, the rancor in the laughter. And when once he had grown angry and told them he didn't appreciate their humor, they had accused him of taking himself too seriously and had spent the rest of the night bowing and scraping to "His Highness."

Since then, Thomas had learned to smile and laugh, keeping his true feelings behind the walls of the fortress of his being where he lived in isolation.

As he rode through the park, letting the horse go where it would, he wondered if, at last, he would be able to open the fortress gates, admit someone he could trust.

Phillip wrote his letter to the "young woman," who in truth was Sir Henry Wallace. The letter was written in a code Simon Yates had devised for the Rose Hawks years ago. It contained the information he had gleaned from Thomas: telling them what he knew about Captain Smythe, the number of troops, where they were located, the prophecy (Henry would get a chuckle out of that), and the Freyan nobleman known only as "Sir Richard." Phillip concluded with his own thoughts about Thomas:

> *Much to my surprise, my lord, I find I like the prince very much. He is not, as we have been led to believe, burning with ambition, although his mother apparently has enough for both of them. Thomas is brave and gallant, modest, intelligent and thoughtful. Should the unforeseen occur and he become king, I think Freya might do worse.*

Phillip read over his letter. When he came to the last page, he frowned. Henry would certainly not be pleased to read such a glowing description of the Pretender. Henry wanted to hear that Thomas was a depraved monster, harboring evil designs upon their beloved country.

Phillip addressed the envelope to its recipient, *Mistress Simone Yates, To Be Left Until Called For,* smiling as he did so. He folded and inserted all the pages except the last one into the envelope. He sealed the letter with his signet ring, then rang the bell, telling the servant that the letter should go out with the evening post.

"And could you light the fire?" Phillip asked. "I'm feeling chilled."

The servants looked surprised; the room was sweltering. Nevertheless, they did as he asked.

When he was alone, Phillip read the comments he had written about Thomas one more time, then tore up the paper. He dropped the pieces into the fire, watched to see that they had burned to ashes, then picked up the poker and stirred the ashes.

This done, Phillip returned to his bed, where he lay awake, disliking himself very much.

TWENTY

Henry Wallace was traveling by wyvern-drawn carriage to the home of his friend Simon Yates. He noted the fact that it was taking an infernally long time for the carriage to catch up with Simon Yates's floating house, but, uncharacteristically, he made no comment. A westerly breeze had sent Welkinstead drifting past the city limits, almost into the country. Henry usually complained if he had to waste time tracking down the house. This time he sat in the back of the carriage in silent perturbation.

Accustomed to the complaints, Mr. Sloan was observing Henry with concern. "You are not yourself today, my lord. I trust all went well in Travia?"

"I have good news on that subject," said Henry. "I am worried about Lady Ann. These confounded healers and midwives tell me all will be well, but what do they know?"

"I keep your lady wife in my prayers, my lord," said Mr. Sloan.

"Thank you, Mr. Sloan," said Henry.

Lady Ann was due to deliver their second child at any time, and while Henry had made all the arrangements for physicians—including the royal physician himself—healers and midwives to attend his beloved Mouse, he did not think he had done enough. The royal physician, three healers, and five midwives all had assured him that Lady Ann was in excellent health and should have a safe delivery.

"What do they know?" Henry muttered again.

What he knew was that childbearing was dangerous and he wasn't about to take chances.

Henry had just returned from Travia, where he had met with a representative of the Travian dragons, a female dragon named Odila. He had arrived in Travia at a propitious time. The Travian government had foolishly sent armed soldiers to demand that the dragons pay their taxes; Odila and the other dragons were furious. Henry had been properly incensed and extremely sympathetic, and had left with assurances that the Travian dragons would undoubtedly accept his offer of titles and land in return for a fortune in gold.

Henry needed to talk to Simon, but he had not wanted to leave his wife at this time. She, however, had ordered him out of the house.

"You are driving me to distraction, Henry," Ann had laughingly scolded him. "Fidgeting about the house all day, then leaping to your feet in a panic to fetch the physician just because I happened to hiccup. Simon will want to hear the news from Travia. You should go tell him."

When the carriage finally arrived at Welkinstead, Henry entered in company with Mr. Sloan and the two went immediately to Simon's office.

"Ah, Henry, your arrival is timely. We've received a letter from Phillip," Simon announced. "I have decoded it."

"Excellent news," said Henry. "And I have successfully negotiated the pact with the Travian dragons."

"Well done," said Simon.

Henry removed his hat and coat and handed them to Mr. Albright, who silently bore them away. Mr. Sloan gave a sheaf of papers to Simon, who passed along the decoded version of Phillip's letter.

"One odd thing about this letter," said Simon.

"What is that?" Henry asked.

"It is only five pages long," said Simon.

"I don't see anything odd in that. Phillip said all he had to say in five pages."

"The oddity is that Phillip wrote a sixth page, but did not send it."

"How can you possibly tell?" Henry demanded.

"His signature is cramped up at the bottom of the fifth page. You see? There is barely room for him to write his name and there was no room at all for a closing."

"And why is this significant?" Henry asked, turning to the last page.

"If you are writing a letter, you know to leave space at the bottom of the last page for your closing and your signature. He did not need to leave space on page five, because he had moved on to page six. But he decided not to send the sixth page and thus had to squeeze in his signature on page five."

"Are you saying there is something sinister in this?" Henry asked, frowning.

"Not in the least," said Simon airily. "I just found it curious."

Henry glared at his friend. "Curious! For God's sake, Simon, give your giant brain a day in the park!"

Simon raised an eyebrow and cast a questioning look at Mr. Sloan, who gave a cough and said, by way of explanation, "Her Ladyship's time . . ."

"Ah, yes," said Simon.

Lowering his head, he began to study the report. Henry perused the letter.

"Ha!" he said. "Phillip says to thank that marine sniper Alan selected for his exemplary marksmanship. The bullet hit nothing vital and our plan worked. Pip managed to immediately gain the sympathy and trust of the Pretender, who conveyed our friend to the house of the marchioness in Verisol."

"Prince Thomas is not a pretender. He is royalty," Simon pointed out. "You can't deny his heritage."

Henry lowered the letter to fix Simon with a grim look. "Stanford is not *my* prince! I don't care how much blue blood he has coursing through his veins. I will not dignify him with the title."

Henry returned to his reading. "Mr. Sloan, this will be of interest to you. I asked Phillip to find out who was in command of the Pretender's army. He is Freyan, a retired marine captain named Jonathan Smythe. Do you know him?"

"I served with several Smythes, my lord," said Mr. Sloan. "The name is a common one."

"Which means it is undoubtedly an alias," said Simon.

"True enough," Henry said, sighing. He continued to read. "Listen to this. According to Phillip, the Pretender told him that a Freyan nobleman has been assisting his foul cause! Phillip says he is known only as Sir Richard."

"We are aware that the prince has supporters in high places in the Freyan government, Henry," said Simon.

"Those you call the Faithful," Henry muttered. He went on reading.

"Phillip mentions a prophecy. Prophecy, my ass!" he fumed. "The marchioness made that up. The woman will stop at nothing."

"Unfortunately, she didn't, Henry," said Simon. "You should really read Jonathan's findings. He discovered the queen's martyred priest prophesied the sign of seven and an ancient evil. Jonathan theorized that sign of the seven could be taken by the Faithful to mean the discovery of the seventh sigil."

"Poor Jonathan," Henry said. "He could never leave well enough alone. As we know, the 'usuper,' Alfred, went on to become one of our greatest kings. He ruled with skill and wisdom for thirty years and died peacefully in his sleep. You're telling me that all the while, some secret society was out there plotting his downfall. Why didn't they act?"

They had secretly smuggled the queen and her children out of Freya, but the king's son died on the journey. Fearing Alfred would find and murder the queen, the Faithful spread the rumor that she and her daughters also had perished. At that time, a daughter could not inherit her father's throne. The Faithful had to wait for a male child to be born. Unfortunately, a hundred and fifty years passed before that happened.

"And now these Faithful are working to place this insolent young upstart, Stanford, on the throne!" Henry snorted again. "Next you will tell me they have secret handshakes and swear blood oaths and hold clandestine meetings in mausoleums!"

Simon gave his friend a sympathetic smile. "You fall back on sarcasm to deflect your anxiety, Henry. I know you are worried, but all will be well with Lady Ann. She came through splendidly giving birth to little Hal."

Henry gave up trying to concentrate on the letter and tossed it onto the desk.

"Lady Ann may have done splendidly, but I was a wreck," he confessed. "I was never so terrified in my life with the exception, perhaps, of when our house was struck by the green-beam weapon and collapsed around our ears. If anything were to happen to my beloved Mouse . . ."

Overcome by emotion, he covered his eyes with his hand. Simon sent Mr. Albright for a restorative brandy, then maneuvered his floating chair to Henry's side.

"You are accustomed to controlling every situation, Henry, but you must face the sad fact that you cannot control this one. You have done all that a man can do and you must leave the rest in God's hands. Right, Mr. Sloan?"

"God holds us all in His hands, my lord, and He has a special care for the little children," said Mr. Sloan.

Mr. Albright appeared at Henry's side with the brandy. Henry drank it eagerly. The liquor would not ease his fears, but the act of drinking gave him time to master his emotions.

He cleared his throat and said briskly, "To return to business. Have you discovered any evidence that there is an organized movement plotting against our queen?"

"Passions ran high during the Cousins War, as happens with conflicts when families are divided in their allegiance. Bitterness remains even after all these years. I have no evidence, but I believe the existence of these Faithful to be entirely possible."

"You are right about bitterness extending down through the years," said Henry. "My own dolt of an ancestor backed the wrong side in the Cousins War and managed to lose everything. My grandfather was bitter over that to the day of his death, but he would have never been part of some secret plot to overthrow the government!"

"I will continue my investigations," said Simon. "If we are finished with Phillip, we should turn to the Travian dragons. I have read your report and I believe their requests can be readily accommodated. Basically they are asking for large tracts of land where they can live in peace, and to be called 'Lord So-and-So' and 'Lady So-and-So.' Considering the vast sum they are willing to pay for land that no human wants, and a few meaningless honorifics, I say it is well worth it."

"I will propose that Her Majesty accept. Of course, I shall have to drum up support in the House of Nobles. I am having dinner with the Old Chap at his club this afternoon. I will bring it up with him," said Henry.

"How is your brother?" Simon asked.

"Still an attorney, still old, and still boring," Henry replied with a smile.

"I believe if I ever needed an attorney, I should like him to be old and boring," said Simon. "Someone like Richard, dull and staid, who takes tea with the judges and attends all-night sessions in the House of Nobles."

"*And* manages to stay awake through hours-long speeches," said Henry.

"Why are you taking this to the House of Nobles? Her Majesty is leasing land owned by the Crown to the dragons. She doesn't need to seek approval," said Simon.

"The nobles will view it differently," said Henry. "They will term it a treaty with a foreign government and demand a vote. Given the turmoil over the lack of an heir, I prefer not to create another crisis. My hope is that I can blind the nobles with the dazzling glitter of dragon gold."

"Good luck with your dinner at the Law Club," said Simon.

"I will need it," said Henry, grimacing. "The food is deplorable. Leg of boiled mutton and mushy peas, washed down by a truly ghastly claret."

Simon laughed. "Give my best wishes to Lady Ann," he called as Henry was departing. "All will go well!"

Henry nodded his thanks and departed.

The Law Club was open only to those gentlemen employed in the legal profession, and if a person met that prerequisite, the gentleman still had to receive a majority vote from the other members. The club was housed in a building that resembled its members, Henry thought, being the grayest, oldest, and dullest-looking building in Haever.

He was greeted at the door by an ancient steward, who said Sir Richard was expecting him in the dining room. The club's interior was shadowy and eerily silent. Heavy curtains covered the windows, and thick carpets blanketed the floors. If a member was forced to speak to another member, he did so in a refined whisper. Several members looked up from their newspapers to glare at Henry for disturbing the silence by clearing his throat.

Richard was waiting for him in the dining room, which smelled of mutton. The dining room was one of the few rooms where one could talk in a normal tone. Richard smiled to see Henry and rose to greet him. The two brothers shook hands and then sat down to their meal.

Richard was fifty-five, nearly ten years older than Henry. The two had never been close. Richard had been away at boarding school when Henry was young, going from there to university and then into the practice of law at their father's law firm. Their father, a judge, had wanted Henry to join the legal profession as well.

"I sooner would have shot myself," Henry had told his friends.

Richard had married a woman who was gray and dull. They had raised three daughters to be gray and dull and had married them off to gray and dull husbands.

The brothers had not seen each other or spoken in years until Henry invited Richard to his wedding out of politeness, never expecting him to come. Much to Henry's surprise, Richard attended. The brothers reconnected and Henry, never one to miss a political advantage, proposed they meet monthly for dinner. Henry used these dinners to enlist his brother's aid in advancing the queen's causes with the House of Nobles.

The brothers had nothing in common except their looks, both having long, thin faces and long, thin, aristocratic noses. Richard was slightly taller than Henry and had thinning hair. Henry still had all his hair and hoped to keep it.

The dinner was unremarkable, as Henry had foreseen, but the claret was a pleasant surprise, turning out to be excellent. The brothers exchanged family news during the meal, with Richard asking after Lady Ann's health and expressing his hope that all went well with the birth, while Henry asked after Sarah, Richard's wife, and the three daughters and their husbands.

After dinner, they discussed the family financial affairs. Their mother's family had always held interests in the wool trade and real estate. She had left her considerable shares to her two sons. Richard had taken over the management of the various businesses. Apparently the businesses needed someone dull and staid to run them, for he had made them extremely profitable, even expanding into wool manufacturing and becoming a partner in an estate agency. Henry was grateful, for he received a percentage of the income, and he did his best to appear interested.

Henry proposed that they have their port in a room where they could talk in private. Richard suggested the game room, since few members ever went there.

"Backgammon too strenuous?" Henry said teasingly.

Richard gave him a puzzled look. "I fear I don't know what you mean, Henry."

"It was a jest. Moving the pieces about," said Henry. "Strenuous . . ."

"Ah, I see," said Richard. "Most amusing."

Henry poured the port.

"What did you want to discuss?" Richard asked.

"Her Majesty has invited several Travian dragons to take up residence in Freya," said Henry. "She will be leasing royal lands to them, so the matter need not come before the House of Nobles for a vote. There's bound to be some discussion, however, and I was hoping you would be able to smooth any ruffled feathers."

Richard had been raising his glass to his lips. He paused, lowered the port without drinking, and stared at Henry with astonishment and consternation.

"Dragons! Living in Freya!"

"Way up north," said Henry, with a wave of his hand. "Way, *way* up north in the Bennenfall Mountains inside the Tristfell Woods. No one will ever know they are there."

Richard was exceedingly grave. "You say these dragons are from Travia. Her Majesty cannot sign a treaty with a foreign nation without sanction from the House."

"Her Majesty isn't signing a treaty," said Henry. "Her Majesty is leasing land owned by the Crown."

"The members will not view it in that light, Henry," said Richard. "We Freyans do not like dragons and with good reason, considering the numbers of our people these beasts have killed over the centuries. Remember the ancient Imhruns . . ."

"The hell with ancient Imhruns!" Henry exclaimed, losing patience. "I am not worried about the ancient Imhruns. I am worried about the deplorable state of the treasury!"

He lowered his voice. "We must do something, Richard, or the country will go bankrupt! The dragons are willing to pay an enormous sum for the privilege of residing here, and we need the money!"

"And so we are to sell our souls," said Richard.

"Oh, for God's sake, don't be so dramatic!" Henry stated. "The way you are acting, you would think Her Majesty had invited the Evil One to take up residence in the palace! Dragons are not coming to Freya to feast on us. They are coming to fill the royal coffers with gold!"

Richard sat motionless in his chair, gazing, frowning, into his untouched port.

"Well? Will you help?" Henry asked, giving his brother a nudge.

Richard blinked, rousing himself.

"I will consider the matter," he said. Placing the glass on the table, he rose to his feet and extended his hand. "Sorry that I cannot stay longer. I have a meeting with a client. I will be in touch, Henry. Wilson will show you out."

Henry gazed at his brother's back as he left the room.

Meeting with a client! The Old Chap never meets with clients. Something I said struck home, Henry reflected. I believe it was the mention of the royal coffers. Richard may be old and dull and boring, but he is a shrewd businessman. He will see reason.

Richard Wallace left the club, but he did not go to meet a client. He returned to his home, where he locked himself in his study, telling his wife and the servants he was not to be disturbed. He remained in his study long after everyone had gone to bed. The only other person still awake was his confidential valet, Henshaw, who waited below in case he was needed.

At about one of the clock, Richard rang the bell and Henshaw appeared.

Henshaw had been with Richard for nigh on twenty years, having taken over the position of valet from his father upon the elder Henshaw's death. He fit into Richard's family well, being short and gray, though certainly not dull.

Richard wrote a few words on a sheet of paper, then handed it to the valet.

"Commit the message to memory. As usual, if anything should happen, you must destroy this paper and deliver your message in person."

"Yes, my lord," said Henshaw.

He read the message, which was startling enough to cause him to raise his eyebrows.

"I see you understand," said Richard. "Thus you know how vital it is that this be delivered with all haste."

"Of course, my lord," Henshaw replied. "You may count upon me."

"I have done so for twenty years, Henshaw," said Richard. "You should be aware that since our plans are now in motion, the danger increases."

"I understand, my lord."

Richard dropped hot wax on the envelope, then sealed it with an old ring made of silver he kept concealed in a box in a desk drawer. The seal was that of a forget-me-not and held special significance. Richard inserted the letter into a leather pouch along with several other letters relating to the family business and handed the pouch to his valet.

"The usual travel arrangements, Henshaw," Richard told him. "Here is money for the journey. Place the letter directly into the hands of the marchioness. Repeat the words of the message to me."

" 'The ancient evil has come to Freya. The prophecy is fulfilled. Make ready,' " Henshaw quoted.

"Excellent," said Richard. "And now, I am going to tell you the nature of the ancient evil, which I dare not commit to paper. Our queen, the descendant of traitors, has committed the treacherous act of inviting Travian dragons to live in Freya."

"Dragons!" Henshaw repeated, shocked. "Why would Her Majesty do such a mad thing?"

"Gold," said Richard, glowering. "She trades Freyan blood for gold. You may assure the marchioness that my information is reliable. My unscrupulous brother told me the news this very night. Given the way he preened himself, I have no doubt this was his idea. And now you must be off. Godspeed, Henshaw."

The valet bowed, tucked the leather pouch under his arm, and left.

Alone in his study, Richard sat down at his desk and began to write. He would be here all night, sending coded letters addressed to various people in all parts of Freya and around the world. Each letter began with the words "To the Faithful," and, when he was finished, he sealed each with the graven image of the forget-me-not.

TWENTY-ONE

Kate sailed away from the Aligoes without a backward look. Her only regret lay in leaving behind the old *Barwich Rose*. She and the crew hauled it onto land in Kate's Cove, hiding it among the trees, and covered it with tarps. She felt as though she were leaving a part of herself behind, for the *Rose* had been her home. She had laughed and played on the *Rose*, learned to sail the *Rose*. Her father's body had been laid out on the deck of the *Rose*.

Kate and Olaf held a private ceremony bidding their ship farewell. They also had to bid Akiel farewell, for he was staying in Freeport to run the Perky Parrot in Olaf's absence. Kate had tried to persuade Akiel to come with her, but he had refused.

"The climate does not suit me, mum," said Akiel. "And I am still wanted in Freya for murder. Besides, the customers would miss my cooking. And do not worry about the *Rose*. I will take good care of her."

Most of Freeport turned out to bid farewell to Kate, including Trubgek. Amelia was the one who first noticed him. She interrupted Kate, who was laughing with friends, and drew her aside.

"Look there, Captain," said Amelia in a low voice, pointing.

Kate saw Trubgek standing at the back of the crowd, his empty eyes fixed intently on her. She shivered in spite of herself, and abruptly cut short the celebration, ordering all the visitors off the ship and Marco to set sail.

The *Victorie* left Freeport Bay and sailed into the Trame Channel. A day's sailing with a fair wind carried them into the open Breath.

The ship was escorted by Dalgren, triumphantly flying overhead. Since the dragon would have to rest during the five-day voyage to Freya, Olaf had added a "perch" to the ship's stern, relating how he had seen the dragons of the Dragon Brigade land on Rosian ships.

Olaf reinforced two spars with magical constructs, then mounted them on the ship's stern, one on the port side and one on the starboard. The spars extended twenty feet out from the stern of the ship. He covered those with planking, forming a platform on which Dalgren could land, so long as he landed gently. From there, he could walk—carefully—onto the deck.

Kate enjoyed the journey to Freya, secure in the knowledge that she held letters of marque. Her one disappointment was that she didn't encounter any fat merchant ships to take as prizes. When they sighted the coastline of Freya, the crew lined up at the rail to cheer and Kate poured Calvados for everyone.

She carried a mug to Amelia, who was talking to Dalgren. The dragon was relaxing on the deck, his wings flat against his sides, his feet curled under his chest, his tail wrapped around his body so that the tip was even with his snout. He had been discussing something with Amelia, something serious, by their attitudes. Amelia smiled to see Kate and offered her congratulations, though she refused the Calvados. Dalgren looked subdued.

Kate placed her hand on his neck. The dragon had been lying in the sun and his glittering scales were warm to the touch.

"We've done it, my friend!" she said with a little tremor in her voice. "We are home. The first of our dreams has come to pass!"

Dalgren shifted his right leg out from beneath his chest so she could sit on his front foot. Amelia had walked over to the rail to admire the view.

Kate knew Dalgren was pleased for her. His eyes warmed and she could see the glint of his fangs in what for him was a smile. But something was troubling him. She could tell that, as well, by the wrinkle in the scales of his forehead and the twitching of his tail.

"What's the matter?" she asked.

Dalgren drew in a breath. "I'm not going to Freya—"

"Not going!" Kate repeated, shocked. She jumped off his leg to face him. "You have to go, Dalgren! You are part of us! You and me. Dragon Corsairs. I can't do this without you!"

"Calm down and let me finish," Dalgren growled. "I didn't say I was never going. The *Victorie* has to go in for refitting and the work won't be finished for at least a month. During that time, you need to find someplace *safe* for me to live."

Kate heard the emphasis on the word "safe." She glanced over at Amelia, who was gazing at the city of Haever, just emerging from the mists of the Breath.

"This has something to do with what Miss Amelia said about Freyans not liking dragons, doesn't it?"

"Freyans *hate* dragons," said Dalgren, his scowl deepening. "I've enjoyed this journey. I have missed being able to fly in the sunshine. I don't like having to go back to skulking about in the night. I'll have to go into hiding when I'm in Freya, just like I did in the Aligoes."

"Not for long," said Kate, trying to persuade him. "The area around Barwich Manor is mountainous and filled with caves and for the most part, no one lives there."

"For the most part," repeated Dalgren in gloomy tones.

"Besides, if people did see you, what could they do to you?"

"Shoot me," said Dalgren bluntly.

"Birdshot," Kate scoffed.

"And how would you like to be peppered with birdshot?" Dalgren demanded. "First it's a farmer shooting at me and then it's the hunt club, only they would be hunting me, not a fox. Then they would call out the militia."

Kate stood regarding him in sorrowful silence. "Where will you go? Back to Rosia?"

"You know perfectly well I have no intention of ever returning to Rosia," Dalgren said grimly. "I am planning to fly to Travia. I have an uncle who lives there."

"How did you come by a Travian uncle?" Kate wondered. "I didn't think Rosian dragons would lower themselves to mate with Travians."

"My uncle was a bit of a rogue. He was the family disgrace before I came along," said Dalgren, his upper lip curling back in a grin. "He not only mated with a Travian dragon, he had the effrontery to become extremely wealthy. My family despises him. Also, while I'm in Travia, I'm going to do some work for Miss Amelia."

"What work?" Kate asked uneasily.

"I am investigating the dragon Coreg," Amelia answered, returning to join the conversation, thereby proving that she had been eavesdropping. "We discussed this."

"You discussed it. I think we should just forget Coreg," Kate said, annoyed. "He belongs to the life that's behind me."

"I have a story of international scope, Captain," said Amelia. "I do not intend to let it drop."

"Then don't involve me," said Kate.

"I do not plan to, Captain," said Amelia. "I have confirmed from various sources that Greenstreet once lived in Travia and it is logical to assume that he and Coreg met there. At least that is a place to start. Dalgren is going to find out what he can about him."

"That should be easy," Dalgren added. "The dragon population in Travia is relatively small. If he lived there, my uncle and his friends might remember him."

Kate said nothing more while Amelia was around, but once the reporter left, returning to her cabin to finish her packing, Kate expressed reservations.

"I don't think it's safe to go asking about Coreg, Dalgren. You and Miss Amelia should leave him alone."

"Coreg threatened me, as well as you," Dalgren said. "Maybe I can find out something that will help Miss Amelia put the dragon out of business. Don't worry. I'll make a few inquiries. That's all."

Kate shook her head. "I still don't like it, but I don't suppose I can talk either of you out of this. When are you leaving?"

"Tonight, after dark."

"I will miss you," Kate said, rubbing his snout. "Don't be gone long. Send me a letter now and again. I'll be staying with Miss Amelia."

"She has told me where to send the mail," said Dalgren. "My uncle keeps a scribe. Several scribes, actually."

"I'll let you know when I find a nice, comfy cave," Kate promised.

"Where I'll have to hide," Dalgren said bitterly.

"Not when I become lady of the manor," said Kate. "You will be under my protection. Lord Dalgren of Barwich. You will be invited to take tea in all the finest homes."

"I may never come back," said Dalgren with the glint of a fang.

Kate counted sailing the *Victorie* into the Freyan port city of Haever as the proudest moment of her life. She wished her father could have seen her. She had not been back to Haever since she was a girl and she was interested to see what had changed and what had not. She remembered being fascinated by the famous flying house of an eccentric duchess as a child, and she laughed to see it almost directly overhead, drifting above the harbor.

She and the crew spent a few days in Haever. She had to report to Sir

Henry and finalize the details of their agreement, including their deal regarding Barwich Manor.

She now was the owner, or at last half owner, of the estate. Sir Henry presented her with a chirograph—a legal contract done in triplicate and then cut in half, with each half having serrated edges. Both parties to the contract received a copy, secure in the knowledge that the contract could be verified by fitting the two halves together.

"The Crown owns the other half of the manor," Henry explained. "I propose that you serve as a privateer for Freya for a term of three years and, at the end of that time, if your service has proven satisfactory, Barwich Manor will be yours—free and clear."

Kate deposited the chirograph in a metal box along with the piece of paper that said, "Fight for your dreams." She put warding magical constructs on the box and then secreted it in the trunk along with the green silk dress. She sat for long moments with her hand on the box, reveling in her happiness—a feeling that had not come often in her life.

The next day, she sailed the *Victorie* to a shipyard Henry recommended, for refitting. The yard was going to upgrade the control constructs and replace the outdated lift tanks that had relied on the Breath of God, converting them to use the more efficient liquid. Parts of the hull also needed replacing, as did a good amount of basic cordage.

Since Olaf was convinced that the work on *Victorie* could not be completed to his satisfaction unless he was there to supervise, he took a room in a boardinghouse near the shipyard, where he could spend the day telling the workmen how to do their jobs.

Kate was able to pay him and Marco and the rest of the crew what she owed them and give them a month's shore leave.

She longed to visit Barwich Manor, but she kept putting off her return to her childhood home. She moved in with Amelia, who owned her own house, a modest dwelling chosen because it was within walking distance of Print Street, a section of Haever where the major newspapers of the day had their print factories and offices.

The energetic Amelia was often away from home, conducting interviews, doing investigative research, attending late-night sessions in the House of Nobles or rallies held by various groups in support of various causes devoted to the solving of various problems. As far as Kate could tell, the solutions involved mobs taking to the streets and breaking shop windows. When Amelia was home, she was busy writing more stories about Captain Kate and her Dragon Corsairs to satisfy the wants of an adoring public.

Kate was soon bored. She traveled to the shipyard to check on the progress of the work on *Victorie,* only to find she wasn't needed or wanted. The shipbuilders and crafters knew their business and Olaf was there to keep an eye on them.

She had been hoping to renew her acquaintance with Captain Northrop, but according to Sir Henry, Alan was away with the Expeditionary Fleet sailing the Strait de Domcaido near Estara.

"You should visit Barwich Manor," Miss Amelia said one morning. "You have been talking about going for days now. You have the money to pay for the journey. And you promised you would find a home for Dalgren."

"I do need to go," Kate said. "It occurred to me that an old abandoned limestone mine near the manor would make a good dragon dwelling."

"Then what is stopping you?" Miss Amelia asked, fixing Kate with a shrewd look over the top of her spectacles.

"I'm stopping me," Kate admitted. "And I don't know why. I have spent so many years longing for my home, dreaming of the day I could go back and yet, now that I can, I feel a strange sort of dread come over me."

"Perfectly understandable, Captain," Miss Amelia said. "You fear the ghosts."

"Ghosts!" Kate laughed. "I don't believe in ghosts, Miss Amelia."

"They are quite fashionable these days. Every noble house has a lady in white who goes tromping about the parapets at night wringing her hands and terrifying the servants. But that wasn't the sort of ghost I meant. I mean ghosts of your past."

"There are no ghosts of any kind in Barwich Manor," said Kate. "My mother would have given them notice, sent them away like ill-mannered servants. But you are right. I have the time and I have the money and I do need to find someplace for Dalgren to live."

Kate traveled the hundred miles to Barwich by post chaise, reveling in the fact that she could afford the luxury. She could afford new clothes, too. Olaf had been scandalized at the thought of Kate going about Haever in her slops.

"At least dress like a lady, if you can't act like one," he had told her.

Kate still found women's clothing restrictive and uncomfortable. She didn't want to make a spectacle of herself, however, especially going back home. She wore a plain gray skirt, cut full so that she could walk without tripping, a demure jacket and blouse, and a hat with a heavy veil. Kate didn't think anyone in the town would recognize her after all these years, but she didn't want to take the chance. The last thing she wanted was to hear someone gush over how much she looked like her mother. Kate adamantly refused to wear petticoats, never mind what Mrs. Ridgeway had to say about them.

Gazing out the window of the coach, she remembered the last time she had been on this road. She had been leaving her home, not going to it. Morgan had received word of his wife's death and come back to take his little daughter to live with him on board his ship. As they rode together from Barwich to Haever on a horse he had hired for the journey, Morgan tried to cheer her by making up outlandish stories about the people they met on the road.

"You see that man coming toward us, the one with the basket?" Morgan had whispered. "He has two heads. He wears one and carries the other in the basket. He puts on the second head at night and goes to the palace to visit the queen."

"Papa, those are just cabbages in the basket," Kate had protested, laughing.

"And how do you know your own head isn't a cabbage?" Morgan had teased.

Kate had worried about that for days. She smiled at the memory, then sighed.

The town of Barwich had grown in the last twenty years. A small company was weaving strong, magic-free ropes, supplying shipyards and hoping to soon secure a naval contract. The company had attracted workers and their families, who had money to spend. Kate was pleased, if astonished, to see the prosperous aspect of the shops on the main street.

She hired a pony cart to take her to Barwich Manor, telling the hostler she would do the driving and she would need the cart for several days. He looked at her oddly. Kate remembered him and she was afraid, even with the veil, that he remembered her. She paid well enough for him to keep his questions to himself, however.

Barwich Manor was located about ten miles southeast of the town. She drove the cart over the road that led to the estate, meeting almost no one on the way, for few people had reason to come to this part of the countryside. The road extended on past Barwich Manor to an old limestone quarry, but it had been abandoned for years. Kate stopped the pony at the head of the long drive leading to the gates of the manor before she had courage enough to drive on.

The lane was lined with chestnut trees. The gardener had once pruned the trees, made certain they were all the same height, with no leaf out of place. Now they had been neglected, allowed to run wild. Their boughs overspread the lane, so that it was dappled with shadow and splashes of sunlight. As Kate drove beneath the stone arches of the gate, her heart beat so rapidly she found it hard to breathe.

When the manor came into view Kate stopped the pony to sit and gaze at it. The once neatly trimmed lawn looked like a hayfield; the flower beds were choked with weeds. The circular drive had almost disappeared. And yet, she was home. Kate wiped away her tears, clucked to the pony, and drove toward the house.

Sir Henry had given her the keys, which he had obtained from the bank. Kate took the pony to what remained of the stables. She unhitched him from the cart, rubbed him down, pumped water from the old well, then turned him out into a pasture to graze.

Gripping the keys tightly, she walked around the manor from the back to the front. Barwich Manor was built in the H shape that had been popular about two hundred years ago. The house was rectangular and stubbornly symmetrical, with wings on either side that flanked the central part of the house, forming the crossbar of the "H."

Gables and turrets, fanciful chimneys, and flying buttresses were the fashion these days. Barwich Manor had none of these and was therefore considered old-fashioned, stodgy, and ugly. At least that's what the estate agent told her, offering that as the excuse for not being able to sell it.

Kate thought the manor was beautiful.

The bank had padlocked the front door. She removed the padlock, pushed on the door, and, gathering her courage, entered the house for the first time since she had walked out eighteen years ago.

She stopped just inside the entry hall. She knew then what Miss Amelia had meant.

"*I* am the ghost," Kate murmured.

The entry hall had been named the Marble Hall for the black-and-white-checkered marble floor that was now uniformly gray beneath a layer of dust. Cobwebs hung in place of the oil paintings of her noble ancestors that had once adorned the wood-paneled walls.

Kate stood in the hall and for a moment her heart failed her. She could not do this. She had made a mistake. She would ride away and never come back.

"Nonsense," she said out loud, daring the ghosts to challenge her. "This is a house. My house. No one lives here, including the past."

She walked through the house, going from the Marble Hall into the great parlor. From there, she entered the drawing room, the dining room, and the library. Her mother having sold the books, the library shelves were empty. She ascended the grand staircase to the barren bedchambers, the empty schoolroom. She visited the chapel, which was at the back of the house on the southeast side. The old marble altar was still there. Her mother probably would have sold it, but it was so heavy Kate doubted if even Dalgren could shift it. In every room, she confronted the ghosts of her childhood and gave them notice to pack up and depart.

Finally, she walked out back to the old mausoleum, which stood beneath oak trees that had been saplings when it was built. Her mother rested inside, sharing the silence and the darkness with the bones of their ancestors. Kate laid some wildflowers she had picked on the steps leading to the iron door. She did not enter. She had said good-bye to her mother long ago.

She needed a place to sleep and she did not want to sleep in her old room, which was crowded with ghosts who apparently were not going to leave without a fight. She left them alone and took the back staircase to the servants' quarters, located on the southwest side of the house.

The servants lived apart from the main area of the house, since servants were supposed to come and go unnoticed. The kitchen was a large two-story room at the back, with a huge fireplace. Kate had often played in the kitchen. When her mother had grown ill, the servants had taken care of the lonely little girl.

Some of the furniture still remained in the servants' hall, for the simple fact that it had not been worth selling. Kate unpacked the supplies she had brought with her, changed into her slops, rolled up her sleeves, and went to work to remove eighteen years of dust, starting with the kitchen.

By the time she had finished cleaning, darkness had fallen. She ate a simple meal and slept in a cot in a room that had once been occupied by the cook. Kate was exhausted and slept soundly, undisturbed by any wandering spirits.

She spent the next day going over the house, inspecting it, making note of what needed to be repaired. The magical constructs were the most critical. Magic had been used in every phase of construction, from strengthening the massive walls to protecting both interior and exterior against fire and water damage. The assault on magic by the Bottom Dwellers had left many fine houses in Freya damaged past repair.

Kate studied the magical constructs on the walls, and although she knew nothing about masonry constructs, she could tell from her experience with contramagic on board her ship whether the damage was extensive or could be reversed. Fortunately Barwich Manor had been designed by unimaginative architects and builders, who had chosen solid construction as opposed to magical flights of fancy. Such houses were "built with more magic than sense," her mother had said, referring to walls made of crystal or delicate, soaring stained-glass spires.

Most of the damage to the magical constructs on the building had been caused by neglect, not by the destructive effects of contramagic. The magic could be repaired, but the cost of hiring masonry crafters and carpenter crafters would be almost beyond reckoning. And that was only to repair the magic. The physical damage was more extensive. Many of the leaded windows were broken, and a leak in the roof had ruined much of the oak paneling in the rooms on the upper floor. One of the chimneys was crumbling. All the chimneys needed sweeping. The ornamental molding in every room needed replacing. And that was just the beginning.

When Kate's list covered both sides of four sheets of paper, she stopped writing.

Discouraged, she sat on the bottom stair of the great staircase and gazed at the Marble Hall with its festoon of cobwebs and cracks running up the walls. She was overwhelmed by the enormity of the task she had set for herself. The house had seemed perfect to a six-year-old child. She now saw the manor as her mother must have seen it—cracked and broken—and Kate understood why her mother had given up.

Fight for your dreams, Lieutenant de Guichen had told her. *Never sound retreat.*

"But what if the fight is hopeless and retreat the only option?" Kate asked herself.

Her mother had retreated, finally losing the battle to madness and death. Kate stood up and brushed the dust off her slops. Giving up was not in her nature.

"This is my home," she said again. "Mine."

Poking around in the attic, she came across some relics of her childhood, including a dilapidated hobbyhorse and an old convex mirror. The mirror had been a gift to her mother from Morgan on one of his rare visits home. Kate had loved it, for when he hung it on the wall, the bulging mirror showed parts of the room that an ordinary flat mirror would have left hidden.

Morgan claimed such mirrors brought luck to a house. Her mother had called it the "witch's eye" and said its distorted view of the room made her flesh crawl. After Morgan had left, her mother had ordered the mirror relegated to the attic.

Kate dusted off the mirror and carried it downstairs. She had decided to hang it in the Marble Hall. The mirror didn't belong there. It would look very small and insignificant in the immense room, but she didn't mind. The mirror was a symbol of hope.

She propped open the front door to let in the fresh air and fading sunlight. She had found a hammer and some nails in the storage room and she chose a place on the wall in the center of the hall. Driving a nail into the wood, she carefully hung the mirror and then stepped back to admire the effect, smiling to see the vast Marble Hall shrink to the size of the mirror.

"Thus may all my problems shrink," Kate said, laughing.

Her laughter abruptly stopped. Inside the mirror, she saw the distorted reflection of a strange man walk through the open door and into the hall.

Kate assumed he was a tramp.

"How dare you barge in here? Get out—"

And then she recognized Trubgek. She was so startled, she couldn't move or speak. She felt paralyzed, like the time he had used his magic on her, except that he hadn't touched her or said a word. She tried to ask him what he was doing here, but failed. She could only stare at him.

Trubgek stood staring at her. He was wearing the same leather jerkin he had worn the last time she saw him. He had the same empty eyes. He looked as if he had simply walked across a street, but he hadn't. He had traveled hundreds of miles to find her.

Kate cleared her throat. "What do you want, Trubgek?"

"Coreg asked me to check up on you," he answered in his lifeless voice. "Make certain you had not forgotten about your agreement with him."

Kate stood silent, thinking. She had dismissed Coreg from her thoughts. Out of sight, out of mind. She had assured herself the dragon posed no threat. He would never go to the trouble of seeking her out in a faraway country. Apparently she had been wrong. Now was the time to take a stand, to say what she should have said back in the Aligoes.

"I did *not* agree to work for your master," Kate stated. "I am sorry if I didn't make myself clear. Thank Coreg for his offer, but I must refuse."

Trubgek said nothing. He walked over and placed his hand, palm flat, on the wall.

Kate was perplexed. Perhaps the man was mad.

"What do you think you are doing?" she demanded.

A tremor ran through the house, as though it shivered. The tremors continued, growing stronger. The floor shook. The walls shuddered. Dust cascaded down from the ceiling, filling the room with a choking cloud. Plaster crashed to the floor. Kate heard a crash from a far room and another somewhere else. The mirror fell off the wall and shattered at her feet.

Kate staggered and had to cling to the wall for support.

"Stop!" she gasped. "Stop! Please!"

The shaking continued a moment longer, long enough for Kate to think the house was going to collapse.

Trubgek removed his hand from the wall and the shaking stopped. The house settled, creaking and groaning. He glanced at the broken mirror.

"Seven years' bad luck," he remarked.

"I'll do it," Kate mumbled, between fits of coughing.

"Do what?" Trubgek asked.

Kate glared at him and coughed.

"Tell Coreg if he has a job for me, I'll . . . think about it. That's the best I can do. My work for Sir Henry comes first."

Trubgek gazed at her, unblinking; then he shrugged, turned, and walked out the door.

Kate stood staring at the spot where he had been standing. He had come and gone so suddenly she began to wonder if she had imagined him. The creaking timbers and slowly settling dust and chunks of plaster proved he had been all too real. Sagging back weakly against the wall, she looked around at the destruction in awe.

She had never seen or heard of any human with the magical power to cause massive walls to shake and huge wooden beams to tremble at the touch of a hand. Kate didn't scare easily, but she had known gut-twisting terror in those horrible few moments when she had feared her house was going to fall down on top of her.

Kate ran to the door, trying to avoid stepping on shards of the broken mirror.

"How did you work such magic?" she yelled at Trubgek's retreating back. "No sigils, no constructs! No human can craft magic like that."

Trubgek kept walking and did not respond.

"Dragon magic!" Kate shouted at him. "Coreg taught you dragon magic! But how did he do it? It's not possible for humans to learn dragon magic!"

Trubgek stopped. He stood long moments, as though deciding whether or not answer. Finally, slowly, he turned to face her.

"Enough pain and anything is possible," he said. His empty eyes flickered. "Remember that."

He continued down the drive. Kate shivered and remained standing in the doorway until he had disappeared from sight. Then she shut the entry door, locked it, and then traced a magical construct on the lock.

The spell was simple. Trubgek would likely make short work of such crude magic, but it made her feel more secure.

She sank down on the bottom stair of the grand staircase and stared into the darkness, wondering what to do.

Coreg had boasted his reach was long, but Kate had never imagined it was this long—that he could reach into her dream.

TWENTY-TWO

A month had passed since Phillip had made his dramatic arrival in Estara. He had recovered from the bullet wound and was now enrolled at the Royal Military Academy.

He fit in well at the academy, but then Phillip had the gift of being able to fit in well wherever he went. He had once fit in well with a coven of blood-draining warlocks, spying on them for the Rose Hawks. His comrades in the academy had been a bit standoffish at first, not certain they trusted a Freyan, but Phillip's genial personality, his easygoing manner, and the rumor that he was immensely wealthy soon won over all doubters.

He and Thomas were spending this weekend with the marchioness in Arcos. He met Thomas's mother, Constanza, for the first time. Phillip had heard much about her, not only from Thomas, but also from Sir Henry Wallace, who considered Constanza if not the Evil One himself, than one of that dread gentleman's close relations.

Phillip carefully studied her and made these observations in a letter to Sir Henry.

> *The marchioness is clever, energetic, and intelligent, though lacking in wisdom and common sense. She believes without*

question her son to be the true and rightful heir to the throne and she will devote her last drop of blood and her final breath to making this come to pass. She will stop at nothing.

Phillip had hoped to perhaps discover the name of Thomas's Freyan supporter while he was with the marchioness, but thus far he had not been successful. She was careful with her correspondence. A glance through her letters when she had gone out for the evening provided nothing more interesting than Estaran court gossip. Of course, the letters could be written in code, but, if so, Phillip saw that it would require someone with a giant brain, like Simon, to crack it.

Constanza's distrust of her own servants meant that he could glean little information from them. Tonight was the last night of the visit, and he was starting to think he would have to report failure when the marchioness summoned both Thomas and Phillip to the music room.

Phillip thought they were to be treated to an evening's musical entertainment, perhaps listening to a pianoforte duet or string quartet. Thomas quickly disabused him of the notion as they walked up the stairs.

"Prepare yourself," he said in a low voice. "For now you will see intrigue at work."

"What do you mean?" Phillip asked, mystified.

"I hope you like the pianoforte," said Thomas with a rueful smile and a sigh of resignation.

The music room was silent, however. Constanza had been impatiently waiting for them and she rose to greet them, kissing her son on the cheek and permitting Phillip to kiss her hand.

"What? No pianoforte music?" Thomas asked, as he was taking a seat on the couch. "Are we to resort to using sign language to keep our secrets safe?"

"He is so droll, Your Grace," said Constanza, speaking to Phillip. "Do you not find him so?"

"I do indeed, Your Ladyship," said Phillip.

"What has put you in such a good mood, Mother?" Thomas asked.

"I have news that will put *you* in a good mood, as well, my son," said Constanza.

"Perhaps I should withdraw . . ." said Phillip, rising.

"Please remain with us, Your Grace," said Constanza. "This news concerns you as well. What do you think has happened?"

She looked from one to the other, her eyes glittering with excitement.

"I am sure I cannot guess, Mother," said Thomas impatiently. "I hope this has nothing to do with finding me a wife, because I would prefer to find my own."

"Don't be ridiculous, my son. The negotiations for the hand of the princess are going well, but that is not why I sent for you." Constanza dismissed the notion with a wave of her fan. "I have received word from Freya. The prophecy is fulfilled!"

Sitting back, she waited expectantly for her son's reaction. "Well, Thomas, what do you say to that?"

Phillip was glad he had not been called upon to say anything, for he had no idea how to respond, at least not until he knew more. He turned to Thomas, who apparently was as much in the dark as his friend.

"Uh, yes, the prophecy . . ." Thomas said with a look of utter confusion.

Constanza glared at him. "'Uh, yes, the prophecy'!" she repeated in scorn. "Is that how you dismiss the prophecy that proclaims you will be king?"

"Mother, please, not that—" Thomas began, embarrassed.

Phillip saw Constanza's eyes flash in anger and he quickly intervened.

"Forgive your son, Your Ladyship," he said in soothing tones. "You know how modest he is. He doesn't like to speak of it."

Glancing around the room, Phillip lowered his voice. "And then, one can't be too careful. . . ."

"That is true, Your Grace," said Constanza, favoring Phillip with a pleased glance and casting Thomas an annoyed one. "Take note, my son. His Grace understands these things. Come sit close to me, both of you, and I will tell you what has occurred."

Phillip and Thomas joined Constanza on the couch, one on either side. Clasping hands with both of them, she spoke in soft and breathless tones. "The second half of the prophecy has some to pass. The ancient evil has returned to Freya!"

"What evil is that, Mother?" Thomas asked.

"Dragons," said Constanza.

She squeezed their hands, then released them to pick up her fan and sit back, to once more observe their reactions. This time, she was pleased. She had managed to astound both of them.

"Dragons!" Thomas repeated, amazed. "In Freya?"

"Are you certain this information is accurate, Your Ladyship?" Phillip asked, skeptical. "Dragons have not lived in Freya for centuries."

"'The ancient evil' returns," said Constanza. "I have this news on the best authority. A member of the Faithful—you will understand that I do not name him—has access to privileged information and he reports that Her Majesty has signed an agreement to lease lands belonging to the Crown to a group of fifteen dragons from Travia in exchange for a vast sum of gold."

"What do dragons have to do with an ancient evil?" Thomas asked.

"To many people in Freya, dragons *are* the ancient evil, Your Highness," Phillip explained, troubled. "Dragons have been reviled in Freya since the days when they nearly wiped out the Imhruns."

"The Imhruns! But that is ancient history," Thomas protested. "Dragons in these days fought the Bottom Dwellers. Undoubtedly their heroics saved thousands of Freyan lives."

"I fear most Freyans will not take such a sensible view of the matter, Your Highness," said Phillip, smiling.

His smile was for show. Inwardly, he was deeply concerned. Constanza's information did indeed sound reliable. Since Sir Henry had said nothing to him about this plan, Phillip reasoned that such potentially explosive knowledge was supposed to be a closely held secret. He needed to find out the identity of this informant, who claimed to have access to "privileged information."

"I do not know that I believe this, Mother," said Thomas. "For one, why would dragons want to live in Freya?"

"I am afraid I agree with Thomas, Your Ladyship," Phillip added. "Even if this is true, I cannot imagine such a proposal will succeed given that a foreign government is involved. The treaty must pass the House of Nobles and they will be in opposition."

"I beg your pardon for differing with you, Your Grace," said Constanza. "There will be a great deal of opposition in the House at first, but several members of the Faithful have considerable influence among the members and they will see to it that the treaty will be approved."

"But if these nobles do not want the dragons living in Freya, why would they approve the treaty?" Thomas asked.

Constanza was impatient. "Must I explain the simplest things to you, Thomas? He is so naive," she complained to Phillip. "By agreeing to invite the dragons to move to Freya, the Faithful are making certain the prophecy about the ancient evil comes to pass."

"Not much of a prophecy, then is it, Mother," said Thomas caustically. "Not if you have to scheme to make it come to pass!"

"Scheme! What have I done for you all my life but scheme!" Constanza flared. "*I* scheme while *you* flirt with pretty women and play at being a soldier! Sometimes I think you do not want to be king!"

Phillip remembered what Thomas had said at their first meeting, and wondered if he would tell his mother that she was right. He did not want to be king. Thomas held his anger in check.

"I am sorry you have such a poor opinion of me, Mother," he said, flushing.

Phillip found his situation a delicate one. As a gentleman, he should not be present during a family quarrel, no matter how much he needed to find out more information.

"I am certain you both will excuse me," he said, rising.

"You do not need to go, Your Grace," said Constanza. "Just because my son is an ungrateful wretch!"

Thomas was angry. Phillip could see his eyes flash, a flush of color on his cheeks.

"The truth is that my wound still pains me at times, Your Ladyship," said Phillip. "I feel a little faint. I believe I will go lie down."

Thomas cast him a grateful look and Phillip bowed himself out.

The hall outside the music room was empty. Not surprising, since Constanza once again had banished the servants. Phillip loudly closed the door to the music room, then softly opened it a crack. He could see and hear both Thomas and his mother quite clearly. Focused on their anger, they were certain not to notice him.

Thus positioned to eavesdrop on his hostess and the man he was coming to value as a friend, Phillip paused, irresolute. He had been given an invaluable opportunity to discover their secrets, and Henry would expect him to take advantage of it.

Still Phillip hesitated. The thought of putting his ear to that door made him almost physically sick to his stomach. He was beginning to loathe this duty, as well as himself, and he started to quietly shut the door when he heard his name mentioned.

"I trust you are pleased, Mother!" Thomas said. He had risen to his feet and was pacing about the room. "You have embarrassed me in front of Phillip!"

"I am certain His Grace will forgive a mother for being passionate about her son. I love you so much, Thomas," Constanza said, embracing him. "I live for you, and it hurts me when you do not take your cause seriously. So many people, including His Grace, have sacrificed so much for you!"

Thomas gave her a remorseful kiss, then gently drew away from her.

"I have listened to you and Captain Smythe and my father discuss landing troops in Haever, marching to the palace, arresting the queen . . . I always supposed the army was, in truth, part of Father's ambitious plan to become ruler of Bheldem. The talk of Freya was, I thought, a smoke screen. I never took it seriously."

Phillip certainly took talk about arresting the queen seriously. His scruples forgotten, he put his ear to the door. He could not hear Constanza's reply, for she had lowered her voice. He heard Thomas, however.

"You will be pleased to hear that I have come to feel differently, Mother. That terrible night when you sent me to fetch Phillip, he was shot and nearly killed. I knelt beside him as he lay on the ground, covered in blood. He looked up at me and said, 'Your Highness.' I realized then that good men like Phillip were prepared to sacrifice their lives to put me on the throne and I was humbled. Phillip believes in me. Perhaps it is my duty to believe in myself."

Good God, what have I done? Phillip asked himself, appalled. Henry sent me to ensure that Thomas did not become king and instead it appears that I have ensured the exact opposite. Thomas never had any notion of being king until he met me! And now he gives the matter serious consideration!

Thomas wasn't happy about it, however. "Know this, Mother. I will not take part in an armed insurrection. If and when Her Majesty, the Queen of Freya, dies—and I pray that she will live and reign in health and happiness for many years—then I will consider coming forward to advance my claim. Not until then."

Constanza pressed her lips together and slapped her fan into her palm. She wasn't pleased, but Thomas had just conceded the victory to her and she wouldn't spoil it by opposing him.

Phillip saw the resignation on Thomas's face, heard the resignation, as well as resolution, in his voice. Phillip felt himself to be in the wrong, eavesdropping on a moment that was intensely personal, revealing Thomas's private, inner feelings. Once more, Phillip started to shut the door and once more, he remained.

Thomas asked, "Do you think I would be a good king, Mother?"

"What a silly question," said Constanza with an affected laugh. "I raised you to be a good king. But what I think does not matter. It is only God that matters and He thinks you will be a good king. And now, I must go to the library to write letters to give the good news to our friends. Dinner will be at eight of the clock."

Hearing silk rustle, and seeing Constanza approach the door, Phillip bolted down the hall and secreted himself in an empty room. Opening that door a crack, he watched Constanza go rustling down the stairs. She was livid with anger. Phillip wondered how she had managed to control herself, for she was known for her emotional outbursts. He saw then that she had been holding her fan so tightly she had crushed the blades. She flung the useless fan to the floor and trod on it, then stamped down the stairs.

Not wanting to bump into Thomas, Phillip waited for him to leave the music room before daring to venture out.

Minutes passed and Thomas did not come. Phillip wondered what he was doing. He crept back to the door of the music room to look inside.

Thomas was sitting at the pianoforte, his hands idly roving over the keys. His expression was grave, his thoughts turned inward. The musical notes he produced were tuneless, discordant.

He is thinking, perhaps for the first time, what it means to be king, Phillip thought. His life will never be his own. He will belong to his ministers, the nobles, his generals, his people. No one will tell him the truth. Everyone will tell him only what they want him to hear. He will be alone, the loneliest man in the world. Poor devil . . . He could use a friend now.

Phillip started to enter. Then he stopped. Here he was, spying on Thomas through a crack in the door. He was filled with disgust. Softly closing the door, he walked off.

"I am not his friend," he said to himself. "I am his enemy."

Phillip wrote to Sir Henry that night, telling him about the dragons and the House of Nobles and how the Faithful planned to ensure the prophecy was fulfilled.

He once again slipped into Constanza's study, this time long after everyone was in bed, in the hope of finding the letters she had written or perhaps a torn-up draft or impression of her writing left behind on the blotting paper. He found nothing except ashes in the grate and a couple of drops of spilled sealing wax.

Early the next morning Phillip set out to deliver his letter. Telling the servants he was taking a gallop before breakfast, he rode into Arcos to give the letter to one of Henry's agents, who promised to immediately dispatch it by griffin courier.

Phillip took his time riding back. He was not eager to return to the task at hand. He could tell himself that he was hoping to save his country from a bloody civil war, but that was small comfort. He was acting ignobly, spying on a man who considered him a trusted friend, and he bitterly regretted accepting this assignment. He regretted still more that he had undertaken it with a light heart, thinking it just another adventure.

Phillip had more or less stumbled into spying while serving with the privateers, the Rose Hawks. Captain Northrop had required information on Rosian ships and their cargoes and the bumbling, dissolute "Pip" had proven extraordinarily adept at persuading people to talk.

During the war with the Bottom Dwellers, Phillip's job had become more dangerous. The dissolute Pip vanished, replaced by an escaped convict, fleeing a death sentence in Freya for murder. He managed by means of this diguise to infiltrate a band of pirates who had joined with the Bottom Dwellers in the Aligoes to raid shipping and capture prisoners for use as blood sacrifices. Alan and the Rose Hawks had posed as a helpless merchant vessel and Phillip had been able to lure the Bottom Dwellers into a deadly ambush.

After the war ended, Phillip had stayed in the Aligoes at the request of Sir Henry to spy upon the viscount, a man who was a boil upon humanity's backside, a wretch who wrote charming letters to the queen while he embezzled her money, traded goods on the black market, and indulged in all manner of vices at the expense of others.

Phillip had enjoyed bringing about the Right Honorable's downfall and he had assumed he would enjoy taking down Thomas. Phillip had believed Sir Henry's view of the matter: Thomas was a pretender to the throne, someone who was plotting to overthrow the rightful queen.

The truth was that Thomas was not a pretender. He was a direct descendant of King Frederick with a better claim to the throne than either King Godfrey's bastard sons or Queen Mary's Rosian sister. Further, Thomas had denounced the use of force to seize the Crown. From the determined expression on Constanza's face when she had left the music room, Phillip guessed that she was not likely to give up her cherished dreams of seeing her son crowned king. Never mind what he denounced.

"I must face the fact that I have come to like and admire Thomas," Phillip reflected, thinking aloud. "The question is: What do I do now? I could stay here, complete my heinous mission, then go back to Upper and Lower Milton, where I would attend balls, play cards, drink to excess, and eventually blow out my brains."

He rode on for another mile and stopped when the manor house came into view, annoying the horse, who wanted to return to its stable and impatiently shook the reins. He could see Thomas out on the lawn, walking by himself, his head bowed, as though he already felt the burden of the crown.

"Or," Phillip added softly, "I could be his friend. . . ."

TWENTY-THREE

Sir Henry Wallace was meeting with Simon Yates on a matter of extreme urgency. Despite the fact that Welkinstead was floating about a half mile over the city of Haever, Henry fancied he could still hear the shouts and cries of the rioters that were clogging the street in front of the palace. The people of Freya were protesting the arrival of the Travian dragons.

Henry blamed himself. He could not help feeling that he had bungled this situation badly. In this he was in agreement with the queen, who likewise blamed him and told him so on a daily basis.

The furor had started with an anonymous letter, published three days ago in the *Haever Gazette* following the successful vote in the House of Nobles to permit the dragons to live in Freya. The letter detailed every atrocity committed by dragons against Freyans from the time of the Imhruns down to the Siege of Denar and concluded with the prophecy of the mad priest: the seventh sigil and the return of the ancient evil (dragons), and heralding the return of the true king. The letter was signed "The Faithful."

The next day, people could talk of nothing else. Lurid illustrations of marauding dragons holding screaming infants in their slavering jaws were splashed across the front pages, side by side with illustrations of Prince Tom standing upon the neck of a dead dragon. Trade unions called upon their members to strike. The Fundamentalist Church spoke out against the dragons, denouncing them from the pulpit, calling them "minions of the Evil One."

"Fulfillment of the prophecy! The return of the ancient evil!" Henry raved to Simon. "These so-called Faithful must be lunatics. As if any rational person would believe such a thing."

"Quite the contrary, Henry," Simon said seriously. "These so-called Faithful are really quite clever. Whether they truly believe in the prophecy or not, they are playing upon the fear and loathing of the populace in regard to dragons to advance their cause."

"Her Majesty is going to speak to the House of Nobles in the next hour. She will explain her reasons for inviting the dragons, reassure the people that the beasts will live in the northwest and they will be of no threat to anyone," Henry said. "Hopefully that will quiet the unrest."

Simon was doubtful. "I am not certain Her Majesty should make that speech, Henry. I know inviting the dragons was my idea, but then I had no idea we would be playing into the hands of those who want to put Thomas Stanford on the throne. Perhaps you could suggest to the dragons that they might wait a year, let all the furor die down."

"The dragons would be deeply affronted," Henry said. "More to the point, their first payment is already in the royal coffers. Or rather, it *was* in the coffers. We have spent it. Have you found out anything more about these Faithful? Who the devil are they? They took the bait we dangled in regard to Phillip. We leaked word that he was interested in joining the pretender's cause and someone recommended him to Stanford. Can't we figure out who?"

"I had several leads, but they all came to nothing," Simon had replied. "These people are extremely careful. Not surprising. They have remained hidden for over a century. Did you talk to your brother about what Phillip reported in his letter, that there are members of the House of Nobles who belong to the Faithful?"

Henry was grimly amused. "I asked the Old Chap about the Faithful. Richard was deeply offended that I would even suggest such a thing. He tut-tutted all through dinner. 'Secret societies! A lot of poppycock. No respectable gentleman would dream of sneaking off to midnight meetings in cellars.' And so on and so forth. He is no help."

"Yet he knew about the dragons, Henry," said Simon, frowning. "You told him. And then there is the name: Richard. The Freyan noble backing Thomas is known as 'Sir Richard.' "

Henry regarded Simon in amazement. "You are not seriously suggesting the Old Chap is plotting to overthrow the queen! We are talking about

Richard! My brother, who has never taken a risk in his life. He refuses to eat blancmange for fear it will make him dyspeptic! As for telling him about the dragons, by the time I had told Richard, the matter had been discussed with the Privy Council and other members of the House of Nobles. Any number of people knew about it."

"I suppose you are right," Simon said. "Still, it can't hurt to talk to him again, ferret out what your brother knows about these Faithful. He might know something and not know he knows it."

"*That* sounds like Richard," Henry said. "And now I must leave for the House."

Her Majesty addressed a session of the House of Nobles. Members of the House also spoke in favor of the dragons, including Sir Richard Wallace. Unfortunately the few who did favor the dragons were drowned out with jeers and hissing.

Henry retreated to his office, where he could think about all this, but managed only to give himself a splitting headache. He was writing instructions to his agent in Braffa—yet another headache—when a breathless office boy tumbled in through the door. "One of your servants is in the front hall, my lord. You are urgently requested to return home."

Henry knew at once that Ann was going into labor. He dashed out of his office in such haste he forgot his hat. He had given his driver orders to keep the carriage in readiness, so he did not have to waste time hailing a cab. Henry had not counted upon the streets being thronged with rioters, however. He sent the coachman to find a wyvern-drawn carriage and was forced to wait, pacing the sidewalk, until the man returned with one.

Henry leaped inside, ordering the driver to make all haste, promising to pay him double his fare. As the carriage flew over the streets of Haever, Henry looked down on the crowds that seemed to be growing larger with each passing day. He knew this furor would soon die down. The Travian dragons were moving into the caves that had been readied for them to live in until they could build their own dwellings. When people realized that the dragons hadn't eaten anyone and that no villages had been set on fire, the people would eventually forget about them. Even anarchists had to eat and feed their families. Eventually the rioters would leave the streets and go back to work. But that was small comfort now.

Henry just had to be patient, wait it out.

The coachman had some difficulty landing the wyvern in front of Henry's house, due to the number of carriages belonging to physicians, healers, and midwives which lined the street. More were arriving every moment.

Henry jumped from the coach when it was still three feet off the ground, dashed up the walk, and burst through the front door, nearly knocking down the footman. Henry found the royal physician inside the entryway, putting on his hat and asking for his cloak.

"Sir Reginald! Why are you leaving? What's wrong?" Henry gasped, assuming the worst.

"Congratulations, my lord," said the physician. "You are the proud father of a beautiful little girl."

Henry blinked, stupefied. "It's over?"

"One of the fastest and easiest deliveries it has been my pleasure to attend," said Sir Reginald.

"How is my wife?" Henry asked anxiously.

"Sitting up in bed and drinking a cup of tea, my lord," Sir Reginald replied.

Henry seized his hand and nearly wrung it off his arm, then ran up the stairs, two at a time. He paused outside the bedroom door to calm his emotions, then softly opened it and peeped inside.

Ann was nursing the baby, singing and rocking her. Hearing Henry, she looked up and smiled at him.

"Come meet your daughter," she said.

"My Mouse, you quite amaze me," said Henry, going to her. "You did not give me time to pace the floor and tear out my hair."

Ann laughed. "I knew you would not survive another long delivery, Henry. So I kept it short."

"Thank you for your consideration, my dear," said Henry.

He bent over to kiss her and smoothed back her hair, whispering how much he loved her. He admired the baby, who had fallen asleep.

"Let me hold her," said Henry.

Ann relinquished her, and Henry walked about the room, gazing down with wonder at the child in his arms. He pointedly ignored the nurse, who hovered in the background, eager to swoop in to rescue her charge.

"The midwife tells me the people are rioting again today, Henry," said Ann worriedly. "Are things very bad? Sister Mabel says the queen has been warned not to leave the palace."

Henry touched the baby's soft cheek with his finger and kept walking, pretending he hadn't heard.

"My beautiful daughter," Henry said. "She takes after you, don't you think so, my dear? Which is much better than taking after her father."

"Don't try to change the subject, Henry," said Ann. "Sister Mabel—"

"—is a gossiping old busybody," said Henry. "You are to concentrate on recovering your health."

"My health is fine. I've had a baby, Henry. I didn't fall down a flight of stairs," said Ann, smiling.

They were interrupted by a soft knocking on the door.

"Begging your pardon, my lord," said the maid, "but Mr. Sloan is asking for you. He says the matter is urgent."

"Tell him I will join him in the library," said Henry.

He gave the child into the care of the nurse and walked to the bed to kiss his wife again. "You must rest, my dear."

"On the contrary, I was thinking of going for a gallop in the park," said Ann. Seeing Henry's startled expression, she added with a laugh, "I'm teasing, my dear. Go save the nation. I will read the latest installment about Captain Kate. I am dreadfully afraid for her. Last week the story ended with her ship caught in a wizard storm, sinking into the Breath, as she was fighting off rival pirates."

"My guess is that she will live to see another installment," said Henry.

Ann made a face at him. "You promised you would bring the captain to tea, my love. I want to meet her."

Henry reiterated his promise and went down the stairs. He used the library for confidential meetings for several reasons. The library was located at the rear of the three-story house and had no windows. The four walls were lined, floor to ceiling, with books that helped to deaden sound. And Mr. Sloan had covered the door in magical constructs. Any one putting an ear to it would receive a nasty jolt.

"I have a daughter, Mr. Sloan!" Henry announced, throwing open the door.

"God be praised, my lord," said Mr. Sloan. "How is Her Ladyship?"

"Splendid. Sitting up, reading the newspaper, and drinking tea," said Henry, shaking his head in admiration. "Women are marvels, Mr. Sloan."

"Indeed they are, my lord. Have you chosen a name for your daughter?"

"We have named her Mary Violet Louise, after our queen, my mother, and Lady Ann's mother." Henry grew somber. "Speaking of the queen, how is the situation in the street?"

Mr. Sloan carefully shut the door before replying.

"Not good, my lord. The police have thus far managed to keep the mob away from the palace. The rioters began hurling paving stones and bricks, breaking windows in the Foreign Office and nearby storefronts. The police are now attempting to disperse the crowd."

"Which means there will be beatings and arrests and that will make the people angrier still," said Henry. "It is a good thing Alan and Randolph are not here. I can hear them now, gloating and saying, 'I told you so!'"

Henry shrugged. "But what is done is done. No going back."

"Very true, my lord. One thinks of the old adage regarding 'spilt milk.'"

"Now, what do you have for me, Mr. Sloan? Good news for a change, I trust."

"I believe it might be very good news indeed, my lord. A message arrived by griffin courier from your agent in the Braffan capital," said Mr. Sloan, handing Henry a letter. "I deemed you should see it at once."

Henry scanned the first part and looked up, astonished. "According to this, Mr. Sloan, the Braffans have five barrels containing the Tears of God in their possession, despite assuring us and King Ullr that the crystals had been lost."

"Yes, my lord."

Henry continued reading. "'The Braffans claim to have stumbled upon the crystals hidden in a storage room. I can believe that. The late, unlamented Lord Bjorn tried to do the same, hiding the crystals away, intending to sell them on the black market."

Henry read through the report twice. "The Braffans intend to hand over the crystals to King Ullr as a 'neutral third party.' Ha! Neutral, my ass! Forgive the strong language, Mr. Sloan."

"You have been under a great deal of mental stress lately, my lord. I make allowances."

"Five barrels of crystals could keep our fleet sailing for months!" Henry said. "According to our agent, 'the Braffans plan to conceal the crystals on board a ferry in the belief that no one will think to look for them on such a humble conveyance.' These Braffan oligarchs are incredibly naive, Mr. Sloan."

"And particularly inept when it comes to keeping secrets, my lord," Mr. Sloan observed. "Your agent did not appear to have any trouble discovering this one."

"One of the many drawbacks to an oligarchy, Mr. Sloan," said Henry. "The more people who are entrusted with a secret, the less likely any of them are to keep it. I fear, however, that our enemies may also find out about the crystals. We must move fast."

"You could send Captain Northrop and the *Terrapin* to Braffa," said Mr. Sloan.

"I don't want to involve the navy in the capture. Alan and Randolph would like nothing better than to attack the Guundarans and provoke a war."

Henry crumpled the letter and handed it to Mr. Sloan, then began to pace back and forth across the library floor. Mr. Sloan picked up what appeared to be a pencil box from Henry's desk, placed the letter inside, closed the lid, and then activated a construct on the underside of the box. Moments later, a small curl of smoke was all that was left of the letter.

Henry stopped pacing.

"This will be a perfect job for our new privateer. Send a message to Captain Kate, Mr. Sloan. Tell her I will meet her at the shipyard."

Kate joined Sir Henry the next day at the shipyard where *Victorie* was being refitted. He inspected her ship and expressed his pleasure at the progress of the repairs. He and Kate walked up and down the boardwalk as Henry explained the job.

"Are you familiar with Braffa, Captain?" Henry asked.

"I am, my lord," said Kate. "I visited Braffa with my father."

Morgan had gone there to investigate the possibility of smuggling the liquid form of the Breath, only to conclude he couldn't make any money at it. The costs of hauling the liquid would far outweigh what he could make selling it on the black market, especially at that time when only a few ships were able to use it. Kate did not mention that to Sir Henry, however.

"Unfortunately, *Victorie* is not yet ready to sail, my lord," Kate continued in disappointment. "I am still waiting on the new lift tanks."

"Your ship will not be required, Captain," said Henry. "This is a mission for you and your dragon, Dalgren."

"Then we can leave upon the instant, my lord. Well, perhaps, not on the instant. Dalgren is holed up in a cave in Barwich. With all the unrest over dragons in the city—"

"Yes, yes, I understand," said Henry.

Seeing his expression darken, Kate wisely changed the subject.

"What is the assignment, my lord?"

Henry explained how the Braffans had discovered five barrels of crystallized Breath, how they planned to hide them on board a ferry and then transport the barrels to a waiting Guundaran ship.

"What I need you to do is locate the ferry with the barrels on board, capture it, and deliver the crystals to Captain Northrop aboard the *Terrapin*. I will provide you with the rendezvous site."

"I understand, my lord."

"How long will it take you to journey from here to Braffa?"

Kate did some fast calculating. "Six days, my lord. How much time do we have before they ship the crystals?"

"My agent estimates a fortnight," said Henry. "The crystals were discovered on a refinery island located some distance from the mainland and there is apparently some sort of problem with their recovery. Once you reach Braffa, you will make contact with my agent, who will provide you with more information. Here is a map of one of the refineries. There are several and I do not know where the crystals are located, but the refineries are all configured the same. Mr. Sloan will furnish you with money for your journey."

Henry regarded Kate intently. "I cannot overstate the importance of this mission, Captain. I do not exaggerate when I say that the very survival of our navy and, by extension, our nation depends upon the acquisition of these crystals."

"I understand, my lord," said Kate, impressed with the seriousness of his tone. "Dalgren and I will not let you down."

Henry smiled. "I have faith in both of you. You must not say a word of this to anyone, not your friend, Olaf; not even Miss Amelia. She can write of your heroics after the crystals are safely upon Freyan soil. My lady wife tells me your stories are more popular than ever. When you come back, she would like to have you over for tea."

Kate returned to the house she was sharing with Amelia and was relieved to find that her friend had gone out. Amelia had a way of asking questions that crept up on a person, and Kate often found herself revealing more than she intended. Amelia had a left a note saying she was out on the street, interviewing the rioters.

Kate hastily packed a valise, taking what clothes she thought she would need, two pistols, a pocket pistol, and a knife. She had to pack light, because she would be flying by griffin to Barwich Manor to meet up with Dalgren, who had only recently returned from his visit to Travia.

Once there, she did not plan to linger. She could still see Trubgek standing with his hand on the wall; still feel her house starting to collapse around her.

Amelia returned home from the office of the *Haever Gazette,* where she had gone to hand in another story on the rioters and to pick up her mail. She found the note from Kate, saying that she was going to be gone for several weeks.

"She has a job from Sir Henry," Amelia guessed. "Good for her. And good for him. The poor man needs something to take his mind off this ridiculous turmoil over dragons."

Sitting down at her desk, Amelia began to sort through the mail, which was plentiful. She had letters from readers praising her work and wanting to know why she couldn't write faster. She had invitations to speak at various gatherings, which she generally declined as they took up too much time. Those went into the wastebin.

One envelope was different from the others and she regarded it with interest. The address was written in the style known as "copperplate," generally used by secretaries and scribes. Most intriguing, it was postmarked "Travia." There was no return address.

Miss Amelia opened the envelope and extracted the letter.

I spoke to a relative of the Talwin clan, who says you are seeking information on a dragon known as Coreg. I can tell you about him. I am in the process of moving to Freya. Do not attempt to contact me. He is having me watched. I will contact you.

The letter was signed with a single name: *Odila.*

Amelia recognized the name at once. Odila was the name of the grande dame of the Travian dragons, and since Dalgren came from the Talwin clan, Amelia assumed that his uncle had been spreading the word. Glancing at the postmark and noting that the letter had been sent two weeks ago, she guessed that Odila could well be in the country right now.

"Good," Amelia remarked in satisfaction. "Now I am getting somewhere."

TWENTY-FOUR

Phillip sat in the tavern El Chancho Feliz, sipping sherry—a drink he detested—while he waited for Thomas.

The two had not seen each other since they had returned from visiting the marchioness. They had been accustomed to meeting daily, but lately Phillip had been avoiding Thomas, figuring if he wasn't around him, he couldn't spy on him.

Thomas had sent a hasty note arranging for the two to meet today, saying that he had something urgent to discuss. Phillip could not very well refuse. He was uneasy at the prospect of seeing Thomas, wondering if he had somehow discovered the truth. Phillip didn't know if he dreaded such an outcome or secretly longed for it.

He could not decide upon a course of action. He had been arguing with himself about this since he realized that he was conflicted about spying on Thomas. At first Phillip thought he would carry on with his mission. Sir Henry Wallace was also his friend, had been a loyal friend for many years, and Phillip didn't want to disappoint him. He argued that Henry had a duty to perform: He was a patriot, fighting to save the country he loved.

But then Phillip would argue that he also had a duty to his country, and that duty was to the true and rightful king, which as far as he could tell was Thomas. Perhaps worst of all, Phillip had a duty to himself. His actions were reprehensible, dishonorable, unworthy of a gentleman.

"But then what do I do?" Phillip would ask himself. "Go skulking back to Freya? Hand myself over to the Estaran authorities? Throw myself in the Breath?"

The internal conflict would generally end with him swearing and lying awake most of the night, staring at the ceiling.

Phillip whiled away the time this afternoon by reading an outdated copy of the *Haever Gazette*. He had arranged for the newspaper to be delivered to him. Since he was a Freyan, no one would consider this suspicious. The newspapers usually arrived with the mail about two weeks late.

This paper contained news about the rioting over the dragons in Haever. Phillip read the queen's speech to the House of Nobles and how the House had passed a bill to support Her Majesty in the matter of the dragons. He frowned over the anonymous letters discussing the prophecy and foretelling the return of the true king and shook his head at the lurid illustration depicting the Evil One riding a dragon landing on the palace grounds.

He smiled to read a small paragraph on the society page:

> *We announce with much pleasure the arrival of a little daughter at the home of Sir Henry and Lady Ann Wallace. We understand that Her Ladyship and daughter are doing nicely and we offer them our hearty congratulations.*

While Phillip was reading, he was also listening to the conversation of several young officers in the tavern, hoping to glean information.

Not surprising, most of their talk involved women and horses, with a great deal of boasting about the merits of both. Today, however, they were talking about King Ullr of Guundar and his "protection" of Braffa, a move that had angered the Estarans as much as it had angered Henry. King Miguel of Estara had worked extremely hard to "protect" Braffa himself and he was outraged at the betrayal.

"Mark my words," Hugo was predicting. "Our next war will be with Guundar."

"Can't come soon enough," said several others, and they drank a toast: "Confusion to Guundar!"

The clocks in the church towers chimed four. Thomas was late by half an hour, which was unusual. Phillip had just taken another sip of sherry when someone jostled his elbow, causing him to spill sherry on his uniform.

"What the—" Phillip looked up to see Thomas.

"Damn!" Thomas said contritely. "I'm so sorry, Pip. I'm clumsy today. Now you'll have to go change."

Phillip was about to say the stain wasn't bad and he didn't need to bother when he saw Thomas wink at him.

"I'll come with you," Thomas offered, adding in a low voice, "We need to talk."

Phillip paid his bill and the two left the tavern. Thomas walked at his side, telling him about a ball he had attended the previous night.

"You should have been there, Pip. I met my future wife," Thomas said offhandedly.

"What?" Phillip was so startled he didn't watch where he was going and stepped in a puddle, completing the ruin of his trousers. "You met the princess? Is the marriage all arranged?"

"Just about. The princess traveled to Estara with the Countess de Marjolaine, who is handling the negotiations. My mother had reservations regarding her. It seems that the Princess Sophia is quite intelligent. She attends university. She is a magical savant and has even written a thesis on something to do with contramagic. My mother does not approve of educated women, but she has concluded that once the princess is married with children in the offing, she will put such nonsense out of her head."

"My dear fellow, you astound me!" said Phillip. "Never mind your mother! You met this young woman, danced with her. What is she like?"

"I could do worse," said Thomas. "The princess is pretty in a pale, nondescript way. She dances well and knows the proper bons mots that enliven the rigors of a quadrille. She is fond of dogs and owns a spaniel named Bandit. She did not say anything too intelligent, for which I was grateful, for then I would have had to dazzle her with my own intelligence."

"You damn her with faint praise," said Phillip.

"Do I?" Thomas asked, smiling. "I don't mean to. She is really a very nice girl. It's just . . ." He fell silent.

"You're not madly in love with her," said Phillip. "But how do you know you could not love her? You have met her only once and that was at a ball. People are never themselves at balls."

"True. And, as I said, I could do worse for a wife," said Thomas, shrugging. "Where were you last night?"

"Believe it or not, I was studying," said Phillip. "The Blackfire War. The Estaran historians have a unique view of it. And might I point out that this is *not* the way to my hall."

"That is because we are not going to your hall," said Thomas.

He led the way through the iron gates of a cemetery. As the two walked among the tombstones, Thomas glanced around to make certain no one was in earshot, then said, "I have just come from a meeting with the secretary of the navy."

Phillip raised an eyebrow. "You are in the army."

"I served in the navy before going into the army. I am supposed to become familiar with all aspects of military science. But that's not what I want to talk about. You have heard about the crystals known as the Tears of God."

"I know a little about them," Phillip replied cautiously, not wanting to reveal too much until he knew what was going on. "The crystals are produced at the Braffan refineries. They act like liquid Breath and keep ships flying."

"*One* crystal can replace six lift tanks filled with liquid Breath," said Thomas. "A warship can fly for months on a single crystal."

"Oh, come now," said Phillip. "I know better than that."

"Well, perhaps I do exaggerate," said Thomas. "Maybe a dozen crystals are required. The fact remains that the crystals are of immense value."

"What of it?" Phillip asked. "The last I heard, all the crystals were destroyed by the Bottom Dwellers when they captured the refineries."

"The Braffans and King Ullr would have us *believe* they were destroyed," said Thomas.

"Some still exist?" Phillip asked.

Thomas paused to glance again around the cemetery. Three elderly women dressed all in black had entered and were placing flowers on a fresh grave.

"Come over here," said Thomas.

He and Phillip walked along a path and ducked beneath the swaying branches of a willow.

"An agent in Guundar reported that when the Braffans were rebuilding one of the refineries, they discovered five barrels of crystals that had been stored in an underground bunker. King Ullr has laid claim to the crystals. He plans to have them transported to Guundar for 'safekeeping.' "

"Whereas the Lord of the Admiralty believes the crystals would be far safer here in Estara," said Phillip wryly.

Thomas grinned. "The Braffans are planning to smuggle the barrels out of the refinery on board a ferry. His Lordship has asked for two volunteers to seize the ferry and take possession of the crystals to keep them safe. I immediately volunteered myself and I said I had a trusted friend who would join me—His Grace the Duke of Upper and Lower Milton."

Phillip didn't know how to respond. The word "trusted" made him cringe. He felt like crawling into one of the graves to join the other worms. He loved the idea of joining Thomas on what promised to be a dangerous and exciting mission, but he also knew that he was duty-bound to immediately inform Sir Henry. And he knew that whatever he decided, he couldn't in good conscience allow Thomas to keep on thinking he could trust the man who was betraying him.

Phillip stood in irresolute silence long enough for Thomas to take note. His manner grew cool. "If I misjudged you, Pip, I understand . . ."

Phillip needed a reason to explain his silence and he said the first thing that came into his head.

"I want to go," he said. "I think it would be great fun. But why are you working for the Estarans, Tom? You are not their king. You should take the crystals for yourself."

Thomas looked so amazed at this suggestion that Phillip had to smile.

"For myself!" Thomas repeated. "Why would I want them?"

"To transport your army," Phillip explained. The more he thought about it, the more his offhand suggestion made sense. "The troop carriers would need to be refitted to make use of the crystals instead of liquid Breath, but I suppose this could be done without a great deal of trouble or expense."

"If I go to Freya, it won't be at the head of an invading army!" Thomas said, frowning.

"Of course not," Phillip hastened to reassure him. "But from what I know of Hugh, King Godfrey's bastard son, not to mention the queen's Rosian sister, you would be well advised to make it known from the outset that you are serious about taking your rightful place on the throne."

"I am an officer in the Estaran army," said Thomas. "I have taken an oath of allegiance."

"You are a Freyan prince thinking of the welfare of your people," Phillip argued. "We Freyans are your people, Tom. Not the Estarans."

Phillip had not intended his words to sound quite so earnest and sincere; he was beginning to think he meant them.

"I never thought of it that way," Thomas said, struck by his argument.

Phillip did some quick calculating. "You wouldn't have to steal *all* the crystals. You have about two thousand troops, plus equipment. That means twelve transports. Now figure one or two crystals per transport and you need only twenty-four crystals. We could always say a barrel broke open and the crystals spilled. If a few crystals end up in our pockets, no one will notice."

Thomas said nothing, but he seemed intrigued.

"King Miguel is your mother's cousin," Phillip continued, making this up as he went along. "He backs your cause because he wants a strong ally when you become king. I do not think he would begrudge you a few crystals."

He had said the last in a lighthearted tone and he expected Thomas to laugh. Instead, Thomas regarded him intently, his gaze troubled.

"My people," Thomas repeated. "You said I have a duty to my people."

"Well, yes," Phillip conceded. "But I didn't mean—"

"I know what you meant," said Thomas, cutting him off. His expression darkened. "I have a duty to my people to be king. And you are right. I am failing them."

Phillip was uneasy. "Tom, I never said that—"

"Hear me out, please, Pip," said Thomas earnestly. "Because of our discussions, I have been doing some serious thinking about the role of a monarch."

Phillip knew this from his eavesdropping, but he couldn't let on. He therefore looked amazed.

Thomas gave a faint smile. "Astounding that I should have a serious thought in my head, isn't it? What you said about King Miguel and what he wants made me realize something. All these people—from my mother to these so-called Faithful—who conspire to put a crown on my head want something. And do you know what that is? They want me to sit on my throne like a good boy and keep my mouth shut."

Phillip tried to placate him. "Tom, I don't think—"

"Take these blasted crystals," Thomas continued, his anger growing. "The Lord of the Estaran Admiralty wants me to risk my life for *his* navy. King Miguel doesn't want an ally. He wants a puppet. My father wants me to advance his cause to rule Bheldem. Captain Smythe wants me to keep out of his way. The Rosians want me to marry their princess and my mother wants to rule Freya. Tell me I am wrong."

"Tom, it is not my place to tell you anything," Phillip said, embarrassed, although he had seen and heard enough to know that these statements were undoubtedly true.

"You have already told me what I needed to hear—that James wasn't a very good king," said Thomas. "I have been reading up on my unhappy ancestor. The poor man let people twist him and turn him until he didn't know if he was on his head or his heels. By the time he realized others were in essence wearing his crown, he didn't have the strength or the courage to take it back."

"So you are going to keep the crown," said Phillip, smiling. "And say the hell with all of them."

"I must let them all know that when I am king, I will *be* king," said Thomas. "I am going to astonish my mother and my father and Captain Smythe. We will steal the crystals, by God, and I will keep them—all of them!"

Phillip was caught up in the enthusiasm, caught up in his own admiration, caught up by destiny.

"By God, we will!" he vowed.

"Excellent!" said Thomas, clasping his friend by the hand. "We have time only to pack a change of clothes and load our pistols. We leave this night for Braffa."

As they left the cemetery, politely doffing their hats to the three elderly women in black, Phillip understood that, cost him what it would, he had made his choice.

He also understood the cost would be dear.

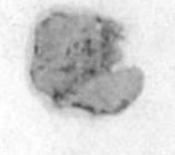

TWENTY-FIVE

Kate and Dalgren flew to the Braffan coastal city of Port Vrijheid, a journey that took them several days. Dalgren had never been to Braffa, but he was pleased when Kate assured him that he didn't have to hide. The Braffans were tolerant of dragons visiting their islands. The Dragon Brigade had helped to drive the Bottom Dwellers from the Braffan refineries and the Braffans remained grateful.

Dalgren took up residence on top of a cliff, much to the ire of a pair of eagles, who had their nest on a mountain peak only a few miles from the dragon. Generally dragons did not like sleeping out in the open, but since Braffa had no suitable caves and the visit was going to be short, Dalgren made do with what he could find.

While he was resting from his long flight, Kate arranged a meeting with Henry's agent. Following his orders, she left a nosegay of violets on a certain grave in an old cemetery. The next day she returned early in the morning and found a single rose on the grave with a note twisted around the stem. The note read: *16 Threadneedle Street, quarter past the hour of four of the clock in the afternoon.*

Ask for Mrs. Lavender, read the note. *You want a hat with a red bird's wing.* Since the meeting was in the afternoon, she had time to go down to the harbor where the ferries docked. She needed to inspect them, learn how they handled, what routes they sailed, and find out if anyone knew anything about barrels of crystals.

Acting on her instructions, Mr. Sloan had procured, among other things, a well-worn black dress, threadbare black cloak, and bonnet, as well as clothes for a fashionable young lady. Kate was not Morgan's daughter for nothing.

This morning, dressed in her widow's weeds, Kate went from ferry to ferry, presenting herself as a grieving young widow hoping to find work to support herself now that her husband was gone.

Ferry owners were kind to her, although they were sorry to tell her they were not hiring. Midday was approaching and Kate was beginning to think her ploy was not going to work, when she was hailed by an older woman who came running up behind her.

"I couldn't help but overhear you saying your good man died in the war, dearie," said the woman. "I lost my own Hans to them fiends. I run the ferry now that he's gone. You poor thing. You look bone-tired. I can't give you work, but I can give you a cup of tea."

The woman invited Kate on board her ferry. They shed a few tears over their lost husbands, then cheered up and drank their tea. Kate said she had grown up on ships and started asking questions about her host's work. The woman was glad to explain.

The Braffan ferries were owned and operated by the individual refinery owners, who used them to transport workers and supplies between the Braffan mainland and the islands where the refineries were located.

The ferries were wide, flat-bottomed boats that could be as small as thirty feet long or as large as eighty. Simple in design, each ferry was equipped with a mainmast, a mizzenmast, a small balloon, and one or two lift tanks, depending on the size of the vessel. A small fore wing and a larger aft wing were mounted on the hull, with airscrews located beneath the wings.

Rows of bench seats for the passengers took up about a third of the deck, with the remainder used for cargo. The helm was located at the front. Since the journey to the islands was short and the Braffan climate generally mild, the refinery owners made little provision for the comfort of their passengers, whose seats were in the open air, as was the helm.

Larger ferries required a crew of two to operate them, with one person at the helm and the other to handle the sails. Smaller ferries could be operated by a single person, such as the woman who had befriended Kate.

By the time Kate left, she had the name of a sailmaker who was hiring seamstresses, and a working knowledge of how to operate a ferry.

Kate hurried back to her lodgings to change clothes. She had been told that Threadneedle Street was in a fashionable part of the city, and thus the destitute young widow had to transform into a smart young woman of independent means. She wore a white blouse and a wine-colored waistcoat, a long skirt and a lacy petticoat. Over these she wore a wine-colored jacket, severely tailored with a slim waist.

She tucked a corset pistol in a reticule on loan from Amelia, pinned her blond curls into a bun, topped them with a small, plain hat, and set out for the address given to her in the note.

Kate had attended clandestine meetings before and was therefore looking for a man wearing a false beard in a church, or perhaps a cemetery or an alley. She was thus considerably startled when 16 Threadneedle Street turned out to be "Mrs. Lavender's Chapeaux: Hats for the Discerning Woman." Kate frowned at the sign and reread the note, thinking she must have mistaken the number. She had not. She was apparently meeting Sir Henry's agent in a milliner's shop, and there was apparently a real Mrs. Lavender.

Afraid of being late, Kate had arrived far too early, and she was forced to find some way to pass the time until the appointed hour. Threadneedle Street was, as the name implied, home to tailor shops, dry goods stores, bootmakers, milliners, and dressmakers. The sidewalks were crowded with well-dressed ladies and gentlemen of the local gentry, accompanied by their servants burdened with their employers' parcels.

Kate strolled up and down the street, trying to remember to take small, mincing, ladylike steps, although she was certain everyone could tell she was nothing but a jackdaw in borrowed plumage. She tried to avoid drawing attention to herself by perusing the storefront windows, all the while keeping surreptitious watch on the milliner's shop, seeing who came and went. Noting the well-dressed women going inside, Kate swore beneath her breath. She would have been far more comfortable meeting the agent in a dark alley at midnight.

When the clock struck the quarter hour, Kate drew in a breath, hesitated for a moment on the sidewalk, then opened the shop door and boldly walked in. A small silver bell attached to the door discreetly announced her entry. Kate paused, looking around in bewilderment, not knowing what to do.

She had never been in a hat shop, and she stared in amazement. The shop was filled with hats of all colors, sizes, shapes, and styles, decorated with all manner of flowers, frills, and feathers. The faint breeze created by her entry fluttered the ribbons and stirred the feathers, making the hats seem as though they were living things.

The shop was quiet after the bustle in the street; the air bore a perfumed scent. When two women holding hatboxes left shortly after Kate entered, she had to step to one side to give them room, and nearly knocked over a hatstand. A young woman in a subdued gray dress hurried to save her hats from destruction and to ask Kate if she could help her.

"I am here to see Mrs. Lavender," Kate said.

The shopgirl nodded and vanished into a back room. Kate could only wait. She had no idea what to expect. A woman in her middle years, stout and dressed in black, emerged from a room in back and walked up to Kate.

"I am Mrs. Lavender, the proprietor," said the woman. "How may I help you, madame?"

"I am looking for a hat with a red bird's wing," said Kate.

"Madame will be pleased to know our winter hats have just arrived," said Mrs. Lavender. "Pray come with me and take a seat."

She gestured to one of three dressing tables tucked away in the back. Kate sat down, feeling nervous. She had mentioned the red bird's wing, as the note had told her. Kate could see Mrs. Lavender's reflection in the glass and she watched her disappear into the back room. Wondering who or what might be lurking back there, she stealthily opened the reticule and touched the corset pistol to reassure herself.

Mrs. Lavender returned alone, however, carrying nothing more sinister than a white hat adorned with red ribbon, red flowers, and the wing of a cardinal.

"I presume Madame would like to try on the hat," Mrs. Lavender said.

"Yes, please," Kate murmured, not knowing what else to do.

Kate removed her own hat, now wishing she had taken more care with her appearance. Mrs. Lavender's silver-gray hair was beautifully coiffed, whereas Kate had pinned her blond curls together in an untidy bun. She sat in front of the mirror, feeling silly, as Mrs. Lavender carefully placed the hat on her head, tied the ribbon under Kate's chin, and stepped back with her head cocked to one side to admire the effect.

"Madame looks charming."

Kate thought she looked ridiculous and tried very hard not to laugh. "I . . . uh . . . don't think so."

"I understand. Madame prefers something more simple and elegant. In green, I think." Mrs. Lavender leaned down to untie the ribbon. As she did so, she said in a low voice, "The name of the ferry is the *Elisha Jones,* leaving from the Midtown Docks at three of the clock tomorrow afternoon."

Kate started, blinked, and stared.

Mrs. Lavender merely smiled, plucked the hat from Kate's head, and disappeared into the back room. A moment later the bell rang, two more customers entered, and the shopgirl went to wait on them. Mrs. Lavender returned with a simple dark green hat trimmed with a darker green ribbon and a hint of white feather.

"With her beautiful brown eyes, green is the proper color for Madame," said Mrs. Lavender. "Begging Madame's pardon, but she should never wear wine. The color washes out Madame's lovely complexion."

The two other women in the shop were laughing shrilly as they circulated among the hats. Mrs. Lavender deftly removed the pins from Kate's hair and rearranged her curls about her face, completely altering her appearance.

Kate gazed at her reflection and was startled to see she looked almost pretty. Mrs. Lavender placed the hat on her head and Kate had to admit that the color green did suit her. She remembered the green silk dress packed away in her trunk. Morgan must have thought the color green looked well on her too.

"You are surprised to see me," Mrs. Lavender was saying, talking under cover of the shrill laughter from the other customers. "I am not your idea of a spy."

Kate flushed. "It's just . . . I didn't think . . . a hat shop . . ."

Mrs. Lavender smiled as she fussed with Kate's hair. "My cover is actually quite perfect. As I explained to Sir Henry, women chatter like magpies when they are trying on hats. I found out about the crystals from the wife of an oligarch exchanging gossip with the wife of a refinery owner."

Kate could understand that. "But how did you discover the name of the ferry? It isn't that I don't trust you, Mrs. Lavender, but this mission is of vital importance."

"A new hat for the young bride of a dockworker of my acquaintance. His wife has expensive taste. Do you have everything you need? Are you well armed? I have quite a lovely Travian double-barreled pistol with the latest targeting constructs."

"With a red bird's wing?" Kate asked slyly.

Mrs. Lavender smiled and said briskly, "If you find yourself in trouble, come to me, day or night. I live above the shop. Take the stairs round the back. Six taps on the window. Count to twenty. Then six more taps."

"Thank you, Mrs. Lavender," said Kate. "I hope that won't be necessary."

Taking off the hat, she gave it an admiring glance, then handed it back.

"I will put it in a box, Madame," said Mrs. Lavender.

"Oh, no! I can't accept it—" Kate began.

"My gift," said Mrs. Lavender. "The color is most becoming. Good luck. And if I may give you a hint . . ." She took hold of Kate's hands and held them to the light. "Next time you walk among the gentry, my dear, wear gloves. Your hands betray you. Women of quality have soft hands, not working hands."

Kate remembered her mother's hands—smooth and soft with pink nails and sparkling rings. She looked at her own hands: sunburned brown, rough, leathery. She hurriedly hid them in the folds of her skirt. Mrs. Lavender placed the hat in a box, shut the lid, and tied it with string.

"What you do is very dangerous, Mrs. Lavender," said Kate. "If you were caught . . ."

"They would hang me." Mrs. Lavender gave a pragmatic nod. "I have been a widow these past ten years, leading a very humdrum existence. I ran my shop, counted the day's receipts, drank my tea, and went to bed. I have lived in Braffa for years, but I was born in Freya and I am a Freyan at heart.

"One day, many years ago, I overheard two women talking and realized I had just found out important information that might help my country. My late husband was a civil servant attached to the Freyan embassy here in Braffa. I contacted one of his old friends and passed on my information. I thought nothing more of it until the day, a month later, Sir Henry Wallace walked into my shop and said my country needed me. I have worked for him ever since."

Mrs. Lavender handed Kate the hatbox. "My life is now so much more exciting and worth living. Good luck, my dear, and remember: six taps."

"Count to twenty and six more," Kate repeated. "I'll remember."

She bid Mrs. Lavender good-bye and left the shop, taking care to keep her hands out of sight as much as possible. She was laughing to herself, imagining what Dalgren would say when she told him he would have to carry a hatbox on his saddle, when she passed a meat pie street vendor and realized she had not eaten anything since breakfast and her stomach was protesting.

Stopping to buy a meat pie, Kate was astonished to see a familiar figure on the other side of the street, walking in the opposite direction.

"Pip?" Kate called. "Is that you?"

The man kept walking.

Kate took a closer look and realized she must have been mistaken. The man, wearing a tricorn, had the same distinctive shock of white-blond hair as Pip, but there the resemblance stopped. This man was wearing expensive clothes and he walked with an air of confidence, quite different from bumbling, clumsy Pip.

Still, he looked enough like her friend that she started to cross the street. Her way was momentarily blocked by a passing wagon and by the time the wagon had rolled on, the man had disappeared.

Kate shrugged. The sun was low in the sky. She was going to meet Dalgren in a field outside the city and she had several miles to walk before dark. Swinging her hatbox by the string, Kate put the incident out of her mind and continued on her way.

Thomas was looking into shopwindows, searching for his friend, who had unaccountably disappeared. Sighting him standing in a window, peering out into the street, Thomas glanced up at a sign hanging above the shop, bearing the gold mortar and pestle of an apothecary.

"Pip, here you are!" Thomas exclaimed, opening the door. "I had stopped to look for the address and the next thing I know, you had disappeared. Now I find you visiting the apothecary. Are you in desperate need of tincture of pennyroyal?"

Phillip shook his head. "Sorry. I thought I saw someone I knew and I didn't want her to see me."

"I take it by the pronoun you saw a woman. Do you know many women in Braffa?" Thomas asked, joining his friend. "Is she pretty? How did you meet her? Why didn't you say something?"

"Because I didn't want to have to answer a lot of damn fool questions," said Phillip, smiling.

"Is she still there?" Thomas asked, refusing to take the hint. He peered out the window.

"I don't see her. I must have been mistaken," said Phillip. "She was someone I knew in the Aligoes, so I have no idea what she would be doing here."

"You never told me you were in the Aligoes," said Thomas.

"I have never told you a lot of things," Phillip said in somber tones.

"You are being very mysterious," said Thomas. "Did this woman steal your heart?"

"Heavens, no!" Phillip replied, laughing. "This particular young woman was far more likely to steal my wallet."

He glanced at his watch. "We have ten minutes to reach the refinery offices before they close for the night."

"Good God, you are right!" Thomas said, frowning. "We must run for it."

The two young men dashed out the door and began walking at a rapid pace down one of the main streets of Port Vrijheid, dodging in and out of traffic.

"Are you sure this is the way?" Thomas demanded after he was nearly run down by a milk wagon.

"Yes. The offices are only a block from here," Phillip answered. "But they own several refineries. Do you know which one we want?"

"I have the name, as well as our credentials. Remember, we are fabulously wealthy Estaran noblemen planning to invest our respective fortunes in the refining of liquid Breath."

"Understood. And since we are prudent, fabulously wealthy young noblemen, we want to see for ourselves where our money is going," Phillip added.

Arriving at the office door, they stopped outside to straighten their hats and catch their breath. Thomas started to open the door.

"Wait! I just thought of something!" Phillip said, dragging him back. "Why did we choose this particular refinery? We can't very well tell them we came to steal their crystals."

"Damn! That's a good point," Thomas said, thinking.

"We could say we took a fancy to the name—as one does when betting on a horse." Phillip paused. "Why are you shaking your head? What is the name?"

"Refinery Number Two," said Thomas.

Both of them laughed.

"I guess we had better come up with something else," said Phillip.

TWENTY-SIX

Thomas and Phillip left Port Vrijheid late the next morning, traveling on one of the ferries. They had dressed with care in clothes that marked them as gentlemen of fortune and quality: knee-length coats in subdued colors, matching waistcoats, white shirts and cravats without frills, close-fitting breeches, and silk stockings.

"Our clothes say that we can afford the best tailors in Estara, while the absence of lace marks us as serious-minded investors," said Thomas.

He and Phillip were the only passengers on the ferry this morning. They strolled about the deck, taking particular note of where and how the cargo was stored and discussing their upcoming mission in low voices.

"So serious-minded that we have a brace of pistols concealed beneath our dull gray waistcoats, two pocket pistols in our dull gray jackets, and powder and shot in our satchels. I hope they don't search us," said Phillip.

"They would not dare," said Thomas. "To do so would be an unpardonable insult. We would be justified in packing up our imaginary money and leaving."

"I am not so certain that would deter them," said Phillip. "The owners quite obviously did not want us anywhere near Refinery Number Two. You note they kept trying to persuade us to visit Refinery Number One."

"Fortunately my lucky number is two," said Thomas, grinning. "In the end, their greed overcame their caution. I like the fact that they tried hard to forestall us. I believe it bodes well for our mission. Our information is accurate. We will find the crystals at Refinery Number Two."

"First we need to know how to operate a ferry," said Phillip. "I happened to get a look at the helm as we were boarding. Seems simple enough, though I doubt even the lucky number two will be able to procure us this particular ferry."

"I suppose one ferry works much like another," said Thomas, shrugging. "We need to find out details about the docking procedure."

"With particular emphasis on *un*docking," said Phillip.

As the ferry neared the island, the ferry operator prepared to lock on to the docking arm. The two wealthy young investors came over to the rail to watch with interest and asked all manner of questions. The operator, accustomed to investors, answered the questions with long-suffering patience.

"Why use a docking arm at all?" Thomas inquired. "Seems a lot of trouble. Why don't ships simply tether themselves to the dock in the usual manner?"

"To protect your investment, gentlemen," said the operator. "Liquid Breath is a valuable commodity. Every pirate that sails the Breath would be dropping in for a visit if the refineries made it easy for them to steal the goods. As it is, the tankers that haul the liquid Breath and the ferries that haul the workers are the only ships in the world specially designed to clamp on to the docking arm."

Thomas and Phillip inspected the arm with interest. Consisting of three long sections of brass-bound timber connected with multiple, jointed "elbows," the docking arm ended in a large iron clamp. The operator explained that the arm could be extended or retracted by means of a series of pulleys threaded with heavy ropes, run by a motor powered by magic, much like the motors on ships that powered the airscrews.

They watched, fascinated, to see the arm reach out, grab the ferry, and haul it in to the dock.

"How does that clamp release?" Thomas asked, craning his neck to gaze upward.

"Simplicity itself, sir," the operator replied. "The large braided rope that runs through the final pulley connects to internal gears on the clamp, creating pressure that causes the clamp to either tighten or release. When the ferry is secured, the dockmaster retracts the arm and pulls the ferry to the dock where it can be tied down. When the ferry is ready to depart, the dockmaster casts off the line, extends the arm, and releases the clamp. A marvel of magical engineering, wouldn't you agree, gentlemen?"

"Wholeheartedly," said Thomas.

He and Phillip bid the operator good-bye and thanked him for his help. They were met on the dock by a man who introduced himself as Master Norgaard, one of the crafters in charge of the refining process. They introduced themselves to Master Norgaard and shook hands.

Phillip nudged Thomas in the ribs and cast a significant glance at the empty dock. Not a barrel in sight.

"The tour will not take long," Master Norgaard was saying. "We should have you off our little rock in an hour."

"Do not rush on our account," said Thomas with a pleasant smile. "We plan to remain here all day. We want to hear every detail."

Master Norgaard frowned. "I am sorry, gentlemen, but we are extremely busy, trying to ramp up production. I don't have all day to spend with you."

"That's a pity," said Phillip coolly. "I, for one, am not willing to invest a thousand golden Estaran rajos after only a measly hour tour."

Master Norgaard opened his eyes very wide. "A thousand rajos?"

"I am investing two thousand," said Thomas.

The master crafter suddenly became extremely accommodating. "Have no fear, gentlemen. We will spend all the time you need."

Master Norgaard walked off and Phillip and Thomas fell in behind him. Taking them at their word, Master Norgaard apparently intended to march them over every inch of the "little rock," starting with a large stone building in the middle of the island.

"This is the dormitory where the workers eat and sleep," said Master Norgaard. "We work fourteen-day shifts, then off for seven."

Thomas insisted on seeing everything in the dormitory, including the kitchen. He even stepped inside the storage closet to look around. He was interested to find among the brooms and dustbins, five barrels marked "ALE" in large black letters lined up by the door.

"Drink a lot of ale, do you?" Thomas asked.

"Those are empty, sir," Master Norgaard explained. "They go back this afternoon to be refilled. We do drink a lot of ale, stuck here on this rock. Now, gentlemen, if you have seen all you need to see to see of the dormitory, we will move on to the refining process."

Thomas cast Phillip a glance.

Phillip understood and, latching on to Master Norgaard, hauled him away, asking him a question about the infirmary. Left behind, Thomas gave one of the barrels a kick, smiled, and hurried to catch up.

"You will be astonished to hear the barrels are *not* empty," Thomas whispered to his friend. Aloud he said, "Before we move on to refining, Master Norgaard, I should like to inspect those gun emplacements."

"They are only gun emplacements," said Master Norgaard.

"Nonetheless . . ." said Thomas.

Master Norgaard rolled his eyes, but he took them over to one of the gun emplacements, which were located at strategic points around the island.

"They were destroyed during the war and had to be rebuilt," he told them. "We have only just completed the work."

"The guns are quite impressive, but where are the gun crews?" Thomas asked. "I want to know my investment will be protected."

"Since the arrival of the Guundaran navy, we have no fear of being attacked, sir," said Master Norgaard. "The gun crews have other duties in the refinery. If the alarm is sounded, the gun crews can reach their stations in a matter of moments. And now, if you will follow me . . ."

He walked off. Thomas and Phillip lagged behind.

"Two of those cannons cover the ferry channel," Phillip whispered.

"By the time the crews reach their guns, load them, and run them out, we will be long gone," Thomas returned.

Master Norgaard took them next to a large floating raft tethered to the island. He pointed out the enormous tubes that snaked down to reach a pocket of pure, liquefied Breath far below the island.

"As far as anyone knows, these pockets are the only source of pure, liquefied Breath in the world," said Master Norgaard proudly. "People have searched for years, but no one has ever located another area where this natural phenomenon exists. And now, I will take you for a closer view of the tanks where the liquid is stored."

Phillip stifled a yawn. Thomas stood staring at the pumps, watching them suck up the cold liquid and dump it into two large round vats.

"They might as well be pumping liquid gold. And now that King Ullr has his grubby hands on it, he means to rule us all by holding the liquid hostage," Thomas muttered. "He can demand outrageous sums of money and governments will pay it."

"I've heard talk Estara might go to war with Guundar," said Phillip.

"No one wants another war," said Thomas. "As King Ullr knows all too well."

He and Phillip strolled over to join Master Norgaard, who was waiting for them beside an enormous tank. They took their time, not bothering to hurry.

"Didn't the Freyans try to gain some sort of influence over the Braffans before the war?" Thomas asked. "I believe I heard my mother talking about it. An old enemy of hers—Sir Henry Wallace. She calls him the queen's spymaster. Do you know him?"

"I think I may have met him at court," said Phillip with a shrug.

"I was just wondering what he was like. According to my mother, he has horns and carries a pitchfork," said Thomas. "Though I rather wish now he had succeeded with Braffa."

"When you are king, you can fund an expedition to discover liquid Breath," said Phillip.

"By God, I will!" said Thomas.

Master Norgaard provided them with a close view of the tanks and the enormous, several-stories-high glass vats where the Breath was distilled. He then gave them a lengthy and involved explanation regarding magic and the distillation process.

Thomas worked to look interested, and kept an eye on the dock. Thus far, it was empty. No sign of the barrels. He was starting to grow worried, and then, at about two of the clock, workmen emerged from the storage room, hauling the six barrels marked "ALE." They began to load the barrels into a wagon.

Thomas nudged Phillip in the ribs.

"I see them. Quit staring!" Phillip whispered.

"Our ferry should be arriving shortly," Thomas whispered back.

Master Norgaard paused in his lecture. "Did you say something, sir?"

"Just wondering about lunch," said Phillip.

"We were hoping it would arrive shortly," Thomas added.

"After a tour of the laboratory," said Master Norgaard.

He led the way to a series of what appeared to be sheds.

"Laboratory!" Phillip groaned. "Whose idea was it to take this bloody tour?"

"Yours, I believe," said Thomas.

"Well, I deeply regret it," said Phillip.

Thomas grinned and out of the corner of his eye watched the wagon carrying the barrels slowly move toward the dock.

TWENTY-SEVEN

Kate sat in the saddle on Dalgren's back, her spyglass to her eye, keeping watch on a narrow ship channel that wound its way among the Braffan islands. Dalgren, his wings barely moving, hovered just above the treetops to avoid being seen.

Back in the Aligoes, he could have remained hidden in the silken mists. In Braffa, the islands appeared to float on a cloud of yellowish gray fog spreading beneath them like a woolly blanket. Above the fog, the air was cold and clear, a natural phenomenon that, like the pockets of liquid Breath, occurred only in this part of the world. No one could say exactly why. The predominant theory was that the change in the Breath was due to higher water content.

Kate's destination—Refinery Number Two—was several miles away. She would have liked to fly over it to reconnoiter, but she and Dalgren had decided the risk of being seen was too great. The sky was clear with only a few thin clouds. And while dragons might be tolerated on Braffa, a dragon spotted flying over a refinery would have been cause for alarm, especially on the day when barrels filled with crystals were to be transported.

Kate counted on the fact that the island on which Refinery Number Two was located would be easy to find, for it was larger than the other islands surrounding it. The refinery was built on the southern end of the island. Unlike the northern end of the island, which was heavily forested, the southern end had been cleared of vegetation.

And Kate didn't really need to see the refinery to know the location of all the buildings and, most important, the gun emplacements. She had pored over the map Sir Henry had provided her, studying it so long and intently she could see the refinery imprinted on the backs of her eyelids.

She would only need to know the layout if something went wrong and she ended up a prisoner, or if the refinery workers grew suspicious and started shooting at her. Kate had learned from her father's unfortunate example that no matter how confident you were in a plan, you always needed to have a way out.

Her plan was simple. She would seize the ferry, arrive at the refinery, load the cargo, sail to the rendezvous with Captain Northrop.

Once again, her idea was to blame this on the Rosians, leaving Sir Henry able to protest Freyan innocence.

"I see the ferry," reported Dalgren, whose eyesight was far keener than hers. "Near that rock shaped like a potato."

"Is it the one we want?" Kate asked.

"It's the only ferry we've seen in an hour," Dalgren returned. "So it better be the one we want. Black and green stripes and a green-and-black-striped balloon."

"That's it," said Kate.

She again raised her spyglass and soon located the *Elisha Jones,* the ferry that was supposed to be picking up the crystals. The boat had all sails set and was chugging along at a good rate of speed.

The operator was coming up on a cluster of islands the locals called the Snake. Here the channel narrowed and began twisting and turning in on itself. Kate had determined that the Snake would be an ideal place for her ambush. The ferry would have to slow its speed to navigate the turns, while thick foliage on the islands would conceal her movements from another ship or ferry, if any happened to be in the vicinity.

Kate did a quick sweep, looking for such other vessels, thinking she might see the Guundaran ship that was waiting to take on the crystals or perhaps even the *Terrapin,* where she was to meet up with Captain Northrop. No other ships were in view, however, not even other ferries.

As Dalgren had said, the *Elisha Jones* was the first they had seen in an hour. Kate wondered if the other ferry operators had been ordered to remain in port as an extra measure of security.

She waited until the ferry was in the middle of the Snake, then told Dalgren to start his pursuit. The dragon skimmed above the trees, flying so close his belly brushed the topmost branches. Kate lost sight of the ferry among the foliage, but Dalgren had eyes on it, apparently, for he held unerringly to his course, approaching the ferry from the rear.

Kate checked her pistols. She had brought two with her, tucked in the broad black belt around her waist, and had a large knife in her boot. She was wearing her slops, a man's calico shirt, and a leather vest. She had tied a bright red kerchief around her head and hung a bosun's whistle around her neck.

The red kerchief and the whistle were for Dalgren's benefit. Kate needed him nearby in case there was trouble, but he had to remain out of sight. He could not hide in the mists of the Breath, since there weren't any. He would have to fly below the thick yellowish fog, keeping watch on the ferry that would be sailing above him. They had experimented, with Dalgren diving into the fog and Kate standing on shore, watching.

Dalgren had returned a few moments later, flying out of the fog, causing it to swirl about his wings in whorls and eddies.

"Could you see me?" he had asked.

"Not a scale," Kate had reported.

"Good! Because I can't fly lower. The Breath is as dark as a cave down there and far colder," Dalgren had grumbled. "I think ice was starting to coat my wings."

"What could *you* see?" Kate asked. "Anything?"

"The mists are thinner at the top, so that, looking up into the sunlight, I could dimly make you out," Dalgren had said. "You need to wear something bright-colored and bring the whistle."

Kate tucked her curls beneath the kerchief. Looking down at her clothes, she was reassured to see the faint traces of the protective magical constructs inscribed on the fabric. The constructs would not stop a bullet or a blade, but the magic would mitigate the effects. Mr. Sloan had recommended a crafter who specialized in such work and, thanks to Sir Henry, Kate could afford to have such work done.

She tossed down the rope ladder and tested it to make certain it was firmly attached to the saddle, then with a pat on Dalgren's neck indicated to him that she was ready.

Dalgren emerged from the trees and flew into the channel. He soared above the ferry, coming so close the wind from his passing caused the boat to rock as though it were caught in a wizard storm. His sudden appearance amazed the two people on board. Both stared, openmouthed, at the monstrous dragon that seemed to have materialized out of the fog.

Dalgren made one pass, then circled back around. This time, he hovered above the ferry.

"I can't go any lower!" he bellowed. "Not without slamming into the trees."

Kate patted him again and began to nimbly climb down the braided leather ladder attached to the saddle. The ladder was a recent acquisition, much easier and safer to use than shinnying down a rope as she had done during the attack on the *Pride of Haever.* Dalgren held as still as he could to keep the ladder from swinging. Kate observed the two men on deck. One was perhaps in his early forties, the other was in his teens, and she guessed by the similarity in looks that they were father and son. Thus far, both had been paralyzed with shock, but when she started to descend, the elder reached for something beneath the helm.

"He's got a pistol!" Kate shouted.

Dalgren snorted two gouts of flame from his nostrils. One missed and set the tops of several trees on fire. The other landed on the deck. The father laid down the pistol and ran to grab a bucket to put out the flames, while the son tried to beat out the fire with his jacket.

Kate let go of the ladder, dropped down onto the deck, and drew her pistol. She picked up the pistol the father had dropped, tucked it into her belt, and ran to the helm, for the ferry had started to veer off course and was in danger of running aground. The ferry was small, with only one lift tank and a single balloon. Kate touched the magical constructs on the helm that sent the magic flowing into the airscrews and brought the ferry back on course.

The two men had put out the flames and now stood with their hands raised. The father was grim, regarding her from beneath lowered brows. His son couldn't take his frightened eyes off Dalgren flying overhead, looking particularly menacing. The father said something and the son flushed and hurriedly tore his gaze from the dragon.

"Do either of you speak Rosian?" Kate asked, speaking Rosian.

Braffans tended to be multilingual, since they had dealings with nearly every nation in the world. The father hesitated just long enough to let Kate know he understood her question.

"Good," said Kate. "What is your name?"

The man clamped his lips together.

Kate sighed. "I have the pistol and I'm an excellent shot. I'll ask again. Your name, sir?"

"Elisha," said the father.

"I'm Joshua," the son added in a low voice.

"And you can call me Rose," said Kate. "I am a privateer, not a pirate, and I can assure you, sir, that neither my dragon friend nor I mean you any harm. So long as you cooperate, you and the boy will sleep peacefully in your beds this night."

"You and your dragon friend have gone to a lot of trouble to steal a ferryboat," said Elisha.

Kate smiled. "As you have probably guessed, I don't want your boat. I want the cargo you are going to pick up at Refinery Number Two."

"Then you've gone to a lot of trouble to steal empty ale barrels," said Elisha coolly.

Kate glanced down at a chart lying near the helm and raised an eyebrow.

"You speak very convincingly, sir, and I would almost believe you, except I see a location marked on this chart some twenty miles north of the refinery. I'm guessing this is where you are to supposed to meet up with a Guundaran warship to deliver those 'empty ale barrels.' "

"I'm picking up another load of cargo," Elisha said stubbornly.

"Not in the middle of the Breath, you're not," said Kate.

She had been watching the boy, and when she saw him cast an alarmed glance at his father, she knew her information was correct.

"Let's not waste any more time." Kate gestured with the pistol. "Sit down on that bench, both of you. Keep your hands where I can see them. This is what we are going to do. You, sir, will wrap this bandage around your knee. When we arrive at the refinery, you will tell the dockmaster that you injured your knee and can't walk and you brought me along, your wife's cousin, to help. Once the barrels are loaded onto the ferry, we will leave. We will make one stop to drop off the barrels. After that, you will never see me or my dragon friend again."

Elisha looked grim. "And what happens if I don't go along? You can't kill me. You need me. The refinery people won't hand over the barrels to a stranger."

"That's true," Kate agreed. "But in that case, a tragic accident would befall you. You would drop your pistol and it would go off. The bullet would strike you in the kneecap. You will survive, but the wound will be horribly painful and debilitating. You might well lose your leg."

"Do what she says, Pa," Joshua pleaded. "It's not worth it!"

"The owners put their trust in me . . ." Elisha said.

"And they betrayed that trust," said Kate. "How do you think I found out about the barrels and what is really inside them? Who knew the secret? And who did the talking? Not you or your son."

Elisha glowered at her, but he rested his hand on his son's shoulder and Kate judged he was at least considering her ultimatum. She had to decide what to do if he proved stubborn, and she steeled herself to carry out her threat.

Dalgren gave a warning hoot. Kate looked ahead to see the channel widening. The ferry was about to sail out of the Snake, which meant they were only a few miles from the refinery. Kate waved at Dalgren, letting him know everything was under control and he could go on ahead and get into position.

Dalgren nodded. Folding his wings close to his body, he dove down beneath the fog and disappeared.

Kate looked back at Elisha and and saw that he had apparently given up the fight, for he was binding his leg with the bandage. Kate gave an inward sigh of relief and used the pistol to gesture to the son.

"You take the helm, Joshua. I assume you can sail this boat?"

"I can sail the ferry through the channel," said boy. "But I've never docked it. Pa does that. He says it's too tricky for me to try yet."

Kate looked to the father for an explanation.

"The heat rising from the land and the vats can cause the wind to shift," said Elisha. "Requires an experienced hand at the helm to keep from crashing."

Kate guessed he was telling the truth. He had no reason to lie and every reason to protect himself and his son.

"I'll stay at the helm," she said. "Joshua, you be ready to help if I need you."

"Do you know what you're doing?" Elisha asked, glowering. "This boat is how I earn my bread."

"I once sailed a three-masted schooner through a cyclone," said Kate. "You sit there where I can keep an eye on you."

She brandished her pistol, then placed it on the shelf beneath the helm. "The hammer is cocked. Say or do anything I don't like and you may yet have that tragic accident."

Elisha gave a grim nod.

Kate steered the ferry toward the refinery. Dalgren, as planned, would hopefully be in place below the fog. He wouldn't be able to see much of what was going on from his vantage point, which was why Kate carried the bosun's whistle. She could summon him in an emergency.

The ferry sailed along the channel, and the refinery came into view. Kate knew what to expect. Each island had two docks—a smaller one to handle the ferries and the large dock for the tankers that hauled the liquid Breath.

Kate sailed toward the smaller of the two. She saw five barrels lined up on the dock, but she couldn't take time to examine them. She was watching the dockmaster. If he didn't feel comfortable, if he thought anything was wrong, he would refuse to extend the docking arm. Kate had a plan for such a contingency, but she hoped she didn't have to use it.

A flag flying from the top of one of the vats fluttered in the breeze, and

Kate could see that, as Elisha had warned, the wind was erratic. She made adjustments to reduce the lift and slowed to a crawl.

"Be ready with the lines," she told Joshua.

Thus far, she had been speaking in Rosian, but now she switched to Braffan. "And just in case you were thinking of tipping off your friends, Captain, you should know that I am fluent in your language as well. Now give the dockmaster a wave, let him know all is well."

Elisha raised his arm and shouted, "The *Elisha Jones* asking permission to dock!"

"I know who you are, Elisha," the dockmaster yelled back with a grin. "No need to be so formal."

He placed his hands on the controls. The motor whirred to life. The docking arm creaked and started to extend.

Kate steered the ferry to meet it.

TWENTY-EIGHT

Phillip and Thomas walked out of the laboratory, thankful to once more breathe fresh air. They stood blinking as their eyes adjusted to the bright summer sunshine. The moment he could see, Thomas looked at the dock. The barrels were lined up, ready for loading.

"What in God's name was making that awful smell?" Phillip grumbled. "I was glad we didn't eat lunch. What time is it?"

Thomas took out his pocket watch.

"Almost time to meet our ferry," he said in a low tone. "As a matter of fact, I think I see one nearing the dock."

"Thank God for some action!" Phillip said. "This day has lasted about a year so far. Should we casually start to stroll that direction? Where is Norgaard?"

"He stopped to talk to a friend," said Thomas. "No, wait. Damn! Here he comes . . ."

"Keep walking," said Phillip.

"Ah, Master Norgaard," Thomas said, half turning. "Our ferry is approaching and we must be shoving off. Thank you so much for your instructive tour."

The master crafter looked alarmed and hurried to catch up. "I fear you are mistaken, gentlemen. That ferry is not the one you take. It . . . uh . . . doesn't go back to the mainland, you see. It stops here, then goes on to the next refinery—"

"In that case, this would be an excellent opportunity to observe the workings of the docking arm," said Phillip.

"Splendid idea," said Thomas, and the two increased their pace.

"I assure you, gentlemen, you won't find it all that interesting," said Master Norgaard.

Thomas stopped and rounded on the man.

"Is there some reason you are trying to keep us from watching the ferry dock, Master Norgaard?"

"One would think you were trying to hide something," said Phillip.

"No, no, nothing like that, I assure you," said Master Norgaard. "I'll just come with you—"

"No need," Thomas said, smiling. "Go enjoy your lunch."

"We will join you in a moment," Phillip added.

Master Norgaard looked from them to the dock and the barrels, then back at them. He frowned, clearly wondering what was going on. He obviously didn't want them anywhere near the barrels.

"Thank you again," said Thomas, shaking hands. "We will make certain to mention your name when we speak to the owners."

"We dine with them tonight," said Phillip, shaking hands in turn.

He and Thomas walked toward the dock, leaving Master Norgaard to gaze after them.

"He suspects something. Is he watching us?" Thomas asked.

Phillip glanced cautiously over his shoulder. "Yes, but he's not coming after us. Uh-oh, there he goes. Heading toward the main office."

"He might be going to alert someone," said Thomas. "We need to hurry."

The two arrived in time to see the docking arm latch on to the ferry and start hauling it over to the dock, where men were standing by, ready to load the barrels. The foreman frowned as he saw Thomas and Phillip approach and ran toward them, waving them off.

"I'm sorry, gentlemen, but only workers are permitted in this area while the ferry is loading. Too dangerous."

"No worries!" Thomas said, stopping just short of the dock. "We are here merely to observe."

"Yes, carry on," said Phillip.

The foreman, shaking his head, went back to his duties.

"I can see three people on board the ferry," Thomas said in a low voice. "Two men and a boy. You cover the man on the bench and the boy. I'll take the man at the helm. When the clamp releases, we make our move."

"For king and country," said Phillip, with a glance at his friend.

"For king and country," Thomas repeated with a grin.

Kate stood at the helm of the *Elisha Jones*. Thus far, everything was going smoothly. She had maneuvered the ferry so that the docking cleat was in the correct position. Now she could only wait as the dockmaster hauled the ferry toward the dock.

Joshua stood by the starboard bulwark, ready to throw out the mooring line. The boy was terrified and kept casting nervous glances in her direction. Kate hoped that no one would notice, or if they did, that they would put it down to the unusual nature of this job.

Elisha sat on the bench, visiting back and forth with a couple of the dockworkers, explaining how he had injured his leg. When he introduced Kate, saying she was his wife's cousin, Kate smiled, but said nothing, concentrating on her work. Docking was a tricky maneuver and no one could blame her for not being sociable. She kept her hands on the brass panel, conscious of the pistol right underneath, and cast a surreptitious glance at the activity on the dock, looking for signs of possible trouble.

Four men stood near the barrels, ready to load them onto the ferry. Two men were handling the docking arm and conversing with Elisha. The dockmaster stood at the controls, manipulating the arm. The foreman strode up and down, keeping an eye on everything and giving orders.

As Kate watched, the foreman bore down on two well-dressed gentlemen who had strolled over to observe the proceedings. They apparently didn't belong here, because the foreman was shouting at them and waving his arms, telling them to back off. The two retreated to the end of the dock, then stood their ground. The foreman obviously didn't like it, but he didn't argue. Giving them a surly glance, he walked back over to talk to the dockmaster.

The two gentlemen clearly didn't belong; Kate studied them intently. Beyond the fact that they were gentry, she could learn little else. Their tricorns concealed their faces. They lounged at their ease in their fine clothes, appeared relaxed, and did not once look in the direction of the barrels. Kate took them as members of the bone-idle rich, here to visit a refinery as they might visit a menagerie, intent on observing the feeding habits of the working class. She had other worries and she dismissed them.

No one was guarding the crystals. Given their immense value, Kate had expected the barrels to be surrounded by men with pistols. As it was, no one was armed with so much as a billy club. Kate wondered uneasily if Elisha could have been telling her the truth, and she had gone to all this trouble, risked her life, to steal five empty barrels.

Kate licked her dry lips and wiped her sweaty palms on her slops. When she caught herself nervously shifting from one foot to the other, she forced herself to stand still.

The docking procedure was interminably slow. The docking arm creaked and rattled as it inched the ferry toward the dock. Kate had to resist the impulse to look over the side of the hull to see if she could catch a glimpse of Dalgren.

"He is there," she assured herself. "Ready to come to my aid. Ready to help me to steal five bloody, empty barrels."

Kate was sweltering, standing at the helm in the hot sun, and she took off the kerchief she had wrapped around her head and shook out her sweat-damp curls. She used the handkerchief to mop her neck and forehead. She could always have it to alert Dalgren.

Finally, after what seemed ages, the ferry docked. Joshua tossed the mooring cable to the waiting dockworkers. The clamp would remain attached to the cleat until the cargo had been loaded.

Joshua lowered the gangplank and the four men set to work, tipping the barrels onto their sides and then rolling them up the gangplank. The barrels appeared to contain something, for the men had to exert some effort to haul them on board. Kate was relieved and, to some extent, reassured.

Elisha directed where and how the barrels were to be stowed, so as to distribute the weight evenly about the small boat. Once the men had placed the last barrel to Elisha's satisfaction, they bid him have a safe journey and left the boat.

Joshua raised the gangplank. The dockmaster shouted that he was going to release the clamp. The workers stood by, ready to free the mooring cable, while Joshua waited at the rail to haul it in.

Kate watched the docking arm, holding her breath. The arm shuddered; the clamp opened like a hand and let go of the ferry. Free of the clamp, the ferry dropped down below the level of the dock and began to slowly drift away.

Kate stood at the helm, ready to send the magic to the airscrews when the ferry was clear of the dock. She was about to yell up to the workers, who were looking down at her, to cast off the line when she heard shouts coming from behind her. She turned, startled, to see the two well-dressed gentlemen racing across the dock toward the ferry.

Another man was running behind them, bellowing at the top of his lungs, "Stop them! They are here to steal the crystals!"

The workers began yelling and tried without success to catch the two gentlemen. No one had been paying any attention to them, and their sudden move had taken everyone by surprise, including Kate, who stared in amazement. Their intent was apparent. They were going to jump onto the moving ferry.

The boat continued to drift, widening the gap between the dock and the ferry. Anyone trying to leap down into the boat was risking either a deadly plunge into the Breath or breaking his neck.

The first did not hesitate. He made the jump and landed safely on his feet, lithe as a cat. The second was about to follow when the foreman grabbed him from behind. He whipped around, socked the foreman in the jaw, and then made an arm-flailing, heart-stopping leap for the deck. He came down hard. His friend was there to steady him.

"You all right?" asked his friend.

"I think so!" was the breathless reply.

"Good, carry on. You cover him. I'll take the helmsman."

The young man who had made the hard landing limped over to Elisha. Kate could see that he was holding a pistol. The other man walked up to her. He had lost his hat in his mad dash; his black curly hair had come loose, and straggled about his face. He glanced at Kate, started to say something, and then stopped, startled.

"You're a woman!"

She stared at him, and the first thought that came unbidden into her head was that he had the clearest, brightest, bluest eyes she had ever seen. The second thought was far less charitable. She had never been so angry.

"And you are a bloody fool!" Kate said through gritted teeth. "What the devil do you think you're doing?"

"My name is Thomas," he said, speaking Braffan with an Estaran accent. "And didn't you hear what they are shouting? My friend and I are here to steal the crystals."

"The hell you are!" Kate said, glowering.

The mooring cable was still attached. The dockworkers were lined up on the dock, yelling down at them, and seemed to be urging each other to jump onto the ferry to effect a rescue. No one appeared eager to do so, however.

Thomas opened his coat just enough for Kate to see the butt of a pistol. "Order them to cast off the mooring line."

"Go to hell!" said Kate.

Reaching beneath the helm, she grabbed hold of her own pistol, and raised it just enough that Thomas could see it was aimed at his heart. Holding him at gunpoint, she ran her other hand over the magical constructs on the brass helm, activated the airscrews, and sent magic to the lift tanks and the balloon.

The ferry began to rise and Kate steered toward the dock. She was thinking fast, trying desperately to salvage the shipwreck of her plan.

Thomas looked at the pistol, looked at her, and smiled. "You know what I think? I think you're here to steal the crystals, as well."

Kate glowered at him. "Maybe I am. If I hand you over, I'll be a hero. They will let me sail away with the crystals and they'll take you and your friend to prison."

The dockworkers were valiantly hauling the ferry back to shore, as the docking arm reached out for the cleat. Joshua stood at the rail, gaping at the two strangers. Elisha was grim-faced, certain this was not going to end well. The second young man, the one who had tumbled into the boat, was watching the ferry creep closer to shore.

"Uh, Thomas, we should—" The young man caught sight of Kate and stopped in midsentence. "Good God! It's you!"

She stared at him. "Pip?"

Thomas stared at both of them. "How do you know this woman? Who is she?" He looked back at Kate. "Who are you? What is going on?"

Kate kept the pistol aimed at Thomas. Taking the other from her belt, she aimed it at Phillip.

"This is what is going on," she said, speaking Freyan. "When we get close to the dock, you two are going to jump off. I'm sorry, Pip. This is business, not personal."

"Kate, let's talk—" Phillip began, but he didn't finish. His gaze shifted to a point over her shoulder, off the bow. His expression altered.

"Thomas! We have a problem."

Kate kept her pistols aimed at both of them. "If you think I'm going to fall for that old ruse . . ."

"Not a ruse, I'm afraid," said Thomas. "A ship's boat is headed this way, filled with marines. You can see for yourself."

Kate glanced over her shoulder. A contingent of armed marines wearing Guundaran uniforms and carrying muskets was sailing toward the ferry. The marines had mounted a swivel gun on the prow of their boat. Kate swore under her breath. The Braffans knew the Guundarans were patrolling the channel around the refinery. That was the reason no one on the dock had bothered to guard the crystals. She should have trusted her instincts.

The ferry was coming close to the dock, and the dockmaster was lowering the clamp. A Guundaran officer on board the pinnace must not have noticed anything was amiss, however, because he waved to them in a friendly manner.

"Hail the ferry!" he called in clumsy Braffan. "We have come to offer you safe escort!"

"What the—" Thomas was perplexed.

"They don't know anything's wrong!" Phillip said suddenly. "Look, Tom, the marines are seated, their muskets at their sides, not aimed at us."

"By God, you're right!" Thomas said. "No one will get hurt if we all keep calm—"

Elisha had no intention of keeping calm. Jumping to his feet, he began bellowing, "Soldiers! Run for it, boy!," and went lumbering across the deck. He grabbed hold of Joshua, heaved his son over the rail, and watched him land safely on the dock. He then cast a bitter glance at Kate, clambered over the rail, and dropped to the dock below.

"Now they know something is wrong," said Phillip.

The officer of the marines began issuing orders.

Kate didn't understand Guundaran, but there wasn't much doubt as to what he was saying. She could hear the sounds of the marines shuffling to their feet and picking up their muskets. The clamp on the docking arm was right above the cleat, opening, reaching for the ferry. Once Elisha told his story, she would be in as much trouble as these two.

"Damn and blast you!" Kate muttered, glaring at Thomas.

She hurriedly thrust her pistol into her belt, then flung her hands into the air and started to scream.

"Don't shoot!" she cried, shrill and hysterical. "Help! Please!"

As she was screaming, she shifted her gaze to look directly at an ax mounted on a bulwark. Thomas followed her line of sight, saw the ax, and immediately understood.

"On my signal, cut the line!" Kate said in a hissing whisper.

Thomas gave her a flashing smile, grabbed the ax, and dashed toward the mooring line. Kate kept one hand in the air and lowered the other to the helm.

"Now!" she shouted.

Thomas slammed the ax into the mooring cable, slicing through it with one blow.

Kate had both hands on the helm. She slid her fingers over the constructs, pressing down hard, flooding every part of the boat with magic that sparked along the leather wires, flowed over the lift tanks, and lit the balloon. As the airscrews whirred, the lift tank glowed a brilliant blue.

"Hang on!" she warned, gripping the helm. "This will be rough!"

Thomas grabbed hold of the rigging. Phillip threw his arms around the mast. The ferry soared into the air, carried rapidly aloft by wind and magic.

Below them, musket fire erupted. Balls whistled through the rigging, clattered on the deck, and smashed into the hull. Kate ducked as best she could, still keeping one hand on the helm. She caught hold of the bosun's whistle, put it to her lips, and blew three frantic blasts.

"I hope you are there, Dalgren!" Kate said softly. "I hope you are there!"

The marines fired again. She heard a thunk, and one of the airscrews clattered to a stop. The ferry lurched and began to list, causing two of the barrels stacked on the port side of the boat to topple over and go rolling across the deck straight toward Thomas, who was still hanging on to the rigging.

Thomas saw his peril and let go, flinging himself to one side, landing on his belly beneath the mast. The barrels rolled harmlessly past and smashed into the benches, where they broke apart, scattering ugly gray chunks of rock over the deck. Kate was crouched beneath the helm, using it for cover. She longed to look for Dalgren, but she didn't dare. He should have been here by now.

"Come on, Dalgren!" Kate urged. "Where are you?"

She braced herself for the next volley of gunfire, but it never came. Instead she heard an angry roar, followed by terrified screams.

"Thank God!" Kate whispered and ran to the rail.

The dragon burst out of the fog, fire flaring from his nostrils. The marines on board the pinnace were thrown into confusion. Some flung down their weapons, while others attempted to shift their aim to the dragon, only to collide with their fellows in the crowded pinnace. A few shots went off. Dalgren ignored them as a human ignores gnats. He roared again, sucked in a breath, and spat a jet of fire at the pinnace.

The helmsman ran for his life, as the helm burst into flame, disrupting the magical constructs. The lift tanks failed, the airscrews stopped. The pinnace crashed into the docking arm, spilling marines, and sending the dockworkers running for their lives.

Dalgren roared again and circled the refinery, glaring down menacingly, letting everyone know the fight was over. Kate put the bosun's pipe to her lips, to give the signal that she was safe, only to drop it.

The balloon had been hit and it was starting to sag, the chambered panels collapsing.

"Look out!" Kate cried.

Thomas was lying on the deck right beneath it. He looked up in time to see the balloon tear loose from its moorings and fall. He disappeared beneath a torrent of green silk and rope.

"Thomas!" Phillip cried, running to help.

"Get this off me!" Thomas shouted, his voice muffled by the silk.

Phillip started tugging at the remnants of the balloon, trying to drag the heavy folds off his friend.

"You could help me!" he yelled at Kate.

"Serves him right," she muttered.

She was making adjustments at the helm. The ferry could still sail, even without the balloon and missing an airscrew. She was increasing the flow of magic to the lift tank when she heard the loud hissing sound.

Kate had sailed on ships since she was a little girl. She knew what the sound meant. She had no need to look.

Putting the bosun's pipe to her lips, she blew three long blasts and two short.

Dalgren would understand the signal. One word.

"Sinking."

TWENTY-NINE

Kate could hear Thomas thrashing about beneath the silk and swearing, and she smiled. If he had breath enough to swear, he must not be badly injured. She hurried over to inspect the lift tank, to see how badly it was damaged. She had to kick aside some of the crystals that had spilled from the broken barrels and thought bitterly that she might as well have been kicking aside diamonds.

She could still hear the ominous hissing sound and tracked it to its source—a bullet hole had pierced the lift tank. Elisha had not gone to the expense of protecting it with magical constructs.

"Not surprising," Kate remarked ruefully. "Poor fellow probably never expected people to be shooting at him."

If anything about this disastrous situation could be called fortunate, it was the fact that the bullet had hit a seam in the metal tank, which had the effect of reducing the size of the hole.

Kate glanced at the regulator that measured the pressure of the gas in the tank. The needle was falling, but very slowly. She had time.

Leaving the tank, she reluctantly went to talk to Pip, who had finally managed to free Thomas.

"Are you all right?" Phillip asked, as his friend emerged, gasping, from beneath the folds of the ruptured balloons.

"Yes, now that I can breathe."

Thomas straightened and looked around. "What was that strange roaring sound I heard? And what happened to the Guundarans?"

"Meet Dalgren," said Kate.

The dragon soared into view, flying up from beneath the ferry. Thomas staggered backward, bumping into Pip, who put out a steadying hand. The two gazed at the dragon in astonishment while Dalgren regarded them with equal perplexity.

"Where did those two come from?" he demanded. "Who are they?"

"No time to explain!" Kate yelled. "A bullet punctured the lift tank! The boat is sinking!"

"Then get off it!" Dalgren growled.

He indicated with a jerk of his head the ladder still hanging from the saddle.

"Not yet!" she cried. "I'm going to try to reach that island. The one that looks like Kristal Island. Where you found the *Victorie*!"

Dalgren's eyes narrowed. He was trying to figure out what she meant. The island on which he had found *Victorie* had been nameless, just another hunk of rock. And none of the islands around here looked anything like the islands of the Aligoes. Kate didn't dare say anything more for fear she would give away her plan.

"Do you know what I mean?" she shouted.

Dalgren apparently did, for he muttered something in his own language. Fire flickered from the corners of his mouth.

"I know! And I don't like it! You need to get off there now!" Dalgren roared. His lips drew back, showing his fangs. "It's not worth risking your life—"

"I'll signal you when I'm ready," Kate called.

She fixed Dalgren with a look and he snapped his mouth shut.

Kate turned to her passengers and was glad to see that both had accepted with equanimity the dire news that the boat was sinking. Both appeared far more interested in the dragon.

"That's your Rosian friend," said Phillip. "The one you told me about."

"Yes, that's Dalgren," said Kate. "Now here's the plan—"

"How can you make out what he's saying?" Thomas asked, interrupting. "I know he's saying something, but his words are so much mush."

"You get used to it," said Kate, exasperated. "Now listen to me! We don't have much time. One of the bullets hit the lift tank. The ship is sinking."

"That much I understood," said Thomas coolly. He looked over at the islands that were yet some distance away. "Do we have enough lift gas to reach land?"

"I'm going to try," said Kate. "But if we don't, we'll have to abandon ship. Dalgren can carry us off."

"Not in his teeth, I hope," said Thomas.

Kate hid her smile. "We climb the ladder."

She pointed to the ladder hanging from the saddle. She had never realized before how flimsy the ladder looked, flapping and twisting in the wind. She herself was a bit daunted. Phillip was appalled.

"Good God!" he murmured.

Thomas regarded the ladder with a critical eye. "What's it made of?"

"Braided leather," said Kate.

"It won't bear the weight of all three of us."

"It doesn't have to," Kate explained. "If we need to abandon ship, one of us can climb up to the saddle, leaving the other two hanging on to the ladder. Dalgren won't have to carry us far. Braffa is only twenty miles away."

The dragon circled overhead, glaring down at her. Every so often, he would shoot flames from his nostrils.

"I don't think your friend likes this plan," said Phillip.

"He doesn't have to like it," Kate said. "He knows what he needs to do."

She went back to the helm, hoping to keep the boat afloat for as long as possible. Thomas walked over to inspect the lift tank.

"Staring at it won't help," Kate told him irritably. "One of you needs to chop down that mast."

Thomas looked at her, startled. "The mast? Are you sure?"

"The damn boat's sinking anyway," said Kate. "Dalgren has to drop down low enough for us to catch hold of the ladder and he can't do that with the mast poking him in the belly."

She concentrated her attention on the helm. Judging by the rate they were sinking and the distance they had left to travel, reaching the island would be a near thing.

"All these beautiful crystals and we're sinking." Phillip picked up one of the ugly gray rocks, then said suddenly, "Here's an idea! The Rosians use these crystals in their warships. Why can't we use them in this ferry? We could place a crystal in the lift tank . . ."

He saw Kate shake her head and his voice trailed off.

"The tank is too small. The gas is leaking too fast. The magical constructs on the tank are designed to work with gas, not crystals. Should I go on?"

"No," said Phillip.

Tossing aside the crystal, he picked up the axe, and began hacking away at the base of the mast.

Kate rested her hands on the brass helm and sighed. She had done about all she could do.

A hand covered her hand. Startled, Kate looked up.

"You should leave the boat now," said Thomas. "I know you're lying. The ladder won't hold our weight. Don't worry about Pip and me. It is our fault you are in this fix."

He was facing a terrible death, yet his touch was warm, his hand firm and strong. His remarkable blue eyes smiled.

He isn't the least bit afraid, Kate realized. Or if he is, he has his fear well under control. Her breath came fast. Feeling her hand tremble at his touch, she angrily tried to snatch it away. She considered telling him she wasn't interested in saving his life, and only cared about completing her mission. But that might give too much away.

"The ladder is standard issue from the Dragon Brigade," she said instead. "Dragon riders perform maneuvers like this all the time. Let go of me!"

"Have you ever done it?" Thomas asked, looking into her eyes.

"All the time," Kate snapped. "You just have to remember to hold on tight."

"Hold on tight." Thomas smiled. He released her hand. "I'll remember that."

"Watch out!" Phillip yelled.

The mast crashed down on the deck, taking the rigging and sail down with it. Kate measured the distance to the island. She was thinking now they just might make it.

She summoned Phillip, who had to climb over the ropes and canvas to reach them, and explained her plan.

"When Dalgren is in position, Pip will climb the ladder and sit in the saddle . . ."

Phillip looked up at the saddle, then at the ladder, and gulped.

"You go first, Kate," he said. "You know how I am about heights."

"I know that on board the *Royal Justice,* you and Alan used to race each other up the ratlines," said Kate.

"Not when I was sober," Phillip protested.

"Anyway, I have to be the last to leave," Kate continued. "I need to stay at the helm to keep the boat aloft until we reach land."

"Why would that make a difference?" Thomas asked. "We still have to abandon ship. From here to the ground is a hell of a long way down."

Kate faced the two, hands on her hips. Her tone was grim. "That is the plan and no more arguments. Pip, you will climb up first. Once you reach the saddle, make certain the ladder is secure. Thomas, you go next and I will be last. Any questions?"

Phillip opened his mouth, caught her look, and shut it again. Thomas might not have even heard her. He was smiling at her, looking at her in a way no man had ever looked at her before. Kate felt her cheeks burn. His admiration was disconcerting and, right now, annoying.

"Pip, go see how much gas is left in the lift tank. The regulator is on the side."

Phillip did as he was told, leaving her alone with Thomas.

"How do you know Pip?" she asked.

"I could ask you the same," Thomas said.

Kate glanced back at her friend: the ne'er-do-well clerk, the scapegrace, the gambler who always lost, the drunken clown.

"I'm not sure I do know him," Kate said. "You look like a soldier, even if you don't dress like one. I'm thinking you're a mercenary, hired to steal the crystals."

"That's as good a story as any," said Thomas.

"Who hired you?"

"Who hired *you*?" Thomas countered.

Phillip hastened back. "The lift tank is almost empty."

Looking down, Kate saw they were over the island. She just needed to nudge the boat along a little farther, to ensure it would land in the thick foliage. She lifted the bosun's pipe to her lips and gave the signal.

Dalgren flew down, flying as close to the ferry as he dared. Phillip stood poised to catch hold of the ladder when it came within reach. He glanced over at her.

"I'm glad to see you left the Aligoes, Kate," he said. "You were mixed up with some extremely dangerous people."

Kate ignored him. "Don't look down. Climb slowly and steadily. Thomas, take hold of the ladder to keep it from swinging. And remember, Pip—hold on tight!"

"Trust me on that!" Phillip said grimly.

The bottom rung of the ladder was now a few feet off the deck. He drew in a breath and caught hold of it. Thomas steadied the ladder for him, but even so the ladder kept shifting and Phillip had difficulty putting his foot into the rung.

Kate was watching the constructs on the lift tank. When the tank was empty, the magic would stop working. The blue glow was definitely starting to fade. The ferry was now sailing over the tops of the trees and they were coming closer than she liked.

She looked back at Phillip, who had at last managed to insert his foot into the rung and was starting to climb, pulling himself up hand over hand. At one point the ladder twisted and sagged. Phillip froze and Kate ran to help Thomas hold it.

"You're going too fast!" she called. "Slow down!"

Phillip gripped the ladder, his knuckles white, his eyes squinched shut. The motion stopped and he opened his eyes and once more began climbing.

"You owe me an extremely large whiskey!" he called to Thomas.

"I look forward to paying!" Thomas yelled.

Dalgren was trying to keep as still as possible, his wings barely moving. He anxiously watched Phillip's progress.

At last Phillip reached the saddle and, after a brief struggle, managed to pull himself into it. Kate looked back at the lift tank and saw the magical blue glow flicker out.

"The tank is empty," she told Thomas. "Now you—"

He grabbed hold of her, his hands around her waist. Hoisting her off the deck, he flung her at the ladder. She had to catch hold of the rungs to avoid falling. While she was clinging to the ladder, Thomas began scooping up crystals as fast as he could and stuffing them in his pockets.

"You— What the devil are you doing?" Kate gasped.

Thomas paid no attention to her.

"The ship is sinking!" Kate cried. "Catch hold!"

Thomas grinned up at her, stuffed a few more crystals into his pockets, then made a leap for the ladder. Grabbing hold, he thrust his foot into the lowest rung just as the ferry dropped out of the sky.

Kate tried to see where it landed. Instead, she found herself looking into bright blue eyes. Thomas put his other foot in the rung, then pulled himself up so that the top of his head was about level with her chin. He had his arms around her, gripping the ladder.

"You are a damn fool!" Kate said. "Risking your life for a few crystals!"

"I only need a few," said Thomas. The wind snatched his words away and blew his black hair into his eyes. He smiled at her. "Why? Were you worried about me?"

"Of course not!" said Kate, squirming. "I had a perfectly good plan and you ruined it!"

"On the contrary, *I* had a perfectly good plan and *you* ruined it," he said.

Kate craned her neck, trying again to see what had become of the ferry, but when she looked down all she could see were laughing blue eyes, partially obscured by black curls, firm lips, and high cheekbones marred by a scar. She had really never hated anyone so much in her life and she wished he weren't so close.

Dalgren was flying toward the Braffan mainland, traveling slowly in an attempt to keep the ladder with the two of them clinging to it from swinging. He kept casting worried glances at them over his shoulder. Phillip, seated in the saddle, was gripping the ladder with both hands.

"Are you all right?" he shouted down anxiously.

"Never better!" Thomas called.

He moved up another rung. Holding on to the ladder with one hand, he slid his other arm around Kate and drew her close, his body pressing against hers.

"What . . . what are you doing?" Kate gasped.

"What you told us to do," Thomas replied, smiling into her eyes. "Holding on tight."

THIRTY

Dalgren carried his three passengers safely to the southern part of the island of Braffa and set them down on a stretch of rocky, barren shoreline.

Kate was glad for the flight to end. She didn't know how much longer she would have been able to hang on to the ladder. Her arms ached from the strain. When the ladder was close to the ground, Thomas jumped down and then assisted Kate, putting his hands around her waist and easing her gently down.

He should have let go of her, but he didn't. He brushed back her windblown curls.

"Who are you, Kate?" he asked with a kind of wonder in his voice.

Kate struck him in the chest, pushing him away. "Back off!"

She called up to Phillip, who was still in the saddle. "You can come down, Pip!" she called.

"Easy for you to say," Phillip called back, making no move to leave the dragon's back.

Dalgren circled overhead, patiently waiting for his passenger to descend.

"Tell me your last name, Kate," said Thomas.

"Tell me yours," she countered, still watching Phillip.

Thomas shook his head. "No one must know I was involved."

"For someone dressed like a toff, are you so notorious?" Kate asked, scoffing.

"In a manner of speaking," said Thomas.

Now Kate was curious. She said teasingly, "Come, tell me. What does it matter? We are never going to see each other again."

Thomas paused, then said in somber tones, "You are right. I don't suppose we ever will."

They were interrupted by a gasping cry from Phillip. Dalgren had apparently grown weary of waiting for his passenger to climb out of the saddle. Circling out over the Breath, the dragon was now gliding back in toward the shore, preparing to land. Phillip ducked down in the saddle and held on for dear life.

Dalgren landed smoothly, coming down first on his powerful hind legs, rocking forward onto his front legs, and slightly crouching to soften the shock of the landing for his rider. Still, landing while on dragonback was jarring and unnerving, even for veterans, as Kate could attest. She and Thomas hurried over to the dragon's side. Phillip was gripping the saddle with both hands, his eyes tightly closed.

"You can come down now," Kate called. "Unless you have decided to join the Dragon Brigade."

Phillip opened his eyes. Seeing that the dragon was sitting safely on the ground, he gave an enormous sigh.

"How the devil do I get off this beast?"

"Climb out of the saddle and drop down onto Dalgren's foreleg. From there, you can slide down to the ground."

Phillip managed to escape the saddle, but then lost his grip and fell the rest of the way, tumbling to the ground.

"Are you all right?" Thomas asked, helping Phillip to his feet.

"Never better," said Phillip, dusting off his clothes. "I think I would have enjoyed the flight if I hadn't been so bloody terrified."

"Dalgren gave an irate grunt. "May I remind you, Kate, that I have not eaten since early morning. I am hungry and tired and you and I still need to find a place to spend the night."

Dalgren emphasized the message with a slap of his tail on the ground.

"I'm coming!" Kate told him. She turned back to Phillip and Thomas. "Speaking of a place to spend the night, there's a village not far from here on the banks of a river. You can likely catch a ride on a barge to Port Vrijheid and from there find a ship to take you home."

Dalgren made a rumbling sound.

"I have to go," Kate said. "I guess this is good-bye. . . ."

She was in a good mood. Her plan had not worked out as she had intended, but it had worked out, no thanks to these two. Phillip looked shaky; he was still recovering from his ride. Thomas was smiling at her with what Kate took to be smug triumph.

A few crystals in his pockets and he thinks he beat me, Kate thought resentfully. I can't tell him the truth. But I can wipe that smile off his face.

Kate sprang forward and kissed Thomas on the mouth.

"Just letting you know that I won and you lost," she said.

She meant to be cheeky, impudent. She hoped to see him amazed, baffled. She didn't intend for him to try to take her in his arms and kiss her . . .

"Sir Henry sent you, didn't he, Kate?" said Phillip.

Startled, both Kate and Thomas turned to stare.

"Deliver a message to Sir Henry from me," Phillip continued, talking rapidly in a low voice. "Tell him I quit. Tell him I was wrong to accept this assignment." Pausing a moment, he added, his voice grating, "And tell Henry he was wrong to ask me to undertake it."

"Pip, I don't understand . . ." Kate began, bewildered.

"I know you don't," said Phillip with a faint, sad smile. "Sir Henry won't either. Good-bye, Kate, and good luck. And Kate . . ." He paused, gazing at her intently. "Be careful."

He kissed her on the cheek. Kate continued to stare at him; then she heard Dalgren snarl in irritation and knew she had to leave. She hurriedly climbed onto the dragon's leg, then pulled herself into the saddle. She wondered about Phillip's strange message and, annoyingly, she could still feel the warmth of that kiss on her lips.

"I marked the location of the wreck," Dalgren said.

"What? Oh, yes. Thank you." Kate looked at Thomas, who was still looking at her.

"That was a damn fool stunt!" Dalgren continued. "You could have been killed."

"It worked, didn't it?" Kate said. She rummaged about in the saddle pouches and pulled out a sack that held her pistol cartridges. After emptying it out, she tossed it down to Thomas.

"You'll need that," Kate shouted. "Unless you want to walk around with your pockets filled with rocks."

Thomas grinned and picked up the sack. He waved at her. She waved back. Dalgren grunted. Kate began strapping herself into the saddle.

"Did you note the condition of the ferry?"

"It crashed into the tops of some trees and broke apart, probably dumping cargo all over the ground. Don't worry," Dalgren added. "No one will find it unless they fly over it, which isn't likely to happen in this godforsaken part of the world."

The dragon shrugged to ease the kinks out of his shoulders and flexed his wings. "Should be an easy salvage."

"For you," Kate retorted, laughing. "I'll be crawling around in the muck all day tomorrow picking up rocks."

Dalgren shook himself in readiness to fly.

"We should leave," he said, peering around at her. "The sun will set in an hour."

"I'm ready," said Kate.

She put on the dragon helm, lowered the visor, and gave Dalgren the signal, patting him on the neck. Dalgren leaped into the air. Spreading his wings, he sailed out into the Breath.

Kate twisted in the saddle to look back at Thomas.

"I wonder who he is . . ." she murmured.

"Who is she, Pip?" Thomas asked. He had been standing in rapt silence, holding the sack, watching the dragon until it vanished over the trees. "I have never met anyone like her!"

"That is because pirates are not generally invited to royal balls," said Phillip.

He spoke absently, hardly knowing what he was saying, his thoughts on the heinous task before him.

"You are telling me she is a pirate?" Thomas laughed. Shaking out the sack, he started removing the crystals from his pockets and dropping them inside. "Come now, you are jesting. And what was all that about Sir Henry Wallace?"

"She *was* a pirate, Your Highness," Phillip amended. "Kate is now a Freyan privateer. She works for Sir Henry Wallace."

"'Your Highness'? Are we so formal now?" Thomas asked.

Phillip was somber and Thomas realized that something was amiss. He emptied his pockets, tied a knot in the sack, and slung it over his shoulder. "We should start walking. The sun will set soon. Wallace is the queen's spymaster. You say Kate works for him?"

Phillip did not budge. "She does. And I work for him, as well."

"I don't understand," said Thomas, stopping. He looked at Phillip, puzzled.

"A man like you could never understand," said Phillip. He kept his head down, did not look at his friend. "I am a spy, plain and simple. I was hired by Sir Henry Wallace to travel to Estara, ingratiate myself with you, make you learn to trust me—all so that I could betray you."

He drew the pistols he had concealed beneath his jacket and held them out to Thomas. "I'm your prisoner. Take these. I surrender myself to you."

Thomas made no move to take the pistols. He seemed lost in amazement. He let the sack fall to the ground. "I don't believe you."

"I am not surprised," said Phillip, shrugging. "I am very good at living a lie. But I am now telling you the truth. Take the pistols."

Thomas was still staring at him. Phillip couldn't bear to see the pain on his face and, worse, the disgust. Turning from him, he hurled the pistols, one by one, into the Breath. The thought came to him that he could throw himself after them and it would be no great loss. Perhaps Thomas divined his thought, for he caught hold of Phillip and dragged him back from the edge.

Keeping a firm grip on him, Thomas marched Phillip inland, far away from the Breath. Phillip stumbled, his head bowed, his vision blurred. At last Thomas halted and, gripping Phillip, forced him to turn to face him.

"Did you?" Thomas asked harshly. "Betray me?"

"Yes, Your Highness," Phillip answered, his voice steady. "I have been passing on information about you ever since I arrived in Estara."

A thought came to him and he raised his head to look Thomas in the eye. "But I did *not* give Sir Henry the information about the crystals. By then, you see, I had made up my mind to tell you the truth. I don't know how he found out about them and sent Kate to steal them. He didn't through me."

Thomas was silent, gazing intently at Phillip, but not seeming to see him. Perhaps he was looking back, trying to recall what he had said, what secrets he had revealed to a man he had thought was a friend.

"How can I believe you?" he asked at last.

"You can't," said Phillip. "And so you must take me back to Estara and hand me over to the authorities. Tell them you discovered the truth, that I am a Freyan spy."

"They will hang you!" Thomas said angrily.

"Undoubtedly," said Phillip. He was suddenly exhausted and he sank down onto a log and lowered his head into his hands.

Thomas walked off and began pacing back and forth. Phillip awaited the verdict. He had no doubt what it would be. Thomas came back to stand in front of him.

"Run," he said, pointing to the forest. "I won't stop you. I won't chase after you."

Phillip gave a faint smile. "Of course you would think me coward enough to flee. I have given you no reason to think otherwise. I will not run. If you do not take me back to Estara, I will go myself and turn myself in."

Thomas glared at him, then walked back and forth a few more times, then rounded on him.

"The Freyans *shot* you!"

"Staged," said Phillip. "I was in no true danger. My friend Captain Northrop brought along a marine sharpshooter."

Thomas stared at him, aghast. The sun dipped into the Breath, filling the sky with flame.

"Damn you! Why did you have to tell me?" Thomas cried in anguish. "You could have gone back to Freya, left me in ignorance." He clenched his fist. "I wish to God you had!"

Phillip had known he would cause pain; he had not known how much. If he had, he might well have run.

"I had to warn you, Tom," he said. "You need to know that you have enemies, people like Sir Henry, who will stop at nothing to keep you from the throne." He gave a faint smile. "You are far too trusting. You should be more careful."

Thomas stood over him, his arms folded across his chest.

"I've heard about this Wallace. He is said to be ruthless. You don't just tell a man like that you quit! He will send his agents to hunt you down!"

Phillip shrugged. "Most likely. He will be furious. I have worked for Sir Henry for many years, ever since the war. I was one of the Rose Hawks, serving in the Aligoes under Captain Alan Northrop. He and Sir Henry are friends. And Sir Henry knew my father, the late duke."

"So that was the truth?" Thomas was astonished. "You really are a duke?"

"Of Upper and Lower Milton," said Phillip. "I couldn't lie about my identity. I know people in the Estaran court who would have recognized me. And, as it was, my title and wealth served as part of the plot to deceive you."

"I can't even look at you!" Thomas exclaimed. He turned and walked away, then suddenly turned and walked back. "How does a man like you, courageous and seemingly honorable, a gentleman of noble birth, become involved in a profession that is so . . . so . . . sordid and degrading?"

"I have often wondered," said Phillip. "I think it is the lure of danger, the excitement: the thrill of taking risks. I grew to crave that as some men crave strong drink."

He paused, then added in thoughtful tones, "To my credit, I did stop some very bad people from doing some extremely bad things."

"And you believed I was one of those very bad people," said Thomas caustically. "What changed your opinion?"

Phillip shook his head. "None of this matters—"

"It matters to me!" Thomas said, his jaw clenched. "And *I* am the one most concerned."

Phillip sighed. "I first started having doubts about Sir Henry's portrayal of you when I read the research undertaken by the crown prince. Jonathan was a friend of mine, as I told you, and I had access to his papers. He proved conclusively that you do indeed have a legitimate claim to the Freyan throne. Still, I withheld my judgment. A man may be born to rule, but that doesn't mean he is fit to rule. The late King Godfrey was, by all accounts, a ruthless, conniving despot. And then I met you. I found you to be noble, honorable, courageous—"

Thomas made an impatient gesture.

"—heedless, reckless, impulsive, and far too trusting," Phillip continued. "The upshot is, I came to believe in you and in your cause. I realized that by betraying you, I was actually betraying my country, not serving her."

Thomas stood frowning at Phillip for long moments in silence. What he next asked was unexpected. "In your bleak appraisal of me, would you concede that I am a good judge of character?"

"Don't do this, Thomas," said Phillip, sighing. "You don't know me. I am expert at deceiving people."

"Am I a good judge of character?" Thomas insisted.

Phillip said nothing.

"Stand up, Your Grace," said Thomas. "Look me in the eye."

Phillip did as he was told. He stood unflinching, facing Thomas, regarding him steadfastly. The worst was over. He could accept his fate with equanimity.

"Answer me this question," said Thomas. "You may have deceived others. Did you deceive me?"

"Yes, I told you—" Phillip began.

"No, no, I don't mean passing along information on how many troops I have or what I ate for breakfast," Thomas said impatiently. "I mean our talks about how we are going to change the world, about my hopes and ideas, my dreams and plans. You led me to believe you share my ideals. Did you deceive me then?"

"I spoke honestly, from my heart," said Phillip. "But that is not to my credit, Your Highness. Part of the art of deceit is to know when to be honest."

"Damn it, you seem bound and determined to make me hate you!" Thomas said, glowering.

"Don't you?" Phillip asked.

"Part of me does," said Thomas. "Part of me wants to shoot you where you stand! The other part of me wonders why in God's name you had to send that message to Wallace and put yourself in danger!"

"Perhaps I was trying to prove to myself I still had some smattering of honor," Phillip replied, sighing. "If so, it failed. I would understand if you shot me."

"I am not going to shoot you," Thomas muttered.

Phillip understood. "Then I am to be hanged . . ."

"And stop talking about hanging!" Thomas shouted. He grew quiet, seething, then added in calmer tones, "The truth is I have come to depend on you, Pip. We work well together, as this ill-fated adventure has proven. I need someone like you on my side, someone who understands me. Someone I can trust."

"You realize how ridiculous that sounds," said Phillip drily.

"The fact that you came to me, that you told me the truth, counts for much," said Thomas.

"I cannot forgive myself, Your Highness," said Phillip. "I don't know how you can forgive me."

"Oh, I don't," Thomas returned, brooding. "Not yet. In the meantime, we will go on as before, act as though nothing has happened. No one can know I was involved in this raid. If you go running to the authorities to confess your sins, all will be known, and God knows where that could lead!"

"Of course," said Phillip, chastened. "I had not considered that. I have caused you trouble enough. I will keep the secret for as long as you tell me to keep it."

"Good," said Thomas, his expression grim. "That is all I ask. And now, we have said enough on this subject. We should find that village."

He picked up the sack of crystals, flung it over his shoulder, and stalked off. Phillip trailed after him. Leaving the barren shoreline, heading east, they walked in silence, searching for the road that led to the village.

Searching for a road that would lead them back to what had been and never would be again.

THIRTY-ONE

Kate and Dalgren returned the next day to the island where she had left the ferry dangling from the treetops. The branches had broken its fall so that the boat remained relatively intact, though it hung at a precarious angle. As Kate had foreseen, most of the barrels had fallen off. She found a couple still snagged among the trees, but the rest lay shattered on the ground, surrounded by spilled crystals.

Kate was eager to start salvaging, fearing the Guundaran navy would initiate a search and discover either the wreckage or Dalgren. The plan was for the dragon to drop Kate off on the island, then spend the day in hiding.

She kept watch on the skies while she marked the location of the crystals, but she saw no sign of either the Braffans or the Guundarans, and she relaxed. The area they would have to search was vast. They might even assume that the ferry had gone down in the Breath and not search at all.

Salvaging the crystals proved to be an arduous task. First Kate had to find them, which meant tromping about in the underbrush. Then she had to pick them up and put them in gunnysacks, ready to load onto Dalgren, who returned for her at nightfall. And since he had no place to land, Kate had to make several trips up and down the ladder, hauling the filled gunnysacks.

Kate crawled through the brush, knocked broken barrels out of the trees, and dumped crystals in sacks, she had time for thinking, for the work was mindless. She wondered a great deal about Phillip and his sudden transformation from drunken bungler to daring, coolheaded thief. Which was the real Phillip? Kate was inclined to think the latter, which meant he had been acting a part the entire time she had known him. Judging by his mysterious message, he was working for Sir Henry and he knew that she too was working for Sir Henry.

She recalled Phillip telling her in Wellinsport that he didn't know Sir Henry and trying to deter her from attacking the ship on which Henry was sailing. Kate was inclined to resent the fact that Phillip had lied to her, and then she remembered that she had lied to him, and she grinned. She supposed they could call it even. But then who had hired Phillip and the mysterious Thomas to steal the crystals? Kate knew it wasn't Henry, because he had hired her. So what was Phillip doing for Henry and why was he quitting?

And who was the mysterious Thomas?

His refusal to tell her his name, and the hints at a dark and secret past, only increased her interest. She could tell by his speech he was a gentleman and she guessed by his bearing and the scar on his face that he was or had been a soldier. He was bold, courageous, resourceful, and daring. She remembered the two of them clinging to the ladder. She had seen admiration in those striking blue eyes—for her. He was attracted to her, in her slops and her calico with her windblown hair.

She now blushed to think of that kiss she had given him. He had thought himself so clever, filling his pockets with crystals, leaving her with nothing. She had he hoped he would be confounded. Maybe he had been, at first, but then he had tried to kiss her back.

"I wonder what it would be like to kiss him again?" Kate mused.

When she caught herself wondering if he would like to kiss her again, she angrily put the mysterious Thomas with the blue eyes out of her mind.

Once she had finally recovered as many of the crystals as she could find, she and Dalgren set up camp in a secluded valley outside Port Vrijheid. The dragon needed to rest before they flew back to Freya, and Kate had one more task to perform.

She fidgeted about until she thought Dalgren was asleep, taking his afternoon nap. Seeing him snugly curled into a ball, his tail wrapped around his body with the tip touching his nose, Kate changed out of her slops and into the dress she had worn when she went to meet Mrs. Lavender. She even put on the new green hat, even though it didn't match the dress, and remembered to wear the gloves to cover her hands.

Glancing at Dalgren, seeing his eyes closed, she stealthily slipped two crystals out of his saddlebags and began to wrap them in a kerchief.

"What are you doing with those?" Dalgren asked.

Kate jumped and looked around, annoyed. "No one will miss them." She stuffed the kerchief with the crystals into the reticule. "I'm going out."

Dalgren's eyes narrowed. "You can't sell them, Kate. The authorities will be keeping watch for you."

"I'm not going to sell them. I know what I'm doing. Just go back to sleep," said Kate irritably. "We'll leave when I get back."

"If you're not in prison," Dalgren grumbled.

Kate returned to Threadneedle Street and entered Mrs. Lavender's hat shop. Mrs. Lavender was with a customer. She gave Kate a welcoming smile, and asked her to wait. Kate went to the window and stood keeping watch. She didn't really think anyone would have recognized her, but Dalgren's ominous words had made her nervous.

"I am sorry to keep you waiting, madame," said Mrs. Lavender in formal tones. "I presume you have come in regard to your overdue account? If you would be so kind as to step into my office, we can discuss the matter."

Mrs. Lavender steered Kate through a curtained door, down a short hall and into a very small office. Closing the door, Mrs. Lavendar gave Kate a swift embrace.

"I am so relieved to see you alive!" she said. "Everyone is saying that the *Elisha Jones* sank and those who had stolen the crystals sank with it! I was afraid we had lost you."

"As you see, safe and sound," said Kate. "But the story about the ferry sinking is good. That means no one will be looking for me."

"You can rest assured of that—in more ways than one," said Mrs. Lavender with a chuckle. "The loss of the crystals is a huge embarrassment for the Braffans and the Guundarans. They will not admit now that the crystals ever existed. And so your mission was a success?"

In answer, Kate drew out the kerchief and unwrapped it, revealing the two crystals. "The story about the *Elisha Jones* sinking is true. I managed to salvage the crystals, but the ferry was a complete loss. I was wondering if you could find a way to sell these and see to it that Elisha has a new boat. He was only doing his job. He shouldn't be the loser."

"Very commendable. Of course I will," said Mrs. Lavender, regarding Kate with a warm smile of approval. "I have friends in the black market who will be glad to pay top price."

"Elisha mustn't know the money came from me," said Kate. "He wouldn't accept it."

"I understand," said Mrs. Lavender. Opening a desk drawer, she tucked the crystals inside and locked it. "I will make up a plausible story. Perhaps the refinery owners will take it into their heads to recompense him for his loss."

"And please send a message to Captain Northrop. Tell him what happened," said Kate. "Now, I must go. Thank you, Mrs. Lavender. Please take care of yourself."

"And you and your dragon. *And* your two daring accomplices," Mrs. Lavender added with a sly smile.

Kate was displeased. "Those two fools weren't my accomplices. They nearly ruined everything." She hesitated, then asked, "Do you know if they managed to get away?"

"They must have," said Mrs. Lavender. "No one has been arrested and, as I told you, everyone is saying the boat sank. And so these two were *not* working with you?"

The ringing of the bell on the door announced the arrival of another customer.

"I must go," said Mrs. Lavender. "I am the only one in the shop today. If you ever need me . . ."

"I know," said Kate, smiling. "Six taps."

"Please give Sir Henry my regards." Mrs. Lavender squeezed Kate's hand and bustled off to sell hats.

Dalgren and Kate flew to Barwich Manor. Kate hid the saddlebags with the crystals in Dalgren's cave, thinking that would be the safest place for them; then she traveled back to Haever and Miss Amelia's house.

Kate found Amelia in an upstairs bedroom, packing her valise.

"Welcome home, Captain," said Amelia, looking up from neatly folding her clothes. "Was your mission successful?"

"It was," said Kate.

"I don't suppose you can tell me about it," said Miss Amelia.

Kate shook her head. "Where are you going?"

"I am traveling to northern Freya to meet with one of the dragons," said Amelia. "Dalgren's inquiries paid off. Please extend my thanks to him."

She handed the letter from Odila to Kate, who read it over and frowned. "This dragon says she has information about Coreg. Are you sure you should be involved in this, Miss Amelia?"

"The story of a lifetime, my dear," said Amelia.

Kate hesitated, then said, "He is more dangerous than we thought. I need to tell you what happened to me when I went to Barwich Manor."

Amelia heard her serious tone and quit folding clothes.

"Trubgek found me," said Kate. "He tracked me to Barwich Manor."

"Tell me everything," said Amelia.

Kate related how Trubgek had come to remind her she was working for Coreg, how he threatened her by nearly knocking down the house. "I told him I would. What else could I do?"

"Nothing, Captain," said Amelia, regarding her with sympathy.

Kate didn't mention that she intended to make money off this deal. She doubted if Amelia would be so sympathetic if she heard that.

"So you see, Miss Amelia, even though Coreg is far away in the Aligoes, he can still be dangerous," Kate said.

Amelia locked the valise and turned to face Kate. "Now, Captain, do I tell you to run away from a little danger? Besides, he is threatening you. All the more reason to bring him down."

"I wouldn't call Coreg a 'little' danger," Kate said drily. "Who is this Odila anyway?"

"The grande dame of the dragons who moved here from Travia. I would dearly love to tell you what I have discovered about Coreg. It is all most fascinating. But I see my transportation has arrived."

Amelia was speaking about a wyvern-drawn carriage that could be seen and heard landing on the street outside the house.

"I do not want to keep the driver waiting," she added. "Wyverns raise such a ruckus. The neighbors will complain."

Kate looked out the window to see the wyverns screeching and snapping at each other, while the driver flicked the whip over their heads. Miss Amelia picked up the valise, hung the reticule over her arm, and hurried down the stairs. She grabbed the umbrella from the stand by the door on her way out, then hastened down the sidewalk and entered the carriage. She leaned out the window to wave to Kate with the umbrella as she left.

Shaking her head and smiling, Kate sat down to write a note to Sir Henry, telling him she had returned and that all had gone well. She sent the letter with a messenger, whom she asked to wait for the reply. While she waited, she took the green silk dress from the valise and put it on, to see how it looked with the new hat. She was admiring herself in the mirror when she heard a knock on the door. Thinking it was the messenger, she went downstairs, only to find Mr. Sloan.

"Sir Henry would like to see you at your earliest convenience, Captain," said Mr. Sloan.

"I'm ready now," said Kate.

Mr. Sloan accompanied Kate to the Foreign Office, and led her up the back stairs and straight to Sir Henry, who rose from his desk to greet her, even going so far as to shake hands.

"You said all went well, Captain," said Henry, smiling broadly.

"Yes, my lord," said Kate, pleased and proud. She lowered her voice. "Mrs. Lavender sends her regards."

"I see you have a new hat," said Henry. "The color is quite becoming. And where, may I ask, are the goods?"

Kate told him about the cave in Barwich, including directions.

"Mr. Sloan—" Henry began.

"I am already on the way, my lord," said Mr. Sloan. "I trust I should send word to the admiralty for ships to return to Haever for refitting."

"With the utmost haste," said Henry, smiling.

"Call out to Dalgren before you go inside his cave, Mr. Sloan," Kate warned. "You wouldn't want to startle him."

"No indeed, Captain," said Mr. Sloan.

"The password is 'Stephano,'" Kate added. "Dalgren will know I sent you."

"Please, sit down, Captain," said Henry after Mr. Sloan had departed. "I want to hear all about your adventures. Everything went as we planned?"

"Not exactly as planned, my lord," said Kate.

"Tell me all," said Henry. Resuming his seat behind his cluttered desk, he leaned back in his chair. "Omit no detail."

"I captured the ferry without incident. The trouble began when we arrived at the refinery," said Kate. "The oddest thing happened. Pip was there."

"Pip," Henry repeated, a puzzled expression on his face. "You speak as if I should know him."

"He was one of the Rose Hawks," said Kate. "He worked for Captain Northrop."

Henry gave a bland smile. "Hundreds of men have worked for Alan over the years. I am afraid I do not know the gentleman. Now, proceed with your tale."

He sat back at his ease, crossed his legs, and regarded her with pleasant expectation.

Kate was confused. If Pip hadn't specifically mentioned Sir Henry and given her that strange message, she would have believed he was telling her the truth. As it was, she knew that he was lying and that he must have a good reason for lying. She began to feel uneasy, but she was determined to know more about what was going on. And she had to deliver the message.

"Pip was with a man named Thomas," Kate persisted. "They were there to steal the crystals."

She tried to think how to phrase the next delicately, not to accuse him of acting falsely, and decided just to come out with it. "Pip sent you a message, my lord."

"Did he?" Henry asked blandly. He continued to smile, but the smile now seemed frozen, his eyes narrowed. "What could this unknown 'Pip' possibly have to say to me?"

Kate saw the shadow in the narrowed eyes and felt as if the scenic trail she had been walking had suddenly dropped her into a ravine. Looking at the man sitting in the chair, she saw the man in the ship's hold who had coolly and deliberately placed the muzzle of his pistol against Jacob's skull and pulled the trigger.

Henry's largesse, his kindess to her, his bland smile and friendly interest, even the homely clutter on his desk, had blurred the sharp corners of that memory. Kate was now almost afraid to say the words.

She still wanted to know what was going on. And she had promised Phillip. She drew in a breath and let the words out all in a rush. "Pip said to tell you he quits. He was sorry, but he should have never accepted the job." She wisely omitted the part about how Henry should have never asked him to take it.

As she spoke, she watched Henry's facial muscles harden, the pupils of his eyes dilate, and his nostrils grow white and pinched. He rose slowly to his feet, not as though he willed himself to stand, but because he seemed compelled to do so.

Amelia had termed Sir Henry the most dangerous man in the world. Kate had thought her friend was exaggerating. Now, looking at his face, she believed it.

Henry placed the tips of his fingers on the desk and slightly leaned over, moving closer. Kate shifted uneasily in her chair and glanced behind her, to gauge her distance to the door.

"The man who was with His Grace—"

"His Grace!" Kate gasped.

"The man you know as 'Pip' is Phillip Masterson, Duke of Upper and Lower Milton," said Henry. "You are certain the name was Thomas."

"Yes, my lord," Kate replied.

"Surname?"

"He would not tell me . . ."

Henry stared at her, his brows coming together. He obviously did not believe her.

Kate tried to explain. "Everything happened so fast, my lord! Pip and Thomas jumped on board the ferry and the Guundarans began firing at us. Dalgren was roaring. The balloon collapsed. A bullet hit the lift tank and the ferry started sinking . . ."

Kate realized she was babbling and stopped, biting her lip.

"Describe him," said Henry.

"Who, my lord? Pip?"

"Thomas!" Sir Henry said through gritted teeth.

Kate swallowed. "Early twenties. Black curly hair and . . . uh . . . blue eyes."

"Striking blue eyes," said Henry.

"Yes, my lord," said Kate faintly.

Henry was livid with rage. Kate cast down her own eyes, so she wouldn't have to look into that terrible face, and shrank in the chair, waiting for his fury to explode and hoping she survived the blast.

She heard him return to his chair and sit back down. He said nothing and Kate at last dared to look up.

Henry was gazing, frowning, at the bookcase. He appeared to have forgotten her. Hoping that was the case, she stood up as quietly as possible, so as not to disturb him, and began to edge toward the door.

"You did well, Captain," said Henry, his voice tight, controlled. "I will be in touch."

Kate paused. She knew she was probably making a dreadful mistake, but she couldn't help herself. With her hand on the door handle, she turned around, greatly daring.

"My lord, who is this Thomas?" she asked.

"Good-bye, Captain," said Henry. "Please close the door behind you."

Kate did as she was told. Once in the hall, she found herself trembling so much that she had to take a moment to compose herself. She looked up and down the hall. She had no idea how to get out of the building, but she could not bear to stay another moment where she was.

Picking a direction, she began to walk. One hall led to another and another after that, and she was soon hopelessly lost and eventually had to stop to ask for directions. A clerk led her to the grand hallway and from there out to the street.

She was surprised to see that the sun was shining. Sir Henry's office had seemed dark as midnight. She decided to walk to Miss Amelia's house. The exercise would help to calm her, and she needed to think. She went over everything, from Pip's message and the astonishing fact that he was a duke to Sir Henry's violent reaction and, strangest of all, his recognition of Thomas, as revealed by his question regarding "striking blue eyes."

The fact that Pip had been an agent for Henry was now obvious. Her first reaction was to be angry. He must have known Henry would be furious when she gave him the message and that he might take out his ire on the messenger. Pip had no right to involve her. After a few moments of silent reflection, Kate wondered if perhaps Pip had involved her for a reason.

She remembered his parting words. "Be careful." She had thought little of them at the time, dismissing them as the usual polite nothings. Now she paid more attention. Thinking back to his tone and the look in his eyes, she realized Pip's words held a more sinister meaning. He was warning her to be careful of Henry.

By the time she reached Miss Amelia's house, Kate was exhausted. She had a key, and let herself in, nearly treading on the mail, which the postman had shoved through the slot in the door. Kate gathered up the letters, as well as the many newspapers to which Miss Amelia subscribed, and went to put them on Amelia's desk.

As she sorted through the mail she found a letter to her from Olaf. The letter was short, saying only that she should come to the port town of Barwich. He had some questions for her about the ship.

"Barwich?" Kate muttered, astonished. "What is Olaf doing in Barwich? The ship is being refitted outside Haever!"

She could think only that Olaf had some urgent reason to talk to her—probably to give her bad news about *Victorie*—and that he had gone to Barwich to find her. Worried about her ship and also afraid that Henry would think of more questions to ask her and send for her again, Kate decided this would be an excellent time to leave the city.

As she placed the mail and the newspapers on the desk, she glanced idly at the *Haever Gazette,* and there was Thomas, drawn in black-and-white, looking back at her.

Kate stared, stunned. The illustrator could not, of course, portray his striking blue eyes in black ink. But he had captured the way Thomas's hair curled back from his forehead, his strong jaw and prominent cheekbones, the slightly hooked nose and—most telling—the scar on his cheek.

She read the caption beneath the illustration.

Prince Tom to Wed Princess Sophia.

Prince Tom. Short for Thomas.

"Bloody hell!" said Kate.

Book 3

THIRTY-TWO

"What are your plans for the day, my love," Alastair, the Marquis of Cavanaugh, asked his wife as he was rising from his seat at the table.

He walked over to kiss her, and Constanza tilted her cheek to be kissed, a ritual they performed every day at the breakfast hour whenever she visited the estate in Bheldem.

"I have an appointment with a wealthy gentleman who wants to contribute to our son's cause," Constanza replied. "Would you like to join us?"

"Unfortunately I cannot, my dear. I travel to Morvindia today to meet with Prince Arlien. His Highness sent for me and since he is nominally our ruler, I must attend."

Constanza made a face. "How tiresome for you. From what I have heard, the doddering old man can't recall his own name half the time, much less the names of his guests."

"The prince is not quite in such bad condition as that, although I do find his tendency to doze off in midsentence to be rather disconcerting." Alastair smiled. "I believe I shall stay a few days to do some grouse hunting, if you do not mind. The Duke of Morvindia and Count Waleran will also be there. It would be well to garner their support."

"An excellent idea, my love," said Constanza in a preoccupied tone, as she sorted through the early-morning post. "I have a great deal of correspondence, as you might imagine, with the time for our son's triumphant return to Freya drawing ever closer."

"You know, my dear, that our Thomas was born in this castle and he has not, to my knowledge, ever set foot in Freya," said Alastair. "Thus making his 'return' impossible."

Constanza looked up at him, her post forgotten in her passion. "Thomas *returns* to claim his birthright! He *returns* to his ancestral home! The Freyan people must view him as their savior, not a stranger from a foreign land. Thus we must always speak of his return!"

"I understand," said Alastair with a smile. "I fear I was teasing you just a little, my dear."

"Ah, do not jest about such serious subjects," said Constanza, shaking her head.

"Where is Thomas? Will he be paying us a visit? He has not been here in months," Alastair said, pulling on his gloves.

"Our son is traveling to Rosia with His Grace, Phillip, the Freyan duke. As you know, I have concluded an agreement with the Countess de Marjolaine for Thomas's marriage to the Princess Sophia. All is arranged. The countess proposed that he and His Grace reside at the palace as her guests. I believe they are also to have something to do with the Rosian navy, as well."

"And how will the Freyans feel about the future king of Freya marrying a Rosian princess?" Alistair asked.

"According to the countess, they view the marriage most favorably," said Constanza. "The Freyans adore the princess. She spent time in that country after the war. I believe she attended university or some such thing where she was known for mingling with the common folk."

"What does Thomas think of this arrangement?" Alastair asked.

Constanza shrugged. "I do not know. I have not asked him."

She returned to reading her correspondence, and her husband departed.

Constanza and Alastair were well matched. He knew she had married him for his wealth and she knew he had married her for her royal blood and her connections in the Estaran royal court. Although they did not love each other, they had managed to produce a son, Thomas.

Following the birth of her son, Constanza made the decision to return to her homeland of Estara to oversee his education. She returned to Bheldem (and her husband) every few months.

Although he did not have much time to devote to his son's cause, Alastair was equally ambitious for Thomas to become king, for the marquis had a cause of his own. He was intent upon overthrowing the aging and occasionally befuddled Prince Arlien, current ruler of Bheldem, and becoming the ruler himself. The marquis already had gained the support of several wealthy Bheldem nobles based solely upon the fact that his son was destined to be the future king of Freya.

After reading her mail, Constanza sent a message to her cook to tell her that the marquis was leaving and that she would be dining alone. She wrote several letters to various supporters of Thomas's cause and then, as the clock struck eleven, she set out upon her morning constitutional.

She took walks daily, no matter what the weather, both for the sake of her health (for she intended to live long as the Queen Mother of Freya) and also, occasionally, to conduct secret business. She theorized that once the servants were accustomed to her daily routine, they would never suspect that she could secretly be meeting someone in a secluded area along the way. Thus far, the practice had worked.

She had received a letter from Sir Richard's trusted valet, Henshaw, telling her he had arrived in Bheldem to discuss a matter of the utmost importance. Constanza wrote back, arranging to meet in the usual place. Having traveled to Bheldem many times before, Henshaw knew where and when to look for the marchioness and he was waiting for Constanza on a walking path that meandered among willow trees and circled a lake, near an old sundial placed at the entrance to a hedge maze.

Henshaw was looking for her and came walking rapidly toward her the moment he saw her.

He made a hasty bow, hurriedly returned her greeting, and moved straight to business.

"The Travian dragons have arrived in Freya, my lady," he reported.

"Indeed," said Constanza, pleased. "Let us walk."

She did not enter the maze, for anyone could be hiding behind the hedges. Instead she embarked along the path that traveled along the outskirts of the woods. Henshaw walked at her side.

"We hear that the dragons are quite pleased with their new home and their new titles," he continued. "We are to call these great beasts 'count' and 'countess' and bow and scrape. Sir Richard believes this to be an outrage and he is not alone. A great many members of the Freyan nobility are incensed. Because these alien dragons have contributed to the royal coffers, they have in essence purchased titles that our own nobles gained by dint of years of loyal service, sacrifice, and dedication."

"I sympathize with Sir Richard!" Constanza said, conveniently overlooking the fact that Sir Richard Wallace had obtained his knighthood because he was a successful businessman who had himself contributed to the royal coffers.

"The dragons plan to build grotesque mansions and devour our deer—"

"If deer are *all* they devour," said Constanza in ominous tones.

"Very true, my lady," said Henshaw. "But there is a problem, one that we did not foresee, regarding your son."

Constanza paused to regard him with consternation. "What is that?"

"Sir Richard fears that the dragons will pose a danger to His Highness when he returns to claim the throne."

"How do you mean? What danger?"

"According to Sir Richard's brother, Henry, the dragons have heard of Prince Tom through the press and asked about the possibility of Thomas gaining the throne. They are worried that should your son become king, he would order them to leave Freya."

"Indeed, he would," said Constanza with an emphatic nod. "His very first edict."

"Sir Richard is of the opinion that when your son attempts to return to Freya, the dragons will try to prevent him by attacking his fleet."

"Merciful Heaven!" Constanza gasped. "The Freyan people would not stand for such an enormity!"

"Her Majesty cares nothing for her people, as you well know, Your Ladyship," said Henshaw. "According to Sir Richard, the dragons could inflict serious damage on your son's fleet, destroy ships and kill many hundreds of soldiers and even attempt to murder your son. His Lordship believes it likely that the army would go down in defeat and all our hopes would end in ruin."

"We must deal with this situation!" Constanza exclaimed, clenching her fist. "Eliminate the threat."

She paused, then added doubtfully, "Although I confess I do not see quite how that can be done . . ."

"Sir Richard has a plan, Your Ladyship," said Henshaw. "He sent me to discuss it with you and to obtain your assistance."

"I am all attention," said Constanza.

The two resumed their walk, their heads together, talking in low voices.

"As Your Ladyship knows, killing a dragon is not an easy task," said Henshaw by way of preamble.

Constanza did not know. She had never given the slightest thought to killing dragons. She did not want to reveal her ignorance, however.

"I have been told that cannon fire is effective against the monsters," she said casually. "A ship's broadside would utterly blast a dragon to pieces."

"I believe that is true, Your Ladyship," said Henshaw, treading cautiously. "The problem is that dragons very rarely put themselves in a position to be fired upon by a broadside. A dragon with its fiery breath has the ability to destroy a ship from a distance, out of the range of cannon fire. Thus the Dragon Brigade has proven to be so effective against our navy."

"I was about to point out that very problem," said Constanza with a lofty air. "But, never mind, proceed. You said Sir Richard has a plan."

Henshaw glanced around and Constanza did the same. No one was in sight, and so Henshaw resumed.

"History tells us that the ancient Imhruns developed magical constructs that they used to kill dragons. Over twenty years ago, during the Lost Rebellion, when tensions ran high between Rosia and Freya, everyone feared a Rosian invasion. His Majesty, the late King Godfrey—God rest him—was ruler of Freya at the time. He ordered scholars to actively search for this magic to defeat the Dragon Brigade. They found references to it in scrolls found in the archives of a museum."

Constanza made an impatient gesture with her gloved hand as of shooing away a gnat. As far as she was concerned, Freyan history began and ended with her great-great-grandfather James I. "What do I care about scrolls and museums and ancient Imhruns? What have these to do with my son?"

"If you will allow me to finish, Your Ladyship," said Henshaw. "The Imhruns had in truth developed magic that could kill dragons. The magic was very crude by today's standards, but King Godfrey hired some very talented crafters to improve it and they succeeded. I do not mean wholesale slaughter, Your Ladyship. The original idea was to assassinate several important Rosian noble dragons, creating an incident that would cause the Dragon Duchies to withdraw from Rosia and the Brigade, a move that would have thrown the political situation in Rosia into chaos."

"Obviously nothing came of this plot," Constanza said, growing weary of the subject. "I fail to see—"

"Please, Your Ladyship, allow me to continue. King Godfrey did not live long enough to put the plot into action. Following his untimely death, his daughter, our current queen, made peace with the Rosians. A few years after that, King Alaric disbanded the Dragon Brigade and Sir Richard believed the threat to our country to be at an end."

Constanza at last understood why she had been subjected to this history lesson.

"The threat has returned," she said, giving Henshaw a sharp look.

"Greater than before, my lady," said Henshaw in grave tones. "His Lordship believes that if an assassin killed one of the Travian dragons, the rest of the dragons would be furious—"

"So furious they might attack the Freyan populace!" Constanza exclaimed. "My son would arrive as the hero to save his people!"

"Your Ladyship misunderstands me," said Henshaw, shocked. "Sir

Richard would never dream of placing the Freyan people in danger. His Lordship's goal is to encourage the dragons to leave Freya so that they no longer pose a threat to our cause."

"Speak to the point," said Constanza. "I presume His Lordship has this dragon-killing magic in his possession. Otherwise he would not have sent you."

"Sir Richard believes he has the means to acquire it, my lady," said Henshaw.

"Then you may inform Sir Richard that he has my approval. He can proceed with the plot to assassinate one or more of the dragons."

Henshaw was rendered speechless. He could only stop and stare.

"Well, what?" Constanza demanded. "Has the cat got your tongue?"

Henshaw found his voice, after a struggle.

"Your Ladyship cannot be serious! Sir Richard cannot be involved with this plot. He was a close friend to King Godfrey and, were it discovered, he could fall under suspicion. His Lordship must be able to profess his complete innocence."

Constanza was irritated. "Then I fail to see why Sir Richard sent you to tell me of this plot if we are not to use it!"

"Sir Richard was thinking that *you* would have the means to put the plot into action, my lady," said Henshaw. "He can provide you with the location of the magical construct, but that is all."

"And does Sir Richard think *I* am in the habit of assassinating dragons?" Constanza demanded in a dire tone that caused Henshaw to back up a step.

"No, Your Ladyship! Certainly not!" he protested. "Sir Richard was thinking that perhaps Captain Smythe—"

"Captain Smythe is the commander of my son's army. The good captain is *not* an assassin," said Constanza coldly.

She was growing to dislike this conversation that was not, apparently, going anywhere. She resumed her walk with a displeased air, leaving Henshaw to hurry to catch up.

"His Lordship knows Captain Smythe to be the soul of honor," said Henshaw. "His thought was that, as a military man, Captain Smythe might have access to . . . er . . . resources."

Constanza slowed, willing to consider this suggestion.

"He might," she conceded. "I can discuss the matter with him if you like, then report to His Lordship. We can proceed from there."

Henshaw mopped his forehead with his handkerchief.

"Such an arrangement will be satisfactory," said Henshaw. "Once the assassin has been hired, the magical construct will be provided."

Upon returning home, Constanza immediately sent for Captain Smythe.

He arrived the following day, riding over from an ancient fortress castle that the marquis had converted into a barracks and military headquarters.

Constanza saw to it the servants were busy with tasks in the lower level of the castle and invited the captain to join her in the library. He sat down in a chair, his back straight, his hat on his knee, and listened in silence, giving no hint of his thoughts as she outlined the plot.

"Well, Captain, what do you think of Sir Richard's proposal?" Constanza asked.

"Sir Richard is right to point out that the dragons could pose a risk to our enterprise, my lady," Captain Smythe replied. "I confess I had failed to take them into consideration."

"I was asking you about his solution," Constanza said. "Assassination."

Captain Smythe frowned. "I cannot condone it, madame. What Sir Richard proposes is cold-blooded murder. No man of honor could condone it."

Constanza glared at him. She often regretted having taken Sir Richard's advice to hire him. She was the daughter of kings and Smythe was a nobody, yet he continually gave her the impression that he was judging her and, worse, that he found her lacking.

"I am not asking you to condone it, Captain," Constanza said tersely. "I am asking you to suggest someone who could be hired to carry it out."

Instead of meekly responding that he would obey, Captain Smythe had the temerity to ask a question of his own.

"Have you discussed this matter with His Highness, my lady?"

Constanza bit her lip. She had no intention of discussing this with Thomas, as Captain Smythe knew. Her son would find appalling the very thought of murdering anyone—including a dragon—and he would absolutely forbid her to proceed, just as he had forbidden her to carry on with plans for an armed insurrection, something else she had not told Captain Smythe. Constanza was extremely thankful Thomas was far away.

"As you know perfectly well, Captain, since you urged me to send him, my son is visiting the royal court in Rosia," said Constanza. "I would have to write to him and I dare not risk the possibility that the letter could fall into the wrong hands. Everyone knows that the spies in the Rosian royal court outnumber the vermin."

Captain Smythe could not very well argue this point. He shifted to another. "Have you considered that His Highness could be implicated in the plot?"

"Not if we take precautions," said Constanza. "Freya is rife with people who are opposed to the dragons. They have formed anti-dragon leagues, and write letters to the newspapers. The assassin can cast the blame on them."

She was growing impatient with the captain. "I do not know why you are so opposed to this course of action. I have heard you say that dragons are minions of Aertheum. Think of this as a battle against the Evil One! Think of the lives of innocents you could be saving! As God's Soldier, are you not required to fight in His holy war against these fiends?"

Constanza was an avid reader of the *Haever Gazette.* She read everything that could have anything to do with her son's cause, and that included the published speeches of Fundamentalist preachers, well known for their hate-filled denunciations of the Travian dragons.

She had the satisfaction of seeing that her words had an effect on Captain Smythe. His frown was no longer disapproving; he looked thoughtful.

"You quote the words of the Reverend Elijah Byrd, my lady," he said.

"I was profoundly moved by those words, Captain," said Constanza. "Your religion and mine differ on many issues, but on this subject we think alike. The dragons are a danger to our people. They are the ancient evil named in the prophecy. This is war!"

Constanza clenched her fist. Captain Smythe was silent and seemed to be deep in thought. She knew when to hold her tongue. She pretended to read a letter, all the while watching Smythe from beneath her lashes.

"I believe I know someone who could be approached regarding this matter, my lady," he said at last.

Constanza was careful to hide her triumphant smile.

"I am pleased you have reconsidered, Captain," she said gravely.

"The man's name is Greenstreet, my lady. He is a black-market arms dealer in the Aligoes. He is reputed to have extensive connections among the criminal classes."

"Can this Greenstreet be trusted?" Constanza asked sharply.

"Insofar as any criminal may be trusted, my lady," said Captain Smythe dourly. "Saying that, I have purchased weapons from him in the past. We are good customers and he would be foolish to betray us."

The captain rose to his feet and stood holding his hat in his hand. "If you like, I can tell you how and where to contact him."

Constanza could not believe she had heard correctly. Rising to her feet in a majestic rustle of silk, she fixed him with an imperious stare. "I hope you are not suggesting, Captain, that *I* should be the one to contact this . . . this criminal?"

"I have already gone against my better judgment by giving you the man's name, my lady," Captain Smythe replied. "I have provided you with the information. You may do with it what you will."

He bowed, hat still in hand. "Your servant, madame."

Before she could say a word, he had walked out.

Constanza glared after him, sputtering in incoherent rage, so shocked and angry that she was momentarily paralyzed. Coming to herself, she decided that she had endured enough of his abuse, his shocking lack of respect. He would not remain in her employ another moment unless he obeyed her command to talk to this Greenstreet.

Halfway to the door, she paused to consider.

After all, do I want such a straitlaced, plebeian fellow handling such a delicate negotiation? she asked herself. *Would it not be better if I went myself?*

Constanza liked to be in control. Smythe was a soldier and she trusted him to do what soldiers did, which was march about and shoot people. She could trust him to barter for shot and powder with this criminal, but could she trust him with something this important? Thomas's life was at stake. If these dragons attacked, her son could be killed.

Her eyes filled with tears. Her lofty ambitions for her son reached to Heaven, but her love for Thomas did not know even those bounds. He was everything to her. His name was the first word on her lips in the morning, the last word she spoke in her prayers at night.

The journey to the Aligoes would be uncomfortable, the meeting with this Greenstreet unpleasant and perhaps even perilous. Constanza shrugged away the discomfort, the danger. She had worked and sacrificed all her life for her son and she would not shirk her duty now. She could trust no one but herself to handle this important mission.

Constanza sent a note to Captain Smythe, requesting information on this Greenstreet, and then ordered her maid to start packing.

THIRTY-THREE

"Trubgek!" Coreg angrily bellowed the name, causing it to rumble through his dwelling. "I heard voices. I didn't summon anyone. Who is here? What is going on?"

The dragon sprawled on the floor in the enormous mansion he had built on the island of Freeport. Although it was huge, Coreg's mansion consisted of only three rooms: the vast, cavernous hall where he lived; the small chamber where he slept; and a single room for his human, Trubgek.

Coreg loathed humans. The only reason he kept even one near him was because he had to rely on a human if he wanted to interact with other humans. He found the need galling. He could manipulate humans, intimidate them, terrorize and control them, yet just because he needed a human to wield a pen for him, he knew deep in his soul that the humans who groveled before him secretly sneered at him.

He would have done without humans if he could, but he couldn't and so he had found the best way to manage the deplorable situation: acquire a human male child, train it to serve him, and keep it around until it grew too old to be of use, then use that one to train a new one. He always named his humans Trubgek—one of the most insulting terms a dragon can use for a human. Coreg had gone through several Trubgeks during his lifetime. He chose boys that were around the age of nine or ten, considering them old enough to be useful yet still sufficiently malleable, and got rid of them when they were old and worthless.

Coreg had exacting criteria. He required all Trubgeks to be crafters, and since crafting was taught by the Church, he would search until he found an unscrupulous monk who would, for a price, let the dragon know when such a boy became available. Coreg would then have the boy abducted and brought to live with him.

The current Trubgek was the best of the lot, being the first to excel in dragon magic. Coreg had long believed that humans had magic "in their blood," as did dragons. If humans were properly taught—and survived the process—they could learn to cast spells that were far beyond the ability of most human crafters, including savants.

The previous Trubgeks had been disappointing in this regard, either dropping dead during the training or proving such dismal failures that the dragon had eventually given up on them. This particular Trubgek had been extremely responsive. He appeared to relish the work, no matter how difficult or painful, and subsequently had developed into the best crafter Coreg had ever produced.

Trubgek had also proven adept at dealing with his fellow humans. He did not appear to be afflicted with a conscience. He obeyed orders without qualm or question. In Coreg's eyes his best quality was that he spoke only when necessary and kept what he had to say short and to the point.

"Trubgek!" Coreg shouted again.

A magical portal opened in the wall at the far end of the room, disgorging Trubgek, who came to stand before the dragon.

"I heard voices," Coreg demanded. "Who is out there?"

"Greenstreet," said Trubgek.

Coreg gave a disgruntled snort. "I grow weary of Greenstreet. He runs to me with every little problem. Is this going to be another waste of my time?"

Trubgek undoubtedly knew what Greenstreet wanted, since part of his job was to keep an eye on him. Trubgek appeared disinclined to answer the dragon's question, however, perhaps because he knew that if Coreg wanted to know, he had only to ask Greenstreet.

"I suppose I have no choice. Send him in," Coreg grumbled.

Trubgek silently departed, then silently returned with Greenstreet, who was puffing from the exertion and leaning heavily upon his walking cane. He did not have to walk through the magical forest, as did other visitors. Greenstreet had only to open the hidden panel in the wall, walk down the stairs and through a tunnel, then enter the portal. With his great bulk, Greenstreet found even walking that short distance tiring.

"Well, what is the matter now?" Coreg demanded.

"Nothing is the matter, sir," said Greenstreet, fanning himself with his hat. "Opportunity."

"Indeed." Coreg was interested. "Report."

Greenstreet glanced around. "Do you mind if I sit down? I have been on my feet . . ."

"Trubgek, a chair," Coreg ordered.

Trubgek walked over to a dark corner where the dragon stored the chairs he kept for human visitors and returned with a chair, which he placed on the floor in front of the dragon. Greenstreet lowered his bulk into the chair and Coreg lowered his snout to the ground. Trubgek faded into the shadows.

"I had a meeting with a marchioness this morning," said Greenstreet, resting his hands upon the cane in front of him.

"A real one?" Coreg was skeptical. Greenstreet had once been enamored of a whore who called herself "Duchess."

Greenstreet chuckled. "This marchioness is very real. She is married to the Marquis of Cavanaugh in Bheldem, extremely wealthy, cousin to the King of Estara. Her son is Thomas Stanford, heir to the Freyan throne."

Coreg was surprised and impressed. He had not thought that, after three hundred years, anything could surprise or impress him. He raised his head.

"A woman of means and noble birth. Why would such a person come to you, Greenstreet?"

"I was recommended to her by Captain Smythe."

"The name sounds familiar," said Coreg.

"The captain has purchased weapons from us in the past," Greenstreet replied.

"Ah, I remember," said Coreg. "The captain is a good customer, as I recall."

"The captain is practically our only customer these days," Greenstreet said, grunting.

Coreg knew this to be sadly true. Following the conflict with the Bottom Dwellers, humans were sick of war. Captain Smythe, King Ullr, and a few of the Westfirth gangs were practically the only people interested in buying arms these days. And of these, Smythe was the only one who paid for the goods on delivery.

"Did the marchioness come to buy more weapons?" the dragon asked. "I have several crates of Freyan-made rifles. I can make her an exceptionally fine offer."

Greenstreet shook his head. "The marchioness came to us because she is in need of an assassin."

Coreg emitted satisfied puffs of smoke from his nostrils and scraped his claws across the floor. "Greenstreet, you have outdone yourself."

"I thought you would be pleased," Greenstreet said, fanning himself with his hat.

Coreg ruled the human underworld, not only in the Aligoes; he had his claws into crime in most other markets as well. He financed smugglers and pirates, bought and sold weapons on the black market, traded in stolen goods of all sorts, from diamonds to coal; and he made money from every human vice imaginable, operating opium dens, gambling clubs, whorehouses. Extremely wealthy, he could buy anything in the world he wanted except the only thing he truly desired: power.

Coreg had long planned to establish a base of operations on one of the major continents, someplace where he could bribe governments to turn a blind eye. He had first attempted to establish himself in Travia, but a dragon named Odila had discovered his nefarious operations and reported him to the Arcanum, an arm of the Church devoted to seeking out wrongdoers. The Arcanum was a powerful force in the world, and Coreg had been forced to flee to the Aligoes.

He wasn't happy here, however, feeling that he was too far from the heart of human wealth and power. Now he had the possibility of sinking his claws into a real live prince.

"How can I be of service to the marchioness?" Coreg asked, almost purring. "Who is the intended target?"

"A dragon," said Greenstreet.

Coreg stared at him, then began to laugh; booming laughter that shook the walls.

"You are a great fool, Greenstreet! Assassinate a dragon! I never heard anything so ridiculous."

Coreg let his laughter bubble into a snarl and thrust his snout into Greenstreet's face. "I told Trubgek you would be a waste of my time. Get out!"

"You should listen," said Trubgek.

Coreg raised his head, startled. He had forgotten Trubgek was in the room. Trubgek never spoke, never interrupted. The fact that he did so now was telling, and caused Coreg to reconsider. He looked back at Greenstreet and said with a curl of his lip, "Very well, then. Go on."

Greenstreet moistened his lips and gave Trubgek a grateful look.

"I said the same thing. I told the marchioness that assassinating a dragon was impossible. She said that it wasn't, and that she had the means to do so. I told her I needed to know more about what she required. She was reluctant to divulge details, but she had little choice. It seems that years ago, the Freyans developed a magical construct that could kill dragons . . ."

Coreg would have laughed again, but a long-forgotten memory stirred in his mind. He had been living in Travia when he had heard a rumor that the Freyans were attempting to develop a secret weapon to kill dragons during some war or other.

He had not believed it. No dragon had believed it. A single dragon could destroy an army of humans. The idea of a lone human assassin attacking a dragon was ludicrous. The human would have to first dismantle magical wards and traps to even enter a dragon's lair. If he made it that far, he would next have to catch the dragon napping, an impossibility, since even slumbering dragons are sensitive to the sound of a mouse creeping across the floor.

Finally if he managed that, he would have to be armed with some sort of weapon that could kill a dragon, another impossible task. Bullets bounced off a dragon's scales, poisons had no effect, swords and spears were practically useless.

But magic . . . now, that could be different.

Coreg shifted his attention back to Greenstreet.

"What was your answer? Did you tell the marchioness I would take the job?"

"I did not," said Greenstreet. "I had to talk to you first. I told her I would give her my answer this evening."

Coreg nodded. "Why does she want to kill a dragon? Did she say? Did you ask?"

"I did," said Greenstreet. "As I told you, she believers her son to be the true and rightful king of Freya. According to her, there are plans in the works to invade, remove the current ruler, and take over. The marchioness fears that the Travian dragons will try to stop her son. If one of these Travian dragons is assassinated, she thinks the others will be frightened and go back to Travia."

Coreg mulled this over. "I suppose there is some merit to this idea. What did you think of this human female? Do you believe her?"

"She tried lying. Captain Smythe had written to me in advance, to apprise me of her coming. I was able to do some checking on her. When confronted, she admitted the truth. She is ambitious, clever, and cunning. She will do anything to attain her goal and that includes murder. She is the type to act first and consider the consequences later."

"Excellent," Coreg said. "Tell her I will undertake to do this job for her. Does she have a victim in mind?"

"She knows nothing about these dragons and could not care less," said Greenstreet. "When I asked, her response was: 'One dead dragon will do as well as another.' Who do you have in mind for the job, sir? The person must be a crafter."

"Trubgek will make the arrangements," said Coreg.

Greenstreet shrugged, happy to let someone else do the work. "What do I charge her?"

"The going rate for assassins these days, whatever that is," said Coreg. "The true charge for my services will come later when her son attains the throne."

"The marchioness appeared particularly anxious that her son has no knowledge of the crime about to be committed in his name," said Greenstreet.

"All the better," said Coreg. "Once I tell him, he will be shocked and horrified and eager to pay to keep the matter quiet."

The dragon paused a moment, then added grudgingly, "You have done well for a change, Greenstreet. I am pleased, though amazed."

Trubgek escorted Greenstreet to the exit, then returned. "Orders?"

"I need to see this construct for myself. After I determine how it works—*if* it works—I will be the one to decide what to do with it."

Trubgek nodded and stood in silence, waiting.

Coreg eyed him thoughtfully, then said, "I was considering having you pick up the construct, but I have changed my mind. I said nothing to that great fool, Greenstreet, but I detect of whiff of something rotten about this job. I suspect this is a trap and you are far too valuable to me to get caught in it. Hire some dog to send down the rat hole and we will see what happens."

Trubgek gave a slight nod of agreement. "Anything else?"

"You know what to do," said Coreg.

Trubgek thought this over and apparently determined he did know what to do, for he left. As Coreg settled down for a nap, he reflected on how pleasant it was that he could hand over responsibility for this job to Trubgek and be confident that he would complete it without fuss or bother.

"A pity about humans and their short life spans," Coreg muttered to himself before drifting off to sleep. "I am going to miss this Trubgek when he is gone."

THIRTY-FOUR

When Thomas had heard from his mother that he was to travel to Rosia to meet his future wife, he had insisted that Phillip accompany him. Phillip had not wanted to go, and tried to make excuses to stay behind. Relations between the two continued to be strained. If they were thrown together among their friends, both acted as if all was well. Thomas would laugh and jest, but there was no mirth in his eyes. Sometimes there was anger, more often unhappiness and disappointment.

"Let me leave," Phillip had said time and again. "I won't return to Freya. I'll go back to the Aligoes."

"You can't go," Thomas had always replied. "People would start to ask questions."

Phillip was forced to admit Thomas was right. But that did not mean he had to accompany the prince to Rosia.

He had no choice in the matter, however. Constanza wrote to Thomas that the Countess de Marjolaine had extended "a most gracious personal invitation" to the duke, adding that Phillip could not very well refuse without committing "a serious breach of etiquette," perhaps even causing an international incident. The two were to attend a ball in the royal palace and from there they were going to be guests on board a Rosian naval vessel traveling with what was known as the Rum Fleet, a name given to ships because they patrolled the Aligoes. The Rosians were intending to rid the islands of pirates and when Thomas had expressed an interest in observing the navy in action, the admiral had invited the prince to join them.

Phillip gave in, and they traveled together to the capital city of Rosia, Evreux. Thomas had planned to fly by griffin, but when Constanza had found out his plans she was furious, writing, "Do you intend to arrive at the palace travel-stained and windblown? They will take you for a tinker and send you to the servants' entrance."

She sent her own elegant and massive two-masted yacht, adorned with the family coat of arms, to carry them to Rosia in style.

Phillip had dreaded the journey, knowing he and Thomas would be alone on the yacht—at least, as alone as a crew of six would allow. The journey would take five days, during which time he and Thomas would be forced into each other's company. His only consolation was that he had his own stateroom, into which he could escape at night. During the day, however, they had only each other.

And as it turned out, in a certain way, they had Kate.

Thomas was infatuated with her. When Phillip mentioned that she was featured in newspaper stories, Thomas hunted down all the old copies of the *Haever Gazette* he could find and read them over and over.

"You realize these tales are about as true as the tales your mother writes about you," Phillip pointed out.

Thomas only smiled and kept reading.

All he could talk about or think about during the five-day trip to Rosia was Kate. That was a blessing, for she proved to be the balm that began to heal the near-fatal wounds their friendship had suffered.

The first day into the journey, the two young men were standing at the rail, gazing into the orange mists of the Breath and talking about Kate.

"Tell me everything you know about her, Pip," Thomas said. "You two met when you were in the Aligoes. Where does she come from? I want to hear the smallest detail."

"Her name is Katherine Gascoyne-Fitzmaurice. She is the granddaughter of a viscount—"

"A viscount!" Thomas said, impressed. "Then what the author says is true. She is of gentle birth."

"—a viscount who shot himself after squandering the family fortune," Phillip continued relentlessly. "Her father was also a gentleman—a gentleman smuggler, swindler, rogue, and thief who died of a cracked skull in a back alley in Westfirth. Kate was raised on board his ship and—"

"—and she is like no other woman I ever met," said Thomas. "You will not diminish her luster in my eyes. The author of these stories describes her: 'bold, courageous and daring with a fatal beauty.' That is how I see her."

"Come now, you cannot call Kate beautiful," Phillip argued.

"Perhaps not, but we saw her at a disadvantage," Thomas said.

"True," said Phillip wryly. "Bullets flying about her head would tend to steal 'the bloom of roses from her damask cheek.' "

Thomas laughed, then said more seriously, "I have spent my life in the company of earls' daughters and dukes' sisters, and Princess This and Lady That. They are all alike. Well bred, well behaved, well dressed, and dull as mushy peas. Kate has spirit and fire and courage . . ."

" 'Kate is a pirate, Mother,' " Phillip said, mimicking Thomas. " 'I am certain you will love her.' "

Thomas grinned. "All right, *that* conversation might be difficult."

"Difficult!" Phillip shook his head. "The word is 'impossible.' Besides, you know you are not serious about Kate."

"Do I know that?" Thomas asked. Leaning his elbow on the rail, he turned to face his friend. "Because I seem to think I am very serious."

"You may think you are, but you are not," said Phillip. "A month ago you were infatuated with some countess or other. You are like a jackdaw attracted to a shiny object."

"You compare me to a crow. Thank you very much," said Thomas.

"Maybe not a crow," Phillip said. "More like a man trying to break out of prison."

He had meant his barb to be funny, but it struck too near the mark. Thomas actually winced and turned away.

He was silent for a long time, then said in an altered voice, "I can dream, can't I, Pip?"

"Of what?" Phillip asked. "Of being a pirate?"

"Of being anything except a king," said Thomas.

"Strange, most people dream the exact opposite," Phillip remarked.

"That is because most people do not know that being king means you are isolated, alone, surrounded by those you dare not—"

"You dare not trust," said Phillip, finishing his sentence. "Such as myself."

Thomas pressed his lips together and gazed out into the Breath. "Look there. The southern coast of Rosia is coming into view."

"The devil take the southern coast of Rosia! Say what you mean, damn it!" Phillip said angrily. "You do not trust me—"

"On the contrary," said Thomas. "I have been giving the matter a great deal of thought. It seems to me you are the one person I *can* trust."

Phillip shook his head. "You have completely lost your mind."

"You told me the truth, Pip, and that for me is a rarity," said Thomas.

"No one ever tells me the truth. My mother and father tell me what they want me to hear. Captain Smythe and Hugh and my friends and all the rest flatter me and tell me what they think I want to hear."

"I tell you I'm a traitor and you find that surprisingly refreshing," said Phillip.

Thomas smiled. "Oddly enough, Pip, I find I do."

Phillip did not return the smile. The matter was not one for levity. He looked fixedly at his friend. "If you can tell me honestly that you once more place your trust in me, Tom, I will be your friend. I will stand with you against all the world, if need be."

"I trust you, Pip. And here is my hand to prove it. We will shake on it," said Thomas, holding out his hand. "And never mention this again."

The two solemnly shook hands.

"Your friendship will undergo its first test in the Sunset Palace," Thomas added. "I am walking onto the field of battle and I would like to emerge unscathed, my honor intact, and no wedding band upon my finger."

"I will be your loyal knight, Your Highness," said Phillip. "Although I fear all I can do will be to administer the coup de grâce and put you out of your misery. Your mother, the princess, and the countess are lined up against you. You are outnumbered and doomed to go down in defeat."

"I am afraid you are right," said Thomas with a helpless shrug. "But, as I said, I can dream. Tell me more about Kate."

The yacht carrying Thomas and Phillip made a grand arrival at the famous Sunset Palace. No one mistook them for traveling tinkers, although Thomas did tell the footman handling the luggage that he could sell him a washtub.

"A bit dented from the journey, but ideal for soaking your feet," said Thomas.

The shocked servant pretended not to hear, and Phillip smothered his laughter in his coat collar.

The personal secretary of the Countess de Marjolaine, a man named D'argent, was there to greet them, saying he would escort them to their rooms, knowing that both of them must want to rest and refresh themselves after the rigors of the journey.

"The countess regrets that she is detained by matters of state, Your Highness. She looks forward to meeting you tonight at the royal ball," D'argent added, guiding them through the palace halls.

"I look forward to renewing our acquaintence with pleasure," Thomas said. "I trust Her Ladyship is well?"

While the two continued to exchange polite nothings, Phillip gazed about the palace with interest. He had never before been in the Sunset Palace, although he had heard all his life about the splendors of the magnificent building. His father had been invited to attend the Rosian court, but he had hated the Rosians and refused to set foot in their country. Later, as one of the Rose Hawks, Phillip had taken part in the capture or sinking of many Rosian ships and he wondered with amusement what the Rosians would say if they knew the elegant Duke of Upper and Lower Milton now walking their halls was a notorious pirate they had attempted to either capture or kill.

D'argent, as though reading his thoughts, turned to politely include Phillip in the conversation. "I believe this is your first time to visit the palace, Your Grace."

"Indeed it is, sir," Phillip answered. "I am overwhelmed by the beauty."

"You should have seen it when it floated among the clouds and caught the rays of the setting sun," said Thomas. "I was nine years old when my mother first brought me to the palace. I was in awe. I could talk of nothing else for days. A wondrous sight."

"It was, Your Highness," said D'argent. "As I recall, you insisted that we take you down to the lower level to observe the lift tanks."

"By God, you're right, D'argent!" Thomas exclaimed. "I had forgotten that. You should have seen them, Phillip. Sixteen enormous lift tanks filled with the Breath of God! The Bottom Dwellers ended all that with their foul magicks."

Phillip had heard about the near disaster. The contramagic of the Bottom Dwellers had eaten away at the magical constructs on the lift tanks, causing them to fail. The palace had begun to sink to the ground; it came perilously close to crashing into the lake below.

"Does His Majesty have plans for raising the palace again?" Thomas asked.

"He does not, Your Highness," said D'argent. His eyes had darkened, his lips compressed, at the mention of the sinking. "His Majesty believes that a king should live among his people, not exist in some exalted state above them."

"I believe that myself, sir," said Thomas, struck by the remark. "I look forward to meeting His Majesty."

"I did not realize the two of you had not met, Your Highness," D'argent said, surprised.

"He was always away doing his duty as admiral of the fleet," said Thomas.

"He will be attending the ball tonight, Your Highness," said D'argent, adding with a slight smile, "You should arrive early if you want to meet him. His Majesty will make every effort to escape as soon as possible."

"A man after my own heart," said Thomas.

D'argent took Thomas and Phillip to their respective chambers. With some four hundred rooms, the palace housed at various times upward of several hundred people, including members of the royal family, guests of the royal family, members of the nobility, guests of the nobility, and their servants and staff.

Phillip and Thomas each had a room. Once there, the two dressed for the ball, Thomas doing so with the assistance of servants supplied by the countess.

Phillip was wearing a full-cut blue silk coat with a waistcoat embroidered in an elaborate pattern of vines and flowers. His shirt was adorned with lace cuffs. He wore a lacy cravat, blue breeches, and white silk stockings. He dressed swiftly, without assistance, and went to Thomas's room, down the hall from his own.

Thomas wore a red silk coat with dark red panels decorated with embroidery and gold thread, an embroidered waistcoat that matched the panels, lace at the cuffs and on his cravat. He glanced at himself in the mirror without interest, dismissed the servant, and then turned to Phillip.

"Make ready, bold knight!" Thomas announced with a flourish. "Prepare to enter the affray!"

"I suggest you offer terms of surrender now while you still can," Phillip said. "Matters will go ill for you if you are taken prisoner."

"So what is our strategy for tonight?" Thomas asked.

"I will go in first with sword and pistol. Your Highness will follow with pike and ax," said Phillip. "Since our foe will be armed with feather fans and champagne, I have no doubt we shall rout them."

"I am serious," Thomas said. "I will, of course, be obliged to dance with Her Highness. I cannot escape that onerous task. But if she attempts to lure me out to the garden for a stroll in the moonlight, you must come to my rescue."

"And how am I to do that?" Phillip asked.

"I don't know," said Thomas. "Say that you want me to meet a long-lost friend."

"Since I know absolutely no one in this country, that could prove difficult," Phillip replied. "I will do my best, however."

"I suppose we should go," said Thomas. He drew on his gloves. "I wonder what Kate would look like in a ball gown . . ."

"Like a pirate in a ball gown," said Phillip.

THIRTY-FIVE

The grand ballroom of the Sunset Palace glittered with jewels and laughter. Chandeliers adorned with myriad crystal prisms shone with magical light and sent rainbows dancing about the room. The fragrance of massive bouquets vied with the ladies' perfume. A hubbub of voices rose to meet them as they waited their turn to be announced on a balcony overlooking the ball. As the herald called out their names and titles, they were to descend a staircase specifically designed to afford the assembled guests time to inspect and criticize the new arrivals.

When Thomas was announced as the Crown Prince of Freya, the din subsided. The gentlemen regarded him with frank curiosity while the ladies whispered about him behind their fans. Conversation resumed when Phillip was announced. No one cared about the Duke of Upper and Lower Milton except to smile at the odd-sounding Freyan name.

The dancing had not yet started. A quartet consisting of two violins, a violoncello, and a viola was still setting up, placing their music on the stands and tuning their instruments. At the far end of the ballroom, banquet tables, covered with white cloths and adorned with flowers, were laden with every type of delicacy imaginable.

The Countess de Marjolaine was waiting for them at the bottom of the stairs. Phillip had heard a great deal about the countess from Sir Henry Wallace. She was his counterpart in the Rosian court. The head of intelligence, she controlled a vast network of spies and agents. Sir Henry spoke of the Countess de Marjolaine with the respect one accords to a noble adversary; Phillip looked forward to meeting her.

He had heard the countess's beauty praised, and he was not disappointed. She was in her middle years and scorned to conceal her age beneath rouge and powder. The fine lines around her eyes seemed only to accentuate their luster and intensity. Her abundant hair, now white, was carefully coiffed. She wore a dress of lavender silk moiré with embroidered panels and with tiers of lace ruffles. The overskirt was drawn back in the front to reveal a white underskirt with more ruffles. She knew Thomas well, and claimed him as a friend, permitting him to kiss her hand.

"Would you like to be introduced to His Grace, Your Ladyship?" Thomas asked politely.

"I would, Your Highness," said the countess and turned her wonderful eyes on Phillip.

Thomas made the introductions. The countess smiled, said everything that was polite and charming, and then led them both to meet the king.

"Which lady is Princess Sophia?" Phillip whispered.

Thomas looked around the room, his gaze roving over bevies of young women clustered together, laughing and talking among themselves and watching the young men.

"I only met her the one time in Estara," said Thomas. "I'm not sure I would recognize her."

"Didn't the two of you ever meet when you were children?" Phillip asked.

"The princess was in poor health," said Thomas. "She suffered from terrible headaches and was not permitted to play with other children. I heard that the headaches were caused by the contramagic of the Bottom Dwellers and that she is fine now. Certainly she was in good health when I met her."

King Renaud turned out to be stern and abrupt, giving the appearance of a man wishing he was somewhere else. He welcomed Thomas with perfunctory politeness and then did not seem to know what else to say to him. Thomas saved the day by speaking of how much he was looking forward to joining the Rum Fleet when it sailed to the Aligoes, and started asking questions about the ship on which he and Phillip were to serve.

King Renaud's true love was the navy. He brightened at the interest Thomas displayed and was pleased to answer his questions. The two began to discuss naval matters, much to the ire of those awaiting their chance to speak to the king.

Phillip did not join in the discussion, but instead stood gazing about the room. He felt a light touch on his arm and turned to find the Countess de Marjolaine smiling at him.

"Have you seen the lake by moonlight, Your Grace?"

"I have not, Your Ladyship," he said.

"Come with me to the balcony," she said. "The view is best from there."

As they walked among the crowd, the countess took his arm and, leaning near, said in languid tones, "I believe you and I have a mutual acquaintance, Your Grace: Sir Henry Wallace."

She looked him full in the face and he saw that she knew everything. He was paralyzed with shock. If she had stabbed him in the ribs, he could not have been more surprised. He had been lulled into complacency by her beauty, her fragrance, her lustrous eyes. He had foolishly lowered his guard, she had struck to the heart, and now he had to fall back and try to recover.

"Sir Henry and I have a passing acquaintance," Phillip said, matching her languid tone.

He could tell by the cool set of her lips and the slight increase in pressure of her hand upon his arm that she knew he was lying.

"People are watching," said the countess. "Keep smiling."

They continued to walk toward the balcony. She nodded and greeted guests. Phillip smiled as ordered, all the while attempting to work out what was going on. The countess had invited him to come with Thomas. Did she plan to expose him? Have him arrested?

No on both counts, Phillip decided. His arrest would create a huge scandal, outrage the Freyan people, and quite possibly end the marriage negotiations. He considered making some excuse and leaving her, but he needed to know precisely what she knew and so he continued smiling as he walked at her side.

They had to pass through double glass-paned doors to reach the balcony. Phillip opened the doors, then politely stepped back to allow the countess to walk in front of him. He shivered in the cool night air and realized he was sweating.

The countess strolled over to the stone railing. He accompanied her and they both stood looking out upon the moonlit lake, feigning enjoyment of a lovely view that neither of them saw.

"King Renaud holds Prince Thomas in high regard, as proven by the fact that His Majesty has agreed to the engagement of the prince and his beloved sister, the Princess Sophia," said the countess.

"His Majesty cannot hold Prince Thomas in higher regard than do I, Your Ladyship," said Phillip.

The countess gave a disdainful smile. Quite obviously, she did not believe him.

"Please inform Sir Henry Wallace that King Renaud would be deeply angered to learn that anything untoward had happened to His Highness."

"I would be glad to deliver your message, my lady, but I am no longer in communication with Sir Henry," said Phillip.

"I find that hard to credit, Your Grace," the countess said. "According to my sources, you are one of his most trusted agents. Sir Henry places a high value on you."

"Your sources are behind the times, Your Ladyship," said Phillip. "Sir Henry might place a high value on my head these days. No longer upon my service."

The countess made a dismissive gesture with her hand, causing the jewels of her rings to sparkle in the moonlight.

"I wonder what Prince Thomas would say if he knew the ugly truth about you."

"If that is a threat, my lady, it is empty," said Phillip. "His Highness knows I was sent to spy on him. I told him. He has been gracious enough to forgive me. I can never forgive myself."

He tried to say the last calmly, but he could not conceal his humiliation. His voice faltered. His lips tightened. His hand, resting on the stone parapet, clenched.

"Interesting," said the countess, regarding him as she might regard some specimen of rare beetle. "You are ashamed."

He looked at her, startled and wary.

"I heard about the dangerous work you undertook during the war. That does you credit."

"Then you believe me," Phillip said.

The quartet began to play. The faint strains of music drifted through the glass doors.

"I withhold judgment," said the countess. "For now, you have been warned. The dancing has started. I must return."

She waited for him to open the doors, then swept past him and into the ballroom. Once there, she gave him her hand in parting. As he politely brought her hand to his lips, he felt her fingers tighten painfully around his.

"I will be watching you, Your Grace," she said softly. "Be mindful."

The countess left him with a smile and vanished amid the glittering, laughing throng. Phillip sank down in a chair to recover, feeling as though he had just been released after having his bones broken on the rack.

"Or perhaps the iron maiden," he said with a shudder. "That would be more apt."

THIRTY-SIX

The room was hot and noisy, and Phillip did not know what to do with himself. He was not in the mood for dancing. He searched the crowd for Thomas, but he could not find him among the swirling dancers.

"I need a glass of wine," Phillip muttered. "Or six."

The buffet table was crowded as gentlemen filled plates to deliver to their ladies. As he approached, the men regarded him with hauteur; he was, after all, a Freyan.

He retreated to the far end of the table, secured a glass of champagne, and looked for someplace quiet where he could be alone. Seeing a servant disappear behind a curtain, Phillip followed. Servants were expected to materialize out of the ether when they were needed and to vanish when they were not. Thus the palace would be equipped with servants' halls—hidden passages through which the servants could walk without offending the sensibilities of their masters. Phillip planned to slip into one of these secluded passages, hoping to find respite from the heat, the noise and the soul-piercing gaze of the countess. For although he could not see her, he could feel her watching him.

He was in front of the curtain when a frantic call brought him to a halt. A hand drew aside the curtain. He saw an eye peering out at him.

"Help me, sir! Please! Help!"

Alarmed, Phillip flung open the curtain to find a young woman kneeling on the floor in the midst of large fragments of broken porcelain, her gown spattered with what he took for blood. Phillip dropped the champagne glass and fell to his knees at her side.

"You are wounded, my lady! Where are you hurt? Who did this?"

"Wounded?" The young woman stared at him, baffled. She followed his horrified gaze to the bodice of her gown and gave a breathless laugh.

"I am not wounded, sir! My gown is stained with chocolate, not blood. Although this might as well be blood," she added with a woeful expression. "For Anna will most certainly kill me."

Phillip could breathe again. "You asked for help, my lady. How may I assist you, since it seems you do not need me to save you from assassins."

"Not assassins," said the young woman, smiling. "A Bandit."

She lifted the tablecloth and pointed to a spaniel who was gulping meringues with a speed that indicated the dog knew he was likely to have his meal interrupted.

"Bandit! You naughty boy! Look what you have done!" the young woman scolded.

Seizing hold of the dog by a jeweled collar, she dragged him away from the stolen treats, then turned her laughing gaze to Phillip.

"You can help me with this Bandit, sir, though I must warn you that if you do, you will be complicit in our crime."

"I draw the line at stealing the crown jewels, but otherwise I am yours to command," said Phillip.

"Good! If you will hold Bandit and keep watch for the servants, I will hide the evidence."

Heedless of her voluminous silk skirt, the young woman began to crawl about on her hands and knees, hurriedly gathering up broken glass and crockery and shoving it underneath the table.

Phillip had a firm grip on the spaniel, who, stuffed with meringues, blinked at him lazily. Tasked with keeping watch for trouble, he found he could not take his admiring gaze from the young woman. She was perhaps nineteen or twenty, with hair the color of chestnuts, large brown eyes, and a winsome, expressive face.

"There! I think that's all," she said, lowering the tablecloth.

"Shh!" Phillip whispered. "Someone's coming!"

The young woman ducked beneath the cloth. Reaching out, she dragged Phillip after her. He scrambled awkwardly underneath the table, accidentally pinching Bandit, who gave a little yip of protest.

"Hush, you naughty dog!" The young woman drew close to Phillip to clamp her hand around the dog's muzzle.

Her eyes met his; they both smothered their laughter. He was dazed by her closeness, her warmth, and the intoxicating scents of chocolate, strawberries, whipped cream, powdered sugar, dog, and roses.

The two crouched under the table until the servants departed. Phillip peered out from beneath the tablecloth. Seeing no one, he crawled out and offered his hand to assist his companion. She regained her feet with some difficulty, for she kept stepping on the hem of her gown.

They ducked behind the curtain and found themselves in a well-lit, narrow passageway. The two of them were, for the moment, alone. The woman looked down at her gown with dismay. The gown was made of white silk, covered in tulle decorated with red rosebuds and, now, chocolate.

She sighed, then laughed and held out her hand. "I am Sophia, by the way. I am forever in your debt, sir. I realize we have not been formally introduced, but may I know your name, that I may properly thank you?"

"Phillip . . . I think . . ." said Phillip, gazing at her, utterly charmed.

He took hold of her hand as best he could while trying to hang on to Bandit. Sophia saw the admiration in his eyes, and her face flushed pink.

Withdrawing her hand, she reached for the dog. "Thank you, Phillip, for coming to my rescue. I can take Bandit. I should go change—"

Phillip did not want this moment to end, and he kept hold of the dog. "Since we are now criminals, my lady, you should at least tell me what happened. When questioned, we will need to get our stories straight."

Sophia smiled, seeming glad for the excuse to stay with him. "I shut Bandit in the closet in my room. I can't think how he got loose, but he is very good at escaping, especially when he smells food. When my maid came to tell me he was missing, I knew where to look."

"Among the desserts," said Phillip.

"I found him standing on the table, eating the meringues!" Sophia said. "When he saw me, he started to run. I made a grab for him and missed. He knocked the platter of meringues to the floor and when I tried to catch him, I overturned a pot of chocolate."

She smiled into Phillip's eyes and he smiled into hers. They unconsciously drew nearer to each other. Sophia's blush deepened and she reached for the dog.

"I can take him now, sir. Thank you for coming to my rescue."

Phillip could think of no more excuses to linger. He was about to relinquish Bandit when, fortunately for him, they were interrupted by the sound of footfalls coming down the passage.

"This way!" Sophia ran across the hall, opened a door, and darted inside. Phillip hurried to join her. She hurriedly closed the door and they were immediately plunged into darkness. Both of them froze, not wanting to bump into anything.

"Do you know where we are?" Phillip whispered.

"I think we're in someone's bedchamber," Sophia said softly.

Phillip smiled in the darkness. He could only imagine what the countess would think if she heard he had been caught sneaking into bedchambers.

"I don't believe anyone is here," Sophia added. "Everyone will be attending the ball."

"I don't hear anything," Phillip agreed, trying to placate Bandit, who clearly was tired of being carried, and squirmed in his arms.

Sophia whispered a word and a soft white glow filled the room, shining from what looked like a pomander filled with tiny sparkling stars. Phillip was impressed. She had conjured the starry pomander out of nothing, or so it appeared. He started to say something, but she put her finger to her lips, cautioning silence, and the two hurried through the bedroom toward the door on the other side. She turned the handle, opened the door a crack, and looked out.

"This leads to a dressing room. Wait here! I'm going to search for a way out," she whispered, and she glided through the door.

At her departure, Bandit apparently thought his mistress was abandoning him, for he raised a dismal howl. Sophia hurried back to console the dog.

"Oh, hush, Bandit, please!" she begged. "Be quiet and I will give you a tea cake!"

Bandit was not inclined to be pacified and kept barking. Phillip began to laugh and, after a moment, so did Sophia.

"I think we should make a run for it, my lady," said Phillip.

They hurried through a suite of elegant rooms and at last escaped into what appeared to be a main hallway. Portraits of men wearing ermine robes and periwigs and women in feathers and jewels adorned the walls. Stands of armor guarded alcoves, and bouquets of flowers adorned tables in niches. Magical light spilled down from floating chandeliers. Sophia dismissed the pomander with a flick of her fingers.

"Now I know where we are!" she said, sighing with relief. "We are not far from my chambers. I can go change my gown, hopefully before Anna catches me. And you can return to the ball. I am certain some pretty young woman is hating me for keeping you from dancing with her."

"On the contrary, my lady, I know only one person in the ballroom and he will not miss my company in the slightest," said Phillip. "I would much rather stay with you. I can watch Bandit while you change. So he doesn't escape again."

"Do you mind very much . . . Phillip?" Sophia said his name shyly.

"I will not 'dessert' you, my lady," said Phillip, grinning.

Sophia laughed. "You are quite dreadful. Very well, to punish you for that pun, you will carry Bandit."

The hallway was quiet, cool, and airy. Thick carpets damped the noise; sounds of music and laughter soon faded behind them. Phillip had no idea where they were, except that they were on one of the upper levels of the palace. Whenever they passed one of the floor-to-ceiling windows, he could see the lights of Evreux glittering in the distance.

They were about halfway down the hall when Sophia suddenly stopped, seized his arm, and dragged him to halt.

"What is it?" he asked.

"Two people are standing in the doorway!" she whispered.

Now that she had pointed them out, Phillip could see a man and a woman locked in a passionate embrace outside a door.

"Give them a minute to leave, then we can proceed," Sophia whispered.

She was standing close to him. Phillip, enjoying her nearness and the touch of her hand on his arm, was happy to give the couple days if they wanted it. At that moment, however, Bandit began to gag and heave, making the unmistakable sounds of a dog about to lose his ill-gotten gains.

"Oh, no!" Sophia said, distraught. "Put him down before he ruins your clothes!"

At the odd sound, the man and woman who had been kissing sprang apart.

"Is someone there?" the man called, looking down the hall.

The statue of a general someone-or-other stood in a curtained alcove. Phillip deposited the heaving dog behind the statue just as the gentleman came walking toward them. Phillip caught a glimpse of the hem of a gown and lacy petticoats whisking off down the hall.

"Oh, Rodrigo!" Sophia gasped. "Thank God it is you! You won't tell my brother, will you?"

"My dearest girl, you should be at the ball," the man said in a tone of fond affection. He made a graceful leg, then, rising, cast a perplexed look at her dress. "What *have* you been doing?"

Phillip stared in wonder, for the gentleman was a wondrous sight. He was dressed in a coat of gold brocade with a gold and black waistcoat, lace cuffs trimmed in gilt thread, shimmering golden stockings, golden breeches and shoes with golden buckles, and a starched white frilly ruff around his neck in place of a cravat. So far as Phillip remembered, ruffs had gone out of fashion during the time of James I.

The gentleman drew out his handkerchief from his coat to hold it over his nose. "Is that the sound of a dog vomiting?"

"Oh, Rodrigo, this has been such a dreadful night!" Sophia tried to explain. "Bandit got loose and there were meringues and chocolate all over the floor and now my gown is ruined and everything was awful until this kind gentleman came to my rescue."

"Very gallant," said Rodrigo. Removing the handkerchief, he tucked it into his sleeve. "I should like to make the hero's acquaintance. Will you introduce us, Your Highness?"

"May I present Sir Rodrigo de Villeneuve." Sophia glanced at Phillip and flushed in embarrassment. "Oh, dear, I do not seem to know your full name, sir."

"Allow me," said Rodrigo, bowing. "I believe we have the pleasure of addressing His Grace, Duke of Upper and Lower Milton, Phillip Masterson."

"Have you two met?" asked Sophia, looking from one to the other.

"I have not had the pleasure, Your Highness," said Rodrigo. "His Grace is obviously Freyan by his dress—quite drab, I fear. I am aware of only two Freyans currently in court: His Grace and His Highness Prince Thomas. I have met His Highness, ergo, he must be His Grace."

Phillip only half heard what Rodrigo was saying. The words "Your Highness" combined with the name "Sophia" were dinning in his ears.

"You are Princess Sophia!" said Phillip.

"You are the prince's best friend," Sophia gasped.

"And you are going to marry my best friend," said Phillip.

Sophia's confusion deepened. She didn't know where to look while Phillip gazed at her in dismay.

Rodrigo gently interposed.

"I hate to mention this, Your Highness, but your dog appears to be currently engaged in eating his own—"

"Oh, Bandit, you naughty thing!" Sophia cried.

"Allow me, Your Highness," said Phillip.

Reaching down to scoop up Bandit, he suddenly remembered where he had heard the name Rodrigo de Villeneuve. Phillip regarded him with admiration.

"If I am not mistaken, my lord, you are the famed crafter who discovered how the seventh sigil could be used to successfully combine magic and contramagic."

"Sir Rodrigo is one of my professors at university," Sophia said.

Rodrigo was highly gratified. "Are you a crafter yourself, Your Grace?"

"Sadly, I am not, my lord," Phillip replied. "I found the treatise you wrote fascinating, however."

"Perhaps we can discuss it sometime over a bottle of wine. But first we must come to the aid of the princess." Rodrigo looked at Sophia's dress. "Chocolate stains, did you say, Your Highness?"

"Yes, chocolate," said Sophia ruefully. "I fear my poor ball gown is ruined."

"Not in the least," said Rodrigo, removing his handkerchief from his sleeve. "Did I never teach this spell, Your Highness?"

"Not in a class dealing with the 'Techniques and Theories of Modern Magic,' " Sophia said, laughing.

"A pity. One of the most useful spells I have ever created," said Rodrigo. "I require two handkerchiefs. Do you have one I could borrow, Your Grace?"

Phillip shifted Bandit, drew out a handkerchief, and handed it over. Rodrigo traced a magical construct on his handkerchief, then decorously draped that over the splotches on the bodice of Sophia's gown. He placed Phillip's handkerchief on top of his, drew another construct, spoke a few words of magic, and the splotches vanished from the gown, only to reappear on the handkerchief.

"Thank you, Rodrigo!" Sophia exclaimed. "You have saved my life."

"One of the first spells I concocted as a child," said Rodrigo.

He handed Phillip back his handkerchief, which was now stained with chocolate.

"Now your poor handkerchief is ruined," said Sophia. "I will replace it, Your Grace."

"On the contrary, Your Highness," said Phillip, tucking the handkerchief into his pocket. "I would not part with it for the world. This will always remind me of you."

"Spilled chocolate and dog vomit," said Sophia, laughing.

Her laughter was infectious, bright and sparkling. Phillip considered Thomas a great fool at that moment for terming this enchanting young woman "very nice," and he longed to ask her what she thought of Thomas. Was she in love with him? She had spoken his name quite calmly, far more calmly than she had spoken his own. Not that it mattered what she thought of him. She was betrothed to Thomas.

"I should return to the ball, Your Highness," Phillip said abruptly.

"Oh, yes, Your Grace, I am sorry to have kept you away for so long," said Sophia. "Here, give me Bandit."

Phillip handed over the dog, who thanked him by giving him a swipe on the hand with his tongue.

"He likes you," said Sophia. "Good-bye, Your Grace. And thank you."

"Good-bye, Your Highness," Phillip said.

Neither made a move to leave, however. Sophia's hand found its way into his hand.

Rodrigo gave a cough and said in warning tones, "The countess!"

Phillip was still hiding in the alcove and couldn't see. Sophia gave a guilty start and dropped both Phillip's hand and Bandit. The Countess de Marjolaine came sweeping down the hall, accompanied by an older woman in the somber garb of a lady's maid.

"Your Highness!" the countess said, with a note of gentle reproof. "Anna and I have been searching for you everywhere. You are to dance with the prince—"

The countess caught sight of Phillip and she stopped talking in midsentence. Her eyes narrowed and her lips pressed together. He knew how this must look—a Freyan agent sneaking about the royal quarters. He didn't know what to say. Sophia had been thrown into confusion at the mention of the prince and she, likewise, was unable to talk.

Rodrigo came to the rescue.

"Her Highness and I were on our way to the ball when an unfortunate mishap delayed us, my lady," he said. "The little dog came running down the hall. I attempted to apprehend the miscreant, but failed.

"Fortunately, as it happened, His Grace had become quite lost in the palace and was searching for the ballroom when he encountered Bandit. His Grace managed to catch the dog and was in the act of restoring him to the princess when Your Ladyship arrived upon the scene."

The countess looked down at Bandit, who was sitting at her feet, wagging his tail. His nose was tipped with strawberries, his ears white with powdered sugar. She looked from the dog to the unmistakable evidence that he had been sick in the corner, and her lips twitched. She seemed to be having difficulty repressing a smile.

Her gaze went to Phillip and her smile vanished.

"Have you met His Grace, Your Ladyship?" Rodrigo asked.

"His Grace and I are acquainted," said the countess.

Her tone was smooth, coolly polite, and piercing as a poniard. Rodrigo twitched an eyebrow. Phillip made a silent bow and said nothing.

Bandit gave a pitiful whimper and once more began to heave.

"Someone might want to see to the dog," Rodrigo suggested.

Anna had been keeping a discreet distance, but now she hurried forward, gathered up Bandit, and carried him away, his howls echoing down the hall.

"Poor Bandit," said Sophia, looking after him.

"Anna will take care of him, Your Highness. You should come to the ballroom. His Majesty has been asking about you," said the countess.

"I hope my brother is not too angry with me," said Sophia.

"He could not be angry with you, Your Highness," said the countess in a tone of affection. She looped a fallen curl back into place and adjusted the roses in Sophia's hair. "We should go now."

"Will you be attending the ball, Sir Rodrigo?" Sophia asked. "Perhaps you could come with us?"

Her question was addressed to Rodrigo, but her gaze was on Phillip. He longed to return to the ball, to ask Sophia to dance. He imagined his hand on her waist as he led her through the steps. Her hand in his hand. Drawing her close . . .

He opened his mouth, only to feel Rodrigo tread upon his foot, warning him to be silent.

"I will join you later, Your Highness," said Rodrigo. "I have offered to show His Grace the way back to his chambers."

Sophia smiled in understanding, as evidenced by the fact that she made it a point to extend her hand to Phillip.

"Thank you for your help with Bandit, Your Grace."

Aware that the countess was keenly observing him, Phillip barely touched Sophia's hand to his lips. He was startled to feel her hand linger in his. A faint blue glow emanated from her fingers. He felt a pleasant tingling sensation on his palm.

Sophia smiled again. Bidding good night to Rodrigo, she left with the countess. Phillip watched her until she was lost to his sight and still he stood transfixed. He felt again the tingling sensation in his palm and looked down at his hand. He was surprised to see a faint mark in the shape of a tiny trefoil knot. He frowned, puzzled.

"You are very fortunate, Your Grace," Rodrigo observed. "Her Highness has given you a Trundler good-luck charm."

Phillip flushed and hastily closed his fingers over his palm.

"Sophia must have learned that spell from a Trundler friend of ours," Rodrigo continued. "Gythe gave me one, as well. Certainly I have led a charmed life ever since. I wish the same for you."

Rodrigo exhibited his palm bearing the identical knot, then said, "May I give you a warning, Your Grace?"

Phillip didn't need another warning this night.

"The hour is late—" he began.

Rodrigo ignored him. "The countess is very close to Sophia and extremely protective of her. Sophia is devoted to the countess. The two of them were captured by Bottom Dwellers and went through a very bad time together. Sophia would do anything for the countess."

"Such as agreeing to marry Thomas," said Phillip. He spoke before he thought and regretted the words the moment they were out of his mouth, for Rodrigo was regarding him with sympathy.

"Her brother, the king, promised Sophia that she would not have to marry anyone she did not love. Prince Thomas is handsome, brave and bold and, by all accounts, an estimable young man," said Rodrigo. "Are these accounts of him accurate?"

"Thomas is the best man I know," Phillip affirmed without hesitation.

"Prince Thomas is to be the future king of Freya," Rodrigo continued. "King Renaud hopes the marriage will ensure peace between the two countries for generations to come. Princess Sophia has been raised in the belief that it is her duty to serve her country. She spoke well of the prince after their first meeting. If she does not love him now, she could grow to love him. How does your friend feel about her?"

"He speaks well of her," said Phillip. He did not add that Thomas could grow to love her. He thought of Kate and the words stuck in his throat. He was aware of Rodrigo keenly observing him. "If you could show me the way to my room, I must rise early in the morning, my lord—"

"Ah, I see," said Rodrigo, looking wise. "His Highness is in love with someone else."

Phillip was startled. "I did not say that, my lord!"

"You didn't need to say it, Your Grace," said Rodrigo with a smile. "I am an expert in *les affaires de coeur.* Ask anyone."

He drew a watch from his pocket and glanced at it. "Dear me, look at the time."

"I am keeping you from the ball, my lord," said Phillip. "I will find a servant."

"If I return to the ball, the Countess de Marjolaine will gut me and grill me like a trout," said Rodrigo. "Besides, I have another engagement not far from your chambers."

Rodrigo enlivened their journey through the palace with an account of the scandalous doings of the noble lords and ladies of the Rosian royal court under the reign of the late King Alaric.

"All that has come to an end under the reign of King Renaud," Rodrigo added with a sigh. "We live a dull, staid life these days, devoid of charm."

He stopped outside a door. "I must leave you now, Your Grace. Continue down this hall. When you reach the end, turn to your left. Your chambers will be the third door on the right."

Phillip thanked him, expressed his pleasure in meeting him, and proceeded down the hall. As he was leaving, he heard Rodrigo softly knock three times. The door opened and a woman's hand, sparkling with jewels, reached out to draw him inside. The door shut behind them.

"So much for a dull, staid life," Phillip said to himself, smiling.

He eventually found his room, though not without difficulty, for he was thinking of Sophia and not watching where he was going. He made a wrong turn and ended up in one of the towers, where he wandered about until a servant took pity on him and guided him back.

Inside his room, Phillip poured himself a glass of brandy and sat in his chair, staring at the tiny Trundler knot on his hand and remembering every word Sophia had said, every touch, every smile. He had no idea of the time, but sat wrapped in pleasant musings until he was interrupted by a knock on the door.

Before he could say, "Come in," Thomas flung open the door and strode inside.

"I'll take one of those," he said, indicating the brandy. "Thank you for abandoning me, by the way."

"I am sorry," Phillip said, pouring the brandy and bringing it to his friend. "I wasn't feeling well—"

"I am not surprised. After gobbling all those meringues," said Thomas, sitting down in a chair.

Phillip stared at him in astonishment. "How do you know about that?"

"The princess told me all about your escapades," Thomas said, grinning. "Her tale of your adventures carried us through an entire quadrille and halfway into a minuet. She seems quite taken with you. She talked of nothing else."

Phillip felt his face burn. "Her little dog . . . And then there was the chocolate on her dress . . ."

Thomas laughed. "You should see your face! Do not worry, Pip, I am not going to challenge you to a duel over her affections. If I cannot love her, I am glad you do. She and I will have something to talk about on our wedding night."

"That's not funny," said Phillip.

"You are right, it isn't," Thomas said. Sipping the brandy, he added in somber tones, "We are in one hell of a predicament, my friend. I am smitten with a pirate. You are yearning after the woman I am to marry—"

"—and as if we didn't have problems enough, there is the Countess de Marjolaine," Phillip said.

"Good God, Pip, have you stolen her heart, as well?" Thomas asked.

"Hardly," said Phillip. He went on to describe his meeting with the countess. "She knows about me and Sir Henry. In fact, I had the distinct impression she knows more about me than I know about myself."

"Ah, that would explain why she lectured me on the need for a king to choose his friends wisely," said Thomas. "I couldn't imagine what she was talking about. As I see, there is only one thing to be done, Pip."

"Throw ourselves off the parapet?" Phillip suggested.

"We would only create a gruesome mess that would be very disagreeable for the servants to have to clean up," said Thomas. "Besides, we have promised to join the Royal Navy on the morrow—or rather this morning—and while you have seen the Aligoes, I have not. I require you to show me around. I particularly want to visit the Perky Parrot."

"You know Kate will not be there, Tom," said Phillip, growing serious. "She has moved to Freya."

"I know," said Thomas, downcast. He added with a shrug, "Still, one can always hope."

Phillip poured them each another brandy, then raised his glass. "Then let us drink to hope. As forlorn as it may be."

"To hope," said Thomas raising his glass. He added with a smile, "And to friendship."

"To friendship," said Phillip.

THIRTY-SEVEN

Olaf had written to Kate that he was staying in a rooming house in Barwich. Kate thought back to the first time she had returned to her childhood home. She had been afraid that people would recognize her, and she had covered her face with a veil. She did not bother with the veil this trip. If people recognized her as Rose Gascoyne's daughter, so be it.

She walked the streets, self-conscious at first, wearing the green silk dress and new green hat. No one knew her; no one spoke to her. Kate began to wonder if anyone even remembered her mother. Of if they did, if they cared. Why should they? Kate asked herself. The Gascoyne family did nothing for these people except rack up debt. I will change all that. Someday I will come into town, lady of the manor, and people will doff their hats and smile and say, "Good day to you, Lady Katherine."

Her pleasant dreams carried her to the rooming house, but Olaf was not there. He had moved out. Kate was leaving, baffled, when she heard someone shouting from a tavern across the street.

"As I live and breathe! Look, boys! It's Captain Kate in a dress!"

"Marco!" Kate said, astonished. "What are you doing here?"

The tavern was known as Pete's Ale House. Kate hurried across the street, glad to see her friends, but wondering why they were in Barwich.

"How are the repairs coming to *Victorie*?" Kate asked worriedly, sitting down with them. "Olaf wrote that he had questions for me."

Marco and his friends exchanged glances.

"The work is slow, Captain," Marco said, shaking his head. "Very slow."

Kate was disappointed. "I had hoped to set sail soon."

Marco sighed deeply. "You better talk to Olaf."

"I want to, but I can't find him," said Kate. She was growing alarmed. "Is something wrong?"

Marco winked at his friends. "Come with us, Captain."

Mystified, Kate accompanied Marco and the grinning crew to the Barwich harbor. The sun was setting, the west streaked with orange and yellow flame. He pointed to a ship, riding at anchor, her yardarms and rigging silhouetted against the glowing sky. Kate recognized the *Victorie.*

"My ship!" she gasped. "What is she doing here?"

"We finished work a week ahead of schedule. Olaf wanted to surprise you and he sent out the word. We set sail in her the day before yesterday," said Marco. "She handled well, only a few minor problems, and Olaf says those can be easily solved. She will soon be ready to venture out into the Breath. Do you know where we are bound? Has Sir Henry told you?"

Kate shook her head. She should probably return to Haever to deliver the good news in person, but the memory of Sir Henry's livid face and those cold, burning eyes still unsettled her.

"I will write to let him know that *Victorie* is ready to sail," said Kate. "We should hear back from him soon with our orders. And we need to bring our crew up to full complement. Where is Olaf?"

"He moved his gear on board the ship," said Marco. "Says it feels more like home."

Olaf was waiting for her on board *Victorie*. He had the rest of the crew lined up to greet her. They piped her on board, saluted, and then cheered. She looked around her ship—*her ship!* The words filled her with pride.

Olaf gave her a tour of *Victorie,* proudly pointing out all the features, from the cannons with their enhanced magical constructs to the lift tanks that used the liquid form of the Breath. The workers and crafters had strengthened Dalgren's "perch" on the stern, reinforced the protecting magic on the hull, and even installed a modern stove in the galley.

"She is as good as new," said Kate, her eyes dimming with tears.

"She is better than new, Katydid!" Olaf said.

Kate wouldn't go that far. *Victorie* still was over forty years old, outmoded by today's standards. Her high forecastle and sterncastle limited her maneuverability and slowed her response time to the helm. Kate loved the old lady, however, and looked forward to once more sailing the Breath, having something else to think about besides Coreg and Henry and a prince who had smiled at her with striking blue eyes while engaging himself to a princess.

He's a prince. Of course he thinks women will throw themselves at him, Kate had scoffed. But then she remembered she had thrown herself at him—literally—and she grinned. *Serves you right for wasting time thinking about him. Mother always said men were the ruin of women. Next time I'll heed her warning. I hope Prince Tom and his princess will be very happy.*

Kate wrote to Sir Henry, asking for orders, and moved back into her cabin on board *Victorie*. She spent her days with paperwork, ordering supplies—food, water, powder, shot—and supervising the changes Olaf deemed necessary. She expected the suppliers to demand payment in advance, but apparently they had already received their money, for the wherries carrying barrels of water and salted pork arrived the next day. After that came the powder hoys, heralded by their crew shouting a warning to put out all fires on board ship.

She had given Henry her address in town "To Be Left Until Called For," and she checked the post office daily. After a week had passed and she had still not heard from him, she began to worry. Since she had been the one to deliver the bad news about Pip, perhaps Henry was venting his wrath on her.

A few days after she had arrived, she and Olaf went into town. Olaf did not like to leave the ship, being convinced, as Marco joked, that *Victorie* would sink if he was not there. He needed the latest charts and maps, however, and he did not trust anyone but himself to acquire them. He and Kate arranged to meet at Pete's Ale House.

Kate stopped by the post office and, finding no letter, went into the floating Trundler village to buy a bottle of Calvados to drink to the success of their next voyage—if they ever took their next voyage. This done, she went to the ale house.

The tavern was mostly empty. The midday crowd had gone and the evening crowd had not yet arrived. A few regulars—grizzled old sailors who spent their days reliving their past glories—greeted Kate. She joined Olaf at a table by the window. From here, they could both see *Victorie*.

"Nothing from Sir Henry?" Olaf asked.

"No," said Kate.

"You didn't do anything to upset His Lordship, did you?" Olaf asked.

"No, of course, not," Kate replied. "Sir Henry was extremely pleased with the success of our last job. I expect His Lordship is just busy, what with the furor over the new dragons and the rioting. Do you want another ale?"

Before he could answer, she went to the bar to fetch two more mugs.

"Seems you have an admirer, Katydid," said Olaf, grinning at her on her return. "That man over there can't take his eyes off you."

"Oh, yeah? Where?" Kate asked, humoring him.

"In the corner, to the right of the bar."

She slightly turned her head and saw Trubgek.

Kate felt a chill, as though she had been plunged into the cold air below the Breath. She managed a smile for Olaf, however.

"I think I'll go back to the ship."

"You haven't touched your ale," Olaf pointed out, startled. He eyed her. "What's wrong, Kate? Something's wrong. I know that look."

"Nothing's wrong," said Kate irritably. "I'll see you on board."

She left the tavern, walked a short distance down the street, and stopped to look in a shopwindow. Out of the corner of her eye, she saw Trubgek come out of the ale house. She turned her back and continued on down the street, trying to maintain a normal pace, though she felt like running.

Risking a glance over her shoulder, she saw that Trubgek was following her and that he was gaining on her. Believing she was safer in a crowd than alone, Kate came to a sudden halt, much to the annoyance of a man who nearly bumped into her. She muttered an apology and turned to confront Trubgek.

"What do you want, sir?" Kate demanded loudly. "Why are you following me?"

Trubgek gazed at her without expression. "Unless you want your business known in the street, I suggest you keep walking."

People were stopping to stare. Kate flushed in anger and turned away. Trubgek fell into step beside her.

"Coreg has a job for you," he said.

"What sort of job?" she asked.

"We can't talk here. I will meet you at the manor."

"I can't go back to Barwich," Kate protested. "I have work to do on board my ship. And I'm waiting for orders."

Trubgek reached into an inner pocket of his leather jerkin and drew out an envelope. Kate saw her name and Henry's seal and the direction "To Be Left Until Called For."

"That is mine! Give that to me!" Kate reached out to take the letter.

Trubgek slid the letter back into his pocket.

"You will hear from me at the manor. Oh, and about that fire in the galley. It wasn't the new stove."

"Fire?" Kate gasped. "What fire?"

He walked off down the street.

Kate slowly walked back to the ship. Once on board, alone in her cabin, she poured the Calvados and sat thinking. She did not have to wait long before she heard the familiar thump of Olaf's crutch on the deck above, then thudding down the stairs.

"Come in," Kate called before he knocked.

Olaf stumped inside. "Is everything all right? You ran out of Pete's like demons were chasing you. That man left after you did. Was he following you?"

"Of course not. Why would anyone follow me? Was there a fire in the galley?"

"A small one," said Olaf.

"You didn't tell me!" said Kate.

Olaf stared at her, startled. "It was only a small fire, Kate. We put it out before it did much damage. I think something's wrong with the magical constructs on the cast-iron damper on that new stove so that it didn't work properly. I was going to look at it tomorrow. Why?"

"No reason. Only I don't think the magic on the stove started the fire." Kate drew up a chair for him. "Here, sit down. Visit with me while I pack."

"Pack?" Olaf, repeated. "You just got here. Where are you going?"

Kate flung some things into the valise, not paying much attention to what they were.

"Since we haven't heard from Sir Henry, I thought I would go to Barwich Manor, talk to Dalgren, tell him about the ship."

"You weren't planning to go anywhere this morning," Olaf said.

"Well, I am now," said Kate, closing the valise. "Is *Victorie* ready to sail?"

"She could be," Olaf replied warily. "A few minor things need to be done, but I could manage those out in the Breath."

"Good," said Kate. "Leave tonight. Tell the port authorities and the crew that you want to see how the ship handles since we've made repairs. Sail to that inlet off Blacktooth Point. The one Morgan used during smuggling runs."

"Why the sudden rush?" Olaf demanded. "We need more men! And what about you?"

"We can manage with the crew we have. Dalgren and I will meet up with you once we have our orders."

Olaf glared at her. "What trouble are you in now, Katydid?"

"Everything will be fine," said Kate.

She picked up the valise and headed out the door.

"Those were the last words your father ever said to me!" Olaf called after her.

Kate traveled the short distance to Barwich Manor and walked into the manor house shouting Trubgek's name. Only echoes of her own voice answered. Annoyed, she searched the manor room by room. She saw no sign that anyone had been in the house since she was last there.

She thought of going to see Dalgren, tell him that Trubgek was back, that Coreg wanted her to do a job for him and that Trubgek had threatened her. She would have liked to see Trubgek make those same threats while staring into the eyes of a dragon.

Kate discarded the idea. If Trubgek was watching her—and she had every reason to believe he was—she didn't want to lead him to Dalgren's lair. She had never known anyone as powerful in magic as Trubgek and while she didn't think Dalgren was in any danger, the dragon had vowed to never attack a human even in his own self-defense. She couldn't take a chance.

And there was another reason. She needed to find out what this job entailed. If it was relatively simple and paid well, she might consider it.

"And I mean paid in bank notes," Kate muttered. "Not paid in threats to knock down my house."

She didn't sleep well that night. She kept imagining she heard noises, and would get out of bed to go roaming through the halls with her lantern, only to discover the house was empty.

When she did finally fall asleep, she woke up to broad daylight. She climbed out of bed, wrapped herself in her dressing gown, and walked into the kitchen. Sunlight streamed into the room, coming through the door that she had left closed and locked and that was now standing wide open.

Trubgek sat at the table.

Kate sat down across from him. "I'm too tired to be intimidated. If you have something to say to me, say it."

"A certain party approached Coreg about hiring an assassin to kill a dragon."

"Kill a dragon?" Kate smiled. "That's ridiculous."

"Coreg thinks so as well, but this party claims to know of a magical construct that was created many years ago for the sole purpose of killing dragons. You are a crafter. Coreg wants you to do the job."

"I may be a crafter, but I'm not an assassin," said Kate.

Trubgek gazed at her with his empty eyes. "You are what Coreg says you are."

Kate opened her mouth to make an angry rejoinder, but then thought better of it. She decided to temporize until she found out what was going on.

"Since Coreg agrees with me that attempting to assassinate a dragon is folly, why are you here? What job does he want me to do?"

Kate paused, then answered her own question. "Coreg wants the magical construct, doesn't he?"

"You will obtain the construct," said Trubgek. "That is the first half of the job. We will discuss the second half once you have the construct."

"I will not murder anyone," said Kate. "Human or dragon!"

Trubgek reached into his pocket, drew out a note and key. He laid them on the table. "The construct will be at this location."

Kate made no move to pick them up. "Why don't *you* do Coreg's dirty work. You fetch the construct. You are a far better crafter than I am."

"Because Coreg is hiring you," said Trubgek. "Will you do it? Or should I tell my master that you refuse?"

"How much does it pay?" Kate asked. She picked up the bosun's whistle she had placed on the table the night before. "And before you answer, you should know that all I have to do is blow on this whistle. My dragon friend and partner, Dalgren, will be here to ask you himself how much this job pays."

Kate leaned forward. "You may be an expert at magic, but are you good enough to go up against a dragon?"

Trubgek gazed at her in silence. He was probably trying to figure out if she was bluffing.

She was bluffing, but could he take the chance?

"Coreg said if you obtain the construct, he will pay fifty Freyan eagles."

"A hundred," said Kate.

"One hundred," said Trubgek.

Kate smiled. "What do I do with the construct once I have it?"

"I will be in touch," said Trubgek. "Say nothing of this to anyone."

He stood up, turned, and walked out the door into the sunshine.

"This is the last job I do for Coreg!" Kate said to his retreating back. "Tell him that!"

Trubgek kept walking and eventually Kate lost sight of him.

The note and the key were still on the table. Kate eyed them.

"I don't believe it. Any of it. I need to know what is truly going on."

Still concerned that Trubgek was lurking about, watching her, Kate waited until nightfall to leave the house. She brought along a dark lantern, but she didn't need it. The night was brighter than she would have liked, for there was a half-moon and the sky was clear. Stars glittered and the mists of the Breath were mere wisps drifting past the moon.

Muffled in a long dark cloak, she walked along the side of the road, keeping to the shadow of trees as much as possible and making frequent stops to watch and listen for the sounds of someone trailing her.

She heard nothing and began to relax and enjoy the brisk walk, glad to release pent-up energy.

She veered off the road and into the woods, finally reaching Dalgren's dwelling—a cavern in the limestone bluffs along the riverbank.

"Dalgren! It's me!" Kate called on entering. Since the hour was late and he wouldn't be expecting her, she wanted to make certain he didn't mistake her for an intruder. She flashed the light about and found him curled up, nose to tail, sleeping.

"Kate . . ." Dalgren blinked at her and gave a gaping yawn. "What are you doing here? I didn't expect you back yet."

"I didn't expect to *be* back," said Kate.

She sat down on the stone floor, keeping her cloak wrapped around her, and set down the dark lantern, leaving it open so that the light illuminated the cave.

"We need to talk," she told him.

Dalgren yawned again. "I just finished eating. I don't suppose this could wait until morning."

"Not after I walked all this way in the dark. I need your advice," said Kate.

She told Dalgren about her conversation with Trubgek.

"A magical construct that can kill a dragon. You can laugh if you want," she added.

But Dalgren wasn't laughing. He had stopped yawning.

"Don't get mixed up in this, Kate," he said. "Tell Coreg you won't do this job."

"So it *is* true," said Kate. "About the magic. I wondered."

Dalgren uncurled his body. His tail scraped across the stone. He stretched, then lowered himself to the ground before he answered.

"There were rumors."

"About dragon-slaying magic?" Kate was skeptical.

"That such magic existed," Dalgren replied. "No one knew for certain. I was in the Dragon Brigade at the time and we considered it possible."

"When was this?"

"During the reign of King Godfrey of Freya. Tensions were running high between Rosia and Freya," Dalgren explained. "War appeared inevitable. The Freyans had always hated and feared the Dragon Brigade and thus it was no surprise that they would try to find a way to kill us or our family members. In the end, of course, war was averted. King Godfrey died. The rumors stopped."

Kate huddled in her cloak. The cavern was cold. She sat, thinking.

"What are you going to do?" Dalgren asked after a moment.

Kate stirred uneasily. "I already agreed to do the job."

"What?" Dalgren roared. The cave filled with smoke.

"I didn't expect you to confirm that someone had actually concocted such a harebrained scheme," Kate said. "Trubgek threatened to set fire to *Victorie*!"

She didn't mention anything about the hundred eagles.

Dalgren eyed her, troubled. "You said Coreg wants to you to get hold of this construct. Is that all, Kate? Or does he want you to use it?"

Kate heard herself saying: *I'm not an assassin.*

She heard Trubgek's reply: *You are what Coreg says you are.*

"How could you think such a thing?" Kate demanded. She was shivering and she rose to her feet and started pacing to keep warm. "You know me better than that! Whatever else I am, I am not a murderer!"

"And yet you are working for Coreg," Dalgren growled.

"The last job," said Kate. "I swear."

Dalgren was silent. Kate could feel disapproval radiating from him. She rounded on him. "I told you that if I don't take this job, Trubgek will knock down my house! He'll set fire to my ship! What would you have me do?"

"Go to Sir Henry," Dalgren advised. "Tell him everything. Let him handle this. He has the means, the resources to deal with Coreg."

"I already thought of that," Kate returned. "Sir Henry would ask questions and I don't have the answers. What could I tell him? That I'm working for someone else on the sly? He would take my house, my ship, and throw me in the gutter."

"Then tell Miss Amelia," said Dalgren. "She could go to Sir Henry. She wouldn't have to reveal her source."

Kate paused. She could tell Amelia. Then she remembered.

"Miss Amelia isn't here. She traveled to northern Freya to meet with some dragon."

Kate continued to pace. Dalgren watched her, his snout resting on the ground. Little puffs of smoke issued from between his jaws. He shifted his body to try to get more comfortable.

"I have an idea," Kate said, talking slowly, thinking it through. "I will do the job. Once I have the construct, I'll take it to Sir Henry. I can say I found it in an old box in the attic. People are always finding things in old boxes in the attic."

"What will you tell Trubgek when he comes for the construct?" Dalgren asked.

Kate wondered if there might be some way to collect the hundred eagles and still avoid handing over the construct. She would have to think about that. In the meantime, she reassured Dalgren.

"I won't have to tell Trubgek anything because when he comes to collect, we will be long gone," said Kate. "Not even he can find us in the middle of the Breath."

Dalgren was troubled. "I still don't think you should have anything to do with this vile construct."

"One last job and I will be free of Coreg for good," Kate said. "Now go back to sleep. Tomorrow I need you to fly to Blacktooth Point, meet up with Olaf and the *Victorie*. Keep watch over them. I want to be ready to leave Freya the moment I give Sir Henry that construct."

Kate felt better having made a decision. She thought over her plan on the way home and wondered about how to earn her money. Morgan would have fobbed off a fake construct. Difficult to do, given that Trubgek was a crafter. She would have to wait until she saw it. She found the note and the key where she had left them on the table and saw no sign that Trubgek had been in the house.

She read the note, which gave a date and a time and an address: *17 Waltham Lane, Haever.* And the instructions: *The package will be inside the house. Take it and leave. Wait for further orders.*

Kate studied the key, thinking it might tell her something. She saw nothing remarkable about it, however; just a plain ordinary house key.

"Sounds simple enough," she said.

Morgan would have said, "Too simple."

THIRTY-EIGHT

Kate had no intention of doing this job without first investigating the house. Haever was a sprawling city of one hundred thousand inhabitants and while she was familiar with the major thoroughfares and prominent buildings and landmarks, she was lost when it came to the multitude of highways, byways, streets, lanes, and alleys crisscrossing the city.

One of Miss Amelia's most prized possessions was a set of maps of the city drawn by a noted surveyor. The project, which took ten years to complete, was published in a large book consisting of twenty-four pages of engravings. Since Miss Amelia visited every conceivable part of Haever in pursuit of her stories, she relied extensively on the maps.

The book was titled *A Plan of the City of Haever with the Contiguous Buildings; From an Actual Survey Taken by Alfred Brock Land-Surveyor, and Engraved by George Oakenshield, Bluemantle Pursuivant at Arms and Chief Engraver of Seals, &c. to Her Majesty.* An alphabetical index listed the names of the streets and where they could be found on the map.

Kate looked for the address, 17 Waltham Lane.

She strained her eyes poring over the finely detailed engraved maps, trying to find the tiny street, and finally located it on the outskirts of the city. She needed to inspect the house in advance, familiarize herself with it and the surrounding buildings. Dressed as a servant in a plain gown of woven striped cotton, a dark linen petticoat and apron, and a short cloak, she stuffed her curls into a frilly cap and set out to view the house. If anyone asked, she was there to deliver a message.

The street was some distance away, forcing her to take a cab. Noting her clothes, the driver asked to see her money first. She paid him and asked him to drop her off several blocks from the house. She walked the rest of the way.

The neighborhood was old and run-down and appeared to deteriorate with each block. Waltham Lane turned out to be short, narrow, and dirty. Kate found four large houses, two on either side of the street. Some attempt had apparently been made to turn the houses into tenements, but that had ended in failure. One was slowly collapsing into a pile of rat-infested rubble. Another was a burned-out hulk.

The two remaining buildings were uninhabited. A few placards stating "To Let" had been placed in the dingy front windows, seemingly with little hope that anyone would respond, for the signs were faded and brown with age. One of these empty buildings was number 17.

The placards gave Kate an excuse to look inside the house. She walked up to the window to study the placard. If anyone noticed her (which seemed highly unlikely, for the street was deserted), she could say she was making note of the name of the estate agent, Cassingham, Schmidt, and Wallace. She wondered idly if this Wallace had anything to do with Sir Henry. She doubted it; Wallace was a common enough name. Still, one never knew. She tucked away the information to ask Amelia.

Kate looked through various windows into rooms, and saw that the house was empty. The walls were water-stained with peeling plaster. No furniture. No curtains. No evidence that anyone had been inside in years. She would have liked to try the key Trubgek had given her to see if it fit in the lock, but, on the off chance that someone was watching, she dared not take the risk.

Kate walked around to the back of the house. A weed-choked yard led to an alley. Boards had been nailed across the back door, perhaps to keep out vagrants. She walked around to the front and surveyed the lane itself.

Trash and dead leaves blew down the broken pavement. The fire in the burned-out building must have been recent, for she could still smell smoke in the air. The only streetlamp on the block was broken. Waltham Lane would be a dark and desolate place at night.

Kate took a cab back home, spending the time formulating her plans. When she entered the house she was surprised to find that Amelia had returned.

"Miss Amelia! I didn't expect you back so soon," said Kate. "Did you talk to the dragon? What did you find out about Coreg?"

"A wasted journey," said Amelia. "Our paths crossed. Odila, the dragon who has the information I need, left the day I arrived, to travel to Haever in answer to an invitation to meet with the queen. After traveling for days, I just missed her."

"So you didn't learn anything," said Kate.

"'What can't be cured must be endured.' That was Mrs. Ridgeway's philosophy. One of Odila's servants was there to meet me with the dragon's apologies and a note. She has rescheduled our meeting for first thing tomorrow morning."

Kate thought this over. She remembered Dalgren's suggestion that she tell Amelia about the magical construct. For a change, Kate decided to act upon it.

"Something happened while you were gone, Miss Amelia. I need your advice."

Amelia was pleased. "A story in the offing! Wait here, Captain. I will make a pot of tea and then hear what you have to tell."

She came back with the tea tray, which she placed on the desk, then sat down and prepared to take notes. Kate poured the tea and told her tale. She described her meetings with Trubgek and the dragon-slaying magical construct.

"This is the note telling me where to find the construct. 17 Waltham Lane. I went to investigate. The house is deserted. By the way, while I was there, I noticed something odd. The agency that owns it is Cassingham, Schmidt, and Wallace. Would that be Sir Henry?"

"I sincerely doubt it, Captain," said Amelia absently. She was perusing the letter. "Sir Henry derives most of his income from his estate in Staffordshire, a gift from Her Majesty."

Amelia glanced at the note and laid it down with a smile and a slight shake of her head.

Kate wondered why she was smiling. "I know you think that working for Coreg is a mistake. But I need to get hold of this magical construct. Dalgren says it could be dangerous."

"Hardly, my dear," said Amelia. "The magic doesn't work. It never did."

She took off her glasses and tapped them thoughtfully on the table.

Kate stared at her in blank astonishment. "The magic doesn't work!"

"It was all a cock-up. A complete waste of time."

"I don't understand," said Kate, dismayed, wondering about her hundred eagles.

"Let me explain. The fiasco began twenty-three years ago when King

Godfrey—a devious man if there ever was one—and a few crackpot members of the House of Nobles got this silly notion into their heads that they could use ancient Imhrun magic to assassinate dragons.

"Godfrey hated Rosia, especially the Dragon Brigade. For years he'd been trying to find a way to get rid of them. A museum curator was examining some ancient Imhrun scrolls when he came across something about dragon-killing magic. He was tremendously excited and sent word to the palace. King Godfrey and his cronies hired crafters, the best in Freya, to develop the magic.

"I was just starting my journalistic endeavors in those days, eager to make my name, when I heard rumors about a secret plot to kill dragons. That was exciting, and I decided to investigate. What I discovered was that crafters worked for months and spent inordinate amounts of money, only to determine that the magic would not work. It had not worked for the Imhruns and it would not work today, even with our modern advancements in magical crafting."

"But if that's true, why would Coreg hire me to get hold of this construct?"

"That is what I find intriguing," said Amelia. "The most obvious answer is that Coreg doesn't know the construct won't work. And neither does whoever hired him."

"Who do you suppose that is?" Kate asked.

"I have no idea. The news about the failure was hushed up, never made public. Godfrey died not long after. I had hoped his loathsome scheme died with him. There were several people who knew about it, however, and given all this rabble-rousing against the Travian dragons, I suppose it was only a matter of time before this ugly idea resurfaced."

Amelia regarded Kate with thoughtful intensity. "Did Coreg ask you to use the construct to kill a dragon, Captain?"

Kate frowned. "Dalgren asked the same thing. Why does everyone assume I am capable of committing cold-blooded murder?"

"I do not think so, Captain," said Amelia. "I merely asked."

"Dalgren does," Kate said bitterly. She jumped up and began to pace about the room. "And apparently so does Coreg, since he hired me. I made it clear to Trubgek that I wouldn't kill anyone. Besides, if what you say is true, then it doesn't matter if I agreed or not, because the magic won't work."

"I would still like to know who is behind this," said Amelia.

"So would I." Kate sighed. She was going to have to give up her hundred golden eagles. She could not see any way around that. In return, however, she would earn goodwill with Sir Henry. Perhaps he might even give her a reward.

She sat back down at the table. "I have a plan. This is our chance to expose Coreg and his entire operation. You are meeting tomorrow with the dragon who has damaging information against him. I'm picking up this construct tonight. It's as if Fate is conspiring with us to bring him down!"

"I do not put much trust in that fickle female," said Amelia. "Still, you do present a cogent argument for acquiring this construct, although I don't like the idea of you going alone. I would accompany you, but I am supposed to meet with Lady Odila at old Castle Lindameer in Durham, north of Haever. The castle is the only place they could find that is large enough to accommodate the dragon. I had planned on leaving tonight and staying in a nearby inn."

Kate smiled inwardly to think of Amelia coming with her as a bodyguard. "Here's my suggestion. Once I have the construct, I will take a wyvern-drawn cab and meet you at this inn. I will have the construct with me. After you've met with the dragon, we will both go straight to Sir Henry."

Amelia was impressed. "An excellent idea, Captain. I will be staying at the Lord Willingham Arms in Durham. I will book you a room and tell them you will be arriving late. And I will send a note to Sir Henry, requesting a meeting."

Amelia wrote the note and sent it by messenger, asking him to wait for a reply. Kate made certain she had everything she needed for the job tonight. She had hired a horse so that she wouldn't have to rely on a cab. She loaded her two pistols and accepted the loan of Amelia's odd-looking pistol, which had two barrels that could each be fired separately.

Hearing the messenger return, Kate hurried downstairs and asked Amelia, "What did Sir Henry say?"

"Sir Henry is planning to accompany Her Majesty on her visit to the dragon tomorrow. He travels to Durham tonight and is staying in the very same inn! He suggests we meet with him there."

Kate's thoughts reverted back to her last meeting with Henry.

"I have an odd question, Miss Amelia. What do you know about this so-called Prince Tom?"

"Thomas Stanford?" Amelia looked up from her writing. "Not much, I am afraid. His stories are quite popular—almost as popular as yours."

Kate smiled. "Does this Prince Tom have a rightful claim to the throne?"

"As I understand it, he has the best claim," said Amelia.

"So then why is Her Majesty so opposed to him?" Kate asked. "Why is Sir Henry opposed?"

"Two words, Captain: power and influence," said Amelia. "The queen views Thomas as a threat to her family and the stability of the kingdom.

As for Sir Henry, he supported the queen's interests when King Godfrey was dying, persuaded Godfrey to name her as his heir. The queen rewarded him by giving him her niece in marriage and making him an earl. She protects him from his enemies, of whom he has many. All that could end if Prince Tom were to take the throne. Henry could be stripped of wealth, lands, title—or worse. He might well find himself in prison or facing execution."

So that explains Henry's outraged reaction to Phillip's message, Kate thought.

"Why do you want to know, Captain?" Amelia asked, fixing her with a shrewd look.

"No reason," Kate said, shrugging. "I was reading the prince's stories. That's all."

"We were speaking of Sir Henry, and you bring up Prince Tom." Amelia laid down her pen to regard Kate with earnest gravity. "Let me give you some advice. I speak from the heart, for I know something of palace intrigue. That world is a pit of vipers, far more dangerous and deadly than you can imagine. Do not get involved, Kate. Do not let Sir Henry or anyone else drag you down into it."

"Rest assured, Miss Amelia, I have no intention of getting mixed up in royal politics," Kate said firmly. "No intention whatsoever."

THIRTY-NINE

After Amelia had left for Durham and the Lord Willingham Arms, Kate took out the book of maps and pored over it, memorizing the route she would need to take to Waltham Lane.

She dressed in her slops, for she felt most comfortable in those, and the calico shirt, with a belt in which to tuck the pistols. She took the additional precaution of placing her knife into her boot. Amelia had provided lock-picking tools, to be used in the event that the construct was locked inside a chest or the key to the front door wouldn't work.

Kate tied her curls beneath her kerchief, put on a dark cloak with a hood, mounted the horse she had hired, and rode off. She was now more curious than apprehensive about the job, figuring that since the house was vacant, this was what Morgan would have called a "dead drop," a time-honored technique long used by spies and smugglers for the secret exchange of goods or information.

The hour was twilight, about seven of the clock. Kate had calculated that she would need at least an hour to ride the twisting and winding streets to her destination, arriving around eight. The meeting was set for nine, but she wanted to be there well ahead of time to keep an eye on the house. She had been a little surprised at the earliness of the hour; such deeds generally occurred around midnight, when no one was about. She had realized, upon seeing Waltham Lane, that she could probably have come at noon.

Her progress was slowed by traffic: horses and carts, carriages and hackney cabs, wagons and pedestrians. It didn't help that some of the streets were missing signs. The traffic thinned out as she rode north and she went from threading her way among the crowds frequenting the theaters to riding alone through empty streets beneath glowing streetlamps. By the time she reached Waltham Lane, she didn't even have the company of streetlamps.

She rode slowly, for with the coming of night, the mists of the Breath were rolling in off the coast. Wisps of fog crept along the pavement, flitting around her like wraiths.

Kate tethered the horse about a block from the house and proceeded on foot, using a dark lantern to find the way. She didn't like showing a light, but there was no help for it.

"Trubgek knows I'm coming anyway," Kate said to herself. "If he's out there spying on me, he's out there. At least he knows I'm on the job."

She flashed the light around, playing it on the buildings she passed and shining it in doorways, but saw no sign of Trubgek or anyone else. By the time she reached number 17, the clocks in the city were chiming half past the hour of nine. She was late. She hoped that didn't matter.

She paused on the sidewalk in front of the house, searching the windows for a glimmer of light that might indicate someone was inside. She saw nothing and heard nothing except water dripping from the eaves as the mists thickened and a light rain began to fall.

Still watchful, she mounted the crumbling steps to the front door and shone the light on the door. The key was cold and wet and she fumbled at the keyhole, but finally thrust the key in. The key turned easily, the lock clicked. She shut the cover on the dark lantern, opened the door a crack, and listened.

The house was quiet and smelled of mold and mildew. She thrust open the door and quickly searched behind it.

Finding no one lurking behind the door, Kate took a step inside, shooting the beam of light about the room. She was in an entry hall with a staircase in front of her, a room to her right, and one to her left. She chose the one to her left. There, on the floor, was a leather saddlebag and an old sword.

Kate could have anticipated the saddlebag, but she was astonished to find a sword and she bent down for a closer look. Setting the lantern on the floor, she studied the weapon, being careful not to touch it until she knew more about it.

The sword was definitely antiquated, crudely made, heavy and clumsy to wield. The blade was dull and notched. She looked for magical constructs, but found none. Any magic the sword's forger might have added would long since have disappeared. The hilt was set with jewels—amethyst and maybe tourmaline, semiprecious and not very valuable.

She turned her attention from the sword to the saddlebag, which, presumably, contained the magical construct. The bag was modern, shabby, plain, and ordinary, with only the usual magical constructs to protect it from the weather.

She checked for warding constructs or magical traps that might have been placed to prevent thieving. Not finding any, she lifted the lantern, opened the bag, and peered inside.

She saw what appeared to be a neatly folded linen dish towel.

"How very strange," said Kate.

She reached into the saddlebag, took out the dish towel, held it up and shook it out.

The linen began to glow a faint blue. Kate gasped and hurriedly dropped it to the floor, fearing the magic might explode or burn her fingers.

The towel lay on the floor in a heap, softly glowing. Kate gingerly touched it, and when nothing happened, she smoothed it out and began to study it.

This wasn't a towel. It was a scroll.

"Bloody hell . . ." Kate murmured, awed.

She had been around magic all her life and she had never seen magic like this. Every conceivable inch of the linen scroll, beginning with the top left corner and extending down to the lower right, was covered with fine lines of magic, the inscription done in a neat and precise hand.

She traced the lines of the magical construct and found, to her growing amazement, that it continued on, row after row after row, until it reached the very bottom.

And there it ended.

The scroll was as long as her arm, extending from fingers to shoulder, and it contained a single magical construct—a construct so complex that Kate could not begin to understand it, much less cast it.

She had no idea what it was meant to do. She knew one thing: Whatever the magic was supposed to do would succeed. The magic was viable. Kate could see and feel and even hear the power of the construct humming, pulsing, eager to be activated.

Amelia was wrong. If this spell was meant to kill dragons, it would work. The crafter would need to be highly trained in the casting of it, however. Kate could make neither heads nor tails of it and she was thankful that she and Amelia had arranged to hand it off to Sir Henry. She wanted nothing to do with it.

She picked up the linen scroll, gingerly holding it by a corner, and started to return it to the saddlebag.

A floorboard creaked. Someone else was in the house.

"Trubgek!" Kate muttered.

The sound had come from behind her. She heard another creak and the sound of breathing, moving steadily toward her. She thrust the cloth into the saddlebag using her left hand. Her right hand stole to her belt and clasped hold of her pistol. Stealthily drawing it, she slowly drew back the hammer.

She caught a glimpse of a man in a greatcoat coming at her in a rush. Kate fired and missed. He lunged at her and kicked the pistol from her hand. Kate made a desperate grab for her other pistol, but he slammed his booted foot down on her hand with such force that she gasped in pain.

Kate fumbled with her free hand for the knife in her boot. Her assailant saw the danger and grabbed hold of the blade a split second before she could reach it. He tossed it away and struck her across the face, leaving her dazed and bleeding. Bending down, he drew a handkerchief from the pocket of his greatcoat and pressed the handkerhief over her nose and mouth. As he bent over her, the scarf concealing his face slipped.

Kate caught only a glimpse, but enough to know the man was a stranger. He wasn't Trubgek.

A sweet, nauseating smell filled her mouth and nose. She coughed and jerked her head, trying to free herself, digging her nails into his flesh. He pressed the handkerchief more tightly over her mouth. The fumes flowed into Kate's nose, down her throat, and into her lungs.

She sank beneath them.

Trubgek was outside the house on Waltham Lane, sitting at his ease on the doorstoop of the burned-out hulk across from number 17. He had been at his post from twilight on. Kate had walked right past him without noticing him.

He watched her enter the house and followed the glow of her lantern as it moved from one dirty window to another. The glow dimmed and he guessed she had lowered the lantern to the floor. He patiently waited for her to come out of the house with the construct. When she did, he would deal with her and take the construct to Coreg.

He was debating what to do about Kate. She disturbed him and he didn't like that. Nothing ever disturbed him. But she knew the truth about his name. She knew that every time Coreg spoke to him, the dragon was deriding him, demeaning him. No one else Trubgek had ever met had either known or cared that his name was an insult. Trubgek had forgotten he cared, until he had met Kate. Her words had set free feelings he had kept chained up in the darkness of his soul.

The light shifted, grew brighter, and Trubgek stood up. Kate would have to walk past him to return to her horse and he would seize her then.

The door opened. Trubgek saw, much to his surprise, a man wearing a greatcoat and a scarf emerge from the house. The man carried a large bundle slung over his shoulder.

Coreg was right, Trubgek thought. It was a trap.

The bundle, of course, was Kate. She was unconscious, her head lolled, her arms dangled down the man's back. In addition to Kate, the man carried a saddlebag and—oddly—a sword.

Trubgek swiftly walked across the street. He did not fear the man would see him, for Trubgek could make himself one with the mists and the rain if he chose. He stationed himself beneath the broken streetlamp outside the house, placed his hand on the pole, and waited.

The man walked beneath the broken lamp.

Magical light flared. The man, startled, lifted his head to stare at the lamp, squinting against the glare. Trubgek got a good look at the face.

For the second time that night, Trubgek was surprised, and that was unusual. Nothing ever surprised him. He recognized the man.

The light flickered and went out and the man continued down the street to Kate's horse. He flung her limp body over the saddle, covered her with a blanket, and strapped her securely to the horse's back.

He gave a low whistle and another man emerged from the shadows. The first man handed over the reins of Kate's horse to the second. The two exchanged a few words; then the first man departed, carrying with him the saddlebag and the sword. He walked around the house and disappeared around back.

The second man led away the horse with Kate, still unconscious, tied to it. Trubgek forgot about her. He kept watch and a few moments later heard wings flapping. Trubgek turned his head to see a griffin with a rider rise from the alley behind the house.

Trubgek watched the griffin until it disappeared behind the rooftops. Truly a remarkable development. One he had not foreseen.

He knew he should return to Freeport, report this to Coreg. But Trubgek had the feeling events were going to move rapidly, and if the events unfolded as Trubgek anticipated, he needed to be here. He had recognized this man and he would have him in his power.

Trubgek decided to wait.

FORTY

The Lord Willingham Arms in Durham was about five miles as the wyvern flies from Castle Lindameer. Amelia arrived at sunset. When the clerk had his back turned to get her key for her, she cast a surreptitious glance at the guest book, curious to know Sir Henry's room number. Finding it proved to be easy. He and his secretary, Franklin Sloan, were the inn's only other guests.

Amelia brusquely refused the clerk's offer to carry her valise, and climbed the stairs to her room. She made herself presentable, then went down to dinner, where she was disappointed to hear that Sir Henry was dining in his chambers. She had hoped to speak to him at dinner, but now she would have to wait.

Upon reflection, she was rather glad. Over her quiet meal, she had the opportunity to compose her thoughts, decide exactly what to say and, more important, what not to say.

When she was finished, she noted the hour. Sir Henry would likely be enjoying a glass of port. Patting her hair into place and arming herself with the reticule, Amelia went to boldly knock upon his door.

Mr. Sloan answered.

"Miss Amelia Nettleship to see Sir Henry," she said as she handed Mr. Sloan her calling card and deftly swept past him into the room.

"Madame! Sir Henry is not receiving visitors!" Mr. Sloan exclaimed, shocked.

"At ease, Mr. Sloan," said Henry. "Miss Nettleship and I are friends of long standing. We can finish the correspondence at another time."

"Very good, my lord," said Mr. Sloan stiffly. He gathered up a bundle of papers, placed them into a portable writing desk, looked his disapproval at Amelia, and departed.

Henry rose from the armchair where he had been sitting and advanced to shake hands. "How do you do, Miss Nettleship? Please, sit down. May I offer you sherry, or ring for some tea?"

"Thank you, no, Sir Henry. I will not be staying long," said Amelia, settling herself on the edge of a chair. "I intend to retire early. And please call me Amelia. Saves time. I have an early meeting tomorrow morning with the dragon, Odila—"

"Lady Odila," Sir Henry gently corrected. "Her Majesty has conferred titles upon all the dragons now living in Freya."

"Ah, yes, thank you for the reminder, my lord," said Amelia. "I would not want to offend."

"I did not know you were meeting with Lady Odila," said Henry mildly. "Might I inquire what the two of you will be discussing?"

"I am researching an article regarding the history of dragons in Freya, my lord," she replied. "Lady Odila has very kindly granted me an interview."

"I fear your article will be extremely short . . . er . . . Miss Amelia," said Henry. He poured himself a glass of port and carried it to the armchair. "Dragons have never before lived in Freya and thus do not have a history."

"They have more than one might think, my lord," said Amelia. "For example, there was King Godfrey's attempt to create magical constructs that could kill dragons."

Sir Henry took a drink of his port and shook his head.

"Good God, Miss Amelia, you astonish me. I have not thought of that fiasco in years!"

Amelia observed Henry narrowly. He was adept at revealing nothing of his true thoughts, but this time, she did not think he was dissembling. He was smiling, albeit with a touch of melancholy.

"Poor Godfrey," Henry continued with another sip of port. "Magic of the ancient Imhruns, wasn't it? I was in Estara at the time, handling a mission of some delicacy for His Majesty, but I heard about it on my return." He gave a rueful shake of his head. "Godfrey was an intelligent man, but he was always falling for crackpot schemes; the crazier the better as far as he was concerned."

"Then, to your knowledge, my lord, the magical construct did not work," said Amelia.

"Work?" Henry laughed. "No, it did not work. Any more than Godfrey's scheme to transmute coal into diamonds."

"Thank you for your time, Sir Henry," Amelia said. "You have been most helpful."

She rose to her feet and Henry rose with her.

"You will be attending the meeting between Lady Odila and Her Majesty tomorrow," Amelia added. "I was wondering if I could ask the favor of meeting with you in private afterward. Captain Kate and I have recently come across some information that I believe could be of value."

Henry frowned. "Where is Captain Kate? She was supposed to have set sail a week ago!" His tone was cool, his brows creased.

"She was delayed. She will join us tomorrow," Amelia answered.

"The meeting is slated for noon," Henry answered. "I should be free around four, the time when Her Majesty is scheduled to return to Haever. Will that hour suit you and the captain?"

"Yes, my lord," said Amelia. "I wish you a good night."

Henry walked her to the door. "Before you go, Miss Amelia, could I ask how you came to hear about the magical construct? I was given to undertand that it was a closely held secret."

"Closely held!" Amelia snorted. "Suffice it to say, I wrote a story about it at the time, my lord. The article was never published."

"I am sure you can understand why, Miss Amelia," said Henry.

"Indeed, yes, my lord," Amelia said drily. "God's anointed king could never be made to look ridiculous."

"Then you understand that you should *not* write about it in this article," said Henry, smiling.

Since Amelia had no intention of writing about the history of dragons, she agreed, although she made a show of being reluctant to acquiesce.

She again shook hands and walked out, pleased with her meeting. Henry had confirmed what she already knew: the construct was a failure. Returning to her room, she started to write down the questions she was planning to ask Lady Odila.

Amelia found herself distracted, however, for she was thinking about Kate and listening for sounds of her arrival. The hours passed, and Kate did not come. When the clock chimed midnight, Amelia decided to give up waiting and go to bed. She was concerned, though not overly so. Kate was someone who could take care of herself.

Amelia woke just before sunrise, her customary time for rising. Mrs. Ridgeway could not abide "lie-abeds" and the girls of her school were all awake and doing their morning exercises at the crack of dawn. Amelia dressed and went downstairs to speak to the servants.

"A friend of mine was supposed to arrive during the night," said Amelia. "Her name is Katherine Gascoyne-Fitzmaurice. Can you give me her room number?"

"I'm sorry, mum," said the servant. "No one came during the night."

Amelia was now worried for her friend. She drank her morning tea and ate her porridge, her customary breakfast, and told herself that Kate could be late for any number of reasons. She might not have been able to find a cab at such a late hour or perhaps she had decided to return to the house, planning to travel today. Amelia settled on these as hopeful possibilities and readied herself for her meeting with the dragon, which was at eight of the clock.

The inn was some distance from the castle, but Amelia decided the walk would do her good, help her to brush away the cobwebs. She set out with the reticule and the umbrella to enjoy the fresh air and the beauty of a day in the country.

Castle Lindameer was an enormous edifice dating back centuries to a time when barons fighting for control of Freya built solid fortifications to help keep what they had. The family that owned it had moved into a much more fashionable palace about the time of King Frederick, but they still maintained the castle, opening it several times a year for large parties. Although they were not particularly fond of dragons, the family could not very well refuse the queen's request to house Lady Odila in the castle on her state visit.

The road that ran in front of the inn led directly to the castle, whose stone fortifications ranged across the top of a hill. Built in a rectangle around an inner courtyard, the castle consisted of ten stone guard towers connected by stone walls, surrounded by a moat that had long since dried up, spanned by a drawbridge that had rusted in place.

The castle's interior was more welcoming. The entry hall had recently been refurbished and was quite splendid, although Amelia found all the furniture covered with sheets and the floor in need of scrubbing. In honor of the queen's arrival, two servants were now engaged in cleaning and talking to each other in Travian.

Lady Odila must have brought her own human servants with her. A good idea, Amelia reflected, considering that the dragon undoubtedly could not have found any Freyans willing to work for her. Amelia stood waiting at the entrance until a maid looked up from her work, saw her, and ran off to tell someone.

A harried-looking man arrived. He introduced himself as Gunthar, Lady Odila's steward.

"You must excuse us, madame," he added, speaking passable Freyan. "We are preparing for Her Majesty's arrival and we have much work to do and few hands to do it."

"I quite understand," said Amelia. "I have an appointment with Lady Odila."

"Her Ladyship informed us she expected you to visit, madame. I have not heard her stir yet, but she is always awake at this time of day. I will take you to her—"

"No need. You are required here," said Amelia. "As long as Her Ladyship does not stand on ceremony, I can find the way myself. Give me directions to her chambers."

"Lady Odila will not mind," Gunthar said, looking relieved. "As I said, she is expecting you. She is residing in the large chamber belowground. Follow this hall until you come to the corner tower. You will need a lantern."

Amelia had studied the layout of the castle prior to her arrival, planning to feature it in her article about Coreg and the interview with Lady Odila.

The baron had used the large underground chamber where Odila was staying to store water, grain, and other supplies in the event the castle should come under siege, a frequent occurrence during that turbulent time in Freya's history. The chamber was accessible either from the castle proper or from a large entryway outside the walls, as wagons would be needed to haul in the supplies, thus providing Lady Odila with easy access.

Following the steward's directions, Amelia hurried along a bleak, dark passageway that led past two smaller towers until she reached the large corner tower. A narrow spiral staircase led to the levels above, as well as down to the dragon's chamber. Amelia lit the lantern and descended the stairs to the ground level.

She did not really require the lantern, for the hallway was well lit with magical light glowing from wrought-iron braziers placed at intervals. Amelia left the lantern hanging on a hook by the door and hastened down the hall. She did not want to be late, and her talk with the steward had put her a little behind time. She could not judge how far she had to go, for the hall did not run straight, but curved to the right, blocking her view.

She began to notice the smell of blood as she followed the curve of the hall. She thought nothing of it, for she had noticed the same odor whenever she had visited Dalgren. Dragons feast on freshly killed carcasses, after all.

But the odor grew much stronger than anything Amelia had noticed around Dalgren. She was not squeamish, yet she was forced to take out a handkerchief and cover her nose and mouth. Picturing the queen having to stop in the hall to vomit, Amelia decided to mention to Gunthar that the servants would be better employed cleaning down here than at the entrance.

Rounding the curve, Amelia stopped short.

Lady Odila's chamber was about twenty feet distant. The entrance was guarded by large double doors made of wood and banded with iron. The doors were closed. A pool of dark liquid had formed beneath the door and was starting to flow in rivulets down the hallway.

Judging by the smell and the dark red color, the liquid was blood.

Amelia thrust her handkerchief into her sleeve, stood her umbrella against the wall, and opened the reticule. She had given Kate her double-barreled pistol, but she carried with her a corset-gun. Drawing it, she cocked the hammer and began to walk slowly and quietly down the hall toward the doors. She tried to avoid treading in the blood, but that proved impossible. The blood had formed a gruesome pond that washed up over the toes of her boots and splattered the hem of her skirt.

Looking again at the massive double doors, she could now see that one stood slightly ajar. Amelia drew in a breath. Holding the pistol in her right hand, she gave the door a shove with her left. The door was heavy and moved only a little, opening enough to allow her to see into the room beyond.

The sight was gruesome, horrible beyond belief. As a reporter Amelia had covered murders, fires, carriage disasters, and dead bodies being hauled out of rivers. She had never flinched.

At this, a wave of dizziness assailed her and she was forced to support herself by leaning against the door. She gagged, swallowed, breathed deeply, gripped the pistol tightly, and stood firm until the giddiness passed. She forced herself to continue to look, dispassionately observing details, before turning away.

She replaced the pistol in the reticule, snapped it shut, then took a moment to decide what to do and to make herself stop trembling. Once she was composed, she walked back down the hall, leaving a trail of bloody footprints.

She was sorry for that, for it might impede the investigation, but it couldn't be helped. She retrieved the lantern and lit her way up the stairs and along the passage. Entering the great hall, she found the steward manhandling a heavy chair, shoving it across the floor. The maids were sweeping and dusting.

"Gunthar," said Amelia. "Stop what you are doing. I need to talk to you."

Alarmed by her tone, Gunthar straightened from his task. The maids turned to stare.

"A tragedy has occurred—" Amelia began.

She was interrupted by one of the maids pointing to Amelia's blood-spattered skirt and giving a loud shriek.

"Stop that caterwauling this instant, girl!" Amelia said. "I don't have time for hysterics."

The maid gulped and stuffed her hand into her mouth. Her shriek subsided to a whimper.

Gunthar had gone rigid. "What has happened, madame?"

"I have some bad news. Your mistress is dead," Amelia said.

"Dead!" Gunthar repeated. His gaze went to the blood on Amelia's skirt and he went white to the lips.

"Listen to me, Gunthar. You must run as fast as you can to the Lord Willingham Arms," Amelia continued. "Ask for Sir Henry Wallace. He is a guest there. Get him alone and tell him what has happened. Do not breathe a word to anyone else. We must keep this quiet for as long as we can."

Gunthar shook his head. "I have to go to my mistress!"

Amelia closely observed him. He had teared up. His eyes were red-rimmed and he was shaking. He appeared to be genuinely grief-stricken.

"You can do nothing to help your mistress now, Gunthar, except to keep this quiet. Think, sir! Queen Mary is due to arrive in a few hours!" Amelia added.

Gunthar blinked at her, dazed, in shock. "We will be ready . . ." He suddenly understood what Amelia was saying. "Oh, God! What do we do?"

"Go fetch Sir Henry. Now! He will know what to do. And, Gunthar, not a word to anyone!"

The steward gave a shaky nod and ran out the door. The maids were weeping. Amelia dared not leave them alone for fear they might flee in panic. She escorted them to the kitchen and made them sit down while she brewed a strong pot of tea. She kept them talking, asking where they slept and if they had heard anything in the night.

"You mean like her screaming, madame?" said one of the servants.

She broke into wails and so did her companion. Amelia could get nothing more out of them for some time.

When they calmed down, they told her that they hadn't heard anything. Not surprising, since the servants' quarters were on the top level, about as far removed from the dragon's chamber as was possible.

"She was a good mistress, madame," one said, wiping her eyes with the corner of her apron. "Never a cross word!"

"We've read some of the terrible things you people have been saying about dragons," the other added indignantly. "It's not true! Any of it."

"I know it isn't," said Amelia. "And you mustn't say anything to anyone. I'm asking you to stay here, at least for the time being. I have to go upstairs to wait for Sir Henry."

"You can rely on us, madame," said one. "We won't talk to a soul."

"How . . . how did she die?" asked the other.

Amelia pretended she hadn't heard and hurried back to the entry hall. Henry arrived not long after, clad only in shirt, breeches, and his waistcoat. He had rushed off without putting on his coat or hat.

"Miss Amelia, I received your message," Henry said, advancing into the hall. "I came as soon as I could and I have brought Mr. Sloan with me. That fellow, Gunthar, is barely coherent. He kept talking about Lady Odila and blood. What has occurred?"

"Where is Gunthar?" Amelia asked.

"He is tending to the horses," said Henry. "What has—?"

He caught sight of the blood that had soaked the hem of her dress and splattered on her skirt. He sucked in his breath.

"Lady Odila is dead," Amelia said. "She has been murdered."

Henry gazed at her from beneath lowered brows. "I know how you journalists love a sensational story, Miss Amelia, but I would be careful if I were you."

In answer, Amelia looked down at the blood that covered her clothes and made a slight gesture with her hands. "There is a vast quantity . . ." She could go no further.

"I see." Henry regarded her intently. He obviously had more questions, but at the moment he had more pressing matters. He turned away from her and began to issue orders.

"Mr. Sloan, ride to the palace. We must stop Her Majesty. Tell her that the Lady Odila is unwell and that the meeting will have to be postponed."

"Yes, my lord," said Mr. Sloan.

"Send a message to Colonel Dalton. Tell him I need a company of marines here as soon as possible. I want this castle sealed, cordoned off."

"Yes, my lord."

"And bring Simon. If murder has been done, I will need him to determine who committed such a terrible crime and, more important, how."

"I know how," said Amelia. "You were wrong, my lord. All of us were wrong. The magic worked."

She had spoken without thinking, which was highly uncharacteristic and only went to prove that she was badly shaken. When she saw Henry's eyes she instantly realized she had made a mistake. He regarded her intently, his lips compressed, his jaw tight.

And it was in that unfortunate moment that Amelia thought of Kate, who had been sent to fetch the magical construct designed to kill dragons and who hadn't come to the inn last night as they had planned. Did Kate do this terrible deed?

The blow was staggering, and Amelia almost gave way beneath it, but managed to keep a grip on herself. She looked at Henry to see if he had noticed her momentary lapse, but he was grappling with his own problems.

"Where are the servants?" he asked.

"I sent the maids to the kitchen," said Amelia.

"I will want to question them, as well as Gunthar. Mr. Sloan, on your way out, tell Gunthar to take my horse to the stable and then go to the kitchen."

"Very good, my lord," said Mr. Sloan.

"I observed Gunthar as I broke the news to him that his mistress was dead," said Amelia. "He appeared to be genuinely affected."

"Appearances don't mean much," said Henry in grim tones. "Godspeed, Mr. Sloan. Return as fast as you can."

"I will do so, my lord," said Mr. Sloan. He left the room with alacrity; shortly, they could hear him outside, talking to Gunthar.

Now that Amelia and Henry were alone, she braced herself for the question she knew was coming and which she had no idea how she was going to answer. She found it hard to meet his cold, piercing gaze, but she stood her ground.

He did not ask the question she feared. Instead, he asked another. "Who found Lady Odila?"

"I did, my lord," said Amelia.

"When you kept the appointment you had with her."

"Yes, my lord," said Amelia.

Henry regarded her another moment, then said abruptly, "I want to see for myself. Tell me where to find . . . Lady Odila."

"I can take you, my lord," said Amelia. She saw he was going to refuse and added hurriedly, "You might have more questions for me."

"Oh, I have questions for you, Miss Amelia," said Henry, glowering. "Very well. Lead the way."

He accompanied her down the hall to the stairs that led to the dragon's chamber. Henry picked up the lantern and they descended the stairs, moving slowly as he flashed the light about.

"Did you see or hear anything upon your arrival, Miss Amelia?"

"Nothing out of the ordinary, my lord," Amelia replied. "And neither did the servants, but then they sleep in a different part of the castle."

"Those footprints?" Henry stopped, shining the light on the floor.

"They are mine, my lord. The blood is . . . everywhere."

Henry said nothing. He hung the lantern on the hook and proceeded down the hall that was still lit with the magical glow. Odila must have lighted the hall for the convenience of the servants and, unknowingly, her killer. Amelia wondered how long the light would last now that the dragon was dead.

Henry said nothing as they proceeded down the hall. They rounded the curve and he saw the blood. "Good God!" he exclaimed, shaken.

The rivulets had combined to form a stream that was slowly spreading. The bloody pool had expanded into a lake.

"The body is through there," said Amelia, indicating the iron-banded doors.

Henry studied the doors for a moment without touching them, then looked into the chamber. Amelia came to stand by his side.

Magical lamps burned, casting a bright light on the ghastly scene. The corpse of the dragon was sprawled on the floor. Lady Odila was a large dragon, about seventy feet in length, and the corpse took up much of the vast chamber. The blood flowed from several huge gashes in the dragon's neck and chest. She had been stabbed repeatedly, and there was no need to search for the weapon.

A bronze sword, protruding from the dragon's skull, had delivered the death blow. The killer had scrawled words on the wall in the dragon's blood.

Death to the Wyrms.

Henry began to softly swear, filthy, ugly words, difficult to hear. He fell silent. Then he said, "I am sorry, Miss Amelia. I did not mean to use such offensive language."

"No need to apologize, my lord," said Amelia. "Lady Odila was tortured. Her death was long and agonizing. You speak what I feel."

"We can do nothing more here," said Henry. "I do not want to disturb anything until Simon has investigated. We might as well question the steward and the maids."

Amelia agreed and they left the grisly scene and walked back up the hall. Henry walked in silence, his head lowered, his hands clasped behind his back.

"You said the magic worked, Miss Amelia. I find it a remarkable coincidence that you should ask me about the magical construct to assassinate dragons last night and stumble across a murdered dragon in the morning."

Amelia made up her mind to tell the truth, or at least enough of the truth to sound truthful. She was not going to implicate Kate in this murder. Not yet. Not until she talked to Kate.

"As you have surmised, my lord, my asking was no coincidence," said Amelia. "I heard that someone was actively searching for King Godfrey's magical construct. I knew from my earlier investigations that the magic didn't work—or at least that is what I was told. I required confirmation. You had done work for His Majesty during that time period and thus I asked you."

Amelia sighed and shook her head. "If you had told me the truth, my lord, we might have prevented this tragedy."

"You think I lied to you," said Henry, frowning. "On the contrary, Miss Amelia, I was assured by someone who had reason to know that the attempts to create such a construct had failed. And I am not yet convinced otherwise. What makes you think an assassin used this magic to kill Lady Odila?"

Amelia stopped walking and turned to face him. "My lord, the answer is obvious. The dragon did nothing to defend herself! The killer tortured her! Stabbed her again and again and she did not roar in pain or anger. She did not burn him to a crisp! She *did nothing*!"

"Can you name this killer, Miss Amelia?" Henry asked.

Amelia met his gaze. "No, my lord."

Henry regarded her in chill silence, then resumed walking.

"You know a great deal more than you are telling me, Miss Amelia," he said. "What was your true reason for meeting with Lady Odila?"

"I was going to bring this information to you after I had talked to her, my lord," said Amelia. "The truth is, I consider my story to be so fantastic I feared you would not believe it. I needed proof."

Amelia told him briefly what she knew about Coreg, leaving out any references to Kate, saying she had heard rumors about the dragon and his vast criminal empire when she was in the Aligoes.

"When I learned Coreg came from Travia, I asked a friend of mine to do some checking among the Travian dragons, to see if any of them knew him. I received a letter from Lady Odila, telling me that she could provide information. She told me in the letter that Coreg was having her watched."

They arrived at the stairs. Henry took down the lantern from the wall and they began to slowly ascend.

"You are right, Miss Amelia, this tale about a dragon criminal overlord does verge on the fantastic," said Henry. "But, as you say, this Coreg is far away in the Aligoes. Why do you think he has any connection to this murder?"

"Because, my lord, I found out it was Coreg who was seeking information about the magical construct," said Amelia.

"And you said nothing!"

Amelia sighed. "My lord, you told me yourself. The magic did not work. I had no idea Lady Odila would be in danger."

"How did you know this Coreg was looking for it, Miss Amelia? Who told you?"

Amelia had known that question was coming. "I would prefer not to say at the moment, my lord."

"By God, Miss Amelia! You either tell me or I will have you arrested!" Henry said, livid with anger.

Amelia nodded. "I understand, my lord. But is that the question you should be asking?"

Henry glared at her. "What do you mean?"

"You were told the magic did not work. My investigations revealed that the magic did not work." Amelia gave him a troubled look. "The question is, Sir Henry—who knew that it did?"

FORTY-ONE

The murder of Lady Odila had placed Sir Henry Wallace in an untenable position. He was the one who had proposed bringing the dragons to Freya, and he would be blamed for the terrible outcome. News of this murder would outrage the Travian dragons and infuriate dragons throughout the world. The scandal would shake a monarchy already on unstable ground. The murder would give credence to the human anti-dragon leagues, those proclaiming that dragons were savage, bloodthirsty creatures who had now killed one of their own and would soon turn on humans.

Sir Henry Wallace listened to Amelia's account of this dragon, Coreg, and was forced to admit that if she had come to him with her tale of a dragon criminal mastermind, he would have found it difficult to keep from laughing. The death of Lady Odila, the fact that she had known this Coreg back in Travia, and that she suspected he was having her watched forced Henry to take a serious view of the matter, although he still found it hard to credit.

As for Amelia, she was shielding someone; that much was obvious. He could not quite believe she was shielding the murderer. She was obviously horrified by the crime. But she knew more than she was telling. A night in prison would loosen her tongue. As for her notion that King Godfrey's magical construct had been instrumental in the dragon's death, Henry didn't believe it. He had good reason to *know* the magic did not work.

He took Amelia with him, determined not to let her out of his sight, and went down to the kitchen to question the servants.

The maids confirmed that neither of them had heard anything, but that proved nothing. Their sleeping quarters were some distance away. Gunthar slept in a different part of the castle, on the floor directly above the dragon's chamber. He had not heard anything, but he admitted to being a heavy sleeper.

"Did Lady Odila ever mention a dragon by the name of Coreg? Either here or back in Travia?" Henry asked with a sharp glance at Amelia. "A dragon she might have known ten years ago."

"No, my lord," said Gunthar. "But I have been with the mistress only about five years."

The maids shook their heads. They had never heard of Coreg.

"Was Lady Odila concerned that she was being watched?" Henry asked.

"Yes, my lord, she was," said Gunthar. "When we lived in Travia, she gave strict orders that no one was to set foot on the property. If I found someone, I was to set the dogs on them. One reason she moved to Freya was to find some peace. God forgive me, I used to laugh at such fancies—"

His voice broke and he lowered his head. The maids began to sob again.

"We could all do with some tea," said Amelia and she went to fix it.

Henry asked a few more questions, more to be doing something than because he believed the servants were involved. He would send someone to check their rooms, of course, but he doubted he would find anything to implicate them. Whoever had done this murder would have been covered in blood. The grisly evidence would have been on the murderer's face, hair, and clothes. Blood was not easy to remove and he could see no trace of it on any of these three. Nor did he see any signs that they had recently bathed.

He decided the best thing to do with them was send them back home to Travia as soon as possible. They would talk, of course, but they could do their talking in Travia, not here. The servants were happy to accept his offer of passage home.

"We didn't want to come to Freya," said Gunthar. "But we didn't want to leave the mistress to the mercy of foreigners."

He gave Henry a baleful look, then took his tea and moved to the far end of the table.

Henry warned them again not to talk to anyone, out of respect for Lady Odila. He refused the cup of tea Amelia offered him, saying he would go upstairs to wait for Simon.

"You will not be able to keep this terrible tragedy quiet for long, my lord," said Amelia.

That is true, Henry reflected bitterly. I cannot keep this quiet. I will have to inform Her Majesty, the other members of the Privy Council, the Lord Speaker of the House of Nobles and key members, some of whom will gloat and immediately plot to use this against me.

"I cannot permit you to write about this, Miss Amelia," he said.

"I have no intention of doing so, my lord," said Amelia.

Henry wondered at this. Here was a journalist with the story of a lifetime and she was not planning to tell it. She stirred beneath his scrutiny, and appeared uneasy.

"You still refuse to tell me what you know," said Henry.

"I will, my lord. I promise. I just need some time to collect my thoughts. This has come as a great shock. I find I think better when I exercise. With your permission, I will take a turn up and down the long gallery." Amelia gave a faint smile. "I promise I will not run away."

Henry trusted she would not leave, not without her story, whether she planned to write about it or not.

"Simon will have questions for you," Henry warned.

"Of course, my lord," said Amelia. "I have long admired Mr. Yates. I look forward to meeting him. I wish it were under different circumstances."

She climbed the grand staircase leading to the upper level. Henry noted that the blood on her clothes was starting to stiffen and harden, as it was on his. He walked over to one of the windows facing into the lane and stood looking out. He had a lot on his mind and all of it extremely unpleasant.

Amelia returned after an absence of an hour to find Henry still at the window.

"When do you expect Mr. Yates, my lord?"

"Not for some time, at least," Henry replied. "He has some difficulty traveling."

"He is without the use of his lower limbs," Amelia said, nodding. "Gunshot wound, as I recall."

"Perhaps you could have the servants make some sandwiches, Miss Amelia," said Henry.

He wasn't hungry, but it would keep her occupied and leave him in solitude.

Simon arrived sooner than expected, accompanied by his servant,

Mr. Albright, and Mr. Sloan. The three had traveled by carriage and they had brought with them Simon's floating chair. Mr. Sloan removed the chair from the carriage. Mr. Albright lifted Simon from the carriage and placed him in the chair.

"Don't fuss, Albright," said Simon, when Mr. Albright wanted to drape a blanket over his legs.

Simon propelled himself into the house. He and the duchess had started designing Simon's chair while he was in bed, recovering from his wound. The chair had been redesigned several times since. Constructed of wood, with a cushioned back and seat, the chair floated over the ground by means of two small lift tanks containing the liquid form of the Breath, one on either side, with a ballast tank on the back. Two small airscrews underneath each armrest propelled the chair.

Simon controlled the chair by means of a brass panel that resembled a ship's helm, which sent the magic to the lift tanks and operated the airscrews. At Simon's instruction, Mr. Albright had built an assortment of wooden cases into the arms. Simon stored various objects, from scientific instruments to a traveling writing desk, in these cases.

"I am glad you could come so quickly, Simon," said Henry, shaking hands with his friend. "I am out of my depth."

"A bad business, Henry," said Simon in a low voice. "A bad business."

Henry introduced Amelia, who had come from the kitchen immediately on hearing Simon's arrival.

"Miss Nettleship, Simon Yates."

"I am glad to meet you, Mr. Yates," Amelia said. "I am an admirer of your work."

Simon shrugged her compliment away. "I would like to proceed to the scene of the murder."

"I doubt Simon's chair will fit in the stairwell. Miss Amelia, would you please take Mr. Sloan and Mr. Albright to see what can be done about transporting the chair down the stairs? Simon and I will follow."

Henry cast a glance at Mr. Sloan, who understood that Henry wanted to speak to Simon alone. Mr. Sloan latched on to Amelia.

"I enjoyed reading your articles regarding those unscrupulous crafters who were using their talents to communicate with the dead, Miss Amelia," said Mr. Sloan.

"They bilked poor widows out of their meager inheritance, Mr. Sloan," said Amelia. "I was glad to bring them to justice. There was one woman, Mrs. A. J. Copley, who was remarkably skilled in creating phantasms . . ."

The three proceeded down the passage. Henry and Simon followed more slowly behind.

"Are you allowing her to accompany us to the murder room?" Simon asked Henry.

"I deem it advisable," Henry said. "As I am certain Mr. Sloan informed you, Miss Amelia came here to meet with the dragon early this morning. It was she who discovered the body. And she has admited to withholding information."

Simon nodded. "Mr. Sloan also said she met with you last night to ask you about Godfrey's magical dragon-killing construct."

"She is convinced the killer used the magic to incapacitate and then torture and kill the dragon," said Henry. "Frankly I think that's nonsense. You and I both know the magic did not work. Are you feeling quite well, Simon? You look a bit peaked."

Henry had been closely observing his friend, noting that he seemed troubled, preoccupied; this was quite unusual for Simon, who generally approached murder investigations with scientific interest and oftentimes disquieting enthusiasm.

"I found the journey fatiguing," said Simon. "Tell me what you have learned."

Henry related the conversation about Coreg. Simon listened without comment as he propelled his chair down the hall.

"The more I think about it, the more I tend to doubt this idea of a dragon criminal overlord."

Simon brought his chair to a halt and sat motionless, frowning down at the blue-glowing constructs on the small brass control panel beneath his right hand.

"Are you listening to me?" Henry asked.

"Yes, of course," Simon said and wheeled his chair forward. "Do not be so quick to dismiss Miss Nettleship's information. Dragons, like humans, are complex creatures, afflicted by similar weaknesses. There is no reason why a dragon should not turn his considerable intelligence to crime. I am certain this Coreg is not the first and might not be the only one to do so. Dragons administer their own justice and thus we humans do not hear about the bad apples."

"I suppose," said Henry, unconvinced.

"That said, I have long been aware of a powerful presence at the center of a vast criminal empire engaged in piracy, smuggling, illicit arms sales, the opium trade, and a host of other evils. The idea that it could be a dragon is intriguing and worthy of serious consideration."

"And what do you make of Miss Amelia's assertion that this Coreg is mixed up with this murder?" Henry asked.

Simon stirred restlessly in his chair.

"A bad business, Henry," he said again. "A bad business. And we are wasting time."

He increased his speed, and began propelling his chair down the hall at such a rapid pace that Henry was forced to practically run to keep up.

Simon managed to maneuver his chair down the spiral staircase, although it proved a tight fit and at one particularly narrow point he became wedged between the walls. After some pushing and pulling, assisted by Mr. Albright, Simon was able to proceed. He slowed his speed as he traveled down the hallway, gazing intently at the floor, the walls and even the ceiling.

"I see your footprints, Henry, and Miss Nettleship's," said Simon. "No others. Is there another way out? I did not have time to study the layout before I came."

"I did, Mr. Yates," Amelia replied. "Lady Odila entered the chamber by means of the trade entrance through which they used to bring wagons filled with supplies. According to Gunthar, once she was inside the castle, she closed the entrance and magically sealed it. There is also a narrow tunnel that leads from the west side of the chamber underneath the walls. The tunnel was built in the event the castle came under siege and the residents needed a way to escape. A rockslide rendered the tunnel impassable about fifty years ago."

"Then the killer came and left by the front entrance," said Simon. "He would have made certain to find out where the servants slept. He knew he wouldn't be disturbed. He must have walked down this very hall."

"But he left no tracks," Henry pointed out. "He could not have avoided stepping in the blood, given the vast quantity."

"He had the foresight to either cover his shoes or he brought another pair with him."

"A professional assassin," Henry observed.

"At least someone who knew what he was doing," Simon said in thoughtful tones.

The blood had cooled and was starting to congeal on the floor. They had no choice but to step in it, with the exception of Simon, who floated above it. Arriving at the banded wooden doors, he called a halt. Ordering them to keep out of his way, he inspected the doors and the surroundings.

"Someone has placed a magical construct on the floor," said Simon. "I can see faint traces of the sigils over there, near the wall. The crafter has attempted to expunge it. Open the doors, Albright. I am going inside. The rest of you stay back."

Mr. Albright pushed open the doors. They gazed inside, silent, overwhelmed by the ghastly sight of the dragon's body lying in a vast pool of blood, slashed, stabbed, and hacked like a side of meat hanging in a butcher shop.

Henry had seen it once and that was enough. He averted his gaze. Mr. Sloan murmured a prayer. Mr. Albright drew a handkerchief from his sleeve and wiped his nose. Amelia stood in pitying silence. Simon was grim-faced and so pale that Henry was worried about him. His hand on the controls of his chair trembled.

"Simon, you are not well—"

"I am fine, Henry!" Simon snapped. "Don't come any closer. I can't have you tromping about, disturbing the evidence."

He entered the chamber. Pausing just inside, he said, "Are you a crafter, Miss Nettleship?"

"To my deep regret, I am not, Mr. Yates," she replied.

"Mr. Sloan, you are a crafter. You feel the sensation, I am certain," said Simon.

"I do, indeed, Mr. Yates," Mr. Sloan replied. "I felt it outside the door, but far more strongly in this room."

"What sensation?" Henry demanded. He was not a crafter and he was sometimes annoyed by Simon's patronizing attitude toward those poor benighted souls like himself who could not see or feel magic.

"The latent effects of residual magic," Simon explained. "A rather unpleasant tingling sensation that can occasionally be felt in the presence of an extremely powerful magical spell."

Mr. Sloan had been looking around the room and now he pointed. "Mr. Yates! I can see traces of the construct!"

"Where, Mr. Sloan?" Simon asked with a flash of his usual energy.

"There, sir, near the wall." Mr. Sloan indicated the direction. "And again on the floor, about a foot from the wall. You will note the faint blue glow."

Simon propelled his chair over to the wall to investigate, while Henry once more cursed the fact that he had been born without a magic bone in his body. He could see, however, that this section of the flagstone floor was one of the few places not covered with blood, owing to the fact that the flagstones had settled over time. Some of the stones had sunk, forming low spots in the floor that were ankle-deep with blood. At this location, the stones stood higher, and either they had escaped the flood or the gruesome pool had receded.

Simon hovered over the faintly shining construct for a considerable length of time, his expression growing increasingly grave. He reached into a compartment on his chair, removed his traveling desk, took out paper, pen, and ink, and began to carefully copy what remained of the construct.

"I will be here for some time and I am afraid you will find this wearying," he said. "I suggest you go back upstairs."

"I'm staying," said Henry.

"So am I," said Amelia.

"Suit yourselves," said Simon.

When he was finished with his drawing, he maneuvered the chair over to the corpse. He studied the sword and drew an illustration of it. Once this was done, he tried to remove the sword, but that proved extremely difficult and eventually he gave up. He placed his hand on the dragon's foreleg, observed the rigidity and the attitude of the body, closely studied the hideous wounds, and made diagrams.

He next floated over to study the letters on the wall, "Death to the Wyrms." He examined each word one by one and made another drawing. When he had completed his work, Simon turned to face them.

"I am finished with the investigation," he said. "We can leave now. Albright, I would be obliged if you would pull out the sword. I should like to take it with me."

"What did you discover, Mr. Yates?" Amelia asked. "Do you know who committed this heinous act?"

"I must go over my notes, Miss Amelia," said Simon. "I will tell you this much, however. Henry informed me that you very astutely noted the extraordinary fact that the dragon did nothing to defend herself. Lady Odila was alive when she was attacked. She saw her death coming. She felt each blow as he struck her, felt the sword pierce her flesh, watched her lifeblood drain away. And she was utterly helpless to stop her murderer."

Mr. Albright blew his nose, then waded through the blood to remove the sword. Mr. Albright was a big man, strong enough to lift and carry Simon. Henry observed that it took considerable effort for Mr. Albright to yank the sword from the body.

Henry shook his head in disbelief. "What you said makes no sense, Simon. Why the devil would the dragon allow herself to be tortured and killed?"

Simon gave Henry a narrow look and flashed a glance at Amelia. Henry understood.

"Mr. Sloan, if you would escort Miss Amelia—"

"Please, my lord, I have one question for Mr. Yates," Amelia said. "I do not ask this idly. The question is of the utmost importance. The answer could assist you in the investigation."

"Ask your question, Miss Nettleship," said Simon. "Although I must warn you that since this involves state secrets I may not be able to respond."

"I understand, Mr. Yates. You said the magical construct cast in this chamber was extremely complex."

"It was, yes," Simon conceded.

"Could an ordinary, everyday crafter cast this spell? Could Mr. Sloan, for example?" Amelia asked.

"No, ma'am," Simon replied. "No disparagement on Mr. Sloan, who is very talented, but the crafter who cast this spell was highly skilled in magic. Not only that, he would have had to be trained to cast this particular spell. I know of very few who—"

Simon stopped, his brow furrowed.

Amelia sighed in relief. "Then it was not Kate!"

"Kate?" Henry stared at her. "You mean Captain Kate? I guessed as much! You have been shielding her!"

"Since Kate is not implicated, I can now tell you everything I know, my lord," said Amelia. "Coreg hired her to obtain the construct and spoke to her about killing a dragon."

"You should have told me!" Henry stated, glowering. "By God, woman, I'll have you up on charges—"

"Calm down, Henry," said Simon.

"I will not calm down," Henry returned. "I'm ankle-deep in blood. I brought this dragon here to be murdered! Mr. Sloan, put out an arrest warrant for Katherine Gascoyne—"

Simon slammed his hand on the arm of his chair and shouted at him, "Henry, be silent!"

Henry had never heard his friend raise his voice, and he stared at him in astonishment. Simon was rarely touched by strong emotion. No matter what the emergency, his placid calm remained undisturbed.

He was clearly disturbed now. He was pale, his eyes feverish in their luster.

"Arresting Kate will do no good, although you should find her, for I believe she is in peril," said Simon. "Both Kate and Coreg are innocent of this crime. The murderer used them to misdirect us. These two are cat's-paws."

Henry found this hard to believe, but he trusted Simon.

"Then who is the cat?" he demanded.

Simon sighed. "You must give me time, Henry. You must give me time."

He slowly propelled his chair down the hall, his shoulders hunched, his head bowed. Mr. Albright followed, carrying the bloody sword.

FORTY-TWO

Kate climbed over the wreckage, trying to reach Olaf and Akiel and the others who were calling to her for help. They were near, but she couldn't find them in the darkness below the Breath. Chill mists clung to her like jungle vines, wrapping around her legs and arms, binding her to the helm. And then the helm changed to Dalgren, bleeding, dying, thrashing about in his death throes. Kate had some vague knowledge that this was all a terrible dream and she tried try to wake up, only to sink beneath the darkness again.

She had the impression of time passing, of daylight and darkness. Each time she woke she struggled to hold on to consciousness and, at last, she managed to seize it.

She woke to find herself lying on a cold stone floor. Her head ached, her right hand throbbed, her throat burned. Bright sunlight stabbed her in the eyes and she turned her head to try to block it. The movement sent a wave of nausea rolling over her. She heaved and then lay still and tried to remember.

Dalgren was dying. Fear jolted through her and she sat bolt upright, only to nearly pass out again. She groaned and clutched her stomach. After another bout of vomiting, she felt a little better. She managed to crawl across the floor, wincing at the pain in her hand, and propped herself up against the wall. She realized with relief that she had been dreaming.

"This is my kitchen in Barwich Manor," Kate murmured, looking around in bewilderment. "But that's not right. I'm not here. I'm in Haever . . ."

Memory began to return, but only in confused flashes: a house, a sword . . . a man, a scarf . . . a handkerchief . . . a linen scroll . . .

The pain in her hand was becoming intolerable. Kate couldn't remember how she had hurt it. She lifted her hand to examine it and stared in shock.

Her hand and arm were smeared in blood from the fingers to the elbow. Horrified, she looked at her other hand. It was covered in blood, as were her clothes.

Kate gagged and she was sick again, although there was nothing left in her stomach to purge. She rested her aching head on her bent knees and tried to fully remember what had happened last night. At least, she supposed it was last night. She couldn't think.

Events were vague and distorted and fraught with terror. She remembered going to a house, finding the construct on the linen scroll, a man rushing at her out of the darkness and after that, nothing.

The blood on her hands was sticky, gumming her fingers. She could smell the iron-tinged stench, and she felt an overwhelming need to be rid of it. She pushed herself unsteadily to her feet, using the wall for support, and staggered out the kitchen door.

She breathed in the fresh air and her head began to clear.

The sun was past its zenith. She had no idea what day it was. She might have been unconscious for a week, as far as she knew. She was desperately thirsty and there was a horrid taste in her mouth. She pumped water from the well and drank from the spout. Then she pumped water into the horse trough, using her left hand to work the pump; her right hand was swollen and bruised. She remembered the man stepping on it.

When the tub was filled, Kate crouched down at the trough and plunged her face into the cold water. Gasping and sputtering, she raised her head again, blinked the water from her eyes, and began to wash her hands and arms. The water took on a reddish tint. Kate shivered and scrubbed harder.

She heard a noise, coming from behind. Terrified, Kate picked up a rock and whipped around, dripping pinkish water.

A squirrel darted out of the brush and bounded away.

Kate dropped the rock and sagged back down to the ground.

Nothing made sense. How did she come to be here . . . covered in blood . . .

She went back to washing her hands and watched the blood swirl in the water. . . .

The magical construct . . . killing dragons . . .

Kate stared at her hands. All this blood. So much blood.

"No! I didn't! I couldn't!"

"Kate!" a voice called. "Oh, my dear! I have been so worried!"

Kate turned to see Amelia running across the yard toward her.

"You're hurt!" Amelia gasped.

"Hurt?" Kate couldn't understand what she meant, and she saw Amelia staring at the blood on her clothes. "This isn't mine. I don't know whose blood it is. I don't know how I got here. I don't know anything!"

Amelia put her arm around her. "Come into the house. The air is chill and you will catch your death."

Kate was shivering and still felt weak and disoriented. She allowed Amelia to help her into the house.

"Do you have any clothes here?"

Kate shook her head.

"I have some with me," said Amelia. "Wait here and I will go fetch them."

She disappeared. When she returned, she was carrying her valise. "You will find a clean shift, skirt, and jacket in here. You are taller than I am, but we are close to the same build, so they should fit. Change out of those wet clothes and I will brew you some tea and fix you something to eat."

The thought of food made Kate nauseous, but the tea sounded wonderful. She went to her room, stripped off the wet, bloodstained slops, her blood-soaked stockings and the bloody shoes. Sickened, she threw them into a corner.

She put on the linen shift. Eyeing the jacket with its myriad buttons, she looked down at her bruised hand and knew she couldn't manage. She towel-dried her wet hair and tied it back, wondering if she looked as bad as she felt. She returned to the kitchen, and wrapped herself in an old shawl for warmth.

Amelia had lit a fire in the big fireplace and was hanging the kettle over the blaze.

"This will warm you," said Amelia and she splashed a generous portion of some liquor from an old jug into a cup. "Apple brandy, or so I should judge by the smell. I found it in the pantry."

"We had a cook who drank," said Kate.

She swallowed the biting liquid and felt warmth spread through her body.

"How did you know where to find me?" she asked.

"I looked for you at the house in Haever. When I couldn't find you there, I realized you might come here. Especially if you needed to escape . . ."

"Escape?" Kate repeated. "What do mean? Escape what?"

Amelia didn't elaborate. She bustled about the kitchen. She cleaned up where Kate had been sick, brewed a pot of strong black tea, and prepared a bowl of gruel. Kate was grateful for the tea, but she couldn't even look at the gruel.

"You need to eat something," said Amelia. "Gruel is plain, wholesome food and will settle your stomach. While you eat, I will bind up your hand."

Kate ate as much as she could and then shoved the bowl away. She poured more brandy into her tea and slowly sipped it.

"What time is it?" Kate asked. "What day?"

"Late afternoon," said Amelia. "Two full days and nights have passed since the night you left to go that house on Waltham Lane."

"I kept trying to wake up . . ." Kate groaned and rested her head in her hands. "How did I get here? And where did all that blood come from?"

Amelia poured herself some tea. "You are in trouble, Captain. Not as much as you might have been, but trouble nonetheless. You must tell me what happened. The truth. Every detail."

"I went to that house. I found a linen scroll with the magical construct." Kate shivered and looked Amelia. "You were wrong about that, Miss Amelia. The magic *will* work."

"Yes, Captain, I know. And then what happened?"

Kate frowned, thinking back. "A man was inside the house. He must have been there, waiting for me. He rushed at me. I drew my pistol, but he kicked it out of my hand. I thought it was Trubgek, but it wasn't."

"Who was it? Do you know?"

"He was wearing a scarf. It slipped when we struggled and I saw part of his face. I didn't know him." Kate turned her gaze on Amelia. "What do you mean I'm in trouble? What has happened?"

"A dragon was murdered, Kate," Amelia said. "Lady Odila. The magical construct was used to incapacitate her. She was viciously attacked and died a cruel death—"

Kate sprang to her feet, upsetting the tea. "I didn't kill her! I didn't!"

"I know, you didn't, Captain," said Amelia in soothing tones. "But whoever committed the murder wants people to think you did. My guess would be that the murderer drugged you. He had an accomplice who transported you here by griffin. I saw tracks outside. He smeared you with blood which, by the way, is probably cow's blood. Then he left you to be discovered."

"Oh, God!" Kate murmured.

She slowly sat back down.

"Tell me about the construct," said Amelia.

"I knew the moment I saw it that the magic would work," Kate said, adding defensively, "That spell was powerful, complex. I couldn't even understand it, much less cast it! You have to believe me!"

"I do," said Amelia. "I have reason to know what you are saying is true. Please go on."

"There was a sword," said Kate. "A very old sword made of bronze with jewels set in the handle. The jewels weren't very valuable. Semiprecious."

She saw Amelia faintly smile at this.

"What happened next?"

"I woke up here," said Kate. "My hands and arms were drenched in blood and so were my clothes."

Amelia sat for long moments in thought, drinking her tea.

"What about your shoes?" she asked suddenly.

"What about them?"

"Did they have blood on them?"

"Yes. I left them in my room."

Amelia smiled, triumphant. "He made a mistake! This proves beyond doubt you are innocent! But now, if you are feeling stronger, we must leave. I have a carriage waiting. My guess is that someone will send an anonymous tip to the constables that they can find the killer here in Barwich Manor. They may already be on their way to arrest you."

"Constables! Arrest?" Kate stared at her in alarm. "What do I do?"

"We must go straight to Sir Henry. Tell him exactly what you told me—"

Kate jumped to her feet. "Sir Henry won't believe me! He will think I did this!"

"No, Captain, he will not," said Amelia. "Sir Henry knows you couldn't because— Kate! What are you doing?"

"You are right. I have to get out of here," said Kate. "Only I'm not going to see Sir Henry."

She hurried to her room, fumbled at the skirt and managed to struggle into the blouse and the jacket.

"Can you help me button this?" Kate asked Amelia, who had followed her into her room. "You said you had a carriage."

"A wyvern-drawn carriage I hired at the inn," said Amelia, deftly buttoning the jacket. "The driver is waiting to take us to Haever."

"Tell him there has been a change of plans," said Kate. "Please don't try to stop me, Miss Amelia!"

"You are making a mistake, Captain. Sir Henry knows you could not possibly have killed Lady Odila."

Kate shook her head. "*I* don't even know I didn't kill her! And it might not matter if Sir Henry believes me. He will be under pressure to solve this murder and bring the murderer to justice. He needs to convict someone and he may not be overly concerned about who that someone is."

Amelia considered her argument.

"You may be right," she admitted after a moment's serious thought. "If Sir Henry thinks his country is at risk, he would stop at nothing to save her. Where will you go?"

Kate hesitated. "To the *Victorie*. After that, no offense, Miss Amelia, but the less you know the better. I don't want you to have to lie for me."

"What about Dalgren?" Amelia asked. "Should I go fetch him?"

"He isn't here," said Kate. "When Trubgek made threats against *Victorie,* I sent Dalgren to keep an eye on the ship and my friends."

Amelia reached into her valise, took out a billfold, and handed it to Kate. "You will require funds."

"I couldn't—" Kate began.

Amelia forced the billfold into her hand. "Consider it payment for the wonderful stories you will bring back to me. I will endeavor to placate Sir Henry."

"I want you and Sir Henry both to know I am *not* running away because I am guilty, Miss Amelia," Kate said. "I need time to sort things out. Tell him I will come back. I promise."

She walked out to the waiting carriage. The evening was cloudy and oppressive. Kate kept expecting every moment to hear the drumming of hooves, the shrill whistles of constables.

She gave the driver directions; then a sudden thought occurred to her.

"How will you travel back to Haever, Miss Amelia?"

"I will take the mail coach," said Amelia. "You are not to worry about me."

Kate climbed into the carriage, then leaned out the window.

"I hope you won't find yourself in trouble with Sir Henry."

Amelia smiled. "He expects nothing less from me, my dear."

"Good-bye, Miss Amelia. And thank you."

Amelia regarded her with earnest concern.

"I beg you to be careful, Captain. I have an idea I know where you are going. You are dealing with dangerous people who will stop at nothing to achieve their goal—whatever that terrible goal might be. I saw what they did to Lady Odila."

Amelia stepped back and told the driver he could proceed. The wyverns had been fed and were sleepy and therefore unusually well behaved. He cracked his whip over their heads, waking them. They snarled and snapped, but he cracked the whip again and finally they took to the air.

Kate looked down to see Amelia waving to her. She closed the window and sat back with a sigh. She had to think up something to tell Olaf and Dalgren. She obviously couldn't tell them the truth.

The journey to Blacktooth Point, located at the southern tip of Freya, took two days. Kate found the trip long and tedious. She worried about what Trubgek would do when he came to Barwich Manor for the construct, only to find that she wasn't there. He had threatened her ship and he might carry out that threat. She tried to reassure herself. *Victorie* was safely concealed in one of Morgan's hideouts. But that was no comfort. Trubgek haunted her like some monstrous creature out of a fairy tale.

When the driver stopped at an inn to rest the wyverns, Kate read the newspapers relating the news of Lady Odila's sudden death, half expecting to see herself named as a suspect.

The official announcement from the palace said nothing beyond the fact that the dragon was dead and the queen expressed her sorrow and deep regret. Other articles termed the death "suspicious" and reported that the Travian dragons in Freya were in an uproar.

Members of the Anti-Dragon League reminded the populace that they had warned that no good could come of bringing such savage beasts to Freya. The dragons had killed one of their own and would undoubtedly turn on humans next and should be driven out of Freya. If the queen didn't order them to leave, the people would take matters into their own hands.

Kate burned the paper, fearful that someone might connect her.

The carriage took her to Alton, a town not far from Blacktooth Point. She paid the driver and dismissed him, intending to walk the rest of the way. A dirt trail led to the secluded location. She knew the route. She had walked this trail with Morgan often enough.

The day was fair, the sun hot. The trail ran along the coastline, about a mile from the Breath. She could see the orange mists in the distance. The land was rugged, rockbound, and barren. No one came here except those who made use of the inlet, and they tended to conduct their business at night.

Kate trudged along the dusty, rutted trail and thought how strange it was that here she was again, walking these same paths she had walked with her father. Was she doomed to always walk the same path? Could she never escape?

She had paid a healer to treat her hand, but she had not yet completely recovered from the effects of the drug, and she had to sit down on a boulder to rest. She gazed out into the blue sky and her spirits rose. She would soon be back with her friends, with her ship, sailing the Breath. Out there in the mists, she was free.

A shadow flowed over her, blocking out the sun. Kate shaded her eyes and looked up to see Dalgren. She waved at him, overjoyed to see him. She waited to greet him when he landed.

Dalgren did not land, however. He hovered in the air above her, gazing down at her. Kate didn't think much about it. Perhaps the wind currents were adverse, make landing difficult.

"I am glad to see you!" she shouted. "Though how did you know I was coming?"

"I figured you would show up about now," said Dalgren.

He sounded odd, not like himself.

"How is the *Victorie*? Is everything all right"

Dalgren didn't answer and Kate was suddenly afraid. "Is something wrong? Has something happened—"

"*Victorie* is fine," Dalgren replied.

"Good," said Kate, relieved. "We need to make ready to sail—"

"Why?" Dalgren asked.

"We have our orders from Sir Henry—" Kate began.

"Liar!" Dalgren snarled.

Kate stared at him, taken aback. "I don't . . ." She faltered and fell silent.

Dalgren hung in the air, his wings barely moving.

"I heard about Lady Odila," he said. "I know you were involved."

Kate felt the blood drain from her face. She gazed at him, stricken. She tried to speak, to explain, but all she could do was say, "No . . ."

Dalgren snorted. "You were hired to find a magical dragon-slaying construct and the very next day, a dragon died, found murdered."

"How did you—" Kate began, but her voice faded away.

Dalgren finished her sentence. "How did I find out? Olaf went into town for supplies. He heard."

"Does Olaf know about Coreg?" Kate asked.

"You mean, did I tell him you were working for that fiend?" Dalgren said, looking grim. "No, I did not. You can do that yourself."

"I didn't want to worry him," Kate explained. "And I wasn't working for Coreg. Not really. I talked to Miss Amelia, as you suggested, and we decided to tell Sir Henry, but we needed the contruct as proof. I went to get it, but I was attacked and drugged—"

"So you admit that you did the job for Coreg. You got the construct," said Dalgren.

Kate sighed. "I did not kill Odila, Dalgren. I swear to you!"

Dalgren grunted. "Swear on what, Kate? The memory of your father?"

"On our friendship!" Kate pleaded. "You have to believe me."

"Why?" Dalgren flared. "When have you ever told the truth to me or anyone else? All that rigamarole about proof and Sir Henry. You lied to me just now, in fact. You don't have orders from Sir Henry, do you?"

"No," Kate admitted. All she could do was repeat, "I am not a murderer, Dalgren! What can I say to convince you?"

"Nothing," said Dalgren. "As Olaf is always saying, you are your father's daughter."

With a flap of his wings, the dragon caught the currents of the Breath and flew off.

"Dalgren!" Kate shouted, running after him. "Dalgren!"

Tripping over a rut, she stumbled and fell. Dalgren did not look back. She watched him fly into the mists until her vision blurred and she lost sight of him.

She angrily blinked away the tears. She had not cried when the crew dumped Morgan's body into the Breath and she would not cry now. This was a misunderstanding. Once she had a chance to explain matters to Dalgren, he would realize he had misjudged her and they would be friends again.

Picking herself up, she walked the rest of her way to the inlet, where *Victorie* rode at anchor. Smugglers had made use of this inlet for years, perhaps as far back as the time of the Pirate King. Some clever crafter had magically whittled away several natural rock formations so that ships could attach lines to them.

The crew was not idle. Olaf could always find work for the men to keep them busy. Everyone stopped what they were doing when Kate came in sight. No one waved or called out a friendly greeting. Marco said something to Olaf, who ordered him to lower the gangplank.

Kate cast a swift glance around. She had nursed a small hope that maybe Dalgren would have a change of heart and that he would be waiting for her.

The dragon was nowhere in sight.

Olaf came hobbling down the gangplank to meet her.

"Did Dalgren find you?" Olaf asked.

"He found me," said Kate. "Is *Victorie* ready to sail?"

Olaf regarded her with concern.

"I tried to convince him to stay, but he wouldn't listen. He seemed really upset, Kate. I think it had something to do with that dragon that was murdered. Was she a friend of his?"

"Did he say where he was going?" Kate asked.

"No." Olaf eyed her. "What is going on, Kate? I know you're in some kind of trouble."

Kate stood on the shore, looking at her ship drifting at anchor. The mists of the Breath twined around the masts and drifted among the rigging. She had lost everything else, including Barwich Manor, for Sir Henry would tear up the deed, just as he would revoke her letters of marque.

Fight for your dreams.

All she had left were her ship and her dreams and her friends.

"Chart a course for the Aligoes," she said.

"The Aligoes! Why would you go back there?" Olaf demanded.

"Because there are only two places in the world Dalgren would go—the Aligoes or Travia. We'll look in the Aligoes first. Besides, I have business there."

"What business?" Olaf asked dubiously. "A job for that fiend, Coreg?"

Kate gave a faint smile. "I have to prove I am not a murderer."

She put her arm around Olaf.

"Once we're safely away, I'll explain everything. The truth, this time, dear friend," Kate said. "No more lies."

FORTY-THREE

The days following the death of the dragon were the worst days in Henry's long career in politics. He likened the experience to being on board a ship under attack, with fires blazing, masts falling, and lift tanks failing. To add to his troubles, Her Majesty was among those firing broadsides at him, lobbing in round after round. As he had foreseen, she blamed him, claimed this disaster was entirely his fault.

Henry had to report to the members of the Privy Council and ranking members of the House of Nobles, which included his brother. Sir Richard looked grim and tut-tutted a good deal. After that, Henry had to meet with the Travian dragons and a delegation of Rosian dragons to assure them that whoever had committed this heinous crime would be captured and punished. Further, he had to try to convince the Travian dragons not to leave Freya and take their gold with them. Finally he had to arrange for the dragons to view the body and remove it from the underground chamber for the funeral.

The newspapers wrote about nothing else. The Freyan populace was united in the demand that the dragons must go. People were expressing their views by surrounding the palace, hurling stones and bottles at passing carriages, and breaking shop windows.

Henry had to continually evade the questions: "How could this murder have been committed? How could a human assassinate a dragon?"

The one saving grace was that no one had as yet mentioned King Godfrey's dragon-killing magic. Henry lived in fear that someone, particularly members of the House of Nobles, would remember and dredge it up. No one did, however; this was a small blessing for which he was grateful.

In the midst of the upheaval, Henry received a note from Simon that, typical of his friend, was short and succinct: *Must speak with you. Immediately.*

"I hope to God he has news on the killer," said Henry to Mr. Sloan, who had brought him the note.

"I have often mentioned it to Him, my lord," said Mr. Sloan. "Perhaps this is His answer."

Henry and Mr. Sloan took a wyvern-drawn carriage to the house, which they found floating somewhere over the east end. Henry arrived with a feeling of relief. At the entrance, they left the noise of the city far below. The silence was a soothing balm to his bullet-ridden soul. He and Mr. Sloan rang the bell. When no one responded, they let themselves in.

They found Simon sitting behind his desk, almost hidden among the mounds of papers, newspapers, pamphlets, letters, and books. He looked up when he heard them, and gave a vague smile.

"Sorry Albright wasn't here to meet you. I sent him on an errand. I thought you might be hungry. He boiled a ham before he left."

Henry and Mr. Sloan both did justice to the ham and potatoes, for they had been too busy to eat regular meals. A glass of wine helped to restore Henry. Simon continued his reading while they ate. Mr. Sloan cleared away the dishes and was about to discreetly withdraw when Simon stopped him.

"If you would remain, Mr. Sloan, you might be of help."

Mr. Sloan sat down.

"You said the matter was urgent," said Henry. "I assume this has something to do with the murder."

"It does," said Simon. "I received this letter from Miss Amelia containing a detailed account of how Kate was approached by a man named Trubgek, who is employed by the dragon, Coreg—"

Henry interrupted, his voice grim. "Kate was supposed to speak to us in person, explain her role in this. Instead she has fled the country. I think we have found our killer."

Simon shook his head. "I know you are in urgent need of a murderer, Henry, but let me again assure you that Kate could not possibly have committed the murder. She is a crafter, but a seagoing crafter at best. Besides, she has a dragon partner, to whom she is deeply attached. She would not kill another dragon. May I continue?"

Henry scowled, but waved his hand in acquiescence.

"Kate agreed to pick up the magical construct. Her instructions were to go to an abandoned house on Waltham Lane," said Simon. "She did so, and found the construct in a leather satchel, along with a sword. Miss Amelia provides a description of the construct: 'Written on a large roll of linen, the construct covered every square inch of the linen from top to bottom, corner to corner.' "

"Yes, yes," said Henry. "Get to the point."

"Kate was about to leave when she was attacked, drugged, and carried off. She woke up in her home in Barwich Manor, covered in blood—"

"Ah-ha!" said Henry.

"She was a cat's-paw," said Simon, looking up. "We were meant to think she committed the murder and do just what you were about to do. Arrest her and close the case."

"Then if she didn't do it, who did?" Henry demanded. "And how? What was this magical construct? Do you know?"

Simon paused, then said, "You won't like what I have to tell you, Henry. This won't be easy for me to say or for you to hear."

Mr. Sloan stirred in his chair. "Perhaps I should withdraw—"

"Please do not leave, Mr. Sloan," said Simon. "Your help could be invaluable. The question is: Why did Lady Odila do nothing to defend herself from her murderer?"

"I assume you have the answer."

"I do," said Simon gravely. "Lady Odila could do nothing because she had been paralyzed."

Henry was incredulous. "How do you paralyze a dragon?"

"By use of a powerful magical weapon. I studied the remnants of the construct Mr. Sloan so astutely discovered. They are part of a complex spell, perhaps the most complex ever to have been created. The magic's sole intent was to kill dragons in their lairs—places where they believe themselves most secure. That was King Godfrey's idea and the construct was, as Miss Nettleship observed, King Godfrey's spell."

"But that spell didn't work," Henry protested. "The project ended in failure."

"So people were led to believe," said Simon. "The truth is the spell worked quite well. You saw the terrible proof."

"I don't believe it! How can you possibly know this?" Henry asked. "How do you know that this spell is the same spell?"

"I recognized the construct, Henry," said Simon. "I know it is the same because I helped create it."

Henry sat, stunned. The biggest shell yet had landed right on top of him, blown up in his face.

Simon sighed. "I warned you this would not be easy."

"You never said a word!" Henry stated, incredulous. "I remember how you and Alan and Randolph discussed it at the time, after I returned from Estara. We laughed over Godfrey's latest fool notion. You laughed with us and all the time you knew. . . . You lied to us!"

"I had no choice, Henry," said Simon. "Godfrey commanded those of us who were involved in the project to keep silent or he would bring us up on charges of high treason."

"You could have trusted us!" Henry cried angrily, bounding to his feet. "We are your friends! We would not have breathed a word!"

He started to pace, but had no room amid the file cabinets and the clutter, so was forced to stand, glaring at Simon.

"I couldn't risk telling you or our other friends, Henry," said Simon. "You know what Godfrey was like: cunning, sly, vindictive. Your career was advancing. Randolph had been made first lieutenant and Alan was just starting to recover from that scandal involving his brother. If Godfrey had suspected that any of you knew the truth, he would have ruined all of you."

Henry said nothing. He was trying hard to master his anger.

"There is another reason I didn't tell you about my involvement, Henry," said Simon. He drew in a breath, let it out. "I was ashamed."

He shifted his chair so that he could look out the large window at the magnificent view of Haever spread out below. After a moment, Henry went to join him, standing with his arms behind his back, hands clenched.

"You had better tell me the whole story," said Henry harshly.

"I was starting out in my career at the time," said Simon. "I had heard the rumors about some plot of Godfrey's to assassinate dragons, but I paid little heed to them. He was always coming up with some fool scheme or other. The king hired two eminent crafters to work on creating the construct. They were successful—or so they thought—until they actually began to train people to wield the magic. At that point, they discovered the construct didn't work. Godfrey brought it to me and asked me to fix it."

Simon shrugged. "I was young. I was flattered. I viewed the problem as an academic exercise. I took the construct apart, discovered the flaw, repaired it, and the construct worked.

"Only then did I begin to question what I had done. I pictured to myself the cruel manner in which the victim would die and I was horrified, both by the construct and the fact that I had worked on it with such callous indifference. I was about to send word to Godfrey that the construct had fatal flaws and suddenly he was here, Henry. The king. He was in this very office, standing where you are now.

"Godfrey picked up the linen scroll and asked me if I had been successful. I was rattled. I was going to lie, but he must have seen the truth in my face, for he thanked me for my work, told me to keep quiet, and left, taking the construct with him.

"I was terrified that he might use it and, I swear, I was going to ask you and the others to help me. I had some vague notion that we could steal it. The next day I received a formal letter from the palace stating that the project had ended in failure and that the construct had been destroyed."

Henry frowned. "But if it did work, as you claim, why didn't Godfrey use it against the Dragon Brigade?"

"I have no way of knowing, of course, and I could hardly ask. Perhaps the king set the plan in motion and it failed. Or perhaps the assassin backed out. The spell is incredibly complex and one has to be within the proximity of a dragon to cast it. If the killer made one small mistake, he would end up the victim. Or it might have suceeded and the Rosian dragons hushed it up. As I said, they deal with their own internal problems themselves. There is even the possibility that the king came to his senses and realized the enormity of what he contemplated. Godfrey wasn't a bad man, Henry, just rash and impulsive."

"So this deadly construct has been floating about out there for years and this is the first I am hearing about it," said Henry.

"I am afraid this gets worse," said Simon. "Could you hand me the sword, Mr. Sloan? It is on that filing cabinet behind you."

Mr. Sloan retrieved the weapon and carried it to Simon. The sword had been cleaned, but Henry was still loath even to look at it.

"Two weeks ago this sword was stolen from a museum," said Simon. "The killer could have used any weapon to kill the dragon. He could have, for example, placed the muzzle of a blunderbuss on her head and shot her between the eyes. Far simpler, much less trouble. Why go to the trouble to steal a sword—specifically a sword that had belonged to the ancient Imhruns. And then, why leave it behind?"

"He forgot it," said Henry.

"A killer who covers his shoes so that he will not leave bloody footprints forgets the murder weapon? For shame, Henry. You are not thinking."

"Forgive me," said Henry. "I have just suffered a severe shock. My best friend lied to me."

"Henry, I am sorry—"

Henry waved off the apology. "Why this sword?"

"The sword and the words on the wall, 'Death to the Wyrm,' both hearken back to the ancient Imhruns. 'Wyrm' is a term they used to mean dragon. The words are a message from the killer."

Henry was puzzled. "But how would the killer disseminate such a message? I have not told anyone—not even Her Majesty—what we saw in that dreadful chamber."

Simon shifted his chair, reached for a newspaper on his desk and handed it to Henry. "Today's early-morning edition. I take it you haven't read it."

"When have I had time to look at a bloody paper?" Henry scowled at it. "What am I looking for?"

"The article titled 'Shocking Discovery.' "

Henry found the article and hurriedly scanned it. "This contains details I have been careful not to make public! Such as the sword and the words written on the wall."

He slammed the paper onto the desk. "Miss Amelia! That woman promised me! I knew I should have locked her up—"

"Miss Nettleship did not write this article, Henry," said Simon. "The style is completely different."

"Then who did?" Henry demanded. "No one has entered that castle. Colonel Dalton assured me this very morning. So who could possibly know such details except ourselves and—"

Henry paused, aghast.

"The killer," Simon finished. "He did not write this to titillate the public. He is sending a message. Note the author's nom de plume."

Henry glanced down at the paper. " 'Imhrun Awaken.' What the devil does that mean?"

Simon placed his hand on the weapon. "The code name for Godfrey's project was: 'Imhrun's Sword.' "

Henry was chilled. "What is the message he is sending and to whom?"

"He is sending it both to his followers and to us. To his followers, he saying 'waken,' be ready to take action. To us, this is a taunt. He can strike with impunity and we cannot touch him."

"I should like to prove him wrong," Henry said.

"I think we can. But it will not be easy. This murderer is like that sea creature known as a man-o'-war," Simon said. "Very little of the creature is visible on the top of the ocean, but it has countless tentacles that reach far below the surface."

Henry sat in thoughtful silence for several moments, turning over in his mind everything Simon had told him.

"I need a drink. Where is the aqua vitae?"

"Second file cabinet, third row, two drawers down. You will find it under 'V,'" said Simon.

Mr. Sloan rose to fetch it, but Henry forestalled him. He needed to do something, even if it was only retrieving a bottle. He located the potent liquor and, not immediately finding a glass, drank straight from the bottle.

He grimaced, coughed. Mr. Sloan procured a glass and silently handed it to him. Henry poured the liquor and took another gulp. Carrying the bottle, he returned to his chair.

"So where does this lead us?"

"To the murderer," said Simon. "And I believe I know his name."

Henry lowered his glass and sat forward in his chair. "Do you, by God!"

"Yes, but there is a problem," said Simon.

"Of course!" Henry muttered, flinging himself back in the chair.

"First I need to explain how the magic works," said Simon.

"Must you?" Henry asked.

"You need to understand the nature of this crime," said Simon. "Besides, Mr. Sloan is interested. Aren't you, Mr. Sloan?"

"I confess that I am, sir." Mr. Sloan cast an apologetic glance at Henry. "I could see for myself, my lord, that the construct was unique."

"The crafters inscribed the construct on a large piece of linen that was itself free of constructs. No magic was used in the process of making it. The caster has to inscribe the spell on the linen in order to cast it. The construct is too complex even for a savant to cast from memory.

"When the murderer came to kill Lady Odila, he placed the linen construct on the floor outside the door, traced over it with his fingers starting from the bottom right and moving to the left. That transferred the construct to the floor, and he then spoke the proper words. As you recall, I found traces of magic at that location.

"The magic would begin to work immediately, forming a gas that would seep beneath the door and inside the room. I surmise that Lady Odila was asleep when the killer attacked and did not wake until he entered. When she was aware he was there, she became alarmed, and started to confront him. I know that because her body was lying on the floor some distance from where she slept."

Henry interrupted to ask, "How did the killer know where to find her?"

Simon spread his hands. "The newspapers reported the queen would be meeting with the dragon who was residing at the castle. Given the size of the dragon, the killer would be safe in concluding she would *not* be slumbering in one of the upstairs bedchambers. He would go to the underground level, the only space large enough to accommodate her."

Henry gave a gloomy nod. "Proceed."

"The dragon had just enough strength to stand up and move a short way before she collapsed. The killer needed to make certain she could not attack him. Therefore he cast the spell again, this time inside the chamber where Mr. Sloan found the construct. At that point, the dragon would have been completely immobilized, although still conscious. This is instructive. The killer truly hated his victim. He deliberately made her suffer."

"So her death was personal," said Henry. "But did he hate her for herself or did he hate her because she was a dragon?"

"An excellent question, and one I cannot answer," said Simon, regarding his friend with approval. He wrote it down. "To continue: The killer was careful to remove all traces of the construct near the door. He was not able to do this when he used the construct a second time inside the room because the dragon's blood had flowed over it. Mr. Sloan was able to discover the construct because the blood had receded."

"You said you know the name of the killer," Henry prodded.

"Only six people could have cast that spell: myself, the two crafters who created the construct, and the three men who were trained in its use. Only six people knew the code name for the project: Imhrun's Sword."

"By God, we have only six suspects!" Henry exclaimed. "Well, five, not counting you. In his arrogance, the fool has given himself away!"

"The killer is not a fool, Henry," said Simon sharply. "Put that notion out of your head. I sent Albright to question the other five people who worked on Imhrun's Sword, find out where they were the night of the murder. Albright discovered that four of these people have unimpeachable alibis."

Henry grunted. "No alibi is unimpeachable."

"These are, Henry," said Simon gravely. "All four are dead."

Henry looked grim. "I don't suppose they all died peacefully in their beds."

"Quite the contrary. One was run over by a carriage in the streets of Haever. Another fell off a cliff while on holiday. A third died in a house fire and the fourth broke his neck while riding. What is even more suspicious is that all the deaths occurred within the last fortnight. In each case, the investigating authorities ruled the death accidental."

Henry poured himself another glass, but did not drink it.

"Why did he kill them?"

"You said it yourself," Simon replied. "The killer feared that if these four people heard about the murder of a dragon, they would recognize the use of the construct and realize the killer was one of their old comrades."

"But what about you, Simon? Why didn't the killer come after you?"

"He didn't know about me," said Simon. "Godfrey brought me in at the end of the project. I never met the other people involved."

"And so of the six who worked on Imhrun's Sword, you and the killer are the only two left alive. You must know his name."

"I do. Isaiah Crawford. He was once a captain of the marines."

Mr. Sloan sat bolt upright. "I served with an Isaiah Crawford, sir. Could that be the same man?"

"I was going to ask you that question, Mr. Sloan," said Simon. "What do you remember about him?"

"Crawford was a devout Fundamentalist, highly disciplined and somewhat dour, and an extremely talented crafter." Mr. Sloan paused, thinking back. "He was selected for some sort of special duty, as I recall, and reassigned."

"He was promoted to captain and trained in the use of the construct," said Simon. "Do you know what became of him?"

"Crawford and I attended the same church," said Mr. Sloan. "I was acquainted with him, but nothing more. I have not thought about him in years."

"So by process of elimination, this Crawford has to be our killer," Henry said. "Have you located him? Do you know where he is?"

"Five years ago, Captain Crawford vanished," said Simon. "Gone without a trace. No one has seen him or heard from him. I admit that the only evidence I have against Crawford is circumstantial, but I believe he is our man. One person could confirm it. Or rather, I should say, one dragon."

"You mean this Coreg," Henry stated.

"According to Miss Nettleship, someone hired Coreg to hire an assassin to kill a dragon. He sent his servant, a man by the strange name of Trubgek, to Kate. Note that the dragon knew about the construct and what it was meant to do because this Trubgek told Kate it would kill dragons.

"Coreg knows who hired him," Simon added. "Even if that person wasn't Crawford, Coreg could provide the information we need to find out who is behind this plot."

"And how do you suggest we persuade this dragon to talk? Thumbscrews? The rack?" Henry shook his head in exasperation and rose to his feet. "Keep investigating, Simon. I must return to the palace—"

Simon was exasperated. "Henry, damn it! Listen to me! I was not jesting when I told you about the sea monster. Crawford is simply one of its tentacles. Think about this, Henry. Where has the construct been all these years?"

"Crawford had it."

"Doubtful. Godfrey would have never given such powerful magic to a lowly captain. He would have given it to a friend, a close friend, someone he trusted. Someone who is still trusted and who might, even now, be taking tea with Her Majesty the queen—"

"Good God!" Henry exclaimed, horrified.

"We need to find Crawford and, above all, we need to know who else is involved and what they are plotting! We have to find a way to persuade Coreg to talk. Offer him something in return for information."

Henry frowned, thinking. "I received a report that the Rosians are sending warships into the Aligoes to root out the pirate infestation. Since Rosian warships would likely have a deleterious effect on business, I could offer Coreg safe haven in Freya."

"Henry, I hate to say this, but the last thing we need in Freya is another dragon," Simon remarked.

Henry gave a bitter smile. "I am desperate, my friend. Unfortunately, I cannot leave Freya now, not during this crisis. Mr. Sloan, you are the only person I trust to undertake this mission. I do not like to ask this of you, however. The risk involved is too great."

"I was going to propose to undertake it myself, my lord," said Mr. Sloan. "According to Miss Amelia, this dragon has already made one attempt on your life."

"True," said Henry. "What with one calamity and another, I had forgotten that. I never did find out why. Perhaps you could ascertain that while you are there, Mr. Sloan."

"I will endeavor to do so, my lord."

Henry smiled. "Thank you, Mr. Sloan. Take the carriage. You will need to make arrangements for your journey. I plan to remain with Simon for a while, so send the carriage back to pick me up."

After Mr. Sloan had gone, Henry walked over to once more gaze out the window, look down at the city he loved, the people he loved, even those who were at this moment rioting in the streets. They were Freyans, all of them. His people, whom he had sworn long ago to protect and defend.

He glanced at his friend. Simon was seated at his desk, but he was not reading or writing or shuffling through papers. He was doing nothing, staring at nothing. Henry understood. He rested his hand on his friend's shoulder.

"You cannot blame yourself for Lady Odila's death."

"Yes, I can," Simon returned. "I should have made certain the construct was destroyed. That would have meant angering Godfrey and I didn't want to risk my career."

"Knowing Godfrey, you could have been risking your life. And putting us at risk," said Henry. "I owe you an apology, Simon. I had no right to be angry with you. You did what you thought you needed to do."

"Nonetheless, I should not have lied to you," said Simon. "As you said, I should have trusted my friends."

He paused, then added thoughtfully, "Well, maybe you and Randolph. Not Alan."

Henry laughed. The two shook hands and Henry put on his cloak and his hat. Simon escorted him to the door, steering his chair among the stacks of books and papers, cabinets and chests, oddments, grotesques and curiosities that filled the floating house.

As they parted, Simon said, "I cannot overstate the importance of finding out what Coreg knows, Henry. I have high esteem for Mr. Sloan, but I cannot help wishing you were going."

"Even though this dragon tried to have me killed," said Henry.

"That small matter." Simon waved it away. "I'm sure the dragon has reconsidered. After all, no one has tried to kill you in at least a week. Don't be such a fussbudget, Henry."

Henry smiled at his friend's raillery. He was glad to see Simon in a better mood.

"I must remain here. I have to try to convince the Travian dragons to stay in Freya. I have to meet again with the Duke of Talwin and the Rosian dragons to calm their fears. I must make arrangements for Lady Odila's state funeral, and just this morning I received word from King Ullr. He never gave a damn about dragons in his life, but it seems he is shocked to the depths of his being by the death of Lady Odila and is coming here to express his outrage."

"Then we must place our faith in Mr. Sloan," said Simon.

"We could not have a safer repository," said Henry.

Bidding his friend good-bye, he climbed into the carriage, sat back, closed his eyes. His ship was damaged, but still afloat. No need to man the lifeboats yet.

FORTY-FOUR

Kate leaned on her elbows at the rail of her ship and gazed out at the northernmost islands of the Aligoes: hummocks of green floating on the orange-pink mists of the Breath. The day was clear, the sun was bright, and in the distance she could see the summit of Fortum, the first of the Six Old Men, which marked the entrance to the Trame Channel. With fair winds, she and her crew could be in Freeport the day after tomorrow.

"Deck!" the lookout called. "Sail to starboard! Two ships!"

"Merchant ships," Kate guessed. "How far? Marco, be ready to change course."

The idea came to her that perhaps she could win her way back into Sir Henry's good graces by picking off a fat merchant. Marco put his glass to his eye. When he located the ships and brought them into focus, he stiffened.

"Those aren't merchants, Captain," he said, alarmed. "Those are warships, and two-deckers at that! Seventy-fours!"

Kate raised her glass to see for herself. Seventy-fours were warships that carried seventy-four guns that each fired a thirty-two-pound ball. Only the Rosian navy had ships that big. Sure enough, she could see the Rosian colors flying from the mast.

"Deck!" the lookout cried. "Dragons!"

Three dragons came into view, flying over the Trame Channel. The dragons flew in formation, one in front and one on each flank. Their flight was slow. They were taking their time.

"Could those be wild dragons?" Marco asked, puzzled. "I never heard of wild dragons living in the Aligoes."

"For good reason, because there aren't any," said Olaf. "That is the Dragon Brigade. We kept hearing rumors that the Rosians were going come to rid the the Aligoes of pirates. Looks like they're here."

"And we are the very pirates they've come to attack!" said Kate, alarmed. "The Rosians will recognize *Victorie*. She used to be their ship, after all."

"So what if they do?" Marco asked. "We are privateers. We have letters of marque."

"They could still arrest us and impound our ship," said Olaf.

Kate was doing some fast thinking. The warships were about four miles away at the entrance to the channel. From their vantage point, the *Victorie* would be partially obscured by the mists. A freshening breeze could ruin that, however, blowing away the friendly mists and leaving them exposed.

"Marco, change course! Get us the hell out of here!" Kate ran to the brass helm. Marco spun the wheel hard to port while Kate reversed the port airscrews. The *Victorie* heeled hard, creaking and groaning under the strain.

"Olaf, have they seen us? Are they chasing after us?"

"Not so far," he reported. "The ships haven't altered course. The dragons are starting to veer off. They're circling back over the lane. I don't think they saw us."

"Let's keep it that way," said Kate.

The *Victorie* retreated, sailing for cover amid the cluster of islands to the south and east of the Trame Channel, seeking shelter beneath a vast canopy of green.

Only when they had left the Rosian warships and the dragons miles behind them did Kate deem them to be safe. She called a meeting in her cabin.

She had told Olaf the truth at the start of the voyage, as she had promised. She had told him everything, from Coreg to Trubgek's threats to the magical construct, to Dalgren's suggestion about Amelia and how she and Kate were going to take the construct to Sir Henry. Kate had even confessed that she had hoped to make money off the deal. Olaf had shaken his head at that.

"But I didn't kill anyone, Olaf. You have to believe me!" Kate had said.

"I do, Kate," Olaf had replied. "I mean that."

"Dalgren doesn't," Kate had said with a sigh. "That's why he left."

"He was just upset, that's all. He'll come to think better of it. Do you know who killed the dragon?" Olaf had asked.

"I am going to the Aligoes to find out," Kate had told him.

By the time Olaf entered the cabin, Kate had decided what she was going to do. She needed to convince him to go along with her. To that end, she poured him a glass of Calvados.

"Sit down, Olaf," she said, smiling.

Olaf eyed the glass, but didn't drink.

"I have an idea, Kate. We sail to Bheldem. We're only five days away. We wait there until the Rosians grow bored chasing pirates and leave. You can talk to Coreg when they're gone"

"I can't wait," said Kate. "Coreg won't stay around for the Dragon Brigade to spot him. For all I know, he's packing his things right now, getting ready to flee. And there's another reason. Dalgren. If he's here, he could be in danger."

Olaf was amazed. "And why would Dalgren be in danger?"

"Because of the Dragon Brigade," said Kate.

"And why would that put him in danger? He served in the Brigade. He probably knows most of the dragons in it."

"And they know him," said Kate. "Dalgren is a deserter. I'm sorry I didn't tell you!" she added, seeing Olaf go red in the face. "Dalgren asked me not to say anything. He didn't want anyone to know. And now I have to find him to warn him. He might not know the Brigade is in the Aligoes."

"I think he might figure it out when he sees a dozen dragons flying overhead," said Olaf dourly.

"Dalgren is my friend!" Kate pleaded. "I won't abandon him any more than I would abandon you!"

"I know you wouldn't, Kate," Olaf said, sighing. "I didn't mean we should let them find him. I'm just not sure what we can do to help."

"I need to warn him," said Kate. "If Dalgren is here, he might have communicated with Akiel. I have to reach Freeport and I think I know a way. We'll hide the ship in Kate's Cove where we worked on *Victorie*. The Rosians will never find us."

Olaf mulled this over.

"That might work, but we have to get there first," he said. "And that's not going to be easy with the Rosians blockading the Trame Channel."

Kate rummaged through her father's charts and maps until she found the one she wanted, and spread it out on the table. She studied it, then drew a line with her finger.

"This is the route we'll take. We'll sail to the north, then head west, avoiding the Trame Channel, and then south through these islands. The

Rosians will concentrate their fleet here and here: the two main shipping channels to the east."

"They could have troops in Freeport," Olaf said.

"Why would they bother?" Kate argued. "Freeport is a backwater town on a bay off the main shipping lane. We will hide *Victorie* in the cove. I will slip into Freeport, talk to Akiel who will know what's going on with the Rosians and if Dalgren is around. After that, I'll meet with Greenstreet. Once I have the information I need, I'll take that to Dalgren, prove to him I am innocent and we can all go back to Freya together. I will make amends with Sir Henry. He will give us our orders and we'll set out to find our fortunes!"

Olaf rubbed his jaw as he studied the chart and gave a rueful smile. "You know as well as I do that those two seventy-fours could sail right through the holes in that plan, Katydid."

"This will work, Olaf," Kate said, adding with grim determination, "It has to!"

FORTY-FIVE

Mr. Sloan flew on griffinback to the Aligoes; an uncomfortable mode of travel, but one that cut several days off his trip. He did not travel directly to Freeport, but planned to stop over in Wellinsport, hoping to gather information. He noted the presence of the two seventy-fours guarding the entrance to the Trame Channel and he saw the dragons of the Dragon Brigade. His griffin saw the dragons as well, and snapped its beak in displeasure.

Apparently the Rosians were serious about their efforts to clean up the Aligoes. Mr. Sloan wondered if their ambitions would stop there.

Mr. Sloan secured accommodations for the night in Wellinsport, then walked to Fort Chessington to pay Sir Henry's respects to General Winstead and find out what was going on.

The general was pleased to see Mr. Sloan. He invited him to have some rum—the local drink—which Mr. Sloan politely declined. They then discussed the political situation.

"The Rosian Southern Fleet, known jokingly as the 'Rum' Fleet, is here in the north, while the Estarans sent their fleet to the Imperial Channel to secure the eastern islands," General Winstead explained, indicating the positions on the map.

"King Renaud invited the Freyan navy to join the Estarans in the south.

Admiral Miller and I agreed it would be wiser to keep our ships here. One never knows," the general added drily. "A defenseless Wellinsport might prove too great a temptation for Renaud to resist. I should not want him to commit some rash act."

"I see the Dragon Brigade is also in the Aligoes," said Mr. Sloan.

"Yes, confound them," said General Winstead. "I have to give the Rosies credit, though. The bloody pirates can't hide from dragons. The Brigade has been spotting their hideouts from the air, then literally smoking them out."

Trusting God would forgive him a small fib, Mr. Sloan lowered his voice as he leaned forward. "You will have read in the newspapers of the tragic death of one of the Travian dragons. The other dragons are extremely upset, as one can imagine. Sir Henry was thinking that he might suggest relocating them to the Aligoes."

"Out of the question," said General Winstead. "Dragons wouldn't like the climate. I hear the Rosian dragons are already complaining about the heat."

Mr. Sloan was confused. "But it was Sir Henry's understanding that dragons are currently living in the Aligoes, sir."

"Can't think where he would have heard that!" said General Winstead. "Is he referring to that complaint from the Travian merchant that a dragon attacked his ship? Bah! You know Travians. He and his crew were likely drunk as skunks, wouldn't know a dragon from a cockatoo!"

"I believe Sir Henry was referring to something the former governor told him regarding his belief that there was a dragon in the Aligoes who was involved with the pirates, as well as smuggling and other illicit activities."

General Winstead laughed heartily at the idea. "I am surprised His Lordship would believe anything the Right Honorable told him. Tell Sir Henry to keep his Travian dragons, Mr. Sloan. We don't want them."

That night, Mr. Sloan sought out several of Henry's agents in Wellinsport, asked them similar questions, received the same answers, and heard the same laughter. The only crime boss in the Aligoes that anyone appeared to know about was Greenstreet. Mr. Sloan's estimation of Coreg went up a notch.

Early the next morning, Mr. Sloan procured an island jumper ferry, known as an island hopper, to transport him to Freeport. The general had informed him that the Rosians had no intention of shutting down trade, and that merchant ships, wreckers, barges, island hoppers, and yachts continued to sail. They had to submit to the occasional search by the Rosian navy, but they were willing to put up with the inconvenience, which was far better than being attacked by pirates.

Mr. Sloan was not concerned about being questioned by the Rosians.

He had papers to attest to the fact that he was employed by a merchant who had sent him to investigate the loss of several shipments of indigo.

He spent his time observing the dragons of the Dragon Brigade fly overhead, searching out pirates. He could not help but admire the grace, beauty, and power of the massive creatures, as well as the courage and skill of their riders. He remembered the ravaged corpse of Lady Odila. The thought that some human could so brutally destroy a beast of such magnificence was appalling.

Mr. Sloan's Fundamentalist faith declared dragons to be the minions of the Evil One. He himself, though, did not entertain the same belief, for which he could find no validation in the Scriptures. The notion had apparently started with one of the founders of the faith, Reverend Elijah Byrd. Although Mr. Sloan agreed with Reverend Byrd on many subjects, the idea of dragons being inherently evil was not one.

The island hopper sailed past several Rosian frigates, which observed them and let them pass. Upon the boat's arrival at the entrance to Freeport Bay, a Rosian naval patrol boat sailed over to investigate them and signaled them to prepare to be boarded.

The boat's owner appeared startled to see the patrol boat, but he complied, throwing lines to the sailors on the patrol boat, who hauled the island hopper close enough that an officer could go on board.

The polite officer apologized for the inconvenience and asked to see their papers and inspect the cargo. He found everything in order, wished Mr. Sloan and the other passengers a safe journey, and departed.

"Well, now that was strange and no mistake," remarked the boat's owner, hauling in his lines. "First time I've ever seen the Rosians patrolling Freeport Bay."

Arriving in the town of Freeport, Mr. Sloan paid the owner of the ferry and arranged to be picked up in two days' time. The owner told him there were no inns in Freeport, but he could recommend a widow who took in lodgers, unless Mr. Sloan preferred the local brothel.

Mr. Sloan thanked him and took down the name and address of the widow. He had no trouble finding the widow's house, for it was located on the only street in town. He made arrangements for his room, then hired a young boy to guide him to Greenstreet's house. Mr. Sloan had considered sending a note and a card, asking for permission to call, then decided that the element of surprise might work in his favor.

The harbor was deserted. The town appeared empty, but it was early afternoon, the time when most people were either at work or staying indoors, out of the heat. The boy led Mr. Sloan to the largest house in the town, appearing very stately and elegant amid a profusion of flowering bushes and large shade trees.

The picture of elegance was spoiled by a big man dressed in slops lounging on the veranda. Sighting Mr. Sloan, the man gave a shout, presumably reporting the arrival of a visitor.

Mr. Sloan was dressed in a well-made, though not ostentatious, frock coat, breeches, stockings, and shirt and tricorn. Assuming he would be searched, he had left his weapons in his room, safely concealed in his valise. He did not go unarmed, however. He carried with him several weapons of a magical nature, among them a calling card whose magic would render a victim unconscious and a watch that could be set to explode by winding the stem and activating the magic.

Mr. Sloan mounted the porch and handed over his card—a real card, not the magic one. Dropping the guise of merchant, he introduced himself as private secretary to Sir Henry Wallace.

"His Lordship has sent me to speak to Mr. Greenstreet on a matter of business."

The big man went inside, leaving Mr. Sloan standing on the veranda. The guard reappeared in a few moments with the news that Mr. Greenstreet would see Mr. Sloan, and ushered him inside.

Greenstreet, in his white coat and white waistcoat, rose from behind his bare desk and made a slight bobbing bow.

"I am pleased to meet you, Mr. Sloan. Be seated." Greenstreet sat down in his chair, leaned back, and laced his fingers over his belly. "How can I be of service to so great a man as Sir Henry Wallace?"

Mr. Sloan took a seat. "Perhaps you could first explain why you hired men to kill him."

Greenstreet looked startled, then chuckled.

"I like a man who is direct, Mr. Sloan. I will be direct myself in turn. That was a misunderstanding; one that, happily, has since been resolved. Please assure His Lordship I bear no malice toward him for killing three of my best men. In turn, I trust he bears no malice toward me. We are men of the world, after all, aren't we, Mr. Sloan? Such things happen."

"Indeed they do, sir," said Mr. Sloan.

He fingered his watch, then reluctantly released it and explained the reason he had come.

"I would like for you to arrange for me to speak to the dragon known as Coreg," said Mr. Sloan.

"A dragon, sir?" Greenstreet repeated, smiling. "I know no dragons named Coreg or otherwise."

His bewilderment might have been convincing, but for the slight start he had given on hearing the name and the sudden glitter of the hooded eyes.

Taking note of both, Mr. Sloan continued as though Greenstreet had not spoken.

"Sir Henry is aware that Coreg has found the presence of the Rosian navy has had a chilling effect on business and he was wondering if the dragon would be interested in relocating to Freya. Sir Henry could guarantee that Coreg would be free to conduct and even expand his various business enterprises without fear of reprisal."

"Let us say for the sake of argument I know someone who might be interested in this offer. What would Sir Henry expect in return?" Greenstreet asked.

"Being a man of the world, Sir Henry would think it only right to reward a person such as yourself, sir, who would be instrumental in arranging this deal with the dragon," said Mr. Sloan.

"A share of the profits," Greenstreet hinted.

"I am not at liberty to say more until I speak directly to Coreg."

Greenstreet shrugged. "That could be difficult."

Mr. Sloan reached into an inner pocket of his coat, drew out several sheets of paper, and, half rising, placed them on the desk.

"I have the details of His Lordship's offer in writing," said Mr. Sloan.

He sat back in his chair, apparently unaware that he had carelessly left several bank notes, each for a hundred eagles, wedged between the sheets of paper.

Greenstreet frowned at the papers and grunted.

"Please take a seat in the hall, Mr. Sloan." Greenstreet raised his voice to a bellow. "Jules!"

Mr. Sloan retired to the hall as the big man entered the house. Jules remained in the hall until Mr. Sloan had settled himself in a chair, then walked into the office, shutting the door behind him.

Mr. Sloan had brought with him his worn copy of the writings of the saints to while away the time. He did not immediately begin to read the familiar verses, however. Mr. Sloan listened, but he could not hear the conversation being carried on inside. Undeterred, he crept over to the door and put his ear to the keyhole.

"Have you seen Trubgek?" Greenstreet was asking. "I need him to take this fellow to talk to Coreg."

"Trubgek hasn't been seen in weeks," Jules replied. "Last I heard he was in Freya."

"The job there ended. He must be back by now!" Greenstreet stated, annoyed.

"I can go look for him," Jules offered, but he didn't sound enthusiastic.

"Never mind. I will take the man to Coreg myself. Why is that sneaky bastard always skulking about when no one wants him, and never here when someone does," Greenstreet grumbled.

Mr. Sloan returned to the chair and was quietly perusing his book when Jules opened the door.

"You're to go in," he said, jerking his thumb in the direction of Greensteeet's office.

Mr. Sloan closed the book and slipped it back into his pocket. He returned to the room to find Greenstreet levering himself out of his chair. The papers had disappeared, as had the hundred-eagle notes.

"You can discuss the matter with Coreg yourself, sir," he said. "I will take you to him. I would summon his servant, but the rascal has gone missing."

Greenstreet picked up a cane to assist him and walked toward what appeared to be a blank wall. Placing the palm of his hand against the wall, he activated what Mr. Sloan observed to be a mundane and unimaginative locking spell. A hidden door slid open in response, revealing stairs that led underground. Greenstreet descended the stairs with much grunting, and Mr. Sloan followed.

The stairs led to a tunnel, which in turn led to another staircase. Mr. Sloan assumed they were going to ascend these stairs, but Greenstreet paid no attention to them. Raising his cane, he rapped several times on a wall, waited, and struck the wall again.

The wall disappeared.

Mr. Sloan raised an eyebrow. Someone had cast a quite good illusion spell. He had been fooled, and that wasn't easy. Mr. Sloan was impressed.

Greenstreet lumbered through the illusory wall and continued down another tunnel for about a quarter mile, by Mr. Sloan's estimation. At the end was another wall. Mr. Sloan eyed it carefully and saw that this wall was real, not an illusion. The only magicks on it were the simple constructs used to light the way.

Greenstreet touched the wall with the tips of the fingers of his left hand. The magical glowing lights went out, leaving them in darkness. Mr. Sloan listened, but all he could hear in the silence was Greenstreet's raspy breathing.

A moment later a dark sphere pulsating with darkness appeared on the wall. That phrase sounded strange even as he thought it, but Mr. Sloan could think of no other way to describe it. Purple flames blazed on the outer rim of the sphere, surrounding a globe so wholly devoid of light that Mr. Sloan imagined it was deeper than the darkness at the bottom of the world.

"Ever see dragon magic before, Mr. Sloan?" Greenstreet asked.

"No, sir, I have not," said Mr. Sloan. "Remarkable."

"I will wager you have never seen one of these either," said Greenstreet.

He fished a small box made of ebony out of a capacious pocket, opened it, and held it to the faint light, revealing a square-cut jewel as large as an egg resting on purple velvet.

"A black diamond," Greenstreet said with a relish.

He removed the diamond from the box and carefully placed it in the center of the pulsing blackness. Mr. Sloan, heard a faint clicking sound and deduced that the diamond was a key to some type of lock. The diamond began to glow with a faint purplish radiance. Greenstreet rotated the jewel a quarter turn to the right, paused for a count of perhaps three, then turned the jewel a half turn back to the left.

"You should take a step or two back, Mr. Sloan," Greenstreet warned.

Mr. Sloan did as he suggested and was glad he had done so, for at that moment the stone wall split down the center, forming enormous double doors. The massive doors silently swung open on well-oiled hinges, narrowly missing Mr. Sloan, who was forced to retreat again to avoid being crushed.

Greenstreet chuckled, clearly enjoying himself.

"Please wait here while I speak to Coreg. Do not enter until the dragon gives you permission," Greenstreet cautioned. "Coreg does not like surprises, and things will go badly for you should he catch you roaming about uninvited."

Mr. Sloan prudently waited in the tunnel. He had no intention of surprising such a host.

Greenstreet walked through the stone doors into a cavernous chamber, bellowing as he did so, "Coreg, it is Greenstreet. I have brought you a visitor! And where the devil is Trubgek?"

Light flared, shining from some unseen source above, illuminating a room that was so vast, Mr. Sloan almost lost sight of Greenstreet. No small feat, considering the man's size. An enormous shadowy figure at the very back of the chamber stirred and reared up. Mr. Sloan assumed this must be Coreg.

Greenstreet and the dragon spoke in low tones; then Greenstreet turned to shout, "Mr. Sloan! You may enter!"

As Mr. Sloan crossed the floor, he cast an appraising eye over statuary, fine paintings, and other signs of wealth. He was interested to observe that while Coreg owned many extremely rare and valuable pieces, he was careless in his treatment of them. The marble statues were dust-covered and dirty. Some of the paintings had been hung upside down and all of them titled at crazy angles.

The dragon does not care about what he owns except as an ostentatious display of wealth, and he has grown bored with even that, Mr. Sloan noted, mentally composing his letter to Sir Henry. He has everything money can buy, so what does he want now?

The answer was disconcerting: Power.

As he neared the monstrous creature, Mr. Sloan was beginning to have second thoughts about inviting this dragon to reside in Freya. Mr. Sloan had his orders, however, and he was bound to carry them out.

Coreg rose to a crouching position. His wings were folded at his sides, and his front claws rasped on the stone floor. His lips parted, his teeth gleamed, his eyes glinted. His clear intent was to impress upon his visitor that he was viewed as nothing more than a toothsome morsel.

Mr. Sloan had been in the presence of dragons before, most notably the majestic noble dragons of the Rosian court. By contrast to them, Coreg with his thick neck and overlarge head looked very common and crude. Mr. Sloan did not consider himself intimidated.

He advanced to stand in front of Coreg and waited for the dragon to speak.

Coreg came straight to the point. "I understand Sir Henry has an offer for me. What is it?"

Mr. Sloan spoke of the Rosian navy, saying that it was Sir Henry's considered opinion that the Rosians planned to be here for some time. He mentioned the disruption to what he referred to as the dragon's "numerous enterprises."

Mr. Sloan then made Sir Henry's proposal: safe passage to Freya, comfortable accommodations, free rein to conduct business.

"Most generous of Sir Henry," said Coreg when Mr. Sloan had finished. "And what does he want in return? Come, Mr. Slope, I know there must be something."

Greenstreet coughed. "Sloan. His name is Sloan."

"Sloan, then," Coreg said with a negligent flip of his tail. "What does Sir Henry want from me?"

"Sir Henry makes no conditions for his offer, sir," said Mr. Sloan, proceeding cautiously. "But he would deem it a favor between friends and compatriots if you were to answer a simple question."

Coreg gazed down at him, eyes flickering. "You have piqued my curiosity. And what is this 'simple' question?"

"Sir Henry has it on excellent authority that you were hired to provide an assassin to murder a Travian dragon named Odila. Sir Henry would like to know the identity of the person or persons who hired you."

"I'll wager he would!" Coreg roared with laughter. Fire shot out his nostrils, echoes thundered around the chamber. His fangs parted in a gaping grin.

Mr. Sloan stood unflinching, waiting for the answer, which he guessed he was not going to receive. His guess proved correct.

"Thank Sir Henry for his concern over my welfare," said Coreg, when he had recovered from his mirth. "I have already made my plans in regard to leaving the Aligoes. A good day to you, Mr. Slope. Perhaps we yet may be—what did you call it—compatriots."

The dragon chortled with laughter again at this last remark—which was some sort of inside jest, apparently, for Greenstreet also chuckled.

"Wait over by the door for Greenstreet to escort you back," Coreg added with a dismissive flip of his tail. "Greenstreet, I need a word with you."

Mr. Sloan departed, walking slowly in a vain attempt to overhear what was being said. The dragon had lowered his head to the floor, however, and was speaking in a gravelly undertone, so that Mr. Sloan could not understand more than a mumbled word here and there. As for Greenstreet, he replied in monosyllables.

Mr. Sloan did not have to wait long before Greenstreet joined him, puffing from the exertion of having to walk across the vast chamber.

"Damn that Trubgek!" Greenstreet muttered, mopping his head with a handkerchief. "This way, Mr. Sloan."

The two left the chamber, and the doors swung shut behind them and returned to being a wall.

"Are you staying long in Freeport, Mr. Sloan?" Greenstreet asked.

"I had not planned on it, sir," said Mr. Sloan in cool tones indicative of his disappointment. "Now that my business is concluded, I must return to Sir Henry."

"You might want to reconsider," said Greenstreet. "Stay a day or two. Enjoy the sights. Freeport is small, but not without its charms. You can find the best food and drink in the Aligoes at a tavern called the Perky Parrot. I also recommend a visit to the Celestial Gates."

Mr. Sloan knew about the Celestial Gates, the name of the local whorehouse.

"Thank you, no," he said.

Greenstreet shrugged. "Suit yourself, Mr. Sloan. I am merely suggesting that you might want to stay on a few days. You could find it to be worth your while."

Mr. Sloan stopped in the tunnel and turned to face Greenstreet. "Speak plainly, Mr. Greenstreet. Has Coreg changed his mind about the offer?"

"I could not possibly reveal a confidence, Mr. Sloan," said Greenstreet, rocking back and forth on his heels.

Mr. Sloan reached inside his inner pocket, drew out his billfold, and removed another banknote. Greenstreet plucked the banknote from his hand.

"Coreg wants to speak to someone first," said Greenstreet, deftly stuffing the banknote up his shirtsleeve. "He has asked me to send for this person and while it might take a few days for him to arrive, the wait could prove to be to your benefit."

"I understand," said Mr. Sloan. "I will avail myself of the pleasures of this picturesque little town."

He and Greenstreet parted on cordial terms. Mr. Sloan spent the remainder of the day acquainting himself with Freeport, which meant that he walked from one end of the main road to the other and back again.

He located the Perky Parrot and viewed it with interest, recalling that Captain Northrop had been known to frequent this tavern and had recommended the tavern as being an excellent place to mingle with the locals and learn all the latest news and gossip.

Returning to the widow's house at twilight, Mr. Sloan ate the meal she provided, which proved to be boiled mutton and cabbage, and decided that tomorrow he would definitely dine at the Parrot. Following supper, he retired to his room, lit the lamp, and sat down to write a letter containing the latest gossip. He knew Sir Henry would be interested.

The lady at first rejected our friend's proposal of marriage outright. Our friend was considerably disappointed and was leaving in despair when he was told in confidence that, upon consideration, the lady might be persuaded to change her mind and give him the answer he so ardently desires.

It is my considered belief that our friend has a rival for the lady's affections and that she is hoping to play one gentleman against the other to determine which has the most to offer her. Our friend plans to remain in town a few days longer, therefore, to see what transpires. I trust he may win in the end.

Yours in Faith,
Franklin Sloan

Mr. Sloan had already ascertained from General Winstead that the mail packets were operating under the protection of the Rosian navy. Amused by the thought of the Rosians protecting Sir Henry's communications, Mr. Sloan posted his letter. He then walked home, taking time to admire the beauty of God's creations, of which even Freeport might be considered one. Arriving back at his lodgings, Mr. Sloan retired to his prayers and his bed.

FORTY-SIX

The journey to Kate's Cove was slow going, with *Victorie* forced to take a circuitous route among the islands, and Kate chafed at the delay. *Victorie* had to navigate narrow channels and sail under, over, or around myriad floating isles. They dared not travel at night for fear of running aground or being struck by the huge chunks of rocks that broke off from the islands and floated about the Breath.

Kate kept a daily record of their journey, marking their location in the log, and although she was disheartened by their slow progress, she had no right to complain. Her plan was working. Most of the islands in this part of the Aligoes were small and uninhabited, containing nothing anyone wanted, including pirates. The Rosian navy would not risk their ships or waste their time on them.

The days crawled by. The pin on the chart Kate used to mark their location drew steadily closer to the pin she had placed in Kate's Cove. When *Victorie* safely arrived at her destination, Kate congratulated herself on not having seen a single Rosian ship or a member of the Dragon Brigade. She was aware the respite was temporary. Kate's Cove might be well hidden, but they were close to Freeport and the Trame Channel and Rosian naval patrols. She doubled the watch.

She was pleased to find the *Barwich Rose* where they had left her, covered by tarps. The ship looked very small and shabby compared to the refurbished and smartly outfitted *Victorie,* but the *Rose* had served Kate well and she was glad to see the old girl.

The crew was eager to continue on to Freeport. Kate had to disappoint them.

"We're going to lie low, keep out of sight until we know what's going on. I'll take the pinnace into town, look things over and talk to Akiel."

Kate eyed the *Rose.* She considered telling Olaf and the crew to haul the ship out of the trees and make her ready to sail. The Rosians wouldn't know the *Rose,* and once she had talked to Coreg and made things right with Dalgren, she could hide *Victorie* until the Rosians had gone and leave the Aligoes in the *Rose.* In the end, she decided to leave *Rose* where she was, on the unlikely chance that the Rosians were sniffing around Freeport.

Kate was eager to be gone. She was forced to wait, however, until the crew had filled the lift tank on the pinnace.

"You're not wearing that, are you?" Olaf asked, frowning.

"What's wrong with the way I'm dressed?" Kate demanded, looking down at her slops and the man's calico shirt.

"Because everyone in Freeport will know it's you," he pointed out. He added with a grin, "Dress like a lady and no one will recognize you."

"Very funny," said Kate, but she had to admit he was right.

She went down to her cabin and put on the green silk dress and the hat Mrs. Lavender had given her in Braffa. The hat had been lucky for her then. The job in Braffa had gone well, not counting meeting Thomas, or perhaps counting meeting Thomas. She still thought about him sometimes. It would be fun to meet him again. She could taunt him about being a prince.

Kate tucked a corset gun in her boot, then displayed herself to Olaf, who swore he would not know her if he tripped over her in the street. She then boarded the pinnace. She had already stashed two pistols beneath the helm. As a last-minute thought, she made a bundle of her shirt and the slops and her kerchief and stuffed them beneath a seat. Hoisting the sail, she sent the magic to the lift tank and the airscrews and set off.

A lady would never sail a pinnace on her own, but Kate couldn't risk any of the crew being seen in town. She decided to dock the pinnace at the old abandoned lighthouse, which was not far from the Parrot, and walk the rest of the way.

She had not really expected to find the Rosian navy hanging about Freeport, which was a considerable distance from the Trame Channel, and she was unpleasantly surprised to see a Rosian patrol boat sailing near the entrance to Freeport Bay.

Fortunately she saw the patrol boat before they could spot her and she steered the pinnace close to the shoreline, in the shadows of the trees. She blessed her decision to hide *Victorie* in the cove.

She was keeping watch on the sky as well as the Breath, and saw two dragons of the Dragon Brigade patrolling the Trame Channel. The channel was miles away, and so Kate wasn't worried about them finding *Victorie*. She was worried about Dalgren, however. She had been hoping he had flown to the Aligoes, back to his old lair, so that she could talk to him. Now she found herself hoping he had gone to visit his uncle in Travia.

At least, if she could see the dragons, so could Dalgren. He would know the Brigade was in the area and he would hole up in his lair by day, fly out only late at night.

She wondered uneasily what the Dragon Brigade would do to him if they caught him. The penalty for humans deserting the military was death. Dragons were more civilized, however. They didn't kill their own kind. But his punishment was bound to be severe. Dragons were proud of the Dragon Brigade, believing it symbolized human/dragon friendship and dedication to their chosen homeland. A dragon deserting the Brigade was tantamount to a human spitting on the king.

Kate tied up the pinnace and stowed it among some trees near the lighthouse, and climbed out, cursing the cumbersome skirt that tangled around her legs. She took a moment to adjust her clothes and partially lower the net veil on her hat over her face. No one was likely to be around this part of the island, for no one ever came here, but she waited and watched for several moments, just to be certain, then walked toward town, trying to remember to take small, ladylike strides.

The path from the lighthouse led her past the Perky Parrot. The hour was near noon and she could smell the savory odors of Akiel's chicken stew drifting out the open windows.

The Parrot had been her home for many years after the death of her father, and memories overwhelmed her, catching her by surprise. She missed the laughter, the good fellowship, and she paused outside, tempted to slip inside to see Akiel and the dear old Parrot, ask about Dalgren, and pretend for a moment that she had come home.

She resisted the urge and kept walking. She couldn't take the chance that someone might recognize her and, in fact, she passed several people she knew on their way to the Parrot. None of them glanced at her and she was amused to think Olaf had been right. None of them knew her as a lady!

As she continued on down the street, drawing closer to the town, her attention was caught and held by a man wearing a dark frock coat walking in the direction of the Parrot. Much about him seemed familiar: the somber way he dressed, his upright stance and military manner.

Kate studied him as he approached, trying to think why she should know him. He drew nearer and she was shocked and alarmed to recognize Sir Henry's secretary, Mr. Sloan.

She knew in an instant that Sir Henry had sent his secretary to find her and drag her back to Freya to stand trial for murder.

Kate longed to turn and run, but that would only draw his attention. Better to keep walking. She tugged at the veil and lowered her head, demure and shy. She and Mr. Sloan would have to pass each other, however, and Kate waited in dread for him to place her.

Mr. Sloan slowed, his gaze fixed on her, and Kate almost ran.

He politely doffed his hat, said, "Good afternoon, madame," and walked on by, continuing down the road.

Kate glanced over her shoulder to see where he was going. Sure enough, he was looking for her. Mr. Sloan opened the door of the Parrot and walked inside.

Kate hurried on, almost faint with relief that she had seen Mr. Sloan before he had seen her. She would have to sneak back tonight to talk to Akiel.

"As if I didn't have problems enough without this!" Kate muttered under her breath.

She turned off the main road down the path that led to Greenstreet's house. She didn't know the big man wearing slops who was lounging on the porch, which was good, for he wouldn't be likely to know her.

Apparently not many well-dressed women paid visits to Greenstreet, for the big man was flustered at the sight of her stepping onto the veranda and seemed to have no idea what to do. He jumped to his feet and self-consciously pulled up his slops, which had parted company with his shirt, then stood staring at her.

"I would like to speak to Mr. Greenstreet, if he could spare me a moment of his time," said Kate.

The big man in slops vanished, going inside, leaving Kate to wait on the veranda. The guard was gone a long time, longer than it should have taken to announce her. Growing uneasy, Kate went over to one of the windows, thinking she would try to peek inside Greenstreet's office, only to be startled when the curtain moved and an eye looked out at her. The curtain fell back into place.

Something was wrong. She was tempted to leave, but the memory of the hurt and disappointment in Dalgren's eyes when he looked at her made her stay.

"He'll see you now," said the big man.

He escorted her into the house and opened the door to the office. Kate swept past him. Greenstreet spoke to the guard.

"You can leave on that errand we discussed, Jules."

The big man departed, shutting the door behind him. Greenstreet leaned back in his chair. His usually empty desk was no longer empty. A tin box, such as might contain letters, sat squarely in the center. Greenstreet's hands were laced over his belly.

"You should not be here, Captain," he murmured.

Kate stared at him in shock. She had hoped to take him by surprise, but unfortunately the surprise was all hers.

"I need to talk to Coreg," she said. "I have money. I can pay for the information. I came here to find out who killed that dragon and framed me for the murder."

"You misunderstand me, Captain," Greenstreet said, opening his eyes and shifting his bulk in the chair. "When I say you should not be here, I mean you should not be *here*—in the Aligoes. The Rosians have placed a bounty on your head: a thousand silver rosuns. A tidy sum. You should feel flattered."

Kate sank down in the chair. Feeling stifled, she lifted the veil and dragged off her hat.

"I don't believe you," she said, moistening her dry mouth.

"You should, Captain. The entire Rosian navy and half the populace of the Aligoes are searching for the notorious Captain Kate of the Dragon Corsairs. The Rosians have been reading your stories and they do not like to be portrayed as fools and poltroons."

"That's . . . ridiculous . . ." Kate said, inclined to laugh. "I want to see Coreg."

Greenstreet opened the tin box, removed several papers, and sorted through them until he found the one he sought.

"I thought you might come to see me and so I obtained this dispatch—compliments of a Rosian officer who has the sad tendency to lose at baccarat—which was sent to all the fleet captains. It is long, so I will summarize. Your ship, the *Victorie,* was sighted a week ago at the entrance to the Trame Channel. The *Victorie* escaped and was last seen sailing southwest on a course that would take her deep into the Aligoes.

"The authorities believe you are going to try to establish contact with a dragon known as Dalgren, a deserter from the Dragon Brigade, who was sighted in the vicinity of Freeport a fortnight ago. Orders regarding you and the *Victorie* are to: 'take, burn, or destroy.' Their orders regarding you are to 'kill or capture.' "

Kate rose to her feet, not knowing what she was doing. She stood a moment, then sat back down.

"Let me see that," she said.

Greenstreet tossed the dispatch to her. Kate tried to read it. The words swam in her vision, made no sense. But she saw the name of her ship, *Victorie*. And the bounty: one thousand silver rosuns.

A bitter taste filled her mouth. A horrid sensation of warmth flooded through her body and ebbed away the next instant, leaving her cold and shaking. A sudden thought flashed through her mind, filling her with terror.

Greenstreet knew the location of her cove. He had been spying on her. He had told her as much when he made the deal with her to attack the *Pride of Haever.* As he was always saying, he knew everything that went on in the Aligoes.

"Where did you send your man?" she asked, her throat tightening.

"You have become a liability, Captain," said Greenstreet. "You are bad for business. The Dragon Brigade had very little trouble finding the cove. They have been keeping watch . . ."

"Oh, God!" Kate gasped.

She bounded from the chair and tripped on the hem of her skirt. Swearing, she hiked it up around her knees and set off at a run. She dashed across Greenstreet's lawn and up the lane. She did not slow when she reached the main street of the town, but kept running. People stopped to stare at her and some even yelled after her. She paid no attention.

Reaching the Perky Parrot, she burst through the door, shouting Akiel's name. The patrons looked up in startlement. Akiel was coming out of the kitchen carrying two bowls of stew. He gaped at her, eyes wide.

"Kate—"

"The Rosians!" Kate panted. Her lungs burned. She could scarcely draw breath. "*Victorie!* They know about the cove . . ."

Akiel dropped the bowls to the floor, grabbed the loaded pistols Olaf had always kept behind the bar, and ran for the door. As Kate joined him, she caught a fleeting glimpse of Mr. Sloan staring at her in profound astonishment. He appeared completely amazed to see her—which meant he had not come here looking for her.

She couldn't waste time wondering, however. Her strength was starting to flag. She stumbled and Akiel caught hold of her and supported her.

"Where are we going?"

"Lighthouse!" Kate answered.

Akiel did not ask any more questions. If there were bounty notices, he had undoubtedly figured out what was happening; maybe he had even been expecting her and wondering how he could warn her.

"Greenstreet said . . . Dalgren was here!" Kate said.

She was trying to decide as she ran if she would hoist the flag to let Dalgren know there was trouble or if she would sail straight to the cove to warn her people and try to escape before the Rosian navy found *Victorie*.

"He was here . . ." Akiel began.

"I need to warn him!" said Kate.

"Mum, wait!" Akiel said, and tried to stop her.

Kate ignored him. She would warn Dalgren. She owed him that much. Entering the lighthouse, she picked up two flags: one was their private signal and the other a flag with two red squares and two white squares meaning "danger." Her hand shook as she tried to attach the flags to the line, causing her to fumble at the snap hooks.

Akiel clasped his big hand firmly over hers.

"Mum, stop!"

"I can't!" Kate said. "I have to warn Dalgren!"

"He isn't here," Akiel said.

Kate shoved him away. "You just said he was! If you're not going to help me, let go of me!"

"Listen to me, mum," said Akiel. "Dalgren gave himself up to the Dragon Brigade yesterday. He said he was tired of running. Two dragons escorted him back to Rosia. He is gone."

Kate stopped fumbling at the hooks and let the flags slip to the floor.

"No," she said. "Oh, God, no! This is my fault. All my fault!"

"Mum, it is not—"

Kate shoved past him. "I have to go warn the others. You take the helm. I'll cast off the lines."

She scrambled down the rock-strewn hill to where she had left the pinnace. Akiel climbed into the boat and ran his hands over the helm, sending the magic flowing to the lift tank. Kate cast off the lines and then jumped in.

"I'm going to change clothes," she warned Akiel, starting to unbutton her jacket.

"Here?" Akiel protested.

"Here," Kate said.

She threw off her jacket, stripped off her skirt, and pulled on a shirt and her slops. She impatiently tugged at her bootlaces, breaking one of them, and thrust her feet into her leather slippers. She had dropped the hat at Greenstreet's and she shook out her curls. Feeling better in her familiar clothes, she took a moment to rest and catch her breath.

She faced forward into the wind, breathing deeply and letting the breeze blow through her hair, cooling her. She let herself think about Dalgren a moment; that was a mistake. Her heart ached and she was angry at him.

"He left me," she said. "He knew I would come, and he left me."

She concentrated on her anger. She was strong when she was angry, and she needed that strength to overcome her sickening, gut-twisting fear.

"I assume you know what is happening," she said, turning to face Akiel.

"I heard about the big bounty," he said. "How did the Rosians find you?"

"Greenstreet betrayed me," said Kate, striving to keep her voice level and calm. "I sailed into an ambush! Olaf and the others don't know they're in danger. I have to reach them in time!"

She paused, looking at Akiel, then said, "You told me Greenstreet was a bad man. I should have listened to you and to Olaf. I will make this right. I swear! I will make it right."

The small pinnace with its single airscrew crawled through the Breath, seeming to barely cause a ripple in the mists.

"Increase speed," Kate ordered.

"The boat is going as fast as it can, mum," Akiel returned. "Probably faster than it should."

Kate could hear the frantic whirring of the airscrew blades and knew he was right. She couldn't take a chance on breaking a blade or crashing. She sat down, then stood up. She checked the four pistols to make certain they were loaded, and thrust two into her belt. She offered the others to Akiel.

He shook his head. "I will not kill."

"The Rosians might not be so considerate," said Kate.

Akiel shook his head again. Kate gave an exasperated sigh and hid the other two pistols beneath the helm. She sat back down and willed the pinnace to go faster.

Whenever the mists parted and the boat sailed into a clear patch of air, she scanned the sky, searching for the dragons she had seen earlier. They were nowhere in sight, and she didn't see any ships, either. She breathed easier.

The Rosians might know where to find the cove, but they still had to navigate the narrow lanes between the islands to reach *Victorie,* and that would cost them time.

"The hell with it! I'll take over the helm," she told Akiel.

Placing her hands on the constructs, Kate sent anger and fear flowing with the magic along the braided-leather lines.

"Faster," she urged. "Faster . . ."

FORTY-SEVEN

Kate followed the shoreline until she reached the entrance of Freeport Bay, planning to return to the cove the way she had come, the fastest route. In her desperate haste, she had forgotten about the Rosian naval patrol boat she had seen earlier. It was still there, prowling about. Swearing beneath her breath, she touched the constructs on the helm, slowing the pinnace.

"We could try to brazen our way past them," Kate said to Akiel. "Talk our way out. They aren't looking for this boat."

"They are looking for *you,* mum," said Akiel. "They have a description of you. I heard the people in the Parrot talking about it. The description is very good, very precise as to detail."

"We'll have to sail the north route, then," said Kate.

She put the pinnace about, doubling back the way she had come. Cursing the loss of time, she steered the boat into a narrow channel that would let her approach the cove from the north. The distance this way was shorter, but would take longer, since she would have to zigzag around several small islands. Even with this delay, she calculated she could still beat the Rosians, whose larger ships would have to navigate the narrow channels.

The pinnace slipped among the islands, sometimes coming so close to the banks on either side that Kate had to duck to avoid being hit by overhanging tree limbs. The heat of the jungle was stifling, and there was no breeze. Mists from the Breath curled around the hull. Kate posted Akiel in the front with a boathook to fend off drifting boulders.

Kate had sailed this route only a couple of times and that was when they had first hauled *Victorie* into the cove. She worried that she might be lost, for it seemed to her that they should have sighted her ship by now.

"We are getting close," Akiel said suddenly, pointing ahead. "There is the upside-down tree!"

By some strange fluke, a cedar tree had sprouted from the bottom of this small island. Seeking the sun, the tree had curved up and over the island's rim. Kate knew where she was now and Akiel was right. They were nearing the cove where *Victorie* was hidden.

"You should slow down," Akiel advised. "Approach with caution."

Kate reduced the magic to the airscrew and brought the pinnace to a crawl. Holding her breath, she listened for sounds that would indicate her ship was under attack: the boom of cannons, the crack of rifle fire. All she could hear was the occasional scraping of branches against the hull.

"I don't hear anything," she said, relieved.

"Neither do I," Akiel said. His expression was grim, his tone ominous.

"What's wrong?" Kate asked.

"We don't hear anything," said Akiel.

Kate impatiently shook her head, not understanding, and then she realized what Akiel meant. They were *not* hearing the familiar sounds of the jungle: monkeys chattering and screeching, birds singing. Kate had heard these sounds so much she had ceased to hear them—until now, when it was far too quiet.

"Animals are smarter than we are, mum. When they sense danger, they flee from it. They do not sail toward it. We should— What are you doing?"

Casting caution aside, Kate sent the magic cascading into the pinnace, speeding through the narrow channel as fast as the airscrew would turn. Vines struck her in the face, branches clawed the balloon and tore at the rigging.

"You are going to wreck us!" Akiel warned.

Kate ignored him. "Once we dock, I will jump out and release the anchor. While I'm doing that, you go on board and sound general quarters. Run out the guns and hoist the sails."

"Which do I do first?" Akiel demanded.

Kate knew what he meant. She had a good crew, seasoned sailors, but their numbers were few. Olaf had repeatedly told her they needed more men, but she had been in such haste to flee Freya that she had left without a full complement. The sailors required to hoist the sails were also needed to man the guns. They couldn't do both at the same time.

"The sails," said Kate; then she stopped talking to listen. "What is that noise? Is that gunfire?"

Akiel cocked his head in the direction of the sound. "No, mum. That is the sound of hammers."

Of course, it was. Now she recalled that she and Olaf had discussed the need for the ship's carpenters to repair loose deck planks and reinforce the railings. She had been so smugly confident that she had outwitted the Rosians that she had relaxed her vigilance. She should have ordered every one on board to keep watch day and night. No one would be paying attention. They would likely never see or hear the enemy approaching.

The pinnace was now close enough that Kate could glimpse *Victorie*'s gray silk balloons through the trees. The balloons would be only partially inflated while the ship was docked, just enough to maintain neutral buoyancy. The crew would need time to shake out the sails, time to raise them, time to fully inflate the balloons.

Time they didn't have.

The pinnace shot out from among the trees and whirred toward the dock. Akiel was standing at the prow, waving his arms and bellowing, trying to make someone see him or hear him over the clamor. One of the crew spotted him at last and shouted at Olaf. He turned and looked their direction.

"Ambush!" Akiel thundered.

Olaf frowned, not able to hear. He shouted something to the crew, and the hammering dwindled to a desultory halt.

"What did you say?" he shouted back.

"I'm docking!" Kate yelled at Akiel. "Hold on!"

Akiel sat down and gripped the gunwales. Kate reversed the airscrew and cut the magic to the lift tanks, and she was still going too fast. The pinnace landed on the shore, bumped, rose up, fell down, bumped again, then slammed into the ground and began to slide. The minute the keel touched, before the pinnace had stopped moving, Akiel was climbing over the rail. He landed on all fours on the dock, jumped to his feet, and began running toward *Victorie*.

"Ambush!" Akiel bellowed again as he dashed up the gangplank. "The Rosians found us. They are on their way!"

The pinnace skidded sideways into the base of the crude docking arm that they had built using the trunk of a pine tree. A spar snapped and came crashing down, narrowly missing Kate, and tangling her in the rigging. She threw off the rope and climbed over the wreckage. Jumping from the rail to the dock, she ran toward the anchor.

The front of *Victorie*'s stern rested in a groove carved into the ground. The ship continued to float, but it was secured to the docking arm by a rope leading from the mast of the aft balloon and to the ground by a heavy cast-iron anchor.

Each arm of the anchor fit over a bollard sunk into the ground. Clamps activated by magic held it in place. Once the clamps were released, the anchor's arms would still hug the bollards, as the tension on the anchor chain held them in place. Kate would then operate the "pump," which took its name from the handle of a well pump. Since the anchor was far too heavy to lift, the pump would cause a metal bar to shoot out of the ground, strike the anchor and knock it loose. The crew would haul in the anchor and the ship would float free.

A crewmember usually handled this task. Kate had not freed the anchor in a long time. The process was relatively simple, however. Magic did most of the work.

Olaf gave the order for general quarters. Drums beat. He portioned out the crew, sending some dashing up the ratlines to release the sails while others raced to the gun deck. The gunports swung open and Kate could hear the rumble as the gun crews started to run out the cannons. Marco was standing at the helm, sending magic flowing to the lift tanks and beginning the process of inflating the balloons.

One of the lookouts and several of the crew started shouting in alarm. Kate looked up from her task. Three dragons appeared in the sky and, at the same time, a Rosian frigate, forty-two guns, sailed out of the mist, rounding one of the small islands that lay to the south.

Kate knew enough about dragon tactics to know the dragons would not attack her ship, not in such close quarters, for they might accidentally set fire to the frigate. The Dragon Brigade was here to keep watch. If *Victorie* fled, they would track the rat to its hole.

Kate turned back to her work, remembering with a swelling in her throat the young Kate who had been so excited to watch dragons flying in formation, high above the cliffs of Westfirth. They had seemed beautiful then, flying so high . . .

So high! Kate gulped with excitement. The *Victorie* might yet be able to escape. Dragons had excellent sight, but they were high in the sky and not even their eyes could pierce the mists of the Deep Breath far below. She would dive down below the mists, sail beneath the islands as she had done when she was wrecking. The voyage would be cold and uncomfortable. The *Victorie* wouldn't be able to stay down long or everyone would perish. Just long enough to throw off pursuit.

The Rosian ship might chase after her, but Kate doubted it. Few wreckers dared sail the Deep Breath. She couldn't imagine that a Rosian naval captain would take the risk, endanger his ship and the lives of his crew. She wasn't worth that much to them.

Kate waved her hand at Akiel, who was on the quarterdeck, leaning over the rail, waiting to give the command to raise the anchor once she released it.

"Tell Marco to take the ship down into the Deep Breath!" Kate shouted. "Sink her! And raise the gangplank! I'll jump for it!"

Akiel understood and ran to relay the order.

Kate knelt down by the first clamp and swiftly deactivated the magical construct by sliding her hand across it, erasing the magic. The clamp popped open, releasing one side of the crossbar.

She heard a bang that sounded like a cannon, but didn't look up. The Rosian navy did things by the book. That was the warning shot across the bow, and that gave her an idea.

Akiel was back at the rail, watching and waiting.

Kate cupped her hands around her mouth and yelled, "Strike our colors! Surrender!"

"Surrender?" Akiel repeated in disbelief. "You just said—"

"We're not really surrendering! I need time to free the anchor!" Kate cried.

Akiel frowned. "I do not like this, mum. This will make the Rosians very angry."

"You don't have to like it, just do it!" Kate shouted.

Akiel shook his head and left the rail, hopefully going to tell Olaf. If Kate had been on board, she could have explained. She could only trust that Olaf and Marco would understand her plan.

She moved to the second clamp and repeated the process, closing the magical construct. The clamp opened. The other end of the anchor's arm was free. The anchor still hugged the bollards, held in place by the tension on the anchor chain.

Kate now activated the magic on the pump and began to work it, pumping it up and down, like water from a well. The metal bar shivered, but didn't budge. The anchor remained attached to the bollards. Desperate to free her ship, Kate worked the pump handle harder, using all her strength. She heard a clank and a grinding sound and the pump froze.

"No! You son of a bitch!" Kate swore at the pump. "No!"

She had to find a way to free the anchor. The crew had hauled the guns back inside and were shutting the gunports as the *Victorie*'s flag—the Freyan flag, the only flag they had—slid down the mast.

Kate smiled grimly. Pretending to surrender: a ploy worthy of Morgan himself. The Rosian captain would be rejoicing, thinking he was going to take *Victorie* as a prize and capture the notorious Captain Kate.

"Not while I'm breathing," she muttered.

Marco must have understood her plan, for he had started the process of deflating the balloons, slowly, chamber by chamber, and he reduced the flow of magic to the lift tanks. The *Victorie* was slowly sinking.

Kate could hear cheers from the Rosian frigate. The captain would have to man a boat and send it over to board *Victorie*. Kate had time, but not much.

She tried working the pump handle again, but it still wouldn't budge. Akiel was back at the rail, staring down at her, waiting. Kate opened her mouth, to yell at him to fetch Olaf.

Without warning, the Rosian frigate fired a salvo from her forward guns straight into *Victorie*.

Kate stared in disbelief. "We surrendered. . . . What is he doing?"

Canisters filled with chain and grapeshot tore into the sailors on deck, sliced through the rigging, and punctured one of the balloons. Such rounds were meant to kill. Men screamed in agony. Smoke from the Rosian cannons billowed around her ship.

"You bastard!" Kate cried, outraged. "We surrendered!"

Apparently the Rosian captain didn't care. They were pirates, after all, not worthy of his time.

Frustrated and outraged, Kate kicked at the anchor. To her amazement, the iron bar shot out of the ground, hit the anchor, and knocked it loose. Gasping in relief, she waved at the watching Akiel, who bellowed at the men manning the capstan to start hauling in the anchor.

Victorie floated free and although Marco had stopped the flow of magic to the lift tanks, the ship bobbed up into the air, leaving Kate stranded on the ground, her head about level with the keel. She ran to the end of the dock, planning to jump on board once the *Victorie* had dropped down to her level.

She eyed the ship and saw that it was again starting to dive, but far too slowly.

"I can throw you a rope!" Akiel called, leaning over the rail at a perilous angle.

Kate shook her head. "I'll board on the gun deck!"

She waited tensely for the Rosians to fire again, but nothing happened. Kate uneasily wondered why, what was going on. She could no longer see the Rosian ship. *Victorie* was blocking her view. She did not think the captain was holding his fire out of the goodness of his heart.

Victorie sank lower and lower. The gun crew opened the entryway to the gun deck. Two men leaned out, waiting to grab her and haul her on board. Kate just needed a few more moments. Once she was on board, Marco would stop the flow of magic to the lift tanks and the remaining balloon. The Rosians had actually helped by puncturing the other one.

Kate was almost ready to jump. The shattering broadside took her completely by surprise. Now she understood why the Rosian captain had waited. He had been maneuvering his ship into position. The frigate had fired all twenty-one guns on the port side simultaneously.

The *Victorie* shuddered like a living thing as the cannonballs smashed into her. Smoke from the guns filled the air. Masts toppled, spars fell, rigging and sails cascaded down onto the upper deck.

She could hear shrieks and cries. The Rosians fired again as the cannons came to bear, raking *Victorie*. The firing continued, relentless. The carnage on deck must be horrible.

Marco had lost control of the helm, for the *Victorie* listed to starboard and started to drift away from Kate. Either that or Marco was dead. Maybe Olaf was dead.

The gun crew was shouting at her to jump. The gap between the ship and the dock was widening. She crouched to make the leap, hands outstretched.

An explosion tore through the gun deck.

Fire belched from the entryway. The sailors waiting for her were engulfed in flame. Kate staggered back, flinging her arm over her face as terrible heat swept over her. Three sailors, their clothes on fire, endeavored to escape by making the desperate leap across the widening chasm. Two missed and fell, screaming, into the Breath. One managed to land, tumbling and rolling on the dock.

He came to rest on his belly, shrieking and flailing about in agony. His clothes and hair were ablaze. Dropping to her knees beside him, Kate was going to beat out the flames with her hands, only to see that his torso was a bloody mass of mangled bone and blackened flesh, pierced by jagged splinters of metal. He looked at her. Blood gushed from his mouth, and his screams stopped.

Kate staggered to her feet. She had to reach *Victorie,* be with her friends. She looked around.

Victorie was gone.

In its place was a ship's boat filled with blue-coated marines. The marines were aiming their rifles at her and one of them was yelling something. Kate paid no heed. She ran to the edge of the dock and gazed down into the Breath.

"Olaf!" she screamed. "Akiel!"

Mists and smoke obscured her view. No answering cries came back to her. She was dimly aware of the ship's boat landing and marines running toward her.

Kate didn't move. She continued to stare into the mists. Then came a splintering crash and her heart lurched.

"Olaf!" she cried desperately.

"Seize her!" someone shouted.

Kate turned to see a lieutenant holding a pistol aimed at her head.

Kate raised her hands. "I give up! All I ask is that you send a boat down there!" she begged, speaking Rosian. "You heard that sound! The ship crashed onto an island. There may be survivors!"

The lieutenant gestured with his pistol. "On your knees!"

"You don't understand!" Kate pleaded with him. "We're not pirates! We're privateers. You can save them!"

The lieutenant gave a grim smile. "Save them for what? The noose? On your knees!"

His marines were lined up behind him. The pinnace that had brought them was empty except for the sailor at the helm. Kate lunged at the lieutenant, struck him full force in the chest, and ran for the boat.

She made it only a few steps. One of the marines clouted her on the side of the head with the butt of his rifle.

She fell to the ground. Pain split her skull. She tasted blood.

"You need to save them," she mumbled and she tried to push herself up. The marine raised his rifle.

"Belay that! We have orders to take her alive," the lieutenant said. "The admiral wants to witness the final chapter in her story. We can call it 'Captain Kate at the End of Her Rope.' "

The marines laughed at the officer's humor and dragged Kate to her feet. They hauled her to the boat, picked her up, and threw her onto the deck. As the marines bound her wrists and ankles, Kate stirred.

"Please, save them . . ."

"Shut her up," said the lieutenant.

The marine struck her in the face; she sank to the deck and was still.

FORTY-EIGHT

Captain Smythe stood on the veranda of Greenstreet's house waiting to be announced. The captain did not pace; he was far too well disciplined. Detached and aloof, he stood gazing into the night sky, hands at his side. The hour was late. He did not know precisely what it was, for no church chimes marked the hour in Freeport. When he had last looked at his watch, the time had been past midnight.

He was wearing a brown coat of military cut, gray breeches, a long-sleeved brown shirt with a wide white collar, black boots, and a broad-brimmed black hat. The army of Prince Tom was not decked out in royal blue or scarlet red. They did not sport brass buttons, frogs or epaulettes. Their uniforms were plain, serviceable, and unremarkable. So far as anyone knew by looking at him, Captain Smythe was a mercenary; perhaps an out-of-work mercenary.

The Rosians were allies of the Estarans and favored the prince's claim to the throne of Freya, but Captain Smythe was not a man to take chances. Thus far, very few people in the world knew about the army in Bheldem. The captain preferred to keep his secret as long as possible.

Greenstreet was one of those few. Captain Smythe had been an excellent customer for almost four years, ever since Sir Richard Wallace had sent him, accompanied by a glowing reference, to Constanza. Since an army marches on its belly, as the saying goes, Smythe had started forming his army by acquiring the supplies his soldiers would need to function—everything from pigs and bullocks and flour, rifles and cots, blankets and bullets.

He could not obtain such things on the open market without causing comment and perhaps starting a war, particularly in Bheldem, where every baron, duke, and earl was convinced his neighbors were plotting against him. Smythe had begun by making small purchases from a weapons smuggler in Freya, all the while letting it be known he was interested in buying in bulk.

Greenstreet had come to hear about Smythe and he had been an excellent customer ever since. Therefore Greenstreet did not keep Captain Smythe waiting, despite the fact that he had called late at night.

When the door opened, the captain walked into the office and took off his hat.

"I apologize for the lateness of the hour, sir," he said.

"Not in the least, Captain," said Greenstreet, shaking hands. "I was up late, going over some of the accounts. But I must say I am surprised to see you. I only sent for you a day ago. I wasn't expecting you this soon."

"His Highness is currently serving with the Rosian Royal Navy. He had some pressing matters he needed to discuss with me and summoned me to attend him. I have been in the Aligoes for several days and I thought, as long as I was in the vicinity, I would stop by. I am sorry to call so late, but I must leave in the morning."

"We do not stand upon ceremony, Captain. Whatever time suits our customers suits us. Please, be seated, sir," said Greenstreet.

Captain Smythe took a seat, sitting with his back straight and stiff, his hat on his knee. He frowned slightly. "Am I to understand that you sent for me, sir? If so, I did not receive the message."

"I did, Captain," said Greenstreet, settling back into his chair. "Well, rather, Coreg asked me to send for you. Not knowing you were in the vicinity, I wrote to you in Bheldem."

"Ah, that explains it," said Captain Smythe.

"Your arrival is therefore most fortuitous," said Greenstreet. "Coreg will be pleased."

"In point of fact, I came to speak to Coreg on behalf of the marchioness," said Smythe.

"Charming woman, the marchioness," Greenstreet said. "She has a man's head for business. No silly feminine sentimentality. Coreg was highly pleased that you recommended him to her. So you came to see Coreg at the very time Coreg wants to see you. It would seem this meeting was fated."

"God be praised," said Captain Smythe in grave tones.

"Yes, well, um, of course," Greenstreet said. He raised his voice. "Trubgek!"

There was no answer. He called again and then shook his head.

"Drat the man!" Greenstreet muttered, forced to again struggle out of his chair. "He was here only a short time ago. Turned up out of nowhere and now he has gone again. I will take you myself. Come with me."

Captain Smythe readily complied. Greenstreet opened the false door and they proceeded down the stairs and through the underground passage.

"While I am here, I am interested in purchasing several more cases of those excellent Freyan rifles you sold me," Captain Smythe stated. "What does the dragon want with me, if you are at liberty to tell me?"

"Coreg has received an invitation from Sir Henry Wallace of the Freyan Foreign Office to take up residence in that country," Greenstreet replied. "Sir Henry has made him a most generous offer. Coreg feels certain his offer would be even more generous if he received information that Prince Tom was responsible for the death of the dragon, Odila."

"Are you suggesting blackmail, sir?" Captain Smythe inquired. He did not ask in a threatening manner, but spoke in a mild tone, merely seeking verification.

"Good heavens! No, Captain," Greenstreet protested. "As an honest business partner, Coreg is simply informing you that another offer is on the table. He is giving you, as an old and valued customer, a chance to make a counteroffer."

"Most commendable," said Captain Smythe.

Greenstreet chuckled and they proceeded down the hall, discussing the Freyan rifles. Arriving at the entrance to Coreg's lair, Greenstreet took out the black diamond.

"If Trubgek were here, you could be admitted at once and we would not have to undergo this tedious process," Greenstreet grumbled. "As it is, I must ask you to be patient, Captain, while I remove the warding spell that guards the entrance."

"I am in no hurry, sir," said Captain Smythe. "I will wait back here, out of your way."

Greenstreet walked toward the door. Captain Smythe moved to stand some distance behind him. Greenstreet placed the jewel in the center of the secret door. The purple flames flickered, the darkness pulsed, and the wall began to creak open.

"Is that you, Trubgek?" Coreg shouted from inside the dwelling. "I sent for you ages ago. Where have you been?"

Under the cover of the noise of the dragon's bellowing, Captain Smythe drew a pistol from his inner coat pocket. Slowly and quietly, he pulled back the hammer, pressed the muzzle against the back of Greenstreet's neck, and fired. The bullet shattered the skull and sprayed the door with blood, brains, and bone.

The sound of the shot had been muffled. The dragon must have heard something, however, for he shouted again.

"Trubgek!" Coreg rumbled. "What was that noise? Did you bring those plans?"

Captain Smythe stepped over the corpse, careful to keep his boots out of the blood, and crept soft-footed a short distance inside the main chamber.

The only light came from a source near the dragon and was blocked by his great body, leaving this part of the chamber in deep shadow. Smythe drew out a dark lantern he had concealed beneath his coat. Taking a linen scroll from his pocket, he placed the scroll on the floor, then opened the lantern and aimed a narrow beam of light on the scroll.

"Greenstreet, is that you?" Coreg rumbled.

Smythe had to concentrate all his thoughts on the intricate and complex magical construct that covered the linen from top to bottom, corner to corner. He touched his index finger to the beginning of the construct in the bottom right corner; then, whispering the words, he traced the complicated construct through the zigzagging pathways of magic as one would negotiate a maze. If he made a mistake, took a wrong turn or had to backtrack, the magic would fail, and that would be fatal.

"Trubgek!" Coreg bellowed irately. "I know someone is here. Find out who it is!"

Smythe felt the floor shake beneath his feet. Briefly glancing up, he saw the enormous body stirring. Coreg had raised his head, was trying to see. The dragon was annoyed at being disturbed and frustrated that no one answered him. Coreg was not afraid. What dragon would be fearful in his own lair?

Smythe smiled and continued working the magic, running his finger over the linen. Wherever he touched, the construct began to shine with a faint blue light. Reaching the end, he intoned the final words and rose to his feet. He would have to wait a few moments to find out if he had succeeded. He needed time. Raising his voice, he answered the dragon.

"It is Captain Smythe, Coreg," he called, placing his body so that it would block the faint glow of light. "Forgive me for calling so late. Greenstreet said you wanted to see me on a matter of some urgency."

"Captain Smythe," Coreg said, sounding surprised. "You are very prompt. Where is Greenstreet?"

"He let me into your chamber, then excused himself, saying he had urgent business," Smythe replied.

Coreg snorted. "He must be off conspiring with the Rosians. Collecting bounties on the sly. The fool imagines that I do not know what he is doing."

"He did not tell me, Coreg," said Smythe.

He glanced back at the linen scroll on the floor behind him. The blue glow was growing brighter, stronger. The magic was working.

"Blasted Rosians!" Coreg continued, grumbling. "I flew to my favorite hunting ground tonight, only to find it crawling with Brigade dragons, gloating over some pirate they had captured. I had to leave before they saw me and now I have had nothing to eat. Life in the Aligoes is becoming intolerable. Which brings me to why I wanted to speak to you, Captain. Come closer! I do not like having to shout."

The magic had seeped through the linen onto the stone floor beneath, and now the stone was beginning to glow. The intricate lines of the construct gleamed. Smythe was reluctant to move, for fear Coreg would see the blue glow and know that he was spellcasting.

"Captain Smythe, I said come closer. Why do you persist in lurking in the shadows?" Coreg roared, snapping his jaws in irritation. "I warn you. I am hungry and thus not in a good mood."

A vaporous cloud began to steal across the floor toward the dragon. The cloud was nearly invisible. Captain Smythe could see it only because he had been watching for it. The spell was complete.

"Forgive me," he called. "I was looking over the order I plan to place, checking my numbers."

"I am no clerk, Captain! Talk to Greenstreet about numbers and orders," said Coreg. "You and I have more important business regarding your princeling."

Smythe walked into the room, taking his time so that he could observe the progress of the vapor as it seeped across the stones, flowing behind him like his shadow.

Coreg had settled back down, crouching at his ease, sprawled on the floor. The vapor crept past Smythe, drawn to the dragon as an iron needle is drawn to the lodestone.

Smythe was not concerned that the dragon would notice the vapor. The last dragon had not noticed it, not until it was too late. Still, as stated before, he was not one to take chances. He walked up to Coreg and stood before him, keeping the dragon's attention focused on him.

"I am all attention, Coreg," said Smythe. "What do you have to say in regard to His Highness?"

The vapor flowed around the dragon and began drifting upward.

"I understand Prince Tom is visiting the Aligoes," said Coreg. "I want to speak to him. You will arrange an audience."

Smythe frowned. "You know that such a meeting is impossible."

"Maybe not quite so impossible, Captain," said Coreg, rumbling deep in his chest. He enjoyed playing with his prey. "I have been picturing the dismay of the people of Freya if they were to discover their future king is a cold-blooded killer."

"I have no idea what you are talking about," said Smythe.

"His mother asked me to hire someone to kill a dragon and the dragon is dead," said Coreg.

The vapor spiraled upward into the dragon's nostrils. Whenever Coreg inhaled, he sucked in the vapor. The magical gas was odorless and tasteless. He would not suspect anything was amiss until he began to feel the first debilitating effects.

"His Highness knew nothing about that plot," said Captain Smythe, drawing nearer.

Coreg chuckled. "And who will believe him?"

The dragon stopped talking. He coughed and grimaced and coughed again. A shudder ran through his body. Muscles twitched, his scales crawled. He coughed yet again and tried to stand. His front claws scrabbled feebly on the floor. His tail twitched. He fell back down with a thud that shook the ground.

Smythe recognized the symptoms of the creeping paralysis, for he had watched the other dragon succumb to the magic. She too had tried to stand up, to come after him. She had managed to make it a short distance before she collapsed, helpless, her feet and tail twitching.

Coreg coughed and cleared his throat.

"As I was saying. Who will believe him?" he said, his voice raspy. "I could be of use to your prince and he, in return, could be of use to me—"

Coreg gave a strangled gasp. His eyes widened in horror. He was beginning to realize, perhaps, what was happening to him. He glared at Smythe and managed to blurt out a single word, investing the word with fury.

"You!" He opened his jaws, tried to breathe fire. His breath wheezed. His head feebly sank to the floor.

Captain Smythe reached inside his coat to a leather baldric he wore slung over his shoulder. He removed the pistol he kept there and advanced on the paralyzed dragon.

"I feared you would try to blackmail my prince."

Coreg could do nothing except draw wheezing, gasping breaths. Drool trickled from beneath his clenched teeth. His body spasmed, shaking the floor.

Smythe walked up to stand directly in front of Coreg. The pistol had been specially designed, magically enhanced to be able to withstand an extremely high-powder charge without blowing off his hand. The pistol had two elongated barrels that could each fire an extremely large-caliber ball.

Smythe climbed onto the dragon's snout.

Coreg struggled and tried to roar, to summon help. The only sound was a muffled whimper. Smythe placed the two muzzles of the pistol between the dragon's hate-filled eyes. The pistol was heavy. Smythe had to use both hands to fire it. He cocked the weapon, held it poised.

"My prince has nothing to say to you."

Smythe fired.

Trubgek heard Coreg call his name.

Standing in the magical forest at the entrance to the dragon's lair, Trubgek watched from the darkness. He had observed Smythe's arrival. He knew why he was here.

Trubgek watched Smythe place the linen scroll on the floor, watched the vapor twist and writhe across the floor toward the dragon. He saw Coreg fall, paralyzed, helpless, and he heard as well as witnessed the shot, for the echoes bounced off the walls. He heard the dragon's feeble, terrified howl.

He watched Smythe drop the pistol into the blood, then walk back to where he had left the scroll. Smythe carefully picked up the scroll and, taking his time, rolled it up, neatly and precisely. This done, Smythe cast a glance in Trubgek's direction. He could not see him, but he would know he was there. Smythe gave a nod, then thrust the scroll into an inner pocket of his coat and left the dwelling by the way he had come.

Trubgek slowly entered the dragon's lair.

The hole in the dragon's skull was massive. Blood ran down the dragon's snout and was forming a pool on the floor. Yet there was still light in the dragon's eyes. Coreg was a fighter and he was fighting for his life. The dragon saw Trubgek and the light in his eyes flickered. He gazed at him with pathetic eagerness.

Trubgek understood. Coreg hoped he was here to save him. The hope was foolish. Coreg must be in horrible pain, desperate, frightened.

Trubgek walked up to the dying dragon.

"What is my name?" he asked.

Coreg could only stare in confusion. He had no idea what he meant.

Trubgek walked closer, treading in the blood.

"The name of the boy you stole from his family. The boy you tortured. The boy who was so frightened and miserable he tried to kill himself. That boy. What is his name?"

The light in the dragon's eye was starting to dim.

"You don't remember," said Trubgek. He shrugged. "Perhaps you never even knew. Petar. My name is Petar."

A shudder shook Coreg, shook the floor, and the dragon died. Empty eyes stared fixedly at Trubgek.

"Petar," he said again.

He bent down, picked up the pistol, and walked away, going back into the jungle whose magic had died with the dragon.

FORTY-NINE

Mr. Sloan had been amazed and confounded by the astonishing sight of Captain Kate rushing headlong into the Perky Parrot, calling for Akiel, and just as fast, rushing back out again.

Mr. Sloan had been so amazed that he had done nothing except sit there and stare. He had eventually come to his senses and hurried out the door, along with several other patrons, to try to see what was going on. By then Kate and Akiel were nowhere to be found.

Mr. Sloan berated himself. He should have done something, said something. He went back to his table, reflecting that, after all, he should not have been surprised to see Kate. Amelia had told Sir Henry that she believed Kate was headed for the Aligoes to try to find out from Coreg who had framed her. Amid his other concerns, Mr. Sloan had forgotten all about Kate. He considered this a serious mental lapse on his part, and sternly took himself to task.

At least, he could ask around and see what he could find out. The other patrons were freely discussing Kate, speculating on what might have occurred. Mr. Sloan was a stranger in Freeport and, as such, did not want to arouse suspicion by appearing too interested. He decided, upon consideration, that the event had been shocking enough to warrant a stranger making inquiries, especially as the cook had fled with Kate, and Mr. Sloan was now one of a number of people who apparently were going to have go without their dinners.

Venturing over to a group of dockworkers, he introduced himself and asked if they thought Akiel would return. The dockworkers considered it doubtful, commiserated with him over the loss of a meal, and invited him to join them. He bought a round of Calvados and soon had his information.

"Likely Greenstreet sold Kate out to the Rosians in hopes of collecting the bounty on her," said one. "He's the one who told the Rosians where to find No-Nose Blake and his crew."

"He's gone too far this time," said another. "Business is business, but friends don't turn on friends."

"Greenstreet better find somewhere else to live," added a third. "Somewhere with a cooler climate. He's going to find this one too hot."

Mr. Sloan returned to his lodging, hoping a summons from Coreg had arrived, only to be disappointed. He wrote another coded letter to Sir Henry, warning him that Kate could be in serious trouble and might have fallen into the hands of the Rosians.

The weather turned foul overnight and the storm continued unabated the next morning. Dark, heavy clouds settled over Freeport, rain came down in torrents, the wind whipped the trees, and thunder rattled the ill-fitting windows.

Mr. Sloan stood at the window in his lodging, watching the dirt street turn into a river. He spent the morning in his room, still waiting to hear from Coreg. The morning passed without word.

Mr. Sloan decided to venture out into the storm. He had another concern, and that was Kate. Telling the widow he could be found at the Parrot, he left around noon.

He had never witnessed a storm so severe. As a marine, he had served in all manner of inclement weather, but he had never seen rain fall sideways. He was forced to hold on to his tricorn, for the wind threatened to rip if off his head. Water ran from his hat in rivulets, soaking through his cloak. He waded in mud and water up to his ankles.

He was drenched by the time he arrived at the Parrot. Some of Olaf's neighbors were now running the tavern in Akiel's absence, and most of the population of Freeport appeared to be here. Everyone was talking about Kate and Olaf and Akiel. Mr. Sloan gathered from their grim looks and lowered voices that the news was not good. A weeping woman in a corner was being comforted by her neighbors.

Mr. Sloan recognized his companions from the previous day, and once he had shed his sopping-wet cloak and hat and found a seat, they told him the news.

"The Rosians captured Kate and sank her ship," one reported.

"Bloody Rosians," several muttered angrily.

"What right do they have to come in here and stick their noses in our business?" one demanded

"Kate is a good soul," said another. "She took care of Olaf and her crew after her pa was murdered. So she helped herself to some plunder now and again? She's a right to earn her bread, same as the rest of us."

"She *was* a good soul," affirmed the woman who had been sobbing. "My boy worked for her. Kate may not have paid him on a regular basis, but if she had money, she saw to it that my lad had money and there was always a hot meal for us here."

People in the tavern nodded and rapped their mugs on the table in a show of agreement.

Mr. Sloan expressed his sympathy and bought a round of ale for the house.

"Are you certain Captain Kate was captured?" he asked, sitting down with the dockworkers.

"The Rosians have been bragging about taking her alive," said one. "That patrol boat that's been snooping around the harbor came in this morning to take on water. The crew was saying as how they had arrested Kate and taken her to their headquarters in Maribeau. Plannin' to hang her."

"Hang her?" Mr. Sloan repeated, shocked. "But the captain is a privateer. At least, so I have read in the newspapers. Her stories are extremely popular in Freya. She holds letters of marque from the queen. Captain Kate has many friends who would be glad to pay her ransom."

"There won't be no ransom, sir. Far as the Rosians are concerned, she's just another bloody pirate."

"The Rosian captain even said as much. According to what we heard, Kate surrendered. She struck her colors, but the captain paid no heed. He shouted for all to hear, 'She's naught but a pirate, lads! Sink her!' "

"Mark my words, sir," said an old man, chiming in from another table. "They're already building the gallows."

"This is Greenstreet's fault," said another. "Everyone knows he's been collecting bounties on his friends. Someone should make him pay."

"Maybe someone did," said another man.

He had entered on the heels of the conversation, bringing a gust of wind and rain with him. He paid for his ale and then joined them.

"Greenstreet's bullyboy, Jules, is dead and Greenstreet is missing."

"Dead? Jules? What happened?"

People crowded around him. The man paused to take a swig of ale and enjoy the sensation he had caused.

"Seems his woman missed him when he didn't come home last night. She went lookin' for him and found him cold and stiff this morning outside Greenstreet's house. Shot through the heart. No sign of Greenstreet."

"Likely he shot him," said one.

"That fat, lazy bastard? More likely he figured he was next and skedaddled," said another.

"He'll keep away if he knows what's good for him," said another. "Folks hereabouts were fond of poor Kate."

Everyone agreed and someone raised his mug to propose a toast. "To Kate!"

"To Kate," said the others.

The old man added, "Her father's daughter, she was. No luck. No luck at all."

The dockworkers departed, going back to work. Mr. Sloan ordered dinner. The food was not up to Akiel's standards, but the navy beans and salt pork was edible, which was more than could be said for the widow's mutton. Mr. Sloan ate his meal and considered what to do.

He was deeply troubled by this news, both about Kate and about the murder of the henchman and Greenstreet's sudden disappearance. Mr. Sloan decided he would go to Greenstreet's house, see for himself what was going on. He was not hopeful, considering it highly likely that both Greenstreet and Coreg had departed. Once he had determined that there was no further need to remain in Freeport, he would travel to Maribeau, find out if the Rosians were actually planning to hang Kate, and do what he could to try to save her.

He considered what he knew of Admiral Alessandro, commander of the Rosian fleet. According to Sir Henry, the younger brother of King Renaud had inherited the worst traits of his father. Not being overly gifted with intelligence, Alessandro attempted to compensate for his stupidity by being stubborn, obtuse, and reckless. Renaud had tried to persuade his brother to resign, but Alessandro refused. To avoid a scandal, the king had surrounded his brother with officers who did what they could to limit the damage the admiral caused.

Mr. Sloan considered it likely that hanging Kate was Admiral Alessandro's idea and that, unfortunately, he might well have the king's support—due entirely to the fiction of Miss Amelia.

Freyans had no love for the Rosians. Bitter over their numerous humiliating defeats at the hands of the Rosians, the Freyan people reveled in Captain Kate's victories over their longtime foes. Miss Amelia knew her readership well, and in each weekly installment, the courageous Captain Kate engaged in battle with the hapless Rosians, whom she gleefully portrayed as bumpkins and poltroons.

Unfortunately, the stories that delighted the Freyans were wormwood and gall to the Rosians. Their ambassador to Freya had even made a formal complaint to Her Majesty regarding the Captain Kate stories. Sir Henry had found this highly amusing at the time. He wouldn't find it amusing when, among all his other trouble, he would have to deal with the uproar when the final chapter about their romantic heroine ended with her "dancing the hempen jig," as death by hanging was known among sailors.

Mr. Sloan considered traveling to Haever to inform Sir Henry, but dismissed the idea. The Rosians hated Sir Henry perhaps more than they hated Kate, if that was possible.

Mr. Sloan would do more good working to save Kate himself. He wondered if there was some other officer in Maribeau who could be persuaded to see reason. He remembered that the Dragon Brigade was in the Aligoes.

"Captain Thorgrimson!" Mr. Sloan said aloud.

He had met Dag Thorgrimson during the Bottom Dweller War, when Stephano de Guichen, then commander of the Dragon Brigade, was preparing to travel to the bottom of the world to take on the foe.

Dag Thorgrimson had been second-in-command. Sir Henry had been impressed by Thorgrimson's diligence, his sense of honor and common sense. When Stephano was made Duke de Bourlet and resigned his command of the Brigade, he recommended that the king give it to Dag.

Mr. Sloan paid his bill and prepared to leave. The rain continued to fall, though not nearly as heavily as before. Mr. Sloan put on his hat and his wet cloak, turned up his collar, and prepared to venture into the storm. Opening the door, he started to walk out just as another man was walking in. Mr. Sloan politely stepped back to allow the man room to enter.

"Thank you, sir," said the man, removing his hat.

As he walked past him, Mr. Sloan had a good view of his face.

"Good God!" Mr. Sloan murmured. The fact that he uttered blasphemy indicated that he was profoundly shaken.

Mr. Sloan glanced back over his shoulder to make certain he was not jumping at shadows. He was not. The man was older, of course, but there was no doubt as to his identity.

"Isaiah Crawford," Mr. Sloan muttered in disbelief. "That man was Isaiah Crawford!"

Mr. Sloan needed time for calm reflection and he proceeded on his way.

Once outside, with the rain drumming on his hat and running down his neck, he kept watch at the window, observing Crawford. Mr. Sloan had not seen or heard of this man in years and now, only a few days after Simon had named him, here he was. Mr. Sloan was not given to given to flights of fancy, but he had the unsettling feeling that, like a conjurer, his thoughts had caused Crawford to materialize.

Upon reflection, Mr. Sloan realized there was undoubtedly a simpler, though more sinister, explanation. Simon had named Crawford the murderer of Lady Odila. Crawford was here in Freeport. And there was another dragon, Coreg—the only one who knew the identity of the person who wanted Odila dead. Crawford was not one to let such a gigantic loose thread dangle.

Mr. Sloan could make a very good guess as to the killer of Jules. Likely Crawford had killed Greenstreet and Coreg, as well.

"I should go to Greenstreet's, verify my suspicions," Mr. Sloan said, thinking aloud.

He watched through the rain-spattered window. Crawford had taken a seat at a table by himself near the fire.

"But if I leave," Mr. Sloan argued, "I might well lose track of him and never find him again."

A plan formed in Mr. Sloan's mind. The plan was dangerous, could even be termed foolhardy. Sir Henry would oppose it. More than that, he would undoubtedly be furious when he found out the terrible risk Mr. Sloan was proposing to undertake.

"I trust you will forgive me, my lord," said Mr. Sloan, apologizing to the absent Sir Henry. "The saints teach us that God works wonders. I believe He has set me in this man's path for a reason."

Mr. Sloan understood that this meant leaving Kate to her fate, and he gave her into God's care, though not without some reservations. With Kate, much as with Captain Northrop, God had His work cut out for Him.

The clouds were clearing and the sun was coming out. Mr. Sloan took that for a good omen. He went back inside and walked up to Crawford.

Removing his hat, Mr. Sloan said, "Pardon me, sir. I cannot help but feel that we are acquainted. Are you not Isaiah Crawford? We served together many years ago in the marines."

The man stared at him; then his stern face broke into a faint smile.

"Sergeant Franklin Sloan. Though I dare say you are no longer a sergeant. Please, join me." Crawford gestured to an empty seat.

Mr. Sloan took off his wet cloak and sat down.

"It is good to see you again, sir," said Mr. Sloan.

"Good to see you, as well, Mr. Sloan. Though I should tell you that my name is no longer Crawford. It is Smythe. Captain Jonathan Smythe."

That name, too, sounded familiar.

Crawford was saying something about having to leave Freya and change his name owing to religious persecution.

All the while Mr. Sloan was mentally scrambling to try to remember where he had heard the name Jonathan Smythe. He recalled a letter . . . A letter to Henry from one of his agents . . . Phillip! Yes, he had sent a letter shortly after he had traveled to Estara to spy on . . .

And then Mr. Sloan knew.

Good God, Mr. Sloan said inwardly, and this time he spoke with reverence. God did truly work wonders.

Isaiah Crawford was Captain Jonathan Smythe. The commander of the armies of Prince Tom.

"And so, Mr Sloan, what are you doing in this part of the Aligoes?" Captain Smythe was asking.

Mr. Sloan did not hesitate. He saw the path before him as clearly as though God Himself was shining the light of His countenance upon the way.

"As it happens, Captain Smythe, I, too, fear I will be forced to leave Freya because of my faith," said Mr. Sloan in sorrowful tones. "My current employer is a blasphemer and an infidel. I fear the loss of my immortal soul if I remained in his service. I would be glad to find different work."

"Something in the military line?" Captain Smythe asked. "You were an excellent soldier, as I recall."

"Thank you, sir, you are most kind," said Mr. Sloan. "I would be glad of a chance to return to active duty."

"Then we are well met, Mr. Sloan," said Captain Smythe. "Well met, indeed."

FIFTY

The surgeon on board the *Soleil* examined the gash on Kate's head. She sat on a stool in the sick bay, her wrists and ankles shackled, barely able to think over the throbbing pain in her head.

The ship was headed for the Rosian port city of Maribeau to deliver the prisoner. Their progress was slow. The ship had been caught in a storm and forced to reduce sail. Kate could hear the rain pounding on the deck, hear the howling of the wind in the rigging.

"You are lucky," the surgeon said.

He was working by the light of a lantern suspended overhead. The light was swinging back and forth with the motion of the ship in the storm winds.

Kate stared up at him. One of her eyes was swollen shut, her jaw ached, and she could barely see for the blood that covered her face.

He gave a tight smile. "What I mean is, the blow did not crack open your skull. To stitch up the wound, I must shave your head." He added with a shrug, "The guards in the prison would do that anyway so they don't have to deal with lice."

He took out a straight razor and began to sharpen it on a leather strop.

"I want to see the captain," Kate mumbled through bruised lips. "My ship crashed on an island below the Breath. There could be survivors."

The surgeon bent over her, putting the razor to her head. "Hold still, please." He started to shave, then paused as a violent gust hit the ship. "Drat this wind!"

Kate grabbed hold of his hand, manacles clanking.

"I want to see the captain!" she repeated.

The surgeon exchanged glances with the marine detailed to guard her, then turned to his loblolly boy and spoke to him in a low voice. Kate heard the words "feverish" and "agitated," presumably describing herself. The loblolly boy dashed off. Kate slumped on the stool. The winds calmed and the rain stopped. The surgeon shaved her head and she watched with dull, uncaring eyes as her blood-gummed blond curls landed in a heap on the floor or in her lap.

"Dirty dishwater," she murmured with a half smile.

The captain took his time. The surgeon had stitched up the wound and was saying it should heal cleanly, when the captain entered the sick bay. Kate was still sitting on the stool and he stood staring down at her with contempt.

"What do you want?" he asked.

What Kate wanted was to wipe that sneer off his face. The bastard had given orders to fire on her ship after her crew had surrendered. Never mind that the surrender had been a ploy to buy time. He didn't know that. She had to swallow her anger, however. She needed him.

"Send a boat to rescue my crew," she said.

"Your crew are in hell," he said. "Which is where you are headed."

Kate shook her head and winced at the pain. "I heard the ship crash. There are islands below the Breath. I know. I was a wrecker. There might be survivors."

"Your ship was destroyed," the captain said. "And you will soon hang."

He turned and started to leave.

Kate tried to jump up, but she tripped over the leg irons and landed on her belly on the deck. She reached out as far as the manacles on her wrists would allow and was able to grab hold of his boot.

"Please!" she pleaded. "I beg you! I don't care about myself. Just save my crew!"

He stared down at her as he might have stared down at a plague-carrying rat.

"Get her off me," he said.

Two marines seized hold of her and dragged her away.

"Sorry, sir," said the surgeon. "She's feverish."

The captain pulled out a handkerchief, cleaned his boot, and stalked out.

The surgeon and the loblolly boy placed Kate on a cot, where she lay with her eyes closed. Her head throbbed, but that was nothing compared to the searing pain in her heart.

"If your crewmembers are stranded on an island in the Deep Breath, they won't survive long," said the surgeon.

"My crew can," said Kate. "Akiel knows a special kind of magic. He will keep them alive. I just need to find them. . . ."

The surgeon only shook his head. "Delirious."

Kate stared at the wooden planks above the cot. Wild ideas roamed her fevered brain. She would overpower the marine, steal his rifle . . . hold the captain at gunpoint . . . sail back to rescue Olaf and Akiel and Marco . . .

They are waiting for me. They know I won't abandon them. They believe in me . . .

She could use the chain attached to the manacles to choke the marine, wrap it around his neck.

First she had to stand up. . . .

She found herself face-first on the deck.

"I have to save them," Kate murmured, as the surgeon and the loblolly boy bent over her.

They laid her back on the cot and there was Morgan, standing over her, gazing down at her.

"How can you save them, Kate?" he asked with a shrug and a smile. "You can't even save yourself."

FIFTY-ONE

The storm rolled into Haever during the late evening hours, bringing dull, plodding, soaking rain, the type that could settle in for days. The pale light from the streetlamps glistened on wet pavement. The horses splashed through small lakes that formed in the intersections, and the carriage wheels flung water high into the air.

Henry's mood matched the weather, gray and somber. He was returning home late from the palace after a meeting with Her Majesty that had not gone at all well.

Queen Mary was an energetic woman, fond of hunting and riding. Even in her middle years, she still rode to the hounds and jumped fence rails with the best of them. She was intelligent, but not a deep thinker. She could not understand that sometimes, instead of charging ahead, she should patiently wait and watch.

"We need to be *doing,* Henry!" Queen Mary had told him, stamping her words with her clenched fist into her palm. "Doing! Not moping about."

Henry had good reason to mope. The Travian dragons had agreed to remain in Freya for the time being, on the condition that the murderer should be swiftly apprehended. Their discontent grew with every day that passed without an arrest. The question of the heir to the throne remained unsettled. The queen remained obstinately fixed on her sister—the one married to the Rosian—and stubbornly refused to listen to the howls of protest rising from all quarters.

King Ullr had been particularly offensive on his trip to Freya. He had gone around Henry and met with the dragons, offering them "safe haven" in Guundar. Despite that, Henry had found some pleasure in Ullr's visit. Henry had asked the king in the blandest possible tone if Ullr had heard the rumors that the Braffans had discovered barrels of a crystalline form of the Breath. Ullr had been furious. He did not know for certain that it was Henry who had stolen the crystals right out from under his nose, but the king certainly suspected as much. The memory of Ullr stomping out of the meeting could still bring a smile to Henry's lips.

His smile was fleeting. The members of the House of Nobles were being more useless than usual. Paralyzed with indecision, they were unable to act on measures that might have eased the financial crisis. Rioting continued in the streets. The Anti-Dragon League was holding rallies every night.

Freya was lurching from one disaster to the next and Henry had been strongly tempted this night to ask the queen just what he should be "doing." She was angry enough with him, however, and he had held his tongue and let her scold him.

The carriage rolled up in front of his town house. The hour was late, the house dark. Since Henry came and went at all hours and sometimes spent the night at his club, he had given orders for the servants not to wait up for him. He entered the silent house, deeply regretting the absence of Mr. Sloan. Henry felt his secretary's absence as he would have felt the loss of his right arm.

He hung his sopping-wet cloak and hat on the coat stand, lit a candle, and quietly walked up the stairs to the second floor. As was his habit, he went first to the nursery. Nanny slept in the back of the room. He could hear her snoring from the hallway and he took off his shoes so as not to wake her and bring down her wrath upon him.

Young Henry had graduated from the cradle and was now sleeping in a bed with wooden side bars to prevent nighttime excursions. He lay on his back, his face flushed, his hair tousled. He clutched a toy wooden soldier, given to him by Alan, from which he would not be parted.

His son had kicked off his covers. The night being damp and chilly, Henry set the candle on the mantelpiece and solicitously drew the blanket up around his son's chin. He removed the soldier and, bending low, kissed his sleeping son on his forehead.

He then padded soft-footed to the cradle where his infant daughter lay on her back with one small fist in her mouth.

"I thought I heard you, my love," said a soft voice.

He looked around to see Ann enter the room. She was dressed in her long white nightdress and nightcap, her hair parted in the middle and neatly braided. Stealing up to him, she twined her arms through his and rested her head on his shoulder.

"I am sorry to disturb you, my Mouse," said Henry softly.

"I was wakeful and listening for you," Ann whispered. "How wet you are! Your shirt collar is soaked. You must change your clothes before you catch your death."

"A little rain will not kill me," said Henry. "Your aunt the queen is the one who will do me in."

"My poor Henry," said Ann. "Is she being very terrible to you?"

"No more than I deserve," said Henry lightly. He would not burden his wife with his troubles.

He kissed Ann's cheek and they both stood gazing at their baby. Her tiny mouth was curved in a bow. Long eyelashes swept her cheeks.

"She grows more beautiful every day," said Henry.

"Henry, she is bald as an onion," Ann said, teasing.

Outside the wind moaned among the eaves. The rain beat on the windowpanes. Henry reached his arm around his wife and drew her close.

"I had a strange fancy, standing here, my Mouse. I imagined my love as a halo of light flowing from me, encircling you and our children, keeping us all safe."

"A lovely fancy, my dear," said Ann.

"I wish it were real," said Henry. "In truth, I feel more like the driver of a carriage that is careening out of control while the crazed wyverns snarl and snap and bite each other."

"Not as bad as that, my love," said Ann. "I trust in your first vision. I believe in you, Henry. Now come to bed. You can do nothing to fix the world tonight."

Henry picked up the candle and held it high, so that a small white halo surrounded him and his Mouse as they walked to their bedchamber.

FIFTY-TWO

The port city of Maribeau had been founded by the Rosians over one hundred fifty years ago, following their victory in the Blackfire War. It was now one of the largest cities in the Aligoes and also one of the wealthiest. Three forts manned by more than a thousand soldiers guarded the harbor entrance and protected Rosian interests in the islands.

The *Soleil* had arrived during the night after a voyage of about three days. Rosian marines escorted Kate from the ship to the prison in the largest of the three forts, Fort Saint-Jean, located on Point La Fierte du Roi.

Kate was the only female housed in the military prison. The commander had to send for one of the nuns who worked in the infirmary to bathe and dress her in women's prison garb—a long white linen gown that extended from her neck to her ankles. The nun took her shoes, leaving her barefoot, to deter escape.

Kate was given a cell to herself with a guard posted outside day and night. The cell was small, only a dozen feet in either direction. The walls were whitewashed stone covered in magical constructs that would prevent any crafter housed in the cell from using magic to escape. An iron-banded, magic-locked wooden door had a small hatch that the guards could open to check on the prisoner. The cell was furnished with a cot with a straw mattress, and a chamber pot.

Kate spent the rest of that night sitting upright on the bed, afraid to close her eyes. Whenever she fell asleep, she would slide into a horror-tinged dream of flame and screams and splintering wood. She would wake with a start and a gasp, bathed in sweat. The next day, she paced her cell for hours, back and forth, back and forth, with occasional stops to yell for the jailer. At first she demanded to speak to someone in charge. When her demands were ignored, she tried pleading and begging. Those did not work either. At least this night, when darkness fell, she was so exhausted she slept soundly.

The next morning, another storm rolled in. Rain drummed on the roof and, above the wind and thunder, she heard the sound of hammering outside her cell. She paid little attention to it. She was thinking of her crew and wondering how long Akiel's spellcasting could keep them alive. A key rattled in the lock. A guard opened the door to admit a Rosian military officer.

Kate looked up. Her head was shaved and bloodied, her face bruised and swollen. The guard walked over, grabbed hold of her arm, and yanked her out of bed.

"Stand up," he ordered.

"Katherine Gascoyne-Fitzmaurice," the officer pronounced in formal tones.

Kate eyed him warily. "That is my name."

"You have been tried in a military tribunal and found guilty of piracy."

"Tribunal? What tribunal?" Kate demanded angrily. "I was not present at any tribunal and I am not a pirate! I am a privateer for the nation of Freya! I hold letters of marque."

The commander smiled, thin-lipped. "If you had letters of marque—which I doubt—they are at the bottom of the world and will do you no good. The punishment for piracy is death by hanging. The sentence will be carried out at dawn tomorrow. They are now, as we speak, building the gallows in the courtyard outside. I will send a priest to you at midnight. May God have mercy on your soul."

He walked out. The guard followed, shutting the door and locking it.

"Keep your bloody priest!" Kate shouted.

She couldn't see but she could imagine workmen crawling over the large wooden structure, pounding nails, erecting beams that would hold the rope, installing the trapdoor on which the prisoner would stand with the noose around her neck. When the trapdoor was released, her body would fall through it, tightening the noose. If she was lucky, the noose would break her neck. If not, she would die slowly, doing the "hempen jig," jerking and writhing in agonizing pain and terror as she dangled at the end of the rope.

She sank onto the bed, shivering. Hugging her knees to her body, she listened to the workmen building her death.

"I am my father's daughter," said Kate through trembling lips. "I meant well. Morgan meant well. When things went wrong, which they almost always did, he would say, with that charming smile of his, 'I meant well.' "

Kate had idolized her parents and she had continued to do so, even as she had come to realize that her mother, Rose, had been weak-willed. Raised to be indolent, she had lived in a halcyon dream from which she could not escape.

Her father, Morgan, had also lived in a dream, confident that the next spin of the roulette wheel or the next shipment of contraband would bring him the genteel life of a gentleman he knew he was meant to lead.

Rose had never loved Kate. Sometimes she regarded her in bewilderment, as though she could not fathom how this child had happened to fall into her life. Morgan had loved his daughter in his own careless way. He could just never figure out how she fit into his dream.

Kate had no reason to be proud of such parentage, and every reason to be ashamed. When Olaf had tried to teach her better, she had laughed at him. She thought back to Stephano de Guichen, who had been prepared to sacrifice his life to save her—a nobody. He had set her an example of what it meant to be honorable and courageous. He had told her to fight for her dreams.

She had fought. And she had lost. And it had all been her fault.

She had been reckless, heedless, and impulsive. She had left herself open to Coreg's threats, put herself in his power. She could tell herself that she had gone along with him because he had threatened her and those she loved. She wondered if that was true. Or was it an excuse to absolve herself of blame?

In the end, she had tried to right the wrongs by seeking evidence to expose Coreg and had ended up being framed for murder.

Her father's daughter. The sound of the hammers beat time to Morgan's song: *There's no luck about the house. There's no luck at all.*

She had meant well. But now her friends were dead or dying and she could do nothing to save them. She couldn't save herself.

Kate pictured the remains of her ship lying among the trees and rocks of some sunken island, like the corpses of the other wrecks she had worked. She imagined Akiel holding Marco's lifeless body, releasing his soul. She imagined Olaf dying, calling out for her. She saw the scrap of paper pinned to the wall of the cabin, the scrap the young girl had kept and treasured for so many years, charred and blackened, soaked in blood.

Kate rolled onto her stomach, buried her face in the straw mattress so no one would hear, and began to sob. Her sobs were gulping and ugly. She sobbed for Rose and she sobbed for Morgan and for her friends. She sobbed until she had no more tears and even then she could not stop. At last she lay quiet, curled up in a ball. The storm had ended.

She heard the watchman call the hours. They passed slowly and all too fast. At sunset, the guard opened the door and placed food on the floor. She ignored it. Not long after, he opened the door and took it away.

Night fell. The hammering stopped. Kate grew cold and sick with fear.

The gallows was finished.

The watchman continued to call the hours. Kate sat unmoving, staring into the dark.

This is what death will be, she thought. Unending dark. Unless, as the saints said, death for the sinner is burning forever in the torments of hell.

At midnight, she heard footsteps and the key rattling in the lock.

"The priest is here," called the guard.

"Tell him to go away," said Kate. Her mouth was dry, her voice cracked. "I am not a believer. I don't want a priest."

The door opened. Light flared. Not one priest, but two, wearing brown robes, stood framed in the light.

"I am Brother Gregory. Brother Sebastian and I have come to pray with you, my child," said one of the priests.

"I don't want your prayers!" Kate yelled at him. "Just leave me alone to die in peace."

"Go in to the poor girl, Brother Sebastian," said the priest. "I will keep the corporal company, if that is permitted."

"I would be grateful, Brother," said the guard. "Here, take the lantern."

The priest took the lantern and shuffled inside. The guard shut the door behind him. The priest lifted the lantern to look for her, and the light hit Kate in full in the eyes, half blinding her. The light was painful and she turned her face to the wall.

"I said go away!" she mumbled.

"But I have come to save you, my child," said the priest.

His voice was soft, low, persuasive, and something about that voice was familiar.

Kate raised her head and looked.

Into striking blue eyes.

ABOUT THE AUTHORS

Margaret Weis attended the University of Missouri, Columbia, graduating in 1970 with a B.A. in literature and creative writing. In 1983, she moved to Lake Geneva, Wisconsin, to work as a book editor for TSR, Inc., producers of the Dungeons & Dragons® role-playing game. She is the author or coauthor of a number of *New York Times* bestselling series, including The Dragonlance® Chronicles, Darksword, Rose of the Prophet, Star of the Guardians, The Death Gate Cycle, Sovereign Stone, Dragonvarld, and the Lost Chronicles. She lives in Wisconsin with her four dogs. Discover more at www.margaretweis.com.

Robert Krammes lives in southwest Ohio with his wife, Mary, and their two cats. He is a longtime member of The Society for Creative Anachronism, an avid Cincinnati Bengals fan, and a backyard bird-watcher.

The two have also collaborated on the Dragon Brigades trilogy, *Shadow Raiders, Storm Riders,* and *The Seventh Sigil*. They are currently working on *Oath Breaker,* the second novel in the Dragon Corsairs trilogy.

ACKNOWLEDGMENTS

The description of the *Pride of Haever* in Chapter Seven is an example of an actual description of real ships taken from *Lloyd's Register of British and Foreign Shipping*. The earliest surviving publication dates from 1764. *Lloyd's Register* "describes, classifies, and registers vessels according to certain criteria of physical structure and equipment, to enable underwriters, shipbrokers, and shipowners more easily to assess commercial risk and to negotiate marine insurance rates." Source: http://www.mariners-l.co.uk/ResLloyds Register.htm

Miss Amelia's prized possession in chapter thirty-eight is her book of maps. The description of this book is taken from an actual book published in October 1746 by John Pine and John Tinney.

The book was titled *A Plan of the Cities of London and Westminster and Borough of Southwark; with the Contiguous Buildings; From an Actual Survey Taken by John Rocque Land-Surveyor, and Engraved by John Pine, Bluemantle Pursuivant at Arms and Chief Engraver of Seals, &c. to His Majesty.*

"This Plan will be contained in 24 Sheets of the best Imperial Paper, being near 13 Feet in Length, and 6 Feet and an Half in Depth, and will extend from West to East, on the North Side, from beyond Mary-bone Turnpike, by Tottenham-Court, the New-River-Head, Hoxton and Part of Hackney to near Bow: From thence, Southerly, by the Easternmost Parts of Mile-End and Lime-House, cross the River Thames to Deptford Road; from whence the Southern Side will extend Westerly, by Newington and Vaux-Hall, to that Part of Surrey which is opposite to Chelsea-College; which Building, together with some Part of Knights-Bridge and Hyde-Park, will be included in the Western Limit."

Such a book would have been of immense value to an investigative journalist! Source: http://www.locatinglondon.org/static/Rocque.html